"What are you looking at?" Damarin asked.

Tchardin was mesmerised by the infinity of Water Side. There was nothing out there to break a kandar's gaze. It seemed to continue forever, and if they were by chance on the side of the island that looked away from Land Side, then it did in fact continue forever. Both Land Side and Water Side were infinite planes. Black Valley—the old city of the kandar—was the only anomaly in the endless dunes of Land Side and their new home—the island of Calendrai—was the only break in the mirror-smooth surface of Water Side.

Damarin followed her eyes. The two stood unmoving for some time.

"I don't know what I'm looking at," Tchardin finally answered.

Half sky, half water, the two halves of the horizon seemed to reflect each other. The view was of one nearly solid sheet of blue permeated by bursts of light from pandinzori. It was the furthest thing from the forest. There was something about one spot out there—Tchardin could actually point to it in the sea of sameness—that called to her.

"What are *you* looking at?" she returned the question.

DAUGHTERS OF TITH

CHILDREN OF THE TREES: BOOK I

DAUGHTERS OF TITH

J. PATRICIA ANDERSON

publishing

Daughters of Tith
Children of the Trees: Book I

Case laminate hardcover with dust jacket, 1st edition

Jacket cover art and design by J. Patricia Anderson
Case laminate cover art and design by J. Patricia Anderson
Maps by J. Patricia Anderson

Published by Root of the World Publishing on May 1st, 2023

ISBNs: 978-1-7782881-1-1 (ebook), 978-1-7782881-0-4 (paperback),
978-1-7782881-2-8 (case laminate hardcover),
978-1-7782881-3-5 (case laminate hardcover with dust jacket)

Root of the World Publishing
rootoftheworldpublishing.com

For Anna.
For so many reasons.

Derkra.

Infinite and flat.

Half land and half water.

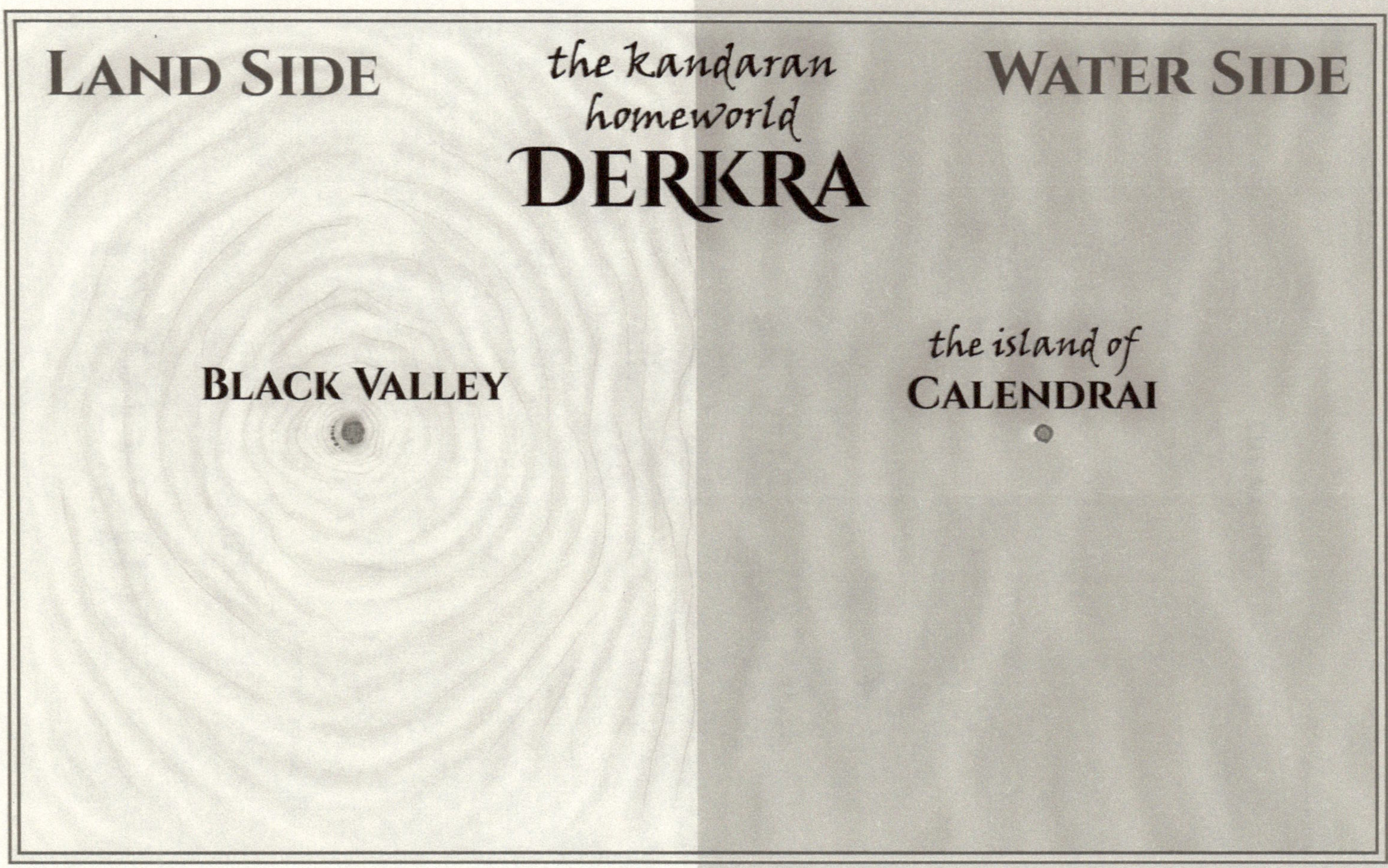

the kandaran homeworld

DERKRA

LAND SIDE

WATER SIDE

BLACK VALLEY

the island of CALENDRAI

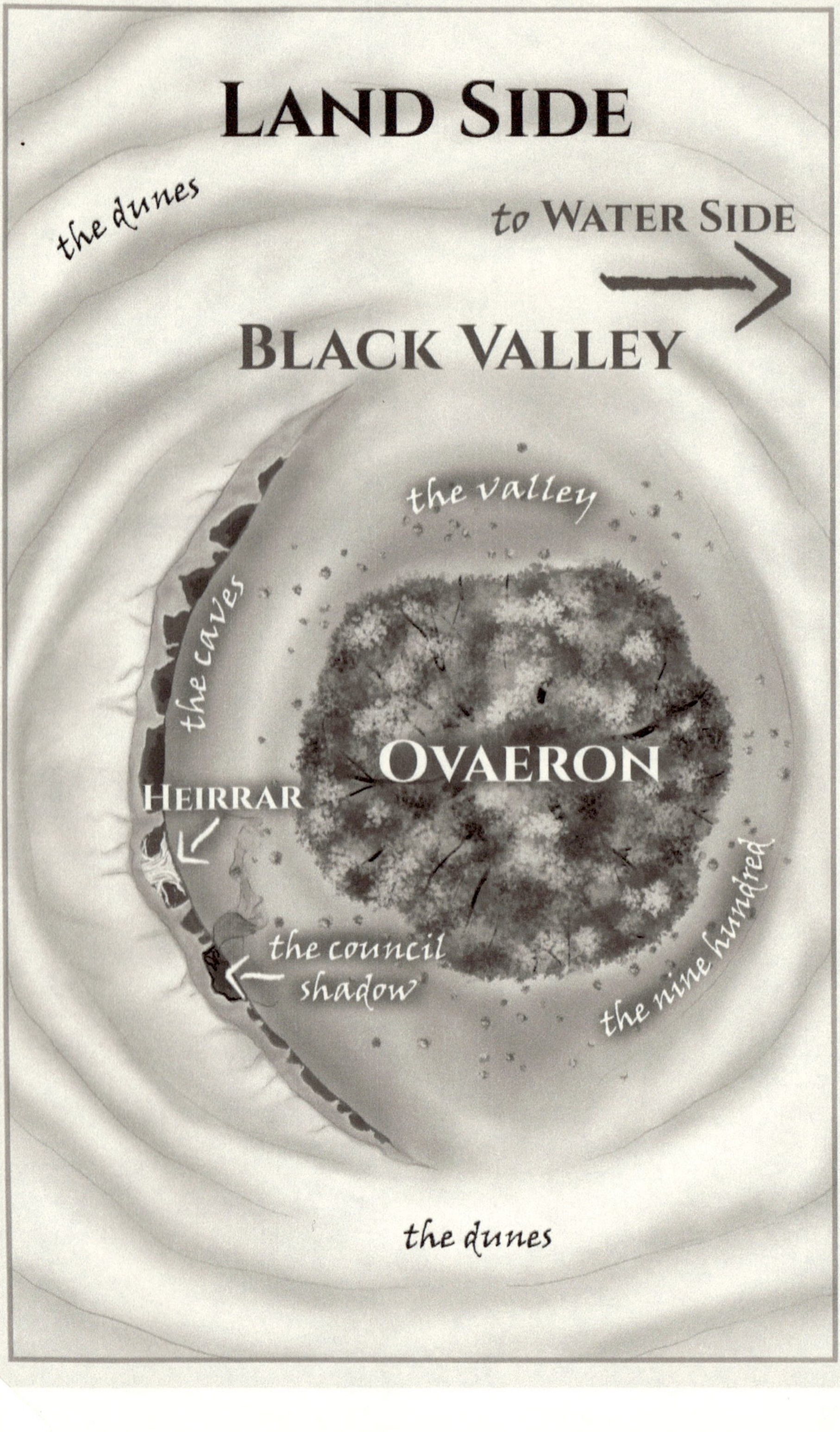

LAND SIDE

the dunes

to WATER SIDE

BLACK VALLEY

the valley

the caves

OVAERON

HEIRRAR

the nine hundred

the council shadow

the dunes

WATER SIDE

the island of
CALENDRAI

the forest
CENS

the sleeping kandar

AHRON

the clearing

the shore

TITH

the council shadow

SIRRHON

to LAND SIDE

PART I

Chapter 1

A SPLASH OF COLOUR lit the darkness in Tchardin's mind. Green was easy to bring up because everything around her was green. The grass that touched her. The moss on the tree trunks that led to the leaves high above. The colour in the centre of her vision slipped to blue as her concentration wavered. She forced it back, watched it spin.

From green she could go to blue or yellow easily. Red and its variants were the most difficult because they were rare in the world around her. She willed the patch of green into yellow and from there attempted orange. She chose not to form the colours into images, instead enjoying their fluid nature.

'Jaydin's looking for you.'

Tchardin struggled for a moment to block out the collective mind but with one thought came many. All the mindvoices of the kandar rushed into her head, buzzing. The colours she'd been cultivating dispersed and were replaced by the image of a tree. She opened herself fully to the collective and sent her mind up the trunk and over the branches—brilliant with light—to find and focus on the leaf of the one who had breached her concentration. *Kadailin.*

'Jaydin's always looking for me,' Tchardin directed towards her sister in answer. *'She wants to be with me when it happens.'*

Physical sensation returned as her mind emerged from the darkness. Grass pricked her cheek. Tchardin opened her eyes and flipped onto her back. There didn't seem to be much point in trying to hide from Jaydin. The light of pandinzori swirled brightly against Tchardin's skin, pulled to her body by the colours she'd been creating. If that wasn't enough to draw attention to her place, the collective would show her position to any kandar who looked. Kadailin's leaf grew brighter in the collective as she drew closer.

Tchardin had chosen a place near Tith's trunk, the enormous tree unfolding above her. She looked up into her father's shadowy canopy and those of his two brothers as she waited. They were kandaran trees. Giants. Five times at least the height of the trees in the forest that ringed the island. Their branches seemed to span the entire sky, interlacing to cover the clearing, silhouetted against the pale blue.

Kadailin's grey aura appeared over the tall grass as she approached, followed by the top of her head and her shoulders. She parted the grass and sat beside Tchardin, far enough away that their auras didn't touch but close enough for Tchardin to clearly trace the patterns on her dark dappled skin.

"Do you think it'll happen soon?" Kadailin spoke aloud now that they were next to each other. Their conversation would be contained and would not clutter the collective, her voice heard by ears instead of minds.

"I think so," Tchardin said, relaxing back into the grass. "I can feel it."

"Quarter life," Kadailin said solemnly. "You're finally going to be queen."

"If things were right I'd be assigned to an Earth."

"I'd already be on one."

Kadailin lay down beside her and they stared into the canopy together in silence. The thought hung in Tchardin's mind. If only it were possible to be assigned to one of the nine Earths now. To go to the humans and fulfill the Purpose as all kandar were meant to. Tchardin sighed.

Her body thrummed softly, just as it did whenever she thought of the change that was nearing. Jaydin had been a nuisance ever since Tchardin started to feel quarter life coming on. The fluttering of her muscles wasn't visible as far as Tchardin knew—Kadailin hadn't noticed it until Tchardin told her—but it was just like Jaydin to notice. Their oldest sister had been waiting for Tchardin's acknowledgement as queen since she was born with the golden aura. A queen could bring the kandar back to the Purpose—back to humans—or so Jaydin said. But the kandar had been exiled to their homeworld, Derkra, for almost four generations. Tchardin didn't see how her acknowledgement alone could change that, despite what Jaydin expected from her.

Jaydin's leaf blazed in Tchardin's mind and she felt her sister's presence somewhere just beyond the high grass. Kadailin's eyes were closed and her thoughts hummed. Tchardin reached a hand out to her slowly and stopped when a jolt ran through her at the collision of their auras. Kadailin's eyes shot open.

"You should leave now if you don't want to be here when Jaydin finds me," Tchardin said.

Kadailin smiled lazily, her mind still somewhere else despite the shock Tchardin had subjected her to. She gave Tchardin a sympathetic glance as she got up and quickly disappeared behind a wall of grass. Tchardin stood to watch her go. Her sister ran through the clearing—displacing the ubiquitous light of pandinzori as she went, leaving it swirling in her wake—and faded into Cens, the forest enveloping her in its shadows.

The collective gave Tchardin warning and she turned to see Jaydin similarly watching Kadailin. The oldest of Tith's daughters could be imposing when she stood completely straight and she almost always did. Of the five sisters only Damarin was close to matching her in height. Jaydin turned her dark grey eyes down on Tchardin.

"We should be talking about the Earths," she said.

Tchardin scanned the clearing for Sandin—the two were always together—and found their second oldest sister neatly shrouded in shadows a few steps away, her dark brown aura barely visible. Sandin had always been the best at physically hiding herself. That ability coupled with the fact that she didn't have a leaf in the collective made her difficult to find. Tchardin smiled at Sandin with genuine humour. She had a special connection with their flawed sister. Sandin had been present at her birth.

"More history?" Tchardin asked, not expecting an answer. It was always history.

"We can speak in Tith's canopy," Jaydin replied.

Tchardin nodded and Sandin led the way towards the colossal trunk, cutting through pandinzori she couldn't see as she parted the grass.

"I know you've been avoiding me," Jaydin said. "The information I'm trying to impart to you is extremely important and you're running out of time to learn it."

"I still don't see how this will help me rediscover the Purpose."

"You will help us return to the Purpose once acknowledged as queen. This is what you need to know before the ceremony."

Sandin leapt onto Tith's trunk and started to climb. Jaydin followed with Tchardin behind her. The climb was immense, but easy. Tith's trunk was covered in moss and his bark was thicker than Tchardin's body and full of handholds. Tchardin moved without thinking, gripping the rugged bark and leaping up from one hold to the next. She had no fear of falling, no need to hold pandinzori close to her in case of disaster. The great tree invited them to ascend his incredible height.

At first they were surrounded only by open space and a dizzying view down to the clearing. Kandar walked through the grass below, made small by distance, and Tchardin saw them by their auras, as smudges of earthy colour. Then the branches started. Like Tith's trunk they were massive, and kandar walked them easily with room to spare on both sides.

Tchardin passed a pair of dodenzinn on a smaller branch. The tevadra and devoshai stood close to each other, their auras joined and blended together. Tchardin resisted the urge to cringe away from the sight. If she came that close to another kandar she would be shocked mercilessly until she moved away. But soon things would be different. She would be able to find her own dodenzinn once she hit quarter life. Kandar didn't feel the missing half of their selves until they were ready to go to the Earths.

Above her Sandin had stopped at a branch large enough to seat the three of them in a circle. She moved gracefully across it, away from Tith's trunk. The branch was unoccupied and Jaydin's notebook lay there, its green cover blending into the moss.

Jaydin mostly carried her notebook with her—held up by pandinzori in the shadows that wrapped her body—but it wasn't uncommon to find it lying somewhere in the great tree, waiting for the tevadra to pick it up again. The two sisters must have been sitting there before Jaydin noticed Tchardin in the grass below. Just looking at it reminded Tchardin of the scale of her future responsibilities. The notebook was a thing of the humans. There was nothing else like it on Derkra.

Jaydin picked it up and opened it.

"We should talk about World Seven," she said, glancing at Sandin who nodded. "I believe I was finished with World Six."

Tchardin nodded as well, her mind already wandering. She wondered absently if World Seven would be any more interesting than World Six. Jaydin had told her World Six was constantly warring, and had been since as far back as Tith could remember. Her sister indicated that was rare for the humans but Tchardin didn't really understand. The only reference for war she had was the kandaran war, and as with all things in the kandar's past, Jaydin was the only one who knew anything about it. Tchardin had asked about rendinzori on World Six, as she always did, and at least that had been interesting.

"You'll want to know about rendinzori on World Seven, of course," Jaydin said.

She looked down at the pages of her notebook but Tchardin knew she didn't need to read them to answer. She must be trying to think of something to say. That probably meant World Seven was lacking in the human power.

"It was lacking, generally," Jaydin said, picking up on her thoughts in the collective. "The humans on World Seven didn't use it directly as those on World Six did. No 'magic'. No enchantments. No bolts of lightning. It's not as interesting if you're looking for rendinzori, but in other ways it's the most interesting of them all. World Seven was restarted just before the kandaran war."

"One of the worlds was restarted?" The option was something the trees told all the kandar about before they were born, but it was never taken seriously. To restart a world was to destroy everything that had been built there, dismiss everything that had been done. To restart a world was to kill all the humans on it. "How could they have justified that?"

"The World Seed was found. There's not much choice at that point. The Earth was burning. There was basically nothing left. Rai—the World Tree—was the last tree standing." Jaydin scanned her notebook and shook her head. "A tevadra called Siltadon was sent to give the Seed to the guardian, Leksten, but I don't know the outcome of the restart."

Tchardin made note of the names of the World Tree and guardian. Rai and Leksten. Jaydin always asked her to repeat them later. "Why don't you know?"

"The kandaran war." Jaydin shrugged. "We were exiled shortly after it ended and there was no way to learn the fate of Siltadon and World Seven then."

Tchardin realised she was straining forward and slumped back. Jaydin would never leave her alone now that she'd shown some interest in human history. But a world had been restarted. It was unbelievable.

"And the rendinzori?" Tchardin asked.

"Lacking in its direct application, as I said. Nothing like World Four or Six. If the humans used it we couldn't see the results. The only thing especially unique about the world before its restart was that it lasted as long as it did. Most of the civilisations on the later worlds would never have survived so much heat."

Tchardin lost interest at the mention of heat and human survival. She didn't understand it, and Jaydin would talk on and on as if she did. She looked over the collective instead. The branches of the tree in her mind were thick and dark but the leaves that coated them glowed with a soft light. Some were dimmer than others—those were kandar she didn't know well—but a few lit up the space of her mind. One of them drew her to it as it blazed. Ryten must be particularly close by, his leaf brighter than it normally was for proximity.

She looked into Tith's branches above. Maybe she could catch a glimpse of him.

"Tchardin," Jaydin said.

A wave of revulsion ran through Tchardin and she looked down to find Jaydin's hand hovering over her arm, their auras passing through each other. Jaydin flinched back before Tchardin could pull herself away.

"It's better if you listen," Jaydin said. "I want you to understand what I'm telling you and to be able to repeat it. If I show you it may be hard for you to explain it to others."

"I can show them in turn."

Jaydin pursed her lips in a way that told Tchardin she was skeptical, but then her leaf flared bright and her thoughts grew loud. Tchardin focused on her sister's blinding leaf in the collective and an image began to form in her mind. Jaydin didn't do this often and it was difficult to receive properly, but it was Tchardin's favourite part of her sister's lectures. The image burst into red and yellow and orange, brilliant with *fire*. The image was familiar somewhere deep in Tchardin's mind but the word was not one she had ever used herself. The image swept over this fire—this burning earth—and came upon a great tree. He was straight and tall and dark against the light of the fire, the only thing in the image that could be said to be alive. As quickly as it appeared the image faded. Tchardin was left looking into her sister's eyes.

"That was Rai," Jaydin said. "The World Tree of World Seven. He should look the same even now on the restarted Earth, though I hope the fire would be gone."

Tchardin resisted the urge to ask for more detail on the fire as she knew that would get Jaydin started on another topic she wouldn't be able to stop talking about.

"I didn't see any humans," she said instead.

"There weren't many left at the end." Jaydin flipped a page in her notebook. "Those that remained had moved underground as the surface of their planet grew hot. More important is how the fires began."

Fires.

Jaydin looked up at her. "You *do* know what fire is, don't you?"

Tchardin frowned. She'd have to be extra careful about keeping her thoughts quiet while listening to her sister speak.

"The image was familiar," she admitted, "but I don't know why I know it."

"You should know it from Tith from before you were born. It's one of the few true dangers to us. Fire and the glass that can grow from it."

Jaydin said something complicated but Tchardin was distracted by the sudden vibration in her muscles. Quarter life was approaching, and with it would come her ultimate confrontation with the High Seat of the council. She knew she could use more information but she had so much trouble understanding Jaydin and the human worlds she spoke of.

Like all kandar of the past, Tchardin was meant to be assigned to one of the nine Earths at quarter life and to go to it with no previous knowledge. She was supposed to see the humans herself and learn from the generation of kandar that had been assigned there before her. Those who had lived with the humans already and learned from the kandar before them. Of course, no kandar had gone to the Earths since they were exiled. Jaydin might have been taught their history while she rested in Tith's trunk, but she'd never been there. She'd never met a human herself. Perhaps that was the reason her words failed to convey meaning to Tchardin.

The thrumming that overtook Tchardin's body was physical, but a yearning entered her mind along with the feeling. The water at the edge of the island called to her. She studied Jaydin's face as her sister spoke. Jaydin said she didn't feel it. No other kandar did, as far as Tchardin knew. The longing for something beyond had come to her early in life, but it had been easy to ignore until lately. Now the feeling pressured her almost constantly.

She got up and walked towards the edge of the branch. Jaydin stopped talking and stared after her. Sandin stirred and watched her too. Tchardin felt their eyes on her back.

"You know it's close," Jaydin said from behind her. "Are you sure you're ready?"

"Every other kandaran queen began her reign with the simple knowledge of the trees." Tchardin kept her gaze on the branches below as she responded. "The knowledge provided to each kandar—including myself—before their birth. I shouldn't need an education to be acknowledged."

"You barely remember what Tith told you," Jaydin countered, plainly disappointed. "This is the history of humanity. You have the opportunity to learn the true nature of the Purpose before you're acknowledged. None of those queens had that. More importantly, none of them were exiled to Derkra."

"You know all of this and nothing has changed."

"I am only kandar." Jaydin frowned. "I have no authority. You will be our queen."

The queen commanded the kandar. Those who sat in the trees or lay about in the clearing and did nothing would be compelled to obey her. But what should she have them do? Even Jaydin didn't know why they were exiled or how to end it. All their oldest sister could do was repeat the past at Tchardin and hope to find something new in it.

Tchardin shrugged. She walked farther down the branch and Jaydin called after her.

"There has never been a High Seat so opposed to an acknowledgment, and she knows all of this too. What I'm offering you is not an unfair advantage. It's what you'll need to match her."

She. Her. The High Seat was tevadra.

No one but the council itself was supposed to know the identity of its members, but it had been obvious to Tchardin for a long time that Jaydin was among their number. She knew too much about them and wasn't careful about letting it slip. She probably would have been dropped from the council a long time ago if she wasn't one of Tith's daughters.

Now she had revealed the High Seat to be tevadra. That eliminated half the population of Calendrai. It wasn't enough alone to figure out who the secret leader of the council was, but if Jaydin would go that far, what else would she say?

"I'm off to the water," Tchardin said instead of highlighting the mistake. "If you need me you can find me at the shore."

"Staring out at nothing again?" There was an edge to Jaydin's voice that Tchardin had never heard before. "Land Side is too far away to see and there's nothing else on Water Side to look at."

Tchardin was about to respond when the tree of the collective mind rippled. A new kandar would soon be born. That would delay her trip to the water, but for a good reason. Jaydin's lips formed into a firm line.

"You should come with me," Tchardin said. "I still don't think one is enough."

"Kandar are born." Jaydin settled herself back on the branch. "It's a fact of Derkra and has nothing to do with me. I don't know everyone here and I don't need to."

"You almost didn't know me."

"I always would have known you."

Tchardin found a clear path to the ground through the tangle below, just about the width of her shoulders. *'Only because of what I am.'*

She stepped off the branch. Sandin jumped up to watch her as she dropped into nothing.

Jaydin reached out to her, her mindvoice fading as Tchardin fell. *'You can't hold it against me that I didn't know what you would be.'*

The lower branches whistled past Tchardin as she rushed towards the ground. She passed out of them and her view to the grass became clear. The pandinzori she'd amassed in the clearing earlier still floated around below. Tchardin closed her eyes and faced towards it. It lit up the dark in shimmering bursts. She felt for it with her mind and pulled it towards her. As she approached the ground she moulded the pandinzori tightly against her body and hardened it. The cushion of solidifying light absorbed the shock of her fall. She landed softly on her feet just outside Tith's base.

'Yes, I can,' Tchardin thought mostly to herself, though it was likely Jaydin would still hear. *'I'm only what you expected each of us to be.'*

She looked up at her great father. Sandin's face showed over the edge of the branch high above, visible as a tiny dot of darkness through the green. Sandin couldn't sense or touch pandinzori, just like she couldn't bring up the collective in her mind or hear the voices of the other kandar as they all could. If Sandin leapt from Tith she would only fall.

Tchardin turned away from her father's trunk and crossed the clearing. The collective told her the new kandar would be born in Cens—the forest that encircled the great trees, beginning at the edge of Tith's canopy and those of his two brothers.

She entered the darkness of the trees and was immediately enveloped in the living forest. As soon as she stepped into its shadows it was as if she stood at the heart of it. Tall, dark trunks framed her path. Thick, dark leaves lined it above and below her. The physical scale of the forest could be seen from the great trees that hung above it, but once a kandar entered it those limits no longer seemed to apply. No one knew how deep Cens really was. Presently Tchardin could see only the trees in front of her, with no glimpse of light that indicated an exit. It would be the same if she looked back, even though she had just walked in.

The downside to being born of a great tree in the clearing was that Tchardin lacked the ability to easily navigate the living forest. Kandar born in Cens knew its quirks and could find what they wanted within it. Tchardin had wandered aimlessly many times when trying to get to the water. Luckily the signal the bearing tree gave off led her towards it.

On her way she tried to collect kandar. Calendrai was sparsely populated and Cens even more so given its undefined size. Tchardin only saw a few others on her way to the tree. Most of those ignored her. Her golden aura would tell them that eventually she would be queen, but for now, no matter how close she was, she was only kandar just like they were.

When she reached the bearing tree she had persuaded just two to join her—one tevadra and one devoshai. Ocien and Torshe. She knew Ocien—having attended the tevadra's birth shortly after her own—and Torshe was Ocien's dodenzinn. Tchardin was happy they'd found each other so quickly after quarter life.

The pandinzori that flowed from the bearing tree pulsated up and down his trunk. The result was an undulating beam of light that reached high into the canopy and spread through a burst of foliage. Pandinzori was made by the trees, and never so much as just before a kandar was born.

The three kandar waited while the collective in Tchardin's mind swayed in imitation of the tree before them. Finally a riveting crack cut through the air and the trunk of the tree split. The wood creaked as it opened wider, wide enough for shoulders and hips to squeeze through. A tevadra walked onto the forest floor and the collective mind grew a leaf. That leaf would stay in the collective until the tevadra went to rest in her father again.

At the same time that leaf came into existence, it grew in Tchardin's mind and in the minds of the two other kandar who bore witness. Tchardin examined its newly formed brilliance. The tevadra's name was Kor.

Kor came forward to meet those who had gathered to greet her. Tchardin smiled. Kor would be happy to see that three had come for her birth. Even happier to see that one of those three had the golden aura.

There had only been one kandar at Tchardin's birth, one tevadra to witness the creation of her leaf. When she had stepped from the great trunk—the sliver that opened for her dwarfed by the thickness of Tith's base—Tchardin had expected the entire population of Calendrai to be waiting. Tith hadn't told her of her aura, but he had told her of his greatness. The kandar were supposed to appreciate that.

When she stepped into the world she'd seen one solitary kandar waiting to witness her birth, the birth of a daughter with the golden aura, she who would be queen. It had been Sandin. Sandin—who hadn't even heard the call of birth go out through the collective, who would never have her leaf. Tchardin had appreciated her sister's presence but she had deserved more. Every kandar did. It was the reason Tchardin went to all the new births.

Ocien and Torshe stayed close to Kor, so the living forest wouldn't separate them from each other before she could be welcomed. Tchardin would have waited to speak with the new kandar but the longing returned, irresistible, compelling her to go to the water.

She backed away from the three kandar until Cens hid them. Then she turned towards the feeling. It guided her through the labyrinthine paths of the forest, allowing her to pass out of the trees with less difficulty than she was used to.

When she broke into the light the sand of the shore spread out before her and her throbbing mind was placated. The longing drew her eyes to a certain point on the horizon as it always did. She scarcely noticed the tevadra beside her until the other spoke.

"What are you looking at?" Damarin asked.

Tchardin was mesmerised by the infinity of Water Side. There was nothing out there to break a kandar's gaze. It seemed to continue forever, and if they were by chance on the side of the island that looked away from Land Side, then it did in fact continue forever. Both Land Side and Water Side were infinite planes. Black Valley—the old city of the kandar—was the only anomaly in the endless dunes of Land Side and their new home—the island of Calendrai—was the only break in the mirror-smooth surface of Water Side.

Damarin followed her eyes. The two stood unmoving for some time.

"I don't know what I'm looking at," Tchardin finally answered.

Half sky, half water, the two halves of the horizon seemed to reflect each other. The view was of one nearly solid sheet of blue permeated by bursts of light from pandinzori. It was the furthest thing from the forest. There was something about one spot out there—Tchardin could actually point to it in the sea of sameness—that called to her.

"What are *you* looking at?" she returned the question.

Damarin didn't answer. Tchardin ripped her gaze away from the water and looked at Tith's third daughter, their middle sister. As usual, the uncanny resemblance to Kadailin confused her eyes for a moment. The two looked like human sisters were said to look, as if they had some common inheritance. But the name of *'sisters'* given to the daughters of Tith by the kandar was only a way of dealing with their strangeness. Kandar weren't meant to have siblings. Tith was the only tree who had ever borne more than one child in the same generation—Jaydin swore to it. Physically Damarin and Kadailin could have been the same kandar. Only their height and auras were different.

Damarin was still, but her eyes were hungry. No kandar had admitted to sharing Tchardin's longing, but recently she'd wondered if she and Damarin were looking at the same thing.

"You're meant to be acknowledged soon," Damarin said, still watching the horizon. "Will you be a great queen to the kandar?"

"I will be a queen," Tchardin answered, not exactly sure what Damarin wanted her to say. "How would you define great?"

"Will you change things?"

Tchardin was reminded of all of Jaydin's expectations. Lead the kandar. Free them from exile. Bring them back to the humans. Fulfill the Purpose. "I hope to."

"Good," Damarin responded. "So do I."

Tchardin looked at the horizon again. So much pressure to change their situation. To return them to the Earths. Yet no one knew how she could do it. Was that all that could make her great? Did she really know what that meant?

She turned away and entered Cens. Maybe she could find Kadailin or Ryten in the trees to take her mind off her impending responsibility.

Chapter 2

Tchardin walked reluctantly across one of Tith's branches towards Sirrhon. A council meeting had been called and she felt compelled to attend, mostly because Jaydin would mention it to her if she didn't. She stopped when she reached the place where Tith's thick branch ran almost parallel with one of Sirrhon's. The place where the council met.

The council had arranged themselves on Sirrhon's branch—the smaller of the two and slightly higher—and dozens of kandar filled the other. A large shadow obscured the council, darkening the members' features and blurring their shapes. They still looked like kandar, but all detail was erased, making it impossible to tell whether they were tevadra or devoshai, let alone who they were. Even the number of them seemed to change on occasion, the shadows sliding over them so they were impossible to count.

The collective itself was dimmed in the area. When a kandar approached the council shadow they could no longer search the tree in their mind to find others. This close, the thoughts that should have buzzed in Tchardin's mind were muted. It made her feel hindered, like she could no longer see or hear as well as she normally did, but only her mind was truly affected.

Jaydin stood with the kandar on Tith's branch, facing the council. She'd been doing that a lot lately—pretending she wasn't a member and supporting Tchardin in the crowd as she approached quarter life. Sandin was there too, although Tchardin couldn't see why. Council meetings took place in the mind. No kandar here would speak aloud for her.

The Voice of the council was already speaking when Tchardin arrived.

'We can no longer ascend to Coralynth. The nine Earths that were entrusted to us by Creator are lost and we languish in exile.'

Tchardin walked into the crowd of kandar occupying Tith's branch. She knew all those around her who were younger than she, having attended their births. Some nodded as she walked by them. The older kandar were less interested in greeting her. Sometimes when she passed one the collective would grow a leaf, and she was shocked to find she had never met them before, but it shouldn't surprise her. Kandar on Calendrai were difficult to find, let alone get to know. By nature they were solitary, and the older they were the more wary of her—some having been present for the births of all four of her sisters before her.

She passed Ryten on the branch and the big devoshai turned to watch her. Jaydin thought he was Tchardin's dodenzinn. Another thing their oldest sister talked about publicly that no other kandar would dare comment on. He was well past quarter life and should have found his other half by now, but sometimes the pairings were strange like that. None of her sisters had found theirs yet and both Sandin and Jaydin were older than Ryten. Tchardin couldn't know hers for sure until she passed quarter life. Then it should become immediately obvious who it was.

She stopped beside Jaydin and listened with the others.

'What are we without the Purpose?' the Voice asked, the words eclipsing all other muted thoughts in the collective. *'What is a kandar without the Earths? What use is a guardian race with no access to those they are meant to guide?'*

Jaydin said the role of the council had changed when they came to Calendrai and found themselves exiled. Back when the kandar had access to the nine Earths the council had chosen which of them were best suited to each world and sent them off to guide it. The council would then be called upon to make decisions on the type and scope of the guidance provided. Under the leadership of their High Seat they had judged how much interference was required and acceptable. The Voice had spoken their decrees. Now all the council did was talk.

'Where is Tchar, the first of us? And Dani, the second? Do they wait on Coralynth for our return or have they left us?'

Tchardin turned to leave. The council's words wouldn't help her change things for her people. Jaydin gestured at her to stay but she had heard this a thousand times before. Some of the kandar watched her go. None followed.

She walked slowly away along Tith's branch. When it met another of Sirrhon's she switched over to his and walked back towards Tith's trunk. The branch curved upwards and she followed its slope until it became too steep to walk easily, then she jumped to another. She walked up and up through the branches until she came to an opening in the leaves.

She looked over Cens and onto Water Side. She searched the horizon for that special place that called her and focused on it. The feeling was even more intense now.

"I think I know what it is."

Tchardin looked for the source of the voice but there was no one to be seen. She studied the collective and found a leaf bright. Then a face resolved out of the shadows. Damarin walked up beside her.

"Damarin," Tchardin said with a little relief, happy to see Jaydin's enthusiasm hadn't forced her to follow. "I didn't see you at the meeting."

"I didn't attend. Just another occasion to make the High Seat feel important."

Tchardin had never seen Damarin at a meeting before, but her attendance would have explained her presence in the high canopy when she was usually at the shore. Damarin followed Tchardin's gaze to the water.

"You feel drawn to a certain point on the horizon, don't you?" she asked. "It's very specific and always the same. You could point to it from anywhere in Calendrai."

Tchardin looked over at her sister and saw in her eyes a yearning for what lay beyond the horizon. Damarin *was* looking at the same thing she was.

"The thing that calls you," Damarin said. "That calls *us*. It's something on Land Side. Maybe it's Black Valley. Maybe even Ovaeron."

Ovaeron. Tchardin raised her eyebrows. The father of all kandar through Tchar, the first of them. The legendary tree had been left behind when the kandar abandoned Black Valley, departing Land Side and the place of their birth to come to Calendrai after the kandaran war.

She focused on the patch of sky that called her. Calendrai was an island city on an infinite plane. You could look out from it in infinite directions and see only infinite water. The likelihood they looked directly towards Black Valley was almost zero. The likelihood they faced Land Side at all was only half.

But Damarin could be right. According to the trees there was nothing else on Water Side that would draw the eye or mind. Why would they both choose this tiny part of an infinite sky to become obsessed with? How could they?

"When you first appeared to share my interest I wasn't sure," Damarin said, "but as you've approached quarter life I've grown more certain."

"Why does it matter what it is?" Tchardin had never wondered what exactly called her from the water. It had only mattered that something did.

"I think we need to go there. Back to our birthplace."

"But why? All the kandar are here now. Black Valley is deserted. Land Side is empty."

"How do you know that?"

Tchardin didn't answer, the response was so obvious. If Damarin really wanted to hear it she could listen to Tchardin's thoughts.

"The word of the trees," Damarin murmured, doing exactly that. "You believe them without reserve, as all kandar do."

"Of course I do." Their names and the knowledge provided by their fathers were the only things the kandar were born knowing. "Their word is all we have to tell us about the world."

"They've been wrong before."

Tchardin was shocked by Damarin's statement. It was the first time she had heard the word of the trees questioned. "About what?"

"Jaydin says before we came to Calendrai the trees told us there was nothing on Water Side but lifeless water. No island. No trees. No pand-inzori. According to our fathers this land we stand on didn't exist."

"But it does exist," Tchardin said.

"It does. The trees told us Water Side was created empty, yet we stand on an island on Water Side now."

Tchardin struggled with the apparent contradiction. The word of the trees was natural law. It was truth plain and simple.

"Do you believe it could be something on Land Side that calls us?" Damarin asked.

"I guess it could be."

"Is it necessarily empty if the trees say it is?"

Tchardin hesitated. The trees said Land Side was abandoned but what Damarin said about Calendrai made their word suspect. Either the trees had been wrong—and Calendrai had always been on Water Side—or Derkra had changed, and Derkra didn't change.

Tchardin searched for Damarin's thoughts in the collective. Thoughts that rejected the word of the trees. To think like that was so contrary to their way of life that Tchardin understood now why Damarin rarely came into the clearing. Just as Derkra didn't change, so kandar didn't question. She only found a slight buzz around Damarin's leaf. No way to interpret its meaning.

"It has to be something on Land Side," Damarin said when Tchardin didn't answer, "and I'm going to prove it."

"You can't. It's impossible to return—"

"It's possible."

Tchardin tried to remember what Jaydin had told her about the move to Calendrai. After the war a tevadra called Carrensing had been called to the water—similar, now that Tchardin thought about it, to her own situation. Jaydin said Carrensing shifted into nothing and found Calendrai on the other side. She had returned to Black Valley to take the entire population of kandar with her, leaving their city of origin on Land Side empty. She had then been called to rest by Tith.

"But we've lost the shift," Tchardin said. "There's no way for us to repeat Carrensing's journey."

"I don't propose we shift."

"How then?"

"Cross the water. Just the two of us, as humans would, on a raft."

"A *raft*?" Tchardin struggled with the unfamiliar word.

"A flat bed of branches—lashed together—that floats on the water. We could easily make one."

Bed? *Lashed*? *Floats*? Tchardin stared blankly at Damarin. Her sister's thoughts grew forceful and an image formed in Tchardin's mind. Bed. Branches. Lashed. Floating. She saw the raft for a moment, then she stared at Damarin in horror.

"You need to spend more time with other kandar, Damarin, you're losing your mind."

Damarin shrugged.

A terrifying thought came to Tchardin. She looked over the water, looked out to the horizon—limitless and unbroken. "Have you tried it before?"

"No." Damarin followed her gaze. Her thoughts had returned to a nearly silent hum in the collective. "I haven't."

Water Side wasn't meant for the kandar. Despite the longing she felt, Tchardin had never considered actually going *into* the water. There were no trees on the water. There wasn't even anything in the water, if Tchardin remembered what Jaydin had said correctly. It was just blue, and clear, and you would sink into it if you tried to step on it.

Damarin leaned towards her. "You can point to that spot from anywhere in Calendrai, anywhere in Cens even?"

"I can."

"I don't think it will be any different on the water."

"But a raft, Damarin? What if it fails?" Tchardin shuddered. Dying in the water wouldn't be the same as going to rest in the trees. They could lose their bodies. Never feel Tith again. Never be reborn. "The water could *kill* us."

"I won't let that happen," Damarin said. "We have to try."

"We don't."

"But why not? Don't you want to go somewhere new? Learn more about our world? Not just from Jaydin—from talking—but from seeing it yourself? Derkra is more than just Calendrai."

"It really might not be," Tchardin said.

Damarin sighed. She looked at the horizon in silence for a moment before turning back to Tchardin. "Have you considered that we may never find our way out of exile from here? We left our birthplace and lost our Purpose. Maybe we have to go back to Black Valley to find it. Isn't that what Jaydin would want you to do?"

Tchardin frowned. Jaydin had been relentless in trying to educate her in pursuit of acknowledgment, so sure Tchardin could lead them back to the Purpose once she was queen. Their oldest sister had never mentioned returning to Land Side but she also hadn't given Tchardin any realistic ways they might help themselves from Calendrai. Four generations in their new home and nothing had changed. What if the reason they hadn't found a way back to the Earths was because they were trapped on the island? Tchardin looked at the water and the longing pulled at her. She felt a need to cross it.

No. Water was not for the kandar.

"I need to stay here, with our people," Tchardin said. "There are no kandar on Land Side and the water is too dangerous. I am to be acknowledged—"

"You may not be. That aura isn't fixed and I've seen it waver before."

Tchardin opened her mouth to respond but stopped. Jaydin tried not to talk about the fact that Tchardin's aura wasn't guaranteed to stay gold but Damarin was right. In the first quarter of her life it had become faint on occasion, but it always came back brighter. She had to be close enough to quarter life that there wasn't time to lose it. She would be acknowledged soon.

"I *will* be queen," she asserted.

Damarin laughed. "What kind of a queen could you be to the kandar in exile? Only an irrelevant queen with no plan to return us to the Purpose." She backed into Tith's shadows and disappeared. *'Find me when you're ready to go,'* her mindvoice added.

Tchardin was left speechless. She looked out at the water again. That argument was more convincing. Quarter life was approaching, but even as the acknowledged queen of the kandar there was no guarantee she could find a way back to the Earths for her people. Maybe Damarin was right. Maybe the answer *was* on Land Side.

***

The shadow over the council broke up slowly. It never fully cleared—the area had to be somewhat shaded for the council members to arrive without being recognised—but it lightened. Jaydin had remained on Tith's branch with Sandin after the rest of the kandar left. She resisted the urge to go to Tchardin.

"You have to wait for her," Sandin said.

Sometimes Jaydin found it hard to believe her sister couldn't hear her thoughts, despite knowing Sandin had no place in the collective.

"It's not like we don't have time," Sandin continued. "Giving her a moment to escape isn't going to break the world."

"It might already be broken." Jaydin sighed. It had been a long time since the human worlds had kandaran guidance and so many had already been so far gone. "I just want to go back to the Earths. I can't help but be impatient."

"You can't go back," Sandin corrected, "when you've never been there."

Jaydin closed her eyes and images of her time with Tith flashed through her mind. Humanity. The Earths that were its home. Thousands of generations worth of history rushed by in a moment.

"Maybe not," she said, "but I *have* seen them."

Jaydin knew what her purpose was. She knew she would be better serving on the Earths with the humans. She knew what most of the kandar had forgotten and couldn't seem to understand. They had been created to fulfill a purpose and that purpose had been abandoned.

The kandaran world, Derkra, was a world of infinite sand and water—endless empty desert and desolate ocean. It was impressive in its scale but not in much else. Ovaeron and Tith were grander than the World Trees on the Earths, but other than those two Derkra had few great trees, and the variety in those it did have was sorely lacking. Images flashed behind Jaydin's eyes. The World Trees. The other great trees that sometimes stood with them on the Earths. The trees that made up the forests that covered great spans of land. Derkra had only one forest. Cens was unique as far as Jaydin knew, in that it was the only forest that could be said to be truly alive, but it was small and plain. There were only trees, moss, and grass contained within it, whereas the forests of the Earths were teeming with abundant plant and animal life. She had seen them. She saw them now.

Waves. Images of violent water, of still water, of the creatures that lived beneath both came to her. The water on the Earths was breathtakingly beautiful. The humans had waterfalls, rivers, lakes, salted seas and deep oceans where Derkra had only Water Side, flat and featureless for as far as they could see. And empty. The waters of Derkra were dead.

The Earths had suns, moons, day and night, light and darkness, where Derkra had only ubiquitous light with no apparent source and floating shadows that chose their places to cling at random. Not that it bothered the kandar. Jaydin was the only one who knew any different. There was no wind to ruffle the leaves of the trees. No mountains or valleys to break up the landscape. Only Calendrai—which was flat where it rose slightly above the water—and the dunes of Land Side which were static and unchanging and had been since the beginning of time.

Even the humans themselves were magnificent by comparison. No kandar could stand up to them now. Pandinzori was used only to save a climb down the trunks of the great trees, when in the past it had been used to create marvels. The members of the guardian race had slowly become more dull, more uniform as time passed away from the Earths. Of course they had, having only Derkra and other kandar to interact with.

The images in Jaydin's mind spoke of things the kandar of this generation had never experienced and maybe never would. By now the humans could have changed the faces of their worlds. Without kandaran guidance everything could have been destroyed. The Earths could even be gone. No one had seen them in generations. World Nine at least... Well, anything was possible. Jaydin stood up.

"I'm going after her," she said to Sandin, who frowned.

Jaydin turned and ran into Tchardin. She recoiled immediately, flustered, as a pulse of revulsion ran through her body from her sister's aura. She must have been too caught up in her thoughts of the Earths to notice Tchardin's leaf grow bright in the collective.

She fought the strong urge to put distance between their auras with her relief. Tchardin had come to her. That had to be better than chasing the future queen all through Calendrai and attempting to force her to learn.

"I was just about to go looking for you," Jaydin said.

Sandin moved closer and Tchardin looked up at her.

"Quarter life is almost upon you—" Jaydin began, but Tchardin interrupted.

"I want to know more about Black Valley."

Sandin raised an eyebrow. Jaydin felt the same but didn't react.

"Why?" Jaydin asked.

Tchardin looked off into the distance, between Tith's leaves, and out to the water. Jaydin was reminded of Damarin.

"You think you're seeing Ovaeron, don't you?" Tchardin's gaze snapped back onto her. Jaydin smiled inside, pleased at having guessed her youngest sister's thoughts without searching for them. "You'll be the queen of Calendrai soon. Your focus should be here. Black Valley is our past."

"I'll be queen of the kandar. Black Valley is the birthplace of the kandar. I thought you of all tevadra—"

"Black Valley is the history of the kandar. Calendrai is our present and our future. Tith told you about Black Valley before you were born. What he told you was enough."

"But why abandon it?"

Jaydin turned away. Those images were blurrier. Tith had told her a lot about Carrensing—the tevadra who had last come to him in rest—but there were pieces missing. Jaydin knew Carrensing had brought the kandar to Calendrai, and she knew the reason for the move had something to do with the kandaran war, but she didn't know it exactly, and that contrasted so sharply with everything else she knew. She wondered as she had many times before if the great tree had chosen to omit that information for a reason.

"You're so close to acknowledgement," she said. "You know the High Seat isn't going to let the ceremony go smoothly. She *will* test you, and not on your knowledge of Derkra."

Tchardin backed away from her.

"We can talk about the shift to Coralynth if you prefer. I've seen how the kandar used to do it. If we could only get back to the path—"

"Why should I be able to open it when no one else can?"

"Carrensing was exceptional in the shift—"

"What does that have to do with me?"

Jaydin didn't answer. This was familiar territory for them. Tith was the only tree to have birthed more than one kandar in the same generation and as far as they knew the only kandar he'd taken in rest was Carrensing. There should have been more, for five tevadra to be born, but Tith had never mentioned them to Jaydin. Another piece of information she was missing. If Tith had made Carrensing into Tchardin, as Jaydin expected—who else would be Carrensing but the tevadra with the golden aura—it was possible she retained some of the tevadra's abilities. Great kandar made great kandar in the new generation.

Jaydin turned away from her two sisters and sat down on the branch.

She motioned for Tchardin to do the same. Her youngest sister complied and didn't say anything. Sandin sat as well. Jaydin focused on the pandinzori around her and lifted her notebook into the light.

She opened it to a random page and scanned it. Not for information—she knew everything contained in its pages as if it were written on the inside of her mind—but for comfort. It was reassuring to see some of her vast knowledge contained in a small, finite thing.

"Why do you keep it?" Tchardin asked.

Jaydin saw the poorly masked confusion on Tchardin's face. Her notebook was the only human thing on Derkra—the only human thing any other kandar of this generation had ever seen.

"I know too much," Jaydin said honestly, for maybe the first time in her life. "It's overwhelming and almost wholly useless because I'm not able to apply it in exile."

Sandin looked concerned. Jaydin realised this information might be new even to her.

"To know all the history of existence when the kandar have always been uninterested in history. Unaware of it, even. To think of how to use it, how it affects us, if at all..." Tchardin wouldn't understand if she continued. Tith had told Jaydin too much before she was born and he had never told her why. "I am only kandar," she said. "Tith must have taught me these things for a reason. Without the Purpose, it seems like this must be it. To record them. To teach them."

"Without the Earths I can't apply them either."

Jaydin shook her head in annoyance. "Something in here must be able to help you return us to the Purpose. Or even one of the other kandar. The problem is they don't care about the things I know. They'll only care when you are queen and *you* tell them to care."

Tchardin's expression was utterly blank. Jaydin looked into her eyes and it was obvious she was lost in her mind. She seemed to look to the water again, the slight buzz of her thoughts passing through the collective. Jaydin placed her hand against the edge of the pandinzori at Tchardin's forearm, so their auras touched slightly.

Tchardin's eyes brightened as the spark of repulsion passed between them. "What if we can't go back until we return to Black Valley?"

Jaydin seethed with exasperation. "Did Damarin put this in your head?"

Tchardin looked away.

***

Kadailin hung off some of Ahron's thinner branches near the edge of Cens, looking down into the forest. She was as far out as she could go and still be supported. The leaves below her were full of pandinzori.

'Kadailin,' her name floated into her mind. *'I need you.'*

She searched the collective for the mindvoice. Definitely Tchardin. Probably being forced to listen to Jaydin's endless droning. Kadailin couldn't help being jealous although she knew it was dull from Tchardin's descriptions of it. Jaydin had never shown much interest in educating Kadailin. No one but Tchardin had shown much interest in her at all.

Kadailin dreaded interrupting their oldest sister. And Sandin would be there too. But she had to go. She could never ignore Tchardin.

Loosening her grip on the branches above, she let those below and around her support her. She reached ahead and slowly pulled and pushed herself through the mesh of small branches until she felt she could stand safely on a larger branch. Then she started to descend. As she got closer to Ahron's trunk his branches grew farther apart and her reach failed her. She jumped from one down to the next until she was past Ahron and into Tith.

She searched the collective for Tchardin and found her close by and slightly below. Jaydin was there too, and Kadailin could only assume Sandin, although she couldn't know for sure since Sandin didn't have a leaf.

Kadailin ran along the large branch until she saw them and dropped down behind Tchardin. Better to surprise the future queen than the other two and she didn't want to land in the middle of the three.

Jaydin frowned at her. "Tchardin doesn't have time for you right now."

"I have to go," Tchardin blurted. Before Jaydin could say anything else she dropped off the branch.

Kadailin smiled weakly at the two tevadra, now clearly angry, and followed quickly after her. When they were in the grass below the three towering trees Tchardin began to walk towards Cens. Kadailin moved beside her and matched her pace.

"I need to go to the water," Tchardin said.

Kadailin tried to stop herself from cringing but Tchardin noticed.

"You don't have to come. I just needed a reason to leave Jaydin."

"I'll walk through Cens with you," Kadailin suggested in compromise.

Kadailin had always wondered who Jaydin thought the bigger disappointment, herself or Tchardin. On one hand, Jaydin had been expecting Carrensing and a queen at Kadailin's birth and had been unimpressed with what she got. On the other, she had gotten a tevadra with a golden aura from Tchardin's birth, but to her great dismay Tchardin was turning out to be more and more like Kadailin despite that. And Jaydin often blamed Tchardin's lack of interest in learning on Kadailin.

"I'm happy we left quickly," she said.

Tchardin made a sympathetic face towards her. "You should spend more time with Jaydin. The things she says might be confusing but at least she has something to say. She couldn't put any pressure on *you.*"

Kadailin didn't respond. She focused on the passing branches to avoid her sister's gaze.

"Or Sandin alone," Tchardin continued. "Or maybe Ocien. I attended her birth—do you know her?"

"Not well."

Kadailin didn't think anything less of Tchardin for attending all the kandar's births, though it was generally considered a waste of time. It was better that she know as many kandar as possible for when she became queen, or at least that was how Kadailin felt. She also still felt bad for missing Tchardin's birth. She expected a lot of kandar did.

Tchardin continued. "Maybe Damarin—"

"No." Kadailin shuddered. Jaydin and Sandin ignored her, but Damarin seemed to hate her. It might be that the two looked so much alike. Every kandar who could be provoked into conversation in their presence said so. Damarin couldn't stand that they shared that small thing. Appearance on Derkra should have been irrelevant, when most kandar only looked at auras, but if even one noticed their similarity that was too much for their middle sister.

They walked in silence for a moment. Tchardin seemed to know exactly where she was going. That was strange. Kadailin had always considered herself to be the best of the sisters at navigating Cens. Maybe even better than Damarin.

"Quarter life," Tchardin said. "Soon to be queen. Then I need to find a way to return us to the Earths. Something no kandar has been able to do since we moved here."

Kadailin looked around, paying attention to their surroundings for the first time since they'd entered Cens. The trees were incredibly dense as always but she had a feeling they were close to the edge.

"I guess that's a reason to listen to Jaydin," she said. "If anyone can figure out how to get us back to Coralynth it must be her."

Tchardin was silent. Kadailin turned towards her. She appeared to be deep in thought. She stopped walking.

"Nothing she's told me has helped," Tchardin said. "But Damarin suggested something I'd never thought of before. Do you think we could rediscover the shift if we returned to Black Valley?"

"You'd have to ask Jaydin."

"Jaydin told me to forget about it."

Kadailin had to admit that seemed reasonable. "There's nothing in Black Valley."

"I'm not sure that's true."

Tchardin was staring hard at something now. Kadailin followed her gaze but didn't see anything, just the trees of Cens and the shadows that littered them. "What is it?" she asked, perturbed.

Tchardin's posture had changed completely. She looked possessed, as if her whole body and mind were being put into wanting something. Kadailin had never seen anything like it.

"Tchardin—" she started, but her sister walked ahead. She followed. An instant later they were on the shore.

Tchardin continued forward but Kadailin shied away from the edge of the water. Everything there was too strange to her. Water Side was a barrier she knew she would never cross and preferred to avoid entirely if possible. Tchardin was intent on her course and Kadailin worried she would walk right into the water.

Tchardin stopped at the last moment and continued her uncanny staring at the horizon. Then Kadailin noticed something even more disturbing. Damarin stood a few steps away and she mimicked Tchardin in stance and gaze. Kadailin stepped back into the treeline and was swallowed by quiet forest. The water was bad enough but Damarin was too much. She turned back towards the centre of Calendrai.

Like most things Tchardin had, Kadailin wished that strange obsession was hers. She wanted something unique, some reason for the kandar to notice her. All her sisters had something special.

Looking at the trees around her and growing calmer as they soothed her, she rethought that. She wanted to be special, that was true, but at the same time she also felt like she had escaped relatively unscathed from Tith. She, at least, was only kandar.

***

Tchardin shook herself and noticed Kadailin had left. She felt the pull of the horizon more now that she might know what it was. She'd been obsessed before but now she needed it. Needed to know.

She twisted away from the water and found Damarin watching her.

"Has it gotten worse for you since we spoke?" her sister asked.

"Much worse," Tchardin admitted.

"It's been unbearable since I've known what it could be. Why do you think I rarely leave the shore?"

Tchardin had always assumed Damarin was particularly antisocial. A kandar with her personality would likely be found in Cens, hiding away from the rest of their people. But Damarin wasn't born in Cens. Being born of Tith would exclude her from the secret world of the forest as it did Tchardin and their three other sisters. So Tchardin had assumed the shore was her substitute. This made a lot more sense.

"Why didn't you say something sooner?" Tchardin asked.

"No one else understands it. When I saw it grow in you as it grew in me I knew I needed to do something about it. That we could do it together. What you felt before was nothing. It'll only get stronger."

Damarin sounded almost sympathetic. The pull overwhelmed Tchardin as her sister spoke. She looked at the forest and back at the water and knew which she would choose. But she would be queen and there was nothing she could do about that.

"I'll go on my own if you won't come—" Damarin said, but Tchardin was already halfway to the treeline.

She broke through it and the forest surrounded her, the leaves and branches crowded her. She tried to focus on the trees, the island, her world, but it was no use. Only one thing consumed her thoughts.

Chapter 3

Sandin sat on the soft forest floor and tried to relax. She leaned back against a trunk and closed her eyes. She needed a moment away from Jaydin and all her sister's worries about Tchardin becoming queen. She needed to get away from the kandar. All of them.

At least when she closed her eyes and shut out the world she was left in quiet darkness. She couldn't understand what it would be like to have all the voices of the kandar in her head constantly. Jaydin said you learned to block them out if you worked at it but Sandin doubted they could ever have real quiet. And pandinzori was supposed to be something you could see behind your eyes, even when you closed them, because it wasn't a physical seeing. For the kandar, darkness was just as elusive as silence.

But not for Sandin. When she closed her eyes she saw nothing. When she removed herself from the clearing she heard nothing. Sometimes she cherished that solitude, but it was also lonely. The other kandar didn't interact much—Sandin was lucky Jaydin spent so much time with her—but they all had that special connection to one another. They were never left alone in their minds.

Sandin was always alone in her mind. No one had been able to penetrate it. That made her very strange amongst the kandar. Jaydin said it might even be human, because as far as they knew the humans didn't connect in their minds. Jaydin said there were too many of them, and on certain worlds it was even difficult for the kandar to connect with all of them and stay sane.

Jaydin had admitted to Sandin once that there was no previous instance of a kandar born without a mindvoice, without a place in the collective mind. Never a kandar who couldn't see pandinzori and therefore couldn't manipulate it. At least not in Jaydin's vast memory that spanned generations. Tith's memory. Sandin would live and rest and no one would ever know what she was. A blip on the history of the kandar that, after Jaydin was gone, no one would bother to remember.

Would it be worse if Tchardin returned them to their Purpose and brought them back to the human worlds? Would Sandin be better off on the Earths? Or would the lack of access to pandinzori make life there impossible for her? Perhaps she couldn't even go.

She opened her eyes to let the world back in. Then she heard footsteps. Two sets. They were playful, erratic. She suspected the kandar who made them talked, maybe even laughed together, their buzzing thoughts making their interaction plain to any other kandar around them, but as usual, for her, there was nothing.

She got up quietly and climbed into the tree she'd been leaning against. As she ascended, his shadows clung to her skin and came with her to hide her. It was her natural state to be shrouded. Jaydin had once said that Sandin's superior ability to blend into the forest made up for the fact that she couldn't identify kandar by their auras or mindvoices, couldn't sense them approaching. She would see them before they saw her. Courtesy of her lack of a place in the collective, they often didn't see her at all.

Tchardin and Ryten passed by below her.

Sandin relied on her vision more than any other kandar. Most of them wouldn't be able to describe the two who passed. They might say Tchardin had dark hair, skin, and eyes, but the finer details of her face and features would be lost to them. Tchardin's golden aura—visible to all kandar except Sandin—and the brightness of her leaf in the collective obscured them and made them unimportant. Take that aura away and any normal kandar would have trouble distinguishing between the youngest of Tith's daughters and half the rest of the tevadra in Calendrai who had similar colouring.

Sandin had nothing beyond the physical to go by, and since kandar looked mostly alike she coveted their unique characteristics. It was almost funny that her closest friend and sister had one of the most distinctive features in Calendrai. Jaydin's hair was as red as Ovaeron's leaves were said to be, though Sandin had never been able to receive an image of the great tree to compare.

Tchardin was not so striking. Only her eyes were out of the ordinary. They were much darker than expected. Almost black. Damarin and Kadailin's eyes were nearly as dark, but those two sisters were distinguished by their darker skin. Tchardin's skin tone was medium brown from a distance and nothing unique, the shadows that wrapped her obscuring a typical dappled pattern. Her black eyes against her brown skin were really her only individual physical trait. If the kandar didn't have such sharp vision Sandin would have missed the difference.

Ryten was much easier to identify because he was huge. As far as Sandin knew he was the biggest devoshai in Calendrai.

Examining them, she thought of humans. Jaydin had attempted to describe them to Sandin many times since she was born because Tith hadn't given her images. It was only through comparison with the kandar that she could understand the things her sister had said.

Adult humans were meant to be a similar size to the kandar, who were born full-sized and never grew. Jaydin said human skin was often a uniform shade, ranging from as black as Ovaeron's trunk to as pale as the lightest grain of sand—two more things Sandin had never seen—unlike the skin of the kandar which came in similar shades but displayed the dappled pattern of light through leaves. Human skin and hair also changed, while that of the kandar never did, not from the moment they were made through their many lives. Humans had no aura to distinguish them from one another, and no shadows clung to them to obscure their bodies. They would be wreathed in swirling and growing pandinzori, as the trees were, because they created it, but Sandin wouldn't be able to see that. She wondered if there were many humans as large as Ryten.

She watched them for a moment longer, perched high above in the tree, covered in shifting shadows. They didn't look up, and there was no way they would notice her unless they did. But if they spoke aloud they spoke quietly enough that she couldn't hear them. She gained nothing by watching them. She jumped down before they could get lost in the trees.

One of them must have heard her land because they both spun around to face her. Ryten stared at her in silence and Sandin recognised the attempt to connect with her mind that was so common among the other kandar. Tchardin had no such trouble.

"Sandin," she said. "What are you doing alone?"

"I don't spend *all* my time with Jaydin," Sandin answered, a little offended though she knew Tchardin hadn't meant anything by the comment. Ryten hovered by Tchardin and avoided Sandin's eyes. "What are you two doing?"

"Staying far away from Jaydin," Tchardin said.

Sandin frowned. If Tchardin didn't want Jaydin to find her she was going about it the right way. Jaydin was hopeless at navigating the living forest. She was probably the least proficient of the five sisters when it came to Cens. The big devoshai beside Tchardin smirked and Sandin turned her disapproval on him. He would be better than all of them because he had been born in the forest. With his help Tchardin could hide forever.

Ryten looked at the ground when he noticed her attention. Sandin ignored his discomfort. It wasn't unusual for the kandar to be uneasy with her flaw.

"You shouldn't be avoiding her," she said. "You should really be with Jaydin when quarter life comes upon you."

"Or with me," Ryten said. He and Tchardin exchanged a quick glance.

Sandin had to restrain herself from expressing the surprise she felt. Jaydin thought Ryten was Tchardin's dodenzinn and she hadn't been quiet about it, but there was always doubt until both kandar reached quarter life. No kandar would mention the possibility to the one they expected until it was a sure thing. Ryten was very bold to say what he said. Especially when there was even more doubt in this instance. But Sandin wasn't sure anyone had told Tchardin that. She raised an eyebrow at the big devoshai.

He looked down at Tchardin and Sandin could tell from their expressions that they spoke silently for a moment. Then he turned and disappeared into the trees. Tchardin was left staring after him.

Sandin reached towards her and stopped when she felt the shock of her youngest sister's aura connecting with her own. It was always strange to feel the result of a contact she couldn't see. Tchardin's eyes regained focus.

"You should come with me to find Jaydin," Sandin finally said. "Your acknowledgement—"

"No."

Tchardin backed away, disappearing into shadow and leaving no trace Sandin could follow. Without access to the collective she would never find her sister in the living forest.

***

Tchardin rushed through the trees, angrily pushing aside branches that blocked her path and mentally apologising to Cens for her haste. The urge to run to the water, to wade into it even, beat strongly in her.

She ran through Cens, ducking branches, darting past trunks. The forest was dark and apparently endless but she felt the edge approaching. Then the world shook.

She fell to her knees, skidding across the forest floor before finally resting. Her muscles clenched involuntarily. The tension that had been building, telling her she would soon be queen was released all at once. Her vision blurred. Her cheek pressed into the grass as she fell. She opened her eyes. Her body no longer hummed. She felt stagnant, yet changed.

A bundle of brown sticks walked past her nose. Tchardin jumped up off the forest floor. She scanned the shadowed ground around her. There was no sign of the strange object. She dismissed it as a symptom of the change.

She was about to continue towards the shore when the council called her. It was insistent—a demand, not a request. The collective pulsed in her mind, and that pulse originated at her own leaf. All the kandar in Calendrai would be called to accept her as their queen, to formally acknowledge her so her aura would matter.

Her vision must still be fuzzy. She thought she saw red in the forest where there had only ever been green and brown. There seemed to be scattered red leaves on the ground and spread throughout the branches. Pandinzori surrounded her, so bright it was almost blinding.

The council called again. She panicked. She wanted to see the horizon one last time before the ceremony. She ran towards the shore. Suddenly the branches parted and let her into the open. Her eyes locked onto Water Side.

She stared at the faint line where the sky met the water, stared at a tiny point on that infinite line. She was losing herself to it when movement below it caught her attention. Damarin was only a few steps away. She stood in the water.

"Damarin—" Tchardin began. Her sister stood knee deep beside a large rectangle of branches that rested on the water. Tchardin recognised the construction from the image Damarin had given her. It was the raft.

Damarin looked up at her calmly. "I told you I would go without you."

"*That* is what you're planning to cross the water on?"

"It's your last chance to join me." Damarin seated herself on the edge of it. Water lapped against the branches but the raft remained afloat. She turned to look off into the distance. "See something new. Learn something for yourself."

"No!" Tchardin practically shouted. "You won't make it on that."

"I *will* make it. We both will, if you come."

"I don't want to die in the water." Faced with the possibility of stemming the ache in her mind with something new, with a potential solution to her impossible responsibilities, Tchardin could only defend against it with the thought of losing her life to the deep. The council called her.

Damarin looked up, tilting her head. "So you'd rather stay and become queen—a useless queen, when the kandar have no Purpose—while I explore Derkra. You'll never get to Coralynth if you stay here."

Tchardin looked away.

"First we'll find Black Valley," Damarin continued, "then perhaps a purpose."

For a moment Damarin's thoughts became clear to Tchardin. She needed Tchardin to join her with an intensity of feeling Tchardin had never experienced before. Almost like this trip was more for Tchardin than for Damarin herself.

"No," Tchardin finally said. "The kandar need me here. There's nothing in Black Valley but the past and Jaydin has the past in her mind. There's no reason for me to cross the water for it."

Damarin shook her head.

"I'm the queen of the kandar—" Tchardin started to offer more explanation.

"Not yet, Tchardin," Damarin cut her off. "Not yet."

Reaching one long leg back towards shore Damarin kicked the raft into motion. Tchardin watched it slowly move away. She wondered how long she would be able to see it for on the infinity. The farther out Damarin got, the more tension Tchardin felt. She watched her only hope of escaping a life of pointless purpose drift off into adventure. Without her.

"Wait," Tchardin mouthed. Damarin turned.

Tchardin looked down at the water, only steps away. She had never touched it in her life. It was too different.

She cleared her mind, tried not to think, and took a step. Then another. She ran. Her right foot hit the water's surface and she sunk down. She shuddered as her momentum carried her forward, deeper and deeper into the water until with one last push she leapt clear of it and landed with both feet on the raft, water rising in a spray behind her.

Damarin stared at her for what seemed like an eternity, while Tchardin fell backwards into the blue. She opened her eyes wide, scrabbling for the thin pandinzori that surrounded her. Damarin reached out and grabbed her hands just before she lost her balance and pulled. In a moment the two were sprawled on the raft together. The wisps of pandinzori Tchardin had gathered swirled around them.

Damarin didn't let go of her hands as they stared at each other, as the pulse of discomfort radiated through Tchardin, as the reality of what had just happened sunk in. Then Damarin's eyes moved away and Tchardin saw the shore diminishing in their depths, reflected.

Tchardin laughed. She couldn't think what else to do. She laughed and she stared at Damarin in terror. Her sister returned the look and laughed too.

Tchardin turned towards the disappearing shore behind them. The height of the great trees on Calendrai was magnificent. Tith, Ahron, and Sirrhon burst from the centre of Cens like the giants they were and seemed to reach out towards them. Pandinzori billowed around the three brothers and spread into the water. The council would be in their branches soon and all the kandar in Calendrai with them. They would be waiting for her. Tchardin tried to put that out of her mind as the call of the council dwindled.

The water around the raft appeared to be deep now. The distance to the shore quickly grew. There was no going back. They settled down flat on the branches and Tchardin watched their father shrink.

When the great trees had begun to fade into the distance she turned to look where they were going. Towards a faint line. There was nothing else to look at. After staring for a while it became confusing. Tchardin blinked, then grimaced.

"My mind feels strange." She closed her eyes tight, an unpleasant sensation building behind them. She opened them again to look at Damarin and noticed her sister was reacting similarly. "What is it?"

"I don't know," Damarin replied. "Maybe the pull is stronger on the water?"

Tchardin looked around them. "Could it be something *in* the water?"

"No." Damarin squinted. "I know it. It's *pain.*"

Tchardin heard the word—a new one to her—and felt it in Damarin's thoughts, and all of a sudden she understood. Her head was splitting. The dull pressure had turned into a full-on stabbing, threading pain.

"Why is this happening?" She grit her teeth. "Will it be like this the whole way?"

Damarin lay back on the raft, her eyes tightly shut. Tchardin lay down with her, trying to remember what the feeling of longing had been like but it was hard. The new pain—a physical pain—eclipsed it entirely.

Damarin opened her eyes and sat up, stock-still. "I know what's causing it," she breathed.

Tchardin gazed at her pleadingly.

"Look around you."

Tchardin did. She didn't see anything of note in the endless blue.

"There's no pandinzori on the water," Damarin specified.

Chapter 4

JAYDIN WALKED A WIDE circle around Tith's base, searching the grass for Tchardin. She kept the pulsing collective in the back of her mind so she would feel if her sister approached the tree. Sandin was behind her somewhere, similarly searching, but the tevadra was undetectable.

"I want to find her before she goes to the meeting," Jaydin said, assuming Sandin was close enough to hear. "I think we should talk one more time before she puts herself in front of the council."

She looked up into Tith's branches to where the kandar would be gathering. From this vantage point, mere steps from his base, it looked as if her father was leaning over her, on the edge of falling onto her. He stretched so far into the sky, his canopy so vast, that it seemed as if he was the sky.

Kandar were supposed to come into Derkra with nothing but their names and the Purpose, yet the tree above Jaydin had told her the entire story of existence. She knew more than any kandar had ever known. All because of him.

'I taught her as much as I could before the council called,' she said to her father. Kandaran trees could answer when the kandar spoke to them if they chose to, but it was rare they did. Tith hadn't spoken to Jaydin since she was born. *'I hope she'll listen better when she's queen.'*

The great tree didn't respond.

Sandin walked up behind Jaydin. "I'll find her. You should go to the council. If you sense Tchardin approaching, just meet her before she arrives."

Jaydin nodded and watched as Sandin ran towards Cens, likely headed to the place on the shore where Tchardin could often be found. Then she vaulted up Tith as quickly as she could. The council members were probably already talking.

There were two shaded figures waiting when Jaydin entered the council shadow. Her body assumed a similar state automatically. The two were clearly having a private conversation as she heard nothing and yet their facial features and body language buzzed with change. They seemed disinclined to include her so she turned her back on them. Things hadn't been the same with the council since Damarin joined.

Jaydin rested against an upright branch and waited in silence as the members assembled. A few of the twenty-nine others acknowledged her as they arrived. Of particular note were Anatoly and Nox, the sons of Ahron and Sirrhon respectively. They had attended her birth expecting greatness and now they supported her place in the council. But they were ageing. Most who thought to notice her were old and would be called soon. The council would suffer a revolution.

Jaydin told herself it didn't matter. If they could gain access to the Earths again the council would need that revolution, and Jaydin was sure Tchardin could bring the Purpose back to the kandar. Then her importance in the council would mean much less. That would be the ultimate victory.

Marr—the council's Voice—arrived. Jaydin followed him through the shadow with her eyes but didn't move her head. She had no interest in speaking to him. He appeared to be searching the crowd. He caught her eye and walked across the branch towards her.

"Do you know where Damarin is?" he asked when he was close enough to speak quietly.

"She must be at the shore," Jaydin responded, making no effort to match his volume. "I haven't seen her since the last meeting."

Some of the other council members turned towards the two at Jaydin's words. Marr glared at them.

"She's missing." There was worry in his usually expressionless voice. "Can you sense her place on Calendrai?"

Jaydin pursed her lips. Of course she could. Everyone knew they'd been close once and that closeness remained in the collective. The council shadow obscured the locations of kandar when they were near, but it only obscured them to non-council members. Jaydin would meet no such obstacle. She closed her eyes and reached out to the tree in her mind, searching along the branches for one of her brightest leaves. She slid over it. Her eyes snapped open.

"I've never seen a leaf like that," Marr said.

"It's dark," Jaydin responded. She looked away from the Voice, holding her thoughts close. If Marr was asking Jaydin to find Damarin despite the state of her leaf he must not know what it meant. Jaydin turned back to him when she had herself under control. Her anger at Damarin for disrupting Tchardin's acknowledgement should obscure her other thoughts. "Send the council to look for her. We can't recognise the queen without the High Seat."

The Voice nodded. He backed away to the rest of the council. A few of them held a quiet conference before kandar left the branch in all directions, some higher into Sirrhon's canopy and some to the ground. Once they were far enough away that they couldn't be recognised they would drop the heightened council shadows that masked them. Jaydin turned to look at the kandar who were massing on Tith's branch.

The Voice rejoined her. A worrisome thought had begun to tickle the back of her mind. She opened herself to the collective again and searched its branches.

"Tchardin's leaf is dark too." A shiver of dread crept down Jaydin's spine. "You should help the others. If you find either of them call us back here. Let the rest of the council know the same." He nodded. *'And Marr,'* she added for his mind alone, *'if we don't find Damarin, if she is lost to us forever, this council is mine.'*

He met her eyes, his thoughts indecipherable, then he turned abruptly and vanished into the leaves below. Jaydin looked towards the waiting kandar again and steadied the collective. The pulsing stopped. The council no longer called. The kandar dispersed in confusion.

Jaydin stood for a while after they left and wondered. It couldn't be what she dreaded. It wasn't fair. Not now. Not when the council called to acknowledge a queen. Damarin might do it—to delay the ceremony—but Tchardin? Even under the pressure of their imposing middle sister Jaydin felt it was a stretch to believe it. Yet it seemed to be the only possibility.

As if in a trance she descended to one of Tith's lowest branches to find Sandin. Her sister must be hidden somewhere in the grass below. Jaydin waited, and Sandin came to her.

"Damarin's leaf is dark again," Jaydin said.

"Now?" Sandin rolled her eyes. "She must be trying to ruin the ceremony."

"Tchardin's is dark too."

"You don't think..."

"Tchardin asked about the old city," Jaydin said. "I knew Damarin would do it for real eventually. She's been talking about a raft. I should have known she would take Tchardin with her. If only to spite me."

"They'll come back."

Jaydin looked over the collective again, hoping to find their leaves bright, hoping at least to find Tchardin's restored, but found them the same. "I don't know if they will. It's different this time, even for Damarin. To take Tchardin just before the ceremony, while the council called..."

"Damarin always comes back."

Jaydin frowned. "If they're on a raft and they get too far out I don't think even Damarin would be capable of returning."

Jaydin felt numb. All that time and effort with Tchardin, wasted. Even her time with Damarin, though it had amounted to nothing. The two could never make it across the water let alone back. Not if they were trying for real. Not if they went too far. The only thing that might help them return from the infinity of Water Side would be Tith's call, and there wouldn't be enough life left to accomplish anything by the time he asked for one of them. They had to return soon or they might not return at all.

"If there was anything in Black Valley Tith would know, right?" Jaydin asked.

Sandin shrugged. "Tith said nothing to me. You're the one who should know that."

"I should have known this would happen when Tchardin asked about our birthplace. Deep down I must have known, but I never thought she'd actually do it!"

Jaydin had felt the same way when Damarin approached her with the idea just after Tchardin's birth. Initially she had thought their middle sister was looking for attention. Damarin had been important once, before their fifth and final sister came into Derkra with the golden aura. Then her obsession with the water began. Her leaf had gone dark for the first time shortly after that.

Jaydin had been alarmed—at the time she'd never seen anything like it—but Damarin's leaf quickly returned to brilliance. When confronted, their middle sister admitted to attempting to leave the island. She said the water called her. It was ridiculous. Her leaf had grown dark on occasion since then but Jaydin never paid it much attention. It always came back eventually.

Jaydin became increasingly certain Damarin would leave the island for good as Tchardin moved closer to quarter life, to becoming queen. She also became increasingly less worried about it. So what if Damarin lost herself to the infinity of Water Side? As soon as Tchardin was born with the golden aura there was no need of a once promising High Seat who now only sowed dissent.

Jaydin had still attempted to dissuade Damarin. There was nothing to be gained by leaving the island and everything to be lost. All kandar were part of the nine hundred—bodies promised first to their dodenzinn and then to the future generations of kandar who would inhabit them—and the nine hundred were supposed to be eternal. The kandaran war had done away with that truth once and for all, but what was left must be preserved. Dying on the water would mean a kandar could never be reborn. One of Tith's daughters—one of Jaydin's sisters—lost forever. Now it might be two.

"Kadailin's here," Sandin whispered, looking up.

Jaydin followed her gaze. Kadailin moved silently across the closest branch above them.

'Come down,' Jaydin said to her.

Kadailin looked at them in surprise, as if just noticing they were there. She appeared reluctant, hugging her body close to the branch, but eventually made her way towards Tith's trunk and descended.

"Do you know where Tchardin is?" Jaydin asked.

"I haven't seen her since I left her at the water with Damarin."

"What were they doing?"

Kadailin's gaze swept the branches below as if she were contemplating flight. Jaydin placed herself firmly in front of her sister.

"I didn't stay for long," Kadailin finally answered. "Why don't you ask Tchardin?"

"You haven't noticed yet?" Sandin asked from over Jaydin's shoulder.

Kadailin looked confused for a moment, then partly closed her eyes. Jaydin heard the buzz of her thoughts as she looked over the collective.

Kadailin opened her eyes in shock. "She's barely there!"

"So this is a surprise to you?"

Kadailin's expression became determined. She raised her eyes to meet Jaydin's. "I have no idea where she is."

"Not the water? Land Side?" Jaydin asked. Kadailin cringed. "She mentioned it to you?"

"Yes," Kadailin started, "but you don't think she would actually try—"

"Damarin's tried it before," Sandin said.

Jaydin nodded. "This time she took Tchardin."

Kadailin looked terrified. "They'll be lost!"

"They probably will be," Jaydin responded. "If they aren't already."

She turned her back on Kadailin. The worst thing about the situation was being unsure of whether or not to hope. Their leaves could grow bright at any moment or they could stay dark, never to be lit again. Even if their leaves never returned to brightness there wouldn't be proof of their deaths unless one of them fell from the collective in someone's mind. The problem was, as the distance grew, the likelihood of any kandar noticing the loss was diminishing. They could remain as ghosts in the collective, just a memory of what they had been, until all the kandar who had known them had gone to rest.

Or they could come back. Jaydin looked away from Tith's trunk, hoping to catch a glimpse of Water Side through the leaves. A raft, of all things. She wondered if it could possibly work.

***

They were surrounded by water now. The three great trees had faded into the distance some time ago and everything was flat. There was no shimmer of pandinzori in the air. Everywhere was the same hue of pale blue. Nothing ever changed.

Tchardin struggled to keep her eyes on the horizon. The feeling of need, of longing, had diminished to nearly invisible behind the horrible pulsing emptiness in her mind. Stronger was the feel of Tith and of the fading pandinzori behind her. She used it as a guide, the opposite of where they hoped to go.

The lack of pandinzori was bad, but Tchardin couldn't decide whether it was worse than the absence of the collective. Full branches of the tree in her mind hung empty of lights. If she focused she could just make out the blackened leaves, but it became harder and harder to do so with her mind in constant pain. Damarin's leaf remained bright—a tiny point in the darkness—and that helped her, but it was little consolation. The silence was oppressive.

Damarin lay still on the raft, her eyes closed and her expression serene. Tchardin didn't know how she managed it. When they started the trip Damarin had seemed just as bothered by the pain as Tchardin was. Now she seemed unaffected by it. Tchardin watched the thick pandinzori that made up her sister's aura with envy.

"Form the colours," Damarin said, obviously overhearing Tchardin's thoughts. "It helps."

Tchardin had been too worried about their situation to think about anything other than the silence and emptiness. She closed her eyes and tried to slip into darkness but gave up immediately. She looked at the horizon instead.

"Can you still feel the longing?" she asked.

Damarin sat up and looked in the direction Tchardin had last felt the pull. "Sometimes."

"What if we're going the wrong way?" Dread crept into Tchardin. "What if we float forever?"

Damarin snorted as if what Tchardin had said was ridiculous. But Water Side was infinite. Tchardin felt it was a legitimate concern.

"We're going the same way we were when we started," Damarin said. "And no matter what happens we won't float forever."

Tchardin looked down into the water. The pain persisted. If they floated for too long, could she endure it?

"How does this raft even work?" she asked instead of alerting Damarin to her thoughts. If her sister had heard them she chose to feign ignorance. "What do we do if we have to turn around?"

"Don't worry so much." Damarin studied the water around the raft. "The raft works because I say it does, and I can get us back if I need to."

Tchardin lay down on the branches, trying to conceal her unease. She thought again about throwing herself into the water. To die, not to rest. To lose her body.

After Tchar and Dani and the nine guardians there were only nine hundred kandar made in the beginning. None had been made since. Their fathers took the bodies back when they needed to rest and re-made them into the new generation. Tchardin had been many kandar and she was supposed to be many more. If she lost herself to the water there would be one fewer kandar on Derkra for the rest of existence. Could she do that to her people?

Of course, there were no longer nine hundred of them. They'd lost a great number in the kandaran war and the events that led up to it. Jaydin estimated Calendrai currently had about three hundred kandar awake and walking around, with maybe another hundred resting in their trees.

One out of four hundred seemed insignificant, but Tchardin owed herself first to her dodenzinn, even before her father or her people. She frowned, thinking of Ryten, or whomever he turned out to be. The kandar believed dodenzinn pairings carried across the generations, though that had never been proven. Jaydin said Tith hadn't confirmed the theory for her, but no kandar had died until the war and Jaydin always seemed reluctant to discuss the recent history of the kandar. Perhaps Tith had been as well.

If Tchardin succumbed to the water her dodenzinn would likely lose the will to live, even though they didn't know each other yet. It was a physical imperative for most kandar, something they couldn't deny when they felt it. If he managed to persevere, empty and weak, he would only do so until he realised he was alone. Then he would destroy himself in turn.

If he didn't realise he was alone—if he somehow made it to his father at the end of his life—he would be reborn, and his new self would be even less likely to know his dodenzinn was lost. What kandar would destroy themselves when they didn't know for sure that their dodenzinn was already dead? At that point, he could be left without his other half for eternity, left weaker than the rest of them, emptier. It was a horrifying thought. Perhaps the kandar continued to believe the pairings persisted just in case it was true.

Tchardin shuddered. She should have considered her future dodenzinn before she decided to leave with Damarin. She had thought only of her own fate on the water, not what it could do to her other half if things went badly. Damarin hadn't seemed to consider it either.

The longing returned with force. Tchardin sat up and locked onto it with her eyes, trying to confirm the raft moved in the right direction.

"I think we're still going the right way," she said.

Damarin nodded. Her eyes slowly sunk shut and she lay down on the raft again and didn't move. Tchardin remained focused on the horizon. How much farther could it be?

***

Ryten adjusted his position on the branch, trying to keep his eyes closed, but softly, not shut tight. He held no colours behind them, only blackness.

'So she isn't dead yet,' a voice said in his mind.

"I'm sleeping," he mumbled aloud.

"Kandar don't sleep," came the terse reply.

He opened his eyes to find Jaydin's face hovering over his, just far enough away to keep their auras apart.

"Some of us do." He indicated the silent kandar surrounding them, draped haphazardly over and throughout the branches.

"Faking it. Just like you were."

Ryten looked at them. They didn't move. Their bodies were limp and their eyes closed in imitation of the human act. An act the kandar remembered vaguely through stories passed down from their time on the Earths. Maybe they *were* faking it. He'd never been able to actually do it. At least he didn't think he had. He wasn't sure exactly what sleep was. Jaydin frowned.

"Sleeping is like being in the belly of the trees," she said. "It's a necessary resetting, but a waste of the time it takes. Be glad you got all of yours over with at once and don't envy the humans."

Envy? Ryten focused on Jaydin's leaf in the collective and found a sense of the word, of what it meant. That happened a lot with her, as she often used words the kandar had no reason to know. Ryten considered the feeling as he came to understand it. Did he envy Creator's children? Did he envy anyone? He was just looking for something to do. They all were.

There were kandar who slept, and kandar who ate, and kandar who shunned the collective mind and spoke only aloud. Leftover actions that belonged with the humans. Ryten only slept. Or tried to. Jaydin often chose to single him out but there were many like him and worse. Most of them hid in Cens and only came out when summoned by the council. Some ignored the call altogether and lay about in Ahron's canopy, shielded from Sirrhon—where the meetings took place—by Tith's great branches.

They had to do something. They weren't supposed to be bored on Derkra, but what was this new sensation if not boredom? Ryten had learned that word from Jaydin as well. *Boredom*. Sometimes he wondered if he'd been so bored before he knew it but he couldn't remember. He did know he had spent almost half a life now looking for things to do.

'Just leave me alone,' he thought privately to Jaydin, realising the disturbance they must be creating for the other sleeping kandar. He closed his eyes again, pushing the light of pandinzori away and descending into blackness.

'I can't do that.' She hadn't moved away. He felt her aura beside his. *'I have to know when she dies. I know she hasn't acknowledged you yet, but as her dodenzinn you'll be the first to feel it.'*

He flinched at that, holding his silent thoughts close. He was an abomination. Jaydin had clearly made note of his recent attentions, but in truth he didn't know who his dodenzinn was. Nearly at half life and he only guessed. The others didn't understand what that meant. What it felt like. He'd even been wrong before. Luckily no one talked about that anymore.

Jaydin's quick buzz of thought—cut off abruptly—indicated she remembered, even if she wouldn't mention it.

'You are *her dodenzinn,'* she repeated, clearly determined to move past his discomfort. *'You might be the only one who feels her death.'*

It wasn't worth Tchardin's death to confirm it. Or Damarin's, for that matter. He had been so sure about Tith's middle daughter once, but she hadn't been sure of him. Unfortunately that hadn't made his own certainty go away. At least until he'd met Tchardin. He sat up. He could never achieve sleep with Jaydin hovering over him like she was.

"You don't have to follow me around," he said, looking down through Ahron's branches and contemplating the drop. "If you leave me alone I'll find you when it happens."

Jaydin stood beside him, ready to follow if he chose to descend.

"You'll find me first?" she asked. "The instant it happens?"

"As soon as I feel it. Once I can walk."

"You would be weak," she said, nodding. "It could take a while to regain your strength. Maybe it's better if I just stay with you, in that case."

He regretted his answer. He already felt weak from the distance between them. Both Damarin and Tchardin's leaves were dark in the collective. He had felt the absence of one of those leaves before, but never both. If Tchardin was his dodenzinn—if either of them were—and they died on the water it was more likely he throw himself in after them than search out their older sister. Jaydin knew that.

But would he feel it? Dodenzinn had been said to feel the passing of their counterparts across worlds. He should easily feel it from just across Water Side. Of course, an unnatural death was rare for kandar—none of the nine hundred had actually died until shortly before the war. When a proper end came, dodenzinn were called to rest together, so they didn't have to live long without one another. If an unnatural act ended a kandar's life it was expected to be very painful for the other half of their whole. Would he walk through that pain to find Jaydin? Or would he choose to end it quickly?

The pain wouldn't even be the worst of it. Ryten already knew he could live the rest of his life feeling as he had for a short time after quarter life. Feeling incomplete. What he couldn't do was wait to be called when he knew he was dooming his myriad future selves to empty life after empty life. And worse, they wouldn't know.

"You'll be allowed to go," Jaydin said, picking up on his thoughts. "There is precedent for that. I won't stop you despite our dwindling numbers. No kandar would."

"I know."

He remembered an instance where he'd been able to sit with Tchardin while Jaydin spoke of the kandaran war. She'd said the kandar who lost dodenzinn during the war had destroyed themselves similarly to ensure they wouldn't be given back to the trees. He remembered as well a thought that came into his mind at her words. Had they really all done it? There could be some kandar out there, of this generation, who passed quarter life and half life and waited still, not knowing if their dodenzinn would ever come to them. You could feel weak, you could feel empty, but would you end it all and risk forcing the same onto your yet undiscovered partner for the rest of existence?

Jaydin sighed beside him. He quieted his thoughts as much as he could. The reason that possibility had occurred to him must be kept silent. He'd wondered ever since if that was the cause of his confusion. Tchardin could be his dodenzinn and things could work out, but he also knew she might not be, and that knowledge in itself made him strange amongst the kandar. They were supposed to *know*. Once he thought he had. Now he knew he didn't. Maybe his dodenzinn was already dead.

"Damarin will come back," he said. "She always does."

Jaydin frowned. "She's never taken Tchardin before."

Ryten recoiled at her words. He got up and slid along the branch, scanning the tree below him for the best way down. Then he dropped off the edge onto another branch, one after another until he saw nothing below him and he headed towards the trunk. He sensed Jaydin following him, only a branch behind. When he reached Tith's trunk he began the climb down but felt it was too slow. He jumped.

Air rushed past him and dark spots in the grass below resolved into the heads of kandar as he approached the ground. The light of pandinzori floated in the clearing. He pulled on it with his mind and the layer that obscured his skin grew thicker. He amassed the brilliance at his feet.

As the green approached, pandinzori billowed below him and his speed decreased until his feet came to rest just above the tips of the tall grass. He felt the solidity of the pandinzori around his lower half, and his feet lay flat as if on the ground. The area below him shone with condensed light.

He let it go. It didn't rush away, but clung to him in wisps as he dropped into the stalks in a crouch. Tith's immense trunk stood in front of him and blocked his view of the clearing. He turned away from the bark and felt an aura enter his space. Sandin confronted him.

He was startled. She could come out of nowhere in a way no other kandar could. Her dark eyes blazed. He felt the subtle pull of her. Sandin had always drawn him, almost as much as two of her younger sisters, but less sharply. Less clearly. He tried to ignore it.

"Is Jaydin following you?" she asked.

Ryten nodded. He avoided her eyes.

"You should go to Del then." She stepped out of the way.

He passed her quickly, grateful to be spared the awkwardness inherent in looking at her for too long. He could lose Jaydin in Cens. Sandin's suggestion of finding his father, Del, was a good one. The tevadra of Tith were slow when it came to the forest and Del was well hidden.

When he broke into the trees he felt relief. He had been born in Cens and he knew the forest better than any of Tith's daughters.

CHAPTER 5

SANDIN WATCHED RYTEN SLIDE between the trees and disappear. Jaydin walked up behind her. Their oldest sister had opted to climb down Tith rather than jump. That was typical. It was rare for Jaydin to use pandinzori. A habit she had acquired by spending so much time with Sandin.

"Help me follow him?" Jaydin asked.

Sandin shook her head. "You need to let him be."

"How else will we know when the water claims the future queen?"

"Even if he is her dodenzinn, which you've never been sure of before," Sandin started, "what good will it do you to know?"

Jaydin stared after the devoshai dejectedly. Sandin had never seen her so frazzled.

"He *is* her dodenzinn," Jaydin said. "He must be."

"But ever since Damarin—"

"I know," Jaydin cut her off. "I know that, but he must be sure now."

Sandin refrained from beginning the argument that had plagued their relationship since Jaydin first started teaching her Tith's history. Their father may have birthed five tevadra but they only knew of one he had taken to rest. Sandin was well past quarter life and she had never experienced anything with a devoshai she could possibly liken to a dodenzinn connection. As far as she knew, neither had Jaydin. She also didn't feel empty or lacking in any way. Maybe dodenzinn were no longer so simple. Maybe a tree could make one kandar into five, and maybe the father of that kandar's dodenzinn wouldn't know to do the same. Even if the pairings didn't persist across the generations, one tevadra becoming five would throw off the balance. But Jaydin knew what she knew. Derkra would never change. Nor would the kandar. There was no convincing her.

Jaydin glared at her. No one could hear Sandin's thoughts but Jaydin must know them just for knowing Sandin.

"Regardless," Jaydin said, "Damarin is with Tchardin."

"What good will it do to know?" Sandin repeated.

"I just need to know."

Sandin sat down in the grass. After a moment of reluctant pacing, Jaydin joined her.

"Tchardin could live on the water for the rest of your life without being called, you know," Sandin said, knowing that Jaydin did in fact know this. Jaydin knew everything. "She's a lot younger than both of us. Even if they don't come back soon, it doesn't mean they're dead."

"They'd still be gone. I need her, Sandin. The kandar need their queen." Jaydin shook her head. "Maybe Tith will call Damarin first. She isn't much younger than you are and kandar aren't called to rest solely based on age. There are more complex factors. She could be called before me. I trust Damarin to find her way back from the infinity of Water Side if it means answering Tith's call. I assume she would bring Tchardin with her."

"Maybe." Sandin was doubtful of Damarin's virtue. "Or she could shove her into the water and leave her to drown."

Jaydin tensed. Sandin reminded herself that drowning was a sore spot for the rest of the kandar. It was one of their greatest fears. To die in the water meant a kandar would never again hear the trees. Never be brought back into Derkra. But Sandin had never heard the trees, and that was her likely end anyway. How could her father call her to rest when she couldn't hear him?

"I don't believe she'd go that far," Jaydin said. "Tchardin has never really threatened her, despite the natural order of things forcing her to take what Damarin wants."

Sandin wasn't as confident. Damarin was ambitious in a way she shouldn't be. She'd always been like that. Jaydin had been ignorant of it for a long time after Damarin was born and might still be, but Sandin had recognised it immediately. The one with the golden aura would be their queen. It had been true since Tchar gave them hierarchy. All the kandar knew that, but Sandin wasn't so sure Damarin accepted it.

Jaydin accepted it so completely she couldn't understand anyone who didn't.

"We'll see," Sandin finally said. Jaydin stood. "I said, we'll see," Sandin repeated. "There's nothing we can *do* about it. We just have to wait."

Jaydin turned back towards the edge of Cens and Sandin was sad.

"It's not worth worrying about," she pleaded with her sister.

Jaydin walked away. Sandin got up and followed. Just as Jaydin was about to enter the trees Sandin reached out and touched her shoulder. Jaydin turned.

An uncomfortable pulse ran through Sandin's fingers at the contact. It was difficult to maintain. Jaydin twitched but didn't break away.

"There are more productive things we could do," Sandin said, looking into Jaydin's eyes.

"Like what? There's nothing for the kandar here."

"Try the shift yourself. Reach out to Coralynth."

Jaydin shook her head. She turned back towards the treeline.

"Just wait—" Sandin tried one more time.

"I've waited too long already."

Jaydin pulled away from her touch and disappeared into the trees. Sandin sighed and lay down in the grass and shadows, hiding from the world. It was ridiculous to obsessively pursue confirmation of their sisters' deaths. No good could come of it.

Sandin believed Jaydin had just as much chance of bringing the kandar back to the Earths if she was willing to continue to make her own attempts. They had failed in the past but she had to keep trying. It was just as likely she was chosen as Tchardin. Tith had given her something arguably better than the golden aura, but Jaydin had never been able to see that.

***

Tchardin's head ached. She didn't dare close her eyes for fear of losing the point they were aiming for. The longing had ceased to be consistent, pushed out of her mind by the endless pain. Behind her, Tith beckoned her back to his strength, his pandinzori. She could still feel that, and she held the feeling tightly, as it was her only real point of reference. One thing had begun to worry her though, more than the water itself.

"What do you feel in this direction?" she asked.

Damarin sat up and looked past Tchardin's shoulder in the way they were going.

"Nothing," she said.

"Exactly." Tchardin looked back at her sister. "Sometimes I feel the longing, sometimes I feel the pull of the horizon, but between those moments I feel nothing."

Damarin squinted at her. Tchardin could almost see the pain behind her eyes, clouding her thoughts. Damarin had spent most of her time concentrating on the colours in her mind in order to avoid the emptiness. Now she was forced to confront it.

"There's no pandinzori ahead of us," Tchardin said with grim conviction. "None at all."

She watched the words sink into Damarin's mind. Her sister looked behind them then, and Tchardin knew she was looking at Tith, though the horizon had been empty of definition for a long time now.

"I don't know if we can truly feel the pandinzori in Calendrai," Damarin said. "I think it's only Tith. Ever since we left the island behind I've seen none but the layer that wraps us."

"But towards Calendrai—"

"You're feeling Tith, Tchardin. We aren't close enough to Land Side yet to feel the pandinzori from Ovaeron's branches. I'm sure we'll see it once we see the sand."

Tchardin held an arm out in front of her and studied the pandinzori that coated it. She was sure it was thinner. "Can this kill us? The lack of pandinzori?"

Damarin looked ahead again. "Losing our pandinzori is what would have caused Tith to call us eventually, had we not left Calendrai."

"But if we lose it and don't go to rest, can it kill us?"

"Yes," her sister said.

"So we're going to die?"

"No." Damarin closed her eyes and settled down onto her back on the raft. "We'll be fine."

Tchardin looked forward again. How much longer would she have to do this? They had half a chance Land Side was even in the direction they were going. Tchardin thought that was improved upon by the fact that both she and Damarin felt the strange longing, but still. Beyond the few paths that would give them the shortest possible journey from the island to Land Side, the trip would get exponentially longer. How quickly could a vessel of the water cross it? And how did that amount of time measure up to the length of a kandar's life?

Was this an impossible journey? Would they travel on and on until they died and never know if they were going in the right direction? That was the worst possible outcome. Tchardin wanted to see something other than the water before she left Derkra in death. Ideally that thing would be Tith. Then she could be reborn.

The longing returned, quietly. It wasn't the rush of intensity it had been on Calendrai. In no way did it equal the feeling of need to return to Tith. There was nothing to do now but continue to endure.

Had she been conscious this entire time? Or had the horizon faded once, to be replaced by its exact image again, ages later? It was impossible to tell when nothing around them changed.

Out on the water Tchardin could only measure reality by two things. By the intermittent periods of longing she felt—both for Tith and for their goal far in front of them—and by the tiny, ludicrous ripples that spread out behind the raft. She'd been watching them. They were always the same.

She'd begun to worry they weren't moving at all. When everything looked the same and the water beyond the ripples remained smooth, and the movement of the raft made no impression on her senses and never had, was there anything to say they went forward? What if the raft had stopped once they were out of sight of Calendrai and rested there? There was nothing she could see to stop it, but similarly no reason for it to continue that she could think of. Other than that it had moved before.

"I don't understand," Tchardin said.

"What don't you understand?" Damarin asked quietly.

"Are we even moving? Nothing around us is changing."

"We're moving." Damarin looked to be thinking hard on something, despite that Tchardin couldn't hear the buzz of her thoughts. She stood up.

"What are you doing?" Tchardin asked, alarmed.

If her sister decided she wanted to drown herself, Tchardin didn't think she could hold on much longer alone. Damarin turned full-circle and examined each direction carefully.

"Does it look the same to you?" she asked.

Tchardin rose to her feet slowly, wary of the instability of the raft when both of them were standing. As she turned herself she noticed a change that hadn't been evident before. Damarin's thoughts told her they had seen the same thing. The horizon cycled through light, to dark, to light again. It was a faint change, but it was there.

"It's Land Side," said Damarin.

Tchardin began to worry again immediately. "If it's Land Side, where's the pandinzori?"

"Black Valley will have pandinzori, but Land Side is infinite, just as Water Side is. We still have to find the city."

They sat down again to wait. This time Damarin stayed alert. New strength grew in Tchardin as the lightness on the horizon became a line of pale yellow sand and clear blue sky. But pandinzori failed to materialise and Tchardin's relief slipped away.

"Where are the trees?" she asked as they floated closer and closer.

Damarin remained silent, the grim line re-appearing across her lips.

"There are no trees," Tchardin repeated. She saw the line of the shore clearly now, and that was all it was. A slightly sinuous line, unbroken by the trunks of trees.

"No pandinzori and no trees," Tchardin continued, a hysterical laugh escaping her lips. "Black Valley is dead and we're going to die too."

Damarin said nothing.

The shore loomed. Tchardin watched it inch closer. When she couldn't take it anymore she launched herself into the water and was only slightly relieved to find it didn't swallow her up. Damarin gasped and reached for her as she dragged the raft onto the sand. Tchardin collapsed as soon as she felt the raft catch.

When she could finally muster the strength to rise, she looked around her. Damarin had taken a place kneeling beside her, looking back over the water, but Tchardin looked forward over the sand. They were on a soft slope and there rose in front of them a mound of sand so wide and so tall it blocked her view of the desert.

"Do you want to climb it?" Damarin asked.

"I think we have to."

Damarin walked up the slope. Tchardin followed, dragging herself through the sand. Her strength faded quickly. The sand slid beneath her feet and every step took the effort of a hundred on Calendrai. She felt the longing for something in front of her again—strongly—but the sensation was bittersweet. She couldn't guess how far away it was and she was starting to doubt their ability to make it there. How long could they last with the press of nothing on their minds and bodies? She looked down at the pandinzori that encircled her thighs as she walked. It was pathetically thin now. Would Tith call her back to rest if she lost it? Or would he try and be too late?

"Now I wish I'd paid more attention to Jaydin," she said as she struggled to keep up with Damarin. "I don't remember enough about the location of Black Valley in the dunes."

"I know it wasn't supposed to be right along the shore," provided Damarin. "There will be trees farther in."

"I really feel it now. The thing that calls us."

"So do I." Damarin stopped and looked back. "I told you we would make it. Now we're almost there."

There was something about Damarin—an assuredness, a certainty to everything she said—that made kandar believe her, trust her. The longing *was* getting stronger. Perhaps Black Valley was just over the rise in front of them. Maybe the dune was somehow blocking the pandinzori that would sooth them back to their former strength. Tchardin missed the collective, and hearing the voices of kandar would go a long way in healing her, but pandinzori was paramount now. Black Valley had to have some.

Tchardin stumbled and fell to her knees in the sand. The slope might be gradual but it was longer than it had appeared. Tchardin could climb Tith and still run through his branches, hoist herself up higher and higher into his canopy then rush back down and sprint to the shore, all without any trouble. The sand sapped her strength, and the absence of pandinzori evidently had a huge effect on her. Damarin was soon far ahead. For some reason the pandinzori that surrounded her sister hadn't appeared to diminish with their journey. It almost looked like it had grown.

Tchardin pushed forward, sinking into the sand with each step. She knew she couldn't go much farther without rest. She was just about to look up and judge her distance to the crest when she ran into Damarin's feet in front of her. She'd been looking down at the sand for some time now, willing step after step to happen, refusing to be confronted with the vast distance left to cover, but Damarin wasn't continuing. They'd reached the top. Tchardin looked up.

In an instant all hope vanished. She folded in on herself, surrendering her body to the sand that had tried to pull her in, and buried her face in her hands.

"What do we do now?" she asked through her fingers.

Damarin looked lost, shocked, as if she had truly known her plan would work and couldn't comprehend the scene that greeted their eyes. The weariness that had eaten at Tchardin across the water and on the climb up the slope finally appeared to touch her sister.

"Give me a moment," Damarin said. "I'm thinking."

Tchardin turned her eyes towards the desert and looked out with Damarin over the endless dunes, the air flat without pandinzori. The sand before them was infinite, melding with the sky in one continuous line, forever.

Chapter 6

THE LANDSCAPE BEFORE HIM was a bleak picture of barren continuity, broken only by the rise and fall of the waves of sand that separated it into infinite, sinuous lines. Humanity would call this a desert. The kandar called it Land Side. It was Derkra. All there was. It was home.

A familiar pang of emptiness resonated through Cien's body. The swath of shining pandinzori that covered a small stretch of sand in the infinity faded into the distance behind him. Black Valley's trees were hidden there, in a deep depression behind the dunes. Every time he left them to wander the desert he felt the loss of pandinzori, felt his strength diminish with it. This time the journey was worth the slight emptiness however, because as he neared the shore, Cien felt a fulfillment unlike anything he had experienced in his existence.

Usually a journey to the water evoked additional pain. Of all the kandar he was the only one who yearned for something beyond the sand, when they all knew there could be nothing there. He had quickly stopped trying to convince the others.

It had been different this time. When he left the caves by Ovaeron he had felt called, not only by the great tree, but also by the water. It had always been a compulsion of his to wander in the direction of Water Side, but this time there was a finality to the call. For once it felt like he would find something other than emptiness waiting for him at the end of the journey.

The dune that confronted him now was a big one. Cien studied the pandinzori against his skin to make sure it was still thick. The sand on the slope would slide under his feet and he would lose most of his strength in the climb. Using the pandinzori that surrounded him would weaken him too, but not as much as the sand. He focused on the light that outlined him and pushed it down to concentrate around his feet. He closed his eyes and spread it into the sand, a shining pathway that led to the crest of the dune. He felt a slight weakening as the pandinzori left him but the climb was easy on the hardened pathway. When he reached the top he elected to leave the path behind. It would be easier to move it onto the opposite rise for the way back than to pull it up and expend it again.

His early trips to the shore had been much harder. In his first quarter life he had been unable to touch the pandinzori around his aura while out in the desert. Using it would have killed him. Those trips often ended while he was still in sight of Black Valley. Many times he had been forced to crawl and slide back, ending up in a limp mess of his own limbs when he finally dropped into the valley. He would lie there while the pandinzori from the stunted desert trees slowly padded his aura and strength came back to him. The kandar who chose to notice at all had been perplexed by his behaviour, having never experienced the loss of pandinzori.

Over time he found he could bring more pandinzori with him into the desert, to counter the lack of a natural source. After achieving this he was able to make it farther and farther into the sand, closer and closer to Water Side. Being wrapped in a thicker coating of pandinzori did nothing to combat the feeling of loss when he wasn't surrounded by it, but it did let him use the excess.

Eventually, it brought him to his goal. He had seen the endless blue during his time in the belly of his father, Roa, as all kandar had before their births, but when he was confronted with the calmness of it, the complete flatness and limitlessness, the emptiness, his mind had changed inside. He was the only kandar to have seen the water with his own eyes. The others simply couldn't understand.

Cien felt that could be the reason why the quiet of the desert didn't bother him. The collective was dark in his mind, but the silence was his. He was the only kandar to have ever been truly alone.

He topped the dune and sent more pandinzori—a thin current—through the air and up the next rise. He looked towards Water Side. There had to be something new to see. The call was different. The yearning was fading. He scanned the three mountains of sand he had left to cross, looking along each one carefully, as far into the distance as he could see. The one closest to the water was the largest. It blocked the shore ahead from view.

He was about to slide down to the next valley when a tiny dark spot far to his left caught his eye. There was a slight depression in the top of the big dune, a flaw in the soft yellow perfection of Land Side. He changed course to walk towards it. It seemed insignificant in scale, but there had never been anything there but sand.

As he climbed one dune and then the next, losing and gaining sight of the anomaly as he progressed, he came to believe it really was the thing he had been searching for. It had to be the thing that called. It was the only change in his journey. The only change he had ever seen.

He struggled with the last climb. His pandinzori had worn thin and in his excitement he had been careless with his expense of energy. He had nothing to spare for the last twenty or so steps of the rise so he trudged through the sand. It had been a long time since he'd been forced to do that.

The small dark spot had grown and resolved into two. Now it looked to be something impossible. He walked the last couple steps to the top very slowly.

They were two tevadra, lying motionless in the sand at the crest of the dune. Cien had never seen skin like theirs before, nor hair. They were very dark. The colours of shadow. There were no kandar in Black Valley with such colouring.

He knelt near them, keeping enough distance to react if they moved, and waited for them to join the collective. His mind ran along each branch quickly, scanning, searching for the leaves that would go with their strange auras. The one had a golden aura. In normal circumstances that would make her the queen, but where had she come from? The other tevadra had a yellow aura. He couldn't find their leaves, when suddenly, something new began to form in his mind. It grew up beside the original collective, and it grew to be much larger. On it were only two leaves—these two—but there was space for many more. A second collective mind?

Then, just when it seemed this collective was a tree of its own, the connection grew. What was once a full tree, his tree, was now only a branch of something greater. The two collectives had joined, but they didn't make a tree. The resulting combination was wrong. The shape and structure were off. It was as if what had been there before was a tree, and this new part of it had also been a tree, but together they made what could only be a branch. Cien shuddered. The collective now appeared incomplete.

The thought unnerved him greatly, but something else took precedence. When they had joined the collective he knew. These two tevadra had called him to the shore. They had always called him, only they had failed to appear until now.

Surely one must be his dodenzinn. He smiled despite the strangeness of the situation, no longer contemplating the impossibility. He had waited so long for a dodenzinn. He had felt empty and weak since his quarter life. But they couldn't both have called him.

He tried to discern which it was by circling them. He shouldn't be unsure. He couldn't be. And yet, he was somehow. As he regarded them more closely he noticed a pair of magnificent eyes looking back at him. The one with the yellow aura was awake.

***

For a moment Tchardin thought she was back on Calendrai, trying to escape her impending responsibility and losing the one thing that had promised her change, if only she would go to it. The feeling of longing was gone. She cried out in her mind for it. Then she realised that what replaced the feeling of longing was one of contentment.

She opened her eyes to a view of the sky. She was on her back on a sheet of pandinzori, floating over the sand. A devoshai walked ahead of her. His grey aura said he held the pandinzori that supported her.

Then she noticed that the smooth back ahead of her was not the dark of the woods it should be. It matched quite well the sand beneath the feet, and those feet didn't sink into that sand but skimmed lightly over it.

Tchardin willed strength into her arms and lifted her head and shoulders to look around her. Desert everywhere. And Damarin. Her sister walked a few steps behind the devoshai who held her. Damarin smiled back at her.

Chapter 7

Tchardin gazed up into Ovaeron's vast black branches. Their darkness framed his ruby red leaves and contrasted with the brightness of the pandinzori they held. His trunk, like his branches, was black and twisted. It curled up into his canopy and disappeared.

He seemed impossibly old. Permanent. She had only ever seen him as gnarled and black, the way Tith had shown him to her. It was hard to believe his trunk had once been perfectly straight and white, but before the kandar it had been.

The first of their people was born here—a tevadra called Tchar. She was Tchardin's namesake, or so Tith had told her before she was born. Tchar had once been human but Creator had picked her specifically for the Purpose and Ovaeron had made her kandar. It was said that while she waited in his belly she had taken the light and life from him and his great white trunk had blackened and shrunk and twisted.

The shock of her birth on the world had formed the valley itself. Ovaeron dug into the sand and held on against the force of it. When it was over, the valley was a deep depression and from it spread the great waves of dunes in the desert. The water similarly had felt the shock, but the waves it caused there had left the shore and floated ever on into infinity. They were probably still out there.

The valley was hidden from the shore by the dunes and the centre of the depression itself was covered by Ovaeron's red canopy. This was Black Valley, named for the dark tree that dominated it and the black sand that spread from his base like a shadow and mixed with the yellow of the desert.

Tchardin tore her eyes away from Ovaeron's trunk and turned to the other trees of the valley. They were the trees of the first kandar. Nine hundred of them.

There had only been ten trees below Ovaeron in the beginning, one of which had given birth to Tchar's other half, Dani. The other nine had birthed the guardians. Jaydin said those ten trees had died upon bearing the seeds that grew the nine hundred—planted by Tchar shortly after Dani's birth. The first two kandar had waited only to relay the Purpose and then ascended to Coralynth.

Black Valley's trees didn't make much of a forest. Spread out over the valley the nine hundred looked sparse, though pandinzori threaded through them. They had light green and yellow leaves and white trunks. This in itself was strange to Tchardin because the trees of Calendrai were dark, both in the green of their leaves and the brown and black of their trunks. The white trunks made it clear these were the fruit of Ovaeron's seeds but not one of them shared his red crown.

Tchardin avoided looking at the white devoshai beside her. His appearance was too strange. He almost blended into the sand. A variety of hues could be seen in the patchwork of his skin if she studied it, but viewed from farther away the myriad shades morphed into a bland yellow.

Tith had told her Carrensing brought all the kandar with her when she left Black Valley to find the island. The trees had told all the kandar of Calendrai that. That was clearly incorrect given there appeared to be at least a hundred kandar in Black Valley. Unlike Calendrai, which hid most of its population in the forest, Black Valley was laid bare before her. Kandar could be spotted easily from the centre. The devoshai followed her gaze.

"There are one hundred and twenty-two of us awake," he said. "We don't know how many rest."

Tchardin scanned the valley. There was no escaping the reality of it. They were kandar, though they didn't look it.

Their skin was one thing, but many of the kandar in Black Valley had hair that was almost white. Worse still were their eyes. It was like she could see through them, they were so light. The devoshai next to her was a colourless thing. They all seemed to be this way from afar.

"How are you here?" she asked.

"This is the home of the kandar. Our birthplace. You say you came from an island on Water Side, but you must know how ridiculous that sounds."

"The island that all kandar were moved to after the war."

"There is nothing on Water Side but water."

"There is Calendrai," Tchardin said.

"I don't know about that," he responded. "The kandar here were born here, in Black Valley, as we always have been."

"But how?"

His expression was blank. Tchardin recognised it from the kandar who spoke the words of the trees. Truth plain and simple.

"When we woke after the war we were shut off from Coralynth," he said. "We still don't know why. Everything else is the same."

So they were cut off too. Tchardin closed her eyes and searched the collective. She'd missed the moment he joined it. She found herself in unfamiliar branches, empty except for his one leaf. His name was Cien and he was part of a second collective? She opened her eyes to find him studying her face intently.

"It's happening to you too then? The tevadra with you didn't react, so I assumed she didn't see it."

"Damarin," Tchardin supplied distractedly. Not a new collective, just a part of the old one, but the tree in her mind that was the collective appeared to be only a branch now. "The other tevadra is Damarin. I'm Tchardin."

"Your name fits you well." He smiled. "You have Tchar's eyes."

Tchardin frowned. It had been generations since Coralynth was lost to them. He couldn't possibly have seen Tchar.

"I haven't met Tchar," he said, catching her thoughts. "I've only seen her through the shift a few times."

Tchardin almost missed the implausibility of the statement because his clear eyes were looking into her. He could open the shift? If he could do that, why had the kandar of Black Valley not gone back to Coralynth? Cien raised his eyebrows. Perhaps her thoughts were not well guarded. "We should find Damarin," she said instead of asking for clarification. That would have to come later.

As soon as they arrived in Black Valley Damarin had insisted on exploring it. Tchardin had been too weak to climb Ovaeron or to walk around the vast depression of the valley so she'd stayed with the devoshai at the base of the dark trunk while Ovaeron's pandinzori gave her strength.

"She can't have gone far," Cien said, looking around them. "She'll stand out well with her colouring. I'll show you around while we look."

Tchardin nodded. As overwhelming as the discovery of the city's state was, she was excited to see what she could learn. She was looking forward to climbing Ovaeron in particular. Tith was her father by birth, but Ovaeron could lay claim to them all.

***

Sandin stalked the soft footsteps ahead of her, unable to see through the thick leaves and branches that cluttered the forest. She'd been searching for Jaydin but Cens was being particularly stubborn and had yet to reveal any other kandar to her. Suddenly the movement ceased. Sandin held herself closer to the ground and ducked through the low branches.

She was confronted with Ocien. Sandin was happy it was someone she recognised. Ocien's huge eyes—a light brown—were fringed with thick black lashes. The tevadra appraised her silently. Sandin wondered if Ocien was speaking in her mind, forgetting Sandin wouldn't hear.

"You need me to find Jaydin, don't you?" Ocien finally said.

Sandin was taken aback. There was no hostility in the tevadra's voice, no annoyance at being forced to accommodate Sandin's unreasonable flaw. It was merely a question.

"I didn't know it was you," Sandin said instead of answering. She didn't want Ocien to think she had sought her out specifically.

"And I didn't know it was you who followed me. At least until I realised that if it were anyone else, I would have known who it was."

Sandin heard a rustling above them. She looked up into the canopy just as Torshe dropped out of the branches and joined them on the ground. He was so average as far as devoshai went that Sandin only knew him by the way he looked at Ocien. The two had only found each other recently, but they already seemed strangely close for dodenzinn.

"What has happened to Tchardin?" Torshe asked.

Sandin couldn't remember an instance like this where she was asked a question by someone other than one of her sisters or Ryten. The kandar weren't inquisitive by nature. From what she had seen since Tchardin and Damarin left the island, few kandar outside the council had made note of their disappearance. Jaydin said that was perfectly normal. If the council didn't directly address the kandar they were left to their own devices. Those usually concerned only themselves and possibly their dodenzinn. Time away from the humans had made them dull and isolated. The closeness between the daughters of Tith was a product of their unnatural situation.

"Tchardin and Damarin have left Calendrai," Sandin said. "They are attempting to travel to Land Side."

Ocien and Torshe exchanged a glance. Sandin expected there were words behind it, but she would never know for sure.

"Tchardin attended my birth," Ocien said. "I was worried when I saw her leaf grow dim. When are they expected to return?"

"They might not return," Sandin answered.

Ocien turned towards Torshe and her expression was sad. Torshe moved closer to her. Sandin saw the moment their auras overlapped by the slight tightening of their muscles. She had learned to look for the physical reactions that went with the invisible.

Sandin turned away to continue her search for Jaydin. She wouldn't ask the dodenzinn for something any kandar could do without even thinking about it. It drew too much attention to how different she was.

"Sandin," Ocien said from behind her. "Jaydin has left Cens. I believe she is in Tith's canopy."

Sandin looked back and shot the two kandar a grateful smile. Ocien didn't seem to notice. Torshe looked off into nothing. Sandin took a step away and already felt crowded by the leaves and branches, a few more and the two kandar would be hidden from view. She hoped Jaydin wouldn't move too much before she made it to Tith.

Sandin leapt from Tith's trunk onto one of his branches and began to search the canopy for glimpses of red. She was glad for Jaydin's hair because unlike some of the small physical anomalies she collected it was easy to see from far away. It wasn't entirely unique but it was rare.

She saw nothing around the first set of branches and climbed higher. On her way up she stopped on occasion to investigate a tevadra she saw, but none turned out to be her sister. Sandin was beginning to think she'd have to re-enter Cens when she saw a fan of red hair spread across a branch below her. She descended towards it, landing near Tith's trunk and walking along it.

Jaydin was lying on her back on the branch, her notebook thrown off to the side, caught on a patch of moss as it slid towards the drop. Sandin approached, allowing her footsteps to make noise to alert Jaydin to her presence.

"Maybe I should become High Seat." Jaydin must have guessed who approached for the same reason Ocien had mentioned in Cens. She could hear Sandin but not sense her.

"You've stopped chasing Ryten," Sandin observed.

"Couldn't find him." Jaydin's voice was emotionless. "But what do you think? Could I lead the council?"

"Of course you could. I don't know why you gave it to Damarin in the first place." Sandin sat down beside Jaydin and her sister looked up.

"Damarin had been pushing for the position since she joined the council and the old High Seat liked her, so I left the decision unanimous." Jaydin shrugged. "I don't know why she wanted it. She knows it's not worth much right now."

"What do you mean?"

"The position is a joke as it is. What's the council supposed to do without the Earths?"

Sandin was taken aback. "But you're a member. I know you find value—"

Jaydin laughed. "I respect the council for what it was. I knew I would join it the moment Tith brought me out onto the island regardless of its current ineffectuality. But I also believed the kandar would get back to the Earths during my lifetime." She sat up and moved next to Sandin on the branch, their feet dangling over the great drop below. "When we return to the Purpose the High Seat will be useful again, but she or he—"

"*He*?" This was the first Sandin had heard of a devoshai being High Seat. She'd assumed they were always tevadra because the two she knew of were tevadra, and things didn't change on Derkra.

"The High Seat has been a devoshai many times," Jaydin answered. "Sometimes it mattered and sometimes it didn't. There's no difference now, between tevadra and devoshai, but there used to be between some."

"Why?"

"We used to go to the Earths."

Jaydin said that as if it should explain everything but Sandin got nothing from it.

"Tevadra and devoshai mostly acted as women and men on the Earths," Jaydin continued. "There can be a difference between those. It was created in a lot of them through the lives they lived from birth. The kandar brought some of that back to Derkra with them. They couldn't help it."

"What about the queen?"

Jaydin frowned. "There has never been a devoshai born with the golden aura. But if there was, he could be queen. I don't see why not."

Sandin was surprised. Jaydin had told her so much already, but there always seemed to be more. "You know a lot more than I realised there was to know."

"You'll know it eventually," Jaydin said. "When we go back to the Earths."

Excitement built inside Sandin. Also a sense of missing something. It was how she sometimes felt when she remembered the lost Purpose. "So why didn't you take the position then? To get us there faster."

"The High Seat has a limited role interacting with the humans. That was the last thing I wanted. But now the kandar have forgotten the Purpose. Damarin didn't do much to remind them of it but I didn't press her because I expected Tchardin would do that. A queen would have reminded them of Tchar."

"And she's gone," Sandin said. Under Damarin the council had only talked. Tchardin would have risen above them as soon as she was acknowledged as queen of the kandar. She would have given their people someone else to listen to.

"They're both gone." Jaydin shook her head. "The one thing the High Seat *can* do in our situation is shape the council to her own purpose. The problem is that most kandar don't have one now. My purpose is and always has been the one given to us by Creator."

Sandin smiled inwardly. She had always known Jaydin could do great things, despite the oldest of Tith's daughters insisting that those great things were for Tchardin to do. She was also glad to see Jaydin obsessing over something other than their sisters' disappearance.

"I only worry because I'm not sure I could get elected now," Jaydin said. "My allies in the council are few and diminishing. I may need more support than is currently available there."

Sandin frowned. "What can we do about that?"

Jaydin looked at her with narrowed eyes. Sandin felt uncomfortable under the gaze. It was rare that those grey eyes were turned on her in that way.

"Will you join me on the council?" Jaydin asked.

Sandin's own eyes widened. "I can't. The council meetings take place in the mind—"

"They don't have to," Jaydin said quickly. "Nox is about to be called. I can see it in him. A spot will open very soon and you should be the one to fill it. I've always said there should be more of Tith's daughters in the council. The voice of another tevadra from a great tree will lend strength to mine."

"Jaydin, you know I can't join it. They'll never change the way they conduct the meetings."

Jaydin looked away, her expression guarded. "Who else is there?"

Sandin contemplated the question. Ryten was of Del—another of Calendrai's great trees, one of those hidden in Cens—but he could be named Shadow if he was Tchardin's dodenzinn. That might not happen without the queen but it was still too great a possibility to reveal the council members to him. As far as she knew Frenn had no children. If Jaydin wanted the child of a kandaran tree that left...

"Kadailin," Sandin said.

Jaydin looked perplexed. Sandin knew she had never planned to ask Kadailin. The council had always been unlikely to accept her.

"She *is* the daughter of a kandaran tree," Jaydin mused after a pause. "Of Tith, of course. The council should be forced to accept her if she expresses an interest in joining. Do you think we can create that interest in her?"

"You might be able to. But will they agree to it? How many members have joined since she was born?"

"I'm not sure," Jaydin said. "I'd say the majority of the council will remember her birth well, but it shouldn't affect her chances. Damarin is gone and I think I can convince Nox to choose Kadailin as his replacement. After that it should be easy."

Sandin wished she could be there to see it, but she was glad not to be a part of the council all the same.

"I still want you though," Jaydin said.

Sandin sighed. She didn't think there was any way Jaydin would let this go. "When you're High Seat you can attempt to change the way the meetings are conducted, but I don't expect it to work. I'll help you in any way I can, but Kadailin will be more useful to you. She could be your Voice."

"We'll see about that," Jaydin said. "For now I'll talk to Nox. Then Kadailin will have to say yes."

Chapter 8

Sitting beside Tchardin in Ovaeron's canopy, Cien felt whole and strong for the first time since he'd passed quarter life. He still wasn't sure which of the two tevadra affected him but at the moment he didn't care. His confusion must have come from meeting them at the same time. It was possible that one of them had yet to reach quarter life and would shortly acknowledge him herself. He ignored his doubts and revelled in the feeling, letting himself hope that from now on his life would be better.

Then something tugged at him inside. Ovaeron called him, pulled him down to a place at the bottom of the great father's trunk where Cien could see the bark opening in his mind. He frowned. The pull wasn't what it had once been—before he found the two dark tevadra at the shore and was given another reason to continue—but it still worried him.

He resisted, as he always had. It would be different if his father called him. When Roa finally called, Cien would go to rest without a thought, but the father of all kandar had never asked for anyone before—as far as Cien knew. There were no stories of it, nothing to tell him what should be done.

The great tree had first called him shortly after he reached quarter life. The same time the water began to call. Pulled in two directions, neither of which made sense, Cien had simply gone on. He intended to do so for at least a little longer. Maybe for a lot longer, now that he had found his dodenzinn. Whoever she was.

Tchardin turned towards him from her place on the branch.

"I was just wondering about hierarchy," Cien said to explain the look that must be on his face. He hadn't told anyone about Ovaeron and he didn't intend to start now. Especially when he was still unsure which of the two tevadra was his.

Tchardin raised her eyebrows. Had he forgotten to tell her about his position? That conversation may have taken place while she was unconscious.

"I'm the acknowledged Shadow of Black Valley," he explained. "And you're to be queen of this island on Water Side."

"I'll be the queen of Derkra," she responded without hesitation. "The queen of all kandar. If you have no queen here who believes the same then I fail to see the problem."

"We'll have to see what they think." He gestured towards the kandar below. The golden aura was supposed to be enough, but they hadn't seen her born.

Tchardin nodded slowly, her gaze passing down and across the valley. Her mind buzzed with distressed thought. Cien felt the same when he looked at her. What was happening now should not be happening.

"You have no queen here?" she asked.

He shook his head.

"And you're the Shadow?"

"For a long time now."

"There's no Shadow in Calendrai," she continued, still staring out at the kandar of the valley.

"Then there is only one of each of us, as there should be." He looked at her, smiling, trying to catch her eye. She had become uneasy and avoided him. If she was his dodenzinn it was clear she didn't know it yet.

"Do you want to see the caves?" he asked. From the look on her face he wondered if she knew the word at all. He couldn't help himself. He laughed. "Have the kandar of your island forgotten where they came from?"

"My father showed me images of Black Valley before I was born, but I don't know what you're referring to."

Cien looked through Ovaeron's red leaves towards the edge of the valley that was farthest from the water. He could just make out one of the black holes in the hardened wall of sand. "Can you see the darkness there?"

Tchardin moved closer to him and followed his gaze. She nodded.

"It's a space in the sand, full of shadows, that we can go into."

Tchardin just stared at him. Her eyes really did look like Tchar's eyes. So dark Cien could see his own eyes reflected back at him. Light, blue, empty.

"I want to show you Heirrar," he said.

"Who's Heirrar?"

"A kandaran tree. The only one on Derkra besides Ovaeron."

Tchardin seemed not to have heard. She leaned over the branch they were sitting on and looked down.

"Damarin's back," she said.

Cien let the collective flash through his mind and focused on the empty branches there. Both the leaves he had from the second collective blazed brightly. A moment later Damarin climbed onto the branch behind Tchardin. He felt even stronger when they were both close by, bringing back his initial confusion.

"Heirrar was Carrensing's father," Damarin said.

Cien didn't recognise the name. The darker tevadra came to kneel between them on the branch.

"I thought her father was one of the nine hundred," Tchardin said.

"You assumed," Damarin responded, "and technically you're right. He was."

The expression on Tchardin's face told Cien he wasn't the only one confused by the exchange.

"She had three, by the end," Damarin said. "Heirrar didn't bring her out onto the earth for the first time, but he *was* her father. If you listened to Jaydin you would know that."

"Who's Carrensing?" Cien asked.

"Carrensing was the tevadra who brought the kandar to Calendrai after the war," Damarin answered.

"Yes," Tchardin said distractedly. "Tith called her to rest when she came to the island."

"Three fathers?" Cien asked, but as he thought about it he realised that might not be strange to these tevadra. All the kandar who had left Black Valley would have been called to new fathers eventually. Someone in their past had once had two trees, no matter who they were now.

Tchardin nodded.

"And Tith is our father," Damarin said.

Cien took the words in stride at first, but then he realised she was talking about both of them. He could accept that a kandar could have two fathers over the generations, but the same father for two living kandar? "Tith belongs to both of you?"

The tevadra exchanged a glance.

"There are five of us actually," Tchardin said slowly, probably waiting for him to protest.

Cien shook his head and made a decision. "An island on Water Side was bad enough," he said. "What you say is impossible, but you are also impossible, and yet you're here."

The two tevadra looked at each other once again and Cien heard the slight buzz of their secret thoughts, but not the meaning.

"The three others are tevadra as well," Tchardin said. "Jaydin, Sandin, and Kadailin. The kandar of Calendrai call the five of us sisters."

"After female human siblings," Cien mused, "because no two kandar have ever been born of the same tree."

"Yes," Damarin said. "Five sisters. Five daughters of Tith."

The information had only just begun to sink in when Cien realised they weren't alone. Miadra walked up behind the sisters. Damarin stood to greet her. As far as Cien knew Miadra didn't spend time with any kandar other than her giant dodenzinn Cotelle. It was strange to see the dark tevadra welcome her as if they were friends. They must have met while Damarin explored the valley.

Damarin and Miadra were of a height. That was where their similarities ended however. Miadra's hair was the colour of sand and it flowed down her back and around her pale white shoulders. Damarin's hair was short and black, standing up instead of flowing down. Light grey eyes beside dark brown eyes. They were a set of extremes. He turned to study Tchardin. She was somehow softer than the two, a merging of their qualities, but she had the darkest eyes of the three.

"I want to see Heirrar," Tchardin said.

"I was just about to take Damarin to him," Miadra said from behind her.

Tchardin turned quickly at the words. Miadra's leaf must have just entered the collective for her. Perhaps she hadn't known the tevadra was there.

"Welcome to Black Valley," Miadra said with a smile. "I didn't mean to startle you."

"It's the collective," Cien provided, coming to Tchardin's defence. "She probably couldn't sense you. I have a feeling this will be happening a lot from now on."

Tchardin laughed. Damarin smiled as if she knew why. Miadra glanced questioningly at Cien. He shrugged.

"Just wait until they meet Sandin," Tchardin said. Then Damarin laughed too.

***

Tchardin avoided Miadra's eyes as she had with Cien when she first met him. The other Black Valley kandar were as unnerving up close as he was. Their eyes were clear in the way the water was clear. You could see nothing in it, or under it, and yet you knew it continued deeper.

Damarin obviously didn't share her malaise. As the four walked towards the caves she spoke silently and intently with Miadra. Tchardin couldn't hear them in the collective but she could tell they were talking by their movements.

She closed her eyes. The sand beneath their feet was hard and lit up with pandinzori. There were paths like those Cien had used on the dunes crisscrossing it, solidifying it. The pattern was so haphazard that they must have only laid the ones they needed and eventually covered the entire floor of the valley.

Some of the pandinzori pathways had begun to dissipate, the shimmering substance floating above the sand. Tchardin watched as someone from their group sent one back into the ground in front of them. It was hard to tell which of them had done it, but the hardening pandinzori had a very slight grey tinge. Cien's aura was a surprisingly dark grey, where Miadra's was lighter. It probably belonged to the devoshai.

The valley sloped upwards softly from Ovaeron's base. They were still under his canopy when Tchardin first saw the caves through the small trees. They spread out across one side of the valley, a line of dark spaces opening towards Water Side.

Cien led them to a large cave near the centre. It grew unbelievably tall as they drew closer. Tchardin could only see shadow inside it until they entered, then the light from outside made the inside visible. They stood in a large enclosed space, the ceiling of which rose much higher than the entrance. There was a tree in the middle of it. Tchardin gasped in shock at the sight of him.

"Why would he grow here?" she asked. No other tree on Derkra grew under the ground.

"We don't know," Cien responded.

Damarin and Miadra walked towards the tree. Tchardin followed slowly. She couldn't see his colour clearly in the dark, but his trunk appeared to be light. It almost glowed in the shadows of the cave. As she got closer she thought, maybe—

Damarin gasped. "He's dead!"

Tchardin ran to her sister's side. There was a large ragged hole in the tree's trunk, the wood splayed outwards in splinters.

"What happened to him?" she asked.

"He was like this when I was born," Cien said. Miadra nodded. "No kandar alive in Black Valley knows what happened to him. My father said nothing about it."

Tchardin stared at the tree in horror. Maybe it had happened during the war.

"There are no stories?" Damarin asked.

"None," Cien said from behind Tchardin.

The tree was magnificent, despite his alarming state. Such a great, straight, white trunk. His branches—bare of leaves—extended to the top of the cave, some entering the rock, spreading cracks. Maybe Jaydin would know what had happened to him. Her memory of the war wasn't as good as her memory of everything else, but it would be worth asking.

Tchardin stared at the tree in awe. This is what she wished Jaydin had focused on. The Earths were inaccessible right now and maybe never would be again. Derkra was more than just Calendrai. The history of the kandar was more than just the Purpose.

"Jaydin doesn't know about this," Damarin said.

Tchardin turned to her sister, holding her thoughts closer.

"If she knew anything about his death, I'd know it too."

Tchardin looked away. Jaydin *had* talked about the history of the kandar, just not with her. Tchardin wondered if their oldest sister would have felt more free to do so if Tchardin didn't have the golden aura, if there was no pressure to prepare for her ascension with stories of the Earths. But Jaydin hadn't told Kadailin anything. Tchardin's golden aura was the reason Jaydin spoke to her at all. Why did Damarin know so much? What had made Jaydin educate her, and why had Damarin bothered to listen? Tchardin turned back to their middle sister in time to see her exchange a look with Miadra.

"We're going to explore the other caves," Damarin said.

Tchardin refocused on Heirrar as echoing footsteps told her Damarin and Miadra were leaving. Cien looked up at the tree's splintered trunk with her. His thoughts buzzed beside hers in the collective.

"Would you like me to show you the shift?" he asked. Tchardin's eyes went to his. "I noticed you were surprised when I mentioned it earlier. Can you not open it?"

"None of us in Calendrai can." How could she have forgotten he mentioned it? He had talked about Tchar. "I've never even seen the shift."

Cien motioned for her to follow him out of the cave and she did, her body tense with apprehension. Seeking the shift was the main reason she had agreed to travel to Land Side in the first place. There had been the longing, of course, and other more selfish reasons too, but if Jaydin ever got the chance to ask why they left that was what she would say. Both to appease her oldest sister and because it was true. The shift was something essential to being kandar and they had lost it. Creator wanted them on the Earths and with the shift they could be.

The pandinzori floating near the cave entrance became concentrated in front of Cien. A strange rift grew in the centre of it and the world appeared to bend in on itself. Then it exploded outwards in a reflective grey circle and Tchardin's eyes were forcibly averted.

When she could look at it again she leaned closer to examine the result. The grey in the circle dissipated. It whitened, then a dark streak divided it. On either side of the streak, in what looked to be pure white sand, were impressions down to something darker. Vivid colours stained the ground there and wafts of white mist grew from them. The dark line led away and out of view.

"It's Coralynth," Cien said. "What looks like white sand is actually snow. The dark line is the path, heated from beneath the earth."

"It leads to the pit," Tchardin continued for him. "Are Tchar and Dani really there?"

"I've seen Tchar a few times. I don't know anyone who's seen Dani."

"And they won't let us through?"

Cien shook his head. Tchardin felt desperate looking at the image. It didn't make sense. Why would Tchar keep the kandar off Coralynth but reveal herself in the shift?

"It's unbreakable," Cien said. "I've thrown my body against it. We've even tried to breach it with pandinzori. The shift to Coralynth is barred."

Tchardin looked at the shift again, considering.

"How do I open it?" she asked.

"The shift is behind the world. You must focus on a tiny point of pandinzori and open it to what's beyond."

Tchardin studied the pandinzori before her. Cien joined her, moving closer to it, and the image faded. The surface of the shift settled. The oval of broken reality became a sheet of slowly spinning grey streaks.

"Don't touch it now," Cien said. "The surface is fragile."

"It doesn't show an image anymore." Ignoring Cien's warning, Tchardin delicately touched the tips of her fingers to the grey. It didn't yield. She looked more closely at the reflective surface and shrunk back at her thoughts.

"Is it glass?" she asked, backing away and suppressing the urge to run. Tith had told her of the dangers of glass before she was born. The glinting, transparent substance created an instinctual fear in her like nothing had before. Like nothing else should.

"No. The surface of the shift is solid water. Something called ice."

Tchardin relaxed. Ice, not glass. She was impressed. How had Cien opened it, by focusing on nothing? It seemed he had taken pandinzori and made its opposite. Not like the loss of pandinzori on the water, but like the complete and utter absence of anything.

"It points to Water Side," he said. "To the shore. Or at least I think it does."

"You opened the shift to a place on Derkra," she whispered. Carrensing was the only kandar known to have opened the shift across Derkra.

Jaydin said the other kandar had travelled through her portal when they left.

"I've done it before, but I've never been through. I can only assume the shift on Derkra would break as it's supposed to, as the shift to Coralynth refuses to do, but I can't make myself risk it for nothing."

The shift disappeared.

"I need to learn to open it," Tchardin said.

"You will learn, but for now it's too dangerous. Explore the city. Learn about us first."

She frowned, but it was true. She had lots of things to think over. "You'll help me when we next meet?"

"Of course."

Tchardin smiled at him. The blue-eyed devoshai looked less strange to her now. She was able to look directly at him without flinching. He turned and walked away, headed in the direction of Ovaeron's trunk.

She watched him until he was hidden behind the green and yellow leaves of the valley, then turned in the other direction. She walked by the cave that contained Heirrar, thinking again about his haunting silhouette. The broken trunk couldn't have happened naturally, shouldn't have been able to happen on Derkra. No kandar would do that to a tree and there was nothing else to act on him.

She walked along the valley wall, peering into each of the caves before pressing on. She was thinking about going back to Ovaeron when she heard kandar talking. The voices came from a small cave nearby. She turned towards it, excited at the prospect of meeting more of the Black Valley kandar. As she got closer she thought she recognised one of the voices. She came to the edge of the cave opening and looked in.

It was Damarin. Miadra was with her. The empty cave amplified their voices.

"Tchar knows the Purpose better than anyone," Miadra said. "She heard it straight from Ovaeron at the beginning of time. If she wanted us to fulfill it she would let us back on Coralynth."

"You've seen Tchar?" Damarin asked. "Through the shift?"

"Many times. She just stands there and looks at me. I know she can see us. She can see what we've become and that we wait, endlessly, for her. I think she's abandoned the Purpose—"

"Or the Purpose has changed."

Miadra nodded. "Creator cares about Its children, the trees say it is so, but they say nothing about Its feelings for us. Maybe It's done with us. Maybe Tchar left us here to give us a life. So we can build a kandaran society on a kandaran world. It would be better than any human society because we, as their guardians, are better than they are. We should be the Purpose, Damarin, not the humans."

"A kandaran Purpose," Damarin said.

Did they know what they were saying? Creator's purpose for the kandar was to guard the Earths, to help the humans. To inspire and protect them. If that had changed, wouldn't they know?

"We've been barred from the Earths for generations," Miadra continued quietly, as if trying to convince herself. "There's no way to return to them."

Damarin looked at her intently for a moment. "You can't believe there's another way? What you've said up until now goes far beyond the thoughts of the average kandar. I'm surprised to find you stop at that."

Tchardin spoke without thinking. "How can there be another way?"

The two tevadra whipped around to face her. She remained standing in the entrance to the cave.

"Little sister," Damarin said quietly. "How could there not be?"

"You don't believe me?" Miadra asked.

"It's hard to believe the Purpose would change without us knowing," Damarin said, her eyes on Tchardin's. "We came here to find a way to the Earths. It doesn't appear you're any closer than we were."

Miadra looked at the cave floor.

Tchardin sat down beside Damarin and her sister smiled at her. Perhaps Damarin felt more at home on Land Side, in Black Valley where the kandar were born. Tchardin couldn't remember seeing Damarin this obviously happy before.

"Maybe..." Miadra said, drawing Tchardin's gaze away from Damarin. "Maybe I *can* think of something. Consider the shift."

A thin thread of pandinzori slid through the sand in front of Miadra, leaving the impression of a circle in the cave floor. Tchardin gasped. She'd never been able to control pandinzori with such fine detail. Jaydin could do it—she did that and better every time she wrote in her notebook—but Tchardin had never seen another kandar try.

"It's the pit, on Coralynth," Miadra said. "How much do the two of you know of Coralynth?"

"Tchar and Dani live there," Tchardin answered. "It's covered in snow like white sand."

Damarin's eyes flicked to her when she mentioned the snow. She'd have to get Cien to open the shift for her sister. Miadra's thoughts buzzed loudly, just beyond Tchardin's ability to interpret.

"We know that the path on Coralynth branches off to nine perpetually open shift portals," Damarin said. "Each leading to one of the Earths."

"Exactly." Miadra's thread of pandinzori sketched a line leading out from the circle. Tchardin almost got an impression of her thoughts before she continued. A hazy image formed in her mind and disintegrated. "When a kandar shifts to Coralynth they find themselves on the path," Miadra said. "From there they can walk forwards to the pit or"—nine lines sprouted off the centre line—"they can shift to any Earth in existence."

"That doesn't mean you can shift to them directly from Derkra," Damarin said.

Tchardin examined the rudimentary image in the sand. Where had Damarin gotten that idea from? Miadra didn't seem surprised. Damarin must have heard her thoughts in the collective and responded without waiting for her to voice them.

"Has anyone ever tried?" Miadra asked.

Then her eyes rose to something behind Tchardin, something immense.

Tchardin turned and faced the largest devoshai she'd ever seen. He was even bigger than Ryten. Taller, and broader, like two of him.

Miadra smiled. "This is my dodenzinn, Cotelle."

CHAPTER 9

JAYDIN WALKED ALONG ONE of Tith's largest branches. She closed her eyes—navigating by the brightness of pandinzori behind her lids—and studied Kadailin's leaf in the collective.

'Kadailin,' she thought to the branches around her, pushing against Kadailin's leaf in her mind. *'I need you.'*

She could hear her sister now as well as sense her. The branches above shuffled softly and a moment later Kadailin dropped down in front of her.

"I want you to join the council," Jaydin said.

Kadailin rose out of her crouch and met Jaydin's eyes as well as she could. She was the shortest of the five sisters by a fair amount.

"Nox is about to be called," Jaydin continued, not waiting for a response. "He has agreed I should find his replacement and I think a daughter of Tith will suit him well."

Now she waited for Kadailin to answer. Her sister stared at her blankly. Jaydin was reminded of a similar moment with Tchardin, shortly after their youngest sister's birth, when her eyes still held the dark emptiness of the banished kandar. It was almost impossible to recognise the future queen for the tevadra she used to be, before Jaydin's attempts at education had taken hold of her mind and made her more interesting. Kadailin had benefited from that education second hand by spending so much time with Tchardin, but she was still the most like the rest of the kandar of all the sisters. Jaydin lamented that she had taken so long to reach out.

Kadailin frowned. Jaydin held her thoughts closer.

"Will you join the council?" she asked again.

"Don't you remember how the council treated me after my birth?" Kadailin asked in turn.

Jaydin returned the frown. She remembered. She had been amongst them when it happened, unable to say anything because the only mind-voices that were permitted to pass through the shadow and be heard by the kandar outside it were those of the Voice and the High Seat. Unfortunately the High Seat hadn't even been in the shadow. She'd been with the rest of the kandar, proselytising.

"Damarin is gone," Jaydin said.

"She may be gone, but they'll always remember the things she said about me."

That was probably true. Damarin had been a force amongst the kandar, but never so visible as when she'd humiliated Kadailin at her birth. Jaydin herself had been responsible for getting the entire population of Calendrai to attend, though she hadn't known their middle sister's intentions. The great number of kandar had incensed Damarin even further and Kadailin's uncanny likeness to her hadn't done the younger tevadra any favours.

Kadailin couldn't know Damarin was the High Seat of the council, but she did know the council remembered the spectacle and had brought it up shortly afterwards, inciting Damarin's second most memorable performance. They still brought it up on occasion.

"They could remember you differently, if you join us."

Kadailin looked like she was about to slip away.

"Damarin is gone, Kadailin. Tchardin is gone. There's no longer anything to measure yourself by other than that you are kandar. Right now that means little. Let's change it together."

Kadailin's eyes met hers again. "What would you need me to do?"

"They're about to choose a new High Seat. I'll need a Voice if I can win the position."

Kadailin's lips upturned in a slight smile. "I don't know if I would make a good Voice."

"And I am not High Seat yet. But I'll need the support of someone I can trust. We were born with a built-in alliance. I think it's time we take advantage of it. As the humans say, blood is thicker than water."

Kadailin nodded at that, then tilted her head. "Blood?"

Of course Kadailin wouldn't recognise the expression. "Sometimes I think it would be easier to talk to humans. As for blood, I could show you right now, but I don't think you'd appreciate a demonstration."

Kadailin shrugged.

"So will you join?" Jaydin asked.

"I guess we can try," Kadailin finally said.

"We should go to the council shadow then. Nox will tell them of his choice and they will accept you."

Kadailin looked nervous when Jaydin turned to leave, but she knew the younger tevadra was interested now. When Jaydin climbed into the branches above them she heard her sister follow.

Tith's largest branch was unoccupied when Jaydin brought them up below it. The council would meet on Sirrhon's parallel branch. Jaydin lifted herself into shadows that flew to obscure her. Then she made the leap between the two trees and entered the shadow proper. Kadailin remained on Tith's branch and looked towards her forlornly. Kadailin was wrapped in natural shadows like all other kandar, but before being formally accepted into the council she could never achieve the level of obscurity that masked Jaydin.

Jaydin focused on the collective to call Nox. He arrived quickly, dropping out of the canopy from high above, pandinzori accumulating below him to cushion his landing. Jaydin had expected this since he was almost always in Sirrhon's branches.

The shadows of the council would cover him to Kadailin's eyes—mask his aura, hide his identity—but from inside the shadow Jaydin could see him clearly. A sense of great age came with him. He felt different than he had when she was born, though he looked exactly the same. The changes were to his mind and aura. The pandinzori around him had been thick and solid once. Now what little remained fit his body loosely and swaths of it failed to come with him when he moved. Jaydin knew that when kandar had been called to rest in the past the pandinzori around them was forcibly repelled. Tith had told her it was so and shown her what he meant in images. For Nox there was less of a repulsion and more of a lack of attraction. The pandinzori that made up his aura was not pushed away, it merely failed to stick.

"So you have found me a replacement." Nox looked towards Kadailin on the branch across from them. His voice was loud in the empty shadow but Jaydin knew it was shielded from those outside. “Are you sure they’ll accept her?”

Kadailin seemed to study the shadow, probably trying to see the details of the two kandar hidden inside it. Jaydin realised it was possible she had never met Nox individually. He knew her, but all the kandar knew her. Damarin had made sure of that.

“They can’t deny her when she’s finally found a reason to join us,” Jaydin said. He looked unconvinced. “I assure you she will only be an extension of myself in the council.”

Nox frowned. “She does not make the Purpose her own?”

“I will do everything I can to encourage it.”

Nox looked away from Kadailin and met Jaydin’s eyes. “I don’t like it, but I trust you.”

“You are right to. There’s no better replacement. You, the son of Sirrhon, could only be replaced by a daughter of great Tith.’

Nox nodded. Jaydin felt him touch the collective, calling the rest of the council.

This wasn’t the usual way a council member chose their replacement. It was almost a gentle coercion, but Jaydin didn’t believe the kandar would know the concept if she didn’t introduce it into the collective herself. Nox was perfectly happy to choose the one she chose for him and none of the kandar would believe it wasn’t his choice. They had each been chosen as a replacement by a previous member of the council when that kandar was called. It had been done that way since the beginning of time. There was no other way it could be done.

It was harder for the kandar to choose replacements now, though. The council members used to represent specific Earths and each member would choose a replacement from the same Earth they represented. They knew those kandar, knew them in ways no kandar knew any other kandar now, when they were so solitary. Jaydin took a moment to wonder which Earth Nox would have been assigned to had he been born in that time. World Five, maybe, because he was so strong, and that had been needed there. She looked out of the shadow at Kadailin again and wondered which her sister would have gone to. She found she couldn’t guess.

She wished she could speak to Kadailin and warn her that the whole council would assemble for this, but she couldn’t make herself break the rules and breach the council shadow.

Marr arrived first. He shrouded himself immediately, joining the two kandar on the branch.

'What are you up to?' he asked for her mind only.

"Nox?" Jaydin spoke loudly into the shadow. A few others climbed onto the branch and gathered around them.

"I'll wait until more of the council arrives," Nox said, similarly projecting. "I have found a replacement and she must be acknowledged."

Marr glanced at Kadailin, then turned his dark eyes on Jaydin. She wondered if he guessed the real purpose behind choosing Kadailin. It was likely he did, but there wasn't much he could do about it.

All thirty kandar who made up the council—all but Damarin, the thirty-first—were present in the shadow when Jaydin reached out to Nox in her mind.

'Now,' she said to him alone.

A dim buzz surrounded the assembled kandar—thoughts sent out over the collective that weren't well guarded. Nox spoke over them. He spoke in the collective so his words would be clear to them all. They would respond in kind, so the conversation flowed smoothly and there was no chance of misunderstanding or interruption.

'My aura fades,' he said. They turned towards the front of the shadow to look at him in one movement. *'Pandinzori does not come to me as it used to.'*

It was obvious Nox was a great devoshai. All those who were born of kandaran trees had a certain presence. Even Kadailin, awkwardly standing alone on Tith's branch, was distinct among the other kandar. The council respected Nox when he spoke. Jaydin would be sad to see him go.

It wasn't sad that he would rest. Not long after leaving he would be back on Derkra as someone else. Maybe even in Jaydin's lifetime. It was sad that he would never see the Earths. There was no chance of that now.

Maybe if she became High Seat he would come back to Derkra and find the majority of the kandar gone—on Coralynth, on the Earths—living as they should. That was her hope. Had always been her hope. If it were up to her, every kandar on Derkra would spend every moment of their lives searching for the Earths. As High Seat, maybe she could finally make that happen.

She forced herself to look back at the kandar, to look outside of her mind which was slowly but surely filling with images of the Earths and the humans who occupied them.

'Sirrhon will call me soon,' Nox said. *'I will need to be replaced.'*

The voices in the shadow buzzed more loudly, a few thoughts were heard above the rest.

'The council is ageing.'

'I will be called too.'

'Not Kadailin...'

Jaydin cringed at the last one. It was insignificant as it was, but if the mindvoices of the council joined and spoke it there was a possibility that Kadailin would be rejected despite Nox's wishes. Damarin's ghost was still causing problems for Jaydin, even if the tevadra was gone.

'I choose a daughter of Tith as my replacement,' Nox said. *'A daughter of a kandaran tree to replace a son. I wish only for the kandar to regain the Purpose. So does Kadailin. Do you join her to the council? Do you accept her?'*

'I accept her,' Jaydin said immediately, as loudly as she could. The council knew she had neglected her sister in the past for the same reasons they had. Let them know she had changed her mind.

The buzz grew in volume.

'A matched replacement.'

'The daughters of Tith belong in the council.'

Jaydin smiled at some of the thoughts that rose above the others, but voices of dissent came with those of agreement.

'Kadailin is weak.'

'Damarin wouldn't allow it.'

Then, *'Damarin is gone.'*

The buzz quieted while they considered that fact. Marr remained silent at Jaydin's side, his thoughts closely guarded.

'I accept her,' someone else said.

'As do I.'

'I accept her!'

The last voice was loud and strong. It was Anatoly's—Ahron's son. Jaydin scanned the crowd for him. His voice would lend weight to hers. The shouts of affirmation coalesced, and one thought boomed over the rest.

'THE COUNCIL ACCEPTS KADAILIN INTO THE SHADOW.'

Jaydin relaxed. The voice of the council had formed—joining all the voices of the kandar in agreement—and it had given Nox his wish. She wasn't particularly surprised, although there had been initial debate. It was a small issue and a lot of the kandar probably felt neutral towards it. In that case their voices would have been joined to the majority to form the final decision.

She turned towards Kadailin, waiting silently on Tith's branch, oblivious to her acceptance. Now all Jaydin had to do was become High Seat.

***

Derkra's ubiquitous light enveloped them as Tchardin and Damarin left the cave that now contained Miadra and Cotelle.

"Cotelle is the biggest kandar I've ever seen," Damarin said, as their distance from the cave took them from hearing range. "He's even bigger than Ryten."

"And very quiet," Tchardin responded. "I couldn't hear his thoughts at all."

Damarin nodded and stopped.

"Can you believe we're home?" she asked, gesturing into the valley. "The Black Valley, Tchardin. Ovaeron—great father of the kandar—is right there in front of us."

Tchardin followed her sister's indication and was struck again by Ovaeron's brilliant red canopy. When they left Calendrai she had thought to maybe find the great tree and possibly some evidence as to the history of the kandar on Land Side, but nothing like this. A whole other population. What would this do to Derkra? What would it do to the kandar?

The kandar had always been one people, in one place, with one authority, and one council to strengthen and balance that authority. She had been swept up in the excitement of it all since they arrived, but now, alone with Damarin, she began to worry.

"How did Miadra mean for the kandar to shift to the Earths?" she asked. "If the path to Coralynth is blocked, how could we get there?"

"The shift is one space behind the worlds." Damarin's thoughts in the collective grew so quiet they seemed to have disappeared. "In the past the kandar followed one path to Coralynth and nine more from there to the Earths. Miadra assumes there must be a way to bypass Coralynth and go directly to the Earths. If it's all connected in one way, perhaps it's connected in others. Tchar has barred us from the path to Coralynth, but she may have neglected any direct paths from Derkra to the Earths because we've failed to find them in the past."

Damarin walked down the slope into the valley. Tchardin ran to catch up.

"And you heard her thoughts on this?"

"Most of you fail to guard them, even when speaking to yourselves in your own minds."

Damarin kept walking as if she was done with the conversation. Tchardin followed her.

"I tried to hear her thoughts," she said. "I couldn't even get an impression of them."

Damarin shrugged. Tchardin would have to concentrate on keeping her own thoughts secret from Damarin in the future, even while speaking aloud.

"Don't you think we should talk about our situation?" Tchardin asked.

They passed a tevadra and devoshai standing together in the sand. Both sets of clear blue eyes followed them.

"Our situation?" Damarin looked back at her over her shoulder. "Why? These are kandar. Nothing changes."

"What about the council? There are two now."

"Join them," Damarin answered without hesitation.

"The two High Seats?"

Damarin stopped walking and turned. She stood beneath the yellow leaves of the first desert tree now, the colour of his canopy mirroring the sand below. "They'll figure it out between them. It's none of our concern."

Tchardin grimaced. "And the Shadow?"

"You haven't been asked to suggest a Shadow yet. Why not ask for Cien? The kandar will vote, of course, but those here will choose their own, and many of the kandar in Calendrai do not favour Ryten."

"None of this bothers you?"

"You still have the golden aura, little sister. You will be queen." Damarin's voice was soothing. "The kandar here can't change that. This world is yours, no matter what's in it."

"You've never felt that way before," Tchardin said, frustrated. "And I'm not worried about becoming queen. I'm worried about all of us, about the kandar. How are they here and how did we not know?"

"If the past couple generations have taught us anything, Tchardin, it should be that we know very little."

"But the trees were supposed to know everything."

"Tith was wrong about Black Valley," Damarin pointed out. "We have proof of that now." She took a few steps and disappeared behind the gnarled trunk of the tree they had stood under. Tchardin got the distinct impression she wasn't invited to follow.

'Where are you going?' Tchardin asked.

'To explore,' Damarin answered. *'To meet more of the Black Valley kandar, maybe climb Ovaeron. We can talk about this later.'*

Her sister's mindvoice faded as her leaf dimmed in the collective. She must be running to increase the distance so quickly. She would be too far away for Tchardin to answer soon. Tchardin's control of her mindvoice wasn't as impressive as Damarin's.

Tchardin looked inward at the collective, focusing on her sister's leaf. It was the only leaf she could see on the original collective, but the Black Valley collective was slowly filling up. Extended eye contact or physical closeness could form a connection and grow a leaf. She'd gathered a few of the Black Valley kandar that way, feeling their leaves grow when she crossed the city with Cien. Some others still had formed when voices came into her mind with inquiries, *'Who are you?'* Those who knew the ones she already had were easier to acquire. They came quickly. A devoshai passed her in the sand—his lightly coloured eyes resting on Tchardin for only a moment—and a bud on the tree in her mind grew and blossomed into a leaf. That one must know someone she had already, and know them well.

Now that she was alone she listened. The noise mounted as the collective grew. She felt more at home, more accepted, and yet she felt overwhelmed. The voices in her mind were strange. While it required some level of familiarity for them to exist at all, it was nothing like what she had with those from the island. Damarin's leaf was incredibly bright when compared to any of those from Black Valley. A faint voice came to her.

'Tchardin.'

She looked at the collective and found it was Cien's. His leaf was surprisingly bright as well. He was the first kandar she had met on Land Side, so perhaps that explained it.

'Cien,' she answered, to let him know she was listening. She waited. Nothing came. He walked up behind her.

She was surprised to find him so close when he sounded so far away.

"Your sister likes to listen to my thoughts," he said, "so I've been trying to be quiet."

"She does that to everyone. Speaking aloud should help but doesn't guarantee anything. The only kandar in Calendrai who can get away from her prying are Jaydin and Sandin. I'm not sure how Jaydin manages it, but at least it's easy for Sandin."

"She must have a very strong mind."

"Maybe she does." Tchardin laughed. "But we don't know. Sandin doesn't have audible thoughts. She has no place in the collective."

Cien looked perplexed. Tchardin was beginning to understand exactly how strange her sisters were. They'd been around for so long in Calendrai that the kandar accepted them as almost normal. But they weren't normal.

"Impossible, right?" she asked. "A tevadra with no mindvoice?"

Cien seemed to catch her meaning. "Just like an island on Water Side."

"And Black Valley kandar after the war."

Cien turned away to look at Ovaeron. "It certainly is a lot of change." He seemed to look past the great tree and towards the water. "I'd like to meet your sisters and see your island. When will you return to it?"

Tchardin had avoided thinking about that since they made it to Land Side. Could they even get back to Calendrai? She assumed the raft was still at the shore, stuck in the sand where she'd dragged it, but Calendrai was not the infinite length of Land Side. Despite the undefined size of Cens, Tchardin had a feeling the island was nothing but a speck in the infinity, if that. It wasn't much to aim for. Could their connection with Tith bring them home safely if they risked the water again?

She also wasn't sure it would be possible to brave the emptiness of the water after making the journey across the equally empty dunes. Whoever tried that would be starting the trip at a severe disadvantage to leaving directly from Calendrai's pandinzori-filled shore.

"Maybe I should teach you to open the shift," Cien said, interrupting her thoughts.

"To shift on Derkra?"

"How else will you get home? You're not going to cross the water again."

"Jaydin says Carrensing shifted to Calendrai the first time," Tchardin said tentatively. "That's how she found the island. Just shifted into nothing."

"Why would she do that?"

"Jaydin says Tith called her."

"Jaydin is one of your sisters? She seems to know a lot about the past generations."

Tchardin frowned. How to explain tevadra that made no sense? Jaydin was as bad as Sandin.

"Our father—Tith—spoke to Jaydin before she was born." She studied Cien's reaction, but he seemed willing to let her continue. "Not in the way all the trees speak to the kandar. He told her everything."

Now Cien looked confused.

"Everything," Tchardin repeated. "All that has happened to the kandar since the beginning of existence, as well as the history of the Earths."

"The Earths." Cien had a faraway look in his eyes. "Are you saying you know the history of humanity?"

"I know some of it, but nothing compared to what Jaydin knows."

"If you know anything of it you know more than I do. More than any kandar here. We only know what the trees told us. There are nine worlds. Nine Earths. Each Earth holds the many humans we must guide. The words of the Purpose. That's all we know."

"I was told the same." Tchardin met Cien's eyes and found them terrifying again. Within the clear blue of them was a wild look she could only recognise from the moments she'd seen Damarin on Calendrai's shore, staring out at the water. A longing.

"And your other sisters?" he asked when his eyes had cleared somewhat.

"They're like the rest of us, as far as I know. Except for Sandin, who heard nothing. Jaydin was born first and she says she knew she would be important. That she would have to use the things Tith told her to get us back to the Earths. But she also knew something else was coming, something more."

"From Tith?"

"Yes. She could feel us in him still. She didn't know we would be four, but she knew we were there."

"I need to go back with you," Cien said. "I have to meet Jaydin and learn about the Earths. And Sandin, to hear the absence of her thoughts."

And Kadailin. She was the most ordinary of the sisters but she was Tchardin's closest friend. Would Cien want to hear about her?

Tchardin jumped when he opened the shift in front of them.

"I think we should try it," he said. "Just on Land Side first."

Panic gripped Tchardin. She watched, paralyzed, as Cien stepped towards the spinning grey. He pushed on it with a hand. Cracks spread from the place his palm rested against the ice, running in white lines from behind his fingers.

"Are you sure it's safe?" she breathed. "No kandar has directed the shift across Derkra except Carrensing."

"I've opened it so many times, just waiting to break through the ice. I've never had a good enough reason to risk it."

"How do you know where it goes?" The grey of the shift told Tchardin nothing.

Cien leaned against the ice. "It aims to the valley's edge. There." He pointed into Ovaeron's leaves above them, in the direction of the water. The sand sloped up and its crest was hidden behind the red.

Tchardin tensed. She couldn't feel the location behind the ice, but maybe she wasn't close enough, and she hadn't been the one to open it. Kandar used to shift all the time, but none had crossed Derkra except Carrensing, and Jaydin had called her a master of it.

"Aren't you going to meet me there?" he asked.

She couldn't move. She only stared at him. "You can't do it."

"I wouldn't try it if I didn't think I could succeed. I feel stronger now than I ever have."

Tchardin raised an eyebrow at that but only had a moment to think before the ice Cien was leaning on collapsed. Water burst out as if alive and wrenched the devoshai through the portal. In an instant he was gone.

Tchardin stood for a moment—a splash of water wet across her face and chest—then she ran. She scrambled across the valley, stumbling when she missed a step on the brilliant paths of pandinzori and found shifting sand under her feet. Kandar stared at her as she ducked by them, sprinting around stunted trees until she was confronted with the rising slope of the valley wall. Her feet sunk into the sand there, slowing her—there were few paths up the slope she could follow. Without closing her eyes she took hold of the pandinzori around her and willed it into the sand. Her feet caught on it and she shot up the rise.

When she reached the top she felt a deep absence inside her. Cien was gone. She stopped. His leaf had gone dark in the collective, darker than any of those in Calendrai.

She sank to her knees and her mouth hung open. The feeling his dim leaf evoked in her was worse than the longing, worse than the absence of pandinzori. She felt like she would be alone forever despite the other leaves in the collective.

Water splattered her and she jumped up, blinking the wetness out of her eyes. Cien fell and rolled across the sand in front of her, tumbling down towards the next valley. Tchardin bolted after him. She caught him in a few strides and became entangled in his limbs as they slid down together, finally sinking into the sand and coming to a stop.

"Cien!" She felt through her mind for his leaf. It was bright in the collective again as it should be. Her aura blended with his as she pulled his head into her lap. She worried something was wrong with him when he didn't recoil from her.

He opened his eyes.

Chapter 10

Tchardin looked down at herself and saw that her pandinzori was thinning. Cien's didn't look much better, but their auras seemed to thicken where they merged. It should be enough to get them back into the valley.

Cien sat up and Tchardin let go of him. He looked around as if confused. Then he burst out laughing. "I'm alive!"

"I can't believe it," Tchardin said. "I felt you leave the collective."

"My leaf fell?"

"No, just—" She tried to remember exactly what had happened. "It grew very dark." She stood and her knees almost gave out as her aura separated from his. She took a step back in the direction they had fallen down the dune. "We should get back into the valley."

"I'm the first kandar to shift since Coralynth was closed to us," he said from behind her. "The only kandar other than your Carrensing to direct myself through the shift across Derkra."

"We can talk about that when we get back to the valley."

She continued to struggle up the hill and Cien walked up beside her. He didn't seem to be having as much trouble as she was. His aura was just as bright and solid as it had been before the shift. Tchardin stumbled in the sand. It had been half that a moment ago. She looked down at her own skin and the pandinzori there was practically gone.

"Do I have to carry you again?" he asked.

"No," she mumbled. The crest of the dune was only a few steps away. When they reached it she could slide down the other side. She felt terrible. She had almost no pandinzori and the collective was dim except for Cien's leaf. She focused on it, but could only think of how she had seen it fade.

She tried to stand up straight and Cien laid a hand on her back. A current ran through her and strength came with it. She knew Cien was smiling but she couldn't meet his eyes. The power he gave her through touch and the incomprehensible despair she had felt when his leaf went dark should mean he was her dodenzinn. But she struggled with the realisation. How had she not known the moment she met him? That was how it was supposed to work. After quarter life she should have known. She pulled away and used her newfound strength to run up the last of the dune and half way down the other side. The air there shimmered with pandinzori and Ovaeron's leaves reached towards her from above. She collapsed in the sand. Cien came to stand beside her.

"So you know now," he said. "We are dodenzinn."

Tchardin didn't answer. He had evidently known before she did. Why hadn't she felt it? She hadn't felt weak on Calendrai, but she had also just attained quarter life.

"Why did you risk yourself in the shift?" she asked. The seriousness of her decision to cross the water without considering her other half was starting to truly sink in. But if she had never crossed the water she never would have found him...

He took a step away. "I thought—"

"If you're my dodenzinn you could have killed us both."

Cien sat down beside her. "I want you to be able to return to Calendrai. I didn't expect the shift to be like that."

He shuddered. Curiosity overwhelmed her anger. "What was it like?"

"Like being torn to pieces behind my eyes. I felt myself—my mind—come apart. I can only assume that was the moment my leaf faded."

"But you came back together?"

"I guess so," he said. "I wanted so badly to be me again. Then I was."

Tchardin sent her mind over the collective's branches. She paused at Cien's leaf to make sure it was still there. She examined it then focused out to see all of the leaves together. His was by far the brightest now. How could that be? She didn't think their connection could become that much stronger from one experience even if they *were* dodenzinn. How could it outshine Damarin's leaf?

She searched for Damarin and almost missed her because her leaf was so dark. Almost as dark as the rest of the collective of Calendrai.

"Damarin is gone," she said.

"What do you mean?"

"Look at her leaf."

Tchardin's mind throbbed from all the change. She had done almost nothing for the first quarter of her life. She had run from Jaydin, longed to leave Calendrai, and lay around with Kadailin in the grass of the clearing. Now she found herself in a second kandaran city with the legendary tree that had brought them into existence. She may even have found her dodenzinn, which meant she never would have found him if she hadn't left Calendrai in the first place. Now Damarin was missing, but missing to where? Maybe this was what it was like to go to an Earth for the first time. Too much change. She put her hands over her face.

'Tchardin?' Cien's inquiry came into her mind.

"I need some time," she said through her fingers. "We can talk later."

She closed her eyes and focused on ignoring the light of pandinzori. Cien's outline faded away as her vision settled into black. Physical sensation left her and she no longer felt the sand against her skin. She didn't know if Cien stayed with her. She felt wholly disembodied. Then there were only the colours.

She brought up green. It was the dark green of Cens to begin with, until a burst of yellow tinged the centre of it, spread throughout it. She slowly forced it into orange then tried to match Ovaeron's leaves in colour. Red was much easier now. She watched the smudge of colour dance, only exerting her will on it when it began to fade.

She thought of creating the scene before her in colour. Behind her lids the leaves would block out the sky. Ovaeron's branches would be interlaced among them, the black striking heavy contrast to the infinite shades of red. From where she was sitting she could probably see a part of Ovaeron's dark trunk rising from the sand, and possibly some of the sand itself in the distance. The red she had brought out of the darkness gradually moved to the top of her vision, leaving a thin line of black at the bottom.

Lighter. The bottom of the red patch melted into orange, then yellow, and covered the strip of black. Her mind sharpened.

She struggled with bringing the black back to slash the red, to support it as Ovaeron's twisted trunk. Black was too strongly correlated with void—the space before the colours. The image she had made was cut in two by darkness.

Tchardin opened her eyes and the scene she had attempted to build was revealed in front of her. Despite the failure to capture it she felt focused and certain of herself again. Cien had left but she could sense him in the collective. He was probably somewhere in the great tree's branches.

She felt an urge to attempt to open the shift. She looked around the valley and watched the kandar as they interacted. None of them were close enough to judge her if she failed.

She took pandinzori from the air and remembered what she had seen Cien do to open it. She forced the light inwards on itself with her mind. Her gaze was pushed away. When she looked back, the pandinzori that had been in front of her was gone. Had it been the shift that forced her eyes away for a brief instant?

She gathered more pandinzori before her. It was like she had to fold it in on itself, but then, once it was consumed, allow what resulted to expand. She pressed the pandinzori lightly, slowly, until it seemed like the next push would shatter it. She nudged it with her mind. It imploded.

She let go of the force she had exerted on the small space, pulled outwards on it. The shift grew in front of her. It grew until it was large enough to see into easily. Its edges were made of pandinzori, so she simply stretched that and it expanded. The result showed no image, just a slowly spinning greyness. She couldn't feel a destination behind it but she hadn't had anything in mind when she opened it. She focussed on it and thought of Coralynth.

The change was subtle at first. The grey became solid and white. The swirl turned into a vertical fall. There was snow falling on Coralynth. She tried to look deeper. There was a slight indent in the bottom centre of the image. The path.

She was so mesmerised by the image she forgot the danger Cien had warned of. She moved towards it. As she got closer she saw that the surface was solid and sensed that the place she was looking at was not actually there, on Derkra, but somewhere behind the world. She walked right up to the ice, until her breath caused hairline cracks to appear in front of her mouth. Would the shift to Coralynth open for her when it wouldn't open for any other? Jaydin had taught her to believe it might. Did she dare to find out?

She pressed on the ice with a palm. It cracked further, the lines becoming thick and white. She drew her hand back, paused, and brought it forward quickly, smashing her fist against the wall of solid water. It didn't yield. She was about to throw her entire weight against it when the cracks vanished and a pair of eyes blazed before her.

They were her eyes. The eyes she had seen reflected back to her in the water again and again. But the face was not hers. The skin was white, lighter even than Cien's skin, so light that the pattern of dapples on all kandar's skin was barely discernible there. So light that the shadows that clothed it were but a wisp. Tchardin jumped away. Half the tall figure was visible now, long and willowy, with dark red hair.

"Tchar," she said.

The first kandar stared at her with her own black eyes, expression unreadable. A jolt ran through Tchardin as another aura collided with her own. The shift vanished.

"She did the same thing to me when I tried to go through," Damarin said.

"Where have you been?" Tchardin backed away from her sister's aura. "I couldn't sense you."

She looked inwards and there was Damarin's leaf, brightest of those lit up in the collective, even brighter than Cien's.

"Wandering in the dunes," Damarin said with a shrug.

"Why?" Why would Damarin subject herself to the emptiness of the desert by choice?

"I wanted to see if I could do what Cien did when he found us. I wanted to bring excess pandinzori with me."

"Did it work?" Tchardin asked. Damarin smiled but didn't answer. Tchardin took that as a yes. "And you've opened the shift too?"

"Of course. Miadra taught me."

Damarin pulled pandinzori out of the air around them and held it in front of her. She effortlessly opened the nothing. Tchardin watched but couldn't see anything different than what she had done, only the process was quicker and appeared more practiced.

The swirling grey of the shift grew dark. Tith's trunk appeared. Behind him the edge of Cens materialised. Tchardin gasped.

"It really does look a lot like glass," Damarin said, misinterpreting Tchardin's reaction.

"Yes, I was worried the first time I saw it," Tchardin responded distractedly. She couldn't take her eyes off the image. "It's Calendrai."

She hadn't realised how much she missed the press of trees. Nothing here was the deep emerald closeness of Cens. Land Side was too yellow, open, and limitless. The image of Tith beckoned to her.

"You didn't think to look at Calendrai?" Damarin asked.

Tchardin shook her head. She hadn't expected to be able to see the island through the shift. She had thought the visualisation of the destination was unique to Coralynth.

"I'm surprised." Damarin closed the portal.

Tchardin watched Calendrai disappear with sadness. She had spent a lot of her young life longing to leave it and now she wanted nothing more than to return.

"I need to go back," Damarin said.

"Now?" Tchardin was startled by the force in Damarin's voice.

"The kandar of Calendrai need to know we still exist."

Tchardin hadn't thought of that. If the lights of Calendrai's collective were dark for her, her own must be dark for the kandar there. They would think the future queen was dead, drowned somewhere in the vast expanse of Water Side. What would Jaydin think of it?

"How will we get back?" she asked. "The raft?"

"I was thinking the shift would be best."

"Have you tried it? Shifted on Derkra?"

Damarin shook her head. "I wanted to talk to you about it first."

What made her think she could do it? Damarin had opened the shift in front of Tchardin with more ease than even Cien had. That was impressive, but did it really mean anything? Navigating the shift was unknown to them. Unknown to all of them but Cien.

"I *knew* Cien had tried it!" Damarin gave her a calculating look. "I felt him leave the collective."

Tchardin's eyes widened. How had Damarin noticed Cien vanish from all the way out in the desert?

"But he came back," Damarin said. "So it's possible."

"He almost didn't make it, Damarin, and he's never been to Calendrai."

"We have."

As if summoned, Cien's leaf brightened in the collective, announcing his imminent approach. Tchardin turned to see him walking towards them.

'If he's done it and survived I can definitely do it,' Damarin said into her mind.

'What if we land in the water?' Tchardin tried hard to hide her words. Cien was focusing on the two tevadra now.

"You will shift to Calendrai?" he asked as he came to stand with them. Damarin glared at Tchardin. "I'm coming with you if you go."

Tchardin hesitated. "Describe the shift to Damarin."

"It's dangerous," he said, "but I think we can do it. I did it and I'm here, aren't I?" Cien laughed. "I believe it can only get easier."

The buzz of Damarin's thoughts disappeared from the collective. Tchardin frowned at her.

"I've opened the shift to Calendrai," Damarin said, glaring back at Tchardin before turning to Cien. "There's an image of Tith, just as there is one of Coralynth. Maybe the trip will be safer than it was through Black Valley. But maybe it will be blocked just like Coralynth."

Tchardin hadn't considered that. Damarin was always a step ahead in her thinking.

"The only way to find out is to try it," Cien said. "All we have to do is open it and touch the ice. The shift will do the rest."

"So once we commit to it we have to be ready," Damarin responded. "If the ice breaks we'll know it's possible, but it will be too late to reconsider."

Tchardin looked at the other two kandar. Should they try it? Were they ready for that?

"We'll do it," Damarin said, "but we should alert the council to our plans first."

Tchardin fought the suggestion internally for a moment. She had bad experiences with the council in Calendrai. Then she thought of how important it was for this council to meet her. During their time in Black Valley neither she nor Damarin had stood in front of them and told them of Calendrai. The number of kandar on the island far outweighed the number here. When the councils were joined things would change more for the Black Valley kandar than for those of Calendrai. She'd need them to accept her fully in order to facilitate that joining.

"I agree," she said. Cien seemed surprised to hear her say it. He was too eager to try the shift to Calendrai. She could tell he didn't want anything to get in the way. "If the three of us attempt this and fail, who will reunite the kandar? Calendrai likely thinks we're dead and Black Valley doesn't know us."

Damarin nodded. "My thoughts exactly."

Tchardin looked to Cien. "Can you call them? Show us where they meet?"

Cien sighed. He grudgingly nodded. She saw the frustration in his eyes.

'We will *shift,'* she thought only to him. It didn't matter if Damarin heard, but she wanted him to know the assurance was for him. *'It's the only way we'll get back.'*

They stood before the second largest cave in the valley wall, one of the two that lay adjacent to the cave that housed Heirrar. The shadow inside it wasn't made up of the normal shadows of Derkra, but of something more. It was the council shadow. The faint outlines of bodies moved through it. As in Calendrai their exact number was uncountable and their features were obscured.

"How do they get in there?" Tchardin asked Cien, who stood beside her. Damarin spoke silently to a devoshai behind them. "How do they enter the shadow without being identified?"

"There are tunnels behind the caves. They enter through other caves and come in the back."

"What do they do now that we've lost the Purpose?" She remembered the council of Calendrai and their endless words.

"They talk," he said. "Sometimes only one kandar listens, but they still talk."

What could they talk about? Perhaps it was the same thing the council in Calendrai went on about. The lost Purpose. The lost Earths. The uselessness of their people now that they were in exile.

Damarin continued to speak with the devoshai behind them. Tchardin looked back at him. The collective was a blur this close to the council, and it hurt her mind to look at it, but she didn't need it to recognise him. He was huge. He had to be Cotelle, Miadra's dodenzinn. She assumed he would leave before they proposed their plan. Only the council was necessary for this meeting.

Damarin moved to stand beside her. Cotelle walked past them and disappeared around the edge of the cave entrance.

"What were you talking about?" Tchardin asked her middle sister when he was gone.

"Nothing interesting."

Tchardin frowned.

"He wanted to know how we got here from Calendrai," Damarin finally said. "I told him about the raft, but I'm not sure he understood. His thoughts are so quiet."

Cien stared at the edge of the council shadow, in the direction Cotelle had gone. "He hides them well," he said distractedly. "How did you even meet him? I don't think I've ever seen him talk to anyone but Miadra."

'Shadow.'

The word emanated from the cave. The deadened tone of the Voice of the Black Valley council was so like that of the Voice in Calendrai that Tchardin shivered. The three kandar turned to face the council.

'Who are these tevadra you have brought before us?' the Voice continued. *'We see that one of them has the golden aura, but Black Valley does not have a queen.'*

'This is Tchardin,' Cien said, *'and the other is her sister, Damarin.'* Tchardin actually heard the buzz of the council's thoughts through the shadow at his words. *'Tchardin will be the queen of Derkra but she has not yet been acknowledged.'*

'This is true,' the Voice responded, *'for we have not acknowledged her.'*

Tchardin felt mild annoyance. Everyone knew she hadn't been acknowledged, not here nor in Calendrai. There was no need to constantly repeat it.

'Tchardin and Damarin come from an island on Water Side,' Cien said, *'where there is a city called Calendrai. They say a large group of the nine hundred moved there after the war.'*

'There is nothing on Water Side but water,' the Voice responded.

'There is Calendrai,' Cien said enthusiastically. *'This means the kandar were not so badly decimated by the war as we've thought. They say there are*

at least four hundred kandar on the island. With Black Valley that could give us close to six hundred of the original nine. We must join with them.'

'So you have come to propose a journey?'

'We want to shift to Calendrai.'

Movement and the noise of thought came from the shadow. *'You propose that kandar shift across Derkra?'*

'I've already done it.'

Tchardin heard the pride in his mindvoice. She looked over at him and his face showed it too. His aura glowed brilliantly and his eyes were bright. She studied his profile as he stared down the faceless council. They were quiet for a long time. Finally the Voice spoke.

'We feel it is too dangerous for kandar to attempt the untested shift to Calendrai. If the shift is possible across the land then it will soon be possible across the water, but work must be done to ensure its safety. You spoke of the number of remaining kandar. We will not allow that number to diminish needlessly.'

"I need to go now," Damarin said from beside Tchardin, her voice too quiet for the council to hear. "I can't just wait here until they allow us to try it."

Tchardin exchanged a glance with Cien. What could they do?

'We arrived here on a raft,' Damarin said. *'That method of travel has already been tested. I will take the raft back to Calendrai.'*

Why Damarin would ever agree to do that again confounded Tchardin. It had been horrible, and it would be worse after crossing the desert. It would be better for them to shift without telling the council.

The shadow rippled as if all the kandar behind it turned inwards to discuss the proposal. Tchardin could almost feel them thinking.

The Voice spoke again. *'It is decided that Damarin will take the raft back to this island on Water Side.'*

Cien looked at the ground. Tchardin felt sad for him, and for herself. It would be a long time before they would see Calendrai, time for Damarin to get there and time again for the council in Calendrai to make a decision regarding her return. She might never even make it.

'One condition,' said a new voice.

Tchardin looked up. The shrouded figures had parted slightly to reveal a single form, centred in the deep shadows. Tchardin could only assume this was the High Seat, although it was unusual to hear the High Seat speak directly.

'Damarin may take the raft back to Calendrai only if she finds a suitable companion to join her. It is too dangerous to go alone.'

Tchardin tried to get Damarin to meet her eyes. They should go together again.

'This does not include the Shadow or the future queen of Calendrai,' the High Seat added. *'Of all the lives we must preserve, those are the greatest.'*

Damarin looked pensive.

'That will do,' she finally said.

Tchardin was taken aback by how authoritative she sounded, as if the decision had been hers. This High Seat, despite being one of two now, would still be second only to Tchardin once she was acknowledged as queen. Right now the High Seat was first. Damarin was only kandar.

The dark shapes inside the shadow retreated. Tchardin waited while they left, the thick shadow inside the cave returning to its natural state, each council member disappearing deeper into the earth.

"Who will you take with you?" Cien asked Damarin.

"I haven't decided." Damarin shrugged, then smiled. "Perhaps Miadra would like to go."

"Not a bad choice."

"I'll think on it more, just to be sure. I'll find you before I leave. Maybe you two can make the journey to the shore with me?"

Tchardin felt like she was being left out of something of great concern to her. She was going to be queen of the island, queen of all the kandar and she wasn't allowed to travel to her city?

"I think we should just shift," she said.

Damarin raised an eyebrow at her. "The council's word is kandaran law, Tchardin, you know that."

"My word is kandaran law."

"Only if it's approved by the council. And only once you're acknowledged."

Tchardin turned her back on Damarin. It was true, but it wasn't fair. She sensed Damarin's aura retreating, leaving her and Cien.

"Come to the top of the valley wall with me," she said once they were alone.

They crossed the valley and ascended the slope behind Ovaeron, this time climbing it on a wide path of pandinzori that Cien laid for them. Tchardin didn't speak while they walked. She heard Cien's disappointed thoughts from beside her and she didn't want to say or think anything too loudly until they were far from Damarin.

When they were at the crest of the dune and Ovaeron's leaves blocked the valley from view behind them, she spoke.

"Cien," she whispered to afford them the least chance of someone overhearing, "I think we should shift to Calendrai together."

Chapter 11

Jaydin ushered Kadailin into the shadow as quickly as she could without allowing their auras to collide.

"It doesn't feel right." Kadailin tried to find a way around Jaydin. "I'm not a member. I don't belong in the shadow."

"You're a part of the council now. You just haven't adjusted to the shrouding yet. That won't happen until Nox is called but you still have to attend meetings with him first."

Kadailin finally allowed herself to be directed onto Sirrhon's branch. Jaydin watched her disappear into the darkness there. She stepped across to join her and Kadailin was visible again, but her appearance was strange.

From outside the shadow the members were obscured, even to other members who had yet to enter. Once a member joined the shadow however, the darkness disappeared and everything was clearly visible to them. Kadailin was different. There was a layer of light between her body and the deep shadows that masked the other council members. There were regular shadows within that light, but they were nothing like the shadows of the council. The effect was that she seemed to glow.

Nox and Anatoly were in attendance already and Jaydin nodded in their direction. She had called the full council before stepping onto the branch but the two devoshai were the first to arrive.

Jaydin took a moment to look over her personal army. Three children of kandaran trees. Four including herself. The tree one was born to had never been a concern for the kandar of the past. The only great tree in Black Valley had always been Ovaeron, until Heirrar joined him, but neither of them had borne any children. Or, they hadn't until Heirrar held Carrensing. Before that all kandar had been created equal. It shouldn't mean anything now but when everything else was the same, any difference was noteworthy.

There were usually only ten or so vocal kandar at the meetings. If the kandar before Jaydin spoke loudly in her favour, they wouldn't have to sway many. The council had to agree to make her High Seat. There was no other reasonable choice.

'Kadailin.' Jaydin directed her mindvoice at her sister's leaf in the collective, keeping her words from the others. *'You know I wish to become High Seat, and you my Voice.'*

Kadailin nodded, her mouth open slightly as she stared at the council members, revealed to her for the first time.

'Now that you're here I can tell you who the current High Seat is.'

'Everyone thinks she's tevadra,' her sister said distractedly.

'Yes,' Jaydin responded. How would Kadailin take the news? *'Surprisingly perceptive. Damarin currently holds the position.'*

'Damarin?' Kadailin turned to glare at Jaydin while the rest of the assembled kandar turned to look at her. The thought had not been well guarded.

Jaydin didn't have time to address Kadailin's outrage before Marr arrived. The devoshai moved through the crowd of kandar to stand near them, his gaze fixed on Jaydin. He was going to make this difficult for her.

She sneered at him. The Voice. More useless than the High Seat in this current generation. The Voice was meant to add another layer of anonymity to the secret position of council leader. The shadows could warp a mindvoice—masking tone, emphasis, and all the other superficial qualities of mindspeech—but they couldn't disguise the way sentences were formed, the order of words, even the choice of words, specific to each kandar. So the High Seat had a Voice to speak for them, and the Voice was changeable, in case they were found out.

Damarin's speech patterns were somewhat recognisable, due to the amount of time she'd spent with Jaydin, but the average kandar probably wouldn't notice. Most of them sounded the same when they spoke now, if they spoke at all, but things had been different before they lost the Purpose. Once, the humans of the world a kandar worked on had influenced their speech. It was often clear immediately which Earth a kandar had been assigned to by the way they described something. Just by the words they used.

The social nature of the kandar had affected their speech as well. Now it was strange to see two kandar talking, but once groups of kandar had spent all their time together, developing unique patterns of speech, adopting words the rest of the nine hundred never encountered. That was when the Voice would have made a real difference.

Now he was just a devoshai with the ability to think more loudly than the rest of them.

"You called this meeting?" he asked.

Jaydin smiled. Nox addressed the council.

'The High Seat and the future queen have disappeared from Calendrai. In Damarin's absence, and in view of the council's expanded duty in a city without a queen, I propose that we elect a new High Seat. How can the council address the kandar without a leader?'

Thoughts buzzed through the collective. Jaydin couldn't detect either a positive or a negative response. Anatoly's mindvoice flashed over the clamour but it was quickly swallowed.

'I propose that our new High Seat be Jaydin,' Nox said, *'and the Voice be of her choosing as is proper.'*

The sound of thoughts rose to near deafening. No individual words could be extracted from the grating, buzzing haze of them. Then Marr forced his way through the group of kandar to the pocket of space around Nox. Courtesy of his position, his mindvoice boomed loudly over the rest.

'As the legitimate Voice I will remind the council that no new High Seat can be named until the previous High Seat has been called to rest.'

It was usually true, but in this case they weren't going to get a body. Jaydin rushed to join Nox and Marr, the kandar parting ahead of her as her aura brushed them. Kadailin snuck in behind her as the press of auras closed again.

'She's not coming back,' Jaydin said. *'You know that.'*

'I do not *know that, and neither do you.'* Marr glanced around at the assembled kandar. *'None of you know anything about Damarin's fate, nor that of Tchardin.'*

'We can't wait!' Jaydin strained her mindvoice to be heard over the rest. *'We need to get back to the Earths. We had a strong High Seat and a future*

queen in the same generation. It looked like we were finally going to get somewhere—but we were waiting then too. Now they're gone and nothing has come of it. We can't wait any longer.'

The kandar looked at each other uncomfortably at her words. Their thoughts were quiet. Nox frowned beside her. No voices were raised in support. Marr opened his mind to speak but Jaydin talked over him.

'We need to do *something. I know that lacking proper position none of you will listen to me. That's why I need to be our High Seat. If the council won't listen, what of the rest of the kandar?'*

Beside her Kadailin looked down at the branch, avoiding the eyes of those around them.

'I don't want the position,' Jaydin said. *'I never wanted it, but I'll take it if I have to.'*

"Not yet you won't," Marr whispered to her.

The look in his eyes told Jaydin he was unreservedly loyal to Damarin. If only their middle sister had been born in place of Tchardin. What a queen she would have made. But they were both gone now. There was no use comparing them.

The collective shivered. Tremors radiated from Nox's leaf. The council was deathly silent. Jaydin couldn't have thought of a worse time for it to happen.

'I am called,' Nox said to them all. *'I must go to Safren. I will return to Sirrhon when she is gone. You are all welcome to see me into my rest.'*

Jaydin searched the collective for Safren's leaf. She must have met Nox's dodenzinn at some point. She found the leaf dim and gently pulsing. There would be few kandar to witness that loss, when the vibrations that told of Nox's calling shook the whole collective mind. Jaydin could already feel herself being tugged towards the place in Sirrhon that Nox would ultimately rest.

The council began to disband. Nox and Marr had disappeared.

"We should find Sandin," Jaydin said to Kadailin. "She won't know Nox is called."

"I can't believe Damarin is the High Seat." Kadailin's eyes darted between the council members as they left the shadow.

"If you knew her at all you wouldn't be surprised."

Jaydin left the shadow and Kadailin trailed behind her.

"The High Seat was terrible to Tchardin," Kadailin said. "And to me. Damarin was even terrible to me as herself!"

Jaydin nodded, scanning the branches around them for Sandin. Their sister had to be somewhere close by. She would be anxious to hear how the meeting had gone.

"Do you even care?" Kadailin asked.

"Of course I do, but there are more important things to worry about right now."

Sandin dropped down in front of them. Jaydin tensed as her sister found her balance on the branch. She worried Sandin would fall. Jaydin could catch her this time, but if Sandin fell when no one was around it might be the end of her. Kandar were resistant to injury, but a fall from the great tree without pandinzori to cushion it? Jaydin wasn't sure she'd survive.

"How did it go?" Sandin asked.

"They won't elect a new High Seat when Damarin's fate is uncertain."

Sandin frowned. "The chances they make it back are slim. No kandar has ever attempted to cross the waters of Water Side. You know that."

"I do," Jaydin said, "but it doesn't seem to matter. Marr demands a body and we'll never be able to give him one. The rest won't risk themselves by speaking up." Sirrhon pulled her more strongly now. "We can contemplate this issue later. Nox is called."

Sandin's face fell. "One less ally in the council."

Nox had been Jaydin's best chance at swaying the council. The timing was terrible. "I still can't believe they did this to us. It wouldn't even matter if Damarin left us with this problem if Tchardin had stayed. Of course they both had to go."

She walked down the branch. She sensed that Nox would enter Sirrhon above them. That was strange as kandar usually went to the base of their trees. Sandin followed her but Kadailin didn't move.

"Aren't you coming?" Jaydin asked. "Nox has given you his spot in the council, the least you could do is see him into his rest."

"This is all your fault," Kadailin said.

"What's my fault?" Jaydin was taken aback. "How is any of this my fault?"

Sandin moved slightly between her and Kadailin.

"Tchardin wouldn't have left if it weren't for you," Kadailin said. "Damarin wouldn't have lured her into danger."

"What could their reckless actions possibly have to do with me?"

"You pushed Tchardin too far and I suspect you did it to Damarin before her." Kadailin's voice was strained when she continued. "I won't let you do it to me."

"You had done nothing until I began to push you."

"Your pushing turned Damarin against her sister. Tchardin could be nothing more than she innately was, because as our future queen she was already the greatest thing Tith could offer you. But Damarin strove to be High Seat? You put that ambition inside her. If she kills Tchardin for it you will be to blame."

"The High Seat and the queen are exclusive. One doesn't replace the other." Jaydin couldn't believe how assertive Kadailin was being. She had never seen anything like this from the tevadra. "Damarin could never have replaced Tchardin without the golden aura. I'm not trying to replace Tchardin."

"Without a queen the High Seat rules. That's what you want, isn't it?"

"She wants what we should all want," Sandin interjected. "To return to the Purpose."

Kadailin appeared to have calmed at hearing Sandin's voice. She met Jaydin's eyes and hers had regained their usual placidity. "The only thing I want is to have Tchardin back, even if she comes with Damarin."

Jaydin looked into the collective to find Safren's leaf gone. "We need to go now if we're to see Nox one last time."

***

"Damarin will take too long on the raft," Tchardin said, "if she makes it at all."

Cien looked across the sand, towards the place he would see water if the dunes weren't in the way. Water Side was infinite in size. There was no certainty Damarin would make it to the island, especially when she had to travel through the desert without pandinzori first.

Tchardin nodded instead of continuing. She must agree with his thoughts. The raft wasn't safe and the journey probably wasn't possible. Perhaps they could get to Calendrai and back before Damarin risked it?

"That's what I was thinking." Tchardin looked at him intently. "But I can't do it alone."

"Don't you think it's better if I go without you?"

"No. I need to go too. If we're going to die it should be together. Just in case."

She left the rest unsaid but Cien knew what she meant. If they were dodenzinn it would be unfair for one to risk the other by risking themselves. Just as he'd done when he shifted for the first time.

"I'm sorry I tried it when I didn't know what I was doing," he said. "I didn't think of the damage I could have done to you."

"The risk is limited if we go together. Do you think you can open the shift to Calendrai? I'd prefer to go through yours since you have more practice with it than I do."

"Can you show it to me?"

"I'll try."

Pandinzori floated to her. She concentrated it around them and awkwardly opened the shift. The circle of grey settled into darkness with a massive trunk at the centre of it. Cien moved closer to the image. The trunk was a deep brown and there appeared to be a wall of shadowed trees behind it.

"It's Tith," Tchardin said. "My father. That's Cens—the forest—behind him."

Cien contemplated the scene. He opened the shift beside it and tried to understand the image. Where it was. What it was. No matter how hard he tried he was unable to locate it in the shift. He couldn't believe something outside of Land Side could exist on Derkra. The water and sand were everything.

He could believe in Tchardin and Damarin, strange as they were. Once something was, it was. This was only an image in ice. He let the shift wink out. Tchardin's portal remained there, with Tith at its centre.

"I can't copy it."

"Well," said Tchardin, "this is as I expected. We'll have to go through mine."

"I should go first, so you can keep it open for yourself."

"We should go together."

Tchardin touched the ice gently from beside him. Nothing happened. She pressed harder but made no impression on the shift.

"Why doesn't it work?" he asked.

Tchardin frowned. "Damarin said it might be blocked, like Coralynth."

"What should we do?"

"Maybe..." she said. The image in the shift dissolved. Grey came back and swirled there. "I think this is the same but without the image."

Cien studied the spinning grey. He didn't recognise the place it pointed to. The feeling it gave was new to him.

Tchardin reached for the ice. This time cracks formed at her touch. The outline of the shift stretched to accommodate both of them. Cien watched, transfixed. The cracks spread. Pain flared in his mind for an instant before fading to a dull ache. He looked back at Ovaeron from the valley's edge. The great tree beckoned to him. The call was muted—as it had been since Tchardin and Damarin arrived on Land Side—but it worried him as always.

He remembered the shift. He had been water. Water that wanted to go everywhere. The water had been his mind.

"Be prepared," he said as she pushed against the ice. "It will be like nothing you've ever experienced."

He felt her hand on his, felt the strength of her aura flow into his body, and looked down to see her black eyes that so reminded him of Tchar.

Water rushed over them.

The water raged. It twisted away and came back again. It wanted only to expand. Expand forever until it was calm. It rushed outwards until it was pulled back, drawn by something that wished to remain together.

Every moment it was torn apart and recombined. Every moment its hold weakened. Then another rush of water joined it and it remembered.

A thought came out of the intruding body of water. It said, *'Cien'*.

'Tchardin,' the first body replied. Then the second body of water dove into the first and the rush of the first grew to be twice as strong. It churned and sped away, moving all together now, to expand, expand even farther than it ever could have alone.

'Wait,' the water said amidst the churning and bubbling and rushing and expanding. *'Wait.'*

As the water expanded it became less. Its power dissipated. The words dissolved. Everything was better than two and two was better than one but one was better than nothing. It couldn't relinquish its mind, its words, its being. What had pulled before, pulled again and the water came rushing inward. All was washed together.

With compactness came intelligence and knowing and for an instant he could see.

Cien pushed Tchardin away from him. He pushed against the barrier in front of him. It gave way.

The first thing he noticed was colour. Translucent blue. Then he saw his thrashing arms in front of him. He stopped struggling and reached in the direction he thought was up, pulled himself through the water. He broke into the air. Pandinzori greeted him.

He was surrounded by water. He fought to stay afloat but his feet found nothing to grip and his arms sluiced through the blue and barely held him up. For a moment he was hysterical and fought the water as he had in the shift. Then he realised he was on Water Side and Tchardin was nowhere to be seen. He stopped moving. Tchardin was gone. He would never feel the trees again. He would drown.

He floated.

"Great," he said.

Something touched his shoulder, making him shiver. What else could be in the water? He looked back slowly and Tchardin's face rose into his vision. Her hand wrapped around his arm and she pulled him through the water. Relief froze him.

'The shore is just behind you,' she said. *'The water isn't deep like this where I left the island.'*

The Black Valley collective was dark in his mind. He searched the new section of the tree and felt a surge of weakness as he passed over the place where Damarin's dim leaf hung. The brightness of Tchardin's leaf revived him.

His back hit something solid and shadows loomed above. He climbed onto the shore behind Tchardin. The ground they stood on was mottled and dark, like her skin. Compared to the shore of Land Side, this strip of earth was tiny. The water threatened at his back.

The trees that stood before him were not the stunted desert trees of Black Valley, with their white trunks and yellowish-green leaves. These were dark and thick, straight and tall. Their leaves were deep green, their trunks a rich brown or black. They harboured so many shadows he couldn't see anything through them.

"We did it," he said.

It was unbelievable. They had shifted onto Water Side. To Calendrai. They had missed, but not by much, and they'd made it.

"That can't be how the shift is supposed to be," Tchardin said.

Cien had to agree. "It was different when I was alone, but still violent. The water reacted similarly to me, tried to rip me apart, but with you there..."

Tchardin cringed. "I wanted to *be* you."

"Yes, that's what it felt like. I wanted to be everything."

He wondered if it could have happened, if he could have absorbed her forever. He had no doubt they could have been trapped there, in the shift, as the water.

"We can ask Jaydin how it was for the kandar in the past," Tchardin said. "For now, we've made it."

A wave of strength passed through Cien. He closed his eyes, bringing up the barren collective. A light had become lit. He opened his eyes to find Tchardin staring at him with her mouth open. She must have seen it too.

"Damarin is here," he said. The tevadra's leaf blazed beside Tchardin's.

"How dare she shift after she told me we couldn't!" Tchardin turned away from him, her thoughts quieting.

Cien looked back at Damarin's leaf. Why had she shifted without them? Tchardin had clearly indicated she thought they should defy the council and shift on their own. Why would Damarin discourage Tchardin and then do it herself?

"Did she follow us?" Tchardin asked.

Cien shook his head. Damarin might have seen their leaves go dark but she had no way of knowing they were here, only that they had left the valley. Considering Cien often left the valley for the dunes, their disappearance was no proof they had shifted to the island. "Maybe. But probably not. She must have meant to do this. We wouldn't have known she'd done it either, if we'd stayed."

Tchardin looked to the trees. "I can sense the others," she said, changing the subject. "I wonder if they've noticed me. Or Damarin."

"Can you talk to them?"

"I can try, but they're far away. I'm not sure I can differentiate. I could be sending thoughts of my return all over the collective and Jaydin might not like that. Better to find them before attempting conversation. Best to find Damarin first."

Cien wondered if his presence would be as impossible for the kandar of Calendrai as Tchardin's had been for him. He looked through the trees and felt Ovaeron's call, dampened by distance. That was a benefit to leaving Land Side he hadn't considered. Now he was surprised he could feel the tree call him at all from so far away.

"Come," Tchardin said. "We should hurry. Who knows what Damarin will tell them if we aren't there."

Cien followed Tchardin towards the trees. When she entered ahead of him she disappeared. He stopped. Her leaf remained bright but she was nowhere to be seen. Endless trunks greeted his vision. Then she walked out in front of him.

"Follow me."

"But you vanished."

"Into Cens. Come."

This time when Tchardin disappeared he followed, despite his discomfort. As he broke through the first set of trunks she reappeared.

"How?" he asked.

Tchardin shrugged. "Jaydin says Cens is alive."

The forest was flooded with pandinzori. By contrast, the pandinzori in Black Valley was incredibly sparse. The trees here were uncountable, which explained the proliferation of it. Cien couldn't even estimate their number. He turned to look back at the water and found it was gone. Trunks, leaves, and darkness seemed to go on forever. "Where did the shore go?"

"It's there, only Cens hides it from you. If you walked back a step you would be out again."

"The forest looks infinite, like Land Side and Water Side. How big is it?"

"We don't know," Tchardin said. "Does it matter?"

Cien shook his head. How many kandaran trees could a forest like this hold?

"The island has at least five," Tchardin answered his unasked question, "but we're not sure exactly how many there are. There could be more hiding in Cens."

"It's spectacular."

"There's so much more to see." Tchardin laughed and ran ahead of him, disappearing between the trunks.

Cien smiled to himself and followed.

She was so well hidden in the forest. He found it difficult to spot her even when he was close enough that the trees allowed him a glimpse of her. Even then, it was only her aura he saw. The dappled darkness of her skin matched the darkness of the trees. He expected he stood out in this place as she did in Black Valley. At least if he lost her she could come back and find him quite easily.

He kept an eye on her but allowed himself to fully appreciate the forest. He had never seen so many trees. How did this forest compare to those on the Earths? This was how he had expected them to be. Or, how he expected them to be now. He hadn't been able to conceive of this before coming here. In fact, he had thought a forest was like the nine hundred in Black Valley, a widely spread set of spare and stunted trees. This was much better. Perhaps Tchardin's sister Jaydin would know how well Cens matched up to its Earthly brothers.

As he was thinking this, Tchardin disappeared into the trees again. She popped back into existence in front of him as he neared. She looked revitalised. Her golden aura illuminated the trees around them, brighter even than the pandinzori that filled the forest.

"Now you will see Tith," she said.

He looked in the direction she had come. How could anything be more impressive than this forest? He followed her through the trees and learned the answer.

Tith was taller than Ovaeron. His trunk was no match in width, but his majesty was just as great. Even in this forest full of trees he managed to be the centre of things. Even with the brothers to his right and left that were nearly as great in size he was the only thing to draw Cien's eye.

"Who are the other two?"

Tchardin pointed to Tith's left. "That is Sirrhon. The council of Calendrai meets on one of his branches. The kandar in attendance amass on one of Tith's at a place where the two run parallel to each other. On his right is Ahron. He is the smallest of them."

Cien was in awe of the trees. He was still amazed he was on an island at all. In a different place. Movement beside him drew his eye. A devoshai walked slowly across the clearing towards them, blatantly staring.

'It's your skin,' Tchardin said.

Cien looked down at himself.

"You have returned," the devoshai said when he was close enough to be heard.

'This is Torshe,' Tchardin explained. Cien could tell her words were only for him. *'His dodenzinn is a friend of mine.'*

She turned to the devoshai as he stepped up to them. Cien studied his aura. Dark and solid. Then the connection grew. Torshe opened his eyes even wider. Seeing the new collective had been a shock to Cien, so he understood the devoshai's dismay.

"Yes, I have returned," Tchardin said to him.

Torshe smiled. "Ocien will be glad to see you're alive. We were told to expect your death, if it hadn't already occurred."

Torshe examined Cien.

"I am Cien," Cien said, feeling the need to introduce himself although the other devoshai would already have his name and a whole new collective to identify him with.

"You are white," Torshe said in bewilderment. He gave Cien a suspicious look and turned to Tchardin again. "Nox is called, in case you knew him. You might make it in time if you hurry."

He sprinted away towards Sirrhon. Cien watched him go and wondered if all the kandar of Calendrai would be so dismissive of him.

"We'll head towards Sirrhon," Tchardin said. "He's Nox's father and I can feel him calling. My sisters will be there."

She walked towards the kandaran trees. Cien watched her glide through the dark grass in the clearing for a moment, some of it waist high. Pandinzori hung over it in wisps. They clung to her as she parted them but inevitably were left behind. Eddies swirled in her wake, marking her passing. She seemed to be heading towards Tith.

"I thought you said we were going to Sirrhon."

'I can't resist him,' came back to Cien. *'We can switch over when we hit the branches.'*

Chapter 12

KADAILIN SHIFTED UNCOMFORTABLY ON her feet. Jaydin and Sandin were standing to either side of her, hemming her in. After her argument with Jaydin, Sandin had attempted to persuade Kadailin that Jaydin really didn't mean any of the things she had done and that she only wanted good for the kandar and their sisters. But Kadailin wasn't sure Jaydin's intentions mattered, given the consequences of her actions.

She fidgeted between the two tevadra. The situation wasn't making her any more comfortable than her sisters were. She hated watching kandar go to rest.

The death of the child of a kandaran tree was sure to draw a crowd, just as the birth of one always did. Most of the council members were arranged throughout the branches around them, hidden amongst the rest of the kandar who had heeded the call. Their leaves had become red in the collective for Kadailin instead of green—now that she knew them for who they were. They circled Sirrhon's trunk at the place where Nox would enter him, high in the canopy.

Nox stood across from the three sisters. Kadailin searched for him in the collective, to get one last look at his leaf before it fell. It was still bright, although the pandinzori that normally wrapped itself around him had gone and his aura was nearly lost. That was supposed to be exhausting, draining. It was supposed to make a kandar long for a place in their tree to rest. His dodenzinn was gone already. That would make things worse.

Kadailin's mind left Nox's leaf and moved swiftly along the branches of the collective. The other leaves rustled as her focus flew by. She felt Jaydin next to her, the light of her oldest sister's leaf glowing brighter than it had before despite their recent difference of opinion. A small red blur drew her focus as she passed. Her eyes snapped open.

"What is it now?" Jaydin asked.

"It's Damarin." Kadailin focussed on the dim red leaf. "Look for yourself."

Sirrhon's trunk creaked and stretched before them, opening just above the branch they stood on. Jaydin spun around to look behind them, then moved away. Kadailin felt torn between joining her and showing the proper respect for Nox. She wanted to search the collective for Tchardin's leaf but that would necessitate closing her eyes again, and the devoshai would enter his father soon. Sandin remained facing the big tree and Kadailin decided to stay with her to watch. The opening in the tree grew as Nox approached the trunk. Then two auras came up behind her. Jaydin and Damarin.

Sandin turned slightly. "Where's Tchardin?"

Kadailin continued to watch Nox as Damarin stepped onto the branch beside her. Their middle sister opened her mouth to speak. Jaydin beat her to it.

"Tchardin is here too." Jaydin smiled. "And she's close."

There was surprise on Damarin's face at the words, but it quickly faded. Kadailin smiled as Nox entered Sirrhon. Tchardin was in Calendrai. Their youngest sister's leaf would be blazing in her collective now, making all the others look dark.

***

Pandinzori swirled around Tchardin in bursts of light. Tith comforted her with his presence. She hugged his trunk, climbing slowly in order to savour him. She was slow for a second reason as well. Jaydin would be waiting for her in the canopy, and the collective told her Damarin was already there.

'This is amazing,' Cien said from farther down Tith's trunk. *'The human forests must have so much pandinzori if this can be found on Derkra.'*

Tchardin smiled, but also felt sad at that. She held a faint image in her mind of a human forest Jaydin had shared with her but she was sure the reality was infinitely more impressive. She might never get to confirm that belief.

Jaydin's voice entered her mind. *'You have a lot of explaining to do.'*

Tchardin sighed, feeling for Jaydin in the collective and finding her very close. *'It'll be worth it. Believe me.'*

'It better be. Hurry now. There isn't much time if you want to see Nox.'

Tith's first thick branch was just above her. Tchardin could see Sirrhon's trunk far to the right of it through his leaves. She leapt onto Tith's branch and gestured for Cien to follow her. She ran along it, searching for a place she could ascend to the next. One of Sirrhon's branches intersected with Tith's ahead and she leapt onto that. Cien followed her as they ran towards Sirrhon's trunk.

'Tchardin!' Kadailin's voice exploded in her mind. *'I thought you were dead,'* she said much more quietly.

'I'm sorry.' Tchardin lifted herself up through Sirrhon's canopy. *'We didn't realise it would look that way.'*

She pulled herself up one more branch and saw the kandar arrayed ahead of her. Sirrhon's trunk gaped wide open and Nox stood inside it. The pandinzori that had made his aura sloughed off him, pulled into the depths of the great tree's trunk by some force they couldn't see. Nox seemed old and weary as he stood there in the growing darkness, in the absence of pandinzori. The sight was unnerving, as it always was when a kandar went to rest. He smiled as his father's bark closed over him. His leaf fell from the collective, its light fading as it dropped through the branches, causing a shiver to run through Tchardin.

The kandar dispersed. Tchardin's sisters moved towards her through the crowd. Kadailin smiled at her until her eyes were drawn to the white devoshai standing behind Tchardin.

Jaydin and Sandin followed Kadailin. Tchardin saw the notebook clutched in Jaydin's hand. Maybe Damarin had already spoken to her. Jaydin's strong grey eyes held Tchardin's before moving on to Cien. Her mouth fell open.

Tchardin regarded Jaydin's shocked expression with amusement for a moment before she saw the darker figure standing behind them on the branch. Damarin. That was less amusing.

"I'm Cien," Cien said, unphased by the series of reactions from the sisters. "I come from Black Valley."

"Black Valley." Jaydin exchanged a stunned glance with Sandin. "How?"

Damarin remained expressionless. Clearly she hadn't had time to tell their sisters anything.

"Black Valley is full of kandar," Damarin clarified for Jaydin. She didn't wait long for the shock to sink in. "They have the shift there."

Amazingly, Jaydin kept the confusion she must feel off her face. Tchardin knew none of this was in her notebook, nor in her head. She and Damarin stared at each other silently. Tchardin thought she could feel the surprise from Jaydin and the smugness from Damarin although she couldn't see it in either of them.

"They can shift to Coralynth?" Kadailin interjected.

Tchardin met her hopeful gaze and wished she could say it was so. Instead she shook her head sadly. "Coralynth is barred, as we knew. To everyone."

"But we can shift on Derkra," Cien proudly announced.

"Not very well," Damarin countered. "They hadn't attempted it until we arrived."

Damarin began to tell the story of their journey to Black Valley. Both Kadailin and Sandin listened intently. Even Cien was riveted as Tchardin hadn't told him much about the raft and Water Side. Jaydin moved beside her.

"There are kandar in Black Valley," Jaydin whispered. It wasn't so much a question as an astonished statement. Her thoughts were so silent Tchardin could hear nothing from her. "And you can open the shift."

"Yes. To both."

"There are two kandaran cities on Derkra."

Tchardin nodded. "Cien is the Shadow of Black Valley."

Jaydin studied Cien. "They don't have a queen."

"Of course not," Tchardin said. "I am to be the queen of Derkra. Of all the kandar."

"Good," Jaydin responded loudly. She talked right over Damarin. "I would like Cien to tell me the history of Black Valley since we've been gone. I need to record it."

Jaydin ignored Damarin's indignant expression at being interrupted and walked towards Cien. She motioned to a higher branch.

"We can explore while we talk, if you wish."

"Tchardin told me Tith gave you the history of the Earths," he said. "I'd like to learn it."

Tchardin didn't think she'd ever seen Jaydin so happy. The oldest of Tith's daughters beamed and led Cien into the higher canopy. Damarin continued their tale of adventure, Sandin and Kadailin immediately returning their attention to her.

'I'm impressed.' Jaydin's mindvoice was still strong although Tchardin felt the distance between them growing. Tchardin looked at Damarin, but if she'd heard she was doing a great job of pretending she hadn't.

Tchardin smiled. *'I thought you'd be angry.'*

'I was angry. I am *angry. But you're alive, and I was wrong in not searching for Black Valley. I thought it was impossible for kandar to live there outside my knowledge.'*

'I didn't really think about it,' Tchardin admitted. She had thought mostly of stemming the ache in her mind. Finding Ovaeron and escaping Calendrai.

'I'm sure Damarin did,' Jaydin responded. Her mindvoice faded into the buzz of the collective.

Tchardin studied their middle sister as she spoke and wondered about that.

***

Jaydin kept her eyes open as she manipulated the thin threads of pandinzori she used to write in her notebook. She didn't remember when she had learned to do it without the focus provided by darkness, but it had been a long time. The improvement in her control could be seen in the improvement of her writing throughout the notebook.

"So," she said, "nothing in Black Valley has significantly changed since the war."

The white devoshai nodded. He seemed to be relatively simple, like the rest of them, but given that he hadn't lived and interacted with the sisters he was refreshingly unique. Jaydin had always thought Tith's daughters escaped the uniformity that had grown in the rest of the kandar because they'd been thrown together through circumstances created before their births. In that way they were like dodenzinn. As far as Jaydin could guess, dodenzinn were a sort of tool used by Creator to force a connection in a people who had no use for connections. She wondered if any of the other Black Valley kandar were the same, or if Cien had found some way to grow on his own.

"As far as I know, I'm the only kandar to leave the valley in the generations since," he said. "None of the others were interested in seeing Water Side."

"But you don't know that, because no one has kept track of the previous generations."

He seemed thrown off by her statement but only for a moment. "We keep no record of previous generations, but through story—"

"They still tell stories? After all this time?"

"Some do. I have—of my travels across the dunes. Few listen, but I believe I would have heard if anyone knew of another who had done what I did."

That was probably true. Jaydin laid a line of pandinzori across the newest page of her notebook, forming it into letters no other kandar could read, preserving his words forever. The thread of light grew black and left a mark when she let it go. To think Black Valley had persisted after they left. It was remarkable.

"I have questions," he said.

His mind buzzed with thought—loud, but difficult to interpret. Jaydin took a moment to examine his leaf in the collective. The Black Valley branch of the collective. Really just a part of the Calendrai collective, the Derkra collective, but seemingly separate now that the kandar were split. She'd always known the collective of kandar should appear like a branch rather than a full tree—how else would the humans join it—but she had been unprepared to see it herself. The collective of Calendrai had been a full tree her whole life, and the lives of all the kandar around her. She had yet to inquire how any of the others felt about the change. They could never have known to expect it.

Cien's thoughts reminded her of his questions. No kandar other than Damarin had ever come to Jaydin with questions. Their people didn't question by nature. She suppressed her excitement, remembering the holes in her memory.

"I may not be able to answer," she said. "But I'll try."

"Tchardin said Tith spoke to you before you were born. That he told you everything."

"He told me most things."

Cien's eyes were greedy. Something else Jaydin recognised from Damarin.

"How did this happen to us? How did we become separated from each other?"

Jaydin looked away from him, filling her vision with her father's leaves and branches. She had always been wary of the empty spaces in her memory. She had always wondered if Tith shared them, or if he had kept things from her on purpose. But the mystery around the kandar's departure from Black Valley—one of the few things Tith had left out—had never been as relevant as it was now. Now she wished she knew for sure which was true.

"That's one thing I don't know," she said. "I know the war divided the kandar both on the Earths and on Derkra. I know we fought each other and many died. My understanding was that all the kandar had left Land Side to come to Calendrai but it's clear that was not the case."

He looked at her with his nearly colourless eyes.

"Do you have any other questions?" she asked.

"Do you think the split could have caused a problem with the pairing of dodenzinn?"

Jaydin couldn't help but show surprise at that. This devoshai was able to question their existence to a level no other kandar in Calendrai had been capable of before first discussing with Jaydin.

"I've wondered that in the past," she said. "Not in relation to a possible split, but in reference to our diminished numbers."

"The split makes it more complicated, doesn't it?"

"It does. I'll have to consider this."

His thoughts buzzed softly now and Jaydin got an impression of them. He thought his dodenzinn was in Calendrai. Then the impact of what he was thinking truly hit her and she clutched her notebook tightly.

She had always considered that she may not have a dodenzinn. She had never felt as if she were missing a part of herself and she had never felt drawn to a devoshai. She had explained this away by assuming he had died in the war long before she was born. All that meant to her was that she could live her whole life and do the things she needed to do without the threat of losing him, without being forced to rest if he was. Maybe she did feel empty, maybe she felt unfulfilled, but how could she recognise those feelings when nothing had ever changed? If she didn't find him before the end she would refuse Tith when he called her. Destroy herself in the water.

There was another possibility, but as always it was too unlikely to seriously consider. Since she felt no need for a dodenzinn she hadn't worried about it. But maybe she did have one. Maybe he was just far away from her. The same could be said for her sisters.

Cien appeared to be lost in thought. Jaydin reached out to his mind again. He thought his dodenzinn was in Calendrai, yet he seemed confused. She was reminded of Ryten.

"Is it possible..." he let his question trail off. He met her eyes. "Is it possible for one kandar to have two dodenzinn?"

"No," she said automatically. "It's not possible. A kandar only has one dodenzinn."

She focused on her notebook to disguise her unease. The truth was that it wasn't supposed to be possible, but it might be. There had always been the question of how exactly Tith birthed more than one kandar when no tree had ever done so before. He had taken Carrensing in rest and no other that she knew of. She had always assumed there were others, unnamed, but maybe there weren't. If the five sisters had actually been only one kandar in the past then technically they could share a dodenzinn. She had dismissed this for the same reasons she had considered her dodenzinn to be dead. She had never felt drawn to any kandar, and of the sisters, at least Damarin had been. If they were made from one kandar she would have expected to feel that too. Cien really was unique to contemplate this.

She studied him, wondering. Not too unique, hopefully. Not if he asked about shared dodenzinn. Back when they had access to the Earths many kandar had loved their dodenzinn—often platonically, but sometimes romantically. They were far from monogamous—they had loved humans too, many humans, of all sexes, both physically and emotionally—but they had only ever had one dodenzinn. Always. Forever. That was the point.

A kandar could touch any human, but they could only really touch one other kandar, at least without getting shocked by their aura. The close connection was singular. Why Creator had chosen to make dodenzinn a tevadra-devoshai pair Jaydin didn't know. The only thing that made sense would be for it to match the human breeding pair, but kandar didn't have children. Perhaps there was a reason beyond her understanding. Tith had provided no insight—it was just the way things were, as with everything on Derkra.

All Jaydin knew for sure was that if things were different, if they could still love, Ryten's confusion could have caused a lot more trouble than a few offended kandar. And now this Black Valley Shadow asked about the same thing. She hoped he wasn't unique enough to love. To be jealous.

Cien stared at her, as if to hear her thoughts. She smiled.

"How did the kandar choose you to be their Shadow?" she asked.

"I'm strong. I've been able to control more pandinzori than the others since the first time I left the valley."

"And what do you do as Shadow?"

His brow furrowed. "Nothing, I guess."

She almost laughed. "They picked you for the right reasons. It's too bad it doesn't matter anymore."

The Shadow was another position that had lost its value away from the Purpose, just like the High Seat, the Voice, and the council itself. Even the queen could be useless in this world, without the Earths, but Jaydin had never been willing to let that happen. The Shadow was supposed to be the protector of the valley, the only kandar who never left their homeworld for the Earths. There had never been an outside threat to Derkra in all of Tith's history, but Tchar must have given the kandar hierarchy for a reason. The Shadow was meant to be strong in case there ever was.

"Maybe it'll matter again soon," Cien said.

"That has always been my hope."

His thoughts buzzed excitedly. "Can you tell me about the Earths?"

"It would be my pleasure. I don't get asked to do that often."

He leaned towards her, almost vibrating with enthusiasm. She had to stop herself from laughing.

"How big are the forests?" he asked.

"They can be huge." Jaydin smiled, seeing them in her mind. "Some cover nearly all the land on their Earth."

His eyes lit up as she answered. It was sad, really. So interested in the Earths and already elected as Shadow. She wondered if he realised he would never see them, even if they found a way back. His father should have told him that before he was born. But maybe he hadn't. Jaydin was less sure of things than she'd once been. "Why don't I show you?"

Cien raised an eyebrow at her. Maybe he had never been given an image. There was almost no reason for any kandar to do it now, when there was nothing to show. She closed her eyes, emptying her mind of Tith's branches and bringing up the darkness.

'Focus on my leaf,' she said to only him. *'Concentrate on my thoughts.'*

She saw it. The great forest on World Four. As big as the world. Endless dark trunks. Infinite shades of green, quivering with life. The sun shone through the leaves from above, a brilliant flash of white. Cien gasped. Jaydin opened her eyes.

"That was...the *sun?*" Cien asked.

"It was. One of them."

"Only one of them..."

"Every Earth has one. The sun is the source of their light and sometimes all of their heat." Cien wouldn't understand any of this—he wouldn't even know what heat was—but they had to start somewhere. "Some suns are great balls of gas and fire and some are merely images painted on the sky."

His eyes were unfocused, as if he continued to look at the image she had given him. "And there were other living things there besides trees."

This time she did laugh. "Yes. All manner of plants and animals."

"But no humans."

"Not in that image. There are relatively few on World Four, and half of them hate the forest."

Cien looked scandalised.

"It's true," she repeated, for emphasis. "The Earths are beautiful but they're complicated. The humans are not all good."

Cien frowned. "I want to know more. I want to know everything you know. We don't know anything about the Earths in Black Valley, or the humans. Only the words of the Purpose, not what it means."

He was exceedingly perceptive.

"Most here wouldn't distinguish between the words and their meaning." Jaydin flipped to an earlier page in her notebook, near the beginning. It could take half a life to teach him everything contained in its pages. She judged that was about the amount of time both of them had left. "It's a lot, but I'd be glad to tell you everything I know."

CHAPTER 13

RYTEN LAY SPRAWLED IN the canopy of an anonymous tree in Cens. He had climbed as high as he could without the branches giving way under his weight. Above him the light of pandinzori mingled with the light of the sky. The living forest wasn't entirely impenetrable. This didn't help a kandar navigate it, but it was pleasant to look at.

A sudden rush of strength flowed through his body and brought his attention to the collective. He studied the tree in his mind and saw the two leaves he had missed so much. Of course they both had to leave him at once, making the distinction between them even more confusing. Then they returned together as well.

Ryten drew pandinzori to him. It swirled around him and made him feel powerful. He stood and jumped to the forest floor, letting himself fall freely and feeling the impact of landing travel up through his toes to his ankles and knees. Something crunched beneath his feet where he fell.

A small set of barbed sticks lay under his foot. They were connected in the centre but were broken from the impact. He knelt down to look at them more closely. Had he killed a plant? It was an instinctive, unconscious act to avoid them, something he had done without thinking all his life. He nudged the pile of damaged sticks with his fingers and it slid freely along the ground. The sticks were connected, but they didn't grow out of the earth. It wasn't a plant. He got up to go, then something below and beside him caught his eye.

There was another bundle of sticks there. He also saw a touch of red. He moved closer to examine it. The red was part of a plant. The rest of the plant was black and lined with green leaves along its length. It ran across the ground and up a tree nearby. It coiled and hung through the branches. There were many more clusters of red leaves throughout it.

As he approached he could see that the second bundle of sticks didn't appear to be attached to the ground either. At least it wasn't attached in the centre as a tree should be. All of its branches led to the ground. He leaned down to look more closely.

It moved. Ryten jumped away as the bundle of branches scuttled across the earth and disappeared behind a trunk. The crushed sticks remained and the red plant as well but there was no sign of the bundle that had moved. He made note of its location and thought to bring Jaydin back to look at it. She might not understand what he meant by moving sticks, but at least he could show her the red plant and the pile of sticks he had crushed with his foot. If anyone would know what this was it would be Jaydin.

Cens seemed to hold him when he tried to leave. He wanted to get out quickly, into the clearing. He had to find Jaydin before he forgot the location of the red-leafed plant. It felt like Cens dragged him around in circles.

Eventually the clearing broke open before him and suddenly Ryten felt even more powerful. The melancholy that had surrounded him lifted and floated away. He almost forgot the incident in Cens in his elation. Damarin and Tchardin's leaves blazed in his mind. They were close.

Then the significance of their presence hit him fully. He didn't have to die. Whichever tevadra was his dodenzinn, she was in Calendrai. Safe.

"What were you just thinking about?" a quiet voice asked from close by. Ocien leaned against a trunk at the edge of the forest. She looked at Ryten's face carefully. "Finally regretting your decision to sleep away your life?"

"Just thinking about Tchardin." That was partly true. "She's returned to Calendrai."

Ocien closed her eyes and Ryten knew she was looking at the collective. "Damarin too."

"Yes, Damarin too." He looked up into Tith's branches. "I have to find Jaydin. I need to tell her something."

"They'll probably all be together."

Ryten walked towards Tith's trunk and left the tevadra standing in the clearing. He began climbing and focused on the leaves in the collective. He looked at Tchardin's and Damarin's, and even Jaydin's, and they all called him from the same direction. He moved up.

Alighting to the next branch he came to, he found himself confronted with something that shouldn't exist. A devoshai with lightly coloured skin stood there with Jaydin. The devoshai looked back at Ryten and there was no similar confusion or shock on his face at the sight.

Ryten stood almost a head taller than the white devoshai, forcing him to look down to meet the nearly colourless eyes. A leaf grew as he stared. A leaf on a new collective. The devoshai was called Cien. Ryten made the connection.

'There are kandar in Black Valley,' he said.

Jaydin nodded. *'Tchardin and Damarin succeeded in their journey and brought back proof of their discovery. A whole other population of kandar remains in our birthplace. Cien here is their Shadow.'*

Ryten's skin prickled. It was one thing for Black Valley to have kandar, but a Shadow? There was supposed to be only one Shadow of the kandar, and it was going to be Ryten. Could there be two?

Jaydin shook her head slightly and Ryten was even more confused.

"I'm going to find Tchardin," he said aloud, choosing to escape the situation rather than make it worse. He sensed Damarin and Tchardin just above them.

"She's just above us," Cien said, as if Ryten didn't already know that.

"Ryten is Tchardin's dodenzinn," Jaydin said. "I'm sure he can find her if he needs to."

Cien's expression was questioning for an instant before his composure returned. Ryten was distracted by a flicker in the collective. Damarin. The sinuous black tevadra dropped onto the branch beside him. She smiled.

It was playful, and Damarin was anything but playful. She looked uncharacteristically happy. She practically glowed. Pandinzori pulsed over her as usual—Damarin always seemed to draw more than the average kandar—but this was something different. Something from inside.

Ryten looked back at Cien. Maybe Damarin had finally found *her* dodenzinn? That would be a relief. It would help him to understand his own situation.

'I did it,' Damarin said.

Ryten looked at the others. Damarin was only talking to him. She beamed. He had to return the smile despite the agitation he usually felt when she was around. She'd been talking about Black Valley for as long as he'd known her. It was about time she felt validated.

'You did,' he said in return, *'and you brought something back with you.'*

Damarin's mindvoice laughed. Her face remained untouched by it.

"I'll go meet Tchardin now," Ryten said aloud, so everyone on the branch could hear.

"I'll go with you." Damarin didn't wait for him to agree before jumping to the branch above them. Then she was gone, upwards, into the canopy.

Ryten stayed a moment longer to watch Cien watch Damarin go. There was something familiar in his eyes as he did. Yes, definitely her dodenzinn. Good. He started to follow, then remembered why he had been looking for Jaydin in the first place.

"I saw something strange in Cens just now," he said.

Jaydin raised an eyebrow at him. "Strange how?"

"I'll have to show you. I'm not sure you'll understand if I don't. It's something new."

"Something new? On Derkra?"

Ryten shrugged. "You never know with Cens."

"That's true." Jaydin looked away and ran her fingers across her notebook. She was clearly interested. He had been right to tell her. "Find Tchardin," she said. "I'll see this new thing later."

Ryten nodded and followed Damarin in the direction of Tchardin's aura. He felt Cien's eyes on him as he left. Maybe all the kandar of Black Valley would help with their confusing dodenzinn situation. A whole second population. Maybe Ryten's true dodenzinn was in Black Valley. He put that thought out of his mind as soon as he found it. The situation was already complicated enough.

He didn't have to go far. A few leafy branches between him and the sisters had obscured them from view. He pulled himself up on the branch as they were engaged in a silent conversation. Tchardin didn't seem particularly happy with it. Nor did Damarin. The two sisters stared at each other with their arms crossed. Then at once they turned those looks on him.

Damarin's gaze softened and Tchardin's turned to the ground. Ryten was hit with a bout of confusion, as he always was when he was near both of them together. At the same time he felt powerful. Pandinzori flew from the trees around him to swirl against his body. The light and strength was comforting.

"I found something in Cens," he said, not sure how to address the fact that both of them had just left him, at the same time, and he hadn't known what to do about it.

"What do you mean you *found* something?" Damarin's voice shattered the resulting silence.

Ryten got to his feet and had to look down at both tevadra. "There was a bundle of moving sticks, and a red plant—"

"Moving sticks?" Damarin looked disbelieving.

"I saw them too," Tchardin said, her focus faraway. "Just before we left for Land Side. I thought it was an effect of the quarter life change."

"You saw the branches move?" Ryten asked. "As if they walked across the ground?"

"Yes, and the red. Little clusters of red leaves."

"Can you show us?" Damarin asked.

"Of course. I remember the place I saw them."

"The exact place in Cens?"

Ryten glared at her. "Unlike you I was born in Cens and can find my way around it."

'What makes you think I can't?' Damarin responded. *'That is a fault of the other daughters of Tith, not I.'*

Tchardin didn't react to the thought. She must be waiting for Damarin to answer him.

"Show us then," Damarin said aloud.

The collective told him Jaydin had left her spot in Tith below them. Ryten contemplated searching her out first but the two tevadra seemed impatient to go. Showing her could wait. It only meant he would have twice as much to occupy his time.

He looked into the branches below and planned a descent. Just as he was about to jump to the branch beneath them, Cien's white head appeared. The devoshai looked up at him and grinned. He lifted himself to join them on the branch.

"What were you all talking about?" Cien asked.

Ryten studied him. He didn't seem confused. Maybe he *was* Damarin's dodenzinn and maybe he was sure of it. No wonder she had always felt pulled by the water. Ryten felt the need to ask about it, but he knew from previous conversations with the kandar of Calendrai that such thoughts of confusion were not normal and were not tolerated. Maybe things were different in Black Valley.

"We're going to see something new in Cens," Tchardin said. "Ryten will show us where it is."

"That sounds interesting," Cien said.

Ryten continued to stare at him. Why not ask if he could finally be sure?

Damarin's voice came to him. *'What's wrong with you? Just show us where it is, if you can.'*

'You know I can,' he answered, flustered. Then it came to him. He might not be able to risk asking the devoshai, but he could ask Damarin. She was the source of his confusion. She'd been there when the kandar learned of it. They had seemed to put it out of their minds but he knew she would never forget. It would be important to her as well. He focused on her leaf. *'Is Cien your dodenzinn?'*

This time her reaction did show on her face. *'What kind of question is that?'*

Cien and Tchardin looked at her. Ryten couldn't know if they'd heard what he said but they must have heard her response. It had been loud. Ryten remembered the previous instances of this conversation and decided to leave before things got worse. He turned around and walked away.

***

Tchardin had never seen such outrage on a kandar's face. What could Ryten have said to Damarin to make her react like that?

"Ryten," Tchardin said to his retreating back, "come with me."

She gestured into the branches below and dropped down ahead of him, leaving Cien and Damarin behind. Ryten followed her. She continued until the two kandar above were hidden in the leaves. They walked towards Tith's trunk.

"What did you say to her?" she asked.

The big devoshai followed her in silence for a few steps before answering. "I asked if Cien was her dodenzinn."

Tchardin stopped walking. The question was inconceivable. No kandar had ever asked it of another. Not as far as she knew. "Why ask that?"

Ryten shook his head and looked away. His thoughts buzzed just beyond her hearing. Tchardin wasn't sure if she should tell him Cien was hers rather than Damarin's. That was also something no kandar would outright say to another. It would become apparent soon, as it always did for dodenzinn pairings. She waited but he didn't answer. His thoughts had quieted but he appeared agitated.

"I've seen Black Valley now," she said, to change the subject. "You will be amazed at Ovaeron when you go there."

He smiled slightly. "Is he as magnificent as the trees tell?"

"More so." Tchardin remembered her first look at the giant. "When I saw him I felt the way I feel when I gaze upon Tith."

"He is the father of all of us."

Ryten walked beside her now, the branch they occupied wide enough for four to walk abreast. He seemed to have calmed. His thoughts were still. Tchardin put aside her worries about his question.

"How was it, crossing the water?" he asked.

Tchardin's head ached at the memory. "Terrible. I wouldn't do it again."

"Then how will we all do it?"

Of course he didn't know about the shift yet. That would be revealed when a council meeting could be called, when the existence of the second population of kandar became common knowledge throughout Calendrai. It had to happen soon. It wouldn't do to have Cien wandering around the island looking so strange without anyone knowing who or what he was.

And the shift. They'd been searching for it for so long in Calendrai, the kandar deserved to know it had been found. They also needed to be told it wasn't the solution to all their problems as they had hoped it would be, at least not in its current form.

"We'll shift," she said, concentrating on the emptiness in front of her. It was more palpable than it had been in the desert, given that the branches nearby closed in the space. Leaves came down all around her and showed her that yes, this space before her, seemingly nothing, was contained. It was something.

She moved pandinzori with her mind and pulled the space in front of her apart, pried underneath it. The emptiness of the shift blossomed before them. Ryten froze on the branch.

"It is glass?" he asked, his body tense.

"No." Tchardin remembered her fear at first seeing the ice that held back the waters of the shift. She was impressed Ryten remembered his father's warnings about the dangers of glass from before he was born. The fear reaction was likely instinctive, but to know the name of it was to remember. Tchardin hadn't had a chance to forget with Jaydin reminding her many times since she started her education about the Earths. "It's ice."

The shift slowly settled into an image of Coralynth. Coralynth was easy to bring up, which made sense, given that the kandar were never meant to shift anywhere else from Derkra. Ryten didn't say anything, but the awe Tchardin saw on his face told her how much progress they had made in such a short time, just by crossing the water. A voice broke her concentration.

"I can't believe it."

The oldest of Tith's daughters approached the image. Tchardin held it steady despite her surprise and Jaydin came close enough to touch the ice. Her sister's loud thoughts buzzed through the branches but their meaning remained obscured.

"The path and the portals to the other worlds," Jaydin said with reverence.

"We can't use it," Tchardin said before her sister could try it. "The ice won't break, but at least we can see it again."

"I knew you'd rediscover the shift for us." Jaydin seemed not to have heard.

"She didn't rediscover it."

Tchardin looked away from the image of Coralynth and closed the shift. Jaydin was released from her trance and looked up to the one who had spoken. Damarin stood on the branch above.

"The kandar in Black Valley had it the entire time." Damarin joined them. Ryten immediately looked like he wanted to leave. "It does us little good as it is."

"There is some good from it," Tchardin said.

"Like shifting between Land Side and Water Side?" Damarin asked.

Tchardin glared at her. "You did it too."

An aura brushed against Tchardin's, sending a pleasant shiver through her. She almost turned, thinking Cien had somehow joined them without her noticing. It was Ryten.

'I'm leaving,' Ryten said into her mind. She was too surprised to tell him to stay before he had already disappeared into the leaves below.

"You didn't shift here together?" Jaydin asked.

"The council in Black Valley told us not to attempt it," Tchardin answered, returning her focus to the conversation. "They said it was too dangerous and we were too important to lose. Damarin said she'd take the raft back but I told her we should shift despite the council's pronouncement. She told me we couldn't."

"The council told *you* not to attempt it," Damarin said. "They granted me permission to take the raft but never specified I couldn't try the shift instead."

Tchardin was shocked at Damarin's audacity. The council hadn't wanted any kandar to try it. She opened her mouth to respond but was cut off by Jaydin's sudden laughter.

"Of course," Jaydin said, turning her steely grey eyes on Damarin. "Of course that's what you'd take away from the council's words of caution to your sister."

Damarin seemed to be trying unsuccessfully to hide a smile. "It's what I always take away from your words of caution. A suggestion, at best."

Tchardin was surprised to see them converse so effortlessly. She tried to remember an instance when they'd spoken like this during her lifetime and couldn't think of any. Sandin said they'd been close once but this was the first Tchardin had seen of it herself.

"I guess I have to accept your interpretation," Jaydin said. "Without it we would still be ignorant of Black Valley's current state."

"Without it you'd be ignorant of a whole lot more than that," Damarin responded.

Tchardin almost missed the look that passed between her sisters. It was only there for a moment, but she believed she read it clearly. Damarin's dark eyes issued a challenge their oldest sister was intent on meeting.

"I had to shift," Damarin said, breaking the tension and turning to Tchardin. "The raft was a one-time risk I wouldn't have taken again. If it makes a difference, I never would have let you risk it either."

"You should have told us," Tchardin said. "Cien and I were worried you wouldn't make it on the raft. That's the only reason—"

"No it's not," Damarin said, cutting her off. "We can both hear your thoughts in the collective."

Jaydin shrugged. "She will be queen. You shouldn't have left her out of it."

"And I've told her before—she isn't queen yet."

"But she will be. As soon as the council can be called to accept her."

Tchardin was annoyed at her sisters for talking over her, but at the same time she didn't feel capable of keeping up with them. Their thoughts were simply a buzz in her mind that meant nothing to her. If they could both hear her thoughts so easily she was left at a serious disadvantage.

"Our world is very different now," Damarin said. "The question is no longer whether one council will accept her, but whether two will."

"I *will* be queen," Tchardin said. Her sisters were silent at that. She wondered if they had taken their conversation into the collective. "The council in Black Valley saw my golden aura just as well as the council here can. The kandar will have to be joined at some point. Whether I have been accepted here by that time or not there will then be only one council left to accept me."

Jaydin nodded.

"The shift was just as dangerous as the raft," Damarin said. "It may be some time before our people can be brought together."

"Yes," Jaydin said, "that reminds me. You'll have to give me an account of your journeys, both to Land Side on the raft and back through the shift. If the rest of the kandar are to make the trip we'll have to find the safest route."

Jaydin brought her notebook out of the shadows around her body. Just the sight of the green book made Tchardin anxious to escape.

"I already have Cien's recounting of the history of Black Valley since we left," Jaydin continued, opening the book. "I also want to add your first impressions of the people and the place."

Tchardin felt the conversation beginning to lead to one of Jaydin's history lessons. She resisted her immediate urge to leave the situation as she realised this was the history of the kandar—something she had been asking to learn about since Jaydin had first started teaching her about the Earths.

"What did he say?" Damarin asked.

"Very little has changed," Jaydin answered. "I wouldn't be able to add much to what you already know."

"Did he say anything about dodenzinn pairings in Black Valley?"

Jaydin narrowed her eyes. "He didn't say anything out loud, but he did ask about the split. His thoughts told me he was looking for confirmation rather than information. Why?"

"Did he ask about Ovaeron?"

Jaydin's thoughts buzzed. "What about Ovaeron?"

Tchardin backed away from the two tevadra on the branch. It might be the history of the kandar but her sisters were clearly more invested in it than she was. Damarin had moved so close to Jaydin that the oldest of Tith's daughters now held her notebook flat against her chest—there was no room between them for her to hold it open. Tchardin waited a moment more to confirm they were no longer watching her before stepping backwards off the branch into pandinzori.

Chapter 14

Tchardin sat in Tith with her legs dangling towards the clearing. She was on the lowest branch before the fall and her view of the grass was unobstructed. She watched the tiny blades dance far below, the occasional kandar tracing a path through them.

She'd left Damarin and Jaydin to their conversation, and she sensed that Jaydin at least hadn't moved far from the place she'd left her. Jaydin's leaf was bright and close in the collective, but Damarin's had dimmed slightly, indicating she might be in the forest below instead of the canopy of the great tree. Tchardin wondered how long it would be before Jaydin came looking for her with more history to force into her head. Or when the council would call her again.

She tried to relax and appreciate Tith's nearness, knowing she might only have a short time to herself. She tried not to think about Ryten and what that feeling of his aura against hers could mean.

The pandinzori that permeated her father's mighty canopy was easily drawn to her body. She closed her eyes and attempted to lose sensation. She brought up a patch of green in the darkness of her mind and watched as it changed slowly into blue. Time passed. The blaze of colour flared red.

She opened her eyes and looked down into the clearing again. Everything appeared to be covered in a slight haze of shadow. She tried to blink it away but it remained. Something was wrong.

'Fire.' The word seeped into her mind. It flowed through the collective. It came more loudly and panicked. *'FIRE!'*

Fire? Where had she heard that word before?

Kadailin ran out of Cens below her. Jaydin followed close behind. Tchardin knew immediately that the panicked voice shouting through the collective was hers. Then she saw it. A thick, dark shadow rose above the forest.

Jaydin seemed to be searching for something in the grass. Tchardin met her eyes across the distance when she looked up into Tith.

'There is fire in Cens!' Jaydin thought forcefully to the entire collective. Her lips moved and Sandin appeared as if from nothing behind her.

Then Tchardin remembered she had heard the word from Jaydin. It was a human thing that had destroyed World Seven. A terrible human thing that ate trees. But on Derkra? How could it—

Living light burst through the edge of the forest, reaching for Tith's lowest branches. Tchardin jumped back towards his trunk. She stared down at the undulating body of translucent reds, oranges, and yellows. She was mesmerised by it. Consumed. There was nothing else like that on Derkra. She didn't notice Jaydin until her sister was right beside her on the branch. Jaydin grabbed her, heedless of the shock that ran through their auras at the touch.

"We need to stop it," she said. "Tell everyone!"

Tchardin looked back down at the fire.

Fire.

"Now, Tchardin!"

Her eyes were drawn to a dark column above the forest. "What is that?"

"What? The smoke? The flames? This isn't a lesson! There's no time. The forest is dying!"

"What would stop fire?"

Jaydin glanced at the surging flames below. "Water," she whispered.

"But how?" Tchardin asked.

"We'll have to move it somehow. Bring it from the edge of the forest."

Tchardin looked at the cloud of *smoke* above Cens just as a massive blue wave grew up behind it and crashed into the tops of the trees. A swath of yellow-tinted pandinzori was left in its wake.

"Damarin," Jaydin said.

'Help me,' Damarin said into the collective.

Tchardin looked at Jaydin in confusion. Her sister returned her terrified stare and jumped off the branch. Tchardin followed her.

The dark haze was everywhere now. It beat at Tchardin as she flew towards the ground. She slowed herself with pandinzori when she approached the grass. Black clouds billowed from Cens in front of her. She parted them with a wave of pandinzori.

She ran by Sandin who stared at the treeline and looked lost. Jaydin landed beside them, pandinzori gripping her and slowing her fall. She shouted at Sandin to stay out of the forest.

Tchardin burst into the trees with Jaydin just behind her. They were confronted with a wall of fire. Tchardin tried to push it back with pandinzori, but the fire swallowed the light. The pandinzori she had used was gone, not just displaced. Her push only contained the fire for a moment before the flames rushed back towards them. The pain of Cens was terrible.

Jaydin motioned for Tchardin to follow and ducked under a fallen tree. *A fallen tree.* Tchardin felt Kadailin nearby and called out to her to join them. She reached out to Ryten as well. To Cien. Then to every light in the collective.

When she opened her eyes again Jaydin was nowhere to be seen in the dark smoke. Tchardin wandered blindly through the dearth of pandinzori and stumbled into a kandar who was running towards the clearing. It was Kor—the tevadra who had been born just before Tchardin left Calendrai.

'We need to put water on the fire,' Tchardin said. *'Tell everyone.'*

Kor didn't even seem to listen before running away. Tchardin almost shouted after her but on some level she understood, and there was no time to waste on those who would run. They needed to save the trees. The trees were everything.

Water poured down on Tchardin from above and white smoke swirled together with black. She had to keep calm and get to the shore to help. The area around her sizzled, but was clear of fire now. She could continue.

But the trees...

They seemed to scream with pain, their trunks blackened and their leaves shrivelled. Tchardin had never heard them speak before, not the nameless trees in Cens. She was certain she heard them now. She cringed at their pain. These trees had given birth to kandar in Calendrai and they were mutilated. Some were clearly dead. How would their children react to this? Could they survive it? If they had to rest, where would they go?

Tchardin broke through the trees in front of her and found herself on the shore. Damarin was there with Kadailin. The two worked in tandem to pull great swaths of pandinzori from the forest to pick up the water. Their eerie similarity had never been more apparent.

Three devoshai broke through the treeline on Tchardin's heels. She recognised Marr, Torshe, and Yulek by their auras. Pandinzori came with them in waves. The air churned with it. Yet they stood there, eyes wide, staring at the water. Just like she was.

A thick column of water, directed by Damarin or Kadailin—Tchardin didn't bother trying to figure out which—flew over her head. Drops fell onto her face. She came back to herself.

"Do something!" she shouted aloud. Yulek snapped out of his awe at the tevadra's work and moved closer to the water. The other two followed. Still they did nothing.

Then the pandinzori that came with them grew into a swirling mass above the five kandar at the shore and was directed into the water. It pulled the water up with it and threw it high into the air.

A darkness extended above the island, roiling and black and gaining in size. It was almost like the smoke from the fire. Tchardin froze again. What was that thing? There was a yellow tint to the blackness, marking the pandinzori as Damarin's. Her sister stood rigid and silent with her eyes closed. The other four kandar stared at her in shock. Then the water that had gone into the sky started to come back down.

"They're storm clouds," a voice said beside Tchardin. "They're making rain." Jaydin pushed past her and into the small group of immobile kandar. "Stop standing around and help!"

Kadailin began to lift water again and Yulek stepped up to help her. *Rain* fell on Tchardin, first in sporadic drops and then in a torrent. She looked up in amazement for a moment more before she was jostled out of her awe by kandar bursting through the trees to both sides of her. Finally the collective was coming.

The fire sizzled loudly where the water joined it, but from outside the forest Tchardin could only see the treeline and the smoke seeping out of it. She couldn't actually see the fire. The rain seemed to be falling everywhere but the kandar throwing water were sending it in blind. The secrecy of Cens was working against it. Tchardin spared a final glance at the kandar at the shore and plunged back into the trees.

She ran into Ryten's solid frame. He looked at her for only a moment before going back to what he had been doing. He took the waves of water out of the sky and spread them over the fire before him. Tchardin wrapped pandinzori around the two of them to keep the rain out of their eyes and push away the smoke. She realised with horror that she could see Tith's great branches from where she stood. There was now a hole in Cens.

Other kandar were spread out amongst the trees around them, mirroring Ryten's actions. It unnerved Tchardin that she could see them. The forest should have hidden them.

She looked up at the water streaming over her head and grasped at the shreds of pandinzori around her. Most of it was already being used. At least the water was easy to direct. It didn't swallow pandinzori as the fire did. Even without the kandar moving pandinzori onto it the fire sucked it in, made it disappear. Tchardin was careful not to let any of the pandinzori wrapped around her get taken by the fire.

A trunk fell in front of them and shook the ground. The tree's leaves burst into sudden flame, dampened by the rain but not quenched. Tith's canopy loomed in the clearing ahead. They couldn't let the fire touch him. If even one of his leaves were to crisp and blacken Tchardin felt like she would die. She thought of the kandar whose fathers had already fallen and tried not to lose focus.

She closed her eyes. The forest around her was dimly illuminated by the disappearing shreds of pandinzori, but a brilliant wall of light shone in the distance. She opened her eyes.

A space in the smoke opened up and showed her solid pandinzori in the clearing. It looked to stretch from the ground to high above the height of Cens and it kept the fire away from the three great trees. The flames reached towards it and ate at it, but whenever a hole bloomed it was quickly filled again. Tchardin caught a glimpse of Sandin through the smoke and for a moment believed it was her doing, however impossible that might be. Then Cien was visible beside her. He looked worn to exhaustion but his eyes were closed, and Tchardin knew it was he who held the wall up. She willed herself to believe Tith and his brothers were safe behind it.

She turned her attention to the water above her head again. Now she used smaller versions of Cien's wall to stop the water in areas that were covered in flames. The water hit the shining substance and fell straight down along it, suffocating the fire below.

The rest of the kandar mimicked her. The fire was slowly dying but it was still all around them.

***

Jaydin's arms were nearly limp as she pulled herself onto the wide branch. It shouldn't have been difficult to direct pandinzori—in fact it needed no physical effort at all, only that of the mind—but Jaydin had used everything she had and more in her attempt to stop the fire. She continued to feebly pull herself up. As soon as she got her hips over the edge she collapsed there. She had never felt physically weak before.

Her body was spent but her mind still raced. There had been a fire in Cens. She turned her head slowly to the side, towards the place where, were she lower in the canopy, she would see clear through Cens to the water.

Fire on Derkra. Destruction on Derkra. The type of thing that ravaged the Earths but had never directly affected the kandaran world. It would be devastating to see any tree die, but the trees of Derkra were their fathers.

She searched the collective for her sisters' leaves. Tchardin and Damarin's blazed much brighter than Kadailin's, but all three were accounted for. She remembered the rain Damarin had brought down on the fire. It was almost as hard to believe as the fire itself.

Sandin sat down next to her. The other tevadra hadn't been able to help in putting out the fire. She had stood quiet and anxious behind Cien's wall of pandinzori in the clearing as the trees were torn down in front of her and the effort at the shore revealed. There had been a moment when they made eye contact through the smoke and rain. Cens wasn't so vast after all.

"All of those who are scarred, but still standing..." Jaydin found she couldn't continue. What she had to say was too horrible, would be impossible for the kandar to understand.

"Many have survived," Sandin said, in a misguided attempt at comfort. "Our fathers are strong."

"They are." Jaydin's lips turned up in a grim smile before she could stop herself. It would only make things more difficult.

She reached for her notebook with trembling fingers and opened it to a page near the middle.

"I haven't told you about Rypien, have I?" she asked. Sandin shook her head. Jaydin scanned the pages. What an awful time for the kandar. "Rypien is the guardian of World Two. Or at least he was when we lost it. A long time ago the people of his Earth carved into the trunk of his father—Fevre—while he rested."

"They cut up a World Tree? Why would they do that?"

"They called it art. I believe they thought it would do no harm, but it drove both Rypien and Fevre mad. Rypien was eventually brought down and rested again but Fevre had to be destroyed. A many-trunked tree called Miran came to replace him."

Sandin looked at the branch they rested on. "So the trees who were touched by fire have lost their minds?"

"It's very likely they have. If a tree is damaged, but lives, and can still carry kandar, he must be destroyed. A damaged tree will bear damaged kandar."

Outrage was plain on Sandin's face now. "We have to kill the trees?"

Jaydin nodded, looking again to where the forest screamed in pain. "It sounds awful, and it will be, but the result of letting kandar go back to those trees to rest and be reborn would be worse. Tith knows this. I know this."

"We can't kill their fathers," Sandin said quietly.

"Other trees of the forest will call them."

"No one will believe you."

"They'll have to. I'll make sure it happens regardless of whether they believe me or not. This is why I'm important. I know this is what has to be done."

"Tchardin's the one who has to tell them," Sandin said. "She's the one who'll have to make them do it."

Jaydin turned away from her sister. "I know."

***

Tchardin stood at Tith's base and looked through the hole in Cens. It was clear all the way to the shore now and was littered with the charred remains of broken trunks and branches. She looked up at the open sky. The storm clouds were gone. Damarin had been forced to let them go before the fire was out and the other kandar had been left to finish the fight without the rain. The remaining fires had disappeared from view when doused with water but they had still been burning in the ground and under bark. The strip was nearly flat now. Everything that once stood there had sunk down to the earth. Not that it mattered how flat it became, how burned down it got. It had all been dead quickly after the fire touched it.

She looked at the trees that lined the dark opening in the forest. What leaves they had left on the side of the fire were yellow, orange, and brown. They were dry and brittle. They clung to the trees but they were just as dead as those that were gone.

Jaydin approached. She joined Tchardin and they stood silently for a moment.

"Kor is dead," Tchardin said. "I guess she threw herself into the fire when her father was burned to the ground."

"Is she the only one?"

"Three that I had."

"Just three? Not Four?"

Tchardin almost rolled her eyes. "Kor was new. She wouldn't have known her dodenzinn yet."

"That will be a problem," Jaydin said. "It may be hard for him to notice her death when he hasn't hit quarter life yet, hasn't felt the effect of missing her." She frowned. "Considering how many trees were taken I'm surprised it was so few."

Silence again. Tchardin looked up, above the average height of the trees of Cens, at Frenn. Or at what was left of him. She had never seen the fifth kandaran tree on Calendrai before. He had been hidden so well by the forest. He was supposed to be the most beautiful of them. Tchardin could see why the kandar said that. Now a third of his canopy was burned and bare.

"Tchardin—"

"Are you going to ask me what I'll do about this?"

"In a way," Jaydin admitted. "But I'm really here to tell you what you need to do."

"That's even worse."

What could possibly be done? Kandar had lost their fathers. At least three of them had felt the need to end their own lives at the loss—or the loss of their dodenzinn. And that was only the number Tchardin had noticed leave the collective. There could be more. There probably were.

"Something must be done," Jaydin said. "You would ignore what happened?"

Tchardin wondered where Cien and Ryten were. Or the rest of her sisters. But she was afraid of the collective, with its missing leaves. She didn't want to look at it again to find them. How were they reacting to this?

"Are you listening to me?" Jaydin asked.

"I'm not even queen yet."

"You should be queen. We should get the council together as soon as possible to fix that. You'll need proper authority if you're going to get the kandar to do what needs to be done."

For a moment Tchardin's mind was incredibly clear. She turned towards Jaydin and could sense what she was thinking. Her sister's leaf in the collective spoke to Tchardin, although Jaydin said nothing.

"No," Tchardin said. "I will not tell the kandar to tear down their fathers and the fathers of their friends. A kandar would never kill a tree."

Jaydin was only quiet for a moment. "It's been done before. And it was a World Tree they destroyed. Out of necessity."

"I don't believe it."

"It was worth the sacrifice, although they waited too long. They resisted, they balked, and it cost World Two dearly. These trees, while they are fathers just the same, are not as great a loss as Fevre was, could never be as great a loss as a World Tree. The kandar who let him live at first recognised their mistake and we should not devalue that by making the same one."

"I can't. I won't do it."

"You've always wanted something to do," Jaydin said. Tchardin looked into her eyes and could tell she was furious. "This isn't a lesson. You don't need to listen. You need to *do* something."

Tchardin turned away but Jaydin continued.

"This is important. It will be history. Fire has never come to Derkra before."

Now Tchardin was angry. "History? You created history, Jaydin. It doesn't exist here."

"It will." Jaydin held her notebook out to Tchardin. "This is the history of Derkra. It is because of Tith that I know what needs to be done to these trees, and it is because of this history that our future selves will know we did the right thing. They will know that those we were before showed us the way and we listened, rather than repeat their mistakes."

"When we're gone no one will care. The kandar aren't meant to remember the past. Who will read your notebook when you go to rest?"

"The kandar will learn to read if they need to, just as I learned to write. They could learn simply if they wanted to."

"No one will ever want that."

"Then the humans will read it. Someone has to. I know it's important." Jaydin charged off.

Tchardin looked down at the blackened earth. Jaydin's mindvoice came to her. *'We have to help the forest, Tchardin. And there's only one way to do that.'*

Chapter 15

Ryten lay in the grass of the clearing. He couldn't bring himself to enter the forest again. He closed his eyes but when he summoned darkness he saw only red, yellow, and orange. Those colours had been so hard to bring up before.

Frenn had been burned in the fire. Ryten had seen it happen. The great tree was still alive but his trunk was scarred and black. One of his branches that nearly swept the ground had carried the flames high into him. Now an emptiness could be seen there. Ryten thought of his father, Del.

From what he knew of Cens his father was far away from the fire, on the opposite side of the clearing. But he could never have been sure, due to the secret nature of the forest. He had waited—while the trees burned and he moved water onto them—for Del's magnificent height to be revealed. Luckily, it hadn't been.

Ryten wanted to go to his father now but the whole forest had become strange. Cens had turned him around and around when he tried as if it were afraid.

He also wanted to go to Tchardin. He'd seen the terror in her eyes while they fought the fire side by side. She would need time to comprehend what had happened. Time he was now taking himself. He closed his eyes again and forced the colours out of his mind. He held it like that—clear, dark—and waited. If he waited long enough things would make sense. They had to.

The grass around him shifted almost imperceptibly. An aura moved past him. He looked at the collective and found it was Damarin. He sat up to watch her, resisting the urge to flee from her presence.

She glided across the clearing, the grass swishing around her. He was surprised to see she wasn't exhausted from the effort she'd put in at the shore. What she'd done had far surpassed his own contribution. Had far surpassed what any of them had done.

She didn't turn to look back at him as she walked. Perhaps she hadn't noticed he was there. He stood watching her for just long enough to see her step into the burned patch of the forest. Then he lay down again and tried to forget what had happened.

***

Cien hadn't been able to move since the fire died down. As soon as Sandin assured him the flames could no longer reach the branches of the three brothers he'd fallen to his knees, then flat against the earth. He didn't think he'd ever been so exhausted, not even during his first attempts to cross the desert to the water.

He had never attempted to control so much pandinzori before. He had never even seen so much. It had come from the three brothers in the clearing. He had pulled and it had come. So much he couldn't believe it.

He had been exploring Ahron's high canopy when Tchardin reached out to him to warn of the fire. He hadn't known what she meant until he landed in the clearing and found Sandin there, frantic. The flames had perforated the thickness of Cens and reached for Tith and his brothers. Sandin could do nothing to stop them. She had left him shortly after he collapsed, but she had returned and sat next to him now.

"Can you not touch pandinzori at all?" he asked. She twisted quickly to look at him, as if he had jostled her out of her thoughts. Silent thoughts that no kandar, no matter how perceptive, could hear.

"I can't even see it."

Cien stretched his legs. He closed his eyes to search the collective just to be certain Tchardin and Damarin were safe. He found their leaves, shining brightly. He sent his mind further to find the other sisters. All four daughters of Tith remained in the collective. He still found it difficult to believe Sandin had never been there.

"You're not a part of the collective," he stated, then regretted it because of the expression on her face. He continued more cautiously. "Tchardin told me you weren't but it's a whole other thing to see it for myself."

She shrugged. "I don't know what to tell you. I'm different."

"I wonder why?"

"Even Jaydin doesn't know." She examined him. "Are all Black Valley kandar this curious?"

"I don't know if they ever had a reason to be."

Cien strained to look over the grass to the forest. His body protested and kept him on the ground. Sandin stood to look for him.

"It's the same," she said. "The kandar have fled from the sight of it. I assume wherever they are they're awaiting a council meeting."

"Your sisters are safe," he said then, realising she might not know.

"I knew Jaydin was fine. I went to find her after you collapsed. I don't think I could have found the others if I tried."

"How did you find Jaydin when you can't sense her?"

Sandin looked pensive. "Her hair is easy to see. Sometimes I can't find her at all, but sometimes I just know where to look."

"Jaydin is strange too. Maybe that's why."

"Your interest in Jaydin's strangeness, your interest in my flaw—it's rare."

"I should think every kandar would be interested. You're different. We're all the same."

Sandin frowned. "Do you know what the other kandar did when I was born? When they found I couldn't talk to them? When they learned I was different?"

Cien shook his head.

"They left. They just walked away from me."

Cien wasn't surprised. Most of the kandar in Black Valley had been in view of his father when he was born. There was nowhere for them to hide. He'd gained many leaves in the collective within the first few moments, but after that, nothing for a long time. "That's normal."

"It may be, and to a normal kandar it probably doesn't matter. But I knew nothing when I was born. Not even my name. I didn't know what I was. I didn't know Derkra, or the name of the place I found myself in when I walked out onto the grass. I didn't even know Tith, who had made me."

Cien could see why she'd been confused, but he couldn't understand that confusion. He'd always known the things he needed. The trees made sure of that before the kandar were born.

"I didn't even know the Purpose." She looked back at him, making eye contact, as if to drive in that point. "The kandar *are* the Purpose."

He looked away. It was true. But the Purpose was lost to them now.

"I'm sure you're thinking something I would pick up on," she said, studying his face, "if I were the same as the rest of you."

"My thoughts right now are unimportant. It's nice to hear something I have no influence on for once."

She sat down beside him again. "Jaydin was the only tevadra who walked towards me rather than away. She told me my name and taught me everything I know about existence."

Cien found himself listening for the telltale buzz of thought that would normally accompany such a speech, but there was nothing.

"It's hard to be alone in one's mind here," she said.

The words reminded Cien of something. "I've been alone in my mind."

She gave him a sideways look.

"On Land Side, in the dunes." He had enjoyed the feeling, but he could see how it would be different if he could never escape it. "I thought I was the only kandar who had ever been truly alone."

"It turns out you're not." They sat in silence for a moment before she continued. "I'm always alone in my mind, but I know the Purpose now. I know I'm one of you and that the Purpose is mine too. I got all of this from Jaydin. I owe her everything."

"Maybe that's why you can find her," Cien said. "Perhaps you have some sort of connection."

"I have no connection with anyone."

Cien chose to interpret that in the kandaran way. She couldn't connect with anyone in her mind. He hoped she had connections outside that. Cien himself was notoriously solitary in Black Valley, but he hadn't had a dodenzinn, and he was the Shadow. There were reasons he spent nearly all of his time alone. He didn't think Sandin's lack of a mindvoice was a good enough reason.

"What about your other sisters?" he asked. "You were the second born. Don't you think Tchardin or Damarin would have gone to you if they had been born before you? Or Kadailin?"

"If Damarin had come before me she probably would have stayed, because Jaydin did. Tchardin and Kadailin both had it just as bad at their births. It shaped them. Maybe it would have led them to pity me, or maybe they would have thought I deserved no better."

"What was done to them?" This was the first Cien had heard of Tchardin's birth being strange.

"I was the only kandar to attend Tchardin's birth. I'm sure she tried to speak to me, ask me why I was alone when she would be queen, but I'll never know what she said. No one heard her first words and no one saw her leaf grow in the collective for the first time. Kadailin..."

Cien waited but she didn't continue. "Why didn't anyone attend Tchardin's birth?"

"The same reason everyone went to Kadailin's," Sandin said. "Damarin."

***

Tchardin sat with Kadailin in Sirrhon's branches. Kadailin had found her there. Tchardin hadn't been able to make herself look at the collective to find anyone's leaf.

"She can't make you do it," Kadailin said.

"I'll end up doing it eventually."

Kadailin frowned. "Why?"

"Because she's right, Kadailin. She has to be. She knows everything."

"She didn't know about Black Valley. She doesn't know as much as she thinks she does."

Tchardin looked down through the branches and contemplated that. They were sitting in Sirrhon because Tchardin couldn't handle feeling so close to Tith when she knew it was possible to lose him. Would Jaydin have proposed what she did if the fire had reached him? Tchardin knew she would have.

"I'll ask Damarin then," Tchardin said.

"Damarin is awful," Kadailin replied. "I don't care that I'm not allowed to tell you. Damarin is the High Seat. She's the one who ridiculed you for so long, who mocked you."

Kadailin must have joined the council in their absence. Revealing the identity of the High Seat wouldn't be a good start for her, but the information explained a lot. The revelation would have surprised Tchardin more before all she had seen—now it seemed almost obvious—but hearing it still stung. The High Seat had not been kind to her, nor to Kadailin. Tchardin placed a hand on Kadailin's arm, feeling a slight repulsion from her aura. Her sister quieted.

"I guess that's why she thought she could disobey the Black Valley council. Or maybe she'd already talked to them."

"When you shifted here?"

Tchardin nodded. "The three of us asked to be allowed to shift to the island. The council denied us but told Damarin she could take the raft back. Cien and I couldn't wait. I told Damarin we should shift without their approval but she said the word of the council was law. I needed to get back to this..."

"So you shifted anyway."

Tchardin smiled for the first time since the fire. "We did. She arrived just after we got to shore. I thought she might have followed us but Cien said she couldn't have known we'd done it."

"I wonder what she would have said to us if you didn't shift. I think she was about to explain where you'd gone."

"I guess we'll never know."

"What makes you think she'll know anything about the trees?"

Tchardin stood. "Jaydin may know less than she thinks she does, but Damarin definitely knows more than she says."

Kadailin remained seated on the branch. She looked up at Tchardin with fear in her eyes.

"I wouldn't make you come with me." Tchardin knew Kadailin had trouble with Damarin. It was probably worse knowing she was High Seat.

"But I should," Kadailin answered. "I let you cross the water without me. I should have gone then."

"Damarin is different," Tchardin said. She dropped off the branch.

She overestimated the amount of pandinzori that would be available in the clearing when she fell. There was barely enough to stop her. Her body jerked in the air as her tired mind tried to hold it all together. She dropped the last distance and landed in a crouch in the grass.

The clearing appeared to be empty of kandar. They could be hiding in the tall grass, but no one walked across it. How would she find Damarin without looking at the collective? She walked towards the hole in Cens.

When she had first emerged from the flaming trees she'd recognised the place Damarin and Kadailin drew the water from. It was the same span of shore where she and Damarin had spent immeasurable amounts of time staring off towards Land Side. It no longer called to her, but she remembered it. She made her way towards it.

Death spread out before her. She almost turned around, but she looked across it and saw a tevadra standing by the water. Damarin's yellow aura blazed against the blue.

Tchardin ran across the black destruction, cringing every time she heard a crack or felt a burnt branch slide under her feet. Cens was not as vast as it once seemed. She made it to the other side quickly.

"Damarin," she said. Her sister turned. There was an odd look in her eyes as she took in the scene behind Tchardin. "I need to ask you something."

"What do you want?"

Tchardin hesitated. "Jaydin says the trees touched by fire have gone mad and need to be destroyed."

"That's not a question." Damarin's dark eyes narrowed.

"I need to know if it's true."

Damarin turned away to look at the water. Tchardin began to regret the question. What could Damarin know about fire, or about damaged trees? There was another way their middle sister could help, even if she didn't know. "I know you're the High Seat of our council, Damarin. If you vote to stop it—"

Damarin looked at her with outrage in her eyes. "Did Jaydin tell you that?"

Tchardin shook her head. Damarin's thoughts grew the loudest Tchardin had ever heard before they returned to their usual quietude. Damarin had realised it was Kadailin who told Tchardin. Tchardin opened her mouth to speak but Damarin spoke first.

"It's true. About the trees. Of course it is. Straight from Tith's history." She turned to Tchardin. "And I know just as much as Jaydin does. About fire. About damaged trees. About everything. I know more than Jaydin does, in fact. *I* know Derkra is changing. Jaydin refuses to see it."

Tchardin stared blankly back at her.

"You really can't see? Not even after our journey together? I could never have expected so much from Black Valley but I did expect more from you."

"I just want to help the forest—"

"The forest isn't our biggest problem right now."

Tchardin looked back at the burnt black path through Cens. She remembered the screaming trees and the kandar who had thrown themselves into the fire. Damarin stepped in front of her.

"Ryten wants to know who his dodenzinn is, even though he's nearly at half life. Cien is close to the same age and he doesn't really know either. They both think it might be you. They both think it might be me. But how can a kandar have two? And how can they not know?"

Tchardin felt betrayed. The dead and dying trees left her mind. The questions Damarin asked were nonsense. Offensive. The kandar were supposed to know their dodenzinn. She knew hers. Or did she?

"Exactly," Damarin said.

Tchardin felt even more hurt and confused. "What do you mean?"

"You're supposed to know, but you don't. Not really. Because things have changed. Ryten and Cien are both yours."

Tchardin took a step back.

Damarin's voice was forceful. "They're both mine too."

"They both belong to both of us?" Tchardin couldn't keep the shock from her voice.

"I guess you have a right to that reaction." Damarin continued talking over Tchardin's disgust. "I felt that way at first too."

Tchardin shook her head. "Derkra isn't supposed to change. We're not supposed to change."

"There was a fire, Tchardin. Derkra's first fire. Look at Cens!"

Damarin stepped to the side then, giving Tchardin a full view of the carnage. The trees were aching and she might have to kill them.

"We need to stop this useless pining for the Purpose. It's time we forgot about the humans. Time we focussed on ourselves."

Tchardin remembered Damarin's conversation with Miadra in the cave in Black Valley. "Forget the humans? Damarin, you're the leader of the council! We *are* the Purpose. There's nothing else."

"How can it be the Purpose anymore?" Damarin's voice was mocking. "Tchar herself bars us from the Earths. Dani is nowhere to be seen. Our forest burns. We're no longer paired. The kandar are split. My position as head of the council is meaningless if I can't make the kandar see."

"What are you saying?" Tchardin asked.

"It's time we built our own world."

"Derkra is our world."

"This? Half sand. Half water. Flat. One forest in all the world? One island in all this water? We can make it better. Start now, from this place of devastation. From this loss."

Damarin was starting to scare Tchardin. "You got this from Miadra—" she began to say but Damarin cut her off with a laugh.

"You think this was her idea? Miadra is smart, Tchardin, and she is rare, but she was almost as dull as the rest of you before I found her. Jaydin may have tried her hardest to discourage me but I will not do the same to Miadra. I will not do the same to you."

"Creator made us to guide the humans. Anything else is wrong."

"Creator has been gone since the beginning of time. Even Tchar never actually saw It. Ovaeron's word is all that remains of Creator and you know how I feel about the word of the trees."

The collective rang out in Tchardin's mind. The ripples originated at her leaf.

"Jaydin calls you." Damarin tilted her head and Tchardin was reminded of the first time the council had called her for acknowledgment. Damarin had challenged her then, to be more than she would have been had she never left Calendrai, and she had risen to it. "What type of queen will you be now?"

Tchardin bristled with indignation. "I will be the queen I was meant to be."

"Oh, Tchardin, you really believe you were meant to be queen just because you were born with a golden aura?"

A tevadra born with a golden aura would be queen. It had always been so.

"What would you do with it anyway?" Damarin turned away from Tchardin to look at the water again. "How can you still not see the problem?"

"Damarin—"

"Jaydin's not going to teach you what you need to know." Her sister looked back and met her eyes once more. "So I guess it's up to me."

***

Cien walked through the charred strip in Cens towards the water. His legs were unsteady and weak from earlier exertion. His whole body shook when he heard the broken, black branches creaking under his feet with each step. Shrivelled leaves hung limp on either side of him.

He looked down as he walked, to avoid tripping in his weakened state. He sensed Tchardin ahead and he crossed the burnt patch because Cens seemed to have gone mad, turning him around and sending him back to the clearing when he tried to pass through it. When he found himself on bare earth again, he saw that both Tchardin and Damarin were there. There was something odd about where they were standing. Ovaeron called faintly from behind them.

"Did you two notice this points straight to Land Side?"

They turned to him. He caught Tchardin's eyes. There was hurt there, and confusion. He looked at Damarin but she had turned back to Tchardin. Pandinzori gathered around the two of them. Their auras were so close in colour it was unclear who was drawing it. Then the shift opened behind Tchardin. It resolved into slowly spinning greyness, pointing nowhere.

Cien was about to ask Damarin what she was doing when she sent a wall of pandinzori towards Tchardin. Tchardin was slow to react and thrown back into the shift. The ice buckled. Water exploded outwards. Tchardin and the shift vanished. A wave of weakness rolled over Cien. He stumbled backwards.

"Where did she go?" He searched his mind for Tchardin's leaf and found it dark. The weakness brought on by this realisation caused him to fall to his knees.

He opened his eyes from the collective to find Damarin looking down at him. The shift was too dangerous to be sending a kandar in unprepared like that. Despite his diminished strength he reached for pandinzori, only to find she had taken all that around him. She pulled him towards her. Their auras collided and he was surprised and enraged to feel renewed strength from the contact instead of repulsion.

Damarin opened the shift again. He fought to stop her. He couldn't let her send him through the spinning grey, but she was too strong, and he was tired. She held him to her with pandinzori and broke the ice herself. Water rushed forwards and pulled them in together.

PART II

Chapter 16

The water seethed. It spun, twisted, dove into itself. It had to expand; expand and expand until it was everything. It had to expand until it was thin and filled all the spaces.

The water was expanding but something was searching. It pulled and it turned and it tried to direct the water but the water had only one purpose. The water would be everything and everything could go nowhere. That which searched was less certain. What was it searching for?

The one purpose eclipsed the other and the urgency faded. The water grew calmer. It was no longer pulled or pushed to search, it only pushed itself outward. The water stretched and rushed, growing more and more still as there was less to stretch and rush. But then there were leaves.

The leaves carved the water. Branches barred it, forced it away from its goal. A faint remembrance formed as the water was brought together, as it churned and raged against the green. Something awoke.

A hand caught a branch.

Weakness gripped Tchardin as she broke from the shift. She landed hard on compact ground and lay motionless there. The collective was dark and silent, empty of lights and voices. She opened her mind to it for the first time since the fire and found no comfort from it.

Where had Damarin sent her that all the leaves of her people had blackened? She felt Cien's absence like she had when his leaf faded in the shift. She knew now she might be feeling the loss of Ryten as well. Could she be somewhere else on Land Side? Far out in the desert? The earth under her fingers could be hard sand but when she opened her eyes she couldn't see it well enough to be certain. She tried without success to study it before realising that would be impossible. True darkness surrounded her—something that shouldn't exist on Derkra. She struggled to her feet, fighting the feeling of despair that had settled on her at the distance between her and her dodenzinn. Or both of them.

Pandinzori blazed around her but without Derkra's ubiquitous light to balance it she was blinded. She closed her eyes to get her bearings, concentrating on seeing only the outline of things in pandinzori. Slowly the world made sense again.

There was a great tree in front of her, his base so wide it blocked out everything else. That explained why the pandinzori around her was so thick. His canopy covered the sky above and it too was full of shimmering light. She walked towards him and placed her hands on his trunk.

'*Who are you?*' she asked the massive tree. He had to be kandaran, so he would tell her his name.

Karel.

Tchardin jumped away from the trunk. Jaydin had told her Karel was the World Tree of World One.

She scanned the canopy above with her closed eyes, then turned to look away from the great trunk. The area behind her was open and flat and pandinzori flowed along the ground at a height just above her head, but there were no more trees to create it. It continued for a vast featureless length then stopped abruptly. Her first thought at the sight was water.

There were areas of higher concentrations of pandinzori between the tree and the water, places where the light blazed brilliantly. Karel—if he really was Karel—loomed above her. She would climb him for a better look.

She placed her fingers into the deep grooves of his bark and began to ascend. His trunk became smoother as she climbed. He was not as inviting as Tith or his brothers—not meant to be scaled—and she was weak. When she slipped she used his pandinzori to catch herself, finding the act possible in her state of exhaustion only because of its abundance. Eventually she made it to Karel's lowest branch and walked along it, the leaves now surrounding her thinning until she was out in the air, on the smallest part of the branch she could manage without falling.

With her eyes still closed, the pandinzori surrounding everything as her guide, Tchardin looked over the world. The void of pandinzori had to be water of a similar scale to that of Water Side on Derkra. It seemed to stretch on forever. Jaydin said World One didn't deviate far from Derkra in its composition—infinite, half land, half water—but Tchardin wondered for a moment if the water she saw *was* Water Side. That seemed more plausible than the alternative. That she was instead on a human Earth. But if she was on Derkra that would mean there was another kandaran tree on Land Side. A tree who dared to name himself after a World Tree.

She backed away into the leaves. She was on World One. In the World Tree, Karel. Had Damarin sent her here on purpose? Or had Tchardin just been lucky enough to make her way through the aimless shift alive, taking the first possible opportunity to escape?

She crossed to the opposite side of the tree, circling his trunk when she came to it and walking along another large branch. There should be a city there, if she remembered Jaydin's teaching correctly. A city of humans. What she saw made her back away in surprise.

There was a monstrous wall of pandinzori in the distance. There was so much it seemed only possible it came from a kandaran tree, but from what she saw there were no trees inside it. Instead, it was full of many small blocks. She felt strangely drawn to them, leaning forward between the branches and almost falling. It had to be the human city. Those blocks were *buildings*.

Then Tchardin remembered the odd concentration of pandinzori below her and looked down from Karel's branch. There was a bright line of it—magnitudes brighter than the rest—leading away from the base of his trunk. Another line came off the base a quarter of the way around. She walked back to Karel's trunk and circled it, putting distance between herself and the city. There were four straight, brilliant lines in the earth leading away from the great tree. She recognised it as the Symbol.

Jaydin had told Tchardin about the Symbol. It was the most obvious manifestation of rendinzori—the human power—on World One. As far as the kandar knew, rendinzori was a power similar to pandinzori, but that the kandar couldn't see. Jaydin might know more but Tchardin had never asked for an explanation of its use, only a list of its obvious results.

She climbed higher into Karel's canopy, high enough that she could see the ground in the distance from a better perspective. She followed one of the lines of the Symbol through the breaks in the leaves and found it had branches coming off it. Those branches in turn branched out farther and so on. Each of the four lines was similar. She knew from Jaydin that they were meant to mimic a tree in profile—the four main lines being the trunks. They represented the paths the travelling people of this Earth had taken when they left the city. Some of the branches appeared to be broken—the lines ending too early to complete the perfect symmetry evident in the others—scuffed away or gouged out of the earth. Tchardin didn't remember Jaydin mentioning that.

She opened her eyes. She must have been ignoring the pandinzori on Derkra her whole life or she wouldn't have been able to navigate through it. It must be the blackness of this world that made pandinzori too bright. She willed it to dim and it slowly faded into the background of her vision. The space around her became clear.

A weak silver light covered everything. The light did little to help her but now she could see the shadows, see the definition in everything. Pandinzori was still there—much greater in brightness than the real light—but it complimented the world rather than distracting from it.

She sat down against a jutting branch and considered her situation. She was on World One. The kandar could shift to the human worlds directly from Derkra. They could get back to the Earths and fulfill the Purpose. All she had to do was return to Derkra and show them it was possible. But how would she get back? And how had she gotten here in the first place?

Damarin could probably help. Her sister may not have done it on purpose, but she had thrown Tchardin into the first human world whether she meant to or not. Tchardin wasn't sure she could replicate what had happened, but she hoped Damarin could. The things her sister had said before she opened the shift made Tchardin leery of her cooperation, but surely the fact that they could return to the Purpose would change Damarin's mind.

First she had to find a way back to the kandar.

She was about to open the shift when a thought came to her. She pulled up the dark collective in her mind, intending to gather what information she could before she left the Earth. She lingered for a moment on Cien's black leaf. What had happened to Cien after she left Derkra? How had he reacted to seeing her thrown into the shift? A wave of weakness washed over her as she observed the darkened leaf. The only way to find out would be to return.

Tchardin focused her mind outwards from Cien's leaf and checked the collective for any sign of the human presence on World One. There was nothing new there. She wasn't sure what she was looking for but she had thought she would know it when she saw it. The guardian of the Earth could help her, but Voronin hadn't shown herself either. Then again, this world was infinite like Derkra. Perhaps the guardian was just far away?

'Where is Voronin?' she asked Karel.

There was no answer but a sense of impossible distance. Tchardin thought it was her own belief at first but the tree seemed to insist when she doubted him.

So Voronin was still the guardian of World One. Jaydin would be happy to hear she lived. Tchardin had never doubted it. The trees said the guardian of a world should never change, but Jaydin worried things would be different when they returned to the Earths. Tith's oldest daughter expected disaster. Tchardin couldn't see anything that implied that would be the case on World One.

She opened the shift in front of her on the branch. It seemed easier now than it had been on Derkra. It was the swirling greyness she expected, so she tried to focus on revealing an image of Calendrai there. Nothing appeared. She felt no sense of the island from the grey. She tried Black Valley with the same result.

Then it occurred to her that Coralynth could be accessible from the Earths. Tchar may not have blocked it outside Derkra. Slowly the grey became the familiar white of snow, but something was different. Directly ahead there was an opening into a yellow forest. When she had opened the shift to Coralynth from Derkra she had only seen the path.

Then she remembered what Miadra had said about the path. There were nine smaller paths branching off the main one, each leading to one of the nine human worlds. She was seeing another shift portal through her own shift. It was the perpetually open portal to one of the other worlds from Coralynth.

Tchardin touched the ice. Nothing happened. She pounded on it. Cracks formed under her beating fist but she was discouraged by its strength. It had taken no effort to open the shift to any other place. It must be blocked here too. The cracks quickly faded when she stopped.

She closed the shift in frustration and noticed that real light threaded through Karel's branches. It was still dim but it was no longer silver. Now it had the look of Derkra's light.

The intricacies of World One were becoming apparent. The buildings she had seen in the darkness were finely detailed in the growing light—not just the uniform blocks they had appeared to be. They were of different shapes and sizes and paths ran between them. *Buildings. Homes.* Jaydin had taught her these words. The humans would be in those buildings. They created them and lived inside them somehow. Tchardin noticed again the mass of pandinzori above them and shivered.

She tore her eyes away and saw in greater detail the lines of pandinzori in the sand below. They were tinted red against the surrounding yellow. Karel's leaves enveloped her in vibrant green and his trunk and branches were a dark grey. Finally she moved through them and saw the water. It was a shimmering plane of blue the hue of which she had never seen, not in her mind nor on Derkra.

What a world. It was already more impressive than Derkra and there would be much to discover beyond her sight. The variety of it—in colour and texture and content—was amazing. The scale incredible. She knew it was infinite, as Derkra was, but it was much more than sand and water. She knew from Jaydin's stories that she could live here forever and never see it all. She was tempted to do so.

But then she remembered the humans. They were probably there, in the buildings, and while this world appeared to still be pristine, there was no guarantee it would stay that way without kandaran guidance. She couldn't leave existence to flounder without them. Not now that she had seen what it contained. Humanity was the Purpose and the kandar were its guide.

Or at least they were supposed to be. Coralynth may be closed to them but here she was, on the first human Earth, without Coralynth. Without Tchar and Dani. It was possible for the kandar to do it on their own.

Tchardin had to face the water of the shift again. She had to go back. The best she could do was to focus on Derkra in her mind and hope the water would take her there.

She drew Karel's pandinzori towards her and opened it into the shift.

***

Kadailin marvelled at her body in the council shadow. She had been a beacon of light amongst the other members at the last meeting she attended. The shadow hadn't accepted her and had clearly marked her as an outsider. Now that Nox had gone to rest she blended with the others.

The collective pulsed in her mind and kandar gathered outside the shadow on Tith's branch. Kadailin was excited to be a part of the ceremony that would finally make Tchardin queen. She had always expected to stand beside her younger sister when the council called, but now she would join her voice to those who would acknowledge her instead.

The collective ceased its beating. Kadailin turned towards Tith's branch with the rest of the council. She searched through the kandar there for Tchardin. An aura encroached on her own, causing a jolt that startled her.

"She's not there," Jaydin said from beside her. "I stopped the call. She's gone again."

Kadailin was worried for a moment before she remembered Jaydin's plan for the scarred trees. If Kadailin knew how to get to Black Valley she would have run from that too. Jaydin's eyes grew hard for a moment. She appeared ready to say something scathing when Marr joined them.

"Tchardin has left Calendrai," he said.

"Damarin is gone as well," Jaydin responded. "The ceremony is impossible if either of them is missing."

Marr twitched strangely at her words. "You called the meeting so she could deal with..."

Jaydin nodded. Kadailin hadn't heard his thoughts but he had to be talking about the fire.

"I'm happy to see you made it through uninjured," Jaydin said.

"You were a great help at the shore," Kadailin added.

He had been one of the first to join her and Damarin at the water's edge. Images of the fire invaded her thoughts. She had been spared the worst of it by Damarin's call for help but what she had seen would not leave her mind.

Marr looked down at the branch. Jaydin tilted her head in question but he refused to look up at them.

"Not enough help," he finally said. "Too many died. Too many were burned."

Jaydin gasped. "Was Gerrin burned in the fire?"

Marr didn't respond. Kadailin had no idea who Gerrin was. She didn't have the name in her mind, but she didn't have many kandar in her collective. Perhaps a friend of Marr's? Perhaps his dodenzinn? She wasn't sure she had ever met Marr's dodenzinn, although he gave off the feel of a devoshai well past quarter life.

"Was he scarred?" Jaydin asked.

Then Kadailin understood. Gerrin must be Marr's father. Before she could help herself she shot a horrified glance at Jaydin and her suspicions were confirmed. She opened her mind to speak to him but a thought from Jaydin stopped her.

'Don't tell him.'

Anger flared inside Kadailin. Jaydin was going to force Tchardin to kill the damaged trees and she wouldn't admit her plan to one of their children?

'I'm serious, Kadailin.'

Kadailin stared at Jaydin. She would give her sister one chance to defend her position. If she wasn't convinced she would share the plan with the entire collective. They deserved to know. *'Why not?'*

'Wait until Tchardin has returned. Until she is queen.' Jaydin held her gaze. *'If you tell him now, when we have no authority here, things could get very ugly. Marr is unpredictable at the best of times and we've never had to deal with something like this before.'*

'But his father—'

'It will only enrage him. Wait for Tchardin. Or better yet, let Damarin tell him. He won't be happy, but he may accept it if she says it must be so.'

Marr watched them as if he knew they were speaking. His unblinking eyes made Kadailin uneasy.

"You should go to Gerrin," Jaydin said to him. "I've cancelled the call. There's no sense holding a meeting when neither the future queen nor the High Seat are in attendance."

Marr seemed to come back to himself for a moment. "The kandar want to know what can be done about the trees."

Kadailin was surprised to find herself speaking. "We should wait for Tchardin and Damarin to return. One of them will have an answer for us."

Marr stood in front of them for slightly too long and Kadailin worried he had overheard their private conversation. Then he turned away and dropped off the branch.

"Come with me to the forest," Jaydin said.

Kadailin stood just inside the edge of Cens and studied the path the fire had taken. The leaves at her feet were crisp and black. She stepped on one and heard it crackle as it disintegrated. She shivered. Jaydin examined the burned trees behind her.

The change in the forest was extreme. Shortly after the fire it had ceased to hide itself, ceased to keep its size a secret. Kadailin saw glimpses of the water all the way around the island from her vantage point inside the trees.

"Are you sure we have to kill them?" she asked.

"I am, unfortunately."

"Will Cens go back to the way it was if we do?"

Jaydin turned away from the trees and frowned at Kadailin. "That, I don't know."

"One of the few things you don't know."

"I'm not sure anyone fully understands Cens. I don't even think Tith does."

Kadailin was sad to see the forest like this. It had always seemed so complicated, so vast. It had even been frustrating at times. Now that it was open to the rest of Derkra it was clear it would only be a short sprint from Tith's trunk to the water's edge. It made the island seem smaller.

They stood in silence for a long while. Kadailin couldn't help thinking back to their argument before the fire.

"You always knew Damarin was the High Seat," she finally said. "I assume you even voted for her. How do you feel about that, knowing she fought to discredit Tchardin? That she treated me so horribly?"

Jaydin studied her for a moment. "You wouldn't understand."

"If you want my help in the council you need to make me understand."

Jaydin paced across the dead leaves. The sound of their dry crunch hurt Kadailin deeper than just her ears. Jaydin saw her expression and stepped back into the trees.

"Before Tith gave us Tchardin, I thought Damarin might be the one I was waiting for." Jaydin's eyes grew bright as she continued. "Sandin was with me when Damarin was born. I described her birth as well as I could, since Sandin couldn't see what made it remarkable and I was unable to send an image to her mind. I've never seen anything like it before or since. Damarin was magnificent the moment she stepped onto the earth. She still is."

Kadailin expected Tchardin's birth was more impressive, but Sandin was the only one to have witnessed that, and as Jaydin said, she couldn't see pandinzori.

Jaydin's sad glance showed she'd heard the thought. "You missed it too."

A wave of guilt washed over Kadailin. "I only missed it because of you."

There was a moment of silence, broken only by the maddening buzz of Jaydin's secret thoughts.

"It probably wasn't impressive, you know," Jaydin said eventually. "If it weren't for Tith's own magnificence, it's likely Tchardin's birth would have been average."

"How can you say that? Tchardin has the golden aura."

"But her mind is nothing special."

"Who are you to judge?"

"I've seen them—" Jaydin started, then shook her head. "No, maybe I haven't seen them but I know them, the kandar of the past, those who went to the Earths. Damarin was like the greatest of them as soon as she stepped from Tith's trunk."

Kadailin didn't respond. She didn't doubt that Tith had spoken to Jaydin and no one else knew anything of the kandar of the past. There was nothing she could contribute.

"I was impressed with her," Jaydin continued. "More than impressed. I let her run rampant over Calendrai and I didn't rein her in. She was interested in the old High Seat and the two became close. I encouraged it. I didn't see the problem. Even though she's done some questionable things I still don't see how I was wrong to do so. She has a drive that nearly all the kandar lack. I thought she could get us back to the Purpose."

"And it took the birth of a future queen to change your mind about her," Kadailin said.

"I had doubts before Tchardin was born. Something had always been wrong with Damarin. It was hard to believe she was the one Tith had promised me despite her greatness. The one who would change everything."

"Did you know you were waiting for a golden aura?"

"No, just, something different. I knew I was born for a secondary purpose. I came to think my role would be to teach. To shape whomever Tith chose to give me. Why else would he tell me the history of existence? But I could never have shaped Damarin, could never influence her unless she invited it." Jaydin stood looking into nothing for a moment. "But the pandinzori she could hold. And the strength of her mind. She would have been assigned to World Four in the past. That kind of mind was made for the Earths." Jaydin must have seen the confusion on Kadailin's face. "You saw her during the fire. You stood with her under the rain. Damarin has the strongest mind in Calendrai."

Kadailin didn't doubt that. She'd been in awe of Damarin when their middle sister made the rain. She had never seen such power. And she had never heard any of this before. Would Tchardin have felt differently about Jaydin's teaching if she'd known?

"I wonder if Cien could match her eventually," Jaydin added, looking out to the water. "That wall he used to shield the brothers was incredible."

Kadailin hadn't seen as much of the wall as the rain, but the three brothers were colossal. To hold up a sheet of pandinzori so great was a feat in itself. "Maybe his birth was as impressive," she mused.

"I don't think it was. He said he gained his prodigious control by travelling the empty dunes of Land Side. I don't think he was born with it."

Kadailin raised her eyebrows in surprise. "I didn't know it worked that way."

"I can see how you wouldn't." Jaydin's eyes became unfocused, as if she looked into her memories, as if she looked at Tith's history. "The kandar of the past grew stronger on the Earths, as they completed the

Purpose. Some of them grew so strong that pandinzori flew from them as it does from the humans. Then it failed to stick and they went to rest." She shook her head, her eyes losing their faraway look. "Mostly we stay the same now, from birth until we rest. But sometimes something happens on Derkra to improve a kandar's ability to draw pandinzori to them. Some of us still grow as we age, even without the Earths. You didn't notice Tchardin was stronger when she returned from Land Side? Nothing like Damarin. Not even like Cien, but closer than she was before."

Kadailin studied the pandinzori that coated her body. Had it grown since she was born? She wasn't sure. She'd never looked at it so closely before. She wasn't sure if she'd noticed Tchardin's growing either. She looked up at their oldest sister. Had Jaydin's grown?

Jaydin smiled when their eyes met. "Why such interest now, after so long?"

Kadailin stopped her study at the question. "You never said a word to me. You barely acknowledged my existence. I couldn't have asked you if I wanted to."

"You could have asked." There was an expression on Jaydin's face that Kadailin didn't recognise. A depth of feeling she'd never seen from another kandar. "Any kandar can ask. Have you noticed that none of them do?"

Kadailin couldn't hold her sister's gaze. She looked through the trees instead. Now that she could see each individual trunk, now that Cens laid them out before her, she could see the kandar standing or walking between them. So many, and they did nothing. They had done nothing since Kadailin was born, probably since before Jaydin was born. Maybe for the entire four generations since Tchar had barred them from the Purpose.

"They don't even ask about the fire," Jaydin continued. "Not where it came from. Not why or how it started. They want to know what to do, in its aftermath, but they don't think to question its origin."

Kadailin turned back to Jaydin. "Where *did* it come from?"

Jaydin shook her head. "I don't know. I can answer a lot of questions, but I can't answer that one."

Kadailin looked down at the burnt earth and the ravaged, blackened leaves that covered it. She would ask her sister questions, even if the other kandar wouldn't. Now that she knew she could. Now that she knew what the answers could mean.

Chapter 17

Cien hit the ground hard, bounced, and rolled down a slope. He landed in soft sand and sunk into it. His mind began to ache immediately. There was no pandinzori around him. The emptiness of the collective assaulted him.

He tried to get up but he was too weak. He paused when he heard the sound of another landing in the sand. A shadow fell over his eyes. Damarin stood above him.

She smiled. How could she tolerate the pain? How could she not be hurting like he was? She'd even been strong in the shift. He'd been torn apart by the water and Damarin had almost consumed him when he was put back together. She'd pushed him out just in time.

There was sand in all directions and no pandinzori to be seen floating through the air. It was incredibly thick around Damarin, thicker than Cien had ever seen around any kandar. His own was pathetically thin. He tried to move it, in case there was a slight excess, but stopped abruptly when it only caused him more pain.

"I wouldn't do that if I were you," Damarin said. "The pandinzori around you is barely enough to keep you alive. There's nothing extra for you to affect."

Cien struggled to rise. He ignored the pain, pushing himself up in the sand. He managed to raise his head and shoulders only to find his body weakened as he moved. By the time he sat up he felt himself slumping down again. His thoughts swirled in his head, threatening to leave him.

"Where are we?" he asked, settling back into the sand.

"Far into the infinity of Land Side." Damarin spun around and gestured at the emptiness. "Farther than you have ever been."

"Why?"

"Because I knew I could handle it, and I knew you could not. You may have travelled a short distance across the dunes without pandinzori but I've been across Water Side."

"Where did you send Tchardin?"

Damarin shrugged. "If the shift had destroyed her we would know. You are her dodenzinn after all."

"You don't know where she went?"

"I wanted her to go to one of the Earths, but I can't be certain she made it. All I could do was point her in the right direction. Can you sense her?"

The Earths? Cien struggled to form the collective in his mind. Nothing came.

"That's probably for the best," Damarin said, acknowledging his failure.

She turned away from him and effortlessly opened the shift. The pandinzori around her remained the same as she controlled it, rather than shrink as it should. There was nothing for her to draw on. Where did it come from?

"How could you send her to one of the Earths from here?" Cien hadn't seen Coralynth behind the shift when she opened it. "The shift was empty, pointing nowhere."

Damarin didn't answer. The shift hung there, a swirling grey oval with pandinzori at its edges.

"You could have killed her," Cien said with difficulty. He didn't think he could talk for much longer. He put all his strength into forming words. "You *might* have killed her."

Damarin looked back at him.

"If I'm right you will get stronger." She ignored the words he had fought so hard to say. "The pandinzori around you will grow, as mine has. Soon you'll be able to sit up, then stand. Eventually you'll walk again. But I'll be back before you can open the shift."

"Why are you doing this?"

"Things need to change on Derkra," she said without hesitation. "They've already started to change. Those who refuse to accept that need to be removed, if only temporarily, in order for the transition to go smoothly."

"Derkra doesn't change."

"How do you know that?"

"It's the way things are," he said, hard-pressed to explain something that was simply true. "Change is for the Earths. For the humans. Not for us."

Damarin appraised him as Cien waited for her to answer. Waited in pain. He couldn't hear her thoughts at all.

"How can you say things haven't changed when the father of all of us calls a kandar to rest?" She looked him directly in the eyes.

Cien stiffened. He had worked so hard to conceal it. He had never told anyone.

"Yes, I know Ovaeron calls you. You may have kept that secret from the others but you couldn't keep it from me. I don't know how you've resisted him this long, but with what's coming I can't have you giving yourself to him. The effect on me..."

"The effect on *you*?" Could she also be unsure? "What effect could I have on you?"

Damarin's eyes bore into him and he shrunk away under her gaze.

"Don't tell me you weren't confused when you found the two of us. When you came to Calendrai and found all five. Don't tell me you couldn't feel it. You are mine as much as you are Tchardin's. You may even belong to more of us, but I'm not sure about that yet." She seemed to contemplate that for a moment, tilting her head. "I've spent more time with Jaydin than anyone other than Sandin has, and while I can't remember things the way she does I know there's never been anything like this on Derkra before."

She turned away. "I'll be back," she said with her face to the shift, "and when I come back we will go farther."

Damarin placed a hand against the ice. Cien didn't understand how she could move so easily when he couldn't even lift himself off the sand. Where had that pandinzori come from? When had she gotten so strange and strong? What change was coming to Derkra?

The ice on the shift broke and exploded outwards. Damarin was pulled into it and Cien weakened even more when she disappeared.

***

Sandin sat in Frenn and lamented the charred remains of his right side. His trunk had escaped most of the damage, but his lowest lying branch near the clearing had caught fire from the ground and carried it into his higher canopy. A third of his branches were leafless and open to view from the sky.

She was surprised how close the huge tree grew to the forest's edge, how no kandar had seen his superior height rising above the forest when they were in the branches of one of the other kandaran trees. Now this height difference was obvious, as it was with Del who clearly stood on the other side of the three brothers.

Sandin mourned the burned trees, but she missed the cohesion of Cens more. She couldn't hear the individual trees' pain as the rest of Calendrai said they could and because of that she had trouble feeling for each one separately. The forest as a whole however, with its power to deceive and conceal, was another matter.

She nestled into Frenn's untouched leaves. He was a beautiful tree. New to her. She wanted to appreciate him properly while she still could. Soon Tchardin would have to kill him and Derkra would lose a kandaran tree.

Sandin didn't blame Tchardin for escaping to Black Valley. She had no doubt Jaydin was right about the proper fate of the burned trees, but it was still a horrible decision to make. It would be even worse to carry out. Her sister should be allowed a small respite and Jaydin seemed to be taking her disappearance well. Tchardin would come back eventually. Perhaps by then she would be ready to accept her role as queen. Once she was acknowledged she could make Ryten or Cien her Shadow and the hierarchy would be complete for the first time since before the war. Then the kandar could work on getting back to the Purpose.

Someone moved below her, between the trees towards the shore. Instantly the shadows came to her and she was shrouded against Frenn's branch, blending into the leaves. In moments she was virtually invisible. A part of the canopy.

The low branches parted a few trees away from Frenn and a tevadra emerged. She was hidden by leaves as she walked quickly in the direction of the clearing but Sandin could make out the short black hair and dark eyes from where she waited. It was Kadailin then, or Damarin if she had returned. The tone of their skin and their facial features were too similar, and it was too hard to distinguish the tevadra's height from this far off. The tevadra that was Kadailin or Damarin stopped.

Sandin grew impatient and moved lower into Frenn's branches. As she descended she saw the tevadra start to walk again, this time in her direction. When she got to a low branch, she dropped to the ground. Damarin was waiting.

"I knew it was you," Damarin said. "I can sense everyone but you."

There was no obvious malice in her voice but Sandin expected it was somewhere in there, hiding behind Damarin's impressive ability to mask her feelings. To mask almost everything in her mind. Damarin hated that Sandin could hide the way she did.

"How did you know it was anyone?" she asked her sister.

Damarin shrugged, and smiled. Then she walked towards the clearing. She appeared to be in a rush.

"Did the others come back with you?" Sandin asked, following her.

"The others?"

"Tchardin and Cien. We assumed—"

"Why?" Damarin stopped and turned to Sandin. They stood in the singed leaves. Sandin leaned her weight from one foot to the other, not willing to press too hard on the fallen foliage. Damarin remained still. "I barely know Cien," she said, "and Tchardin and I have done exactly two things together in our lives. Stared out hopelessly at the infinite water, and crossed it to find what called us. No more than that."

Blunt, but true. The tevadra weren't exactly close.

"I have to call a council meeting," Damarin continued. "Something needs to be done about these trees."

"Jaydin wanted Tchardin to handle that, but we can't find her. We thought she was in Black Valley with you."

"I didn't see her. She and Cien may have been there but I had no reason to search them out."

"Why did you go then?" Sandin asked.

"I needed to meet with the council."

As High Seat of the council in Calendrai, it made sense that Damarin would want to meet with the members in Black Valley. Perhaps she was even trying to take over. That gave Sandin pause. Damarin was a nuisance in her position as High Seat, but maybe the one in Black Valley was worse.

Damarin stared at her, her dark eyes searching for Sandin's thoughts. Sandin was glad her sister would never find them. The tevadra wouldn't like them.

Damarin turned to go. Sandin followed.

"Are you going to talk to Jaydin before you call the meeting?"

"I suppose I could. You need me to find her for you?"

Sandin almost stopped. "No. Now that Cens is opening up to us I don't think I'd have much trouble."

Damarin looked around them then and Sandin thought it might be the first time she had noticed the thinning of the trees. "I guess you wouldn't."

"I think you should show her the shift."

Damarin scanned Cens, probably to gauge the damage caused by the fire. It wasn't only trees that had died. It may have been the entire forest.

"Of course," she said. "All the kandar must learn to shift."

Sandin smiled. She had been waiting her whole life to watch Jaydin open the shift since she could never do it herself. Then her smile faded. Damarin couldn't get what she wanted. There was one kandar who could never learn to shift.

***

Ryten lay in a slight groove in one of Ahron's branches. It cradled him and he avoided slipping off the branch because of the dip. The kandar arranged in the branches around him were still and silent. There were more of them now, after the fire. Supposedly they slept, but as Ryten continued to frequent this place he became less and less convinced they could achieve something he found impossible to do.

Damarin and Tchardin had left Calendrai again. It was starting to bother Ryten that they would make such dangerous decisions without consulting him, when his life might be equally affected. Worse yet, no one had taught him to shift, so he couldn't follow. Cien was gone too and that confused him even more. If only there was a way to just stop. Stop thinking and hearing and seeing. To sleep.

One of the sleeping kandar sat up and stretched. Ryten recognised his aura and knew his name was Maxim. Maxim took one of Ahron's leaves off a branch. Ryten was still unsure how he felt about that. Some kandar had convinced themselves they could eat, but there wasn't anything in Calendrai to eat but grass and leaves. Did Ahron feel the missing leaf?

Ryten thought of a leaf falling from the collective and shuddered. If the tree experienced a similar feeling to a loss in the collective every time one of his leaves was taken from him that would be reason enough to bar the kandar from removing them. The problem was that no one knew. Tith could have told Jaydin about it, but Tith had never lost a leaf. The kandar wouldn't touch him. How could he know what it felt like?

Ryten also wasn't sure it would matter if Tith said they should stop. Without the Purpose to guide them, the kandar would do whatever they wanted. Until Tchardin took control of their actions they were free. There were no rules. They had never been needed before.

"Maxim," he said to the devoshai, who had just stuffed Ahron's leaf into his mouth and was pulling off another one. "Why do you eat?"

Maxim turned the second leaf over in his hand and joined it to the other in his mouth. He settled himself on the branch as if to ignore Ryten, but eventually looked over. "Why do you sleep?" he asked in turn.

"I don't sleep." Ryten had never felt like arguing about this before. Now his unhappiness and confusion at Damarin and Tchardin's disappearance spurred him to question his actions. "Nor do you. Kandar can't sleep."

The devoshai's blank look gave him away, but a moment later he smiled. "You must be unable to achieve the necessary concentration."

Ryten laughed. "I don't think it's supposed to require concentration."

None of the kandar around them moved, dedicated to the illusion to the end. Maxim looked to them as if to search for support. Ryten felt a surge of strength. The collective flashed in his mind.

"You shouldn't take Ahron's leaves," he continued, pushing the image away.

"I can do whatever I want," Maxim answered.

'Ryten,' came into his mind. He looked around. The voice was Jaydin's. He turned back to Maxim.

'Ryten!' Jaydin said. *'We need you here. Now.'*

'I'm having an important discussion,' he said in her general direction. *'I would expect you to support me, now that I'm coming over to your side of the argument.'*

'There is no argument.'

'What do you want me to do then?'

Maxim stared at him suspiciously from the other branch. He must be able to tell Ryten was talking to someone but not what he was saying.

'I want you to learn to shift,' Jaydin said. *'Maybe you'll have more success than I have since you want to go to Black Valley so badly.'*

Finally. Ryten nodded at Maxim and stood to climb higher into Ahron. The devoshai didn't press the issue. Ryten rushed through the leaves towards Jaydin's aura and belatedly realised Damarin was there too. Her leaf had reappeared in the collective while he was talking to Maxim.

He came out almost directly in front of Sandin. Her eyes widened at the sight of him. He knew his were the same. They stared at each other until Jaydin came between them. When he turned away from Jaydin, Damarin glared at him.

'Found her finally?' Damarin showed no outward signs of talking to him. He ignored it. *'Is Sandin your dodenzinn now?'*

Where had this hostility come from? It had never been this bad before. He felt like pushing her off the branch. He wouldn't do it—he'd never touch her without her consent, without her acceptance of his status as her dodenzinn. But he wanted to. More than that, he wanted to demand that she consider him when endangering herself, but he had asked before, and it had accomplished nothing.

'Tchardin is my dodenzinn,' he said. *'I know that now.'*

'Say it all you want,' Damarin thought to him as he turned back to Jaydin. *'You have no idea.'*

"I can open it," Jaydin said.

Ryten noticed the hole in the world that floated in front of them. The portal showed Coralynth as he had seen it with Tchardin before the fire. Its surface was ice, not glass. "Can you open it to Black Valley?" he asked hopefully.

"I've only been able to get grey that doesn't seem to point anywhere. No image as Damarin can. I'm hoping you can do it."

"How do I do it?"

The pandinzori in the branches around them flew to hover in front of Damarin. It collapsed in on itself and exploded into the shift. Ryten took a step back. It started out grey and spinning, but slowly a tree appeared in the centre of it. *Ovaeron.*

"The rest of you should be able to bring it up," Damarin said with a smile. "I'm not sure why you're having trouble."

"I want Ryten to try," Jaydin said. "His need for Tchardin should help him."

Damarin's dark eyes flicked to him. He turned away from her.

Chapter 18

Tchardin looked through the grey branches that surrounded her into yellow leaves. The entire forest appeared to be yellow. It had to be the one she'd seen through the shift to Coralynth from World One. She had lost herself to the water at first, but once she found the yellow leaves she had known who she was. This time, instead of taking hold of them and pulling herself out, she'd continued.

She had made note of the place the leaves broke the water and spread herself thinner, wider, looking for Calendrai, Black Valley, anywhere on Derkra. She reached but could find nothing else. Only when she felt like she would lose herself completely had she surged back towards the leaves and forced herself out of the shift.

She sat high in Miran's branches now, the World Tree of the second human Earth. He was wider than he was tall and those that surrounded him—those that looked like only brothers—were in fact a part of him. The tree himself was a forest. His roots grew into seemingly separate entities that encircled him. What were many trees above the earth were one tree below it.

Due to his diminutive height and the fullness of his foliage, she could see nothing of the surrounding area from his branches. This was as good a place as any to think.

Her aim had been to shift to Derkra. The shift wouldn't resolve into an image of Ovaeron or Tith from World One, but she had figured that by entering the spinning grey she could go back. Without specifying where the shift should point, could a kandar go anywhere? It seemed not. She'd only been able to find this one place to leave the shift. Everywhere else had just gone on and on forever.

The shift was also incredibly violent. Tchardin had felt a much greater control this last time, but she'd still been torn apart many times before she knew herself again. How had the kandar used this as a means of transportation for so long? She had to be doing it wrong.

'Miran,' she said to the World Tree, trying to remember the name of the guardian of World Two. She thought back to Jaydin's lessons and it came to her. *'Where is Rypien?'*

Miran's answer swirled through the forest. A similar sense of distance came from his trunks as had come from Karel when asked about Voronin. It wasn't as great as it had been—World Two wasn't infinite in size—but it was still immense. Tchardin despaired. Would she never find someone to help her?

'Where are the humans?' she asked.

The answer was close. Very close. Tchardin whipped around to look through the branches. It almost felt as if Miran said they were among his trunks.

She needed to move, on to another Earth or at least away from here, to avoid the humans who would inevitably find her if she stayed. But it was hard to make herself get up and leave the tree. Things here were new. The yellow leaves were beautiful. She'd felt the same way on World One and had wanted to stay. She should at least look around before she left.

She dropped down from Miran's central trunk. As soon as her feet hit the ground her eyes were full of light that blinded her. She flinched and backed up. There was a line of brightness across her chest. It trembled as she moved and its shapes were like the dapples on her skin. She pushed shadows over it.

It hit her again when she stepped forwards. She passed through it but was left with purple spots over everything she looked at. She was reminded of something Jaydin had told her. It must be the *sun.* She turned until the light was behind her and looked ahead. The purple spots faded slowly from her vision.

A whispered thought entered her mind. *'We need rain.'*

Tchardin blinked and the spots renewed themselves. She looked for the source of the thought but saw only Miran around her. There was nothing in the collective.

'The air is too dry.'

Were the trees talking to her? The voice echoed strangely, as if it were many voices in quick succession, all saying the same thing. She continued to walk through the forest of Miran's limbs.

Rain, the voice had said. Jaydin had taught her that rain was water that fell from the sky and Damarin had shown it to them during the fire, but what was *dry*?

The world changed when she came to the edge of Miran's trunks. There was something wrong with the other trees. Their leaves were yellow too, but they drooped. Some fell. The ground was carpeted with them. Those that had fallen were torn and crisp. They crackled under her feet.

'The earth is too dry.'

Dry. Tchardin pulled away from the branches that reached towards her, covered in dead yellow leaves. *This* was dry. She ran. The voice followed her, speaking new words to her. Terrible, deadly words.

'There is nothing to drink. Nothing to eat.'

Tchardin ran through the trees, farther away from Miran, but the voice stayed in her head. Suddenly the forest ended. She came to an abrupt halt in front of a depression in the ground. The light filtered through the branches behind her and filled the space.

'The lake is dry.'

Tchardin knew instantly that what lay ahead of her was once a *lake*. A lake was water and there had been water here before. Big water, but not so great as Water Side on Derkra. Nothing like that existed here. Dry was the absence of water.

'We need rain,' the voice repeated.

Tchardin walked into the lake. Dead leaves lay inside the edge of it. She walked far enough out that she no longer stepped on them. There, the earth itself was cracked beneath her feet. It was lined with dark shadows in beautiful patterns. She almost forgot her fear of it as she traced them with her eyes. Then the voice returned.

'The children are dying.'

The children? There would be no kandar—no children of the trees—on this Earth. What did the voice mean? Creator's children? Humans themselves?

'The future dies with them.'

An image flashed through her mind. Small bodies appeared. They were too small to be kandar, too softly shaped. Kandar were born fully grown, had always been and always would be fully grown. These were less developed, and their skin—which clung closely to them—was a uniform colour throughout. They were less wild, less natural than the kandar. Tchardin was startled by the image. The voice spoke of human children. They were starving.

The voice was horrible. It was all-encompassing and strange. Tchardin felt nothing in the collective when she heard it. The tree in her mind was dark as it had been on World One. Miran had said the humans were close. It had to be a human voice she heard.

She tried to remember what Jaydin had said about World Two. All she could think of were the stories related to rendinzori. She knew the people of this Earth practiced something called *weather magic*—though she didn't understand it—but she was sure Jaydin had said nothing about a voice.

'My partner is dying.'

Another image lit the space behind her eyes. A partner was something like dodenzinn. Tchardin thought of Cien and Ryten unbidden. She saw them shrivel up and disappear.

'I'm dying,' it said.

Tchardin closed her eyes, scratched at her face with her fingers. Anything to rid herself of these thoughts she could not ignore. They were loud, and with them came a feeling. A sense. A terrible knowing of what was to come, and what was to come was the end.

When a kandar spoke into her mind she heard only words. This was something else. The end the voice spoke of was not the end of a kandar—to be able to rest and return. There would be nothing more for this human when death came.

'We need *rain.'*

Tchardin stumbled back to the forest. Where were these humans? What was she supposed to do when she found them? Why didn't the rain come? She ran back through the trees.

The kandar were supposed to help the humans manage the Earths that had been given to them by Creator, but what did that really mean? For the first time Tchardin felt unprepared to fulfill the Purpose. She doubted even Jaydin would know what to do.

She slowed when she noticed the voice had left her mind. It was quiet again, but she still felt the despair. It stuck in her and festered there. She needed to find the humans. She needed to find rain for them. She came out of the forest to a clearing. A true clearing, not like the one in Calendrai which was covered by the branches of the great trees. This clearing was open to the sky. It was full of grass.

All the grass was dead. Tchardin stopped for a moment and looked at the place. It must have been beautiful and green once. She could have spent the rest of her life slowly moving across it, touching each blade. There was so much detail here, even after its death, that Derkra and even Calendrai itself looked plain.

Now when she looked at it she only felt sad. The words of the voice weighed heavier on her mind. This meant more to the humans than it did to her. She could live here—there was still pandinzori wrapped around the dead and dying trees, covering the clearing—but they couldn't.

She walked across the open space. There was a spot of light in the sky, and from it emanated the beams that assaulted her. The sun. She kept it to her side and tried not to look at it.

'It has never been this bad before.'

A new voice, similar to the first, but definitely different. Then more voices. The air was suddenly thick with them. Tchardin cringed but kept walking towards their apparent source. The voices clawed at her.

'We. Will. All. Die.*'*

She fell to her knees in the lifeless grass. It was brittle against her. The humans needed rain. The trees needed it. The grass needed it. She closed her eyes and brought up the images Jaydin had given her. Her vision went black behind her closed lids. She saw the rain in her mind as it had been when she first learned its meaning. She remembered the gathered darkness above Calendrai when Damarin called it. The pandinzori of the clearing was drawn towards her. In the void of her vision, she let herself see it.

A drop struck her hand. She kept her eyes closed and felt pandinzori join her from above. Another drop hit her cheek. Water from the sky. Like the water that was used to drown a fire, enough water to fill the lake. Two more drops across her chest. Then they came in earnest. She opened her eyes to find that reality mimicked the image in her mind. She stood up and looked into the falling water.

The spot of light was gone, and instead the clearing was dark. The sky roiled above her, black and grey. The rain grew heavier. The drops ran down her body and into the earth. The voices in her head quieted, the film of despair dampened. All she could hear was the sound of the rain and the occasional abrupt crash from the sky.

Then there was a noise to her right. Quiet, under the rain, and quick. She turned. A human child ran towards her from the trees. Pandinzori grew out of the child in massive waves.

Tchardin ducked into the dead grass. There was easily as much pandinzori around the child as had been used in Cien's wall to block the fire in Calendrai. Could the child manipulate it? Tchardin remembered rendinzori and was both intrigued and afraid.

'Little girl,' one of the voices in Tchardin's mind said. It was calm now. *'Little girl, play in the rain that will save us all.'*

The girl didn't look at Tchardin. She looked at the sky. She raised her hands above her head and spun in circles until she fell to the ground. There was a smile on her open mouth and the rain fell into it. Her black hair dripped water as she moved. She was the most beautiful thing Tchardin had ever seen.

The shadows that wrapped Tchardin thickened as she watched the child carefully. Raindrops fell heavily around her. The girl got to her feet.

Tchardin opened the shift. She needed to leave, but she only stared at the spinning greyness. She had made no plan to engage it this time. Everything had happened so fast. Could she control the water right from the beginning? Or would she feel her body and mind being ripped apart again, and maybe never recovered? Where would she find herself when she broke out of it?

She looked for the child and panicked when she realised she'd lost sight of her. A thought came into her mind, much lighter than the thoughts of the original voices.

'Rainmaker,' it said.

Tchardin looked down and found the girl at her feet. From across the clearing it had been hard to judge the state of her small brown body, but now Tchardin saw that her bones stuck out under her skin and her eyes were sunken. She met the girl's gaze. Those starving eyes were strange, almost yellow, like the leaves. Tchardin moved slightly and the girl's eyes were brown. Then green.

The collective stirred in her mind. A new branch formed and joined with the two that were already there. On that branch a leaf grew. Tchardin was already amazed to find that humans had leaves too, when more leaves bloomed around it. There were five of them. They were small, indistinct, and the first was the brightest. The rest varied in strength but they all hugged the first. The little girl's name was Alyx, and her leaf was a blaze in the dark collective. Dimmer leaves grew out from the five. Eighteen in total. Tchardin held the girl's eyes as the collective grew in her mind.

Then she wondered if the humans were supposed to see her.

She turned away and bolted from the clearing, leaving the shift to vanish behind her. When she entered the trees she pried the air in front of her open and plunged through the ice.

Compactness.

The thought flowed with the water and the water hated it.

Solidity.

The water tore at the idea, rushed this way and that way to dislodge it. The water expanded, forcing the thoughts to thin before being pulled back by them. It rushed together.

I am.

The water was Tchardin, and Tchardin was looking for something. She was looking for an anomaly on the smooth, continuous infinity of the shift. She was looking for an escape.

A branch cut at her. She gripped it.

Tchardin jumped up instantly as her body sunk into something. It wasn't like water, which gave little resistance, or like sand or earth, which gave too much. This let her fall while also trying to keep her. For a moment she was terrified.

A coating of white dust clung to her when she stood. She recognised it as snow before it became water and slid down her body. It fell from her hair and impaired her vision. She brushed the water out of her eyes and shuddered, remembering the little girl from World Two. She could still see the girl's eyes. Her strange and wonderful eyes. But did World Two now know of the kandar? She could almost hear the terrible echoing voice in her head.

"The voice of humanity?"

Tchardin spun around to find a devoshai standing in front of her.

He was different from any she had seen before. He seemed big, but not like Ryten or Cotelle. His apparent size came from his intense presence and the unbelievable amount of pandinzori that followed him. She also felt that he was old. It was a strange combination. He gave off a sense of great age, but he held onto pandinzori as if he were in his prime.

His aura was white. It made him hard to see in the white around them. The patterns on his skin and hair too, were white. How had he come to be on the Earths?

"They still have it?" he inquired.

"Have what?"

"The voice. On World Two. They still speak as one?"

Tchardin looked at the devoshai in confusion. "Who are you?"

"I am Kordic, guardian of World Three."

"The guardian of an Earth," Tchardin whispered. She looked around her, searching for the World Tree. Spots of white fell through the bare branches above. She didn't see leaves on any of the trees that surrounded them. Were they dead?

"The great Zemko—World Tree of this Earth—is not dead," Kordic said, gesturing to the trunk directly behind him. "He only sleeps."

Zemko was an average-sized tree, indistinct from the others that stood with him. Nothing about him would have told her he was kandaran. If Kordic hadn't pointed him out, Tchardin doubted she would have found him.

As she studied the World Tree the guardian joined the collective in her mind. He was not a leaf on a branch as the other kandar were, nor a cluster of leaves such as the girl from World Two had given her. He was a seed, hanging from a fourth branch in the collective. The true guardian of an Earth.

"The guardians of World One and Two were far from their fathers," she said.

Kordic shrugged. "We go where we wish."

She was saved. A guardian of a human Earth could tell her how to get back to Derkra.

Kordic's expression grew confused. "I have not returned to Derkra since my birth and yet I know how you came here. You must return the same way. Through Coralynth."

"I came from World Two," Tchardin said. "I searched the shift and there didn't seem to be anywhere else to go."

Kordic looked at her closely. "I do sense World Two on you. I can almost hear the voice of the people. They do not talk like that here anymore." He looked pensive. "But you cannot have shifted directly from World Two. The shift is from here to Coralynth and from Coralynth to all the worlds. There is no other way."

"There is," Tchardin said. Damarin was at least correct in calling the kandar intolerant of change.

"Are you here to watch the world while I rest?" Kordic ignored her protest. "You are young enough. New to the Earths. There must be someone around here who can show you World Three's intricacies. I will not be with Zemko for long."

"What?" Tchardin hadn't thought the guardians ever rested.

"Tchar did not call on the kandar to aid me?"

"Tchar hasn't spoken to us since the war."

"The war?"

Tchardin tried to remember if Jaydin had told her which worlds the kandaran war had touched. She couldn't. "The kandaran war?" she tried.

"War is of the humans. The kandar do not war." Kordic looked her over and shook his head. "I do not know what is wrong with you. It would be best if you left this Earth and returned to Coralynth. You will only cause more harm than help here." He turned away from her.

"Wait," she said.

"I cannot help you, and it appears you are not here to help me."

"No one will come to help you if I can't get back to Derkra. There are no kandar here, and those on Derkra don't know how to return."

He turned back and tilted his head at her. "The kandar are not on the Earths?"

"Not for generations."

"It has been a while since I have seen them. Maybe that is why..." he trailed off, and started to walk away again.

Tchardin had never been so blatantly ignored in her life. It didn't matter that she was unacknowledged. The golden aura said she would be queen.

"Guardian," she said to his retreating back. "I am to be queen of the kandar. You will help me."

'Little queen,' he said as he continued to walk away, *'I have known many of you in my lifetime. I still have them here in my head. There has only ever been one guardian of World Three, and that is I. If you want my help, you will walk with me.'*

'The hierarchy says I'm above you.' Tchardin ran to catch up and fell in beside him as he skimmed over the snow.

"Yes, but where have you been? I have kept this world alive for all of time, and what have you done? You have rested, many times. You say the kandar have shunned the Earths. They have abandoned Creator's children and it is taking a toll."

"We didn't choose to. Tchar barred us from Coralynth."

"I do not believe it." He said it with conviction, but he stopped walking. Tchardin stopped beside him and her feet sunk into the snow.

"Open the shift then, to Coralynth," she urged. She hoped failure would convince him. It would be even better if he succeeded instead and could go through the shift to Coralynth. Then maybe she could follow.

The shift grew easily beside them. Tchardin looked through the ice and saw the snow that covered the path on Coralynth. Just beyond the path there was a dark place. The trunk of a big black tree was centred in the portal across from the one Kordic had opened.

"Here is Coralynth," Kordic said, annoyance in his voice. "Here is the path and the shift to World Four across it, just as it has always been."

So the black tree was Tairasyn, World Four's World Tree.

"Go through," she said.

The guardian stared at the shift, then said, "I have nothing to say to Tchar. Things are bad right now but nowhere near dire enough for me to leave. Especially if I am alone here."

"Please, just try it. You can come right back if it works."

Kordic looked unimpressed, but he pushed lightly against the ice of the shift. It cracked. He stopped. "See, it is—"

Tchardin reached past him and smashed her fists against the ice. Kordic pulled her away from the shift before she could throw her body against it.

"What are you doing? Do you not know never to enter another kandar's shift?"

Tchardin was surprised she couldn't feel his aura against her. There was no repulsion from him, as there would be from another kandar on Derkra. He glared at her, but then seemed to realise nothing had happened. Tchardin looked at the panel of ice. The cracks were gone.

"I didn't know not to enter another kandar's shift," Tchardin said, "because the kandar have forgotten how to shift."

Kordic stared at the now smooth ice. He let it disappear.

"I fell into World One from Derkra," Tchardin continued, "the first kandar to set foot on a human Earth since the war ended and Tchar barred us from her mountain. From World One I found my way to World Two and now to Three. I need to get back to Derkra so I can show the kandar there's another way to the Earths. So I can show them we can fulfill Creator's Purpose without Tchar. Without Coralynth."

Kordic shook his head. "It is not that easy."

"I assure you I came straight through."

"Not that." He sat down in the snow and motioned for Tchardin to join him. She settled into the white and found it was soft and moulded to her body. "Even if the things you say are true, they are not the problem. If the kandar have truly lost access to Coralynth and Tchar's great wisdom, and if none of your generation has experienced the Earths under the supervision of the generation before yours, then you will never be able to properly guide the humans."

"That can't be—" Tchardin started, but found herself believing him. She hadn't known what to do about the rain on World Two, about the terrible voice, and she had let the little girl see her...

"You showed yourself to a human child?"

Tchardin's gaze dropped to the ground. "I did."

"But you were in camouflage, of course."

Tchardin frowned. She met the guardian's eyes and was lost in them for a moment. They were blue, and so deep, so knowing. So old. She shook herself and looked away. When she looked back Kordic had changed.

The devoshai who had been sitting before her was gone. In his place sat a withered human man. His skin was as white as Kordic's had been—white as the snow—but it was no longer smooth. It was lined with deep impressions, filled with shadow. His blue eyes were sunken now but still sharp. There was white hair on his jaw and less on his head, and the hair from his face trailed down over his frail chest, almost blending in. The shadows that had hidden parts of Kordic's muscular body from view had fled and the entirety of the man was laid bare. Pandinzori wrapped him in a white aura as it had the devoshai.

"It has been a while since I have done this," he said. Tchardin was shocked to hear the same voice from this shrunken human as had come from the powerful guardian. She found him still in the collective, still the same seed. "There is a respect but also a dismissal that comes with great age for humans. Some would heed me, many would not."

"How?" Tchardin asked. "How are you doing that?"

"The same way you are."

It took a moment for Tchardin to understand. She looked down at herself. Pandinzori still coated her as it did Kordic, but the shadows that had clothed her were gone. Her skin was a uniform shade of medium brown. It was smooth where Kordic's was lined, but it was human skin just as his was.

"How?" she repeated.

Kordic smiled, deepening the lines in his gaunt face. "Lucky for you it is instinct. Lucky for all of us, really, since you have already exposed yourself to a human. Eventually you will learn to control it as I have, call it whenever you wish. For now—as long as you do not fight it—it will come up without being called when in the presence of humans." He chuckled. "Or in the presence of an imitation."

Tchardin raised her fingers to her face. She traced her features to look for change before realising she had never bothered to study them before.

"Yes, your face too. You still look like you did. Only, there is less of the forest you were born to, less of the trees."

Tchardin's eyes widened as a realisation hit her. "We can come back to the Earths. There is no danger—"

Kordic cut her off. "You think that is all it will take?"

Tchardin frowned. It seemed she didn't know what it would take. Her journey through the Earths was making that very clear.

Chapter 19

Damarin walked away from Jaydin on the branch. When the distance between them was great enough Jaydin glanced at Kadailin beside her.

"Did she speak to you when she passed?" she asked.

"She welcomed me to her council."

"Yes," Jaydin said. "She would. The council is hers, and things will be different here now."

Damarin had called the full council for this meeting. The kandar needed to be informed of the developments in their world as soon as possible. Many were still ignorant to the existence of a whole other population of kandar. There was also the fire to address.

Damarin appeared to be conversing silently with Marr. The two stood next to each other, looking into the crowd. Damarin's expression gave no indication of the silent words she was saying, but unfortunately for her, the Voice was less disciplined.

Marr had been stoic until a moment ago, when his eyes had widened suddenly. He turned to Damarin—who outwardly ignored him—before his face grew calm again. Damarin never gave anything away, but those she conspired with were always weaker.

Could Damarin have told him the fate of the trees? Then Damarin turned towards Jaydin with dark eyes and lowered brows. Marr must have told her about Jaydin's attempt to become High Seat.

'Council,' Marr's mindvoice boomed over the collected thoughts that cluttered the air, bringing Jaydin's attention back to the meeting. *'Your High Seat will speak to you.'*

The mindvoices of the council buzzed a greeting, but it must not have met Damarin's expectations because her dark expression remained. Then the questions started and it grew worse.

'Where did you go?'

'Do you know what happened here when you were gone?'

'Did you see the fire?'

Jaydin rolled her eyes at that one. Whoever had asked that had clearly been cowering on the other side of Calendrai when the flames were brought under control by Damarin's rain.

'What will we do about it?'

'My father was burned.'

Jaydin cringed as similar thoughts rose above the rest. Dodenzinn or friends with burned trees. How many fathers had felt the touch of the fire? How many would have to die?

'The fire isn't the only reason I've called you here.' Damarin's mindvoice silenced them. *'I've called you to tell you there are kandar in Black Valley.'*

Jaydin shook her head as the thoughts of the council erupted to twice the volume they had been before. Not exactly the way she would have told them. Damarin had to be trying to shock them.

'What is she doing?' Kadailin asked.

'I'm not entirely sure.'

As the buzzing calmed Jaydin could hear that most of the council voices were raised in protest.

'Black Valley has been empty since we left it.'

'The trees tell us it is so.'

'How do you know this?'

Damarin focussed on the question. *'Many of you made note of my absence of late. I crossed the water, travelled to Land Side. I've seen Black Valley myself.'*

The thoughts quieted. They had known she was gone. Gone in a way that indicated she was far away, but not necessarily dead. Jaydin noticed Damarin failed to mention Tchardin had been her companion on the journey.

'And the city lives?' a voice from the crowd emerged.

'Yes.' All eyes were turned towards Damarin and the council was silent. Jaydin knew this was where her sister had always wanted to be. The complete centre of attention. *'There were kandar in the trees when we left it. They still live there now.'*

Their thoughts buzzed.

'They have the shift,' Damarin said.

If the voices had been loud before, they were deafening now.

'We have the shift too!' Jaydin couldn't help interrupting, straining her mindvoice to be heard. Damarin glared at her.

'I don't want them idolising the old capital,' Jaydin said for Damarin's mind only. *'Calendrai is the home of the kandar now.'*

'But Black valley is where it came from,' Damarin said to everyone in response to Jaydin's outburst, ignoring her private comment. *'Where it has always been. Is it coincidence that we came here and lost everything we used to be? Black Valley is our source.'*

Jaydin was about to argue again when Damarin continued.

'We should return there,' she said. *'All of us.'*

Chaos in the collective.

'What about the future queen?' someone asked.

'Where is Tchardin?'

'How do we get there?'

'I can't cross the water.'

'I won't.'

'Can they shift to Coralynth?'

Jaydin had been silent since she spoke to Damarin, but that thought silenced the rest of the council. Kadailin fidgeted at her side.

'I have opened the shift to Coralynth,' Damarin said. *'I have seen the snowy mountain and the path. I have seen Tchar herself.'*

'What?' Jaydin asked. The council was still silent, although now they looked at Jaydin. She had spoken the question to everyone.

'Yes, Jaydin, I've seen her.'

'Where?' Jaydin couldn't stop herself from asking. *'How?'*

'Through the shift, on Coralynth,' Damarin said. *'Standing in front of me, looking at me, and blocking it.'*

Jaydin felt unable to speak. If what Damarin said was true their exile was intentional. It wasn't a mistake that Tchar kept them off the Earths. It wasn't a misunderstanding. Tchar knew they were trying to go back and she was actively stopping them. But why? How could they return to the Purpose if Tchar was set against them?

'None of the kandar can shift to Coralynth,' Damarin continued as if she had never mentioned Tchar. *'But Black Valley is our home. Cens has been devastated. It dies in front of us. Nothing can be done to save it. It's time to leave.'*

Damarin looked at Jaydin again. What was this? Retribution for her attempt to take over the council?

'Think on it,' Marr's mindvoice exploded over the rest. *'This meeting is over.'*

The Voice walked towards Jaydin and Kadailin. Jaydin stepped in front of him and forced him to stop. He looked at her, his face emotionless.

"You would leave Gerrin?" she asked.

He physically pushed her aside, his aura sending a ringing warning through her body. As he brushed by, his voice floated into her mind. She could tell she was the only one hearing it.

'Better than letting you kill him.'

"What's going on?" Kadailin asked.

Jaydin steadied herself from the impact of Marr's aura. "I have to talk to Damarin."

Damarin took the same path Marr had taken to leave the council. When she was close enough Jaydin moved to meet her.

"I need to talk to you," she said quietly. Damarin nodded and left the shadow. *'Stay here,'* Jaydin said to Kadailin.

"What are you trying to do?" Jaydin asked Damarin. The council shadow still shrouded them. It swirled over their bodies, hiding them from each other.

"I'm trying to bring the kandar home. Tchardin would do the same."

"How do you know that? Have you seen her since the fire?"

"I haven't. She must be somewhere on Land Side with Cien." Damarin's face was hidden but Jaydin got the distinct impression she was amused. "The fire in Cens was hard on her. Then your plan for the trees nearly destroyed her. We can handle things here while she's gone."

"*We* can handle things?" Jaydin laughed wryly. "It sounded like you were going to handle things all by yourself."

Damarin snorted. She walked away. Jaydin followed.

"You're only the High Seat, Damarin. Tchardin will be our queen. You can't make such an important decision without her."

Damarin rounded on Jaydin. As she did she let the council shadow fall. "Tchardin is already in Black Valley. Perhaps she doesn't plan to return."

Jaydin shifted awkwardly under Damarin's intense gaze. She let the shadow go as well.

"Then you need to find her and convince her to come back to us." Jaydin wanted to continue arguing but Damarin was the only kandar in Calendrai who could shift to Land Side. "If she wants what you want, it's in your interest to bring her back. If she doesn't, you'll have to let it go."

"We'll see," Damarin said, "but there are things we can do while she's gone to lessen the burden for her return."

Maybe Tchardin would agree with Damarin, but Jaydin couldn't see how bringing the council to a frenzy would lessen the load for anyone. She wished more than anything that she could shift to Black Valley and find Tchardin herself.

"I understand." Damarin had obviously overheard the distress in her thoughts. "I'll go to Land Side right now to find Tchardin."

"You will?" Jaydin asked, hating the pleading tone in her voice.

"I'll find her, but I can't guarantee I'll bring her back. Not yet. Unlike you I can wait until she's ready to be a true queen."

"As long as you aren't trying to take her place here," Jaydin said, meeting Damarin's eyes and holding them. "Then I can wait too."

Damarin smiled. "I was only exposing the kandar to the idea. As you said, nothing can be done about it until Tchardin returns."

She walked a few steps away and began to descend through the foliage. Her leaf dimmed in the collective as the distance between them grew. A few moments later it was dark.

Sandin dropped onto the branch next to Jaydin.

"You were watching?" Jaydin asked.

"Of course," Sandin replied. "I'm always watching."

Jaydin examined Damarin's dark leaf in her mind, then moved to Tchardin's.

"What were you talking about?" Sandin asked.

"Damarin has gone to Black Valley to find Tchardin for me."

Sandin raised her eyebrows in surprise. "Why don't you go?"

"I can't shift there. You saw me try it."

"You opened it without a problem and Damarin showed us Ovaeron."

"There was only grey when I tried."

"But we saw Ovaeron," Sandin insisted. "Why can Damarin do it when you can't?"

"Damarin has a mind like—"

"Yes, you've told me Damarin is exceptional. But the shift is for all kandar. All the kandar but me. There's no reason you can't open it to any place Damarin can."

Sandin was right. She should try it again. Just to be sure.

"Just think of Ovaeron," Sandin said. "More than any of us, you know him. If you can't see the city, see the tree."

Jaydin considered that. She brought up an image of Ovaeron in her mind as Tith had shown him to her before she was born. She had trouble believing the city remained, but the tree certainly did. She arranged pandinzori behind the image and pulled open the shift.

It was difficult at first, to keep the image in her mind superimposed over the hole in the pandinzori in front of her. Ovaeron's black branches disappeared into the darkness and his trunk melted into the sand. Slowly she brought him back. She concentrated on the emptiness and tried to fill it with the image. She wanted to see Ovaeron. She wanted to go to Black Valley. A gasp from Sandin let her know it had worked. She opened her eyes.

"Ovaeron," she whispered. The image she had held in her mind stood before her in reality, suspended above the branch. She put her hand against the ice that looked so much like deadly glass, stroked the red tree through it.

Sandin gripped her other arm, shocking her. "Jaydin—"

"Maybe eventually you can come with me." Jaydin turned to see hope in Sandin's eyes. "But not this time. Not the first time."

She pressed her fingers against the image, preparing herself to be dragged into the water, but nothing happened. She turned back to look at it. Her fingers were rigid against the pristine ice. Not one crack had formed.

Sandin moved to her side, reached for her. "It doesn't work."

"It has to."

Jaydin let the image dissipate to spinning grey. She could still feel the tree. Ovaeron was no longer visible in the shift, but he was there, behind the ice, behind the water.

"Maybe..." She placed her hand on the ice again. This time it cracked under her palm. "Maybe the image is the problem."

Tchar must be blocking the shift between the two cities as well, but her influence only affected the image. Jaydin shook Sandin off as the ice buckled. Pandinzori grew between them and she gave her sister the slightest push away. If Tchar was blocking the path through the image in the shift but not the path through the spinning grey, did that mean there were other places they could go directly through the shift? She began to wonder. Then the water took her.

***

Tchardin recognised the smoke before she really saw it. It touched her eyes and nose in the same way it had in Calendrai. Images of fire cutting through the trees rose in her mind and she almost turned around.

"It is not that kind of fire," Kordic said.

He walked ahead of her through the snow. She stepped in the footprints he left and hid herself behind him. The guardian was himself again, powerful and swift in his movements. His body no longer hunched as it had when he looked human and his incredibly white skin was mottled and masked with soft shadows. A dark shape loomed against the snow ahead of them, silhouetting him. It was a stand of trees. Tchardin had never seen trees like these before.

Kordic walked between the low branches of one of the trees and disappeared inside. Tchardin didn't follow. The tree was nothing special in size. His shape was odd but not particularly beautiful. She stopped because the trees here appeared to have leaves that held up the snow when none of the others did. Clumps of white hung in the darkness of their branches.

'Come in,' Kordic's mindvoice came to her. *'Before someone sees you.'*

"What is this tree?" she asked, moving under his branches. She looked up and was reminded of one of Black Valley's caves. Shadows filled the inside of the tree.

"A tree like any other. Is it the shape that gives you pause? The leaves?"

"The leaves," Tchardin admitted, looking more closely at them. "They are not true leaves."

"Just because they do not look like leaves to you does not mean the tree is wrong. These trees are ever-green. You do not have snow on Derkra, so you do not need them."

Tchardin frowned, but let the argument go. Kordic knew more about this Earth than any kandar ever would. "Why are we here?"

'Quiet now.' He held a thick branch aside for her. *'I have brought you here to see the humans.'*

Initially Tchardin saw nothing in the small space that was revealed to her, but then, in the distance, a woman walked by.

Tchardin pushed up against the opening, brushing past Kordic to hold the branch herself. She felt a slight change in her body as it settled into a human mask. She focused on the sensation and tried to memorise it.

'The humans of World Three,' she said.

'Only a very small number of them. It is just a village.'

There were more of the blocky structures she'd seen on World One. More buildings. A *village*. The woman Tchardin had glimpsed walked along a wide path of snow between two of the buildings. She was wrapped in dark shadows, so dark there was no indication of what lay beneath.

'It is clothing,' Kordic corrected. *'For the cold. For modesty.'*

Tchardin looked back at him in confusion. He had also assumed a human image.

Kordic sighed. *'Underneath all of that they look like we do now. If you were to approach the village undressed as you are, they would believe you had lost your mind. No human of World Three would walk the winter forests without clothing.'*

The pandinzori under the tree condensed around him. Tchardin was amazed how quickly it changed. Lines of light swirled over his body and before she could understand what he had done he was wrapped in darkness.

'Clothing,' he said. *'Specific to this region of World Three.'*

Tchardin was too excited to be annoyed at his tone. She studied the lines of light that remained in the clothing he'd created. She'd never seen pandinzori used for anything close to that intricate. She didn't think she could recreate what he'd done.

'Just another part of human appearance you know nothing about,' the guardian said, motioning for her to look back at the village.

Tchardin turned to the opening in the branches. The village was a beacon of light, flooded with pandinzori that rose high into the sky. Some of it floated towards them, probably drawn by Kordic who had appropriated nearly all the pandinzori in the tree to be his own. The woman she'd been watching disappeared behind one of the buildings.

'Houses, specifically. Most of them. Some are communal buildings.'

Tchardin looked back at Kordic again. He had lost his human guise but the clothing remained. It appeared to have grown to accommodate his much larger frame and the twisting shadows that should cover his body clung instead to the cloth.

'Most of these buildings are houses,' he explained. *'Humans live in them. This is a village, full of houses, and in each house there are humans. Do you see why appearance is not enough?'*

He seemed to slump, his expression becoming dark. Then the shift opened beside them. Tchardin turned to see Coralynth and World Four's black World Tree in the shift across the path. Kordic gave her a sad look and moved close to it to pound on it. This time there weren't even cracks.

'Tchar,' Kordic said towards the portal. *'Tchar, answer me.'* The surface of the shift remained the same, the image unchanging. Kordic waited in silence. Eventually he closed it. *'I cannot believe she would do this. She has to be watching. Perhaps I will have more success when you leave.'*

Tchardin was stunned. *'Can she hear you from here?'*

'She can, and she can also see us if she wishes to.' Kordic looked away from her, through the branches of the tree and out to the village. *'I think you will have to continue.'*

Tchardin followed his gaze and saw a man emerge from one of the houses. She resisted the urge to gasp. That was what Kordic—and Jaydin before him—had meant by the humans living *inside* the buildings. The man walked between the houses and into the snow. His clothing was almost identical to Kordic's. He disappeared from view where the branches blocked him from her. Tchardin pushed farther through the strange leaves and saw him again.

Then she saw the fire. The base of it was wide and long but it didn't move or grow. The flames that rose out of it were of a height with the man. He sat down beside it, the light playing across his face and clothing. The pandinzori that spiralled off him flew towards the fire and was consumed, but the loss didn't seem to affect him. There was always more pandinzori around him. He didn't seem afraid. She flinched when she thought of being so close to fire.

'You think I have to shift on?' she asked.

'I do.'

'Can I get back to Derkra from here?'

'I do not know. No kandar has travelled the shift in this way before. You have failed to find Derkra in previous attempts. You may struggle to find it now.'

'If I can't get back to Derkra where will I go?'

'World Four, if I had to guess. If you have travelled the first three worlds in sequence you could be following some sort of path.' The guardian looked down at her and his eyes were hard. *'I do not like the idea of letting you out of my sight on these Earths when you know nothing, when you have no idea of the Purpose.'*

'All kandar know the Purpose,' Tchardin said.

'You may think you do, but without proper guidance in it you will never understand.' Kordic backed away from the opening in the branches and sat against the trunk of the tree. Tchardin reluctantly moved towards him and away from the village. She felt her appearance become kandaran again. A very slight weight had lifted from her body.

"I do not want to let you go," the guardian said aloud, "knowing you may wander through the final six Earths before finding a way home. But someone must bring the kandar back. Things here are bad. I cannot leave this world alone during such a trying time. I cannot go in your stead."

Tchardin felt terribly unprepared to journey through the rest of the human Earths. "If I continue and find myself on World Four, Five, Six, what then? How will it lead me back to Derkra?"

"You should try to return to Derkra every time you travel the shift. If you fail to find it you should at least learn something. The Earths will change you as you experience them. If you travel through all of existence and still lack an answer"—the guardian paused—"call for Tchar, as I did."

"I can speak to her?"

"Tchar is one tevadra, just as you are, despite her place on Coralynth. She cannot listen to all of us at once but I believe she will listen to you after what you have done. Whether she chooses to answer..." Kordic hesitated. "When she does not answer a guardian, I cannot guarantee she will answer at all. But I believe you can find your own way. If she does not answer, you will have to."

Tchardin looked at the ground. It was free of snow under the tree and it almost looked like the forest floor in Cens despite the difference in the leaves that coated it. "So I must go."

Kordic nodded. "You must go. When you find yourself on Derkra again you must bring the kandar back to each of the Earths. Find their guardians. Learn the Purpose. Do not engage the humans until you understand them."

Tchardin froze. What about World Two? She had reacted to the humans there, done something. Would her actions there have consequences beyond helping the humans? Kordic looked at her expectantly and she knew he had heard.

"I made rain for them," she whispered, watching Kordic closely for his reaction. "On World Two. That's when I ran into the little girl. They needed it so desperately."

Kordic's expression turned neutral. "Had you seen rain before?"

"Only once. On Derkra."

"I am surprised you were able to create it."

Tchardin blinked at the emotion in his voice. He was genuinely surprised. Then she saw that he raised an eyebrow at her. Not the beautiful, clean arch he had a moment ago, but a bushy, unruly thing. Kordic was human again.

She looked down at her body and it was a uniform colour, exposed. It was so quick to change. Kordic seemed pleased for a moment but then his eyes narrowed.

"I had to," she said, worried he disapproved. The voices had essentially demanded it of her. "They just... They made me."

Kordic laughed. "It can seem that way. They are insistent, are they not?"

Tchardin didn't know how to answer so she just stared at the small human shell of the big guardian. He had spent all of time with the humans. She barely knew anything about them.

"You will learn," he addressed her thoughts. "If you are able to bring rain from the sky when you have only seen it once before there may be hope for you yet. Unfortunately, until you understand it you are also dangerous."

"Did I hurt them? With the rain?"

"That is unlikely. It is also unlikely you helped."

"But they asked for rain."

"And you gave it to them. That was good. Then you left. Whether the rain continued for long enough to make a difference we cannot know, but I expect it did not."

Tchardin heard the voice in her head again, saw the dark cluster of leaves around Alyx in her mind. Would the little girl die? Would they all die?

"I need to go back," she said.

"It would take more than one rainfall to fix what is wrong there." Kordic frowned. "Better you go on. Bring all the kandar back to address it, as they are meant to."

Tchardin looked at the dark leaves she had gotten on World Two. She had only met one human and yet she had many leaves. "Why did she give me more than one leaf? There are lots of leaves in the collective from when I met her, small things, dim, but more than one. Why?"

"That is something essential to the Purpose," Kordic said. "The more leaves a human carries with them the better. But that will not help you right now. Bring me the kandar, then you will learn."

Tchardin felt defeated by Kordic's attitude. She was queen of the kandar, or she would be when finally acknowledged, and she knew so little about the humans they were made to guide. She knew almost nothing about the Earths and according to Kordic, wouldn't understand if she were told. The small amount of history Jaydin had been able to force her to learn wasn't going to help her when confronted with this. The guardian looked up at her through his bushy human eyebrows, his eyes sunken into deeply lined flesh.

"I will tell you this," he said, "but only so you make less of a mess on the worlds as you journey through them. Avoid the humans if you can. That is most important. However, if you do encounter them, you may need to know what you are capable of, if only to stop yourself from going too far. I will teach you more about pandinzori."

Tchardin stared enviously at Kordic's clothing. "I could make myself clothes."

"You could," Kordic said. "But if you wear the clothing of this world I cannot guarantee you will not look just as strange to the people of the other Earths as you would if you were bare as a newborn babe."

The Earths were so complicated. Tchardin looked down at her skin again and wondered what Alyx had thought of her. The little girl hadn't seemed to think her strange.

"Do the kandar still say pandinzori is for the Earths?" Kordic asked, pulling her attention back to him.

Tchardin nodded. She had always wondered about that expression.

"They have always said that, and it is true. On Derkra you learn how to move things on and in the earth with pandinzori. You learn how to open the shift. There is simply no use for anything else. But you can create things. Change them." Kordic looked to the snowy ground at the edge of their hiding spot inside the tree and pandinzori accumulated there. The snow rushed away as water. Crushed brown grass was revealed beneath it.

"You made the snow into water!" Tchardin said, impressed, but Kordic wasn't finished.

The grass grew green under his pandinzori. Stalks rose from their flattened state and stood tall and straight. Bursts of coloured leaves exploded among them, reaching for the lowest branches of the tree. Tchardin gasped. There were purple leaves and yellow leaves, but they weren't like the yellow leaves on World Two.

"They are not leaves," Kordic said. "They are flowers."

Tchardin bent to study them. There were currents of pandinzori in them and throughout the newly living grass; concentrated threads of light like those in Kordic's clothes. The lines of light flowed through the flowers and down to the ground. The dead grass around it had no such light.

"Rain, grass, flowers, these are simple things," the guardian said. "You can use these things on your journey if you wish. To truly fulfill the Purpose, you would need to do and make more complex things. Appropriate clothing is one of them. That requires much more knowledge than you have at this point."

"What else could I do?" Tchardin asked. "What else could I make?"

Kordic considered for a moment. Then looked back down at the pandinzori.

"You can make anything you wish to happen, happen. You can create anything other than trees, kandar, and humans. I will go slow this time. Maybe you should close your eyes so you can see better."

Tchardin did so, but before she did she noticed Kordic didn't close his. He hadn't closed them to make his clothing either, or to bring the grass back to life and make the flowers. She was amazed he could control pandinzori so well with them open.

The patterns within the pandinzori at their feet grew more complex. Tchardin focussed on keeping only the small patch of light bright in the blackness behind her eyes. Then the threads of pandinzori that twisted before her began to coalesce. A shape was forming in the grass. She tried to listen to Kordic's thoughts in the collective but no matter how hard she focused she could only hear a slight buzz. The patterns of light before her were mesmerising. She found herself losing concentration.

Tiny points of colour formed and spread over the shape. They were pinks, whites, and greys. Tiny, impossibly fine lines and small spots. Had she brought those into being? Was she looking at the pandinzori under the tree or at the colours in her mind?

The word *fur* came to her. An odd sensation ran across her skin, as if something very soft caressed her. Then the small shape had eyes—blue as Cien's—and Tchardin knew that whatever it was, it would be alive.

Something brushed her shoulder and she waited for another new word, another new idea, but it was Kordic. She opened her eyes and examined the thing he had made. It had legs and arms like she did, though they were formed differently, and it was covered in long white fur. It also had two long appendages—

"Those are its ears," Kordic supplied. "Not all living things are the same or even similar. You will meet many of different shapes and sizes on the Earths."

"What is it?" Tchardin asked.

"It is an animal, a creature. It is called a rabbit. They are common here."

Tchardin was in awe of it. "How did you make it?"

It had seemed as if she brought the colours together in her mind, and then there it had been. She knew now that they hadn't been her colours. They had been Kordic's.

Kordic smiled. “Yes, it is the same way you control the pandinzori around you. You see it in your mind. If you can see it in your mind you can make it real.”

Tchardin put her hand out to the rabbit. The little white creature didn’t move when she touched it. Its fur felt strange against her skin. It was the sensation she had gotten when the word came to her, but more solid, more real. A similarity struck her. She raised her other hand to her hair and wrapped it around her fingers. It was soft, like the rabbit’s fur, but her fingers got caught in it. She pulled down but they wouldn’t go through. This had never happened before. She pulled harder.

“Stop,” Kordic said to her. “That is unnecessary.”

“What’s wrong with it?”

“It is knotted. Your hair is human hair while you are in camouflage. It reacts to the world around it.”

Tchardin stopped. “Is that why you look so old?”

“I am old,” he said. “But yes, humans age. Wind weathers them. Water clings to them. Dirt gathers on their skin. They grow small with too little nourishment and large with too much. Your camouflage knows this, even if you do not. Here is another thing.” Kordic raised a finger and drew it down Tchardin’s arm in a line.

She followed it with her eyes and noticed her arm was covered in tiny bumps. They appeared to be a part of her skin. She looked down at her chest and found the same was true there.

“What are they?”

“Your body’s reaction to the cold. From them,” he said, gesturing towards the branches that hid them from the village, towards the humans. “They react that way, so you react that way.”

“It’s too much. I don’t understand.”

“You do not need to. Not yet. Your body will take care of itself for now.”

How? How would it do that? Tchardin felt the urge to close her mind to the guardian and disappear from the external world for a while. The colours called to her. Kordic put his hand on her shoulder.

“More importantly,” Kordic said, kneeling in front of the rabbit. It had stayed in its place, motionless. “They will not all be like this. You can see the pandinzori in this one because I created it—its body and its mind.

Any creature, any thing made with pandinzori will show its structure in pandinzori. Then you can control it more easily."

The currents of pandinzori that had created the rabbit hadn't faded when Kordic was done. They had stayed inside the animal. Tchardin could see them if she looked beyond the colour. "How do I control it?"

"See it in your mind, move it with your mind, just like the pandinzori that covers the earth."

"What about the ones that aren't made of pandinzori?"

"You can push them with pandinzori, lift them, break them, but you cannot control the separate parts of them without harm. You should not go inside them, should not affect their minds until you properly know how."

"So with the humans..."

Kordic got to his feet. His eyes remained on hers. "You can only move them with pandinzori as with anything that is not made of it. But you must remember not to expose yourself."

"What about their minds? We're supposed to guide them. How can I guide them with physical force? Without them knowing me to be different?"

"Avoid them for now, as I said. Then come back to learn with the rest of the kandar."

"What if I do encounter them?" Tchardin felt like she was getting close to the Purpose. All she needed was for Kordic to explain it to her. The guardian stared at her intensely.

"Listen to them. Act as they do. Do not try to change them or affect them in any way. Their individual thoughts can be confusing, but if you listen properly, if you distance yourself from them as you did from me when I made the rabbit, as you did when you learned of fur, you will hear their emotions, their ideas, their individual purposes. If you listen as the kandar were meant to listen to humans, they will tell you what they expect of you."

"What if they can tell I'm not human?"

Kordic looked away. "You have too many questions."

"What if they know what I am?"

"Then you destroy them. If they threaten you in any way. If they threaten the kandar. Humans or animals. If it means your life, or discovery, do not hesitate."

Tchardin was almost stunned into silence. "Kill a human?"

"It has been done before. I need you to make it to Derkra. The kandar need to return to the Earths. Things here are not good, and I cannot guess what it is like on the later worlds." Kordic met her eyes again. His were sad. "You are not ready for anything more complicated, so yes, if you must, you kill them."

Tchardin pushed the branches apart to look at the village. The pandinzori that had filled it before was brighter now, almost blinding. She searched for a human to look at but she had trouble focusing on the shapes behind it. She turned back to Kordic in confusion.

"It is nearly night," he said. "The darkness comes. The humans will sleep."

Night. Tchardin saw the blackness behind her eyes. It must have been night on World One when she arrived there. She let the branches swing slowly back to their original position. She looked at the patch of grass where the rabbit had been created and found the creature gone.

"Did you kill it?" she asked apprehensively. Kordic shocked her with his laugh.

"I let it go. It has a purpose now, so it left us."

"What is its purpose?"

"To run free." The guardian smiled. "To be a rabbit like any other."

Chapter 20

Tchardin stood in front of the ever-green trees with Kordic at her side. The sky above the village had gone dark and the humans had disappeared into their houses. Kordic said they wouldn't come out until the sun returned. Until *day* returned.

"What's wrong with this place?" Tchardin asked.

Kordic said the Earth was having problems but Tchardin had been too afraid to ask about them until now. All she knew from Jaydin was that the people of this Earth actively sought out those who used rendinzori and destroyed them. It hadn't seemed to have any other problems before the kandar lost it. Now she was afraid the people here might die like the ones on World Two.

"There is a plague." Kordic didn't look at her when he spoke. Tchardin closed her eyes to understand what he meant and immediately wished she hadn't.

Plague. She found herself leaning towards the village again. The humans there didn't look like the ones her mind had just shown her, in their twisted, unnatural poses, with their skin torn and weeping. These humans were perfect. They drew her to them, almost irresistible. She wanted to help them before they got to that point.

"I want to stay here and learn from you. I want to help the humans."

"I am certain it will come to this village regardless of whether you stay or go," Kordic said. "I see nothing in those here that would stop it. It may yet come to the whole world."

Tchardin shuddered.

"I am afraid you cannot stay," he said. "The Earths were not made for you. The Earths were made for them, and they need all the kandar, not just their queen."

Kordic turned away from the village and took a human image again. He looked up at her.

"I do not know how you got here without Coralynth, but you have shifted through three of the worlds so far. If you have to shift through all nine to get to Derkra, at least you will know them when you bring the kandar back."

"I'll bring them to you to learn," Tchardin said. "Then I'll find the other guardians so we can learn from them too. We will come back to the Purpose."

Kordic's old-man lips were chapped and cracked, but they curled up in a smile that held so much emotion it could never be found on the face of a kandar. "I will wait at the foot of the World Tree, Zemko. I will watch this village and the others nearby. After you have returned to Derkra, when you show the kandar the Earths, come back to see me."

Tchardin opened the shift. It settled into grey and she took a step towards it. On to World Four, or Derkra if she could manage it. Kordic caught her arm and his grip was strong despite his apparent human frailty. When she turned to face him his eyes were wide.

"You will really go into that?" he asked. "Into nothing?"

"It's the only way I know."

Kordic nodded and let her go. She looked down into his eyes—lower than hers in his human guise—and they were familiar. Kandaran. The emotion that touched his face didn't extend that far. Tchardin wondered if the kandar were capable of feeling it.

She broke the ice on the shift.

She knew who she was immediately. The water surged into her but she didn't lose herself to it. She had a strange sort of control over it. She had no body, no limbs, only the undefined shape of the water, but she could move. She flowed. Then suddenly she could see.

All around her was a brilliant blue. As it swirled away it grew darker. It was un-ending. There was nothing in it for her eyes to focus on, if she had eyes. She wasn't sure. It seemed to be a seeing that eyes could not achieve.

A dark shape floated into her vision. It took her a moment to recognise it as an arm. Her arm. She turned her gaze downwards and found her body, suspended in the blue. There was water in her mouth. There was water in her nose. She panicked.

She thrashed wildly. No matter how she moved, how she twisted her body or pulled at the water, she couldn't gain any traction. When she had done the same on Water Side her body had been projected forwards, but here it was useless. She closed her eyes—now that she had eyes—and willed herself to be the water again.

Tchardin knelt in the grass and held her throat. She opened her mouth and waited. There didn't seem to be any water in there. Would it matter if there was? She had never had water inside her before. She got to her feet.

She stood in front of a wide black trunk. It had to be Tairasyn, the World Tree she had seen through the shift from World Three. His bark wasn't as flawlessly dark as Ovaeron's. It was edged with grey where it separated from his trunk. He had dull green leaves coating massive twisting branches, one of them nearly sweeping the ground ahead of her, and he stood in a forest that was full of shadow. It lacked the cohesion of Cens but made up for it in darkness. It didn't create the illusion of continuity. It looked like it really did go on forever.

The touch of humans on this Earth was immediately evident. There was a low wall spanning three sides of the area Tairasyn's foliage covered, separating him from the forest. It was built in a similar way to the houses on World Three, with uniformly shaped rocks stacked on top of one another. Tchardin followed it around the clearing with her eyes before her attention was drawn to the earth it partially enclosed.

Around Tairasyn, inside the walls and partly concealed in the dark earth, were the remains of trees. Tchardin could see their roots pulled up where some had tried to hang on and the shredded stubs of what remained of their trunks where they had been torn apart, just above the ground. In other places there were deep furrows where roots must have been removed entirely. She backed away from them and found herself against Tairasyn's trunk. The World Tree gave a cry of distress when she touched him. A scream for his guardian.

She opened the shift. She had to escape this world. She didn't want to encounter the thing that had caused the devastation, nor did she want to see any more of it. And the guardian. What could have happened to him for his father to cry out in anguish? The greyness of the shift spread out before her, hiding the ruined trees from view. She stared into it. What would happen with the water this time?

Something landed softly to her right. A light rustling followed, approaching. She let the shift go. If the disturbance was created by a human she couldn't let them see her leave the world.

As she turned to look she found an animal. It was a large one, much bigger than the rabbit Kordic had shown her. It ducked near the ground and its body moved gracefully as it slid quietly towards her. Its limbs were long and slim and it was covered in beautiful spots, in a range of colours that were new to her. It had simple oranges and yellows, browns and black, but the colours melted into each other, an impossible number of shades between them. Delicate patterns of light decorated its skin under the spots. The creature was made of pandinzori.

Tchardin walked to meet it. The animal stopped and regarded her with its clear yellow eyes. It remained in a crouch, its entire body tense. Tchardin closed her eyes and touched the pandinzori that made up the creature. She could control the lines that lived inside of it, if only she could see it in her mind. She pulled. The animal's body twisted.

With her eyes closed she saw only the light of pandinzori. The spots faded away with the rest of the world. Now the animal was only a pattern—an intricate design—made by kandar in the far past. She tried to move the animal forward, pulling and pushing its lines with her mind. It made a terrible noise.

Tchardin flinched and let the animal go. A flash of pandinzori invaded her concentration just as the animal disappeared behind a bush. She opened her eyes.

A human boy jumped over the wall in front of her and landed in a crouch. He stared up at her, his body immobile. Pandinzori spiralled off him as his eyes darted between Tchardin and the bush that hid the creature.

Looking down at her skin, Tchardin felt safe in her human disguise. She was uncovered and the boy was not, but Kordic had been right in noting the difference in clothing between the worlds. She was better off the way she was. The best course of action now must be to remain in the clearing as if she were a human like any other. She studied the boy. A new branch grew in the collective when he joined it. He brought many leaves with him to cluster around his own.

His name was Rann. His thoughts were clear. He was Sparr—a child of the forest—and he loved the animals. The leopard Tchardin had injured—one of the great cats—was beautiful and in pain. Despite the danger to himself, he would do what he could to help it.

Loved? Injured? She closed her eyes to see the lines of pandinzori in the creature's body behind the bush. It was a *leopard*, his mind had said. Love was a complex emotion she didn't understand even with the thoughts his mind gave her. The simplest explanation was that he cared for the creature. He loved it and he believed Tchardin had harmed it. Could she have done something wrong?

Rann spoke.

"Be calm," he said towards the leopard, but his words went into Tchardin's mind as well. *'Be calm,'* was given to the collective at the same moment the words left his mouth. She saw his lips move again. "I'll protect you."

'I'll protect you.'

The tension ran out of Tchardin's body at the words. The boy wasn't looking at her, wasn't speaking to her, but she was touched by the words as if he was. As if his words had more power than words should. Could all humans speak this way? Alyx's words had entered her mind on World Two but the girl hadn't spoken with her mouth. Only her mind had spoken to Tchardin.

The leopard emerged from the leaves that had hidden it and Tchardin saw its body relax as hers did. Could it understand him? Did the boy speak into the mind of the cat just as he did into hers?

"Come here," he said.

'Come here.'

The leopard moved towards him. It turned to look back at Tchardin and she could have sworn it knew what she had done. She felt similarly pulled. She advanced on the boy.

Rann was focused on the leopard. As Tchardin neared he looked up into her eyes. There was terror there, but as Tchardin looked longer she began to see some of the leopard in him as well. He knew the animal's pain, its discomfort, its shock at being physically manipulated with no attention paid to its mind. No effort given to soothe it. She saw what she had been doing to it, what it had taken for Rann to stop her, to fix it. Then the leopard was gone from his eyes and there was only a young boy who was afraid.

"Be calm," she said to him, and as she did she pushed the words into his mind. She spoke to him in the same way he had spoken to her and to the leopard. His fear intensified. Her words may have sounded the same, they may have seemed the same to Tchardin, but they must have been different to Rann.

His lips didn't move when his mind spoke this time. *'Forest Spirit,'* his thoughts said.

Forest Spirit?

'Run,' a new voice said into the collective.

The boy fled. The leopard followed him at a slower pace, its body less graceful than when it had entered the clearing. They went over the wall of stones and disappeared. Tchardin looked for the source of the new voice but couldn't see anyone around. She should be able to leave now.

When she tried to turn away from the wall she found she couldn't move. Something bound her, tightening across her body until she was completely still. She looked down at herself and couldn't see anything that held her. The pandinzori that surrounded her floated across her false human skin in its natural way. There was no disturbance in it.

A man appeared from behind one of the walls. He walked into the manufactured clearing through the open side, shedding pandinzori in great waves as all the humans she had met seemed to. He stared at her intently with his hands raised in front of him, his fingers curled as if he held something. Tchardin remembered what Jaydin had said about World Four. Many of the humans on this Earth actively and directly used rendinzori. *Magic*, they called it.

She fell to her knees on the ground, struggling against the invisible bonds. Whatever entangled her came with her, allowing her body to bend as she fell, but negating her control over it. She must be able to break the man's rendinzori apart with the pandinzori that lit her, but if she did that he might learn what she was. Then he would need to be destroyed. The idea of killing a human still shocked her.

She stopped struggling when he approached. He stared down at her for a moment, his eyes brushing her bare skin, then he drew a line along her body in the air with his hand. The ties that held her dissipated.

A smaller branch grew out of the World Four collective, apart from Rann and the leaves he had brought. The man's name was Hunter. His leaf grew on the new branch and with it came a bundle of others. He had many more than Alyx, but not so many as Rann. There were varying levels of brightness in his cluster. His leaf was the brightest, but there was another that came close to matching it. He knelt beside her.

"I've got you now," he said. "Finally."

His words sounded different from those spoken by Rann. Tchardin understood them just as well, but she sensed they were said differently, that perhaps the boy would not have understood.

Hunter raised a hand in front of her body, his fingers spread, and turned to scan the cleared area. Tchardin stared at his hand. What could he do to her with rendinzori? And how could she stop it if she couldn't see it? He turned back and looked her in the eyes.

"You come with me," he said slowly. Now he spoke like Rann, but his words didn't enter her mind.

Tchardin felt lost already. The man had caught her and held her in rendinzori and then he had freed her. He had spoken differently than the first human she had met on this Earth but now he spoke the same. She met his eyes and concentrated on the haze of his thoughts. They became clear.

He was the Royal Hunter. He had spent the last ten years of his life searching the evil forest for one such as herself. One with no obvious ability. One of the Sparr. All had evaded him. His eyes dipped to her skin again. Now some depraved ritual under the wicked tree had delivered her to him. Now he would be free of the forest.

Sparr? Like Rann?

"My Spardic must be rusty," he said quietly. "Come with me," he repeated.

His thoughts told her the difference between the words he had first spoken and those of Rann. Hunter had spoken Arkan. Rann spoke Spardic. They were different *languages.*

He reached down and pulled her gently up by the arm. Tchardin was shocked to feel nothing as his hand passed through her aura. Just like it had been with Kordic.

"Why?" When she spoke she spoke like Rann.

"The king wants you."

Tchardin looked into his mind to see what the *king* was. His thoughts led her to the brightest leaf he had added to the collective. She examined it.

The leaf was that of Tezroi Ferroen. He was the king of Arkaiyan. The king was to the humans what Tchardin would be to the kandar as queen. But the role functioned differently. Tchardin would command the kandar, but rarely. By contrast, the king was everything to this place. Hunter wanted to bring her to him.

He led her past the ruined stumps to the far wall. An animal waited for them there. This one was not made by kandar, as no pandinzori threaded through its skin. It was a big grey creature. A *horse.* The horse was attached to a wooden structure. Hunter's mind called it a *cart*, and in the cart there was a *cage*. It was meant to confine her.

Tchardin smiled faintly. The spindly thing could never hold her. She wouldn't need pandinzori to escape it. She could tear it to pieces with her hands. Hunter felt differently. He seemed certain the cage would contain her. He would use it to bring her to this king.

Hunter led her into the cage and gave her a large square of dark cloth to cover herself. She knelt when he closed it behind her and examined the construction. She had been right. It was made of small branches, woven beautifully together, but not strongly. She could break it apart without pandinzori and flee into the trees whenever she wanted. Hunter wouldn't be able to follow her and she could shift on to the next Earth.

The cart began to move and she became aware she was gripping the branches that made up the cage. The skin of her hands was a uniform brown and there was earth ingrained in it. She studied the imperfections there. Human hands, to gather dirt. She pulled the cloth that covered her closer against her body.

How had she come to be here? Kordic had specifically told her not to let this happen and yet it had seemed impossible to resist as soon as she saw Rann. She was reminded of the way the voice on World Two had affected her. The humans made her forget everything else. Their lives were so immediate, their thoughts so overwhelming. How did the kandar handle themselves when this was their place? It was so different from their lives on Derkra.

She should leave. But she didn't want to. What had Kordic said exactly? That the Earths would change her? That she would need to change to return to Derkra? Perhaps she needed to stay to learn the things that would get her home. Hunter was taking her to meet his king, the most important human in this world in his mind. She hadn't exposed herself and she hadn't needed to kill anyone. She should be able to spend some time learning more about the humans of World Four and their ways.

The sound of water came to her as the forest opened before them. She was confronted with memories of the shift. She remembered being immersed in it and having no way to get out, full control of her body in it but none of her surroundings. She covered her face with the cloth.

"Afraid to be out of the trees?" Hunter asked.

Tchardin ignored him. She was beginning to understand why Kordic was worried about the kandar interacting with humans when they had no guidance. What did this man want from her?

"Afraid to be out of the evil trees when no Arkaiyan would willingly enter them." He laughed. "Your life is about to change, my dear."

She looked at the water that gave off the noise, trying not to flinch as she thought of what it could do to her. It flowed to one side of them. It was a *river*. She had never seen such thin water, to be contained between two stretches of land covered in forest. The trees hung over it in some places ahead of them. They were travelling uphill and she could only see so far into the distance. She closed her eyes to shut out the world and thought of the colours.

She brought up red instantly. It burst into the black as soon as she calmed herself. That was a change already. It had been so hard to do before. She always strove to bring it up eventually, but confronted with the swirling blaze of colour she wasn't sure where to go from there. She slowly expanded it to fill her vision and watched it. A perfect sheet of red. She let it fade into yellow.

As if from a great distance, through the numbness of her body, she felt the cage level off. She opened her eyes.

The forest was gone. In its place were shredded stumps, just like the ones she had seen around Tairasyn. Far ahead the earth rose into the sky and the water went with it. No, that wasn't right. She opened her mind to Hunter's loud thoughts at the sight. The earth reared up in *cliffs* and between two of the highest was a *waterfall,* a great waterfall, as tall as Ovaeron if she had to guess. It was the source of the river they followed. At the height of the cliff, on either side of the waterfall, bare rock had been shaped into a majestic *castle*. The *halls* and *towers* were carved deep into the cliffs and extended to disappear behind the water. The castle continued below the city as well. There were rooms beneath their feet.

"Castle Arkaiyan," Hunter said. "Your new home. I bet you've never even seen it before."

The forest continued on the tops of the cliffs, high above the city. At the base of the cliffs it surrounded the city in a semicircle, outlining a wide strip of grass that had been razed of trees. The entire area was full of pandinzori. Tchardin knew then that the king would be in the castle. Hidden behind the rock, behind the water. Hunter would take her deep into the earth to meet him. These were the people who had cut down the trees.

She pushed against the branches of the cage. They were thin and should be weak, but when she gripped them, braced herself against two sides of the cage and pushed with all her strength, they didn't even bend. Hunter turned back at her struggle and looked on impassively.

What was this wood? These were not tree branches, not in a natural sense at least. She looked closer but could see no difference in them. It had to be rendinzori that strengthened them. That must be why Hunter had so much confidence in the cage.

What *was* rendinzori? She'd asked Jaydin about its application so many times but they had never discussed how the power should be dealt with. She settled down in the cage again. Rendinzori couldn't be that powerful. She must be able to break the cage with pandinzori.

The edge of the city was close now. They were nearing the end of the brutalised forest, still following the river. The castle loomed above them in the distance.

They passed through the cleared area around the city and came to a great wooden wall. Hunter waved at someone Tchardin couldn't see and the *gate* that barred their way swung open. The cage shook as the cart transitioned from grass to a rocky path. Tchardin stabilised herself and focused on the slim branches of the cage again. This time she pushed more calmly to avoid drawing Hunter's attention. The branches didn't yield at all. Pandinzori floated around her and through them. Hunter couldn't possibly notice if she broke just one of them.

People emerged from houses as they approached. Hunter jumped down from the cart and walked in front of the horse to clear a path. It was too late to escape. Tchardin would meet the king and take her chances for escape later, when there were fewer humans watching. She didn't want to kill them all.

The collective exploded with light. Leaves grew at a rate that made it clear they would quickly surpass the number she had from the kandar. As they grew in her mind they overlapped. For every new human who gave her a leaf, the leaves they shared with others blazed brighter, as if she knew each of them better for having known the others. The human collective was even stranger than she thought. With each leaf she gained, the brightest of them increased its light. They all knew King Tezroi Ferroen.

She chose a tiny branch woven into the cage at eye-level. She closed her eyes and concentrated on it, ignoring the murmurs and thoughts of the growing crowd, pushing the brilliant collective into the back of her mind. It was one of those branches that could be found at the very top of a tree and was incredibly fragile. She plucked it with her fingers. Even it didn't move by physical force. She took hold of a fine thread of pandinzori—no wider than the branch itself—hardened it, and pulled it towards her. It cut cleanly through. She smiled.

That was all the reassurance she needed as they entered the shadow of the cliffs. She would free herself when it was safe for the humans. Until then she would remain a voluntary captive, and meet a king.

Chapter 21

JAYDIN GROANED WHEN SHE landed in hard sand, more from relief than from pain. She'd been sure the water destroyed her, that she was no longer herself, but Ovaeron's leaves had drawn her out in the end. She'd never felt happy to be alive before. She wasn't sure she had ever felt anything so strongly.

She opened her mind and searched the dark collective for any sign of light. The kandar of Calendrai were gone, but she had expected that. What she hadn't expected was to find complete darkness. Not one leaf was lit. Where were Tchardin and Damarin? Where was Cien?

She was shocked. Shocked at their disappearance but also at the loneliness, the silence. It was the first time in her life that she was alone in her mind. Then she realised this must be what Sandin felt like all the time.

She almost missed Ovaeron in her distress, but that was impossible. The sand at her feet was dark, but the giant exposed root that curved to her right was darker, blacker, and it drew her eye with a power as great as Tith's. She stared at it for a moment before her gaze was led inevitably up, into the canopy of deep red leaves that stretched above her. Tith might be taller than Ovaeron but the vastness of his branches was hidden by his brothers. Ovaeron stood alone and sheltered the valley with his leaves. From here his canopy was the only sky she could see. A blood-red sky, full of shadow.

He was Ovaeron, father of all kandar, who had given Tchar to Derkra, who had grown the ten seeds that had spawned the first trees, those who had borne Dani and the nine guardians. Those ten trees had then borne the seeds for the nine hundred, the original fathers of all the kandar of Black Valley and of Calendrai.

Jaydin approached Ovaeron's trunk, walking along the sinuous line of the great root closest to her. She was going to touch him, her father who was not Tith. When she came to his trunk she extended her hand and brushed his bark. A tiny spark of repulsion hit her and she withdrew, confused. Then she noticed the kandar watching her.

A small crowd gathered around Ovaeron's base. Their skin was lightly coloured, like Cien's, and they stood in stark contrast to the sand at their feet. Jaydin backed away from Ovaeron and towards the kandar. It was amusing how much better she blended into the dark sand than the kandar who lived on it, for her body was one of shadow. Looking out from her place at the tree's roots she knew it would not be so on the rest of Land Side. These kandar were made for the yellow desert. She was not.

None of the kandar spoke to her as she approached, but leaves grew in her mind on Cien's branch of the collective and quiet thoughts swirled around her. She didn't know these kandar. She was at a loss of what to do. She focused on a new leaf.

'Ondra,' she tried, not sure which kandar she was speaking to. *'Where is Tchardin?'*

No one answered. The kandar stared at her as if they'd never seen colouring like hers before. Had Tchardin not established herself here? Had they not even met Damarin, who was darker than she?

'Or Cien?' A few of the kandar reacted to that, but still they didn't answer. She tried to focus on one leaf in the collective at a time, search it for quiet thoughts, but they were so dim. The meaning that must be there was too quiet for her to hear.

It reminded her of her birth. She had been born in front of the entire population of Calendrai. They had stood around her and stared much as these kandar did now. None had spoken to her. When they'd realised she was nothing special—that she was nothing more than a daughter of a great tree—they had left without a word. Even then they'd been waiting for something, although they hadn't known what.

There wasn't much she could do if these kandar refused to answer. She could only wait in silence. Slowly, the crowd dissipated. Surely someone who knew the Shadow well would help her. She just needed to find the right kandar. She followed their retreating backs onto the yellow sand of the valley.

The valley was vast compared to Calendrai. It was open and sparsely covered by the nine hundred. They were tiny, twisted trees. Jaydin caressed their leaves as she passed them, wishing she could have seen the ten others that were gone now.

Sand slid uncomfortably under her feet as she walked. Her strength waned as she adjusted to the smaller amount of pandinzori available to her. The valley was familiar in such a strange way. She knew it as if she'd been there before, but it was all in her mind. Her body didn't know the place. Her feet didn't know the sand and her aura didn't know the sparseness of light that flowed there. She wondered if she would feel the same if she ever made it to an Earth.

She passed more light-skinned kandar who glanced at her but refused to speak. They left barely glowing leaves in her mind that failed to fill the silence. How could she feel so alone, be so unhappy in such a legendary place? It wasn't what she'd expected.

A red leaf grew in her mind. She stopped, turning back to see if she could identify the kandar who had left it. There was no one there. She must have passed someone in a tree, or someone sprinting across the valley. The Black Valley collective had the same quality as that of Calendrai then. The council was available to her. Could she call them?

She sat down in the sand, leaning against the nearest trunk, and concentrated on the new red leaf. She only had one. It was dim enough that she didn't think she could locate the kandar who had given it to her. That might also make it difficult to call the council. She focused on the leaf to know it, so she could call it up without pressing her mind against it too forcefully. The kandar was called Verron. A devoshai. When she was certain she knew his leaf well enough to try, she unfocused her mind, pulling it away from the individual leaf and viewing the collective as a whole.

It was incredibly bare. She could clearly see the red leaf glowing softly amongst the green ones. She pulled on it with her mind. She had to call to it, call to all the red leaves in Black Valley without calling Verron specifically. She found it actually helped that the leaf was dim. She couldn't get a hold on the devoshai himself so it was easier to make the call general. She concentrated. Verron's leaf pulsed. Jaydin opened her eyes. That should succeed in calling them.

Then she realised she didn't know where the council met. But the kandar were so easy to see here, where there was no true forest. Maybe if she watched them closely enough she could discern a pattern in their movement? Follow a member to the shadow?

There was no one around her now. Some of the group that had gathered to stare at her after her arrival still paced around Ovaeron's base, but none approached her. A few kandar seemed to wander aimlessly across the valley. Many climbed through the great tree, their auras glowing faintly amongst his leaves. There was no wave of movement, no sign that any of them had a purpose to their actions. Perhaps she wouldn't be able to follow them.

She turned away from Ovaeron and nearly ran into a tall tevadra. She was about to attempt a conversation when she noticed the tevadra stared at her intently. Maybe it wasn't an accident.

"Who are you?" The tevadra's leaf grew in the collective.

Her name was *Miadra*. A second red leaf. Another council member. Jaydin's identity would be equally available at this point, but she knew the question was not in regards to her name.

"I am a member of the council in Calendrai."

"Why did you call us?"

The collective ceased its beating. The council was no longer called. Jaydin looked around them and noticed a devoshai approaching from Ovaeron's direction. She watched him while she spoke.

"I'm looking for my sisters and no one will speak to me. I know they saw the council when they were here."

The devoshai joined them and his leaf grew in her mind. Also council. She had to tilt her head to look up at him. He might be bigger than Ryten.

"I am the High Seat of the council." Miadra didn't specify she was only the High Seat in Black Valley. "This is my dodenzinn and Voice, Cotelle. Your sisters are not here. Perhaps they shifted back to your island just as you shifted to us?"

Jaydin pursed her lips in annoyance. "What about Cien?"

"You know the Shadow?"

"I met him in Calendrai."

Miadra's thoughts in the collective were silent. She might be as good at that as Damarin. "We haven't seen him since."

Jaydin was beginning to realise the tevadra wasn't going to help.

"Did you talk to Damarin about what will happen with the two councils?" she asked instead. "You're High Seat of the Black Valley council but there can only be one…" she trailed off. Perhaps it was unwise to alert Miadra to the fact that Damarin would likely win the position if it were between the two of them.

"I would give it to her," Miadra said with a laugh. "If she wanted it."

Just as good as Damarin. Jaydin held her thoughts closer. "You don't think she will?"

"We've worked out a better arrangement." Miadra turned away from Jaydin as she said it. She motioned for her big dodenzinn to join her before walking away. *'Soon you will see.'*

***

The pandinzori that coated Cien was strange to him now. It had started thin in that first place and it had thinned further from there. It thinned to a point where he knew he would die if it stayed like that for long. He had lain in the sand and worried about Tchardin, yearned for the power she would give him if she was near. He thought of Ovaeron—who called him—and of his father, Roa, and the fact that he might never again speak with him in rest. He had thought of what it would be like to die as a human did. To never return.

Slowly he had felt better. The pandinzori around him swelled and he found he could walk. Just as Damarin had told him he would. He walked and walked towards Ovaeron's distant call until he fell between two dunes and couldn't climb the next. There, he had waited.

The pandinzori that coated him grew thicker through it all, until he could touch it with his mind and use a small amount to make the sand move. Then he tried to open the shift. He tried over and over again until he was exhausted but his pandinzori just wasn't great enough.

Eventually it grew. It grew close to ample enough for him to use and only then had Damarin appeared.

"You doubted me?" she'd asked when she saw the look of surprise on his face.

He had doubted her. How could she have known he was so close?

"I wonder if you will doubt me again."

She had opened the shift—the pandinzori that was wrapped around her much thicker than it had been before—and forced him to join her when she went through. The shift had sought to destroy him, Damarin's presence had sought to consume him, but both had failed and he was dropped into the sand in agony. Damarin was gone before he could say a word, depleting his strength even further when she left.

The second place was worse. Cien was so far out in the desert now it was possible this sand had never seen pandinzori before he was thrown here.

He knew he could get to his feet now, but he hadn't tried because he was conserving energy. He also wasn't sure how Damarin had known to come back in time to stop him from shifting. If she watched from somewhere across the dunes he wanted to look weak until he was able to stand and shift all at once.

He felt Ovaeron's call intermittently and could point to it through the dune to one side of him, but there was no way he could walk that far now. Shifting was his only chance. When he was strong enough he would open the shift and point it anywhere as long as it was closer to the valley. Any place in the direction of Ovaeron's call. It was possible Damarin could only find him in the infinity of Land Side because she knew where she had put him.

He could see the collective now. The tree remained dark and empty but Tchardin's leaf was still there. Was it bright for the kandar in Calendrai, or those in Black Valley? Or was it dark for them all? Could she be wandering the dunes as he did? Or could she still be trapped in the water of the shift? He should feel it if her leaf were to fall and so far it remained. He could only hope that meant she was safe. Then he considered what Damarin had said. If Tchardin's leaf was dark for them all, had she made it to an Earth?

An Earth. The image Jaydin had given Cien of the forest and sun on World Four came to him for a moment, a fleeting glimpse of green and blinding brightness. What could Tchardin be seeing if she were on an Earth? Cien was confronted with the yellow endlessness of the desert around him and frowned. It felt like a long time since he'd seen a tree outside his mind.

The slight valley he lay in was slowly filling with wispy pandinzori. A feeling of calm came over him. He was no longer in pain. He might have enough. He closed his eyes and took hold of the pandinzori that surrounded him. He did it very carefully, cautious not to expend any extra energy, and began to form the shift. Water sprayed across his face.

A surge of strength came to him. He was almost able to use it before the pandinzori he'd gathered left his mind and blazed a light yellow. He struggled to regain control of it but Damarin was too strong.

"How?" he asked, knowing she was behind him in the sand. He turned to her. "How do you know?"

"I check on you." She walked up beside him, flooding the air with pandinzori. It was all a lighter shade of her yellow aura. All carefully controlled. "You can't deceive me by lying in the sand. I can see your pandinzori."

He had to admit she might be right about their connection, although it made no sense. There was a clear difference in his strength when she left him compared to when she reappeared. Maybe with the strength she gave him—if he could make her wait, stay longer—he'd have a chance of escape. His power had grown since the first time the shift threw him down in the sand.

"You believe me now?" she asked. "That we are dodenzinn?"

He laughed in exasperation. "It seems you must be right. But how can it be?"

"Change, as I said before." She shrugged. "You know Ryten is a part of it as well, don't you?"

Cien remembered a comment Jaydin had made when he first came to Calendrai. "Jaydin thinks he's Tchardin's dodenzinn."

"He thinks so too."

Damarin came to stand in front of him, looking down at him in the sand. He just had to take enough of her pandinzori to bolster his own. He concentrated on the vast amount she held. Her control was impressive. He had to stall her.

"What have you done to Ryten, then, if he is the same as me? Is he in another place on Land Side?"

"Ryten remains in Calendrai, unaware of this, as all the other kandar are."

"Why am I here?" He had seen her throw Tchardin into the shift—

"That's not the only reason," she said before he could think of another. "Ryten's safe. You are not, with Ovaeron calling you. Ryten has no reason to rest. I know he'll still be there when I return."

Cien felt the great father call him. He wouldn't rest. Not yet, even if he made it back to Black Valley.

"He calls you now?" Damarin asked, looking down at him. "I asked Jaydin what it could mean."

Cien refused to meet her eyes. Why had he not thought of asking Jaydin himself? If anyone would know what was happening with the great tree it would be her. But he had been too afraid to admit it, even to Jaydin. "What did she say?"

Damarin smirked. "The only thing she could have. Guardian. What else?"

Cien wasn't surprised to hear the words, he had thought them many times himself. The World Trees held the guardians of each world, and what was Ovaeron if not the World Tree of Derkra? But why would Derkra need a guardian, and why would Ovaeron call one now? Cien looked in the direction of the distant pull and wondered, most importantly, why him?

"Change," Damarin said. "Change so clear you should have seen it before I started this." She followed his gaze. "I wonder what Jaydin would say if she knew the great father was actively calling. I didn't reveal your secret."

Cien felt relief at that, though he didn't know why. Damarin already knew. What difference would it make for one more sister to know? He closed his eyes and hoped Damarin would see it as a reaction to her words. The pandinzori that floated closest to his aura was hers, but he felt like he could take it. How much did he need?

"I'm surprised you didn't tell her," he said. "If you wanted her to see the change."

"I'm not ready to involve Jaydin in this just yet."

She opened the shift. He flinched. He needed more time.

"Does Tchardin know Ryten claims her as dodenzinn?" he asked.

"He claims us both, just as you do," Damarin said in response. "But that's enough of this. You should know by now that I can hear your thoughts. It's even easier to hear them out here, without the rest of the collective to obscure them." The shift remained open to spinning grey. She took a step towards it. "You're getting too strong. It's time we go on, to the next place."

"Please," he said, surprised at the emotion in his voice. "Take me back to the kandar. To Calendrai, or Black Valley. This is wrong!"

He was forcibly lifted from the sand and pulled towards her. He didn't try to fight it this time. He could only hope he'd do better next time, but he knew it would be harder.

The water rippled and coiled and roiled and ran. A small current sought to escape it. Cien remembered who he was just as the immensity of Damarin caught him. She encircled him and twisted him and forced him out of the blue.

Cien fell into the sand and was shocked at how weak he became almost instantly, even though it had happened to him twice before. Damarin landed on her feet behind him. She didn't even stumble.

"I have to do this to you," she said. "I'm doing it for the kandar."

He couldn't turn to watch her leave. He couldn't move at all. He knew she had gone when he felt even worse. How could he survive this? It was unbearable.

He concentrated as best he could on the pandinzori around him. He knew how dangerous it would be for him to touch it, to move that which made up his aura. He had known that since his first attempt at crossing the dunes between Black Valley and Water Side. If what Damarin said was true—and it seemed it could be true—if he were her dodenzinn, he might be able to destroy her by sacrificing himself. She wouldn't die outright, but she could lose all motivation to live.

But if he could end her, did she deserve it? Maybe not yet. Maybe not ever. He had never thought of harming another kandar and it repulsed him that he thought of it now. But what else was she doing but destroying him, little by little? He didn't think he could do it yet, but he would remember the option existed.

Then something else occurred to him. He took his mind off the meagre pandinzori surrounding his aura. If what she said was true, he would also be sacrificing Tchardin.

***

Sandin lay in utter darkness, her eyes closed, no light behind them. Ocien sat on the branch beside her. The tevadra had climbed up to join her while Sandin had her eyes open and Sandin periodically checked to see if she remained there.

Sandin had never thought she would appreciate the presence of another kandar as much as she did right now. She had spent a lot of time away from Jaydin—despite the kandar believing they never left each other—but they had never been this far apart. She was truly alone for the first time since she was born. She might be alone forever, if Jaydin failed to safely make it to Black Valley and back. Ocien's presence comforted her.

"Jaydin's leaf hangs in darkness," Ocien said, "but it is still in my collective, at least."

Sandin opened her eyes to see the other tevadra watching her closely. No one could hear Sandin's thoughts, but she enjoyed the moments they came so close. It made her feel like kandar.

"She went to Black Valley to find Tchardin," Sandin said.

Ocien turned away to look out over the water. "So this time she went after her."

Sandin followed her gaze. She had never been drawn to Water Side like Tchardin and Damarin, but now that the trees in Cens were exposed she took advantage of the exceptional view. The branch they occupied hung out over the shore, the thinnest of its offshoots almost reaching the water.

"Yes," Sandin said. "This time she did."

The water was blue and infinite, stretching away as far as she could see. Sandin had never been drawn to it but she had also never had a reason to cross it. Until now.

Chapter 22

Tchardin stood with Hunter in front of a small red *door* set in stone. She was fully covered by the sheet Hunter had given her now, due to the reaction of a woman who had stopped them as soon as they entered the castle. Tchardin still remembered the woman's scandalised thoughts. Hunter mopped his brow with a crinkled square of cloth.

"I've been searching for you for ten years," he said. "I don't know what I'll do when Tezroi sees you."

Tchardin frowned at him. The red door opened. Behind it was a big round man with a blank expression. He looked at Hunter, who Tchardin noticed was on the ground, his forehead against the stone, and he looked at Tchardin, who was confused. He nodded and stepped out of the way. King Tezroi Ferroen walked through the door.

The king came towards her with his arms open and Tchardin knew why she had let herself become so involved in this human world. Bursts of light exploded in her mind as leaf after leaf grew there to surround his own. The leaves she had gained in the city were nothing when compared to this new light. It enveloped all the other leaves of this world in its glow.

This was a man the kandar should know. If she were to spend her time on the Earths fulfilling the Purpose, a glowing man such as this—radiating pandinzori and centred in a cluster of leaves so huge it filled his branch of the collective—was the type she would search out. That had to be part of what Kordic had kept from her.

"You've done it!" the king declared.

Hunter rose to his knees and glared at Tchardin. She got the impression she should also be on her knees but she didn't see why.

"Your Majesty—" Hunter started.

"We've known each other for too long, Hunter, you know my name."

"King Tezroi." Hunter's voice trembled slightly. Tchardin looked down at him and noticed his clothing had darkened around his neck. He wiped at his forehead with his hand, the square of cloth forgotten. "I found her for you, at the base of the evil tree."

"For Arkaiyan, Hunter, not for me. For all of us."

Tchardin felt the strength of the pandinzori around the king. It swirled between them, pulling her towards him. She closed her eyes for a moment, revelling in the power.

"Forest child." The king spoke Spardic, as Rann had.

His hand brushed her shoulder through the thin sheet Hunter had given her. She flinched and opened her eyes. Tezroi's face was inches from hers. Hunter's eyes had grown unfocused and he swayed where he knelt. The big man behind the king remained expressionless.

"Your Majesty—" Hunter said.

Tezroi waved a hand in Hunter's direction and the man was quiet instantly. Tchardin thought she heard his mouth snap shut.

"Your name?" the king asked.

His eyes were a light blue—the colour of Derkra's sky over Land Side. His skin was pale but his hair was black, as if he had been made to stand out. Kandaran bodies were built to blend in and no tree would create such stark contrast in them. The other humans she had seen in the castle were more softly coloured, with lighter hair and darker skin. None had such striking colouring.

"Tchardin," she said.

Hunter gasped. The big man averted his gaze.

"Tchardin," Tezroi whispered. He spared a glance at Hunter whose face seemed to have lightened a couple shades, before turning back to Tchardin. "Was it prophesied amongst your people that you would come to us?"

She regretted giving her name. All three men had reacted too strongly to it. What answer did the king want? After a moment she shook her head.

"Well, Tchardin won't do, and you know that. If you weren't such a rarity I'd have you thrown over the falls."

Tezroi looked at the two other men in attendance, first at the big man beside him, only for a moment, then at Hunter.

"Has she spoken to anyone else?" he asked.

Hunter shook his head emphatically.

"Then it will be Tchar," the king said.

Tchardin couldn't help the expression of surprise that passed over her face. He would name her for the first of the kandar?

Tezroi didn't appear to notice and continued, "Because I prefer it to Din. You will remember that she gave Tchar as her name. Perhaps it will be Tchardin when things have progressed, but certainly not yet. We would have a riot in the dining hall."

The big man chuckled. Tchardin looked into his mind. The Sparr were named in Spardic. 'Tchardin' would be an Arkan name. 'Tchar' and 'Din' would be acceptable in Spardic. The big man found it ridiculous that she could be called Tchardin someday. He thought of Tezroi's statement as a joke. She would remember this. Names were important here. Jaydin hadn't thought to mention that but Tchardin certainly would when she got back to the kandar.

Tezroi smiled, and his smile was wide and warm and it touched his eyes. They seemed to sparkle. The variety amongst humans in expression was amazing. Nothing like the severe lack of it in the kandar.

"Now we must have you dressed," he said.

Tezroi extended a hand towards her and Tchardin stared at it. They stood like that for a moment before the king withdrew his arm and gestured for her to follow him. She walked past the big man who closed the red door behind them, separating them from Hunter.

Tchardin pulled at the cloth that had been draped over her body. Or not so much draped as stretched over her, pulled tight so it was nearly as restrictive as Hunter's rendinzori had been. It was purple. She had never seen her body in a different colour before.

It was called a *dress*. And it was terrible.

The castle, however, was wonderful. It was full of vivid colours and complex textures, and its halls were bathed in pandinzori. Tchardin was starting to forget any idea of escape. Kordic had been wrong about her ability to help the humans. She hadn't yet found out what problems there were to solve on World Four, but she was now confident she could make a difference alone. It was as Kordic had said—the humans gave her everything she needed to interact with them if she only listened to their thoughts.

Now she followed the king down a small dark tunnel, lit by floating orbs of light. She examined the colour of the stone as she walked. It was many beautiful greys.

The tight space opened up to a huge stone room. Voices assaulted her and she did her best not to flinch away from them. She followed Tezroi onto a raised section of stone, set slightly above the rest of the room. There were hundreds of humans below them. Each lay with their head to the ground as Hunter had when Tezroi walked through the red door. They didn't speak aloud, but their minds battered her.

There were more colours in the room than Tchardin believed existed on Derkra. The noise was intense but it began to make her feel safe as she adjusted to it. She was encapsulated in thought, a part of the people. It was the first time she had felt that way since she left the collective behind in Calendrai.

She wished her sisters could see it. She wished Cien and Ryten could be there with her. What if Damarin could experience this? How different would their middle sister be if she had seen the Earths? If she could be here, feeling this, would she wish so strongly for change on Derkra? For more? That was what the Earths were for. More than her other three sisters, even more than Jaydin, Tchardin wanted to show this to Damarin. She *would* show it to her, when she brought the kandar back.

King Tezroi placed his hand on her arm. She shivered at the lack of impact his touch made on her aura.

"Tchar," he said, "this is my queen, Jaycee."

Tchardin hadn't noticed the other human when she walked out of the tunnel—there had been too much else to take in—but she wasn't surprised. Of course this man would have a counterpart. A second half. A dodenzinn.

Jaycee was swathed in bright red fabric. Her clothing was a dress, just as Tchardin's was, but Jaycee's seemed to have been made to increase her size rather than contain it. Tchardin's purple dress was tight to her form most of the way down. Jaycee's flowed outwards. Tchardin was reminded of one of Kordic's flowers.

There was something strange about her. There was another there. Jaycee had a second voice in her body. A *baby*. As Tchardin thought this

Jaycee's right hand brushed across the folds of her dress, those that hid her stomach. It looked to be an unconscious movement. The baby was growing there, behind her hand.

King Tezroi's expression grew serious. He turned towards the rows of silent humans who filled the hall. "Rise, Lords and Ladies of Arkaiyan."

The people stood like a bright wave. Like flowers growing and opening. The room was full of pandinzori that rippled as they rose. There didn't seem to be an empty space anywhere in it. Tchardin reached out to it with her mind.

"It is with great news that I interrupt our feast tonight," Tezroi said. "The Royal Hunter has found us one of the Sparr."

All the eyes in the room turned to Tchardin. The people were quiet.

"I feel no ability in her." The king walked a slow circle around her. "But is she truly a child of the forest?"

The crowd roared. At first Tchardin was overwhelmed. Their thoughts filled the hall and their words hurt her ears. Then she heard what they were saying.

"Test her!" they shouted.

Tezroi's voice rose above them somehow, like the Voice in the council. "There have been pretenders before..."

"TEST HER!" The words were omnipresent in the hall.

King Tezroi turned to her and said quietly, "Hunter assures me you are the real thing. I believe you are the real thing. But we have to be certain."

The people still shouted. They pressed against the platform. Tchardin looked down on them and the colours of their clothes and their faces melded together for a moment. The one thought in her mind was, '*test her*'.

The king took her by the arm and swept her through a doorway. Jaycee followed close behind. The hall they passed through this time was full of shadow. They walked deeper into the earth.

The passageway led to another large open space. The *animal hold*. Tchardin scanned the expansive room. Humans were filing onto *balconies* around them, on either side of a great hole. A *pit*. Across from her, at the far end of the room, there was a platform. It mirrored the one she stood on with the two humans. On it was a tall black shape. The black shape was made of pandinzori in the same way the rabbit and leopard had been.

Tezroi followed her gaze. "He is Lowren. The dragon."

Hunter walked up beside them.

"Lowren? But, your Majesty—"

"I was not suggesting the dragon for the test, Hunter. I think Einen would be more appropriate for today."

Hunter retreated from them. Tezroi extended an arm in the direction of the dragon. He made a flicking motion with his fingers and walked into the pit. Tchardin suppressed an urge to reach for him. He walked on nothing, straight through the air. He beckoned for her to follow.

Jaycee remained on the platform and nodded slightly in dismissal. Tchardin followed Tezroi into the pit. It felt as if her feet remained on solid ground but the pandinzori that floated around her was free and did not support her. The king must be using rendinzori to hold them up.

As they approached the middle of the pit, the black shape at the end of the hall moved. Massive planes of skin stretched and slid across it. Tezroi's mind called them *wings*. They parted and a luminous green eye turned towards them. Lowren was wrapped in its wings, lines of pandinzori bright throughout them. The dragon was very intricate. It would have been difficult to create. It would be difficult to control.

They walked downwards, the invisible floor beneath their feet sloping into the pit until they reached the visible ground. From there Tchardin saw many caves in the stone walls at varying heights.

"I call Einen!" The king's voice boomed through the room, reverberating off the walls. The crowd of people above them grew silent, waiting.

A huge cat emerged from one of the caves and bounded towards them. It was bigger than the one Tchardin had seen near Tairasyn. This one was striped—orange and black—not spotted. A *tiger*. Tchardin braced herself as it approached. The tiger wasn't made of pandinzori. It was real. She gathered pandinzori and prepared to expose herself.

Just as the tiger was about to reach them, just as Tchardin hardened the pandinzori around her body, Tezroi raised his hand, palm towards the creature, and Einen bounced backwards as if repelled.

"Now," Tezroi said in his resonant voice that filled the hold, "you will tame him. You will teach him to love you as the animals of the forest love your people. You will prove to us that you are one of them. Sparr. A child of the forest. A daughter of the Spirits."

Einen prowled the far side of the pit. Instinct told Tchardin the animal's movements indicated he was angry. The king stepped away from her in the opposite direction. Tchardin moved to follow him but came up against an invisible wall. The king met her eyes and smiled.

She turned away and found the tiger right there. He leaped towards her, claws extended to rip her apart. She threw herself to the ground as he soared over. His agile body compacted audibly when he crashed into the invisible wall and he let out a roar that seemed to shake the room. What could those claws do to her in her camouflage, with her image of a human body? She realised she didn't know what they could do to a kandaran body either.

She got to her feet and ran towards the far wall of the pit. The dress restricted her and tangled in her legs. What did these humans want her to do with this creature? Tezroi had said to tame him, to make him *love* her. That complicated word again. She looked back and found that despite her speed there was no way she could outrun such a magnificent animal. Not without pandinzori. Not while appearing human. Einen rose and bounded after her.

The thoughts in the hall were so loud it was overwhelming. She had to separate them, understand what they meant. Tezroi had said they wanted one of the Sparr, but how could Tchardin prove she was like Rann? She stopped when she got to the far wall and found nowhere to go. Einen was only steps away. She would have to reveal herself.

An image grew in her mind as she turned towards the big cat, pandinzori billowing around her. The voices of the people coalesced and showed her the things that had been done in this pit. Humans of all ages rent to pieces by fierce claws, torn apart by savage teeth. The only thing that could have saved them were words. She solidified the pandinzori around Einen before he could leave the ground and shouted, "Stop!"

She pushed the word into the tiger's mind as she spoke it. She expected most of the Arkaiyans wouldn't understand the language, but Tezroi would, and he was listening for it. Einen stopped abruptly.

Tchardin was careful not to move her hands when she stopped him, for it seemed to her the Arkaiyans used rendinzori with certain motions. Her body trembled. The big cat was close enough that he would have found her had he jumped. His razor-sharp teeth glinted in the light. Her human body knew this threat, even if her kandaran mind did not.

His pose was unnatural. He looked uncomfortable in the way the first cat had been, though she hadn't realised it at the time.

"Be calm," she said, mimicking Rann. Einen's tense body relaxed. She let the pandinzori around him go. "Come to me."

The big cat advanced, but now she felt no danger in his movement. He stood placidly before her, his huge head at the same height as hers. She reached out to touch him and looked into his eyes. She had spoken into the mind of this creature that was not made of pandinzori. This great animal that had sought to destroy her. His fur was soft. She stroked him.

Tezroi walked towards them. The king seemed to consider the tiger safe now. Einen's eyes told a different story. The big cat hated the king. He hated every person in the hold except Tchardin. There was an instinct in him that told him to do so. The people of Arkaiyan seemed to feel the same way about the animals.

The king slowed as he approached. What would he do with her now that she had passed his test? She knew she had succeeded by the smile on his face and the silence of the crowd. Suddenly she was wary of him.

She had become enraptured by human life again. This felt real, like it was her place in the world to pass this test and suffer the consequences. But she was kandar, and the kandar needed to come back to the Earths. Tchardin looked into Einen's eyes again and wondered. Perhaps it was finally time to move on.

The king spoke but Tchardin ignored him. She scanned the walls of the pit, studying the caves that marked them. What would it take to disappear into one of them? If she could get away from human eyes she could shift without worry of discovery. Einen watched Tezroi. The tiger's lips drew back from his teeth and he made a low, angry sound.

"Go," Tchardin said in Spardic, propelling the word into the animal's mind. Einen met her gaze. All she needed was a distraction. "Attack the king."

Einen spun towards Tezroi. Someone in the crowd screamed.

Tchardin put everything she had into pushing Einen forward. *'Give me a distraction,'* she said to the tiger. *'Help me escape.'*

The king raised his hand again and laughed as Einen was repelled by a wall he created in front of him. A wall Tchardin couldn't see, and could do nothing about without pandinzori. Tezroi pushed the air with his hand and the tiger was flung away, his claws skittering uselessly along the stone.

The king turned his back on Einen and waved to the crowd. The people cheered him, shouted his name and called their admiration down to him. Einen came to a stop on the other side of the pit. He got to his feet and approached Tezroi again from behind. Surely the king would turn and stop him. Einen began to run.

Tchardin moved towards the wall, but the king didn't turn. The people shouted at him, but still he faced them and ignored the threat of teeth behind him. Tchardin hesitated. She didn't want the king to die. That had been the whole point of her distraction. Tezroi turned just as Einen was about to leap towards him.

"Einen," he said. Tchardin froze, all thoughts of escape leaving her. She had heard the name in her mind. Tezroi spoke Spardic and he spoke to the tiger just as Rann had. "Stop!"

The big cat stopped just before him. Tezroi stood close to him for a moment—close to those teeth that would have claimed him—then prodded him with invisible rendinzori, directing the tiger towards a cave in the wall.

The people stared down at them. Their thoughts swirled in Tchardin's mind. Arkaiyans couldn't speak like that. It was a thing of the Sparr. The people were in awe of their king. Tchardin didn't understand. Now that the danger had passed they began to shout. The king held up a hand and they quieted, but their angry thoughts continued.

"My people, do not blame Tchar for what she does. The Sparr have but one weapon against us and she uses it admirably."

Tchardin felt the hate coming off their bodies and pressing against her.

"Now, now," the king soothed, "did this not provide the proof we needed? She *is* Sparr. No Arkaiyan would attack me, no matter how dedicated they were to their cause."

That seemed to convince them. They remained silent. Tchardin saw Jaycee's eyes from the edge of the platform. The queen turned away and disappeared.

"Now that she has tamed the tiger, perhaps the dragon?" Tezroi asked the people anxiously leaning over the balconies high above.

There were many shouts of 'yes', a few of 'no'. Tezroi laughed and motioned towards the dragon. Tchardin recognised a similar movement to one Hunter had used. It was the motion that had released her from the bond he had placed on her. Lowren didn't move at first. Then Tezroi called him.

The dragon opened his wings and stretched them to their full extent. A third of the back wall was framed against them, so vast was their spread. The people closest to the end of the hall screamed and piled into those around them, trying in vain to put space between themselves and the dragon. Lowren paid them no notice. He lifted his great head and roared. Tchardin admired the tiny lines of pandinzori that lived inside him, behind his skin. His thick, scaled arms remained wrapped around an object that was revealed when he opened his wings, his mighty claws gripping it tightly. It shimmered in the points of light, familiar to Tchardin in some strange way.

She released the pandinzori around her. The glittering object appeared to be a glass cage, intricately built in a similar way to the wooden cage Hunter had used to hold her. If it was truly glass and not ice, that cage was infinitely more dangerous than the one used to trap her. That cage—combined with Tchardin's control of the pandinzori in the room—could kill them all.

A dark shape was confined in the cage, behind the dragon's claws. When Tchardin recognised it she almost grasped pandinzori again in shock, but now she knew the cage was definitely glass. That stopped her.

The dark shape was a devoshai. Shadows wrapped him and his skin was mottled black and brown. He was not in camouflage.

Lowren released the cage and lifted into the air. Tezroi guided the dragon towards them with gestures. Tchardin heard the screams and shouts of the people as Lowren flew near them. She heard their thoughts—of her, of Tezroi, of Lowren. She heard all these things, but her mind was with the devoshai. The dragon alighted in the pit in front of them. The air he brought in his wings blew over Tchardin. Tezroi took her arm and lifted her with him and suddenly they were in the air, nestled between Lowren's black wings. Tchardin didn't react to any of it. They approached the cage.

Tezroi led her off the dragon's back and into the air. They walked on nothing until they came to the platform. Lowren flew over them before disappearing into one of the largest caves. The people were silent.

Tchardin's skin crawled as she was brought to the glass. The pandinzori that surrounded her was thick now. She didn't want to get too close. Tith hadn't told her exactly why glass reacted with pandinzori. Did it need to be manipulated to affect it? Or would it react to her aura? Jaydin probably knew but Tchardin had never gotten the details.

The devoshai in the cage was similarly lit by pandinzori, so it must need to be manipulated to be affected. How had he come to be in this glass prison?

'I know you.' His mindvoice came to her though his leaf was not yet in the collective. It was ragged, disused. *'I would know you anywhere, despite your camouflage. Despite that you pretend.'*

Tchardin was taken aback. *'That is the purpose of kandar—'*

'How does it feel to have pandinzori wrapped around you in the presence of glass? If you must come so close, do not touch it with your mind. I have many things to do before I die.'

Tchardin noticed Tezroi was talking to her.

"Impressive, isn't he?" The king had a huge smile on his face, that same beautiful smile he had given Tchardin when he first laid eyes on her. She felt differently about it now. "He is Zyphen. A Forest Spirit. The crown jewel of my collection."

'How long have you been here?' Tchardin took a step towards the devoshai. The king flinched as if he was afraid despite the glass that kept the devoshai captive.

'Many times again the length of your life.'

'Why aren't you in camouflage?'

'They know what they have.'

'But if you looked human now—'

'No,' his mindvoice seemed to growl the word. *'Do you know nothing? There was a time when they knew we could hide amongst them and all it did was endanger us further. Some remember, but most have forgotten. I will not remind them. You should not either.'*

She was close to him now, and she felt as he began to join the collective. *Ruon*. That was his name, not Zyphen, as Tezroi had named him. Tchardin stepped back in horror as a seed grew in the collective. Not just a devoshai, but a guardian. Like Kordic. The World Tree's frantic screams came back to her.

'Yes, little queen,' Ruon said. *'These humans hold the guardian of their world in glass. They destroyed many of us with it centuries ago and if they have their way my fate will be the same, only slower.'*

"I've never seen him like this," Tezroi said from a step behind her. "He must see the forest in you."

Ruon continued right over the king's remark. *'You will free me.'*

'How?'

'You will free me and we will kill these humans.' His eyes were black with rage.

'The glass—' she said, but the guardian only glared at her.

'You will find a way.'

He did need to be freed. It was atrocious that the guardian of a human Earth had been taken captive by those he was made to protect. But to kill the people of Arkaiyan? To kill King Tezroi? Tchardin had sent Einen towards him, but she had only meant to escape without revealing herself. She had done it to avoid having to kill him. She couldn't kill such a magnificent man.

'Yes.' Ruon's mindvoice was clearer now, stronger. *'That one will be the first to die.'*

Chapter 23

KADAILIN BROUGHT UP GREEN. The colour swirled slowly against the black void of her vision. It filled the space behind her eyes and calmed her. She focused and forced yellow to invade it. Bright strips grew along its edges, spiralling into its centre. She opened her eyes.

Feeling came back to her as she did. Tith's bark was rough against her shoulders where she leaned on it. She was alone with him now. The only one of his daughters to remain in the collective. The only one in Calendrai besides Sandin, who he surely couldn't sense. She wondered if he noticed.

Kadailin certainly did. The collective felt empty, though it had barely changed. She sent her mind over it unconsciously, instinctively finding the dark spaces that held her sisters' leaves. She stopped at Tchardin's, the leaf that had always been brightest in her collective.

"Do you think it'll be much longer?"

Kadailin had to search the tall grass ahead of her to find the mass of shadows that spoke. The only reason Sandin was visible at all was that she stood. If the tevadra had ducked into the grass Kadailin would never have seen her. She looked down at her own body and noted the meagre covering her shadows provided.

"Jaydin?" Kadailin asked. Sandin nodded. "She didn't even tell me she was leaving."

Kadailin wasn't sure how long her sister's leaf had been dark. It hadn't seemed long to her, but she had spent a lot of that time with the colours in her mind at Tith's base. Sandin had probably spent the entire time worrying.

"We should go after her," Sandin said.

"I've never travelled the shift before."

"Neither had Jaydin when she left for Black Valley."

Kadailin turned her head and pressed her cheek lightly against Tith. She shuddered when she thought of the endless water that separated them from Land Side. There were no trees in that great expanse, nothing to take a kandar if something were to go wrong. To shift to Black Valley was to cross that water. If they missed and came out in the blue...

"Jaydin can take care of herself," she said.

"I need to go after her," Sandin insisted. "You know I can't do it alone."

It was unfair that Sandin couldn't go after Jaydin on her own, but Kadailin wasn't going to be the one to help her. It was too dangerous. She hadn't gone after Tchardin and if there was anything that could motivate her to cross Water Side their youngest sister's disappearance should have been it.

"We'd die." Kadailin pushed herself upright and walked towards Cens. Sandin followed her.

"So you don't think Jaydin made it?" Sandin asked.

"I didn't say that."

"Then why can't we make it?"

Kadailin stopped before entering the forest. If Cens had been its former self she could have lost Sandin moments after walking under the first set of trees. Cens was much different now.

"I don't want to cross the water," she said. "You don't understand what it would be like to lose Tith."

"You're right about that." Sandin looked away from her, through the sparse trees towards Water Side. She hid her disappointment well, but Kadailin knew it was there. "Let me walk with you at least," Sandin said. "If Jaydin returns she'll find you first."

Kadailin was surprised to hear that. "Why me?"

Sandin laughed. "Of course it'll be you. How would she find me?"

Kadailin had to laugh at that too. She stepped into Cens, though there was barely any difference between the forest and the clearing now. Sandin followed her.

"I hope the forest can be saved," Kadailin said. "I miss it."

"I do too."

Kadailin looked at the ground as she walked. The trunks were easy to avoid without looking up—there was always pandinzori around them—and she stepped over roots instinctively, enjoying the beautiful patterns they made in the earth. She knew the water wasn't far from the clearing, now that they could see it. It felt like they had been walking too long. A smudge of colour caught her eye.

She stopped and knelt in the grass. There was a tiny patch of red leaves there. They were a shade she only knew from the time before her birth, from memories of Ovaeron given to her by Tith—something that didn't belong on the island. The shape of them was new to her as well. She cupped them in her hand. Sandin knelt with her.

"Was this here before the fire?" Kadailin asked.

"I've never seen anything like it."

"Neither have I." Kadailin sat back on her heels. "I'm not even sure what it is."

The red leaves covered the ground ahead of them. There appeared to be hundreds of patches laced through the grass. How had they come to be on Calendrai?

"I saw them in Cens before the fire," a voice answered her unspoken question.

Kadailin searched for the speaker. It was hard to identify who spoke when the words didn't come from the collective.

Ryten appeared beside them.

"You've seen this before?" Sandin asked him.

"They hung through the trees when I found them before the fire. I'm pretty sure these are the same."

"Where did you come from?" Kadailin asked. The devoshai had seemed to appear out of nowhere.

"I heard you, from Del. Just over there." Ryten turned away from them and began to gesture but stopped abruptly. Kadailin followed his eyes and saw nothing but average-sized trees framing the water.

"He was right there," Ryten said. "I jumped down and walked over. I can still feel him."

Kadailin got up and walked in the direction he had pointed. Ryten couldn't be confused about the location of his father. That was impossible.

Then she noticed the change. She had been facing the water when she started walking but now she looked into the clearing. Del's huge trunk stood before her, with Tith and his brothers behind it. Sandin exclaimed in surprise and Kadailin looked back. She could see the two kandar—Ryten standing and Sandin kneeling in the bright leaves—but it was clear they couldn't see her.

"I guess Cens is recovering." She walked back to them, watching their faces for a sign they could see her again.

"Good," a new voice said when she rejoined them. "We might need its protection soon."

"It's Jaydin," Sandin said. "I recognise her voice."

The oldest of Tith's daughters appeared as if from nowhere, just like Ryten had. She smiled in Sandin's direction.

"I saw the three of you here before I lost sight of Kadailin," Jaydin said. "Evidently you couldn't see me."

"Is it just this place that does this?" Ryten asked.

"Where's Tchardin?" Sandin asked at the same time.

Jaydin looked between them. "I don't know the answer to either of those questions and I have many of my own after visiting Black Valley."

"Tchardin wasn't there?" Kadailin asked.

Jaydin shook her head. "None of them were."

"How?" Ryten asked.

"I have a feeling it has something to do with Black Valley's High Seat, but I'll need to go back to find out more."

"Damarin wasn't even there?" Kadailin asked in disbelief. "I thought she shifted there for you."

"I'm going with you," Sandin said.

Ryten opened his mouth to speak. Jaydin held up a hand to stop him.

"That's all I can say for now. It was very strange." She knelt in the grass. "But this"—she ran her fingers through the red—"is also very strange."

"It's what I wanted to show you," Ryten said, "before the fire. It's not exactly the same. The leaves I saw before grew in the trees on long black branches. There were also moving branches—"

"These are flowers," Jaydin said. "Those were likely flowers as well. Maybe they hung through the trees on vines."

Flowers. Kadailin looked closer at the red leaves. *Vines.*

"Moving branches?" Jaydin continued. "I don't know what that could have been. Can you see them in your mind?"

"Yes," Ryten said, "but—"

"Concentrate."

The two kandar closed their eyes. Kadailin did the same, focusing on Ryten's leaf in the collective to see if she could catch some of the images herself. They flashed in her mind too quickly for her to absorb.

"I think they were spiders," Jaydin said, before Kadailin could calm herself enough to try again. "A little lacking in definition, but spiders nonetheless."

"Spiders?" Ryten asked.

"What are they doing here?" Jaydin said, seemingly to herself. "Flowers are odd enough, but I could see Cens conjuring them on its own. Spiders!" She shook her head.

Kadailin stared at the ground. Flowers. Fire. *Spiders*. What was happening to the forest?

Jaydin stood. "This is unnerving, and I'd like to stay to look into it further, but I have to go back to Black Valley. I just wanted someone here to know I had made it. Now I have to figure out what they're up to."

"I'm coming with you this time," Sandin said. "You have to let me."

"You can't all leave," Ryten said.

"Kadailin will stay." Jaydin locked eyes with Sandin. "They both will."

Sandin's mouth set into a firm line. Kadailin knew Sandin would find a way to Black Valley on her own if Jaydin didn't take her.

'You have to let her go.' Kadailin spoke to Jaydin but let Ryten hear. *'She won't wait here for you again.'*

'It's too dangerous,' Jaydin answered. *'I don't know what the shift would do to her and I don't know how the Black Valley kandar would react to her strangeness.'*

"I'm not afraid," Sandin said.

Kadailin and Jaydin turned towards Sandin in unison.

"I don't need to hear your thoughts to know what you're saying. Kadailin thinks it's too dangerous. I don't care. No matter what happens I'd rather be with you."

"Actually," Jaydin said, "Kadailin was advocating on your behalf. She says I shouldn't leave you here if you want to go."

"I want to go."

Kadailin knew it was decided from the look on Jaydin's face. Their oldest sister would take Sandin with her. The shift formed in the air beside them. Kadailin flinched as her mind mistook the smooth surface for glass. It was ice, she knew, but that didn't help her instinctive reaction.

"You're sure?" Jaydin asked. "You could die. We both could."

"We'll be fine," Sandin answered.

Jaydin nodded. She turned to Kadailin.

"If Damarin returns before we do, make sure the council knows something strange is happening on Land Side. Don't let our sister lie again."

Ryten averted his eyes. It was harder to pretend not to hear something when it was spoken aloud rather than through the collective.

"I won't," Kadailin said, but she wasn't sure she could live up to the promise. She could only hope Jaydin would return before Damarin did.

Ryten's gaze came back to them as Jaydin and Sandin walked towards the spinning grey. Kadailin concentrated on Jaydin's leaf in the collective. It would be gone again soon.

The ice of the shift ruptured under Sandin's fingers and the two sisters were swallowed up. Jaydin's leaf went dark but there was no sign Sandin had left. Kadailin noticed Ryten was now staring at her.

She couldn't think of anything to say to the devoshai. After a moment in silence he walked towards Del and disappeared.

***

Ryten turned away from Tith's last remaining daughter in Calendrai and walked farther into the forest. He studied the red on its floor as he walked through the sparse trees.

The flowers had clearly proliferated since the fire, but what of the spiders? Could he find one to show Jaydin when she returned? To show the other kandar? Did these strange additions have anything to do with the fire? Did they have anything to do with the seemingly healed patches of the forest that appeared now?

His mind filled with questions and he was grateful for them. Now Sandin was in danger. He was worried for the silent sister, more worried than he should be. The more he interacted with Tith's daughters the less sure he became of his decision to name Tchardin dodenzinn. They all seemed to draw him to some degree. That made things even more difficult. He wished Damarin and Tchardin had never left Calendrai.

He could follow them if he wanted to. He had opened the shift for Jaydin and seen Ovaeron through the ice. He was sure he could do it again, but what good would it do him when they were nowhere to be found on Derkra? How could their leaves hang dark to him in Calendrai and remain dark for Jaydin when she was in Black Valley? Where else could they be?

The clusters of flowers ended where he stood. The forest floor ahead appeared to be normal so he turned in the direction of the water and continued his search. Tchardin had told him she saw the flowers too, on one of her many trips to the part of the shore that faced Land Side. She had also seen a spider. She had mentioned them shortly before the fire, when Damarin was so insistent Ryten would never be able to find them again in Cens. Damarin knew him better than any kandar and her reaction to his discovery still surprised him. He had never been lost in the forest before. He knew it too well, and she should have known that.

He looked up and found he faced Del again. Cens must be turning him around. He had known the forest as it once was, but the fire had changed it.

He came to the base of his father's trunk and looked up. Del towered over the other trees as Ryten towered over the other kandar. While in Del's belly he had been given images of Black Valley with Ovaeron at its centre, and he'd seen Tith and his brothers looming over Calendrai, but nothing could eclipse the image of Del just after his birth when he had looked up at his father for the first time. The tree hadn't described himself and Ryten had been shocked to find he had been born of such a great trunk.

He could seek comfort in Del's branches or he could search the rest of Cens for spiders. He could also look for other places where the forest wreaked havoc on direction. He brushed his father's trunk as he passed and the great tree responded with a pulse.

There was no obvious sign of the red flowers in the grass beyond Del so Ryten continued to walk away from his father's trunk, scanning the forest floor for anything new.

Chapter 24

Tchardin was escorted through another door of the hold in a daze. The crowd cheered deafeningly as she and Tezroi disappeared from view. They went farther down, deeper still into the earth. The orbs that lit the sloping tunnel whipped past her as they descended. Ruon's voice haunted her.

"They cheer us," Tezroi said. "They cheer for you."

Did he know what a dangerous thing he kept in his castle? What a beautiful thing he had imprisoned and poisoned with hate? Tchardin had to stay with the humans now. She had to get them to free their guardian. Then she had to find a safe way to get him away from the Arkaiyans before anyone was killed.

She followed Tezroi into a chamber where the tunnel levelled off. The stone of the walls was covered in a thick red fabric, patterned with gold. Tezroi led her through the room and into yet another. The walls of this one were coated in shimmering purple. It was almost the same colour as the dress Tchardin had been forced into. Tezroi sat her down in something his mind called a *chair* and paced towards something he called a *bed*.

"Did Hunter capture Ruon?" Tchardin asked.

Tezroi's pleasant expression grew confused. Soft lines marred his beautiful face. "Ruon?"

She had forgotten Tezroi named him Zyphen. "The Forest Spirit." The kandaran guardian of World Four.

"Zyphen?" Tezroi laughed. "No, that would have been beyond Hunter. Zyphen has been with us for many generations. He was taken after a massacre of our people by the Forest Spirits. We were more powerful then and the repercussions were not considered in the blindness of rage. By the time our eyes were opened again, it was too dangerous to release him."

So he did know how dangerous his captive was. It seemed the people of this Earth knew of the kandar and had renamed them to fit their own history. The king looked at the floor for a moment and was silent. He had said Ruon was captured after a massacre. There was only one time in Jaydin's vast history that kandar had killed so many humans. Ruon must have been taken because of the kandaran war.

"But that is the past," Tezroi said. "I wait for retaliation, as my father did, and his before him, and yet it has never come. It seems the Spirits have abandoned Zyphen. They continue to hold sway over the forest and the people of Arkaiyan and until today it seemed as if they always would."

The king smiled and removed his red coat. "Hunter introduced himself to you?"

Mentioning the man's name had been a mistake. Tezroi was suspicious of something.

"He named himself," Tchardin said. "Nothing more."

"Excellent. I have trusted Hunter completely, but you could make me doubt him. There isn't an Arkaiyan alive who doesn't want a Sparr. Not only for the power it could someday give them, but also for the beauty of your race. Hunter knows our cause is greater than the simple pleasures of the flesh, and that is why I have trusted him, but until now he has not been tested."

Tchardin remained silent. The king came to kneel before her. She saw his pale chest through the thin fabric that covered him. His skin was almost silver. He took her hands in his. The humans seemed fond of touching.

"You're the first we've found since the plan was formed. The first we've been able to take." The king stared into her eyes intently. "We will make an heir that no one could ever deny. Of the city *and* the forest. As strong as the Spirits themselves."

He was waiting for something. Tchardin smiled faintly to encourage him to continue and he did.

"If you help us you can live in the castle for the rest of your days. This world will be yours."

Pandinzori flooded the room and blazed like the collective in Tchardin's mind—full of leaves given to her by this man. She was caught up in his words, caught up in his power. This was the type of human the kandar were meant to sway, to fix the worlds. But what did he want from her?

"She might not want to help, Tez. She'll probably run as soon as she gets a chance."

Jaycee strode into the room from where she'd been standing in the doorway and sat heavily in a chair across from Tchardin. The king turned to her.

"Why wouldn't she help?" he asked in Arkan. "We'd be creating the most powerful Arkaiyan since Ferr."

"An *Arkaiyan*, Tezroi," Jaycee answered in Arkan. Tchardin pretended not to be listening. "She's Sparr. And besides, a baby should be an expression of love, not a puppet to exploit. Why should she make one with us?"

The king got up and walked over to his queen. He knelt in front of her in the same way he'd been kneeling before Tchardin. Instead of taking her hands he spread his fingers over her belly. She put her hands over his and smiled.

"Ours is a child of love," he said. "This one could be too."

Tchardin focused on the second voice inside Jaycee. The baby. It was only a bud in the collective, not yet a leaf, and there was something strange about its presence. It bridged the gap between the two humans. It was somehow made of both Jaycee and Tezroi. Tchardin looked deeper. Then she understood.

Tezroi wanted to put a second voice inside Tchardin. He hoped to create a human child. He expected her to understand, to be enticed—not by his body, but by his plan. He expected her to want to be a part of it. Despite her protestations, Jaycee expected the same thing.

"I won't," Tchardin said.

The two humans turned their attention back to her. Tezroi's face fell. "Why not?"

Tchardin shook her head. She didn't feel ready to give an explanation. It wouldn't sound human enough.

"You've seen the union of our races, haven't you?" the king asked.

Jaycee squeezed his hand. "Those would have been different, Tez. Lazy. The Sparr have nothing to fear from the forest or the Spirits. They'd have nothing to gain from the power."

"Jaycee, please," the king said. "Tchar, you've seen them, out in the forest?"

Should she have seen them? If she were what he thought she was? She focused on the collective, on Tezroi's leaf, to hear his thoughts. Humans didn't seem to guard them. Tezroi's mind had only words. No images. He had never seen this union he spoke of. His only experience with it was far in the past, long before his own birth, in the form of a story.

A boy had been born in the forest with power beyond that of the Sparr. From his mother—who was Sparr—he inherited the ability to speak to the trees and animals. From her he gained their love and the grace of their protection. From his Arkaiyan father he inherited his power to manipulate the physical world. His name had been Ferr, and unlike those who had come before him, he had gone to Arkaiyan to complete his destiny. The rest—and there had been many in those days—simply faded into the past, never having left the forest. Ferr had gone into the city and taken it for himself.

Ferr's line persisted to this day. Over time their Sparr qualities had been diluted, but their Arkaiyan talents had been kept strong by the succession of powerful city women and men chosen to give them children. Tezroi was the distant result. Jaycee carried Tezroi's future child. They would be strong by the standards of the city, but there was no guarantee they would have the speech.

If Tchardin were one of the Sparr and she gave Tezroi an heir, the result would be an Arkaiyan ruler with both the ability and the will to traverse the evil forest unscathed for the first time and see what was on the other side.

Tezroi looked at her expectantly. She nodded.

"And what do your people think of these children? Are they revered? Loved?"

"No." She couldn't be sure, but the impression she'd gotten from the story of Ferr was that these children were unwanted. Their mothers were abandoned to raise them alone, and the rest of the Sparr saw them as cursed.

"This one will be," the king said. "I promise you that. This child—our child—will be loved as well as their sibling. By both of us."

Tchardin was getting drawn in again. She almost felt as if she *were* a human of World Four. As if she were Sparr and the situation truly applied to her. She looked into Tezroi's eyes and saw a heat there, an emotion far beyond her comprehension. It pulled her back to herself. She was supposed to be helping Ruon.

"Ferr's blood still runs through my veins, although it is weak," the king continued, imploring. "Our child would be more you than me. Perhaps they would rule both Arkaiyan and the people of the forest. Bring us back together after centuries apart."

Out of the corner of her eye Tchardin saw Jaycee smile sadly. She searched the queen's thoughts. The child wouldn't be a product of the forest, regardless of their blood. They would be the opposite. Raised as an Arkaiyan, raised to hate and fear the trees, they would never love their Sparr ancestors. If they came to rule them it would be done harshly and with loathing.

Tchardin thought of the expanse of stumps that surrounded the city. If she gave Tez his hybrid child would they cut down the whole forest? She shook herself. She wasn't Sparr. She wasn't even human. She couldn't give him a child. She was kandar.

A loud scraping sound interrupted them, as if something dragged across the stone ceiling above.

"They're unsettled," Jaycee said in Arkan. "You must have excited them with the test earlier."

Tezroi nodded, then turned to Tchardin and switched back to Spardic. "The animals live above us. They guard us from all but a certain type of attack." He smiled as he said it. His thoughts told her he was remembering her pathetic attempt to escape him earlier. "Normally they sleep when we do, but—"

The sound came again, drowning out the king's words.

"It's Lowren," Jaycee said when it was quiet again. "Should I try to calm him?"

"I'll do it," Tezroi said. "You should rest."

He leaned over her and their lips touched. Tchardin could only think of the shock she would get if she tried to do that to another kandar. There would be no such shock from a human.

"Keep the newest addition to our family entertained while I'm gone," he said in Arkan.

Jaycee smiled. Tezroi strode out of the room and the queen stayed where she was. Tchardin could tell she wanted to accompany him, but her body was heavy now. The baby took her strength.

"I'm sorry about Tez," Jaycee said. "He's so enamoured with this plan he forgets reality. You're a person with a life, not just an answer to our prayers. Do you have children already? A family?"

Tchardin felt the anticipation in Jaycee's thoughts—several responses being readied for her answer. She shook her head. It was simplest to say no.

"That makes it possible," the queen said. "You'll have as much time as you need to decide. Despite his grand plans I can tell you Tezroi won't force you. Neither of us will." She smiled and Tchardin found no threat in it. "I know what your life in the forest is like. Dirty. Hungry. Dangerous. The castle is luxurious and safe. Stay here with us. That is all you must decide for now. For the rest, wait until our child is born, if you wish. See us as parents. See us as lovers, friends. To each other. To you. Both of us."

Jaycee's thoughts swirled in the room. Tchardin's best interpretation was that with time, the queen expected her to be a sort of dodenzinn to them. She expected Tchardin to join their family and love their child as her own, love them as her partners. The king and queen were generous, and kind to their people, but the darkness inside them—the hatred of the trees and the humans who lived among them—was strong. Tchardin frowned.

"Yes," Jaycee said. "It's more complicated than that. It would have been easier if Hunter had brought us a man. Asking you to carry for us makes it more dangerous for everyone. Choose carefully. You can't change your mind once the decision has been made. We can't let you run back to your people with a royal heir in your belly. Especially when we know they'll be more powerful than any of us. Ferr was a blessing, of course, but this time it will be done right."

Jaycee stood and walked to Tchardin.

"Just think of it." Her face lit up as she spoke. "A true Arkaiyan with the power to tame the deadly forest that holds us. To free us from it once and for all. The child you make with Tezroi could rule this land and match the Forest Spirits."

Tchardin looked at Jaycee's swollen belly. "What about your child?"

Jaycee's arms encircled her stomach protectively. The act seemed unconscious, instinctive. Tchardin knew she wouldn't—couldn't—let Tezroi put a human child in her, regardless of the couple's plans, but could she feel that way about it if he did?

"They will be yours as well, if you choose to stay," the queen answered. "And yours will be mine. They will grow up as siblings. Perhaps they will rule together."

Another loud noise from above shattered their conversation.

"What's going on up there?" Jaycee gestured and the world opened beside them. Tchardin's eyes widened involuntarily. It was the shift.

The open shift resolved into a view of the animal hold. Tchardin was amazed Jaycee could make an image appear. She knew if she opened it now to the same place she would only see grey.

The image in the shift twisted and moved through the hold—another thing the kandar couldn't do. It came to rest on Ruon. His eyes seemed to bore into Tchardin through the portal. As if he could see her from where he was. He beat his fists against the cage.

"You would think he'd learn." None of Tchardin's fear showed on Jaycee's face. "The glass holds him. He cannot use his shadow magic while contained there."

Jaycee was wrong not to worry. There was something new in Ruon's composure. Tchardin hoped she wasn't the cause of the change. He should be set free, but not when he was like this. There was no clarity in his eyes, no reason. Kandar were made to protect humans, not to kill them, regardless of what those humans had done.

A shadow flew across the cage. Ruon ducked away from the glass. The image in the shift showed the black dragon passing above him.

"Lowren." Jaycee frowned. "Once Tezroi has control of him he'll put Zyphen in his place. The Forest Spirit fears the dragon."

Tchardin doubted that, despite Ruon's reaction. She respected the dragon—it would clearly take great control to tame him—but even she wasn't afraid of him. If she had any trouble she could simply destroy him. Free of the glass, Ruon could do the same. If he was anything like Kordic he could do it without closing his eyes.

Where was Tezroi? Tchardin brought up the collective by instinct, expecting to be able to find the king by focusing on his leaf. There were so many lights. She struggled to concentrate on Tezroi's regardless of its brightness. She was about to give up when she noticed a glow in the corner of her mind. She opened her eyes in surprise.

Damarin was on World Four. Her leaf was lit alone in the branches of the Calendrai collective. She must have found a way to follow Tchardin to the Earths. How long had she been here? Tchardin was about to close her eyes to study Damarin's leaf for a location when she noticed the dragon in the shift.

He flew towards the cage and the shine of his scales blazed in Tchardin's eyes. They glittered from the many floating points of light in the hold. She squinted. Ruon ducked in the glass lattice just as Lowren's razor teeth clamped down on the cage. The glass shattered. Jaycee screamed.

Tchardin stood. She'd have to expose herself, use pandinzori to get to the guardian before he killed anyone, and use it to stop him. Then she remembered the glass. What could she do to subdue him with so much of it nearby? Ruon would want her to kill with him. She'd have to convince him to leave, draw him away from the castle. The glass might stop her from using pandinzori, but it should also stop him. Maybe Damarin was close enough to help. Jaycee reached for her.

"We have to go up," Tchardin said.

"No," Jaycee whispered. She held Tchardin's dress tightly. "No. Tez is the strongest of us. We can't help him now."

The queen's thoughts were loud and full of fear. Jaycee didn't expect to leave the castle alive. She wanted to join Tez in the hold but she felt she couldn't make that decision for her unborn child. If she was going to die she would do it here, in the safest possible place for her baby.

The image in the shift moved to the floor of the hold.

"The guards are arriving," the queen said. "We can only hope the glass will hinder the Forest Spirit."

Maybe the Arkaiyans could handle the guardian without Tchardin. The glass would be just as dangerous to Tchardin and everyone else in the castle if she went up to the hold. It would be better for the guards to recapture Ruon than for her to accidentally kill them all trying to dissuade him.

Fifty or so women and men spread out on the floor of the pit.

"Where's the king?" Tchardin asked.

The image in the shift slid sideways.

"There," Jaycee said.

Tezroi stood on the platform at the front of the room. His arms were crossed and he looked down on the guards below.

"He looks calm," the queen said, "but he isn't. He has a shield up, a strong one. I can feel it."

"Will it protect him from the Forest Spirit?"

"Maybe." Jaycee raised her hands and clasped them in front of the miniature image of the king. "I can strengthen it."

"You can do that from here?"

"If I can feel it I can affect it."

Tchardin was impressed. As far as she knew the kandar couldn't manipulate pandinzori through the shift.

"Oh, no," Jaycee whispered.

A blinding flash of light lit the shift. It poured over Tezroi until he was so bright he disappeared. Jaycee's body went stiff, her hands drawn so tightly together her skin paled. Tchardin's eyes were forced away. The room shook. Tchardin found herself on the ground, her cheek pressed into softness. She didn't remember falling.

Jaycee remained upright, the shift still open in front of her. The pandinzori in the hold was gone. It had been turned into light when the glass reacted to its manipulation. Tchardin searched the collective for the brightest leaf Arkaiyan had. The king had survived the blast.

She saw him in the shift. He knelt on the platform with his hands held out in front of him. The platform was untouched but the surface of the walls to either side of it had been scoured away. Pandinzori grew around his body to fill the void in the hold. Jaycee's hands parted and dropped to her sides.

The queen moved the image away from Tezroi as he got to his feet and spun it around the room. The platform at the other end of the hold—that which had held the glass cage—was gone. The image moved into the pit. The bodies of guards were strewn everywhere.

"The Forest Spirit must be dead," Jaycee said. "If the guards have fallen he can't possibly have survived."

Tchardin examined the figures lying in the hold. Pandinzori grew from them. "Some of them are alive."

She searched the collective for Ruon, hoping the blast had been caused by his escape from the castle. She should be able to tell how far away he was by the brightness of his seed. It blazed when she found it.

The shift showed Ruon leap out of one of the tunnels and force pandinzori through a guard who stood to block him. Tchardin flinched as the body of the man disintegrated in a shower of red. The guardian passed through the blood and disappeared from the image. Jaycee shrieked. The shift faded and resolidified as the queen got herself under control.

"I'm going up there," Tchardin said. Damarin had probably arrived on World Four at Tairasyn's base, as Tchardin had, and was too far away to be aware of any of this. There would be no one to help with the guardian. "Where's the Forest Spirit now?"

Jaycee gave her a sideways glance. Tchardin could tell she was petrified. Resigned, the queen motioned and the shift moved.

The image in the shift skimmed around the room. Without the glass to hold him back Ruon would be incredibly powerful. Hopefully there was some glass left after the explosion. Even the possibility that it hadn't all been destroyed might limit the guardian. Tchardin remembered the things Kordic had done with his eyes open and shivered. Ruon had to be stopped before things got worse.

The guardian had ascended to the centre of the pit and floated on nothing. Tezroi was nowhere to be seen. The surviving guards fled to the tunnels that ringed the pit. A shadow passed over the shift.

"What was that?" Jaycee motioned and the shift moved back in the direction it had come. "There's another one," she whispered.

Damarin must have been on World Four for some time, to come this far. Tchardin's middle sister joined Ruon in the pit, surrounded by pandinzori and looking fully kandaran. Why did her camouflage not conceal her? She must not know her appearance should be hidden from the humans. But Tchardin remembered the first time she had encountered a human. Damarin's camouflage should have been instinct.

Despite her sister's appearance, Tchardin was hopeful. Damarin was strong. Probably not as strong as Ruon, but certainly stronger than Tchardin. There was something about her that made the kandar listen when she spoke, that made them look to her. Perhaps Ruon would feel the same. Damarin could help Tchardin stop him. Then they could return to Derkra together.

Jaycee widened the shift until they could see both Ruon and Damarin. "They'll destroy us all."

The two kandar stared at each other as the remaining guards massed below them. Indentations appeared in the pandinzori that surrounded them but were quickly filled again. Tchardin guessed it was rendinzori from the guards that did it. So far the kandar didn't react to it. They didn't need to. The effect was barely noticeable.

Tchardin could try to speak to her sister, tell her to calm the guardian, to take him away from the castle, but she didn't want Ruon to hear her. She watched them in silence instead.

Ruon nodded. It was almost imperceptible through the shift, but Tchardin saw it. Then she saw Damarin smile. She relaxed.

The yellow-tinted pandinzori around Damarin shot downwards with purpose and obliterated the guards below.

Chapter 25

The shift disappeared as a rain of leaves fell in the collective. Jaycee climbed onto the bed. She rocked back and forth, crinkling the purple fabric.

"I need to see what's happening in the hold," Tchardin said.

She searched the collective for the king's leaf. It remained bright. The guardian hadn't found him yet. Damarin's leaf drew her mind away from the World Four collective. Why would her sister kill those guards? They couldn't have harmed the two kandar.

"I knew that monster would be the end of us," the queen said. "The first time I was brought to the hold to see him I knew. But what could we have done? There was no way to free him. He was always going to destroy us."

Tchardin tried to pull the queen to her feet but Jaycee's legs tangled in her dress and she fell to the floor. She huddled there at the end of the bed.

"Those arrogant idiots," Jaycee continued quietly, her face in her hands and her voice muffled. "They killed us. Hundreds of years ago they doomed us all."

Tchardin had to stop the two kandar before things got worse. She couldn't match them in strength so she'd have to convince them with words. Or at least convince one of them.

"Jaycee," she said, kneeling in front of the queen. "We have to help the king."

"My Tez is dead."

"I promise you he's alive."

The queen had hidden her face in the folds of her dress but now she looked up. Her eyes were rimmed in red. "How can you know?"

"I just know."

Jaycee let out a sob that turned into a laugh. She buried her head in her hands again and her shoulders shook gently.

"I'm going into the hold," Tchardin said. "Come with me."

"I don't see why you would help us, even if you could. You Sparr are more like the Spirits than you are like us."

"People are dying," Tchardin said. "I have to do something."

"*My* people are dying. Arkaiyans are dying. How does that concern you?"

Tchardin couldn't believe what she was hearing. "You're all the same," she said before she could stop herself. "I have to help."

She got to her feet and turned towards the door leading from the room.

"Wait," the queen said.

Jaycee's thoughts were loud. She had expected to die, but Tchardin's insistence that they fight made her hope they might live. There could be a chance for her child. A chance for her king. If a powerless Sparr woman could fight, so could she.

Jaycee stood and moved towards one of the walls of the room. She took something small and dark that hung there, pulling it down and holding it against her chest. Her thoughts quieted. "Follow me."

She strode towards another of the purple walls and gestured with her free hand. The fabric flew away, revealing a small tunnel in the stone. She ducked into it. Tchardin ran to join her.

"Hurry," Jaycee shouted from ahead.

They followed the dim passageway as it wound upwards through the earth. When they turned a corner Tchardin saw light at the end of the tunnel. Jaycee stopped. She clutched the dark object in her hands. Tchardin recognised the softness of fur. It was a black fur *bag*. The queen lowered it and opened the shift.

Everything was red. Tchardin didn't understand what she was seeing until Jaycee moved the shift away from the floor of the pit. It was blood. The stone shone with it.

"Are they all gone?" the queen asked. "Am I too late?"

Tchardin felt a flash of emotion she had never experienced before and knew it was *shame*. The queen was ashamed of her fear, ashamed of her reluctance to help her people before the fight was over. The image in the shift pulled away from the blood. It soared above the platform—saved from the glass explosion by the humans' rendinzori shield—and the shredded balconies until Damarin and Ruon appeared, dark shapes floating above the red and grey.

Jaycee met Tchardin's eyes. There was a question in her gaze.

"The king escaped," Tchardin said. "He's alive."

The queen was silent for a long time before she spoke. "Then he must be in the tunnels too. I need to look into the pit."

The shift closed and they walked towards the light. Tchardin became aware of a slight buzzing of thought in her mind. The two kandar were speaking. They came to the end of the tunnel and Jaycee leaned forwards slightly to look up into the hold. Tchardin looked across the pit. There was so much red. Could any of the humans have survived? Pandinzori swirled into the room from somewhere. It didn't simply hang in the air—it flowed and mixed as if it had a source. There were other openings in the wall across the great stone floor, covered in blood. Pandinzori emerged from one of them. She focussed on the shadows there.

"Guards," she said.

The queen followed her gaze. "Brave and stupid. They should leave, while the Spirits rest."

Tchardin looked up at the two kandar hanging motionless in pandinzori above a damaged balcony. She closed her eyes and looked into the collective, concentrating on their buzzing thoughts with everything she had. Ruon's voice formed in her mind.

'—will kill him before I leave. That is non-negotiable.'

Damarin must be trying to convince him to go. Perhaps Tchardin wouldn't need to do anything. She switched her focus to Damarin's leaf but didn't hear her sister's response.

'If you want my help you will make time for it,' the guardian said.

"We have one chance now," Jaycee said, still looking up at the kandar. "It's risky, but we're likely to die anyway."

'What of the other tevadra?' came Ruon's mindvoice. *'The queen?'*

Damarin turned her back on the guardian, her expression unreadable. Tchardin tried even harder to hear her sister's words. Damarin would know Tchardin was in the hold now if she hadn't known already, if she hadn't followed her to get there. She would have looked for Tchardin's leaf as soon as Ruon mentioned it. Damarin's thoughts remained inaccessible.

Jaycee's hand gripped Tchardin's elbow. "Glass is our only weapon in the fight against the Forest Spirits," she whispered. The queen held the black bag towards her. "Simple glass beads."

Tchardin flinched at the words. *Glass beads*. The queen parted the fur of the bag and tilted it towards the pit, towards the brightness of the room. Tiny points of light appeared, reflected. Tchardin closed her mind to the pandinzori around her—tried to lose awareness of it—and lost touch with the collective at the same time. The queen sealed the lights away in the blackness and Tchardin backed away from her. She couldn't help looking up at the two kandar in the pit again, oblivious to the danger below. Jaycee's eyes followed hers. Understanding dawned in them.

"Wait," the queen said. "We're safe. As long as the bag is closed the Spirits can't touch them."

"How can that be?" Tchardin couldn't see the glass anymore but she knew it was there, in the bag. How could any covering protect them? If Ruon or Damarin saw Jaycee and directed pandinzori their way—or if Tchardin manipulated it by accident—they'd be killed.

"This is Avren's fur," the queen said.

Tchardin searched her mind for an explanation, but the queen provided one in words.

"Of course you wouldn't know him by that name, being of the forest. His fur is a barrier. Our magic can't touch him. It's the same for the Forest Spirits. When the glass is inside they can't affect it."

"What will you do with the beads?" Tchardin asked.

The queen drew out a handful of the glittering glass spheres and Tchardin tried to ignore the pandinzori that swirled from her hand to encircle them. Jaycee placed the closed bag against the wall of the tunnel, hidden in shadows.

"If Tezroi is alive—as you say he is—he'll have them too." She ignored Tchardin's question. "I wish the guards had been trained in their use but it's been more than a hundred years since we've faced Forest Spirits."

Tchardin had wanted to help Jaycee save the king, not attack the kandar. Especially with Damarin there. "I don't think this is a good idea."

"It's our only chance."

Above them, Damarin turned away from Ruon. Yellow pandinzori gathered in front of her. Tchardin took a step out of the tunnel. She needed to warn them. More than that, she worried she might never get back to Derkra if Damarin left without her. Something sparkled in the air.

'Glass!' Tchardin thought as loudly as she could.

The pandinzori around the guardian lost the darkness of his aura and he fell out of the air.

'Let go!' his mindvoice shouted, his words flashing through the collective. Damarin didn't move.

The beads flew by him, passing through the pandinzori he had held, and impacted Damarin's. For the first time, Tchardin clearly saw the shape of another kandar's mind.

Damarin's yellow pandinzori ignited. It formed a ragged half-sphere on one side of her and the brightness of it was seared into Tchardin's vision. Then, just as quickly, it disappeared as if nothing had happened.

"It works!" Jaycee shouted. "Tez is alive!"

Damarin fell out of the air. She fell until she came level with Ruon who had stopped himself safely below her. He caught her in a sheet of dark pandinzori and her body hung there, unmoving. Tchardin frantically searched the collective for Damarin's leaf and found it. She relaxed slightly against the tunnel wall.

Ruon's thoughts boomed in Tchardin's mind as he looked wildly around the room. *'You cannot let the glass meet your pandinzori. It will take anything you hold when it touches!'*

Damarin's response was hidden.

'Go back to Derkra,' Ruon said. *'You will heal there.'*

Her body twitched.

'Go now! I can handle this on my own. I have dealt with them before.'

Damarin righted herself. Her eyes were wide as she took in the damage. She lifted an arm out of the shadows that surrounded her body and held it in front of her. It was dark and wet and ragged.

"They bleed just like we do," Jaycee said.

'What's wrong with my skin?' Damarin didn't hide her thoughts.

'Something very human,' the guardian said. *'Blood and muscle and bone. The result of it will be human too if you stay.'*

'Something human? I'm not in camouflage. My skin is kandaran. How can it react this way?'

'It is a thing of this place,' Ruon said, his eyes still searching the hold.

'It's rendinzori,' Damarin answered herself.

Ruon nodded. He spun slowly in the air, seeming to examine each of the entrances to the balconies. Tchardin remained silent, afraid to draw his eyes in their direction lest he lash out.

'It was the king who sent the beads,' he said. *'I know it was.'*

Damarin's gaze turned towards the pit. Instinct made Tchardin flatten herself against the wall of the tunnel. She lost view of her sister. She saw Jaycee instead. The queen stood just inside the shadow of the tunnel, staring at the glass beads in her open hand.

"I should help Tez," she said.

Light flared in the pit. A loud crack followed. Tchardin looked up at the kandar again, reminding herself not to touch pandinzori in fear. The pandinzori around Ruon and Damarin was reduced but there was no visible hole in it. There was instead a great emptiness between Ruon and the far wall of the room. The guardian must have seen the beads before they got close and affected the pandinzori around them, letting go before it reached the kandar. The pandinzori he used had disappeared in the blast.

"Leave!" the guardian shouted aloud. Jaycee stepped back at the sound. *'Now!'* followed from the collective. *'If you stay here, with an injury like that, with their eyes upon you, you will die.'*

Damarin's eyes remained huge and dark in her bloodied face, but now there was anger in them. Blood flowed down her side and ran off her foot to join the blood of the guards on the ground. The shadows of her body covered its origin. Could she really die from it? Tchardin understood the threat of the glass beads but not of this blood.

'Meet me in the desert once you have killed your king,' Damarin said. *'The future queen of the kandar will have to find her own way home.'*

Jaycee moved. Tchardin saw a glint of light as the glass beads left the queen's hand and rushed silently into the pit. Jaycee motioned upwards and the beads changed direction, aimed for the feet of her sister and the guardian. Tchardin thought to catch them in pandinzori, destroy them before they reached the kandar, but every moment of hesitation brought them closer together.

'Go,' she thought quietly, directing the word at Damarin alone.

High above, her sister opened the shift. Ruon nodded.

Jaycee flinched when Damarin disappeared. The beads sparkled in the light and Ruon's searching eyes flashed in their direction. He dropped out of the air and the glass passed harmlessly by him. He landed in the blood on the stone floor as an explosion of light rocked the hold above.

"Where are you, Tezroi?" he shouted.

He was level with the tunnel Tchardin and Jaycee hid in. Tchardin pulled the shadows of the tunnel around them but she was sure the guardian would find them if he looked. She heard the thoughts of the guards in the tunnel on the other side of the pit for the first time since entering it. They huddled together and filled the air with despair. They too were easy to see, and even easier to hear, but Ruon's eyes and mind were focused upwards, searching for the king, searching for glass beads. He didn't pay them any notice.

"If you will not come out to face me I will bring your castle down around you!"

Pandinzori began to fill the room again. Did it come from Tezroi? More guards on the upper level of the pit? Jaycee and the others had managed to refill the bottom half of the hold with their own pandinzori since they arrived but the upper half had only held that of the two kandar. It had been used up in the explosions.

Jaycee reached for the black bag. "He's so close."

The queen's thoughts were excited. She believed they had scared Damarin into leaving. Now there was only one Spirit left. She was beginning to believe they could win.

"No." Tchardin held Jaycee's hand away from the bag. "It's not safe. He's going to do something."

Pandinzori was everywhere. It filled the pit and entered the stone of its walls.

"But—" Jaycee said.

The earth shook. Tchardin was rocked off her feet by the movement. Jaycee crashed into her. The queen screamed behind the roaring of the earth. Tchardin's head connected with the side of the tunnel and red filled her vision. Her human body bled, just as Damarin's kandaran body had. The guards across the pit thought to steady themselves with rendinzori but couldn't get a foothold. Some of their thoughts were silenced as part of the tunnel they hid in collapsed. Leaves fell from the collective.

Maybe Jaycee could do what the guards had failed at if Tchardin helped her. The small black bag leapt up and down with the shaking of the room as if it were alive, but the glass beads were hidden from view. Would the black fur act as Jaycee said it did? Tchardin reached for the pandinzori around them and found the guardian held it. The black bag was able to block it. She pushed against Ruon's mind. His resistance was weak. He must be holding all the pandinzori in the pit. Exerting that much control, it seemed he couldn't protect this tiny bit from Tchardin. She partly solidified it.

Jaycee's feet met the ground and she had time to raise her arms above her head. Tchardin felt pressure as the queen used rendinzori to hold them steady. Their tunnel remained intact. Ruon passively sought to take the pandinzori from Tchardin. She concentrated on resisting him. Jaycee shouted with the effort of holding up the tunnel. Cracks formed above them.

The shaking stopped. Jaycee dropped her arms and fell to her knees. The rumbling noise that had accompanied the shaking remained. Ruon stared straight up. Tchardin leaned out of the tunnel and followed the guardian's gaze. The roof of the hold was riddled with cracks, like the ice of the shift before it gave way. The dark fissures spread through the stone. The queen watched with horror on her face. The sound of the groaning rock covered the shouts of the remaining guards in the pit but Tchardin heard their thoughts. They had calmed for a moment when the shaking ceased. Now they were terrified again. The tunnel had collapsed behind them. There was nowhere for them to go.

An immense rock dropped from the roof of the hold. It was followed quickly by another. Tchardin was swept from her feet as the first one landed. Ruon threw himself into the air, away from it. Tchardin steadied herself on hands and knees for the next. A shower of smaller rocks followed. The black sky poured in with them.

"The river," Jaycee whispered in awe.

Water. So much water. Falling in on top of them. Tchardin remembered the futility of struggling against the shift. The guards' thoughts in her mind reinforced her own. She was paralysed with fear.

"Move," Jaycee said.

The queen got to her feet unsteadily and stepped in front of Tchardin. She dropped the short distance into the pit and raised her hands. The deep blue rushed towards them, so high it would cover the tunnel. Tchardin forgot her fear when she saw the tiny woman in red standing before the wall of water, braced to block it. This wasn't the shift. Tchardin wasn't helpless here. Pandinzori filled the pit and flowed through the approaching wave. A moment and it would cover them.

The water crashed against empty air in front of Jaycee. The queen must have created a shield. She was tossed against the wall of the hold, her upper body forced into the tunnel towards Tchardin. Jaycee shouted soundlessly behind the crush of waves as her hands were pressed back against her chest. Her shield held. Water rushed around it on all sides. A thin layer flowed over the queen's feet. It splashed over them from above.

Tchardin felt for the pandinzori she had held before and pushed. The water coming over Jaycee's shield sprayed into the air. The tension in the queen's body reversed itself. She was no longer being crushed, but straining forward. She forced her arms out straight in front of her and stepped away from the wall. Tchardin followed with her mind, letting the queen hold enough of the weight to feel as if she were doing it alone.

But Jaycee didn't believe she was doing it alone. Elation erupted from the queen's leaf in the collective. She thought Tezroi was helping her. The king's leaf was still bright. He had survived both the shaking earth and the river.

Tchardin turned her eyes to the roof of the hold. It was slowly crumbling under the weight of the water. Would the river empty itself into the room? Would there be an end to it? Jaycee's elation dampened and Tchardin understood there wouldn't be at the same time the queen did. Eventually they'd have to escape the pit or drown. Jaycee couldn't handle this herself.

Tchardin felt a slight relief of pressure as she let her camouflage drop. Shadows came to her body from the corners of the tunnel until she was swathed in darkness again. She looked down at her skin that was not covered by the dress and smiled faintly at the familiar pattern there.

The entire room was flush with pandinzori again, as it had been when Tchardin was tested. It flowed against the crumbling ceiling and around and through the water that poured in above them. All Tchardin had to do was harden it. Replace the rock the river had run on. Remake the roof of the room in pandinzori. Stop the water completely.

The thoughts of the guards disappeared as the last of their leaves fell. She had to hurry. She closed her eyes and realised she had manipulated the pandinzori in front of the queen without doing so. Perhaps she was stronger than she thought.

The room was brilliantly lit against the darkness behind her eyes. Ruon's black aura was a shadow in one corner of the hold, high above the slowly rising water. He stood in the remains of a doorway that had once led to a balcony above the pit.

Tchardin moved towards the pandinzori against the ceiling with her mind, climbing through the light that filled the hold, using it to extend her reach. She tentatively pushed at it and found Ruon's mind didn't claim it. She had never attempted to control so much pandinzori before.

She made a wall, like she had during the fire on Calendrai. This wall was much bigger, and required more concentration, but she found it to be the same. She pushed it into the water, just below the stone. The flow parted easily.

No more water fell into the pit. The bottom of the river was visible through pandinzori as it passed above the hold. The water level in the room began to drop. It ran off into the tunnels around the pit and was no longer being replenished. Tchardin took full control of the water in front of them.

Jaycee must have felt the pressure disappear because she lowered her arms. When she turned her expression was one of confusion, but it quickly changed to outrage. Tchardin released the water and used that part of her mind to harden the pandinzori around Jaycee, keeping her in place. A wave rushed past the queen.

'I thought you might be there.' Ruon's mindvoice came to Tchardin. *'If you are capable of this you could have freed me.'*

Jaycee twitched. Tchardin held the pandinzori around her firmly, treating it like the pandinzori she held against the ceiling of the room. The queen's eyes followed her, unbound by the thick air that kept her still. There was hate in them.

'This is different,' Tchardin said to the guardian. *'There's no glass left to stop me.'*

She grabbed the black bag from the water in the tunnel. Jaycee's hatred turned to panic as she saw Tchardin with the weapon. Tchardin pushed the queen's thoughts to the back of her mind. Ruon waited above, level with the remaining platform at the front of the hold.

Tchardin leapt to meet him. She tried to mimic the way Damarin had flown through the air but it didn't work. She didn't move.

'You are too slow,' the guardian said.

Ruon forced her mind away from the pandinzori around her. She fought him, but couldn't risk losing control of the pandinzori that supported the river. He pulled her towards him, regarding her impassively. His expression showed none of the concentration Tchardin was sure was plain on her face. She gripped the black bag at her side, partially obscured by shadow, and hoped her plan would work. He released her and she held herself up in the air.

"You cannot fly," he said. "You could not match the tevadra who did free me."

"I know her."

"She told me. *Sisters*. How strange."

Tchardin moved the fur bag in front of her, hidden in darkness. If she opened it, Ruon would be forced to act as she did or die. They would both lose the ability to control pandinzori until they got a safe distance away from the glass.

"I won't let you kill any more humans," she said. "You have to leave the castle."

Ruon's eyes met hers for a moment and she saw annoyance in them. He scanned the hold again. "The king is not dead yet. How can you wish to protect him now, when you have seen the weapon they have? What they do with it?"

"He's human." Tchardin held the bag out in front of her. "That is the Purpose. I am queen of the kandar and I command you to let go of pandinzori."

The guardian's eyes widened slightly when his gaze went to her hands. She was about to open the bag to scatter the beads when a sliver of light caught her eye. She reacted and let herself fall. She only fell for a moment before the guardian caught her. Light exploded behind him. He wrested the bag from her hands and dragged her bodily through the air.

"Another earthquake, Tezroi?" he shouted. "Is that what you want? Show yourself!"

Tchardin saw the telltale glint of light in the emptiness that warned of danger. Ruon saw it too. Another great swath of pandinzori lit up beside them and disappeared with a crack. He dropped the sealed black bag to the ground. Tchardin helplessly watched it fall.

"I am here," a voice rose in the pit. The king stood in the doorway that had led to Ruon's former prison, at the opposite end of the hold. "You've killed too many of my people, Zyphen. I won't let you take any more."

Tezroi strode into the open air. He held a larger black bag of glass beads. The king couldn't know his advantage but it was clear to Tchardin. There was no pandinzori left between him and the kandar. If Tezroi released the glass, Ruon would only be able to stop it when it reached them. Or let go.

'I am not Zyphen.' The guardian's black mindvoice filled the hold with hate. *'I am Ruon, guardian of your puny world.'*

Pandinzori spread around the king. Ruon's eyes followed it. Tchardin realised he was stalling. The king could fill the room again if he waited too long to attack.

"Whoever you are," Tezroi said, "you will leave or die."

Ruon seemed about to reply when the king ripped the bag in half. Hundreds of glass spheres floated before him. Tezroi raised his hand and they shot forward, spreading out in the air.

Ruon laughed. Tchardin let go of the pandinzori around her but she didn't fall. She realised with horror that the guardian had trapped her there, in pandinzori he controlled, as Tezroi's glass beads sped towards them. She fought him but couldn't escape. She tried to let the ceiling fall, wash them all away with water, but Ruon had taken control of that too and gave no indication of letting it go. He was going to kill himself and take Tchardin with him. She watched—able to close her eyes but unwilling to—as the glass approached. The mass of beads had entered the void of light, flying through empty air.

Movement behind the beads drew her eye. The pandinzori around Tezroi darkened. It swirled up around the king and settled against his legs and chest. Ruon held it. The guardian's control was astounding, to move so much pandinzori so precisely from that far away, when it wasn't connected to him. It should be impossible. But the guardians were stronger than the rest of the kandar because they were whole beings, not half, like those with dodenzinn. What was impossible for Tchardin could be possible for Ruon.

Tezroi's eyes widened when he realised he was stuck. He struggled to move but he didn't stop the glass beads. They flew on, moments from impacting the active pandinzori around the kandar. Tchardin closed her eyes tightly in anticipation and was confronted with a brilliant wall of light. The pandinzori around the king rushed towards them, darkened by Ruon's control. The first of the glass beads shattered. Then another. Pockets of darkness formed in the wall of light. The reaction started, but it didn't advance on the kandar.

Tchardin gasped and opened her eyes. Ruon still held the pandinzori around them, but it wasn't connected to the pandinzori that touched the glass. There was the barest sliver of emptiness between them when the impact was made. That emptiness grew increasingly quickly as the glass reaction ate up the pandinzori in a blazing rush back towards the king.

There was only a moment for Tezroi's expression to change from concentration to shock before the brightest light in the collective winked out and a leaf fell. Jaycee's leaf pulsed with thoughts of anguish when the king disappeared behind the blast. There was no shield to save him this time. Ruon laughed again.

He released Tchardin. She pushed against him to take as much pandinzori as possible but found he'd only left her enough to remain in the air. He held everything else so strongly she couldn't believe it. She had never felt a mind like his.

"Finally." The guardian smiled. The anger he had carried when she first met him seemed to diminish. "I have planned his death so many times but I never thought it would end like that."

Jaycee's murderous thoughts were hard to ignore. Tchardin pushed them to the back of her mind. She'd tried to help the humans, but the king was dead and there was nothing she could do about it now. Ruon had been too strong. They'd never had a chance.

"You could have killed us with him," she said.

"I could still kill you."

Tchardin tried to move away from him but came up against the pandinzori he controlled.

Ruon waved a hand in dismissal. "I will not, but know that I could. We were never in any danger."

"But the glass—"

"It is nothing when it does not surround you." The loathing returned to his eyes. "As it does in a cage."

"They didn't know what they were doing. They don't know the kandar as we are, only as something monstrous they created. If you'd been in camouflage—"

"That is enough. You will live because Damarin wishes it and I owe her my life. You have the golden aura, and you may call yourself queen though you remain unacknowledged, but it is faint, and it can fade. I am a guardian and I have lived forever. There is no reason for me to heed you."

"You're still kandar," Tchardin said, disbelieving. Her position was absolute while the aura remained, despite the lack of affirmation from the council. "I'll be the queen of all the kandar in existence."

"Go to Derkra and claim it then." He opened the shift. "I go to a new purpose. The humans of World Four do not deserve a guardian. Let them fend for themselves."

He put a hand against the ice. The pandinzori in the hold lost its grey cast as he let it all go. The river fell in above them. Tchardin turned towards it as the guardian's seed went dark. She reached for the pandinzori closest to the ceiling but there was nothing to carry her mind over the extreme distance. The pandinzori that had filled the room was mostly gone now. It remained in the bottom of the pit and along the ceiling, but not in the centre. Her mind couldn't grasp it. She took the pandinzori below her and pushed herself through the air towards the water. She had to get closer.

When the pandinzori around her connected with the mass on the ceiling she closed her eyes to take it. She hardened it, stopping the river where it burst through the open rock. A voice below threatened to break her concentration.

"You were one of them all along!" Jaycee shouted up at her, her words echoing in the empty pit. "This was all part of your plan to destroy us. To kill my Tez!"

Something brushed against the pandinzori Tchardin held. She opened her eyes but kept control of the light in the back of her mind, slowly forcing the river above the rock. Jaycee collapsed on the floor of the pit. Her body shook. She gestured feebly towards Tchardin. The queen tried to bind her with rendinzori but Tchardin had pandinzori firmly controlled and the attempts failed.

Tchardin looked up through the water into darkness, saw the black sky above it. She couldn't hold it forever. She'd be forced to drop it immediately if Jaycee noticed the bag of beads Ruon had let fall to the floor of the hold.

'Jaycee,' she thought to the queen, not bothering to yell. *'The water will return when I leave. You need to find somewhere safe—'*

The queen's thoughts rang out in the emptiness. Emotion overwhelmed Tchardin. Jaycee hated her, cursed her, wished her dead a thousand times. The queen believed she could have protected Tezroi, could have held a shield around her king and blocked out the light as they'd done before, but she felt Tchardin had stopped her. She wept—her body wracked with sobs for her lost husband and people, and for her child. She held her stomach as she had before but she worried the baby was gone. The earthquake had thrown her against the stone of the tunnel too many times. She waited for Tchardin to drop the river on her. It would take her to join her lost family. Tchardin struggled to hold herself together under the barrage of pain. She focused on keeping the water contained.

She looked into the collective. Jaycee's leaf was now the brightest on World Four. It lay at the centre of the Arkaiyan leaves and beside it, faint, was the bud of her child, the one that had linked her to Tezroi.

'If you won't leave to save yourself, leave to save your baby.'

Jaycee cried out.

'Your child lives,' Tchardin said. *'I didn't lie about Tezroi and I don't lie now. I was never a part of this, but I* will *leave, and the water* will *fall.'*

The queen fled. Her thoughts slowly faded from Tchardin's mind, but she doubted she would ever forget them. Tchardin surveyed the damage to the hold while she waited for Jaycee to escape to a safe distance. She wasn't sure how long it would take but she expected the queen to go up in the tunnels, while the water would first go down.

The shape of the great room was completely different than it had been when Tchardin arrived. Its walls were cracked and scraped, the balconies and platforms were gone, and the ceiling had crumbled until it was only water, held up by pandinzori. Glass was a horrible weapon when used against the kandar.

Tchardin thought of Derkra. So simple and beautiful. There was no glass there and no destruction. Or there hadn't been, until the fire. She opened the shift, thinking of Calendrai, remembering Tith's welcoming leaves. She had to be able to shift there now. Hadn't she seen enough?

She broke the ice.

Part III

Chapter 26

Something landed in the sand. Cien wasn't strong enough to shift on yet. He hadn't even moved. Damarin had arrived much earlier this time. He used the strength her presence gave him to angle his prone body so he could see her.

She knelt in the sand. Her body trembled, mostly hidden in dark shadow. Her lips moved slightly as if she spoke and her eyes were shut tight. He strained to hear her. He put all of his gathered strength into it.

She regained her composure quickly. "You don't look as bad as I thought you would," she said.

She stood and walked towards him. Her skin was darker than it should be and gleamed in the light. Red dripped down one of her legs onto the sand.

"What happened to you?" he asked.

She looked down at herself and shivered. "Nothing that won't fix itself now that I'm back on Derkra."

She raised her right arm out of the shadows that concealed her and stared at it as if to will it back to normal. One side of it was dark and ragged and red.

"I've never seen anything like that," Cien said. Was this the source of her discomfort upon arrival?

"It happened on World Four. Glass is a powerful weapon, but this doesn't feel like anything. My discomfort comes from killing humans."

Cien's eyes widened.

She looked down at him. "They'd convince you they're more than kandar. They're not—they can't be, given how they were made—I know that now. But their minds seem so complex, and they make so much pandinzori..."

She trailed off and her eyes lost focus. Cien studied her leaf in the collective to understand her meaning but only got a sense of confusion from her. Killing humans. On the Earths. If Tchardin was on the Earths, he hoped she hadn't been involved.

"How much farther do you plan to take me?" There must be a point where even she would be incapacitated. He had to get back to his people.

Damarin dropped her arm into the shadows that disguised her body and sighed, responding to his unspoken thoughts instead of his question. "I'm sure such a place exists, but it's a long way from here."

"What will you do when we reach it?"

"I'll find a new way to keep you, if I have to." She stood above him and seemed her usual confident self again. "If I find myself too weak I could just wait it out with you in the sand. Things should change with or without me now."

He wasn't ready to go on. If she forced him through the shift this early he was sure he would die. He lowered his gaze, unable to meet her eyes.

A soft thump rippled through the sand. Cien jerked his body upright. He didn't believe for a moment it was rescue. Someone was helping her.

A devoshai Cien had never seen before stood at the crest of the nearest dune. His aura and skin were dark, almost black. Cien was relieved at the sight of him. He couldn't have handled the betrayal had her accomplice been one of his people, one of the light-skinned Black Valley kandar. The devoshai had even more pandinzori around him than Damarin did. He descended the slope to join her.

"Who is this?" the devoshai asked.

"This is Cien," Damarin answered.

"I am the Shadow of Black Valley," Cien said.

The devoshai ignored him. "You were serious then?"

No emotion touched his face or voice when he spoke. Cien felt him enter the collective.

"Completely," Damarin responded.

She indicated they should move away. Cien watched the two backs retreat as he considered the newest addition to the collective in his mind. *Ruon*. The devoshai was a guardian. What was he doing on Land Side? The guardians were never meant to come to Derkra. They were required to stay with their Earths.

Their conversation continued for a while and Cien thought only about somehow drawing on the obscene amount of pandinzori that surrounded the guardian. Ruon turned away from Damarin and strode back to Cien.

"I am Ruon," he said, "guardian of World Four. I will be the Shadow of Derkra now."

Cien recoiled from the words. Damarin had taken Cien away from his people, confined him to the desert and near death, but no one could take his position. The kandar had chosen him. "I am the Shadow of Black Valley for life. There is no Shadow of Derkra."

"There are two kandaran cities now, are there not? I will be the Shadow of all the kandar."

"This is getting out of control," Cien said to Damarin. "A guardian has no claim on Derkra."

"He will make trouble," Ruon said as if Cien hadn't spoken. "Why not just kill him?"

Cien saw a flicker of fear in Damarin's eyes.

"We need to keep him alive," she said.

"Why?"

"Because the future queen of the kandar is his dodenzinn."

Cien almost blurted out the real reason. Ruon's next words stopped him.

"You want to rule the kandar, yet you keep the queen and Shadow alive. I do not understand."

"You don't need to," Damarin said, meeting Cien's gaze.

"Rule the kandar?" Cien asked.

"There may be no other way to get them to listen."

"You'd need the golden aura for that."

"I might," she said.

Cien was furious. Damarin turned to walk away. He struggled to rise, to follow her, but found himself surrounded by solid pandinzori. The guardian glared at him.

"He would not afford you the same grace," Ruon said. "He wishes you harm, you know."

"Of course he does." Damarin turned back. "I'm not worried."

"Are you sure you want them alive? I could just bury him." The immense swath of pandinzori that surrounded the guardian began to spin and pick up sand. "It would be so easy."

Damarin's smile vanished. "No," she said, holding the guardian's gaze. "Both he and the future queen must live. For now."

Ruon dropped the sand around him. It was as if the whole thing had been done unconsciously, as if he didn't know what he did. "You will continue to hold him?"

Damarin shrugged. "This has worked so far."

"You cannot keep him out here forever. If you take him far enough and he survives, there will be a point where he grows strong enough to return despite you, and once he does he will be difficult to deal with. Even for me."

"Do you have a better idea?"

The guardian's dark eyes lit up and a smile came onto his lips. "A glass cage."

Instinct made Cien move. He willed the pandinzori that pressed his aura to be his and somehow, perhaps through desperation, it worked. Power flooded through him. He opened the shift towards the great tree's call. His strength waned as Ruon pushed back against his assault but the portal remained open. He lunged towards it, away from the two kandar who would put him in a cage, who would confine him in glass.

Ruon caught him before he could enter it, trapping him in a wall of pandinzori. Cien tried to take the power for himself but this time the guardian resisted and Cien's fragile mind slipped away. The shift vanished. He fell to the sand and stayed there, all his stored strength used up.

"You may be right," Damarin said. "He's getting too strong too quickly."

Ruon seemed truly happy for the first time since he had arrived. The pandinzori around him swirled in intricate patterns. His control was astounding. "A glass cage it is, then."

Damarin nodded. "But how?"

"Leave that to me," the guardian said.

***

Sandin heard a voice. The voice wasn't in her ears, but in her mind. She didn't even have ears. She seemed to be only a mind. A vast blue mind.

'Sandin,' the voice said. *'Sandin! If only you could hear me.'*

'I hear you,' she answered. The voice sounded like Jaydin's, but somehow different.

'Then let me go and come towards the leaves.'

'What leaves?' Sandin thought, but for some reason her thoughts were words.

'Ovaeron's leaves!'

Her vision was ubiquitous. Everything was blue and unmoving and huge. The scale was incomprehensible. She didn't see any leaves and she didn't see the source of the voice. She saw everything and nothing.

'What's happening to me?' she asked.

'Focus, Sandin. Concentrate on my voice. Look through yourself—through the water—and find me. Find the leaves.'

Sandin searched for Jaydin's voice. Blue twisted past her, flowed with her, pushed against her, pulled her forwards. The blue was water. She was water. She was chaos. And there was Jaydin—a tiny current—struggling to separate itself from her vastness.

'Sandin!' Jaydin said. *'Find the red leaves and take us out of here.'*

Jaydin's voice was frantic but Sandin felt complete control as she expanded herself and searched out the leaves. They were small—on the same scale as Jaydin's tiny thread of water. Sandin hadn't been able to see them in her previous, colossal state, just as she hadn't recognised herself as water.

'They're here.' She directed Jaydin towards them effortlessly.

"Sandin," a voice said.

Sandin opened her eyes. Jaydin stood over her, her face full of concern.

"Was it really you?" Sandin remembered the power, the vastness of herself. "In my mind?"

"It was." Jaydin studied her for a moment, the concern fading. "I really hoped you would still hear me."

Sandin sat up on the black sand, feeling her body around her again. A huge, dark trunk stood before her and blocked her view of the valley. He must be Ovaeron. His size was incredible. He was wider even than Tith. She twisted herself to look around.

"Are you surprised?" she said as she took in the new sights. "Why would one trip through the shift change me?"

"I guess I'm not surprised. Just a little sad. You have a powerful mind. I'm impressed."

Sandin smiled, but hid it from her sister. The statement filled her with joy, though nothing would come of it. She may have controlled the waters of the shift, brought them through unscathed without difficulty when her sisters considered the shift to be dangerous, but what good was a powerful mind if it couldn't touch pandinzori?

She got to her feet and looked over the sand. The valley was entirely new to her. She hadn't had an image of it provided to her as it had been to the others before birth. She only knew what Jaydin had described of it and that hadn't been much. Her mind reeled from the experience of the shift and from the reality of being in a place that wasn't Calendrai.

A devoshai walked past. He stared at them for a moment, then he turned to Sandin with his eyes wide.

"I thought my time with this was over," she said to Jaydin, "after all of Calendrai had heard about me."

Jaydin stared at her too. "I'm not sure it's that. You're drawing a surprising amount of pandinzori."

Sandin shook her head. The devoshai couldn't be so shocked by pandinzori. Jaydin was just accustomed to her flaw. Sandin turned away from her sister and stared right back at the devoshai until he kept moving. Word would spread of the tevadra who didn't exist in the collective. How strange she was. How different.

They would probably still stare. The kandar here were lightly coloured and Jaydin and Sandin would stand out like the dark trunks of the trees of Cens when they ventured into the yellow sand. At least it would be easy to see Tchardin and Damarin as well.

"Are they here?" she asked.

Jaydin closed her eyes for a moment. "No. It's just like my previous visit."

"Should we wait for them?"

"I sense Miadra on the other side of the valley." Jaydin turned to look in the direction Sandin assumed she could feel the tevadra. "Maybe she'll be willing to tell me exactly what's going on. As a member of the council I deserve to know."

Sandin nodded.

"You should explore the valley while I speak with Miadra," Jaydin said. "Acquaint yourself with its secret places. We may be moving here soon."

Sandin was surprised. "I thought you would just speak in your minds. I wouldn't be able to hear."

"I can't be sure she'll welcome you to sit in with us, as you're not a member of the council."

"I'm also not part of the collective."

"I know that," Jaydin said softly. "And Miadra should know it too when she sees you, but if she doesn't trust it I don't want to antagonise her."

Sandin realised she wasn't going to win the argument. "I guess I'll be wandering around, getting stared at."

"I'll find you later. If you see Damarin, bring her to us."

"I'll try."

Jaydin left the black sand beneath Ovaeron. She had never banned Sandin from anything before. It hurt a little, despite the fact that Sandin understood the necessity. This was a new place. The kandar might behave differently. Sandin turned away—more conscious of her strangeness than she had been in a long time—and studied the valley.

Black Valley was laid bare before her eyes. The stunted trees hid nothing and the valley was bright and without deep shadows. It didn't seem complex, but at least it was new. Perhaps it held secrets she couldn't see from the base of the great tree.

On the far side of the valley she saw a wall, broken up by black holes. They were the most interesting thing she could see and the most likely to hide her. She picked a large, dark space and headed towards it. As she walked across the valley she studied the kandar that inhabited it.

They all had light hair that matched their skin. The darkest hair she saw was several shades lighter than her own, which was light by Calendrai's standards. They had beautiful green or blue eyes. There were no blue-eyed kandar in Calendrai.

The lightly-coloured eyes followed her wherever she walked, widening upon discovery of her flaw. At first she tried to memorise faces, to distinguish one tevadra or devoshai from another, but without names to go with the faces she found it too difficult and gave up quickly.

The black hole she headed towards hadn't looked so big from a distance but now it was huge. Calendrai had nothing like this. The island's size was hidden by the forest, and anything in Cens could only be seen from up close. The black hole appeared to have a lighter shape inside it. Something tall and sinuous, like a tree.

Sandin craned her neck to see the top of the hole until movement in her peripheral vision caught her eye. A dark shape fell into the valley from the edge of the desert. It was a tevadra. The short black hair and dark skin told Sandin that unless Kadailin had changed her mind and come to Land Side, it had to be Damarin.

Sandin ran towards her. The tevadra rose and walked towards Ovaeron. The confidence in her stride confirmed her identity. There was a slight flash of surprise in her expression when she noticed Sandin's approach.

"How did *you* get here?" Damarin asked.

"I shifted with Jaydin."

"I'm amazed she was able to bring you through."

Sometimes Sandin was disappointed Damarin couldn't hear her thoughts as she did with all the other kandar. She was about to explain that she'd been the one who got them to Black Valley safely when she noticed a streak of red in the sand behind her sister. She looked more closely and there, behind the shifting shadows, were large splotches of deep red, almost black against Damarin's skin.

"What is that?" Sandin asked with alarm. It reminded her of something Jaydin had told her. "Are you bleeding?"

Damarin looked down at herself. "This is blood?"

"Don't pretend you don't know it." Sandin was shocked at Damarin's body. How could such a thing have happened? "I know Jaydin's told you about it too. But I didn't know kandar could bleed. I thought it was purely human."

"I don't know." A crimson pool had grown at one of Damarin's feet. "I have things to attend to now, if you don't mind."

Sandin blocked her from leaving. "How did it happen?"

"I made a mistake. One I will not allow myself to make again."

What could Damarin possibly have done to bleed? Sandin wondered but could come up with nothing.

"Have you seen Tchardin?" she asked instead. "You said you'd be looking for her."

"She's not here."

"And Cien?"

"I haven't found him either."

"Where were you, then?" Sandin asked. "Jaydin came to Black Valley and found all three of you gone. I was in Calendrai with Kadailin and she assured me none of you had returned. When I came here with Jaydin she couldn't sense you."

Damarin gave Sandin an exasperated look. "I was in the desert."

"Doing what?"

"Searching, of course. Where else could they be?"

Sandin turned away to look past the valley wall. If Damarin's leaf had darkened when she left Black Valley for the desert, Cien and Tchardin could be out there too. But where? And why?

"Is that all?" Damarin asked.

Without waiting for an answer, Damarin brushed past her and strode towards Ovaeron. She left bloody footprints in the sand. If Damarin had been searching for Tchardin and Cien in the desert, why was she bleeding? There was nothing out there.

Sandin went after Damarin and walked alongside her.

"I know you're thinking about something," Damarin said. "It bothers me that I can't hear you."

Sandin suppressed the urge to tell her sister what she was thinking.

"I've been thinking too," Damarin continued. "Would you like to know what about?"

Sandin didn't answer. Maybe Damarin knew where Tchardin and Cien were, and was only pretending to search for them. Where else could the blood have come from if not another kandar?

"Are you kandar, Sandin?" Damarin asked.

The words snapped Sandin out of her thoughts. "You can't be serious."

"I am." Damarin's voice was low and she sounded sincere, but the question was ridiculous.

"Of course I'm kandar. How could I not be?"

"But how do you know?"

"We're in Black Valley," Sandin said, "birthplace of the kandar. All those that pass us are kandar. All those that live here are kandar. Look at me!" Her strangeness had just been judged countless times and here was Damarin—who knew her, whose father was her father—insulting it further. To ask her if she was kandar? It was the cruellest thing anyone had ever done to her, even if Damarin didn't mean it to be. "Look at my body. I have an aura just like you do. Look at my skin. The shadows that cling to it—"

"So you were born here, and you look like us, but what if you'd been born on an Earth?"

Sandin was silent in her rage. The question meant nothing to her.

Damarin was relentless. "If you woke on the floor of a human forest and knew nothing but your name—as you did when you woke beneath Tith—what would you be then?"

"Jaydin told me my name. I was born knowing nothing at all."

Damarin's expressionless veneer cracked for a moment. Sandin was surprised to learn her sister didn't know that.

"You're evading my question," Damarin said.

Sandin rolled her eyes. "I'd still be kandar if I were born on an Earth."

"I don't think you would be. I'd be kandar if I were born on an Earth, as would any of us born with the collective in our minds and the knowledge of what we are, but not you. You can't see pandinzori, can't touch it. Your camouflage would wrap you and you'd believe yourself to be just as human as any of them. Jaydin had to tell you you were kandar for you to know it. As for what you've become since your birth..." Damarin paused and stopped walking. She looked into Sandin's eyes. "Maybe you're one of us now. Maybe you're more, or less. I'm unsure."

"I was born of a tree, Damarin. Our father, Tith. I am kandar and have always been kandar, regardless of my flaw."

"It may not be so simple anymore." Damarin turned to face Ovaeron. "Things are changing. I will prove it beyond a doubt soon."

Sandin shook her head. Clearly there was no reasoning with Damarin. What she had said was nonsense. The people of Derkra were kandar, and Sandin had been born on Water Side, just as Damarin was.

"Jaydin wants to talk to you," she said, changing the subject. "You must be able to sense her here. She should be with Miadra."

"I'll find Jaydin later. At first I was annoyed at your presence, but perhaps it's better she's here to see this."

"What are you going to do?"

"I could tell you, but you'll see soon enough."

Damarin took off across the sand, running towards Ovaeron. Sandin followed. She might not have access to pandinzori and she might not have the collective, but she was just as fast as any other kandar. She kept pace with Damarin, then began to gain on her. Her younger sister stole a glance back at her, and suddenly Sandin ran into a wall.

It was a shock to stop so quickly. There was nothing in front of her. She shook herself and ran again. She hit another wall. This time it pushed her back, the sand coming with it. Damarin was stopping her with pandinzori.

Sandin leaned into the invisible barrier but she knew resistance would accomplish nothing. She skidded across the valley as it pushed her, her shoulder braced against a solid mass of air and sand. The kandar watched her. She was pushed past a pair of devoshai and the sand parted in front of them. They ignored it.

She was pushed all the way to the far edge of the valley, where she finally stopped struggling. She slumped to her knees, exhausted, and was pushed a short bit further before the force dissipated. She lifted a hand to feel for it but if the pandinzori remained there it had gone back to its natural state.

It was the first time pandinzori had been used against her so forcefully. She couldn't have stopped it. She couldn't even see it. Maybe Damarin had a point. Was she truly kandar?

***

"Did you find your future queen?"

Jaydin kept her eyes on Cotelle's huge frame while Miadra spoke, oblivious to her dodenzinn's intimidation factor. The two had softened since their first meeting but Jaydin still felt they viewed her as an intruder.

"We haven't been able to sense her anywhere," Jaydin said. "Her leaf remains hanging in the collective but there is no longer any light to it."

Miadra frowned. "Then it's just as likely she's dead as alive. Even if she lives, why should she become queen when she abandons the kandar?"

"Because she has the golden aura." Jaydin felt silly saying that. It was so obvious it shouldn't need to be stated, but the obvious appeared to have changed at some point without her consent.

If Miadra didn't accept what she said it would be hard to convince the tevadra of her authority on the subject. It was written in her notebook. It had been told to her directly by Tith, as it had been told to all the kandar by their fathers, but that didn't seem to matter to Miadra. Just as Jaydin was about to try again, the earth moved.

"What—" Miadra said, but her voice was cut off as the collective exploded with thought.

Jaydin looked across the valley and took a moment to resolve what she saw with what should be there. The whole of the earth literally shook. A thought came into her mind. A memory. *Earthquake.* Her legs buckled as the earth surged beneath her feet.

Cotelle sheltered Miadra against the wall of the valley under his massive bulk and the two remained relatively stable, but Jaydin was bounced and dragged across the desert like a leaf in the wind on the Earths. She solidified pandinzori around her and watched it continue from stillness. The noise was deafening. None of the other kandar would know what to do, but did she?

It was an earthquake. On Derkra. When would it end? Was there anything to be done with pandinzori that could stop it? Sandin was in Black Valley. What would happen to her sister if it got worse? She wouldn't be able to protect herself. The thoughts of the collective were full of fear and confusion.

As quickly as it had come, the shaking died down. It hadn't vanished, only moved on. Jaydin let go of the pandinzori around her and watched as the tremor rocked across the valley, through Ovaeron who shook tremendously—shedding a red haze onto the sand as his leaves fell—and past him in the direction of the water. Miadra and Cotelle joined her as the roaring got louder. A shelf of earth rose into the sky beside Ovaeron.

Jaydin ran towards the great tree to get a better view. She shot by kandar who were only just getting to their feet after the immense quake had passed, keeping her eyes on the monstrosity that was being drawn from the sand. It was becoming a mountain, wreathed in pandinzori and growing taller by the second.

Jaydin vaulted up Ovaeron's trunk, pulling herself over his bark until she reached a large, low branch. She leapt onto it and threw herself towards the next. When she was high enough she ran along a branch to emerge amidst the leaves into the blue sky. But there was no sky to see, for the mountain—now reaching to half Ovaeron's height—blocked her view to the water.

Yellow pandinzori encircled it. There was a blazing mass of it between Ovaeron and the mountain as if the first tree of existence had been the builder.

Jaydin's mind raced. She thought of earthquakes and mountains on the Earths and knew this was not a natural fusion of the two. Earthquakes could force the earth into the air but in this case it was all wrong. Derkra had shuddered at the force of the mountain emerging from the earth. It hadn't pressed it out.

Then she saw a tevadra hovering slightly above ground between the base of the tree and the mountain. The pandinzori that was drawn from Ovaeron and the nine hundred swept first over this tiny spot of a kandar below. Jaydin opened her mind and looked at the collective. It was Damarin who stood there, as if she had built the mountain. The yellow colour of the pandinzori should have told Jaydin its master but what was happening was impossible. The sheer force of mind it would take to change the face of Derkra was beyond any kandar. It should have been beyond Damarin.

What could Jaydin do? She couldn't stop all that pandinzori on her own. She certainly couldn't put the mountain back into the desert. The damage was done. She watched Damarin, looking for some clue as to how her sister had done it.

The mountain stopped growing in height—finishing where its crest levelled out with Ovaeron's crown—but pandinzori still pulsed into and around it, swirling dark and grey. Then Jaydin noticed the pandinzori no longer ran through Damarin at all, but onto the peak of the mountain.

She climbed higher into Ovaeron. Kandar stood amongst his leaves—blank looks on their faces—and passively watched while more pandinzori than they had likely ever seen brushed by them and out to the mountain. As Jaydin climbed she thought she felt the mind that drew the pandinzori. Some kandar she didn't know. She broke out of the canopy and saw him.

A devoshai—dark as any from Calendrai but unknown to her—stood at the apex of the mountain. Jaydin knew immediately that he had the power to build this, even if Damarin did not. By his mind the pandinzori entered the rock and the mountain hollowed. Caves formed in it, darker shadows against its darkness, and suddenly the mountain was on fire.

Jaydin jumped back into Ovaeron's leaves by instinct. Liquid red and yellow burst from the caves, swallowing the pandinzori outside them. The stone blackened, and melted, then hardened—a crust forming on it as it burned a path down the side of the mountain.

She was terrified the fire would engulf Ovaeron, and only this forced her out of his shadows to monitor the spectacle. Her mastery of pandinzori would be of little help if Damarin or the dark devoshai sought to burn the valley, but she could try. She had to.

The fire didn't pour from the mountain for long, but it came quickly, forming a pool of incandescent red in the sand before it hardened into black rock. Some of Ovaeron's fallen leaves had been swallowed up by it, and those that were left formed a carpet of mock fire that extended it outwards and covered the black sand at the tree's base. Luckily the real fire hadn't approached his trunk.

'Miadra,' she whispered in her mind, searching out the tevadra's leaf in the collective that trembled with voices. She put all her power into connecting with the High Seat, despite their possible distance. It turned out Miadra wasn't far, just below Jaydin in the tree. *'Call a council meeting. Now.'*

There was no response. Then the collective pulsed along its red leaves. The entire council was called. Relief flooded through Jaydin and she settled back against one of Ovaeron's branches. A small pulse of discomfort seemed to radiate across her aura at his touch. She frowned, but ignored it, looking to the caves. She would find Sandin later. This time Miadra had to let her in.

Chapter 27

Jaydin stood apart from the small crowd of kandar in the cave. In Calendrai she would have waited with Anatoly or Kadailin but here she was alone. The Black Valley council members gathered in groups and spoke silently amongst themselves, glancing at her from time to time with unreadable expressions. She listened to the slight buzz of their thoughts but was unable to discern any meaning. They were surprisingly calm given what had just taken place in the valley.

Jaydin flinched as the memory of liquid fire invaded her thoughts. The creation of the monstrous rock was one thing, but fire? How had the devoshai done that? It should have been impossible, even with the mind he appeared to possess. Shouldn't the fire have swallowed the pandinzori he used to create it? She wondered if he would make an appearance at the meeting. Or if Damarin would.

The Black Valley council meetings took place in one of the larger caves in the valley wall. Jaydin stood with her back to the cave opening and felt exposed, despite the shadow that masked the entrance. At least Miadra had led her here through a tunnel under the ground that filtered into the back, so her arrival had been hidden.

Miadra stood by one of those tunnels at the back of the cave. The tevadra was surrounded by the largest group of kandar and appeared to be conversing with them. Their thoughts were impossible to distinguish over the dull roar in the room.

Cotelle stood by himself against one of the walls. He was easy to pick out because of his size. He and Miadra exchanged a glance over the heads of the council and Jaydin focused on their leaves in an attempt to catch their thoughts. She heard nothing until Cotelle's voice echoed through the cave.

'Silence, everyone. The High Seat will speak now.'

Their ability to communicate secretly over the thoughts in the cave was impressive. The kandar here were reserved—as a small group their thoughts sounded nothing like those of the rest of the collective—but they were still loud, and Jaydin hadn't detected even a trace of Miadra and Cotelle's words. Now the council became silent.

"Yes," Miadra said, moving to stand alone before the group of kandar. "I think you should hear what I have to say in my own words."

Jaydin was surprised to hear Miadra speak aloud. Perhaps it would be easier to get Sandin to join the council here than in Calendrai. She took a step towards the High Seat but decided to see how Miadra handled the meeting before saying anything herself. Jaydin would be nothing to these kandar. Miadra was their leader.

"You've all seen our new valley"—the High Seat paused as quiet thoughts buzzed over the assembled kandar—"I think I can confidently say it's all we hoped it would be. A clear sign that our world is changing. That our purpose will change."

"Wait," Jaydin heard herself say. This wasn't what Miadra was supposed to be telling them. She should have denounced Damarin for her destruction of Land Side, should have soothed the kandar in the face of their fear. The devoshai closest to Jaydin turned to glare at her.

'Who are you?' came to her, floating over the collective. The words had no obvious source. The kandar who spoke to her was unknown.

'The High Seat speaks,' another said.

Cotelle looked at Jaydin too.

"The mountain on Land Side is just the beginning," Miadra said. "Soon we will have everything the humans have."

Jaydin took another step towards the other kandar. Many of them had turned now and they looked at her like an enemy. She had never seen such anger before. She had thought the kandar incapable of expressing so much. A voice entered her mind.

'You've come,' it said.

The voice was Damarin's. All thoughts of the impossible situation Jaydin found herself in left her mind. She focused on her sister's leaf. Damarin was close, but Jaydin hadn't seen her in the crowd.

'Yes,' she answered, relying on the collective to pass her words to Damarin, *'I'm here. How long did you think you could keep this up without me finding out?'*

'A little longer, at least.'

Jaydin looked through the last pocket of kandar in the cave. Damarin was not among them. Her leaf indicated she was close, but she didn't seem to be at the meeting. A dark spot in the corner of Jaydin's eye drew her gaze. She turned.

A tevadra stood in the sand of the valley just outside the council shadow. Her identity was exposed to any kandar who wished to see and she looked through the shadow straight at Jaydin. She stepped into the darkness. Miadra stopped talking. All eyes fell on Damarin.

"It is with pleasure," Damarin said, "that I once again welcome you to my council, Jaydin."

Jaydin was stunned. Damarin had just broken the only real rule the kandar had on Derkra, and she had done so in spectacular fashion. Jaydin might let the names of council members slip on occasion, but she had never exposed herself or anyone else in a way that couldn't be disputed. If any kandar had been watching from the valley Damarin had just made it clear she was a council member. The secret didn't matter much without the Earths, but the act of keeping it was still held sacred.

"You're forgetting that I was the one to introduce you to Calendrai's council," Jaydin said, still trying to understand exactly what was happening. None of the council members said anything about Damarin's unconventional entrance. "I was a member long before you were even born."

"And yet it was never yours."

"I never wanted it."

"I thought as much." Damarin stood just inside the entrance to the cave, framed by the light from the valley. "That's why I was so surprised to find you trying to take my place when I returned to Calendrai. Maybe you're changing."

Jaydin shook her head. Damarin and her talk of change.

"You certainly hold more pandinzori than you once did," her sister continued. "Everyone in here seems to."

For the first time since she'd entered the cave, Jaydin noticed the power available to those around her. Pandinzori was sparse everywhere on Land Side—even in Ovaeron's branches—and yet the shadow was full of its shimmering light. She blinked. If she had noticed that before she might have remained silent. The looks the kandar had given her combined with the pandinzori they held frightened her.

The kandar moved apart, opening a path between Damarin and Miadra. The two of them might share an idea, but what did the High Seat think of this intrusion? The Black Valley council was supposed to be hers.

'It was *hers,'* Damarin answered her thoughts, *'and it will be again, in due time. She knows that.'*

Damarin moved towards Jaydin, her features emerging from the darkness of silhouette. There was something strange about her skin. It couldn't be what Jaydin thought it was. It looked like blood.

"What happened to you?" she whispered.

There was nothing on Derkra to cause that. Damarin looked past her to the kandar of the council. The shadows around her grew thicker. Jaydin followed her gaze. The kandar of Black Valley might not know what it was. Perhaps Damarin didn't want them to.

"What's really going on here?" Jaydin asked, louder.

"I've been meeting with the Black Valley council since I first arrived here with Tchardin. I'm sure you've figured that out by now."

"You're the High Seat in Calendrai. It's only natural you would—"

"I'm more than that now. I have to be, if I'm going to lead our people."

"Lead our people?" Jaydin turned back to the council in shock. She expected a similar reaction from them but saw nothing. If anything they were excited. "In what way? The High Seat can only advise. Tchardin will be our queen by kandaran law, by the hierarchy given to us by Tchar on Coralynth."

"That"—Damarin gestured to the cave opening and out to the mountain beside Ovaeron—"is my Coralynth. The new Coralynth. It doesn't belong to Tchar, only to the kandar. It belongs to Derkra. That is where the laws will be made now."

So the mountain was supposed to be some sort of display of control? Of course the kandar of Black Valley would be ignorant to what it really was, but did the council know?

"That isn't Coralynth, Damarin. That is something very different."

"A fire mountain," Damarin said. "A volcano. I remember what you told me."

"Then you remember they were used to destroy, when kandar killed humans in the war."

"I do. It's perfect really. The kandar need something to help them move on. A sign, as Miadra said."

"To move on from what?"

"Creator's Purpose." Damarin smiled.

Jaydin's mind filled with the few images she had of the kandaran war. Kandar burning humans with fire from the earth. Kandar burying humans under mountains of snow and ice. Kandar killing kandar. She pushed the images away.

"This desecration has nothing to do with the Purpose," she said, "and nothing to do with Tchar and Dani's home. You can't even claim ignorance. You know that just as I do."

"I know everything, just as you do. You made sure of that. Perhaps we feel differently about it because I didn't get to hear it from Tith. I heard it from you, and with it I heard the flaws in it."

The flaws? How could there be flaws in Jaydin's memory? What she had learned from Tith—what she had passed on to Damarin from him—was simply the truth. There were holes in it, and Damarin knew that, but what Jaydin *had* passed on was complete and perfect. She was about to respond when she noticed the kandar at the back of the cave were moving. Even Miadra had left her spot at the centre of the crowd. Pandinzori gathered there. The kandar parted to let a devoshai through. Jaydin froze.

His presence was immense. He wasn't physically big like Ryten or Cotelle, but he was imposing in a way she had never experienced. His dark eyes met hers and she shivered. When he got close enough to join the collective she knew why.

The devoshai was Ruon, guardian of World Four and as old as existence itself. The stories Tith had told of him failed to capture his magnificence. The magnificence of a guardian, powerful beyond measure, beyond the kandar because he was whole, with no dodenzinn to hold half his strength. She was in awe, but she was also afraid. He had helped Damarin build a mountain on Derkra and filled it with fire. What was he doing away from his Earth?

'The humans drove me away with their atrocities.' His mindvoice was like a black whisper. *'I would have abandoned my Earth a long time ago, had I been able.'*

'Abandoned?' Jaydin asked before she had a chance to think. *'But you couldn't have. You're a guardian, you—'*

'I am here,' he spoke over her.

Now the brightness of pandinzori in the cave was impossible to bear. It was intensely concentrated around the guardian. He seemed to draw it away from the other kandar.

"Ruon is going to help us change the Purpose," Damarin said. "Coralynth was his idea."

"Yes," Ruon said. "Land Side is much improved."

Jaydin glanced at Ruon then closed her eyes to see the collective more clearly. She held Damarin's leaf in her mind, crimson and blazing, and tried harder than she had ever tried before to speak only to her.

'Damarin.' She had to keep the guardian out of her mind. *'Send him back to World Four and stop this now, on your own, before I'm forced to intervene.'*

'What could you possibly do?'

There was one thing she could do. Something only she and Ruon would truly remember, but something Damarin should understand. She could only hope the full weight of the threat would come through.

'There are three times as many kandar on Calendrai as there are in Black Valley. If you make me bring them here it will not be to join you.'

Damarin laughed. Jaydin opened her eyes at the sound. The council members watched them in silence. Ruon tilted his head.

'You would start another war?' Damarin's mindvoice was serious despite her outburst.

'Only if you make me.'

The two tevadra locked eyes.

'It means that much to you?' Damarin asked. *'Enough that you, Jaydin—who was shown the lifeless bodies of kandar spread across Black Valley and through the Worlds, who was shown what we can do when we want to destroy—would give that back to the kandar when they've forgotten it?'*

Jaydin only hesitated for a moment. *'You've already given them part of it. The Purpose is all we have, Damarin. If you take it away, what then is a kandar worth?'*

Damarin pursed her lips. *'I asked that question once.'*

'You did, but I don't want the answer you found.'

'So you want a war instead? Over the Purpose?'

'I want you to realise you can't win a war. And that I will do whatever it takes to stop you from destroying us.'

'Can't win a war? Oh, sister, I have a guardian with me. And if he isn't enough, there are more kandar here—in this council—that will follow me, than there are in all of Calendrai who would follow you.'

'You underestimate me—'

'No, Jaydin.' Damarin frowned. *'You overestimate the kandar.'*

Ruon took a step towards her. For a second Jaydin was worried. She had been caught up in the argument and wasn't sure how loudly they were speaking. He might have been able to hear them. He stared at her, his expression unreadable. How devoted was he to Damarin's cause? Could she die here, now, before she had a chance to warn the kandar in Calendrai? Damarin's words echoed in her mind. Was she overestimating their people? Would a warning even matter?

'She could be a problem,' Ruon said. Jaydin was surprised he let her hear.

'She will be,' Damarin replied, *'but not as big of a problem as she wants to be. And I need her. Just like the others.'*

Ruon looked away from Jaydin. He scanned the assembled kandar in the shadow.

"Let us leave," he said.

"This isn't over," Jaydin said, but the council members were already heeding his words.

They didn't leave through the tunnels in the back of the cave, but moved past her, exiting the shadow through the exposed entrance. They walked, alone or in groups, through the barrier between the secret space of the council and the very open sand of the valley. They didn't bring any shadow with them. Jaydin forced herself not to look away.

Miadra was the last of them to leave. When she was gone, Ruon followed. He looked back at Jaydin as he left. Damarin moved beside her.

"Your skin," Jaydin said. "Did he do that to you?"

Damarin laughed. “We haven’t come to that yet.”

“He’s dangerous.” Jaydin wrenched her gaze from her sister’s body. Who could have done that to Damarin if not the guardian? Who among the kandar would know how? “He’s a threat to Derkra itself. A guardian has no place here.”

“Every kandar has a place here. It’s only the humans I propose we exclude.”

Jaydin’s skin prickled. “We were created for them.”

Damarin didn’t answer, but for once Jaydin clearly heard her think. Her red leaf blazed in the collective and Jaydin was given images of all the time they’d spent together. Damarin was the only kandar who really cared about the things Tith had told Jaydin. Their middle sister had never simply listened, like Sandin did, and never run away like Tchardin. Arguments came to Jaydin from ages ago, before Tchardin’s birth, before Damarin was High Seat. How could Jaydin have known all those words would ultimately lead to this? Had Damarin known they would?

“I’ve been wondering,” Damarin said, her thoughts quieting. “Has Tith told you any more since you were born?”

Still asking, still searching for knowledge. “You need more to use against me?”

“I wouldn’t have to if you’d join me.”

Now it was Jaydin’s turn to laugh. She went to leave but Damarin’s hand broke through her aura and landed on her shoulder, stopping her. Waves of unpleasantness rolled through Jaydin’s body.

“Sandin’s name,” Damarin said. “Did Tith give it to you to give to her?”

Jaydin closed her eyes. She resisted the impulse to break away from Damarin’s touch. Their middle sister had always wanted to know everything, needed to know it. Jaydin held her thoughts close, confident she could hide them from Damarin. Tith hadn’t spoken to her since she was born. Jaydin had given Sandin her name when she realised the tevadra would never get the one Tith meant for her. This, Damarin would never know.

“You’ll never learn another thing from me,” she said, turning back. She lifted Damarin’s hand off her shoulder and let it drop. “I will stop you. I promise you that.”

Now her sister’s eyes met her own. “Look at their pandinzori, Jaydin.”

The council members spread out in the valley. Pandinzori covered them thickly and twisted between them, writhing across the sand and spiralling around the small trees when it met them. The scene was amazing. Their behaviour was appalling. Jaydin was struck silent.

"It's already too late," Damarin said. "No one can stop me now."

Jaydin brushed past Damarin and out of the cave, leaving the dark tevadra alone in the shadow. She refused to follow the rest of the council and expose herself by walking across the sand, so she turned to the valley wall.

Sandin walked out of a small cave in front of her when she rounded the corner, startling her. Jaydin let the council shadow drop.

"Is that the council?" her sister asked.

Jaydin frowned as she watched the white backs disappear between the scraggly trees of the valley. She tried to ignore the storm of pandinzori and the dark guardian who followed them. "Not anymore. Not as far as I'm concerned."

"What happened?"

"We're going back to Calendrai," Jaydin said, ignoring the question. She wanted to put distance between herself and Damarin as quickly as possible. She began to walk along the valley's edge and Sandin fell in with her quietly. "Something must be done about this but we can't do it here. Not yet."

Jaydin's brisk pace quickly brought them into view of the mountain.

"What is it?" Sandin asked, stopping. They looked up at its foreboding height.

"Coralynth," Jaydin said, and heard the venom in her own voice. "That's what Damarin called it. Coralynth. It's a volcano. A fire mountain. Brought to Derkra by the guardian of an Earth."

"A guardian? Why would a guardian come to Derkra?"

"I don't know why he came, but I know it's wrong. The guardians are supposed to stay with their Earths forever. There hasn't been a guardian on Derkra since they first left, just after they were born."

"What could be happening on the Earths to make him come here?" Sandin asked.

Jaydin turned back to the cave. The shadowed entrance seemed to pump pandinzori into the valley. Jaydin was struck with a thought, remembering the times her sister's leaf had grown dark before she first went to Land Side with Tchardin, and how many times it had been dark since. "Damarin," she whispered.

"Damarin?"

"I think—" Jaydin said, overwhelmed for a moment by the words she planned to speak. "I think Damarin has been to an Earth."

Chapter 28

Ryten looked out from his father's branches into open air above Cens, towards Tith, Sirrhon, and Ahron. Now that the forest failed to conceal his height it was evident Del was much taller than those that surrounded him. It had always been obvious he was kandaran, as he had a name all kandar knew, but it had never been so clear he was magnificent.

Unable to find any spiders in Cens, Ryten had sought out the sleeping kandar in Ahron's branches. He had hoped to find peace there but in the end he had found too much of it. The indifference of the kandar had begun to grate on him. None of them cared that their future queen was gone, and some seemed not to have noticed at all. He'd been unable to sleep, unable to ignore them, so he'd retreated to solitude in Del.

A voice floated into his mind.

'Have you heard anything from Tchardin?'

He searched the collective for its source and found the voice belonged to Ocien. He looked down and saw her making her way up through Del.

'Ocien,' he answered, acknowledging her presence. After a few moments she pulled herself up beside him and sat down to share the branch. "She's still missing."

"They've all gone to Land Side now," she said. "All but Kadailin."

"They have." At least some of the kandar had noticed.

"Maybe we should go there too."

Ryten lay back against one of Del's branches. "You would leave the forest?"

"Torshe says it's not much of a forest anymore."

Ryten was surprised to hear that. Torshe was Ocien's dodenzinn, and while the devoshai had never liked Ryten, they shared the bond of being born in Cens. Ryten didn't think he could leave. "Your fathers are here."

Ocien looked away. "I just heard Jaydin will kill the damaged trees. I've also heard Tchardin is dead. That Damarin will rule in her place."

The first parts were shocking but the last part was impossible. "Who said that?"

Ocien didn't reply. Ryten closed his eyes and watched the pandinzori in Del's branches flow. Colours came to him unbidden. After an indeterminate amount of time he opened his eyes and said, "The council will deal with the fire and Tchardin is not dead. I would know if she was."

"Are you sure?"

"I'm sure." Even if he wasn't, it couldn't hurt to say he was. If the kandar were saying the things Ocien said they were, someone needed to be certain of something.

Ocien gave no indication of having heard him. She stared out at the three brothers and her thoughts buzzed softly. Ryten joined her. It wasn't such a bad way to spend his time while he waited for Tchardin to return. She couldn't be dead, and Damarin would never rule in her place. Tchardin had the golden aura.

"Jaydin has returned," Ocien said.

Ryten saw the tevadra before he had a chance to search the collective. She appeared between the trees below them as if from nowhere. Ryten remembered the hidden spot they'd found in Cens the last time she was on Calendrai.

He dropped off the branch. It wasn't as far down as a drop from Tith, but it was still dangerous. He used pandinzori to shield himself from the branches that flew at him until he was free in the air. Then he slowed himself. Jaydin spoke to him before he made it to the ground.

'Ryten,' she said as he descended. *'You need to learn to shift. Not only to open it, but to travel through it safely. And Ocien,'* she shifted her gaze to look above Ryten, *'it would be best for you to learn as well, if you wish to. I have to go back to Black Valley, but before I do I'm going to ensure the skill doesn't remain solely with them.'*

"What's happening?" Ryten asked as he landed in the grass in front of her. Ocien dropped down beside him.

"If the worst comes to pass, we could go to war again."

Ryten exchanged a glance with Ocien. "Is it Damarin?"

"It is," Jaydin said.

"And Tchardin?"

Ryten knew the answer from the look on Jaydin's face. The future queen was still missing.

Sandin appeared at Jaydin's side and Ryten was startled despite that the trees didn't hide her like they used to. He looked into her eyes for a moment before Jaydin spoke again.

"The trees," Jaydin whispered distractedly, looking up into the leaves. "We need to do something about them soon."

Ocien's leaf gave off a quick buzz of thought before she silenced herself. Her eyes remained wide.

"So you've heard," Jaydin said. "What exactly has Marr been saying about me?"

"Marr?" Ryten asked.

"It was Marr who told me Jaydin plans to kill the trees," Ocien said. "He has told every kandar whose father was burned in the fire."

"Your father was damaged?" Jaydin asked.

"No, but Buran was."

Ryten's brow furrowed in confusion but Jaydin clearly understood. *'Torshe,'* she said to Ryten alone. *'If he goes to rest in his injured father he'll go mad and Ocien's future selves will have to live without a dodenzinn. Worst of all, they might never know he was gone.'*

Ryten understood that fear. *'What should we do?'*

'We have to kill the trees, regardless of who's affected. It's the only way to fix the forest and save the kandar. I hope another tree will call him. If one does not, at least they'll have a choice, at the end.'

It was extreme, but Ryten knew Jaydin was the only kandar equipped to predict the consequences of the fire. If Torshe was allowed to return to Buran and was reborn insane, the new generation would have no idea how to deal with it, and no way of knowing who his dodenzinn would be. If Buran was destroyed instead, and no tree claimed Torshe when Ocien was called, the tevadra could choose not to rest and die with her dodenzinn.

Ocien's gaze moved between them. Ryten wasn't sure if she could hear them or if she was only insinuating she knew they were speaking. Jaydin turned towards her.

"The damaged trees are as good as dead already. In fact, they're worse. Buran is broken inside. If you let Torshe return to him he will be broken too. Possibly forever."

Ocien looked at the ground. Her thoughts buzzed quietly around them.

"If you believe Tith spoke to me before I was born," Jaydin said, "you must believe me when I say this is the only way."

"I believe you," Ocien finally answered, "and Torshe will believe you too. But you must let us do it. Torshe would never allow another to harm his father."

"Your help would be appreciated," Jaydin said. "We need as many kandar as we can get."

"Why should we do this now?" Ryten asked. "Don't we have more important things to focus on? Like Damarin?"

Jaydin crossed her arms. "Those kandar could be called at any time. I wanted to wait for Tchardin and the council but it looks like we'll have to do it ourselves."

"But—"

Jaydin held up a hand to forestall him. "It *will* help us with Damarin. If there is a war we may need somewhere to hide. A healthy Cens could save us as none of the Black Valley kandar would know how to navigate it."

Ryten looked through the thin trees and frowned. "Do you think it'll come back?"

"After it's been purged? I don't know. But I doubt it'll come back like this."

Ryten wasn't sure what to think. They'd just have to hope the forest regained its previous impenetrability when they removed the dying trees.

"I'll find Torshe," Ocien said. "He'll want to learn to shift."

She turned away and ran through the trees. Ryten watched her go with apprehension. Things could get complicated when she returned with her dodenzinn. Torshe had been particularly vocal about Ryten's confusion.

"Torshe will be an asset to us," Jaydin said while she similarly watched Ocien leave. "He'll do what needs to be done. More than that, the two of them portray very well the way we used to be. What we should be. And they care."

"They care?" It was exactly the type of thing Jaydin would say, and Ryten didn't understand it at all.

"You must see how important that is now? I've been thinking, and outside you and my sisters, two is more than I thought we'd have. The rest will wait, oblivious, while those of us who care either save or destroy their world in front of them."

"Only two? You must have allies in the council."

Jaydin shrugged. "I had a strong ally, but there are few left who would follow me without Nox at my side. Especially with Marr actively turning them against me. The council may be useless to us now. I'll talk to Anatoly and Yulek before I leave. They might help, but I can't guarantee it. Perhaps Fensen as well, though she is likely to ignore me."

Ryten was uncomfortable with hearing so many names from the council.

"I never said they were council," Jaydin answered his unspoken thoughts. "And even if they are, the only real reason to keep their identities secret was to protect them from backlash for their decisions about the Earths. That doesn't exactly matter now."

That was true. Ryten had never considered why the identities of the council members were kept secret. It had only mattered that they should be.

"You'll teach me to shift?" he asked. "More than the first time you tried?"

"I have to go back to Land Side." A slight smile formed on Jaydin's lips. "Sandin will teach you."

Sandin seemed to be paying attention for the first time since she arrived. Ryten tried to hide his surprise at Jaydin's words. How could Sandin possibly teach them to shift when she couldn't touch pandinzori? Jaydin laughed, obviously catching his thoughts.

"I'm going back with you." Sandin narrowed her eyes at Jaydin.

"Not this time. You need to teach the kandar here to move through the shift safely."

"But you'll need me for that."

"I can manage on my own. I made the journey once without you. I can do it again."

They stared into each other's eyes in silence. If Ryten didn't know better he would have thought they were still talking.

"Is war likely?" he asked, breaking their silence.

Jaydin pursed her lips. Her thoughts buzzed just beyond his reach.

"I'm not sure," she finally said. "That depends on Damarin. But I hope not. The first and only kandaran war was devastating. We must do everything in our power to avoid it this time. I really thought the threat of it would be enough but I was wrong."

A sense of dread crept into Ryten's mind. It happened every time the kandaran war was mentioned. He didn't know what Jaydin knew about the war—she routinely refused to share images of it with the few kandar who asked—but he knew it must have been terrible. Nine hundred kandar had been born on Derkra at the beginning of time. Now there were four hundred or so on Calendrai and many less than that in Black Valley. The war nearly halved their number over the course of less than a generation.

"It would be better to hide in the trees until a resolution can be found," Jaydin continued. "Or until Tchardin returns."

"You still expect her to return?"

Jaydin looked up at him. "Don't you?"

Two auras approached. Ocien had found Torshe and brought him to them. Ryten turned towards the feeling and saw the devoshai striding through the trees, Ocien just behind him. Torshe spoke immediately.

"Damarin wishes to start a war?"

"Perhaps," Jaydin answered.

The dodenzinn stopped in front of them. "Why?"

At that Ryten realised he hadn't bothered to ask. Jaydin's announcement of Damarin's intentions hadn't surprised him.

"She proposes we abandon the Purpose completely," Jaydin said. Ocien's mouth hung open but Torshe was stoic. Jaydin continued, unfazed. "She has desecrated the face of Land Side and brought human dangers to Derkra. There is fire in Black Valley now, just as there was here. There is a guardian on Land Side—"

"A guardian?" Ryten asked.

"Ruon—of World Four."

Ruon. A guardian. Ryten shivered.

"What is he doing here?" Torshe asked. There was evident anger in his voice.

At first Ryten thought Torshe was referring to the guardian, but when Jaydin turned to glance at him before answering he realised that wasn't the case. Torshe was talking about Ryten.

Jaydin stepped between the two devoshai. "Any kandar who cares enough to preserve our way of life should be included. We need as many as possible—"

"If what you've said is true," Torshe interrupted, "he needs to die."

Ryten's body tensed. Jaydin appeared to study him.

"There is time for that later," she said, "if it proves to be necessary."

"He is Damarin's dodenzinn—"

Jaydin cut him off. "I know what you were implying, Torshe."

Ryten looked at the ground. He tried so hard to forget it, and when Tchardin was around no one mentioned it, but now there was no reason to avoid it.

"Then you know why he must die," Torshe said. "If Damarin will bring war to the kandar it's worth the sacrifice, even if he isn't, just to be sure."

Ryten relaxed. There was a sense of rightness to the words. If he truly was Damarin's dodenzinn, would he sacrifice himself to end her? To stop a war? To save the kandar? Torshe was willing to kill his own father to help their people. Surely Ryten could do less.

"But what if he's Tchardin's dodenzinn instead?" Jaydin responded. "As he believes he is?"

"Tchardin is gone," Torshe said.

Ocien glared at him.

"She may be absent but I don't believe she's dead," Jaydin said. "Not this time. This time I choose to believe she will return. When she does, the kandar will know her as queen and the problem will resolve itself."

Torshe opened his mouth to protest further and Ryten stiffened. Jaydin continued before he could say anything. "I've dedicated my life to our people, to bringing us back to the Purpose. Damarin seeks to destroy that. I would do anything to end this conflict. Anything to stop a war. Do not doubt I apply this same attitude towards Ryten, and towards any of you."

Ryten was surprised at the threatening tone of Jaydin's voice, but Torshe nodded, and desisted.

"We'll deal with the forest soon," she continued, "but for now, Ryten will teach you to open the shift."

Ryten turned away from Torshe but he was certain the devoshai's dark gaze remained fixed on his back. He closed his eyes, focusing on thoughts of elsewhere, and pried the pandinzori that floated before him apart. The shift opened in front of him, a grey oval. He allowed himself a small smile despite the confrontation that had just taken place. At least he could contribute something.

He looked back and could tell Jaydin and Torshe were talking. From the expressions on their faces he guessed they were discussing Buran. Sandin's eyes were locked onto the shift. Ocien stared into the distance.

"You will go to Black Valley again?" Torshe finally asked aloud.

"Yes," Jaydin said. "I need to know how many kandar are involved in this. You two stay with Ryten. You must learn to shift. If I don't return soon, one of you should come after me to assess the situation."

"Why wouldn't you return?" Ryten asked.

"If I don't return"—Jaydin looked at Sandin—"things have gotten out of control and direct action may need to be taken. I won't start a war without reason, but if it becomes necessary we do need to win."

The four kandar were silent. The implication was clear. Damarin could hold Jaydin, kill her if she felt threatened, and then they would have to act. But what would they do without Jaydin? Most of the kandar on Calendrai didn't even know what was happening on Land Side. Ryten knew more than most, but he had to admit he didn't fully understand it.

Jaydin's eyes passed over each of them in turn. When Ryten met them she spoke.

"Practice opening the shift. Teach any kandar who would learn. I'll send Sandin back to help you before I leave, and Kadailin if I can find her. When I come back we will deal with Cens." She took a step towards Ryten. *'Protect my sisters while I'm gone,'* came into his mind.

She turned and ran towards Tith. Sandin followed. Ryten had to smile at the thought—given only to him—despite the weight of her previous words. It seemed Tchardin wasn't the only little sister Jaydin cared about. He wondered, not for the first time, exactly where on that scale Damarin lay.

Torshe approached him as he watched the sisters leave. The smaller devoshai came so close their auras almost touched.

"If it's proven that Damarin is my dodenzinn while we're still in conflict," Ryten said, "I will gladly destroy myself to end it."

"It was proven to me the moment you said it," Torshe replied. "At the time it was only happy news. But now"—he shook his head and looked at the ground—"just know you're only alive because Jaydin knows more than any kandar on Derkra. Her reasons to keep you around, whatever they really are, are good enough for me." He turned his back on Ryten and began to walk away. "For now."

Ocien stayed with Ryten when her dodenzinn left.

"He'll be fine," she said when he was far enough away not to hear. "Marr's words have gotten to him. His words are getting to all of us."

Torshe disappeared into a hidden patch in the forest and Ryten wondered if they were spreading. Where was Marr and what exactly was he saying?

***

Tchardin floated through the shift. A wall of ice preceded her and kept the water off her body. There were leaves in the distance. She moved towards them.

When she had entered the shift from World Four she found herself immobilised again. She could see her body around her but was unable to control her movement through the water. Twisting and turning had done nothing. Finally, in a panic, she had decided to treat the water like pandinzori.

Ruon and Damarin had moved through pandinzori without physically moving. They had slid through the air in the pit, surrounded by light. Tchardin hadn't been able to do it when she tried, but now there was no other option. She had willed herself forwards.

It worked. The sheet of ice that broke the water in front of her was something she had brought up later. The water flowing past had been too disconcerting. She couldn't feel it and it had seemed like she wasn't moving at all. Now her movement was evident. The leaves approached. They had to be Tith's leaves.

At first she had expected Ovaeron's. If Derkra could be said to have a World Tree, Ovaeron would have been it. But the leaves ahead of her were green, not red. If she was moving towards Derkra she was headed for Calendrai. Unfortunately the leaves seemed too dark and too small. She hoped it was only the distance.

Suddenly the leaves that had been so impossibly far away were right in front of her. They swayed in the unmoving water, seeming to appear from nowhere. Instead of grasping them and leaving the shift she stopped. The ice formed a bubble around her. This wasn't Tith. The colour was wrong and the shape was strange. It had to be another World Tree.

How could she have come to another world? She had tried so hard to go home to Derkra. She felt a moment of despair. She had been calm as she travelled through the water, once she had come to understand it, but now the prospect of leaving it for another experience like that on World Four terrified her.

She turned her bubble in the water. Endless blue greeted her eyes. Tith and Ovaeron were nowhere to be seen. Tairasyn's leaves were gone as well. If she abandoned this chance to leave the shift would she ever find another?

Maybe Kordic had been right. Maybe she *was* following some kind of path. She studied the leaves. They might take her to World Five if she touched them.

She sent herself forward. The ice that had protected her from the violence of the shift dissolved as the leaves gripped her and pulled her back into the world.

Tchardin found herself on strange grass. It was short, reaching only to her ankles. She knelt in it and studied the blades. It seemed to have been severed to make it that length. She got to her feet.

There were colours here that she had seen for the first time in the court of Arkaiyan, in the peoples' clothing. Now they bloomed before her in a variety of shapes and sizes. Red, yellow, and orange flowers that reminded her of fire, blue sky the colour of the shift, and trunks the dark umber of Tith's bark lived here. She would never have to create colours in her mind with this in front of her eyes.

She stood on a small square of grass, surrounded by flowers and guarded by a wall of short trees that blocked her view of anything else. She walked along the wall of trees, careful not to tread on the flowers at her feet. The trees reminded her of those on World Three—ever-green. Their leaves were so thick she couldn't see through them. She wanted at least a glimpse of the wider world before she shifted on, if only to gauge its condition.

There seemed to be an opening in the branches ahead of her where the edge of a wooden gate could be seen. When she came to it and tried to look through, her eyes were forcefully lowered. It felt as if her gaze slid off whatever was in front of her. She tried to look again but the unnerving sensation made her turn away.

She closed her eyes to re-orient herself. She was able to look through the opening with her eyes closed, but the space in front of her was black, empty of the light of pandinzori. She only knew of one thing that could be that dark. Water. But why couldn't she see it when her eyes were open? She turned back to the square of grass. Better to just shift out of this world than to be trapped in this walled area. There was evidently something wrong here as well, and if she didn't intend to meet the humans there was no other reason for her to stay.

Her experience on World Four had reminded her of Kordic's words. The humans might be new and interesting but they were also dangerous. She knew almost nothing about them. If she had to travel through the rest of the Earths she should take the guardian's advice and avoid them.

She drew pandinzori from the wall of trees. A large stream of it flowed from one corner of the space. The burst of power hit her hard and she was shocked by the strength and abundance of it. She walked past the opening in the branches to investigate, keeping her gaze pointed ahead. There was a tiny tree there. He came up to her hips and his leaves were miniatures. She touched the slender branches and was surprised to find he spoke to her.

He was Irah, the World Tree of World Five. He was even smaller than Zemko had been. Smaller than any tree she had met. A kandaran tree could never be so small, but the fact that she could hear him made it true.

'Where is your guardian?' she asked him. *'Where is Koska?'*

There was a crash behind her. She spun around. A small woman stood between the trees on the other side of the yard. She held something that looked like a thick, straight branch in her hands, but it didn't seem to be made of wood.

"If you break any of those branches I'll kill you," the woman said in a low voice. "That tree is worth more to me than my life. You have five seconds to decide if you feel the same."

So much for avoiding the humans. Tchardin noticed the slight pressure that indicated her camouflage had settled over her. She was happy she'd continued to wear the purple dress. She took a step away from Irah.

The woman approached her, squinting as she did. Her skin was brown and her dark curly hair was laced with grey. An older woman then. Tchardin backed away.

The woman stopped. "Oh," she said, in an entirely different voice, "it's just you."

The woman let the branch drop to her side and picked something out of her clothes. She put it to her face and it framed her brown eyes in thin black circles. Tchardin recognised glass. She flinched but refused to be affected. It was so little, and so close to the woman's face. Now that she knew its secrets it couldn't be used to hurt her.

"That's odd," the woman whispered, almost to herself. "You don't look anything like her, but you felt the same." The woman looked around, examining all four faces of the green wall that contained them. "That cut above your eye looks bad. I can clean it for you, if you need help."

Tchardin lifted a hand to her forehead. Her fingers came away dark and sticky. She'd forgotten about that. It had happened when she hit her head during Ruon's earthquake on World Four. Why didn't her human body eliminate it? She attempted to search the woman's mind for an appropriate response but the collective remained dark. The woman hadn't joined it yet.

"Or coffee? A hot drink couldn't hurt."

Tchardin shook her head. She didn't need the woman's thoughts to know she didn't want anything to drink. She contemplated the trees that bordered the grass. Could she climb them? Jump over them without giving herself away?

"I could use the company," the woman continued. "Hard to come by these days."

She shrugged when Tchardin didn't answer. Tchardin watched her carefully as she walked to the wall of trees and fiddled with something in the opening that had diverted Tchardin's eyes before.

"The gate's locked," the woman mused. "Just like last time. Climb over the hedges, did you?"

As Tchardin came around the edge of the dark trees she braced herself for the disconcerting experience, wondering how the woman tolerated it. When she saw what the woman was looking at she gasped. Instead of having her eyes pushed away, this time she saw the gate. Past the gate there was an expanse of grey ground, framed on either side by short rectangular buildings and small trees. The empty space that had forced her eyes away was no longer empty. The woman turned away from the scene and Tchardin's eyes were pushed down again, repelled by the uncomfortable sensation of void.

The woman joined the collective. She joined alone, her presence bringing no others with it—something Tchardin found strange even after such a short time with humans. Tchardin closed her eyes and focused on the woman's solitary leaf only to find that it wasn't a leaf.

It was a seed.

Chapter 29

Jaydin knelt in the sand and clutched her notebook to her chest. Once again she struggled with the feeling that the shift was different than it had been. The kandar of the past couldn't have used it as often as they had if it was so dangerous. She wished Tith had told her more about it. She looked down at her notebook.

It had been a risk to bring it. She could have lost everything, but the risk had paid off. She wasn't sure she'd be leaving Black Valley this time and she wanted to record what she learned for the future generations of kandar. What was happening with Damarin was a mistake that could easily be repeated.

She stood and held the notebook against her hip with pandinzori as she moved slowly across the desert. She was looking for Miadra—the tevadra's aura played lightly on her mind from Ovaeron's direction—but she was also taking stock of the situation. She needed to know what the Black Valley kandar were up to.

It didn't look like much. The kandar she passed lounged in the sand or climbed trees. A few walked purposefully across the valley but Jaydin guessed there was no actual purpose behind it. More likely they sought a dodenzinn or were just wasting time. She might only have to worry about the council. And Ruon and Damarin.

Damarin had used pandinzori against Sandin. Jaydin shuddered at the thought. It would have been a much bigger risk to bring her powerless sister than it had been to bring her notebook.

She searched the collective for Tchardin's leaf without much hope. It was as dark and still as it had been on Jaydin's two previous visits to Black Valley. Damarin's leaf was the same, but Ruon's seed was lit. Others grew in brightness as she approached individual kandar and dimmed as she left them behind.

One of the leaves she found was surprisingly bright. It was red and it belonged to a devoshai called Kaio. She turned to find his eyes on her. His expression was angry.

Another red leaf blazed in her mind. She spun around, expecting a second angry face. Instead she was confronted with a massive chest. Cotelle stared down at her from his immense height. She sought his thoughts but found herself barred from them.

"Miadra wants to talk to you," he said, before turning to walk away. "Come."

She had to run to catch up with him, his stride was so long. Kaio's eyes finally left her when the nine hundred came between them. Jaydin turned to the big devoshai and watched his back as he walked, probed his leaf in the collective. She looked for secrets there, for the reason for this change in the council. He was the Voice and Miadra's dodenzinn. He would know the tevadra's motives.

She heard nothing. Not even the telltale buzz of thoughts too quiet to decipher. Either he wasn't thinking—which was unlikely—or he was hiding it amazingly well. She was still pushing against his mind when Miadra joined them.

The High Seat stood before one of the caves. A white figure loomed in the darkness behind her. Jaydin forgot about Cotelle and Miadra and moved closer, wondering. Could it be the tree she thought it was? Tith's stories of Heirrar were vague, but he had spoken of the white tree at length. An important tree. One of Carrensing's three fathers.

Miadra noticed Jaydin's study of the cave.

"He is Heirrar," she said. "He's kandaran. Like Ovaeron."

Jaydin took another step towards the darkness. Heirrar. Grown from Aurine's World Seed. To think what could have happened to World Nine after the Seed was taken. Miadra stepped in front of her.

"Why have you returned?" the High Seat asked.

Jaydin would have to examine Heirrar later. Seeing the tree had not been her purpose in coming to Land Side.

"How could you let Damarin do that to the council?" she asked in turn.

Miadra must have been expecting the question. She answered quickly.

"She has found a way for us to have a future, here, on Derkra. Tchar has turned her back on us. Now we will do the same to her."

Miadra already sounded like Damarin. Jaydin frowned. "Where is Damarin now?"

Miadra sat in the sand. She motioned for Jaydin and Cotelle to join her. Cotelle took a place next to Miadra. Jaydin looked at the white tree in the cave once more. It could wait. She joined the dodenzinn.

"You must know where she is," Jaydin said to the two kandar.

"I think you already know," Miadra answered.

Jaydin hesitated. "Has she left Derkra?"

Miadra smiled. "Damarin is on the Earths."

Jaydin had been dreading that confirmation. There were only three ways a kandar could disappear from the collective on Land Side. Death, the desert, or the shift. She had been leaning towards the desert until Ruon appeared. Why would a guardian leave his Earth without contact from Derkra urging him to do so? Of the kandar on Calendrai, only Sandin knew Jaydin held this theory. She'd hidden it away from the collective.

"You've found a way to Coralynth?" Jaydin asked.

"Why should we need to?" Miadra responded. "Coralynth is here now."

Jaydin had to force herself not to look towards the mountain. A false Coralynth. Nothing more. Then the deeper implications of what Miadra said began to sink in. Jaydin trembled. "We can shift to the Earths directly from Derkra?" Could they possibly have been so close the entire time?

Miadra nodded.

"So Damarin has shifted from Derkra to one of the nine human Earths." Jaydin was both impressed and terrified by the revelation. There was a way to bypass Coralynth. "Have you been there?"

"No," the tevadra said. "I have no interest in going."

"But she's rediscovered the Purpose. We can go back to the humans." That a kandar would choose to remain on Derkra when they could go to the Earths was beyond Jaydin's comprehension. It was what she had been striving for her whole life. How had Damarin not come to Jaydin first when she discovered it? "We were made to guard them, to guide them."

"They can't be the Purpose anymore," Miadra said. "Tchar has kept us from Coralynth, barred us from the human worlds."

"You have the Earths! That's all that matters. If Tchar had meant for the kandar to abandon our Purpose she'd have blocked us completely."

Miadra shook her head knowingly and smirked. Cotelle smiled lazily off into the distance.

Jaydin looked around. "You truly think we were meant for this?"

Black Valley was an expansive pile of sand. The kandar milled about it with nothing to accomplish and Damarin wanted them to stay like that forever. Miadra and Cotelle agreed, and the Black Valley council followed them, as if there were some higher purpose behind it.

"There is a greater purpose to it," Miadra interrupted her thoughts. "*We* are the greater purpose. Derkra doesn't have to stay like this. Black Valley doesn't have to be a pile of sand."

"That is how our world is, Miadra—"

"It doesn't have to be."

Jaydin's fingers tightened around her notebook in the shadows that hid her body. It was how it always had been, how it was meant to be.

Miadra turned to Cotelle. Jaydin thought they must be speaking but there was no sound of their thoughts. Then she realised something. They weren't speaking. They were just looking at each other. Conveying meaning with their eyes, with their lips, with a tilt of the head. Like the kandar of the past. Like humans.

Jaydin frowned at the dodenzinn. How had they become so different from the other kandar, isolated on Land Side since they lost the Earths? Perhaps Damarin had inspired this in them.

"It was a part of us before she came," Miadra said, overhearing. Her eyes were alive when she looked back at Jaydin. "We joined the council to do something for our people. We felt like wandering the valley endlessly from our births to our rest wasn't enough. Then I became the High Seat and found there was still nothing for me to do."

"That's because your position means nothing without the Earths. Neither the High Seat nor the Voice can accomplish anything without the Purpose. The whole council exists only as a tradition now—"

"Damarin has changed that," Miadra said. "With her words and with her presence. When she walked up to me in the valley just after she arrived, her skin dark as the council shadow, I couldn't believe I was seeing something new. Something else. Something other. She taught me there is more than Black Valley on Derkra, and there could be more yet."

Jaydin shook her head. As High Seat and Voice, Miadra and Cotelle were just kandar elevated above the rest for a Purpose that was lost. Jaydin continued the tradition because she knew it would be needed when they returned to it. Miadra and Cotelle had come to believe they should find a new one.

"I wonder," Miadra said. "How do you think Calendrai came into existence?"

Jaydin had heard this from Damarin before. "Calendrai has always been on Water Side."

"Then why do the trees say 'and Derkra was half water and half sand, forever, and there was nothing in the water and nothing in the sand, but one great tree'. The story of Derkra's beginning doesn't include an island on Water Side. Ovaeron and the city around him are all we started with."

"An island can't just come out of nothing," Jaydin said. "If Calendrai is there now it was there in the beginning. Creator built it along with the rest of Derkra."

"Without telling Ovaeron? Without telling Tchar and Dani? I don't think so."

"Then how?"

"Damarin would say Carrensing created it."

Jaydin thought of the false Coralynth rising out of the sand. "With pandinzori?"

Miadra shook her head. "Not like that. You're the authority on our history, I hear. There is no pandinzori on Water Side and you say Carrensing shifted out into nothing. That Tith called her."

"He did. From Calendrai."

"Which means he was there before she shifted."

"Which supports the prior existence of the island."

"But it only had to exist when he called her, or shortly before that," Miadra insisted. "Why don't the trees mention Calendrai in the beginning? They explicitly state there was nothing on the water. Does your history make mention of it at all before Carrensing discovered it?"

Jaydin closed her eyes and put her hand to her head, holding her notebook against her face. There was only so much of this she could take.

"What is that?" Miadra asked.

Jaydin opened her eyes to find both Miadra and Cotelle staring at the green cover of her notebook. Miadra's eyes glittered with intensity.

"This," Jaydin said, too exasperated to avoid the question, "is my notebook. This is where I keep our history and my thoughts on it."

"It's not a thing of the kandar," Miadra said.

It had taken long enough for this reaction to cease in Calendrai. Now Jaydin would have a whole other set of kandar to explain her unique circumstances to. She began to understand what Sandin felt like. "It's a thing of the Earths."

"How did it get here?" Miadra asked.

Both Miadra and Cotelle's gazes were riveted to the notebook. Jaydin flipped slowly through the pages. She thought back to her birth—to before her birth when Tith had told her the story of existence.

"It was there when I was born. I came from Tith to a great crowd of kandar expecting Carrensing come again. I knew too much to believe that's who I was. I knew too much to even remember it all for long. After the kandar departed I climbed high into Tith to think. I found it there."

"It was just there? No mention of it from Tith?"

"None."

Cotelle and Miadra exchanged a glance.

"Rendinzori," Miadra said reverently.

"Rendinzori?" Damarin was clearly teaching Miadra, just as Jaydin had once taught Damarin. "Of the humans?"

Miadra nodded. "Your notebook must have been created with rendinzori."

"What makes you think that?"

"How else?"

"That's not a reason!"

"It's as good as any you've given us."

Jaydin took a moment to think. "The notebook being created out of nothing is ridiculous enough but it doesn't prove anything about Calendrai. A whole island, full of trees. Five kandaran trees! Only Creator can bring a tree to life. The kandar know that and Tith affirmed it."

"Tith was wrong," Miadra said with conviction. "The humans can and have brought trees to life with rendinzori. Now the kandar will use it to build our own world."

"Nonsense."

"Why should it be nonsense? It wasn't just pandinzori that made Coralynth."

Jaydin narrowed her eyes in confusion.

Miadra sighed. "The false Coralynth then, the fire mountain there. Just as we don't believe Calendrai was made by pandinzori. Just as your notebook came into being by a force we do not know, a force we cannot see."

Jaydin had wondered about the fire in the false Coralynth, wondered how the pandinzori around it wasn't swallowed in its creation. "You're implying Ruon used rendinzori on the mountain? To make the fire?"

"He did," Miadra insisted.

"But how do you know?"

"How could pandinzori create fire?"

"How do you know kandar are even capable of using rendinzori? How do you know what it can do?" Jaydin was dizzy with questions. The whole conversation was questions and Jaydin was used to knowing the answers to everything. There was an evident contradiction here. Kandar had manipulated the fire from volcanoes on the Earths in the past, but that fire had already been there. The fire on Derkra had been created by the guardian. Miadra's explanation could be the answer, but it seemed like the tevadra was making it up. Jaydin wondered for a moment if this was what the other kandar felt like when they spoke to her. At least she had a valid source for her information in Tith. "Where did this idea come from?"

Then Miadra smiled, as if Jaydin had finally asked the right question. "It came from Siltadon."

Jaydin raised her eyebrows. Siltadon must have been dead for generations. Dead as long or longer than the kandar had been barred from the Earths. "You know who she was?"

Cotelle leaned forwards, waiting.

"Who she *is*, Jaydin," Miadra said. "Siltadon is the tevadra who restarted World Seven, and she isn't dead."

***

Tchardin focused on the seed in the collective again. A guardian's seed. This woman was not Koska, changed and reborn. She was clearly a human. Tchardin pushed against the seed with her mind. Even with her eyes closed, even with no other leaves lit up in this world, she couldn't learn anything from it. The woman who had brought Tchardin into her home didn't seem to have a name.

"I'm Irah," the woman said, "if it matters to you."

Irah, like the World Tree. Tchardin held her thoughts closer. Had the woman heard her? Humans weren't supposed to be able to hear thoughts, as far as she knew.

"The tree's name is Irah too," Tchardin said before she could stop herself.

The woman frowned at her. "What a strange thing to say."

Irah turned back to her search of the small room. She was clearly looking for something but without her thoughts Tchardin didn't know what. One wall of the room held an empty space like that in the garden. A void. *"Sit by the window,"* Irah had said. Tchardin quickly turned away before it could push her eyes down. It faced the world on the other side of the garden, and it showed Tchardin nothing—rejected her gaze—just as the gate had.

Irah's thoughts were too closely guarded for Tchardin to learn anything on her own. They were more similar to the thoughts of the kandar than to those of any of the humans she had met up until now. Tchardin didn't know how to interact with the woman without knowing what she expected, but she wanted to understand. What had happened to Koska—the first true guardian of the Earth—and how could a human have taken her place?

Tchardin was startled by a loud crash as Irah dropped something on the floor.

"I'm sorry," the woman said. "I'm very tired."

Irah's posture told Tchardin that without her words. She didn't have anywhere near as much pandinzori around her as the other humans Tchardin had met. Tchardin wondered if that was the source of her exhaustion. It would be so for a kandar.

"Tired?" Tchardin asked.

"I barely sleep now."

Sleep. A word Tchardin knew but didn't fully understand. She couldn't forego the opportunity to learn about something that was so important to humans. Something the kandar didn't have. She also couldn't just ask what it was. The woman would expect her to know.

"Why don't you sleep?" she asked instead.

"Memories of the Bug and the Aftermath. Still. Always. I have terrible nightmares about them; both when I'm asleep and when I'm awake."

Tchardin waited for the images and meanings of Irah's words but nothing came to her.

"Nightmares?" There were so many things she didn't understand.

Irah cringed. "I'll never forget them. I don't think anyone could."

Tchardin decided to continue the conversation for as long as possible, to see what answers she could find about this strange world. She could always just sit and listen if it became too complicated.

"You're young." Irah didn't sound like she wanted an answer. Tchardin smiled, since she would have been lost for one. "You missed it, didn't you?"

"Missed what?"

"The Bug. If not, you must have just been born. Do you remember it?"

"No," Tchardin said. "I...missed it." It was best to repeat the woman's words back to her.

"Lucky," Irah said, "and unlucky. At least I had a childhood. Being born in the Aftermath must have been hard."

Irah sat in the chair next to Tchardin and placed the objects she'd been searching for on a small table. Tchardin stared at the three white balls the woman had deposited between them, uncertain as to their function. Irah picked up and examined various other objects from the table. Her eyes flitted to Tchardin's forehead.

"Tell me about the Bug," Tchardin said.

Irah studied something in her hands. "I'm sure you've heard too many stories about it to be interested in mine."

A response came to Tchardin. "My sister used to tell me stories all the time, but I didn't want to listen."

"What's changed?"

"You're not my sister."

Irah laughed. It was the first time Tchardin had seen her smile.

"Alright," Irah said, "but you have to sit still. I'm going to clean that cut."

"What is that?"

"Bottle of peroxide. Better than gold in these times, but it's going to hurt." Irah twisted the bottle open in her hands.

Tchardin stared at it until Irah spoke. Then the woman's words pulled her in.

"I was young when the Bug emerged. My parents and I were up north. We avoided it for a time—fewer people in larger spaces meant less sickness—but it killed them in the end. I only made it because they were determined to save me."

Tchardin struggled to deal with the emotion she saw on Irah's face. It was terrible, just as Jaycee's had been at Tezroi's death, but it was further away, deeper, less raw. Ingrained. That made it worse for some reason.

"Up north?" she asked.

Irah nodded. "I was born at the end of the Plagues. The cities that remained weren't safe anymore. Too many fanatics. Some believed the world had already ended. Those groups were bad, others were worse. God was vengeful, they said. I was an eleven year old girl and I was meant to die for my sins. We were all supposed to die." Irah pressed one of the white balls against the opening of the bottle in her other hand. "They were mostly right. A lot of them died, maybe all of that kind, but not me. If you ask me God died with them. The Aftermath might have been worse than the Bug."

She reached for Tchardin's face with the white ball. Tchardin backed away from it. She remembered that word. *God*. Jaydin had told her the humans liked to believe there was a greater power specific to their worlds. Often many for each world. Like Creator, but only for them. Most of the time they were wrong, but World Five's God had been real.

"Who was God?" Jaydin would be interested to hear what an actual human had to say on the subject. If God had died before this woman believed Tchardin was born, Tchardin had no reason to know who they were.

"Ha!" Irah slapped her thigh with her free hand and laughed again. "I guess it's true. He must be dead if you don't even know him."

Tchardin watched the white ball closely but smiled. The frightening expression had left Irah's face. Tchardin was amazed how well she was doing despite being unable to hear the woman's thoughts. It helped that she only had one human to deal with. Things had escalated quickly in the castle on World Four. The more humans there were to speak to one another the more complicated things became.

"Tell more of the story," Tchardin said.

"Only if you stay still and let me do this. Someone out there will think you're an easy target with that much blood on your face."

Tchardin remembered the dark stickiness she had felt on her forehead. She didn't know how to make her camouflage fix it. She met Irah's eyes and nodded.

Irah reached out and held Tchardin's chin with her free hand. Tchardin was relieved there was no shock from touching humans as there would have been from another kandar. She relaxed against the woman's fingers.

"The faces I remember..." Irah brushed Tchardin's forehead with the white ball as she held her head steady. "There were so many of us before the Bug. There used to be even more once, back when my grandparents were young. But God had been out to get us for decades, they said. The Plagues halved the world's population."

"The Plagues?"

"Do you not know of them? Disasters of epic proportions—earthquakes, volcanoes, tsunamis—accompanied by severe weather of all kinds. Then drought and famine. I was born in the famine."

"How many people were there before?" Tchardin asked, thinking of the immense number of leaves Tezroi had given her. Leaves that were dark with distance now.

"Oh, many millions. A few billion maybe."

Tchardin's eyes widened at the numbers. She hadn't heard of such numbers before. She wished more than anything that Irah's mind could show her what she meant.

"I know! It's almost unbelievable." Irah seemed to grow sad again. "But the Plagues, and the Bug..."

Tchardin could tell the woman didn't want to continue on that path, even without her thoughts. "How did you survive? Up north?"

"We ran from it. We ran deeper and deeper into the cold. Away from the infected mobs that fled the cities." Irah paused, her hand fixed in front of her, the once white ball hovering in front of Tchardin's eyes, red and black now. "It wasn't just me and my parents. There were others. A whole group of us, lost in the snow and the trees, numbers dwindling, first slowly, then so fast it was a blur. First to the cold, then..." Irah's hand shook against Tchardin. "We took in a small number of women and children. They seemed fine at first, but then they got sick. They were barely human by the time it killed them. After that I saw a lot of death. But the seeing wasn't the worst of it. I swear I could *feel* them dying. I could feel death. We kept walking, but there wasn't any hope in any of us. I wonder if the rest of them could feel it too."

Tchardin nodded. Maybe they could, like leaves falling in the collective.

"The feeling intensified after my father died. When my mother followed I just knew that was the end. Of all of us. All of humanity gone from the face of the earth. Just like they said." Irah turned towards the window. "But the world came back."

Tchardin followed Irah's gaze and the world did come back. She was distracted for a moment by the brightness, the range of colours. Then she noticed she was looking at glass. She turned away—the urge to escape strong in her—but the woman sat placidly and looked out. Irah didn't seem to think the glass was a threat to her or to anyone. Her reaction to it was very different from those of the Arkaiyans.

Tchardin slowly turned to look again. It was just like the glass that covered Irah's eyes. It couldn't hurt Tchardin now that she understood it, and Irah had given her no reason thus far to use the pandinzori around them.

The window showed a similar view to the one through the gate. Grass and flowers were visible. Short trees intermittently lined the grey ground that stretched away into the distance. The more Tchardin looked at it, the stranger it seemed. Where were the other humans? Where were the animals? There was no movement in the world at all.

Irah looked away and Tchardin saw the nothing again. Her eyes were forcibly averted. Irah must be very powerful to remove Tchardin's view of the world, of the glass. Just like the other guardians with their pandinzori. Irah was the first human she had met with such control over rendinzori though. It had to be rendinzori that did it. Whatever it was.

"I don't know why the Bug didn't kill me," Irah finally continued. "But I survived the cold because they gave me more than my share of food. They gave me their blankets and they gave me their own body heat. They kept me dry and out of the wind, away from the wild animals that waited for us to die so they could live. They kept me safe. When they think their world is ending, people try to save the children. Especially the girls. And I survived.

"I woke up in a hospital. Terrified. I still don't know where it was or how I got there. Everything was blurry back then. I think that's why it feels more like a dream than reality. Like a nightmare. Everyone I knew died. All the people we were with."

"All of them?" That would explain why Irah's seed hadn't brought any leaves to the collective.

"Yes. I'm alone. I've been alone for a long time, but worse than that I remember the feeling of being truly alone. The only one to survive. It haunts me. I can't shake it." Suddenly she laughed. "The last woman alive. Ridiculous, right?"

Tchardin was beginning to believe it might not be so ridiculous. The nothing at the gate and the window. No movement on the Earth when she could see it. Maybe Irah truly was alone. She gave the woman a faint smile. Irah didn't continue.

"What did you do then?" Tchardin asked. "After you woke up alone?"

"I grew up." Irah shrugged. "It was terrible and confusing. A waking nightmare. When things settled down I got myself this little place. Now I garden and try to stay alive."

"What about the other people?"

The woman looked out the window. Tchardin followed her eyes, trying to take in as much of the outside world as she could before Irah made it disappear again. There had to be other people.

"What about them? They live their lives and I live mine. It's rare someone breaks into my garden. Or it used to be. Two in such a short time..." Her eyes lost focus as she trailed off.

The first of those two had reminded Irah of Tchardin. Had that been Damarin? If her sister had been to World Four she could have been to World Five.

"Did you grow up with family?" Irah asked. "You mentioned a sister."

Tchardin's skin prickled. Again. Had Irah heard her thoughts? Could a human this powerful access the collective? No, Tchardin had mentioned a sister earlier. She had brought up Jaydin when they spoke of stories.

"I—" Tchardin paused. *Family.* "I have four sisters."

"Five of you? That's impressive. And all girls. Your mother certainly did her part. A noble cause, rebuilding the human race. I have great respect for those women, though I could never have been one of them."

Girls. Women. Tchardin was reminded that on the Earths, she was a woman. She had been a woman on World Four—when Tezroi asked her to make him a child—and she was a woman now. She would be on every Earth. She remembered Jaycee's round belly. "You couldn't have children?"

Irah laughed. "Who knows? I didn't try very hard."

She looked at Tchardin with a calculating stare for a moment before her gaze went soft. Without thoughts to go with the extreme range of expressions Tchardin was lost.

"It's not that I don't like children," Irah said, placating. "Babies are sweet and fine. Little kids are impressive, the way they learn. Even teenagers, not too bad. I just couldn't accept that it had to be all on us to repopulate, you know?"

The edges of Tchardin's mouth lifted in what she hoped was an understanding smile. The conversation had become impossible to continue without the woman's thoughts to guide her.

"You must feel it too. I have to admit I don't know if it's worse now or better. When you reach a certain age people stop looking at you for that and you forget. It was really bad in the Aftermath. Men were looking at me before I bled. As far as I can tell that wasn't a new thing, but it'd become less acceptable in the years leading up to the Plagues." Irah sighed. "Women had just begun to claw their way out of the hole society had been digging for them since its inception, only to find it being filled in on top of them."

It seemed that on this Earth a woman was treated very differently from a man. Tchardin frowned.

Irah looked away. "Your cut looks better now. You should go back to your life before I get any ideas about daughters I could have had."

Tchardin was about to protest when she realised she really did need to go. There could be four more Earths between her and Derkra and she had to tell Jaydin about this. World Five, at least, had suffered in their absence. Suffered beyond belief, if she was right about this woman and her Earth.

"I need to continue a journey." Tchardin thought of Irah, the World Tree. Perhaps he would have answers for her. "I'd like to see the garden again before I leave."

"You like the flowers? Is that why you broke in?"

"No." Tchardin laughed. "I mean, I do. They're beautiful, but I want to see the little tree."

"Ah. That one." Irah's eyes lit up. "Special, isn't it? I've been working on it for as long as I can remember. Trying to get it just right."

"Working on it?"

"Shaping it, to look like the original." Irah stood, once again peering out the window. "The light won't last. Shall we?"

***

Kadailin watched as Ocien cleared the forest of the dead leaves that littered its floor. They had continued to slowly fall around the burned area. Ryten walked by her, a wall of pandinzori before him, pushing the leaves out to the shore.

"Are you sure this is what we need to do?" he asked her as he passed.

"I only know what Jaydin told me," Kadailin answered. "We need to remove the damaged trees. It makes sense to me to remove the leaves as well. They were part of the trees."

Ryten shrugged. "Whatever you say."

Kadailin was really just putting off dealing with the scarred trees. She could see Frenn from where she stood. It was clear even from what was left that he had indeed been the most beautiful tree in Calendrai, though his trunk and many of his branches were charred black now, his fallen leaves mixed in with a multitude of others Ryten pushed across the forest floor.

She walked towards the great tree. Jaydin and Sandin sat under him, their heads close together. They had been like that since Jaydin returned from Black Valley a third time.

Kadailin felt a concentration of pandinzori to her right and turned to see Torshe appear from the shift. The devoshai tumbled into the leaves and lay sprawled there, a somewhat dazed look on his face. Kadailin shuddered. She found the ice and the water behind it terrifying, but

Jaydin was adamant that she learn too. She didn't know how much longer she could put it off.

Her sisters whispered to each other. Kadailin was too far away to hear them but Jaydin's thoughts buzzed loudly and Kadailin found them tempting. She had never heard her sister's secret thoughts before. Jaydin was usually too good at masking them, having spent so much time with Damarin.

Kadailin approached. The pandinzori around the two swirled away in vast quantities. Kadailin was mesmerised by it. She had seen something like it around Sandin before but never around Jaydin. When she was about ten steps away Jaydin's buzzing mind became impossible to ignore.

Behind Kadailin's eyes the image of a silver-skinned tevadra appeared. The tevadra in the image was seated in the sand of Land Side. She held a bright red seed in her hand. Kadailin knew without thinking that the tevadra was *Siltadon* and that the red seed she held was the World Seed of World Seven.

Chapter 30

Cien blinked. A moment ago his vision had been dark. He didn't think he'd opened his eyes but now he could see. Faceted blackness greeted him. It shone with a strange red light. The last thing he remembered was the yellow of the desert. He wasn't conscious of a transition.

"Be wary." The voice was Ruon's. "You lie on glass."

Cien's cheek pressed into jagged stone. Something wet touched his lips as he moved against it. His right arm was underneath him, crushed against the sharp rock, his left thrown out before him, as if he had been tossed to the ground without any control over himself. He closed his eyes. His mind pulsed with pain, but he remembered.

Damarin had moved him a fourth time. He had recovered quickly and was about to stand when Ruon appeared. The guardian walked towards him at the centre of an expansive beacon of pandinzori that lit up the dunes of Land Side. Cien shuddered as he remembered the horror of the guardian's aura against his, through his, as Ruon's fists and elbows, knees and feet had sought him out. At first Cien had been surprised. Affronted. He hadn't known how to react. Other kandar didn't belong so close to him. The guardian's aura didn't create the sense of revulsion that would come with another kandar's, but he shouldn't have touched Cien at all.

Ruon also shouldn't have been able to hurt him. Not physically. That was a human thing. But the guardian had seemed so sure. He was forceful, determined. At first Cien had only felt a sense of disgust, but then... He shivered. The pain in his body was gone now, but he would always remember it.

Pandinzori surrounded him. Its blinding light lit up the space behind his eyes. He shied away from the power, afraid of what Ruon had said. *Glass.* Could he really be lying on glass? On Derkra? He'd been without pandinzori for so long. Out in the sand. Alone. He wanted to grip it with his mind. Pull it to him. But if he was lying on glass that would kill him. He attempted to stand.

"Do not move," the guardian said.

Cien froze. A massive crack ripped through the air. The black wall before him exploded with reflected light. He flipped onto his back just in time to see fire fall from the sky. Not the sky in truth, but a stone sky. He was in a cave, like those in Black Valley. The section of ceiling just past his feet had opened up and burning liquid rock fell through. It fell in a broken line from one wall to the other, trapping him behind it. He stood just in time to avoid the fire as it hit the cave floor and spread out. It darkened and hardened immediately upon landing but continued to fall and cover the ground.

He found Ruon's face behind the fire. The black devoshai stared at him from across the cave, his expression devoid of emotion. Rage welled up in Cien. He would take hold of the pandinzori around him and walk through the fire. The fire would swallow it, expose him eventually, but he'd learned something from his experience on Calendrai. With enough pandinzori he could do anything. The fire could only take so much. Ruon must be lying about the glass. Cien was about to move when the liquid fire between them began to solidify.

This time it was different. The jagged, reflective black rock he stood on was strange to him, the faceted wall behind him a wonder, but this he recognised immediately, instinctively. The air seemed to pulse. Cien forgot his anger and dropped to his knees.

It was glass. The sheet of haphazard pillars that formed was darker, deeper than the image in his mind, but it was undeniably glass. It reached from the cave ceiling to its floor.

He backed away from it until he ran into the faceted wall. He turned from that in terror and was confronted again with the pillars of translucent rock. His feet scraped against the same rock beneath him. He looked down and saw they were slashed with red. He was trapped. He didn't know what to do with the pandinzori that revolved around him. It spread out from his skin and pierced the glass. It swirled to Ruon and back again. Cien tried desperately not to focus on it, not to take hold of it with his mind. It soothed him, caressed his skin. The strength it gave him was there, but he couldn't touch it with his mind. The guardian peered in at him.

"I did not expect you to wake so quickly."

Cien felt another blaze of anger. Without the glass his chances against the guardian had been slim. He might have made it through the fire but Ruon would have wrested his pandinzori away and thrown him to the ground again, helpless. There was no matching the guardian's strength, his control over pandinzori. Now, Cien was guaranteed a draw. Surrounded in glass, it would only take a small amount of concentration to destroy them both.

He considered it for only a moment. Tchardin had to be alive somewhere. He would have felt her leave the collective if she had died. Killing Ruon with glass, and therefore himself, would only mean killing her too. Or killing Damarin. Or both. He turned around and around in the cage, looking for some kind of relief. Eventually he slipped on the slick floor and fell, clutching himself as he had done in the desert.

"You will not do it?" Ruon asked. "For your absent queen? Then you will stay here forever."

A sound escaped Cien's lips. "Why, Ruon? What is this?"

"It is your glass cage. Crude, and very much unlike my own, but it will do."

"Your own?"

"On World Four." The guardian knelt before him, only one of his eyes visible through a space in the glass. "There is a whole cavern full of them in Castle Arkaiyan. Buried deep beneath the earth. One for every Forest Spirit they believe exists. One for each of us."

The eye disappeared. Could they be on World Four? "Where are we?"

"We are in Black Valley."

Cien closed his eyes. If they were in the city why hadn't the collective lit up? He ran his mind along its darkened branches, searching for light. Ruon's seed glowed, but all else was dim. He couldn't remember if it had looked like that in the desert, or if the leaves were slightly brighter now. It didn't matter. He couldn't reach them.

"Look," Ruon said. "Look out from the glass."

Cien hesitated. The glass that trapped him was no more dangerous than the glass at his back or the glass that supported him, but it actually looked like glass. It matched the image in his mind. Somehow that made a difference. He got to his knees and leaned forward until his aura brushed the cage. He shrunk back but nothing happened. Slowly he got to his feet, his eyes on the glass until he came to a break in it and through that could see the guardian.

Ruon stood in the centre of a roughly circular space. He was framed against the light of its entrance. The cave reminded Cien of the one that held Heirrar at the edge of the valley, but the walls here were covered with leaves. A red light emanated from a thick line of liquid fire along one of the walls. Cien turned away from that, reminded of the fire that had fallen from the ceiling. He looked instead at the leaves. Some of them were truly red, not just made to look that way by the fire. Dark shapes moved through them.

"What are they?"

Ruon followed his gaze. "Red flowers. The creatures that move amongst them are spiders."

How could these things have come to Derkra? "Did you make those? Like the cage?"

"No. This magnificent structure is mine, and the fire and glass are mine, but not them."

The glass in front of Cien glowed red in places, reflecting the fire. "Why would you bring this to Derkra? How could you?"

"It is my masterpiece. My contribution to Damarin's new world."

Cien was taken aback by the words. "You're proud of this?"

The devoshai smiled. The expression was sinister on his face. "You would not be? I have taken something the humans of World Four have used against the kandar since its inception and made it my own."

"Do you hear yourself? It's a weapon designed to fight us, to kill us, and you would bring it to the kandar?"

"I control it now."

"How?" Cien asked.

"I had a long time to watch the Arkaiyans create it. To listen to their minds while they did. The rock was to be made in a specific way and I needed the fire to melt it. So I built the volcano and all that is contained within. We stand now in the belly of the new Coralynth."

"You said these were the caves of Black Valley."

"No, Cien, I said only that we were in Black Valley. These caves form the fire-hollowed veins of a great mountain at the edge of the city. It is Coralynth, in memory of the days when kandar were Creator's slaves and two of our number held the reins on high."

"You can't call this Coralynth—"

"We will not go there again," the guardian continued, ignoring his words, "and we will not return to the Earths unless it is to take what is rightfully ours."

Cien could believe they were on Derkra. He could believe he was in one of Black Valley's caves, could even believe Ruon had changed it. The part he couldn't believe was the mountain. Coralynth. To alter the face of Derkra was inconceivable. Ruon frowned.

"I wish I could show you what we have made. I wish you could know it to be true. But neither you nor your cage will ever leave this place. That is how it must be."

He turned and walked away.

"Ruon," Cien said to the guardian as he rounded the corner and out of sight. Pandinzori swirled in his wake and sent prickles through Cien. The light of Ruon's seed faded. Cien began to feel incredibly alone. The empty collective had haunted him in the desert, but here, behind glass, it was devastating. *'Ruon!'*

Nothing.

A tremor radiated through Cien's skin. The collective pulsed. A desperate thought came to him. He should have known he was on Derkra because Ovaeron still called him.

'Ovaeron,' he said. *'I am called, Ruon, by the first tree of existence. Ovaeron asks for me. Would you keep me from him?'*

The guardian reappeared. He lingered in the entrance to the cave, surprise plain on his face. "The father of all of us has asked for you?"

"He's been asking for a long time now."

"Perhaps he knew what was coming to you and wished to spare you from it. But it is too late now. The trees cannot save you."

The pandinzori around Cien seemed to spin. He closed his eyes to it, only to find it brighter, more present. He opened them again and glared at the guardian. "So I will die here, without a father, never to be reborn."

"No." Ruon's eyes lit up for a moment, a rare burst of emotion. "You will not die in this cage. If you stay here, as you are, you will live forever."

Then he left. Cien thought of calling out to him again, but now he had no hope the guardian would free him. Yelling would only wear him out, make him more likely to grasp at the pandinzori around him. He closed his eyes.

The room in front of him was bathed in bright pandinzori. The glass, amazingly, wasn't visible as pandinzori floated through and around it. On the other side of the room the fire devoured the light. Cien wondered if the cave would eventually be rid of pandinzori. Then maybe he would find peace. He almost laughed. If pandinzori had grown around him in the desert it would come to him here. It would continue to torment him even if the fire sought to swallow it all.

Someone approached. Cien looked over the collective as a light appeared. He opened his eyes to see Miadra standing just inside the entrance to the cave. She leaned against the stone across from him and stared.

The pandinzori around Cien swirled through the cage to meet hers. He tried not to look at it, instead focusing on the tevadra. He was worried his mind might unconsciously grasp it, attempt to hold it to his body and inadvertently pressure the glass into reacting.

Miadra remained against the cave wall. What if she manipulated the pandinzori around them? Ruon said he had spent time in a cage of glass and Cien trusted him not to make a mistake. At least more than he would most kandar. Miadra would be as new to this as Cien was, and she wasn't confined in it. He tried to put it out of his mind but the thought kept coming back. She had a power over him now, greater than that of the guardian—who had left, whose seed had darkened in Cien's mind. Cien and Miadra were linked together by death in the air.

"You think I would make such a grave error?" the tevadra asked. "I would never do such a thing when our world is on the brink of change. I must live to see it rebuilt."

She walked to the centre of the cave, away from the leaves that covered its walls.

"Free me," Cien said. "I am your Shadow."

The tevadra paced. She didn't acknowledge his words. He wondered if Ruon had told the kandar he planned to be Shadow in Cien's stead. He hoped that wasn't the case.

"You are only kandar—"

"Only kandar?" Miadra walked up to the glass. He flinched when her aura touched it. "How can you be so sure?"

"Then you are council."

She nodded. "But I am more even than that. I am your High Seat, and therefore your equal. Below only Tchar and Dani and the queen of the kandar."

The revelation didn't surprise him. He felt like nothing could surprise him again. "My dodenzinn will be queen."

"I would say Damarin will be."

The smile that accompanied the statement did surprise him. For a moment he wondered if Miadra knew Damarin claimed him. But she couldn't know unless Damarin had told her, and he didn't believe Damarin would do that. It was too big a change.

"You saw Tchardin's golden aura," he said. "I was there. You can't deny that."

Miadra shrugged. "Tchardin is gone. She was gone before she could do anything for the kandar. Damarin remains, and she has found us a new Purpose."

"Tchardin isn't dead. Until she dies or loses the aura she is our future queen."

"Why can't I choose? We chose you to be our Shadow. Why can't I choose my queen?"

Cien turned in his cage. This wasn't going to help him escape.

"Look at me," he said, desperate. "Look at this glass, on Derkra. How can you do this? Ruon has lost his mind. Damarin may have as well, but you, Miadra, you are a kandar of Black Valley and I am its Shadow." He couldn't believe she could stand there and watch this. "Like you said, you chose me."

"You don't understand, Cien. This is bigger than you. Rendinzori will bring a complexity to our world that the kandar will struggle to accept. As things change for us there will be those who fight that change. There will be those who slow its progress. Tchardin, as a symbol of Tchar and our past, is one of those kandar whether she wants to be or not, and therefore so are you. It's hard to turn dodenzinn against each other."

"I don't even know what rendinzori is."

"It's human," she said. "And it's more powerful than pandinzori, in its way. Creator gave it to them and now we will take it for ourselves."

"But this..." He almost touched the glass with his fingers. She was so close to it now. How could she not see?

"Would you rather die?"

He didn't answer. It would be so easy to say yes. After the desert. After the glass. But his death wouldn't only be a release. It would mean the death of his other half.

"I wouldn't kill you," Miadra continued. "Not here. Not unless you could be given back to your father. There are too few of us left. If the kandar had found a way to detain those who worked against them during the war maybe more of us would have lived."

The words shook Cien. "Is that all this is to you? A way to hold me so I don't get in your way?"

"Really, that's all it is."

"I don't think you know what you're doing to me."

"It's easier this way. You will be called to rest naturally in time, never having interfered with our plans, and your future self will awaken to a changed world. But the world will never have changed for him, nor for any of those he comes to know. It will only be as it always has been. Just as it is now. Maybe the kandar have no history—maybe they don't remember—because nothing has ever changed. That doesn't mean it shouldn't."

Cien remembered the guardian's eyes. "I will never have a future self."

"Of course you will. That's why we've put you in there. So you don't need to be destroyed. We'll try to do the same for Tchardin—"

"I can't die if I don't leave," Cien interrupted. "You won't release me, so I can't leave without destroying my body. If I stay here I'll never be anyone else."

Miadra seemed perturbed by that. "Why would you think that? You will die in there, just as all kandar die eventually."

"No," he said. "Ruon says I'll live forever."

"Forever?" She paused for a moment, her thoughts swirling in the collective. "Then there's plenty of time to let you go."

"No," Cien said again. "Unless you release me before I'm as far gone as Ruon, I'll be just as dead as any who were destroyed in the war. Release me now."

Miadra's eyes were unfocused. Her thoughts buzzed and he realised she wasn't listening. "There could be another war, you know."

"Over this? You can't let that happen."

"And this will save you." Her vision cleared. "After it's over, when everything has changed, I'll release you. Then you can rest and come back to us."

"No, Miadra." His body tensed. He wanted to throw himself against the glass, throw himself at her. He wanted to strike at her, to do what Ruon had done to him, and he wanted to do it to every kandar who had agreed to let this happen. But the glass held him back on every side.

He looked to the ceiling and noticed the cage was rock there, not glass. For a moment he thought of escape but the memory of fire falling from above came back to him. There could be more there. If he managed to break through it could burn him. He wouldn't be able to use pandinzori in defence. "This is unbelievable."

Miadra smiled. "Maybe you just need to see the change. Look around you. Things are already different." She turned away from him and walked to the wall of the cave. She stood in front of the leaves and plucked a flower from among them. "Do you know what these are?"

"Red leaves, flowers. Spiders. What do I care? Those things don't belong here."

"They do now, and more will come."

She placed the red leaves against her tongue and closed her mouth. Pandinzori swirled around her. Cien tensed.

"You would eat?" He hadn't thought she was the type.

"The kandar will be the Purpose soon," she said around the mouthful of red.

Cien averted his eyes. He had seen kandar eat on Derkra before, but it still made him uneasy. It was unnatural.

"Why can't we finally have what the humans have had since the beginning of time?"

Rendinzori. A human power, she had said, but more powerful than pandinzori. She swallowed the flower. They had lost the humans—lost the Purpose—to become more human themselves?

"Is that what you want?" Cien asked. "To be human? To use this human power—"

"No." A line of red trailed from the corner of her lips. "We're better than them. That's what this is about."

"Will you sleep now?" Cien asked, ignoring her protest. He was too angry to listen. Pandinzori flew from him. "Will you waste away pretending like those of us who've forgotten the Purpose? Lying around in the sand, stuffing your face with the bodies of our fathers. I'm sure that's what Creator meant for us."

"Enough!"

They stared at each other. The pandinzori between them was wild. Then Miadra stumbled. She regained her footing but confusion flashed across her face. Cien watched her through the glass and wondered what she would try next. She closed her eyes.

"I think," she said quietly, "I do need to sleep."

"Of course," Cien said. "Of course you do."

Kandar who played human were just wasting time. Creator had made them the way they were for a reason. Pretending to eat, to sleep, just to find something to do when they could be searching for a way back to the Purpose was wrong. Now Miadra would adopt this flaw and call it change. He was stuck in a glass cage to stop him from interfering.

She stumbled back to the cave wall. When she reached it her body slumped and she slid down to rest on the ground. "Cien," she said, but the word was slurred. "See. See the changes that have come to us."

He looked above her to take in the leaves. They rustled with the spiders' movement. He looked to her side to see the fire, liquid and burning a path through the stone. Then, directly before him he saw the glass. Last he considered her motionless form, huddled and still on the floor of the cave. Her eyes were closed and she pretended to sleep. There was nothing good about this change. If any of the kandar deserved to be in a cage, if any of them deserved his fate, it was Miadra and those who followed her. Again he wished to attack the glass. Break through it to the other side. If he could only escape he would make them pay for what they had done.

Movement drew his focus. He pressed himself against the glass, oblivious to the danger it presented. Spiders streamed down through the leaves and swarmed over Miadra. She didn't react to them.

Cien was mesmerised by the flow of the creatures. They poured from the cave walls like black water. Miadra's skin shivered with them. They slid in and out of the shadows that caressed her and still the tevadra did not stir.

'Miadra.' She didn't respond. "Miadra!"

Then in the back of his mind Cien felt a leaf fall from the collective. The tree went dark. Miadra was gone. The spiders streamed off her body and left it lying there. The pandinzori that had made up her aura went with them.

What had happened to her? Kandar didn't just fall dead like that. Cien knew extreme loss of pandinzori or excess physical harm could end a kandar before they were called but neither of those things had been applied to Miadra. Her body was pristine. The same as it had been in life, only somehow emptier.

Perhaps something had happened to Cotelle? Cien checked the collective and found the devoshai's leaf just as it winked into bright existence. Cotelle was coming.

Cien spun in the cage. He searched for something, anything to help him escape. There had to be a way. Something he could use against the glass. Something he could break it with. There was nothing. He dropped to his knees on the rough black floor. Cotelle would be angry. Cotelle could easily kill him by accident. He heard a noise.

The big devoshai rushed into the cave, shouting incomprehensibly. When his eyes locked onto Miadra he became silent. He walked slowly towards her small, still body and knelt there. He gathered her up in his arms and lay with her.

Cien watched from a slit in the glass near the ground. A flitting shadow drew his eyes across the cave. Damarin stood in the entrance. She leaned against the wall much as Miadra had and looked down on the two silent kandar. Her skin had gone back to its previously flawless state. Now his looked as hers once had.

'*What happened?*' her voice came into his mind. Cotelle didn't react to the words.

'*Miadra is dead,*' Cien responded, trying to hold his voice directed just at Damarin. He was careful to avoid applying that concentration to the pandinzori that surrounded him.

'*That is quite clear. How did she die?*'

'*I'm not sure.*'

And he really wasn't. One moment they had been discussing the humans and rendinzori and the next Miadra had eaten the flower and begun to slump to the ground.

'*She ate a red flower?*'

Cien was amazed at how well she could hear him. If Damarin could hear his silent thoughts then Cotelle should be able to hear him too.

'You're not concentrating enough on keeping them silent. The collective is full of the private thoughts of kandar if you care to listen. I simply pay attention in the right way.'

It was useless to even speak to the tevadra. Cien stood behind the glass and waited for her to continue.

'So Miadra ate a red flower,' Damarin mused. Cotelle was kept out of the conversation. He had to be. *'And she slept?'*

Cien concentrated. It was hard through his fear and anger. *'She pretended to sleep, as useless kandar of that nature do.'* It was the tevadra's own fault she hadn't moved when the spiders covered her. She could have easily done so. Unless she really was asleep. But she couldn't have been. He didn't believe it.

'You did this, didn't you?' Damarin said.

Cien snapped out of his thoughts. Damarin's eyes were wide and her mouth was slightly open. It was the most extreme emotion Cien had ever seen on her face, and it did not abate.

'You killed her.'

Cien turned his eyes to Cotelle. He hoped the devoshai hadn't heard that last thought of Damarin's, although it wasn't true. How could he have killed Miadra from a cage of glass?

'No use denying it,' she said. *'Although I know what it feels like to be responsible for death. At least she can come back. Not like a human.'*

Cien met her eyes and recognised her expression. She looked the same way she had looked when she arrived in the desert with Ruon.

'I didn't kill her.'

'You did.' Damarin laughed.

Even if the thought was silent, laughing couldn't possibly help the situation. *'He could kill us in an instant, Damarin. What are you doing?'*

The pandinzori in the cave seemed to pulse in Cien's mind. He blinked and it was still. Fear was going to kill him if Cotelle didn't do it first. His instinct was to reach for pandinzori to protect himself. Damarin was far gone if she thought to provoke a devoshai who had just lost his dodenzinn, let alone another in a cage of glass.

Cotelle's eyes darted from the silently shaking Damarin, her laughter quieted, to Cien behind the wall of glass.

"How did this happen?" he asked. It was barely loud enough to hear.

Damarin smiled. Cotelle stared at her.

'Damarin,' Cien warned with a quiet thought.

"How does a kandar just die like this?" Cotelle's voice wavered when he spoke.

Damarin walked calmly to the wall of the cave and picked a red flower from the vines. She held it against herself.

"Miadra wanted rendinzori on Derkra," she said. "You both did."

Cotelle turned to Damarin. "Rendinzori did this?"

"You know it did." Damarin dropped the red flower onto the cave floor and crushed it with a foot. "See how they've changed."

She stepped away from the deep red smear. The shadows against the cave wall shifted. Then the spiders came. Hundreds of them. They flowed over the spot on the rock and when they left there was no sign of the red that had brought them. Most disappeared into the vines but a small group broke off. They scuttled towards Damarin.

Cien found himself wishing they would cover her as they had Miadra. Flow over her until she was dead. He also hoped she'd somehow escape. If they were dodenzinn he needed her alive.

When the spiders reached Damarin's feet, yellow-tinged pandinzori swept over them. Cien ducked. It was so close to the cage. He almost reached for it himself. Instead he covered his head with his arms and sunk to the ground. There was nothing he could do.

"Into the fire," Damarin said. "Only rendinzori could have changed them. Rendinzori made them, but they had no purpose. Now they do, thanks to Cien."

Cien got to his feet behind the glass. He watched Cotelle for a reaction. Damarin looked down at the devoshai. His arms were wrapped around his dead dodenzinn and he hadn't moved since Damarin dropped the red leaf. Cien was amazed he could be so calm around the glass and pandinzori. But maybe he wasn't calm.

"You don't think he could do it?" Damarin asked Cotelle.

Cotelle's gaze shifted to Cien.

"So much pandinzori," he said. "He almost looks like Ruon."

"It's true." Damarin examined Cien. "And did he have as much when Ruon brought him back from the sand?"

Cotelle shook his head.

"Then we have learned something." Damarin looked at Miadra's body in the devoshai's arms. "Will you take her place? Help me build our new world?"

Cotelle shook his head again. Cien thought he saw the devoshai's eyes flash with anger.

"I shouldn't be surprised," Damarin said. "You're just as intelligent as she was. Just as invested in change. You could have been High Seat yourself, yet you chose to be her Voice. When I came to Black Valley you let her speak for you and not just through you. Why?"

The big devoshai didn't return her gaze. "It doesn't matter now. She was the only thing that mattered."

Cotelle's thoughts grew loud and Cien was overwhelmed with an emotion he didn't understand.

Damarin gasped. "You actually loved her. Jaydin told me love was gone from the kandar."

"Love?" Cotelle asked.

"You don't need to know it. Love is for humans."

"So was rendinzori," Cotelle responded.

Damarin looked back at Cien. "I guess we have to take some of the bad with the good." She turned to walk away without another word.

Cien barely noticed Damarin leave the cave. He watched Cotelle carefully for signs of instability. He wasn't sure what he could do if the devoshai decided to kill them both with the glass, but he had to try something to stay alive. Damarin wanted to keep him alive, so why had she left them together?

Cotelle stood and paced in the cave. He held Miadra's body against him and cradled her in his arms. Cien watched him warily. The devoshai approached the liquid fire.

"Did you do this?" Cotelle asked, after he had stopped near the edge of it. "Did you kill her?"

"No," Cien said with conviction. "I did not."

Cotelle glared at him. "I could destroy both of us right now, you know."

Cien was already tired of being afraid. The direct threat was too much. "So could I."

"But you won't. You can still live. My life is here, in my arms."

"Tchardin is lost to the sands of Land Side or missing somewhere off Derkra. She may never return." And Damarin was actively confining him in glass.

"So half of you is free," the big devoshai said. "Missing, but alive. Half of me is dead."

Cotelle held Miadra's body out before him and stared down into the orange glow. Cien wanted to look away but his eyes were riveted to the scene. The devoshai took another step forward. It looked like he meant to walk into the fire.

"Stop." Cien was shocked to find the word leave his lips.

Cotelle turned towards him. "Why?"

"You have her body." Miadra may have been complicit in Cien's imprisonment, but he couldn't watch them disappear into the fire. Kandar weren't meant to die forever. "She can still go back to her father."

"I'm not called."

"How can you not be?"

Cotelle shrugged. "I'm not. I feel nothing. Her father might take her, but what if my father won't take me? I won't let her be reborn alone."

"Give her to the trees and wait then. It'll be hard, but you'll be called when your life was meant to end. It has to be so. It always has been."

Cotelle turned back to the fire. He was at the very edge of the rock now. Cien didn't understand why he was losing him. The answer to Cotelle's problem seemed so clear.

"That has to be enough," Cien said, "knowing you'll be together again and again forever."

"The longer I wait, the less likely I am to be called."

"Why?" Cotelle would be called. All kandar were.

"You don't know what's happening out there, do you?" The devoshai took a step away from the fire and towards the glass. Cien realised neither direction was safe. "The council is ready to change things. There are those in Calendrai who do not agree, and war could come to the kandar."

"War," Cien whispered. "Miadra mentioned the possibility."

"If it's anything like the first one, am I likely to survive it?"

"Then keep Miadra out of the trees until it's over. Until you can be certain you'll both be whole when it ends. Or don't let it start in the first place! You can't just give up."

"I could hide her body somewhere, but what if I'm destroyed in the new war? What if the kandar find her body and remember her father, assume I've been called to mine? What if he takes her?"

"And you will be gone." Cien was starting to understand the devoshai's dilemma. If only one of them was given to the trees, they'd never know their dodenzinn was lost.

Cotelle nodded. "Or what if I am whole and they place me in my father, but they never find hers? What if her body is destroyed and I am dead, unable to stop them from doing as they will with mine?"

"There has to be a way to guarantee you'll both be given to the trees."

"I don't believe there is."

Cien couldn't think of anything else. Cotelle stared at him.

"Then end it," Cien said. "You were right. It's the only sure option."

Cotelle didn't move. Pandinzori slid past the glass between them.

"End it for all three of us."

Cotelle still didn't speak. The longer the devoshai remained silent the more hopeless the situation seemed. Cien looked at the pandinzori around them, at the glass he stood on, the glass that held him. How long could he be expected to live like this? How long before he lost his mind completely? At least Miadra had said she would come back for him, when everything was done. He hadn't believed her, hadn't thought it would matter, but she had said it. She was gone now.

"If Tchardin is still alive she probably won't survive a war," Cien said.

"She's alive." It was a statement, not a question. "If you die here she could be left alone in her future. Would you let that be possible?"

"No." Cien said it without thinking, then realised his answer contradicted his request. Until he had felt her leave the collective, until he had seen her body destroyed, there was always a chance she could go back to her father, whether through her own will or another's. If she did he would have to join her. He couldn't let her be reborn alone, especially when her new self wouldn't know. And then there was Damarin to consider. She might deserve it right now, but what about those she would become? It was the same with Miadra and Cotelle.

"If Tchardin does return to her father," Cotelle said, "and we are still alive, I will free you myself and see you returned to the trees. Until then, you must remain here. You owe her that."

"But you will go into the fire," Cien said, confused.

The big devoshai almost smiled. "I won't. Not yet. I owe Miadra just as you owe Tchardin. She'd want us to be together again, in her new world. Even if it's flawed. Even if it killed her. She wouldn't have given up. I shouldn't either."

He disappeared from Cien's view, hidden by the glass. Cien moved closer to the pillars to watch him, though it sent shivers through his body to be so near it. He lifted a foot at the thought, cutting it on the sharp black glass beneath him.

Cotelle carried Miadra towards the entrance. Cien was overwhelmed by the image. First Miadra had promised to save him, in a way, and now she was dead and her dodenzinn had done the same. Yet they were the cause of all this, as much as Damarin was.

When Cotelle was almost out of sight Cien got angry again. The devoshai's dodenzinn might be dead before her time, and he faced a crippling decision as to what to do with her, but he had options. He could leave the cave. He could destroy both Miadra's body and his own and ensure no harm would come of the situation. But he also didn't have to. They might still get to be reborn. Cotelle could choose.

Cien had no control over what would happen to his body if he was killed, and even less over Tchardin and Damarin's. His only option was to end it himself and that wasn't an option at all.

"You helped her start this," he called after the devoshai.

"I didn't know it would end this way," Cotelle answered without turning. His voice was soft, resigned. Perhaps he knew why Cien said what he did. "I didn't understand what we were doing."

Cien almost let him leave at that. Then he remembered Damarin's words about rendinzori, Miadra's thoughts on those who opposed them.

"Miadra did," he said instead. "So does Damarin."

The big devoshai paused for a moment but didn't speak. Cien last saw him silhouetted against the light from the entrance, Miadra's limp body hanging in his arms. Then he was alone again with his pandinzori and his glass cage.

Chapter 31

Tchardin knelt before Irah and stroked his miniature leaves. *The original,* the woman had said. How could Irah not be the original? He was the first tree of this Earth.

"You should have seen my inspiration," the woman said from behind Tchardin. "It was the best part of my parents' property up north. I used to climb it all the time. A magnificent tree. The largest I ever laid eyes on. It must have been more than a thousand years old."

That description fit a World Tree much better than what stood before Tchardin's eyes. Irah should have been huge. This tree felt immense but didn't look it.

'Are you the first?' Tchardin asked the tiny tree. *'Was there another?'*

The answer arrived as a feeling in her mind. He was confused. The tree knew he should look different. He knew there had been a change he didn't understand. But he was adamant he was the World Tree, Irah, and always had been.

'And Koska?' Maybe Irah would know what had happened to his original guardian, the proper kandaran one.

The answer this time was extreme distress, then calm. She sensed respect from him. If the woman had a seed in the collective and Irah wasn't upset at its presence she had to be the true guardian. Koska must have been lost sometime after the kandar left the Earths and this human woman had unknowingly come to replace her. If the World Tree accepted this, Tchardin would have to as well.

"I'm probably the only one left alive who's seen it," Irah the guardian continued, oblivious to Tchardin's silent conversation. "I'd love to see it again..."

Tchardin turned to look at her, still kneeling. "Why can't you go back to the original?"

Irah walked to the opening in the wall of trees. Tchardin got up and followed her.

"Even if I could travel this world by myself. With all the changes, I wouldn't know where to find it."

Tchardin looked out from the gate. Again she was unsettled by the absence of other humans, of animals. Of movement. The scene was too quiet, too still. For Derkra it would be normal, but for an Earth it looked dead. Irah didn't seem to find anything wrong with it. Tchardin closed her eyes and immediately opened them again.

She had to turn back to the yard to conceal her shock. There was no light outside the gate. She remembered seeing a black space there when it had shown her the void, but with a view of the world she expected pandinzori. There were trees out there. How could they not have pandinzori around them? She looked at Irah and wondered what the woman's world was. Was it only an image? Tchardin had worried there were no other humans on it, but was there nothing else at all? Perhaps Jaydin would understand.

"I have to go now," Tchardin said.

"Will you come back? You can stop by anytime you'd like. To talk. Or to see the garden. You don't have to break in."

Tchardin hesitated. She planned to return to Irah—just as she planned to return to Kordic and World Three—if only to figure out how to deal with this Earth, but she couldn't guarantee she would. She worried that if she said so, Irah would wait for her. The woman was already lonely. Tchardin couldn't bear to disappoint her if she didn't come back.

"No," she said. "I probably won't."

Irah looked at her with a sad smile.

"I'm sorry," Tchardin added.

"Nothing to be sorry about. You have to look out for yourself. Just promise me you'll come back if you need help."

Tchardin smiled and touched her forehead. It was no longer sticky with blood and her hand came away clean. "I will."

Irah motioned for her to move back, stepping to the side as the wooden frame of the gate swung open. Tchardin walked into the space it had occupied. She'd have to leave the yard if she wanted to shift. She couldn't do it in front of Irah, despite the woman's possible status in the hierarchy as a guardian. Irah was still a human.

Tchardin forced herself to step through the opening. The void of pandinzori hit her and reminded her of Water Side. Her mind began to ache, her body to weaken. She took a few steps on the grey ground but didn't like the sensation against her feet. It was too hard and too flat. There was grass to one side of it so she moved onto that. The sensation against her skin was more familiar, but still somehow off. At least the world was more than an image.

"Wait," Irah called after her. "You never gave me your name."

"It's Tchardin," she said, turning back to the woman. She was too tired to search for an acceptable human name. She wondered about Irah's, spoken to her but not reflected in the collective. Perhaps the woman had gotten it from the tree.

The pandinzori around Tchardin thinned. She turned away and began to walk, looking back at intervals to see if the guardian had left the gate.

The grey pathway seemed to go on forever and the view to either side of it was always the same. Tchardin was getting farther away from Irah but not really going anywhere. She didn't think she would ever leave the guardian's gaze as long as the woman continued to watch. How would she shift without Irah seeing? How would she go on to the next world? She looked back and saw Irah waiting still, standing at the gate without stepping out.

Tchardin turned to the right, away from the grey strip. The grass she walked across was even stranger than the grass just outside Irah's yard—sometimes she couldn't even feel it against her feet—but she had to get away before she had too little pandinzori to shift.

She approached one of the other buildings and found it to be nothing like Irah's home. This one was an almost featureless white rectangle with blurred edges. She turned back towards the guardian. Now Irah leaned out of the gate to keep her in sight. If Tchardin walked past the building Irah wouldn't be able to see her. Its unfocused corner was only steps away. She closed her eyes and walked through the blackness.

She had walked into water.

She nearly lost herself to it for a moment, but it was nothing like her earlier trips through the shift. She recovered quickly and stayed in her body as she had between Worlds Four and Five. A curved wall of ice preceded her as she moved through the water and left a trail of frozen shards behind.

Tchardin stopped to look around, her ice shield growing to completely surround her. She floated within the sphere of it. Infinite clarity. The water was clear with nothing behind it.

She glided forwards, searching for the next tree. Leaves appeared before her, breaking out of nothing and swaying in the water. These were a light green with jagged edges. Black splotches marred their surfaces. Some had holes through them.

She didn't get a good look at them before her body accelerated. She caught a branch as she swung by.

She was pitched into World Six. She rolled on the ground and landed gracefully with one knee against earth. Her exit from the shift improved with each world she visited.

It was dark on this Earth. It must be night. Faint silver light filtered down on her, but there was no true light ahead of her. She was confronted with a wide wall of blackness, lit only by blazing pandinzori. Its presence comforted her after Word Five. She moved forward to investigate, her hands stretched out to touch the wall. Her fingers brushed it and she pulled away.

It wasn't a wall, but a trunk, so wide as to seem flat. It was Veradon, the World Tree. His base was wider even than Ovaeron's. Jaydin had said he was the largest World Tree in existence, but Tchardin had been skeptical. How could any tree be greater than Ovaeron? Now she saw it was true.

She turned to examine her surroundings. She stood in a quiet forest. There were no humans in sight so she opened the shift and thought of World Seven.

As the grey oval grew she remembered seeing World Four through Coralynth from the shift on World Three. She might be able to see World Seven if she looked again from here. The swirling grey first darkened, then lightened to lines of white. It snowed on Coralynth. There was a slight indent in the snow where the path wound towards the mountain. Across the path she saw an image of a tree she recognised. It was Irah, the World Tree, and before him knelt Irah, the guardian. The image was of World Five, not World Seven.

Irah stroked the tree's leaves. She left the image briefly and returned with a short red cylinder. She tipped it towards the tree and water ran onto his roots. When she turned there was also water on her face, streaking down from one of her eyes. She stood and walked away.

'Tchar,' Tchardin said in no particular direction. *'Tchar! I don't want to do this anymore. I want to go back to Derkra.'*

There was no response. The first kandar didn't appear in the shift, and Tchardin was left staring at the miniature World Tree through the snow.

'I can't help them alone.'

Jaydin would have been the better kandar to travel the Earths. Or even Damarin, despite her actions on World Four. One sister had made it her life to return to the humans, the other had found the way. Tchardin wondered for a moment if Damarin had shared that discovery with the rest of the kandar. Perhaps they were searching for Tchardin. Maybe it would be best to stay where she was. One of the kandar would figure out how to return to Derkra directly, if Damarin didn't already know.

Tchardin let the image of Coralynth fade to grey and thought of World Seven again. There were only three Earths left. If she hadn't run into any of the other kandar yet, there was no way they'd figured out how to visit specific Earths. At best they were chasing her, if they had come to the Earths at all. The only thing she could do was continue.

The ground around her trembled. The surface of the shift shivered and cracks appeared in the ice. She studied it, wary of the fact that something outside her power had broken it. Looking at its fractured face she wasn't sure what she'd been thinking of the moment the ice settled. She closed it and began again.

Another shock ran through the earth. She was thrown off her feet. When she recovered she turned towards the trunk of the great tree. She couldn't open the shift if she couldn't stand. Veradon would sway with the movement of the earth, but she could compensate for that. She would find a safe place to shift in his branches.

Her fingers sunk into his bark when she went to climb him. She recoiled from it, disbelieving. She searched his base for a solid place to start but everywhere she touched was unnaturally soft. Something was wrong with the tree. She couldn't climb him like this. Her hands and feet would leave gouges in the wood.

Another tremor hit her, this one small and from far away. The buzzing of thoughts grew in her mind. She looked behind her.

Shadowed figures raced through the small trees that encircled Veradon. At first glance they looked like kandar. The colour of them and the way they moved was familiar to Tchardin, but they had too much pandinzori. One of them stopped and turned in her direction. She abandoned the tree and ran.

They were humans. Humans with kandaran skin. It was mottled, like the shadows thrown by leaves, but it was green. Dark green and light green and brown and black, and they had no faces. Where their eyes should have been was only a span of black reflection. They were misshapen. Their backs and legs bulged and their hands were joined by a length of dark material that couldn't be a part of their bodies.

Tchardin ran behind the trunk of a smaller tree and stopped. The purple dress she wore from World Four was torn now in numerous places. Maybe the strange kandaran skin was also clothing, but it seemed too monstrous to be a choice.

The earth rumbled. She ran again. There were thoughts from above. She looked up and saw humans in the trees. One of them fell from the sky between branches, leaving a blaze of pandinzori in the night. She had to get away. They were too much like kandar. They had to be dangerous. Even the people of World Four hadn't scared her so much.

The stretch before her was clear of trees. She looked over her shoulder as she continued to run, checking behind her. There didn't appear to be anyone in pursuit. The humans in the trees must not have noticed her as she silently sped past.

All of a sudden she found herself on hard, flat ground. Tall, straight walls rose on either side of her. They climbed so high they seemed to close in above her. She recognised them as the sides of enormous buildings, but they were easily as tall as the World Tree. At her back was the forest, full of humans.

She stopped. Set into the walls, starting high above her head and continuing until they were too high for her to see clearly, were uniform rectangles of light. They looked to be windows, like the window in Irah's home. Pandinzori floated out of them. Another tremor hit the forest and a number of the lights disappeared. The place pulsed with hysterical thought.

Tchardin felt uneasy. She couldn't see the humans who generated the thoughts and the buildings continued ahead of her into the far distance. They were broken in places on one side or the other, but her impression was of an unending corridor with no escape.

She didn't care if a human saw her. She prepared to open the shift. Light blossomed above her as she gathered pandinzori. She looked up. The tops of the buildings blazed with a red and orange glow. Higher, above them, somehow flattened against nothing in the sky, there was fire. A massive boom followed, but there was no tremor through the hard ground. She refocused her attention and opened the shift.

Something crashed into her. The force sent her flying through the ice.

The water was hostile. Tchardin struggled to resist as it rushed at her from every side, trying to consume her, striving to break through the ice shield she had built around herself. She felt its want, its singular need for her. It was as bad as the first time she travelled the shift, when Cien had gone with her. She didn't know why.

She approached a visible disturbance in the water. At first she thought it was only more of the violence that had assaulted her since her entry, but as she got closer she noticed it was too slow, too regular to be the same. The water seemed to flow around something she couldn't see. The pattern was familiar.

Could they be leaves? Transparent branches covered in waving water? She pushed through the angry blue to examine them. Something pierced the bubble around her. The ice disintegrated.

Tchardin's mind ached as she rolled herself over in the grass of World Seven. It had been several shifts since she succumbed so fully to the water. The fight to get out had been exhausting.

The leaves spread above her told her she was in another forest. She turned over and saw a woman lying a few steps away. A shiver ran through her body. The woman had the same mottled green skin as the humans on World Six.

The woman didn't move. Tchardin got up and quietly walked over to stand above her. The woman's presence explained the violence of the shift. Just like Cien had sought to join with Tchardin in the water, so too had this human. Her body remained still.

Perhaps she hadn't made it. Tchardin looked closer. There was pand-inzori sloughing off her skin. If she had been kandar that would have signified she was close to death, but for a human it was normal. That must mean she was alive. What would happen if a human woke in a new world? A leaf formed in her mind.

Reva, the collective told her. Reva was a citizen of Argyle, and she had spent her short adult life killing other humans. The gun in her hands had been given to her when she was fifteen, on the day she failed to prove her magic. Only some people could throw fire, but everyone could carry a gun. It had been heavy then. It was heavy now, but for different reasons.

Reva brought other leaves with her—dark with the distance between the worlds—but they were all the same. One story, many names. World Six was a world of war, as Jaydin had said. Reva was one of its soldiers. Tchardin's eyes were drawn to the black branch the woman carried. A *gun.* It was similar to the one Irah the guardian had been carrying when she threatened Tchardin in her yard. Now Tchardin knew what it was. She looked down the length of it to where the woman clutched it. Reva's hand twitched.

Tchardin jumped and ran behind a nearby tree. There was nothing she could do if the woman was waking. She'd have to see how Reva reacted to the new Earth and decide what to do with her then. She watched from around the trunk.

Reva scrambled to her feet. She held the gun in both hands and propped it against her shoulder. She turned in a slow circle, her knees bent, her body tense. Her thoughts were erratic and Tchardin had trouble deciphering them. She wondered what the woman was doing. A forest was a safe place. Then she remembered the forest they had just come from.

Eventually Reva paused. She lowered the gun and gripped at her strange black eye with one hand. She pushed it back over her head. The kandaran skin came away and Tchardin was relieved to see her true face. It was just like any other human face she had seen. Reva's mind said the shed skin was a *helmet* and the eyes were *goggles.* It had been clothing after all.

Reva placed the helmet and goggles on the ground and looked around her again, this time with less trepidation. Tchardin looked around too. She gasped.

Despite being in a seemingly untouched forest, there was glass all around them. One of the trees nearby wasn't a tree, but a travesty. It was entirely glass and it grew right out of the earth that way. Off to the side of it was a solid glass block. Most of the trees were wood and green but she saw others that were glass, scattered through the forest.

Tchardin was horrified, but Reva's thoughts radiated awe. Her mouth hung open and she spun slowly, looking up into the sparkling canopy. Tchardin tried to clear her mind so she wouldn't touch any of the pandinzori, but it was hard with the human generating so much.

"I'm dead," Reva said. "I must be. The firebombs..."

The World Tree caught Tchardin's eye. He was unmistakable. Much larger than the trees that surrounded him, with a beautiful straight trunk of a rich dark colour. She remembered his name was Rai. As his trunk grew up it became wreathed in emerald leaves. Tchardin's gaze followed it upwards to take in his whole height.

After the first few sets of branches the wood grew into glass. Tchardin was revolted. She thought of the translucent leaves in the shift and knew what they meant. At the same time she noticed the pandinzori around her was brightening. She looked back at the woman and found a maelstrom of light. The amount that came off her was more than Tchardin had ever seen around a human. Her eyes grew wide.

There was glass all around them. The World Tree had grown into glass. Reva was filling the forest with pandinzori. It was only a matter of time before Tchardin made a mistake and killed them both.

"It's beautiful." Reva dropped the gun. "It's so peaceful..."

A streak of light drew Tchardin's gaze. A figure sprinted across the grass behind the human. It was a tevadra, out of camouflage, shadows wrapping her body. The glint came off a long shard of glass in her hands. The tevadra sprang upon the woman's back and drove the glass into her skin, just above her shoulder.

Red sprayed across the tevadra's face. Reva screamed. She raised her hands to push the glass away. They were cut to pieces. Her body slumped and her leaf faded and fell but the tevadra cut at her again and again, breaking the shard between her bones. Tchardin watched in silent horror. Then everything was still.

The tevadra stood and approached Tchardin, her body slick with blood that was swallowed by the shadows that clung to her. "Why did you bring her here?" she demanded. Her voice was strained, disused.

A seed grew in Tchardin's mind. The guardian of World Seven was supposed to be a devoshai called Leksten. The name that came with this seed was Siltadon. Jaydin had mentioned the tevadra, but Tchardin couldn't remember why.

Then the guardian was right in front of her. She was as tall as Tchardin but the opposite in colouring. Under the blood she was a silver-white, like Kordic had been. Almost colourless. Her clear blue eyes darted around them as she spoke.

"They think only of glass. Why would you bring her here?"

"I didn't mean to," Tchardin responded. "She ran into me while I was opening the shift. The water got both of us. I never thought a human could make it through. Why did you kill her?"

The guardian was livid. It showed on her face and looked strange on a kandar. "You came from another Earth? Not Coralynth?"

"Wait." Tchardin remembered why Jaydin had mentioned this tevadra. "You're the one who restarted this world." A tevadra straight out of Jaydin's history, alive and in front of her.

Siltadon took a step back. "I am its guardian."

"But you restarted it."

"How do you know that? It was a long time ago." She turned away, the broken shard of glass gripped tightly in her hand. Blood ran down its edges. "Too long for the kandar to remember."

"There is one who remembers," Tchardin said.

Siltadon turned back to face her. Tchardin watched the glass warily.

"She *remembers*?" Siltadon shook her head. "And she told you?"

Tchardin was about to answer when she realised Siltadon had said 'she'.

"She did." Perhaps the guardian was listening to her thoughts of Jaydin.

"And how many others?"

"How many others what?"

"How many know?"

"Not many."

"How many?"

Siltadon's insistent tone was insulting. Tchardin resisted the urge to point out her golden aura. So far the guardians hadn't reacted well to that, despite Tchardin being higher on the hierarchy than they were. Jaydin must have told Damarin about Siltadon, and Sandin as well. She didn't think there were others.

"I think there are four of us who know, including Jaydin."

"Four," the guardian said, seeming to look past Tchardin and into the distance. "That's not so many."

Tchardin turned around to see what she was looking at. Glass and green and pandinzori greeted her eyes. She turned all the way around to look in every direction. There didn't seem to be anything else to look at. Glass and green for as far as she could see, broken only by Reva's blood-soaked body.

"What happened here?" she asked. "What happened to the trees? To Rai?"

The tevadra didn't answer.

"Jaydin said the Earth was burning. So you must have restarted the world successfully."

Siltadon looked her in the eyes. "No," she said, her voice faltering. "I failed."

CHAPTER 32

SANDIN BRUSHED ASIDE THE grass that fell in her face and looked up into the canopy of Cens. She lay on her back beneath Frenn, hidden in deep shadows, thinking. Jaydin talked to Kadailin a few steps away. Her younger sister had asked about Siltadon.

"Siltadon was born of a tree on Derkra," Jaydin said, "in the Black Valley, like any other kandar of her time. She was assigned to World Seven when it was already dying."

"It was dying?" Kadailin asked.

"The humans had set their Earth on fire. Liquid heat had burst from the core of the planet to cover everything—"

"The planet?"

Jaydin sighed. "An Earth is called a planet when it's spherical." Silence. Sandin muffled a laugh. She remembered how difficult the concept had been for her the first time. She wasn't sure she entirely understood it even now. "Round," Jaydin continued. "A round Earth. It wasn't flat and infinite like Derkra, but continuous, in a circle."

"Why was it like that?"

"I assume that's what Creator planned for it, but it wasn't always that way. All the worlds started as Derkra is and some of them gradually became round over time. As of the last time we visited the humans, Worlds Five through Nine had spherical Earths. Worlds Eight and Nine even had other planets."

"Other Earths?"

"Not exactly. There's only one Earth in each World. The other planets didn't have humans on them."

"Could they have?" Kadailin seemed completely absorbed.

"They might have, eventually. They might even now."

Sandin saw where this was going. Jaydin would never stop elaborating if Kadailin didn't stop asking her to. Sandin had seen the same thing with Damarin. There wasn't time for it now. She sat up in the grass. "Back to Siltadon."

Both tevadra turned to look at her, Jaydin with an irritated expression on her face. Her notebook was nestled in the grass between the two.

Jaydin turned back to its pages. "The people of World Seven were all but gone at that point, and the forests, hundreds of years since gone."

"No trees?" Kadailin asked. Sandin glared at her. "How could they live without trees?"

"They don't always need them, as hard as that is to believe. As long as the Root of the World lives they can survive. And on World Seven the Root was intact. Even Rai, the World Tree, hung on. His trunk was straight and strong and he stood on one of the last pieces of hard earth that remained above the fire. The people lived below him, deep within the rock."

Sandin looked at the burnt strip and saw Ocien and Ryten quietly speaking over the blackened leaves. She wondered if they could hear Jaydin from where they stood.

"The kandar worked hard to save it," Jaydin continued, "Siltadon more than most. She was a friend of Carrensing's and Tith told me a lot about her. They tried, but in the end it was hopeless. World Seven was the first world of existence in need of rebirth."

Kadailin cringed at the harsh words. Sandin understood that reaction. To restart a world meant to begin again with nothing. All the people who had lived through the fire would have been killed. Erased. Jaydin ignored Kadailin's look and adjusted her notebook in front of them.

"How did they decide to restart it?" Kadailin finally asked. "That's a terrible decision to make, even if there weren't many humans left."

"Siltadon found the World Seed at Rai's base. There's no clearer sign that a World Tree has given up on his Earth. He was about to die, and the Root could have died with him. Then it would have been too late for World Seven."

"What did Siltadon do with the Seed?"

"She brought it first to Tchar, then before the council. Each bade her restart the world. The kandar on World Seven were called back and

Siltadon left Derkra for Coralynth. From Coralynth she was seen leaving for the burning Earth one last time. That's all we know."

"Nothing is told about the rest of her life?" Kadailin asked.

Jaydin shrugged. "No kandar had set foot on World Seven since before the war, and she never came back to her father. Tith couldn't even say what had happened to the Earth."

"But Damarin knows?"

"So Miadra says."

Sandin studied the tall grass around her. She was thinking again, in her silent mind. She had been doing a lot of thinking since Jaydin returned from Black Valley the third time. Damarin's words came back to her.

"Are you kandar?" her sister had asked, and Sandin had known the answer. Or at least she had thought she did. She looked above her and had a nearly clear view of the sky through the sparse leaves. Much too clear. There should be more branches, more trees.

Miadra had told Jaydin that humans could create trees. She had said the idea came from Siltadon, alive on World Seven since so long ago. If that was true then the humans could use rendinzori to perform feats even the kandar were incapable of. Sandin followed Frenn's blackened trunk farther into the high canopy. She looked at the sky again. She ran her eyes over her sisters' bodies and examined the air that surrounded them.

"Can the humans see rendinzori?" she asked.

Jaydin took a moment before responding. "I'm not sure, but I don't think so. Most of them don't even use it directly. Or knowingly. It's complicated."

Sandin had been hoping for certainty. "Can the kandar see it?"

"From what I was told, no."

"But Miadra says we can use it."

"She believes we can."

Sandin looked around her again. "How then? Without seeing it? How can we use it?"

Jaydin sighed. "I don't know. I'm sorry, Sandin, but this is new to me as well. Tith told me of rendinzori but only in a human context. He never said if the kandar could use it or how we could learn to do so."

Sandin found herself frustrated with Jaydin's vast knowledge for the first time in her life. She had never been one to ask questions of her older sister. Not like Damarin and certainly not like Kadailin. But now she wanted to know something important, needed to know it, and Jaydin couldn't give her any answers.

"You want to use it?" Kadailin asked.

Sandin's eyes locked onto Jaydin's. "Why shouldn't I?"

Jaydin met her gaze but remained silent. Her grey eyes were soft for once.

"It could be dangerous," Kadailin said, her focus shifting between the two of them.

Sandin was about to respond when Jaydin spoke.

"She deserves to feel like one of us."

"But rendinzori isn't pandinzori," Kadailin responded. "You said it yourself; Tith only spoke of it in human terms."

"Nevertheless, using something to manipulate the world would be better than remaining helpless," Jaydin said. "Am I right, Sandin?"

"As close as you can be." Sandin lay down in the grass again, wanting to hide from her older sister's pitying gaze. She regretted telling Jaydin how Damarin had pushed her around with pandinzori, how the earthquake had made her fear she would die. "Could we go to World Seven? To ask Siltadon about rendinzori ourselves?"

Kadailin gasped. Jaydin shushed her.

"You know I would give anything to see the Earth as it is now," Jaydin said. "Any of the Earths as they are now. If we could get there we could fulfill the Purpose."

Sandin wondered what it would be like for Jaydin to meet Siltadon, a kandar who had actually lived her history. "Then we should go. If Damarin can do it, so can we."

Her sisters didn't respond. Sandin watched the grass sway above her as she waited, but still they didn't speak. She sat up.

Jaydin and Kadailin stared at each other intently. Sandin had seen the rest of the kandar do this often enough to know they were speaking together. Excluding her. It was rare for Jaydin to be so blatant about it.

"What is it?" Sandin asked, refusing to be ignored.

Kadailin turned to her. "You implied Damarin has been to an Earth."

"How else could she know about Siltadon," Sandin said.

Kadailin ignored her. "Could Tchardin be on an Earth?"

"We don't know where she is," Jaydin said.

"But she could be," Kadailin insisted.

Jaydin frowned. "She could be. Tchardin disappeared around the same time Damarin did and we now know Damarin went to an Earth. They may have gone together. But I doubt—"

"And Cien?"

"I don't know." Jaydin raised her hands in front of her defensively. "They could also be out in the sand. Or even out in the water."

"They have to be on the Earths," Kadailin said. "Someone has to go. We need Tchardin. She would fix everything if she were here."

Jaydin fidgeted with her notebook in the grass and refused to look at either of them. Sandin had never seen her act so strangely. Their oldest sister had always been so confident.

"Even if they are on an Earth," Jaydin said, "the next thing you'll ask me is how we get there, and I'm going to have to tell you I don't know again."

At that, Sandin realised her frustration with Jaydin's uncertainty was nothing like her sister's frustration with being unable to provide the answers.

"So what do we do now then?" Kadailin demanded. "What's the point of learning about Siltadon if we can't go to her when Damarin can?"

Jaydin shrugged. "We can't get to the Earths on our own, but I won't go back to Black Valley until I know it's safe, and I don't trust the council of Calendrai with what we've learned so far."

"Tchardin could need our help," Kadailin said. "We have to find out how to get there."

"We don't know that for sure," Jaydin answered. "Maybe she and Cien are together. Maybe they're fine."

"I thought you were supposed to know everything," Kadailin said.

Sandin shot her a look. Kadailin ignored it.

"I don't really know everything," Jaydin said. "I just know so much more than the rest of you that it feels like everything, even to me."

The admission seemed to have shocked Kadailin out of her outrage. "What do you mean? I thought Tith told you our history."

"He told me most of it. Basically all of it. And the things I don't know really wouldn't matter if we could just return to the Purpose!" Jaydin stood up and paced. "What exactly started the war? Why did Tchar banish us? And why did Tith keep this from me? Does he not know, or did he hide it from me on purpose?"

Sandin opened her mouth to speak but both sisters turned away from her. They moved at exactly the same moment and they looked in the same direction. Someone else must be talking to them. Sandin followed their eyes but didn't see anything of particular note. "What is it?"

A tevadra she didn't recognise walked onto the burned leaves. Jaydin ran towards her. Kadailin rose to her knees but didn't follow.

"What's happening?" Sandin asked again.

"Moradi is called," Kadailin said. "Her father is one of the damaged trees."

The tevadra stopped in front of Jaydin. Torshe joined them and Ocien approached. Sandin didn't see Ryten anywhere.

"Will you tell me what they're saying?" Sandin asked.

Kadailin seemed to be concentrating on something. "Jaydin is explaining the problem to her. I've told her to speak aloud so you can hear. Perhaps Moradi will follow her lead."

A creaking sound split the air. Sandin searched the edges of the burnt patch for the trunk that had caused it. That would be Moradi's father, opening to let her rest in him. Sandin's eyes had settled on a tree across the clearing with bark so burnt it was nearly black when Jaydin's voice rose over the sound.

"You can't rest here," Jaydin said loudly, clearly exasperated. "Your father isn't well."

Kadailin said, "Vurel is my father." Her voice was strange and Sandin turned to her in surprise. It took her a moment to realise Kadailin was repeating the words Moradi must be saying into the collective. "He has called me. If you wish to stop me from returning to him you'll have to kill me yourself. I am meant to die as it is and you won't touch him while I'm alive."

"You can wait," Torshe said. "It will be hard, but another tree will call you. Just as another will call me after Buran is gone."

Kadailin spoke close to Sandin's ear. "She's thinking. Loudly, but not loud enough for me to hear specifics."

"We'll have to kill him with you inside if you go," Jaydin said.

Moradi's face changed then. The tevadra's eyes became focused and she glared at Jaydin as she responded.

"You would," Kadailin repeated in the same toneless voice she had used before to indicate she was speaking for Moradi. "I have heard what you would do."

Sandin felt useless sitting at the edge of the trees and watching. Maybe she could help persuade Moradi to leave her father. She stood and took a step towards the group of kandar. A hand gripped her arm. A jolt of revulsion ran through her as the invisible aura collided with her own.

"Wait." Kadailin had risen behind her and was looking away. "Things are about to get much worse."

Her sister let go of her arm and Sandin followed her eyes again, feeling lost. There she found Marr. When she looked back at Jaydin and Moradi all the kandar in the burnt patch had turned to him.

"There's so much pandinzori around them," Kadailin said. "I'm afraid of what will happen. If you get too close you could get caught in it."

She left the most important part unspoken. Sandin wouldn't be able to defend herself.

"Maybe you should hide," Kadailin continued quietly. "Get behind Frenn. I'll let you know what's happening if you can't hear for yourself."

"I want to help."

"You can't," Kadailin insisted. Sandin was surprised at the strength of her words. Their eyes met for a moment but Kadailin quickly lowered hers. She continued in a softer voice. "If something happens, Jaydin will forget everything to save you."

The kandar in the burnt patch were silent now. Silent and still. If they spoke at all, none of them spoke aloud. Maybe Jaydin was doing so on purpose to divert Marr's attention away from Sandin. If the devoshai hadn't seen her when he entered the burnt patch he might not know she was there. But he would notice Kadailin eventually.

Sandin backed away from the edge of the forest until she was out of sight. Kadailin followed her, facing the rest of the kandar the whole time. Frenn's trunk was thick and curved, but Sandin could still see Jaydin and Moradi around him. Marr was lost from view, along with Ocien and Torshe, which meant they probably wouldn't see her. Vurel's trunk yawned wide.

As Sandin strained to watch she noticed Ryten had joined the rest of them. He was wrapped in shadows and leaned against a dark trunk with his arms crossed. He was close to Jaydin and he looked in Marr's direction.

"They speak in their minds now that there are so many of them," Kadailin whispered from the other side of the trunk. "They're discussing Jaydin's plan and Marr is being nasty about it. Moradi seems to agree with him. He's had a lot of practice getting kandar to listen in the council."

"So has Jaydin," Sandin said.

Moradi took a step back, away from Marr. She stood beside Jaydin. Sandin wondered if she was changing her mind. Then the tevadra took another step. Neither Jaydin nor Ryten looked at her. They must be intent on the discussion with Marr.

"Jaydin's going to lose this one," Kadailin said. "Marr's too angry. Maybe if his father hadn't been burned—"

Sandin didn't listen to the rest of her words. Moradi was past Ryten now. The tevadra turned and ran.

Sandin ran after her. She wasn't the closest but there was no other way for her to help. "Moradi!" she yelled as loudly as she could. "Stop her, Jaydin!"

Jaydin turned towards the tevadra but it was too late. Moradi ran into Vurel's open trunk and it began to close around her. The tevadra's eyes disappeared behind the bark just as something solid shoved Sandin hard.

She crashed into Frenn's trunk. She crumpled to the ground, the world going black. Her vision returned and the air solidified around her and lifted her with it. She strained uselessly in an attempt to escape, but she was unable to move at all. Kadailin appeared in front of her.

Sandin was jerked back and forth in the air. Someone must be fighting Marr for control of the invisible pandinzori that held her. She relaxed her body, the world whipping past her, and tried to think of what she could do. She saw Jaydin for a moment. Her sister faced away from her. Then she fell to the ground, free.

"Run!" Kadailin shouted.

Sandin picked herself up and ran past Frenn into the sparseness of Cens.

***

Kadailin watched Sandin sprint away with relief. Now to make sure Marr didn't follow. She turned towards the others. Ryten stood in front of Marr with his back to Kadailin. He faced the devoshai, whose eyes were closed, and the two were enveloped in the thick pandinzori that filled the clearing. Ocien and Torshe were behind Marr, and behind them was Jaydin.

Vurel's trunk was being forced open.

Jaydin strained against him with her mind. A sheet of reddish pandinzori, as thin as a hand, was caught between the edges of his bark. It stopped him from fully taking Moradi. One of the tevadra's eyes was visible again, closed and pushed up against the inside of the tree. Some of her hair hung through. She didn't move.

The pandinzori widened slightly as Kadailin watched. To resist a tree. To force a father to abandon his daughter. Kadailin could only assume that would take all of Jaydin's concentration. Ocien and Torshe must be controlling the pandinzori that surrounded them, protecting Jaydin from Marr. Ryten was protecting Kadailin and Sandin.

He was pushed back a step. Kadailin focused on the pandinzori in the clearing, but it was difficult to tell which parts of it belonged to which devoshai, or if any of it belonged to the two dodenzinn. They all had similarly coloured auras, and the pandinzori that was clearly attached to one or the other spiralled through the other bits and would be impossible to separate. She wanted to add her strength to Ryten's, but she wasn't sure she'd be fighting Marr if she tried to join the fray. She could end up fighting her allies for control of pandinzori they held. They could already be fighting each other. The only way she saw to help would be to overwhelm them all, and she knew she couldn't do that.

Ocien and Torshe remained still, but Kadailin could tell from their expressions that they fought with all their strength. She wondered if they were really fighting Marr or if they were inadvertently fighting each other. Or Ryten. Their superior numbers were not an advantage.

The pandinzori around them condensed as more of it flowed from the forest. That must be the answer. She could take uncontested pandinzori from the trees and use it to attack Marr. She reached for the pandinzori closest to her, but someone already had it.

In an instant Ryten was swept away. Marr must have realised the same thing she did. The pandinzori Ryten had held flew in all directions and created chaos in the clearing. Black leaves filled the air. Ocien was thrown to the ground but Torshe held on. He turned towards Jaydin and Kadailin knew he wouldn't be able to help anyone else while he focused on her. Kadailin struggled to take hold of the pandinzori around them, to do something to stop Marr, but failed.

A wall of light formed in front of Marr and he sent it across the burnt ground. He walked behind it in Kadailin's direction. She resisted it, creating a pocket of her own pandinzori around herself, but her actions were useless when Marr's pandinzori surrounded even her bubble of safety. She was stuck in it. Marr passed her and ran when he got into the trees. A moment later she was free.

Jaydin turned her head. The pandinzori that held Vurel's trunk open thinned. Ryten stood up at the edge of the forest.

'Don't let go,' he said to Jaydin as he ran to follow Marr.

Jaydin turned back to the tree. "Torshe," she said. "We're doing this now. It can't wait any longer."

The pandinzori around the three kandar shifted. There was a ripping sound. One of the dodenzinn took the tree next to Vurel out of the ground completely. His blackened branches shed what leaves they still held as he leaned in the air, his roots bringing the earth with them. He shrieked into Kadailin's mind. The sound reminded her of the fire.

"Go after them, Kadailin!" Jaydin shouted over the din. "Help Ryten."

Kadailin looked to Ryten's disappearing back as he sprinted after Marr. Another tearing sound rent the air and more screams followed. She was paralysed by indecision. If she stayed she'd have to kill the fathers of kandar. If she left she might have to fight Marr.

'Please,' Jaydin's voice came to her.

'I'm going.' She took off towards the three kandaran trees in the clearing before she could change her mind. *'I'll come at them from the other side.'*

Chapter 33

Sandin vaulted onto the trunk of the nearest tree and scaled him, dragging herself into his leaves. She hoped her sisters and the others could keep Marr in the burnt patch but if they failed she had to put some distance between them, and she couldn't hide from him on the ground. She ran along the largest obscured branch until it bent under her weight, then she leapt to the next tree.

Leaves whipped her skin as she ran. She shivered when she thought of the assault she had suffered by pandinzori. It had been a lot worse than the time Damarin used it against her. She had never believed her sister would harm her. She didn't know what Marr meant to do.

The leaves she ran towards thinned until she saw clear sky. Not all of the trees in the forest were close together. A moment later the branches bowed beneath her and she leapt into the blue. The next tree was farther away than she had ever had to jump. As the green approached, she braced herself.

She crashed through the thin branches at the edge of the canopy, reaching for those that would hold her. The fall was loud. She scrambled to get a solid grip, to stop herself from sinking farther. As she tumbled through the leaves she saw a devoshai standing amongst the trunks below. She wrapped her arms and legs around the thickest branch she could reach and froze.

The top of the tree continued to sway, but she was concealed from the floor of the forest. She saw only leaves below her. The devoshai could have been anyone, but she didn't want to take the chance. If it was Marr—if it was anyone who would tell Marr what he had seen—she was in trouble.

The branches to one side of her seemed to bend slowly towards her. She watched them with wide eyes. Were they really moving or was it just a product of her fear? If they were moving something had to be affecting them. They grew still and she hoped it had been nothing. Then they were torn out. The remaining branches swung wildly in their wake, clattering against her skin. She clung to her branch and held on under the onslaught.

She was trapped. If she moved he would see her. She had to wait, with no indication if pandinzori was massing around her or if Marr had moved on. The air was quiet. The leaves ceased to quiver. She closed her eyes.

She was dragged through the tree. She couldn't move her upper body, couldn't even open her eyes. Her head and arms were surrounded by calm as her lower half was buffeted by the canopy. She tucked her legs in, held them close to her body but she was unable to protect herself, unable to shield herself from the forest. The mass of pandinzori that carried her swung to the earth. She thumped to the ground, landing on her knees.

The force that had wrenched her out of the tree dissipated and the branches that had come with her fell and exposed her. She opened her eyes. She could move again, but her body was slow. Her legs were covered in gouges that ran red. She was bleeding, just like Damarin had been in the desert.

Marr walked towards her. She tried to stand but her legs wouldn't work. What could she do? What would he do to her if she did nothing? She fought the urge to close her eyes, waiting for invisible pandinzori to take her again. He walked right up to her and smiled. Then he paused and turned back towards the burnt patch as if waiting for something. Sandin scrambled backwards as best she could. Maybe he would go back to Jaydin.

Suddenly Marr was swept into the closest trunk. His body gave off an audible crunch as it collided with the wood. Ryten appeared through the trees and ran to the devoshai. Sandin finally got to her feet. She limped away, staring at the trees in desperation. Pandinzori would be everywhere. Without the shadows of Cens, without the intervention of the forest, she would never escape Marr's influence on it. Ryten would need to hold him off long enough for her to hide. To find some place dark enough, secret enough in the open forest to save her. But was there such a place? If only Cens had been healed she could escape.

She limped more quickly, her awkward gait finally turning into something resembling a run, but she was forced to stop too soon, still in the open. A dark tevadra approached, running much more quickly than Sandin could manage. She saw the short black hair, the dark eyes, the determined look, and cringed. Was it Damarin?

"Sandin!" the tevadra shouted. Kadailin's voice. She stopped beside Sandin and reached out to her, causing an uncomfortable pulse as their auras collided. "What did he do to you?"

"No time," Sandin said. "Ryten is back there with him, somewhere in the trees. I need to get away from here."

"Go. Hide. We'll keep him here while Jaydin fixes the forest."

It was smart of Jaydin to start killing the trees. If Cens could be healed in time Marr would never find Sandin. Kadailin's eyes narrowed and Sandin turned to see Marr and Ryten behind her. Her sister stepped between Sandin and the two devoshai. Sandin ran as best she could.

She looked over her shoulder at the kandar as she staggered away, trying to judge the best direction to run. Kadailin slid across the ground slightly, her feet slipping as something invisible rammed into her. The other two moved quickly now, darting around each other. Suddenly, all three disappeared. Sandin stopped.

They were gone. She looked down at her bleeding legs. Had the damage caused by the canopy affected her mind too? There was no sound in the forest now, nothing around her. When she looked back she saw the burnt patch in the far distance. If she looked towards the clearing she saw the massive trunks of the three great trees.

For a moment she was confused, but then she saw the colour in the grass. Flowers. Tiny points of red grew in the green around her. She was reminded of the strange place in Cens they had found with Jaydin. Maybe the fighting kandar couldn't see her. She would have to move on if they could, but if they couldn't, moving would only expose her. It would be different if she could run, and even easier if she thought she could climb, but this might be the best she could do. Slowly, she retraced her steps.

A moment later the forest was revealed. Kadailin was right in front of her. Her sister's back was to her and Marr forced her in Sandin's direction. Marr's eyes locked on Sandin before she could step back. He shouted wordlessly and Kadailin was thrown into her. Sandin landed on her shoulder with Kadailin on her legs. Her sister rushed to her feet, but Marr was gone. Kadailin turned to look at Sandin with confusion on her face. Sandin motioned for her to be quiet.

Kadailin looked around wildly before the same realisation must have come to her. Sandin hoped Ryten would keep Marr from following them, but there was no guarantee he would be able to, or if he even understood where they'd gone. Kadailin must have thought of the same thing because she motioned for Sandin to stay and braced herself before running back out of the space.

Sandin watched her go in anxious silence. She stood with difficulty and limped to one of the trees. She leaned against him. She didn't like that she couldn't see or hear what was happening outside the hidden place, but Cens had saved her. Perhaps Jaydin was succeeding at healing the forest. Sandin needed it to come quickly. Kadailin and Ryten seemed to be holding their own, but she didn't want them to be forced to fight for her.

She looked up into the branches of the trees around her and hoped Cens could shelter her, hide her, as she should be hidden. Could protect her sisters, Ryten, Torshe, and Ocien. They would need the forest more than she'd thought if war came to Calendrai. They needed it just as badly now.

***

Jaydin braced in the crisp black leaves, her body tense as she stared at the tree in front of her. Gently, slowly, she eased more pandinzori into the fissure in his bark. It cracked.

'Just break it,' Torshe's voice came to her. *'He's as good as dead already.'*

'I don't want to hurt Moradi.' Jaydin was annoyed the devoshai would divert her attention. The work she was doing was precise. It required more control than she had thought she had.

'She's dead too,' Torshe responded.

Another great tearing rent the air. Splinters of wood flew against Jaydin's body. She tried to ignore the screaming of the trees.

'She won't stay that way forever. Not if I have anything to do with it.'

She didn't know if removing the body would save it, but she had to try. There had to be a childless tree in Cens that would take a kandar.

She glanced to either side of Vurel. One of the trees that had stood beside him had been uprooted by Torshe. Another was half-way out of the earth. Ocien worked on the other side of the clearing. Frenn would have to be last. It would probably take all three of them to pull him up. Jaydin wasn't even sure they could do it alone. They might need Ryten and Kadailin as well.

She flinched as she remembered Ryten's last words to her. *'I'm following,'* he had said. *'He's hit her with pandinzori.'* She hadn't heard from Kadailin yet.

Vurel's trunk groaned as Jaydin's control slipped. The tree shuddered, resisting her, pushing against the pandinzori that held him open. Moradi's head hung through the hole in his bark. Jaydin cringed as she thought of what would happen to the tevadra's body if she let her control slip too far, if the trunk snapped shut...

'You have to do it now, Jaydin,' Ocien said. *'We need your help.'*

Jaydin grimaced. The purge of the burnt patch was taking too long. They needed to clear it quickly so the forest could heal. The thought was desperate, and there was no reason to believe it but that she needed it to be true. To protect Sandin. To protect Kadailin and Ryten who had risked themselves to go after her.

But something troubled Jaydin. What would they do with the bodies of these trees? Would the forest heal with its dead strewn about it? Seeing the destruction, hearing the screams of their fathers, it almost felt like the fire all over again. How would Cens see things?

Jaydin focused on the trunk in front of her. It was right to kill the damaged trees. She remembered what had happened with the guardian of World Two as if she had been there herself. If Moradi was reborn like that, or Torshe—or worse, both at the same time—she wasn't sure Derkra could stand against them. Humans were better at that sort of thing, and World Two had still suffered greatly at its guardian's madness.

Moradi's shoulders slumped through the ever-widening gap. Maybe Jaydin could pull her out now. The space that had let her shoulders through should be wide enough for hips. Jaydin closed her eyes. The pandinzori around Vurel blazed in the darkness. She pushed it behind the tevadra, formed it to her body and hardened it, pulling towards herself. At the same time she held the trunk open. Slowly Moradi's body slipped through the crack.

'I have her.' She pulled the tevadra through the air, all the way to her feet, and let her body go in the black leaves. Vurel's trunk snapped shut. The pandinzori that had surrounded him grew, pulsating up and down his great height in a column of undulating light.

'Help us,' Torshe said.

Jaydin relaxed for a moment, her mind relieved of the stress of holding the tree open. She turned to look at the progress the other two kandar had made in the clearing. There was shattered wood everywhere. Green leaves mixed with the black on the ground. The earth had been torn up in many places where Torshe and Ocien had ripped roots out. Jaydin refocused her attention on Vurel.

An eerie screech filled the air as she took hold of the pandinzori at the base of his trunk. It escalated to screaming as she began to pull. This type of control was simpler than the control she had needed to extricate the tevadra, but it was much more painful. The tree had been devastated to see his daughter go, but now he would die. That was entirely different.

His roots gripped the soil as she pulled. It felt like they moved, dug deeper, held on against her. She pressured him and all at once they seemed to let go. The wood broke, the soil gave way, and Vurel rose into the air. He crashed against the tree beside him. Jaydin let him fall to the earth, his bulk tearing the branches off the trees around him as he rushed to the ground. She turned to the next burned tree, steeling herself for the terror that would fill the air, when a faint voice spoke in the back of her mind.

'Marr just disappeared.'

It was Ryten. Jaydin panicked. *'You lost him?'*

'Sandin and Kadailin too. Right in front of me.' The faint voice paused. *'Cens just closed around us.'*

Jaydin studied the collective in her mind. Marr's leaf was still bright, as was Kadailin's. As usual she was worried by the absence of Sandin's. If her sister had a place in the collective Jaydin would never have worried about her so much. Ocien and Torshe continued to pull trees from the ground. How could Cens have healed while they did this to it?

Then, as she watched Ocien tear a blackened trunk from the earth, flawless leaves and branches closed in around her. The screaming stopped. The air quieted. It was almost as if the events of a moment ago had never taken place, but then Jaydin looked down and found Moradi's body still between her feet, blank eyes staring up at her.

"It's healed," she said to no one in particular. She didn't look up until Torshe and Ocien broke through the trees some time later.

"How?" Ocien asked. "After what we did? How did that bring it back to peace?"

Jaydin shrugged. "I have no idea."

"Is it just here?" Torshe asked. "Is it just this place that has recovered?"

"It's all of it," a third voice answered.

Ryten appeared beside her. Jaydin looked past him to wait for Sandin but her sister didn't join them. "She's not with you?"

"I couldn't find her. I hoped she would find me once the forest healed."

"But she's safe." Jaydin waited for confirmation.

Ryten's expression told Jaydin he didn't know. He frowned. Jaydin sensed Kadailin approaching.

"You walked through normal forest to get to us?" Torshe asked Ryten.

"As if it had never burned."

What had happened to the bodies of the trees? Had Cens absorbed them and made them new? Or had they disappeared? What had happened to Frenn, and the other trees they had left standing? Were they healed or were they gone? What about Buran—Torshe's father?

Kadailin walked out of the trees. Sandin followed her, visibly limping. Jaydin was flooded with relief, until she saw her sister's injuries. She ran over to her, examining the cuts that had been carved into Sandin's calves and thighs. Sandin's knees were a mass of bruises. Jaydin looked up at Kadailin in question but her sister just shrugged.

"I'm fine," Sandin said. "I'm just glad you healed the forest."

Then Jaydin noticed Marr's leaf was gone. It hadn't fallen, only dimmed to darkness. It looked like Tchardin and Damarin's leaves. "Marr has left Calendrai."

"Good." Sandin sat down where she'd stood, her eyes coming to rest on the tevadra that had started the whole mess.

Jaydin looked down at Moradi. The tevadra's body was limp and empty-looking.

"Moradi." The other kandar turned towards her, stopping their silent conversations. "Does anyone know her dodenzinn?"

There was no response.

"Tchardin would," Kadailin finally said.

Jaydin sighed. "Ocien, take her body to the clearing. If she has a dodenzinn he might be looking for her."

"If he's not already at rest," Ryten said.

"If he has gone to rest we'll find her a new father. If he hasn't and we can find him, maybe he can help."

"What if he was already resting in one of the burnt trees?" Ryten's thoughts buzzed loudly. "What if some of the other kandar were?"

Jaydin turned away. Kandar already at rest. They could have been resting in the trees burnt to the ground in the fire or those torn from the earth in the purge. Had she failed to realise that because she didn't want to?

Torshe stepped up to her side "We barely killed any. There are so many trees and so few kandar, it's unlikely there were any at rest in them."

Jaydin gave him a weak smile. She would have to hope he was right. It was starting to seem impossible to protect the kandar from lost dodenzinn. She looked back at Moradi. "If any were already at rest"—she sighed—"we'll just have to hope Cens healed them along with the trees."

Torshe spoke quietly to Ocien and the tevadra nodded. Pandinzori surrounded Moradi again. It almost looked like an aura. She was lifted into the air and Ocien disappeared into the trees. The floating body followed.

Jaydin looked at the four remaining kandar. If she spoke in her mind only three of them would hear her.

"Thank you," she said, turning to Torshe. "For protecting me and for helping me with the trees." She glanced at Ryten and came to meet Kadailin's gaze. *'And for going after Sandin.'*

Sandin rolled her eyes and Jaydin smiled. Her sister could always tell when she was using her mindvoice to exclude her.

"That was hard," Kadailin said, breaking the moment. "Pandinzori is difficult to fight with."

Ryten nodded, but kept silent.

"How did the kandar fight a war against each other?" Kadailin continued.

"They were better with it than we are," Jaydin answered. "They'd had a lot more practice."

"Let's just hope it doesn't come to that," Torshe said. "I never want to do that again."

Jaydin agreed. She had felt the power in the burnt patch. It had been contained, and the kandar had been inexperienced and fought each other when they should have been fighting Marr, but they could still have done a lot of damage.

"And the forest," Kadailin said. "I saw you starting to pull the trees out when I left, but I can't believe you managed to get them all so quickly. And Frenn!"

"We didn't," Torshe said. "We never finished clearing the trees. We didn't touch Frenn."

Jaydin let the devoshai explain. She was tired of thinking about it.

"Can we talk?" Sandin asked her quietly.

Jaydin looked at the other kandar. Kadailin continued to speak with Torshe. Ryten appeared to be in his own world, looking straight ahead with his thoughts buzzing. Jaydin nodded. They moved away until the other three faded from sight.

'We'll be right back,' she said in their direction. No need to scare anyone after what they had just been through.

"I have to talk to Siltadon." Sandin didn't waste a moment. "After this, I have to."

"After what?"

Sandin was shaking. Jaydin looked at the cuts and bruises on her body with concern—for that to happen to a kandaran body—but her sister waved her away.

"All of it," she said. "Marr. The helplessness. The forest. Jaydin, there's pandinzori all around me, all the time. I need some sort of defence against it. And Cens..."

"What about Cens?"

"Torshe said you never finished killing the trees."

"I was never sure that's what it needed. I only knew we needed to remove them."

"I think I helped it heal."

Jaydin found herself looking down at her feet, at the grass and earth that surrounded them. It had been black and burnt a short time ago, and she had stood amongst shrieking, falling trees.

"If not Siltadon, then Miadra," Sandin continued. "Maybe even Damarin. I need to know if it was rendinzori. I need to understand what happened."

Jaydin opened her mouth to respond.

"I needed it to heal, Jaydin. Don't you understand? I wanted it more than anything. And then it did. You never finished fixing it but it healed. To save me."

Jaydin focused on the branches that crowded them. Thick branches, plentiful, and covered in emerald leaves. They were just as they always had been before the fire. Something must have helped Cens to heal. If not, then why now, after all this time? It may have been the purge but that had been incomplete, and it had been traumatising. The way the forest was reacting to the gruesome death of even more of its members was contradictory. It might have healed eventually, once all the damaged trees were gone, but not in the midst of their assault. She could see that now.

Miadra had said Jaydin's notebook was made with rendinzori. She had implied all of Calendrai was made with the human power. Damarin had built a mountain in the sand and Ruon had filled it with fire, two things no kandar had ever done before on Derkra. Rendinzori was invisible. Maybe it could have been Sandin who helped the forest heal. At the very least it could have been rendinzori.

A red leaf flared in the collective. Jaydin started, worried it belonged to Marr or Damarin, but found it lit alone. It was a leaf on the Black Valley branch of the collective. The kandar who owned it approached. Jaydin focused on it to find their identity.

Cotelle.

She ducked through the branches, running back to the other kandar. Sandin followed, confusion on her face. When Jaydin burst through the leaves Ryten turned towards her in alarm.

"What now?"

Jaydin didn't have time to answer before the big white devoshai appeared. He stared into the canopy when Cens finally showed him to them. He was so distracted he was frozen in place before he could take another step, wrapped in solid brownish pandinzori. Jaydin wasn't sure which of the kandar held him but she was relieved to see it done.

"This magnificent forest," he said, his mouth free of pandinzori. "How can you have this here when we have only the nine hundred?"

The others looked questioningly to Jaydin. She examined the devoshai and noticed the pandinzori of his aura pulled away from his skin. That would make him weak. It was amazing he had been able to shift to Calendrai in that state. If they had to restrain him again they shouldn't have any problems. Each of them individually should be able to overpower him. She shrugged. The pandinzori that had held him dispersed.

"This is the forest Cens," she said. "It has always been here."

Cotelle looked at the assembled kandar one by one until his eyes fell on Sandin. "Your sister. The one who does not join the collective."

"Her name is Sandin," Jaydin said.

Cotelle's eyes were wide with wonder as he examined his surroundings. His gaze settled on Ryten. From what Jaydin had seen in Black Valley and what she knew of Calendrai the two were the only kandar of that size.

"Why are you here?" she asked.

His gaze left Ryten and came back to her. "If you still want to go to the Earths, I can help you."

***

Tchardin followed Siltadon through the trees. The guardian continued to carry the bloody glass shard she'd used to kill Reva, though she gripped it less tightly. Tchardin was still shocked by the human's death.

Her unease was heightened by the glass all around them. More than one tree had suffered the same fate as Rai, and many were completely made of glass. At one point they had walked by a group of glass buildings. Their halls had been full of coloured cloth and they had almost been more beautiful than they were terrifying, glinting in the sun. She hadn't seen any humans in them.

"Where are the humans?" she finally asked, breaking a silence that stretched back to the beginning of their journey.

"There aren't any."

Tchardin waited for more but Siltadon just kept walking.

"That can't be right," Tchardin said, thinking of Irah the guardian. "There has to be at least one."

Again Tchardin waited but Siltadon didn't answer. She looked more closely at their surroundings as they continued. Until this Earth she had seen a sort of progression in the worlds, as if the touch of humanity was more and more present as she made her way through them. There were very few signs that humans lived here.

They came to a large body of water at the edge of the trees. There was a small island just off the shore. Tchardin felt a moment of sadness as she thought of Calendrai and what it had looked like when she'd left it with Damarin. Pandinzori stretched across the water to the island.

Siltadon led her along the shore until the water lightened in colour. Then she dropped the jagged piece of glass and walked into the water. Tchardin stopped. Siltadon turned and gestured her forward.

"It won't go above your shoulders."

Tchardin stared down at the calm water. It couldn't be as bad as the shift. It couldn't be as bad as Water Side on Derkra. There was pandinzori along the path they would travel, and if it was deep Siltadon would disappear into it before Tchardin had any trouble herself. She followed the guardian into the blue.

The water lapped around her shoulders at one point, pulling her gently from side to side, but other than that it was shallow. It remained on her purple dress when she left it—unlike the water of the shift—and dripped down her legs through the shadow.

As soon as the guardian stepped onto the island, pandinzori flowed to her, becoming a light grey haze where she controlled it. It separated into thin strips and streamed over her arms and around her legs. Once the tendrils had touched her they flew to the trees nearby, caressing their leaves and lining their branches. The control it would take to separate the light like that was beyond Tchardin. She was mesmerised by the danger it presented and couldn't look away. Siltadon opened her eyes and the pandinzori around them slackened, growing lifeless.

"There's no glass on this island," the guardian said. "It's one of the only places near Rai where I can safely touch pandinzori."

Tchardin hoped Siltadon was right. She couldn't see any glass from where she stood but it wouldn't take a lot. As she looked over their surroundings she noticed colour in the grass. There were small red flowers there. They spread across the ground and climbed the trees on black vines. Tchardin got the sense she had seen them somewhere before.

"I would have gone mad without this place," Siltadon said.

Tchardin turned back to the guardian. It seemed Siltadon was at least a little mad by now. Her reaction to Reva had proven that.

"Why are there no humans on this Earth?" Tchardin felt safer with the guardian now that she could touch pandinzori. She reached out to it with her mind and found she could hold more than she expected.

"You're going to shift back to Derkra, aren't you?" the guardian asked instead of answering.

"When I can. Tchar has barred the kandar from Coralynth, so there's no easy way to get home."

"So you *did* come here directly from another Earth."

"It's the only way now."

"It can't be."

Tchardin frowned.

"Damarin tells you she *remembers* everything but she can't remember the most important thing?" the guardian whispered, seemingly to herself.

Tchardin tensed. *Damarin*. Siltadon hadn't been hearing Tchardin's thoughts of Jaydin. Damarin had come here too. The guardian paced between the trees.

"When did Tchar close the shift to you?" Siltadon asked. "How long has it been?"

"A long time. Four generations by the longest kandars' lives."

Siltadon's eyes clouded and her thoughts buzzed, as if her mind had gone elsewhere for a moment. Then her eyes widened. "I *knew* she was lying."

Tchardin could tell the words hadn't been directed at her. Why would Damarin lie to Siltadon about the lost Purpose? Tchardin turned away from the guardian and opened the shift.

"I need to go now," she said.

"Take me with you."

Tchardin hesitated. A guardian wasn't supposed to leave their Earth. Damarin had invited Ruon to Derkra, but Tchardin didn't believe he would have actually gone, despite his feelings about the people of World

Four. He'd shifted away from the castle, but he couldn't have shifted to Derkra.

"You have to stay and guard the Earth."

The world might need to begin again. Tchardin wasn't sure how to accomplish that, or if it was possible, but if there were no humans they needed to try. Maybe Jaydin would know what they could do. World Seven would need a guardian then. If Ruon was on Derkra when Tchardin returned she would send him back to his Earth too.

"You are the queen of the kandar," Siltadon said. "You can free me from this purpose."

Tchardin shook her head. "Only Tchar can release you."

"Please. I want to go home to Derkra. I was never supposed to be a guardian."

Tchardin stepped towards the shift.

Siltadon's eyes settled on the slowly spinning grey. "If I tell you what happened here, will you let me leave?"

Tchardin paused. Maybe if she heard Siltadon's story she could figure out how to help the Earth. If not, she could bring that information back to Jaydin. At the very least, Damarin must already know it and it was becoming clear her sister might not use her knowledge to get them back to the Purpose. Tchardin closed the shift and turned to Siltadon. The empty shore of the mainland was visible in the distance behind the guardian. She needed to know how it had gotten that way.

"Tell me what happened," she said.

Siltadon sat down in the grass and Tchardin joined her. The guardian ran her hands back through her hair—something Tchardin had never seen a kandar do—and looked up at the sky for a moment before speaking.

"When I was sent here the people were terrified. They were desperate. Their hysterical thoughts covered the Earth. We had to work in that every day, searching for solutions when it seemed nothing could be done."

Tchardin flinched away as an image of the burning Earth came to her. Not the type of image Jaydin had given her, where she had felt removed from the fire. This one was personal and the hopeless thoughts of the doomed humans came with it. The image dissipated when Siltadon continued.

"I tried so hard to save them," the guardian said. "So many of our people believed it impossible. They left the humans and went back to Derkra in defeat. They left the people! Thousands of people. Children!" She looked away. "I was one of the last to try. In the end they couldn't be saved, no matter how much I wanted it. I restarted the world, but something went wrong." She frowned. "The council said I could stay, become a part of the new world, but I should have listened to Leksten. I wanted to believe. I wanted to help them, but he was right. The restart wasn't enough."

"Leksten," Tchardin said. "The previous guardian of the Earth."

Siltadon nodded distractedly. Tchardin couldn't believe she was getting the opportunity to hear about the beginning of a world from a tevadra who had actually been there. "What happened? When you restarted it?"

"I entered Rai with the Seed. The fire disappeared and the round Earth became like Derkra. Infinite and flat. Half land and half water."

Tchardin looked around her. Somehow this world had gone from the desolation of Derkra's deserts and dead waters to become green and alive.

"It was half *land*," Siltadon corrected. "There was no infinite desert. It was always green and beautiful around Rai, right from the beginning. There was sand, far away, but not everywhere." Siltadon looked towards the World Tree. The only parts of him visible from the island were the glass branches and leaves that stretched well above the rest of the forest. "It quickly changed."

Tchardin looked back to the mainland. "The glass?"

The guardian seemed unwilling to go on. She blinked and shook her head, pulling her knees against her chest. Her thoughts were obvious but unintelligible.

"Rai told you this?" Tchardin asked.

"No."

"Then how do you know?"

"I saw it."

Tchardin tried to remember what Jaydin had said about the beginning of the Earths. Were the kandar supposed to be able to watch?

Siltadon stared at her. "You have to let me return to Derkra. There are things I need to do on the other worlds."

"Tell me what happened to the people. There must have been humans."

Siltadon looked away.

"Did you kill them? Like Reva?" Tchardin was beginning to think the answer to that was yes. She thought of all the new humans that could have been on the Earth, eliminated, leaving only this dead, empty place. It was worse than World Five. It made her angry.

"I didn't kill them," Siltadon said.

"I don't believe you."

"They were killing themselves. I had to help, eventually, but it would have happened without me."

"So you did kill them."

"I tried," the tevadra relented. "They made others. They always made others."

"But in the end you succeeded. That's why there's no one here."

"Until you brought that one with you from another world."

"And you killed her too."

Siltadon smiled faintly. "Just in time."

Tchardin was trying to make sense of it all. "So the restart failed because you killed them?"

"It failed because they were rotten. Right from the core. Right from the beginning. It failed, ultimately, because of me."

The tevadra had lost her mind. Tchardin was about to get up and open the shift again. Leave the mad guardian with her broken world. Jaydin could sort it out when they came back to the Earths. There had to be something in her notebook or her head that could help them deal with this. But something Siltadon had said stuck with Tchardin.

"You said they made others?"

Siltadon frowned and closed her eyes. "It started with only two, in the beginning, but they made more. Every time their numbers dwindled, every time I got close, there were always more. Until the end."

Tchardin thought of the bump under Jaycee's dress on World Four, the faint bud that had joined her with Tezroi. "Children?"

"Yes." Siltadon opened her eyes to stare at Tchardin. There was a deep sadness in them that echoed the look in Jaycee's eyes at the death of her king. "And no. I could have kept up with children."

Tchardin remembered Alyx, the little girl who had seen her on the second Earth. She thought of Siltadon killing small, defenceless humans and shook her head in disgust. If it hadn't just been children, then what else? "Then how? What do you mean?

"They made fully formed humans. Fully grown, like kandar, out of nothing."

Like kandar? Siltadon's thoughts buzzed.

"They made all of this too," the guardian continued, looking back to the mainland. "The glass, the trees, this island. The very shape of the Earth. All of it, and it's just as rotten as they were."

Chapter 34

Cien slumped against the black glass wall at the back of his cage, his feet resting on its smooth base. At first he had tried to avoid it but standing in his drying blood on the jagged floor had become tiresome. He looked down at the blood, shining in places, matte and flaking in others. At least it covered the glass.

He closed his eyes and tried to see the image of the human forest Jaydin had given him. He had gone from the desert to this dark cave of glass without once seeing the green of his father's leaves or the vibrant red of Ovaeron's. The image grew clear for a moment, helping him forget where he was, but when the flash of the sun broke through the leaves in his mind the brilliance of pandinzori encroached on his awareness. He opened his eyes.

There was pandinzori all around him now, flowing across the floor of his cage, against the back of it, through the bars. The line of fire on one side of the cave constantly strove to consume the light, but it wasn't fast enough. A thought could kill him, and the only thoughts in the cave were his own. No one else had come to him since Cotelle left with Miadra's body.

He looked over the empty collective. He had tried to talk to them—his people who waited in the valley—but their leaves were dim, and no one had heard. This time he was surprised to find a faint glow permeating the branches.

A shadow appeared against the true light of the entrance. Ruon's seed grew bright. The guardian walked into the cave and leaned against a wall, the flowers and spiders suspended above him. Cien looked at the bars of his cage. Would Ruon be so relaxed if he was in the cage and Cien was outside it? The guardian was still close enough to be affected if Cien touched pandinzori, and he didn't seem to be bothered by that.

Ruon said nothing. He wasn't even looking at Cien. He stared straight ahead, his thoughts quietly buzzing. Cien's focus returned to the bars. He had to do something other than stand alone and think.

"You were caged once?" he asked. "On World Four?"

Ruon turned his head as if he had only just noticed Cien was there.

"I was. For longer than you can understand."

Cien didn't feel any pity for the guardian. He would have once—he knew that—but not now. "How did you escape?"

"I did not escape. I was released. It is the only way."

Cien pushed off from the glass wall. He paced, his feet cut into by the jagged floor. If a guardian had been unable to escape a cage of glass, how was he supposed to do so? Especially with the collective dark. There would be no one to rescue him. Suddenly it occurred to Cien that Ruon might be the only one to visit him in the foreseeable future. If the guardian left, he'd be alone with the glass and his thoughts again.

"The humans put you in that cage?" he asked.

"Yes."

"And they let you go."

"No."

Cien saw his future in Ruon's stilted responses. Still, it was better than being alone.

"Miadra is dead, you know," Cien said, just to continue the conversation. "She died in here."

"The High Seat. I do know."

"And you know how she died?"

"Yes."

Cien continued to pace. "Do you know what's happened to her dodenzinn?"

"Perhaps he has chosen to die with her."

"No. He wouldn't."

Ruon shrugged. "I have not seen him since."

Cien turned away. Cotelle was his only real hope of escape. It wasn't a great hope, but it was something. The devoshai couldn't be dead. Cien began to wonder why Ruon remained to talk to him. Was it just to torture him? To revel in his suffering? He turned back to the bars and jumped, startled. The guardian had come right up to them. His face was no more than an arm's length away.

"Do you feel it yet?" Ruon asked. "The power?"

"Power?" Cien struggled with his disbelief. "I have no power in here."

Ruon's eyes remained fixed on Cien. "But you must feel it, nonetheless. If you killed the High Seat from behind that glass it is coming to you. Just as it came to me."

"What are you talking about?"

"I noticed it after Tairasyn called me back to him the first time. When I could not answer him, though I wanted to, that first time."

"Tairasyn?"

"My father. The World Tree of World Four. The second time he called I did not want to go. I wanted to leave the cage, as I always had, but I did not want to return to the trees."

"Why not?" There was a constant pulsing in the back of Cien's mind. He hadn't wanted to go to Ovaeron before all of this happened, but now he wasn't so sure. His reasons to stay alive would be beyond the guardian's understanding, because guardians didn't have dodenzinn. If Ruon had been held behind glass, why wouldn't he want to go back to his father to rest and forget?

"Because of the power," Ruon said in response to his thoughts. "Just look at the pandinzori you could command."

There was an unnatural amount of pandinzori in the cave, but Cien didn't want anything to do with it.

"You are the only other kandar who has ever been caged," Ruon said. "The only other kandar who will be forced to ignore his father when he is called back to him. You are, in a way, the only one like me."

"And you think that's why this pandinzori comes to me?"

"Yes. Pandinzori and rendinzori."

There was that word again. Miadra had mentioned it before she died. A human power. Cien wanted nothing to do with that either. "So you want to watch me. See what I become? What this makes me?"

"Damarin has her reasons and I have mine. I already know what it will do to you, but maybe this will prove it to the others."

"Prove what?"

Ruon's eyes glinted in the soft red light. "That the trees are as bad as the humans. They only limit us."

No kandar should ever say such a thing about their fathers. "You would have the kandar just"—Cien paused to think about it—"live? Forever? Never rest?"

"If we are to achieve our true potential..." Ruon turned away and walked back to the far wall of the cave.

Achieve their true potential? Abandon the humans and then abandon the trees. What was their true potential? Insanity? To be like Ruon? But no, apparently it was power. What power could the kandar need beyond what they already had? And it would come to them if they never returned to the trees? Cien felt Ovaeron's call. He looked at the bars of glass that blocked him.

"So eventually," he said to the guardian's back, "if I stay here, I'll be as powerful as you are."

"You could never truly match me," the guardian said, without turning. "Even if you survive it, you will always have one weakness I never had."

"And what is that?"

"A dodenzinn."

***

Siltadon paced through the trees and Tchardin watched her warily. The humans had made all of this? Made the trees? Made the Earth? But Creator had made the Earths...

"Humans did this," Siltadon said, looking back at her. "With rendinzori. Just like the first time, just as with any of the Earths."

"What do you mean?"

"Creator made the Earth. It made the Root of the World and the World Tree, and It made the first two humans, but It didn't make anything else. What this world became—what the humans became—had nothing to do with Creator."

"How do you know that?"

"Rai told me, when I was inside him, before he abandoned me to this nightmare. The restarted world began in the same way it did the first time. With two humans and not much else."

Rendinzori. Trees and earth from rendinzori. From humans. Tchardin looked around. It was clear these things had not come from pandinzori.

They weren't full of the lines of light that formed the objects and animals created by kandar.

"Creator only made two humans?" Tchardin asked. "Two humans for the whole Earth?"

"Yes."

Tchardin remembered the hundreds of humans she had seen and heard on World Six. She remembered the people Irah had spoken about on World Five, the ones who had fallen to the Bug. Millions of people, Irah had said. Maybe a billion or more. Tchardin thought of the Arkaiyans and the Sparr, the villages of World Three, and the great voice of World Two. Even World One had held too much pandinzori for only two humans. If Creator had only made two for each Earth, then the humans had made themselves. With rendinzori. It was remarkable.

"No!" Siltadon shouted. Tchardin reached for the pandinzori around her by instinct. "No. You don't understand. Damarin agreed with me."

So Damarin *had* talked to Siltadon about this. Tchardin backed away from the guardian.

"There were only two humans," Siltadon said. "One kandar makes one kandar makes one kandar for the rest of existence. Creator made nine hundred of us and there will never be any more. If It only made two humans, the rest were something else. Something less."

"What else could they be?" Tchardin asked, stopping her retreat. "Pandinzori can't make a mind, but rendinzori clearly can. If a human can make a tree as you say they can, if they made these around us, why not another human? Even if they came from rendinzori they were all just as human."

Siltadon looked at the ground. She closed her eyes and her thoughts exploded in volume. Tchardin was buffeted with feeling. With pain. Siltadon had loved the people of World Seven. She had loved all humans. Every single one. She could never have worked on World Six like her closest friend, Carrensing, where the kandar were required to kill so many. Siltadon had spent her time fruitlessly trying to save them instead. But when they had come back after the restart there had been something wrong with them. They couldn't be allowed to spread. To cover the Earth.

"You're looking for an excuse," Tchardin said. "If they weren't human you didn't do anything wrong. You—"

"I didn't do anything wrong." Siltadon's thoughts grew eerily quiet. "They would have killed themselves without me."

The guardian walked towards her and Tchardin turned away. Siltadon put a hand on her shoulder and Tchardin shivered at the lack of shock.

"Now," Siltadon said. "You will free me from guardianship."

"No." Tchardin pulled away from the guardian's grip. "You are the guardian of this Earth. It's your purpose to stay here."

She couldn't possibly let Siltadon leave World Seven after hearing what had happened to the people who inhabited it. Siltadon had proven she wasn't reformed when she killed Reva.

"You can't travel between the worlds," the guardian said. "Not without me. You'll soil them all."

"How?"

Siltadon's expression was haunted. "You want to know why the restart failed?"

"I do."

"We carried parts of them with us when we went to more than one Earth. We spread their ideas. The humans who came onto this Earth remembered the threat of glass from me, and they embraced it and grew it to cover the world."

Nonsense. How could the kandar have caused this simply by fulfilling the Purpose? Tchardin moved away from the guardian. Surprisingly, Siltadon didn't follow. Tchardin opened the shift and put a hand on the ice.

"I should have listened to Damarin," Siltadon said. "She told me Derkra is changing."

Tchardin turned back to the guardian. "What did she say to you?"

Siltadon shrugged. "Maybe the hierarchy doesn't matter anymore. Maybe I don't have to ask you for permission to leave."

Tchardin couldn't believe Damarin had said that. "You can't leave your Earth. That is my word as the future queen of our people. I will rule Derkra soon, regardless of anything Damarin may have told you."

Siltadon looked away from her now, towards the mainland. Tchardin followed her gaze and expected she was looking at the glass tips of Rai's great branches again, just visible in the far distance above the lesser trees around him.

"You know I've killed thousands of humans," Siltadon said. "And you believe they possessed thousands of equal or greater minds to those of the kandar." The guardian met Tchardin's gaze and her clear blue eyes were hard. "You say there are four of you who know this."

Tchardin turned back to the shift as the guardian continued.

"That's not so many, for one who has done what I have done."

***

Jaydin watched Cotelle's face as they stepped into the clearing, into view of Tith and his two brothers. The big devoshai stared up at them, his eyes full of awe, craning his neck to take in as much of their great height as he could from the ground. He was so much more expressive than the average kandar.

Ocien stood near Tith's trunk in the distance. Jaydin could only assume Moradi's body was in the grass beside her. She and Cotelle had lost track of the other kandar in Cens as they'd tried to exit, but Jaydin wasn't worried about them anymore. As long as Marr's leaf stayed dark she believed they would be safe. Still, Cens had been strange, and more difficult than before. Cotelle seemed to have enjoyed it. They walked slowly towards the great trees.

"Why would you help us?" she asked.

Cotelle never took his eyes off the giant trunks. "The kandar need to understand what Damarin wants for us."

"I know what she wants. She's wrong."

"How can you be sure?"

"It's not what we are. Not what the kandar should be. Tith taught me that."

Cotelle shook his head. "I don't believe all the kandar should go back to the Earths, but I do think you will need to, to change your mind. The others wouldn't understand what they were seeing."

Jaydin was still surprised to hear him speak so much. He had said maybe five words to her before he came to Calendrai. Why hadn't Miadra accompanied him? Could they agree about this? Once again her eyes were drawn to the pandinzori that slipped across Cotelle's skin. It didn't seem to hold there anymore.

"Are you called?" she asked.

His eyes finally left the brothers and came to rest on hers.

"You will explain it to them," he said instead of answering, "when you return. You will call the council and tell them the Purpose has changed."

"And what if I don't believe it has?"

"Then maybe we were wrong." Cotelle shrugged. "I don't expect that to happen. The kandar could do so much better with the things Creator granted the humans. I believe you'll be able to see that."

"That can't be all of it." Jaydin looked him over. "Why would you come to us now, when things have already progressed so far? Damarin's winning. You're winning. Why help us?" It didn't make any sense. "What if I don't see what you saw?"

"I don't want anyone else to die."

Jaydin was struck quiet by his words. He wouldn't know about the kandar who had died in the fire and he wouldn't have known about Moradi until he arrived. It had to be someone from Black Valley. The pandinzori around him slipped.

"There's one thing I ask in return," he said.

She looked up at him.

"You were right. I am dying."

Jaydin nodded. She should have understood that from his aura immediately, but she was surprised at his age. He seemed far too young.

"Miadra is already gone," he said.

Jaydin was immediately sad to hear it. The tevadra had been smart and curious, even if she was wrong. Better than the kandar who didn't care.

"I still have things to do," Cotelle continued. "This is one of them."

Jaydin gasped. "You would ignore the call? She could be reborn alone—"

"I know that. That's why I've kept her away from her father. I am not yet called—"

"How can you not be?"

He shrugged. "She wasn't either."

So she had been killed. This was getting worse and worse. Jaydin could see where it was going.

"If I die the wrong way—" he said, his voice faltering.

"You want me to get rid of her. Destroy her body."

"Yes. That's what I need from you."

They were approaching Tith and Jaydin saw the depression in the grass where Moradi's body must lie. There was no way to know what had happened to her dodenzinn. He may have gone to his father before the confrontation in the burnt patch, in which case Moradi would need to be joined with him in rest. It was also possible they had yet to find each other, or that he had died in the fire, or one of the purged trees, or been born on Land Side in Black Valley. Or, even worse, that he had died in the war generations ago and there would be no clue in Calendrai as to what had happened to him. If they found Moradi a new father, would they be relegating one of the pair to eternity without a second half? Had that already happened during the war, leaving Moradi without a dodenzinn?

"Why me?" she asked. "Why not some kandar from Black Valley? Someone you trust?"

"I trust you. With this I would trust you even if I didn't believe you could change."

"Why?"

He looked at Moradi's body, now within view. Then he looked back at Jaydin. Ocien watched them. Jaydin frowned. He was right. She'd do anything she could to stop more of this from happening.

"Teach me to shift to the Earths," she said. "I'll take care of Miadra if the time comes."

Jaydin stared up into Tith's branches as she contemplated the thing she was about to do. Her great father stretched across the sky, as beautiful and powerful as ever. She followed his trunk down to the grass and found Sandin, Kadailin, Ryten, Torshe, and Ocien seated below him, watching her. Cotelle sat off to the side with Moradi's body.

Jaydin scanned the clearing for other kandar, but only Ocien and Moradi had been there when they entered it. It remained deserted. The rest of the kandar of Calendrai seemed to have gone back to Cens.

"We have to go to World Seven," Sandin said.

Jaydin had to admit it was tempting. With what Miadra had said about Siltadon, and the fact that the world had been restarted. The only world to have ever been restarted and no kandar from Derkra had seen the result. Except Damarin, if Miadra and Cotelle were to be believed. And Siltadon herself, but Jaydin still wasn't sure how that was possible.

"Can we do that?" she asked Cotelle.

"Any world you want. Damarin has been to most of them."

Was World Seven truly their best option? Sandin stared at her hopefully. Jaydin couldn't see any reason why another Earth would make a better choice. Tith had only told her so much about rendinzori and now Miadra was gone. Cotelle wanted Jaydin to see for herself, and she definitely wasn't going back to Damarin at this point. World Seven might be their only hope of understanding what was happening on Derkra.

"I will go to World Seven," Jaydin said to the assembled kandar. "I will find Siltadon if I can and speak with her if she is willing."

"And Tchardin?" Kadailin asked.

"I will go to one Earth and if she is not there I will go to another, and another, and another until I find her. Anything to bring the future queen back to Derkra."

"Then open the shift," Cotelle said, "and think of World Seven."

Jaydin took hold of the pandinzori in front of her with her mind. She effortlessly opened it to what was behind. That part of the process had been getting easier since she had first travelled to Black Valley. Grey swirled before her. She thought of the Earths. She thought of World Seven. The grey continued to churn.

"I don't see anything."

"You won't." The big devoshai stood from Moradi's side. He walked over to her and peered into the shift. "You have to go straight through the grey."

Further proof that Tchar may have only blocked the images in the shift. Jaydin studied the empty portal. "How do I go to the proper world if all I see is grey?"

"Damarin said it was the same as any other shift. You see an image of the place you're going in your mind."

"But I've never seen the Earths." Images of the burning World Seven surfaced in her mind but she blinked them away. "Tith showed me images of them, yes, but not as they are now." She looked at the kandar around her and they all looked back at her expectantly.

"What about Rai?" Sandin said. "Just as you did with Ovaeron to get us to Black Valley, you can do with Rai."

Jaydin saw him in her mind. Rai shouldn't have changed when the world was restarted. The World Tree that had grown the World Seed should remain when all else began again. She thought of Rai and focused on the shift. She concentrated on his straight height, his emerald leaves—ever-green—and his name. The shift remained grey. She shrugged at the other kandar.

"That's really it?" Kadailin raised her eyebrows in disbelief. She turned towards Cotelle. "This is how you propose we get to the Earths?"

Cotelle nodded, his eyes never leaving the shift. "I've seen Damarin do it."

"I'll try it," Jaydin said. It was no different than when she had gone to Black Valley.

She looked at the shift and couldn't believe an Earth was behind it. She had been trying to find a way back to Coralynth for her whole life and it wasn't even necessary. As soon as Tchardin had brought Cien to them from Black Valley she could have opened the shift and resumed her duty. They all could have.

"I should be recording this." Jaydin remembered having her notebook at the edge of the burnt patch, under Frenn's trunk, before Moradi appeared. It had been left there in the confusion. All those notes, all the memories, Tith's words, gone. Maybe it was lying somewhere in the newly healed Cens, but it would take forever to find it. They didn't have that kind of time now. She took a step towards the ice.

"You can't go alone," Sandin said. "It's too risky. You don't know what you'll find there. What if something happens and you can't come back?"

Jaydin stopped. "I can't make anyone else take the risk. We don't even know if it will work."

"I'll go," Ryten said.

Jaydin sighed. "You can't. If you're Tchardin's dodenzinn, we need to make sure you're still around when she gets back."

"We need you just as much," he said. "We need your memory."

"My memory is exactly the reason I need to go. None of you would know what to do there."

"I can go," Sandin said.

Jaydin frowned, but when she looked at her sister she knew there was nothing she could do to stop her.

"You said yourself how good I was in the shift," Sandin said. "How strong my mind was. I can protect you. I can make sure we end up where we want to go."

"But you can't open the shift. You won't be able to take us back if something happens to me."

"I might be able to. You've said the humans of World Four can open the shift. That means rendinzori can do it. Maybe Siltadon can teach me."

Jaydin was skeptical of any kandar's ability to teach another kandar to use rendinzori, but she was also getting excited. The prospect of meeting Siltadon—a tevadra straight out of Derkra's history—whether she could help Sandin or not, was something Jaydin had never believed possible.

"I will go as well," said Torshe. Ocien was silent at his side.

Jaydin looked at Moradi's body. They might never find the tevadra's dodenzinn but Ocien and Torshe had found each other. Even if Torshe's father had fallen to the purge, even if Cens had destroyed or changed him, they still had a chance.

"No," she said. "You two need to stay together, here with Ryten."

Torshe opened his mouth to protest but Jaydin raised a hand to silence him. Cotelle stared at her. His expression was blank but she had to believe he approved. She wondered for a moment if maybe he would join them.

"What about me?"

They all turned. It was Kadailin who had spoken.

Jaydin was about to say no again, but the look on Kadailin's face deterred her.

'I want to find Tchardin,' Kadailin said for Jaydin's mind alone. *'I don't have a dodenzinn yet and I may never find one, but we sisters belong together just as Ocien and Torshe do.'*

They were nice words, but they didn't change Kadailin's nature. She wasn't the first of the sisters Jaydin would go to for help. She was probably the last. Or she had been. Jaydin thought of Kadailin's support in the council, her help in protecting Sandin, her interest in Siltadon and in World Seven. All of the questions she'd asked...

"Alright." Jaydin looked into the swirling grey. "The daughters of Tith will go to World Seven."

"We'll get away from this glass. I promise you, just stop. You have to control yourself!"

She was so focused on Kadailin she almost jumped when Sandin entered her vision. The tevadra put a hand on Kadailin's shoulder, melding their auras. Jaydin cringed. The shock of that contact could have caused Kadailin to lose it. Instead, their sister let the pandinzori around her go. It floated freely away. She removed her hands from her eyes and the two sisters stared at each other. Jaydin watched in silence. Sandin let go of Kadailin and walked around the glass tree to join Jaydin, calm as ever. Kadailin slowly followed.

"We can't touch pandinzori here," Jaydin said. "Not around the glass. Your instinct will be to use pandinzori to protect yourself but that will only get you killed."

"It just floats through the glass," Kadailin said. "Why doesn't it react?"

"It's safe when a mind doesn't hold it."

"How will we leave if you can't touch pandinzori?" Sandin asked.

Jaydin frowned, she hadn't thought of that in her terror.

"We'll find a way when the time comes," she said. "Now relax, both of you."

Jaydin tried to take her own advice and calm down as she looked around them. This was not what she'd expected but it was still one of the Earths. She allowed herself a small smile. Once she started she couldn't contain it and it quickly grew.

"How can you smile about this?" Kadailin wrapped her arms around herself and stared dejectedly into the canopy above. Parts of it sparkled in the sun.

Sun. Jaydin beamed, watching the points of light break through the leaves. When she looked back at her sisters Sandin was smiling too.

"I never thought we'd get back," Jaydin said. "I wanted so badly to believe we could do it, but most of the time I didn't. And here we are. This is all I ever wanted."

"This isn't everything you wanted," Sandin said.

"This can't be what you wanted," Kadailin said at the same time.

"It's certainly a start." Jaydin peered into the forest ahead of them. "This is an Earth. A real human Earth! Don't you understand?"

Sandin nodded, still smiling. Kadailin frowned.

"We can go back to them now." Jaydin's eyes were drawn to the glass tree that had nearly caused them so much trouble. "But it will be dangerous. How could this have happened?" She didn't expect an answer. Kadailin and Sandin wouldn't be able to explain it, but maybe she could, from somewhere deep in her memory.

There were glass trees scattered around them and a glass panel stretched through the earth to the left of them. She followed it with her eyes. It led through the brush to a massive, dark trunk.

"Rai," she said.

She pushed through the leaves until she could look up at him. The tree's base was still far away but it was clear he was gigantic. His trunk wasn't as thick as Ovaeron's, but it was straight and perfect like Tith's. In fact he looked a lot like Tith from the ground. The smaller trunks that surrounded his only made him look more magnificent. Jaydin took a step towards him, craning her neck to see through the lower canopy and up to his branches which must extend above them.

A seed grew in the collective, but there was no one around.

"What is it?" Sandin asked, reacting to the look on Jaydin's face. Her sisters had followed her.

"A guardian," Kadailin whispered.

A guardian. Jaydin waited for the name to come with the seed. It would be Leksten, she knew, but just to see it, to feel him. To meet him. It would be nothing like her meeting with Ruon, when she had known he was wrong to be on Derkra. This was a true guardian, loyal to his Earth. He had to be close if his seed was added to her collective.

Siltadon. The seed didn't belong to Leksten. Jaydin's mouth dropped open. She searched for the tevadra but could see nothing. Miadra had said Siltadon lived, but Jaydin had been skeptical. Now the tevadra was the guardian of the Earth? What had happened to Leksten?

She looked up through the lower canopy to Rai's great height and her shock was amplified. A few sets of branches above the tops of the others, the World Tree became glass.

"Look up at Rai." Jaydin turned to her sisters. "Look at the glass."

Kadailin gasped. Sandin put a hand on her shoulder.

Jaydin motioned for them to back away into the trees. She tried to direct them to a space without much glass. Siltadon had to be close to them but she was still hidden. Sandin's eyes were wide with excitement.

"Siltadon's the guardian," Jaydin said to her. "That isn't right."

"What do you mean?" Kadailin asked.

"Leksten is the guardian of World Seven."

Kadailin backed away from Jaydin with a frantic look on her face. Jaydin frowned but then she saw that Sandin was also looking past her.

"He was," said a raspy voice from behind her.

Jaydin turned around. Siltadon stood a few steps away. The new guardian bridged the small gap between them. She was almost as tall as Jaydin. Her skin was very white, her hair nearly the same shade. Her seed was bright in the collective. Siltadon had restarted a world and she was still alive. Jaydin had found it hard to believe she could live so long without being called back to her father, but now Rai was her father, and as guardian she would live forever.

As far as Jaydin knew Leksten should have remained the guardian when the world began again. If they had come to World Seven and found Leksten made anew, given a different appearance or name or even if he had been remade a tevadra, Jaydin could have accepted that—no one knew what would come after a world was restarted—but Siltadon had lived in the time of the kandaran war. She had been real in the past, a part of Jaydin's history, and she had not been remade. Here she stood, guardian of an Earth. A tevadra from Derkra. One of the nine hundred. What had Rai done about her dodenzinn?

"What are you doing here?" the guardian asked.

"Siltadon," Jaydin whispered, unable to keep the awe out of her voice. "You lived before the war. You stood on this Earth when it burned. You carried the Seed. You—"

"I know all of that," Siltadon said. "I was there."

Jaydin stared blankly back at her.

"More of you." Siltadon's eyes narrowed. "Did you come from another Earth?"

"We came from Derkra," Sandin answered.

Jaydin had almost forgotten Sandin was there. That either of her sisters were there. She took a step back to stand in line with them. Siltadon's eyes fell on Sandin. They widened.

"What is *that*?" she asked.

"What is what?" Sandin said.

"Not in the collective," the guardian mused, seemingly to herself. "Humans, kandar, they all join the collective."

Sandin raised her eyebrows.

Jaydin cast a cursory glance around at the mention of humans. Where were they? Should she and her sisters be hiding themselves? Or was Siltadon trusting in their innate camouflage to obscure them? Jaydin couldn't wait to see it happen, to see her sisters in their human skins. She hadn't mentioned that to the other kandar on Derkra, besides Damarin—who had asked. It hadn't been relevant until now.

Siltadon stared at her. Jaydin had so many questions for the tevadra. What had happened when she restarted the world? Where had the glass come from? Where were the humans? When could she see them? The guardian could also fill in the holes in Jaydin's knowledge, tell her the things Tith hadn't known about the kandaran war or had hidden from her. Siltadon's blue eyes remained fixed intently on her. Once again Jaydin wished she had her notebook to record it all, but there were more important issues to deal with. She'd have all the time she needed to talk to the guardian after they had dealt with the situation on Derkra. All the time she needed to get the kandar back to the Purpose.

"There was a tevadra here," she said. "Damarin. Did you meet her?"

"Yes."

"Did she talk to you?"

"She did." Siltadon smiled. "She wanted me to help her."

Jaydin frowned. "With what?"

"She wanted me to return to Derkra and raise the kandar up. She told me Tchar and Dani were dead or gone, that humanity was no longer the Purpose and that existence should be ours."

Jaydin thought of Ruon in the Black Valley council meeting. One guardian was already too much. She was glad Siltadon hadn't joined him.

"But why?" Siltadon seemed to be talking to herself. "We're no better than them. I let this happen. We all did." The guardian shook her head and ran her hands through her hair.

"What happened here?" Jaydin asked. "What did you let happen?"

"No," Siltadon said. "No one else will know."

She must be talking about the restart. A lot of humans would have died when Siltadon brought the Seed back to World Seven from Coralynth. Tith had explained that the tevadra had loved the world and its people.

Jaydin remembered the screams as she pulled Vurel out of the ground, as she killed him. It had been necessary, but terrible. So too was the restart of a world. Maybe Siltadon wanted to forget what she had done. Jaydin could understand that.

"Did Damarin speak to you about rendinzori?" she asked.

"Rendinzori," Siltadon hissed. Her blue eyes lit up. "Rendinzori to make a world."

"Yes," Sandin said from beside Jaydin. Her voice was excited again. Kadailin was silent and still. "To make trees. To build a mountain full of fire."

Siltadon stared at Sandin with confusion on her face. Jaydin was about to repeat what her sister had said when the guardian spoke.

"Only humans can do that."

Siltadon turned away from them and Jaydin took the opportunity to exchange a glance with her sisters. Sandin's excitement faded. She looked to be deep in thought, but Jaydin knew there was no way to hear it. Kadailin just looked scared. Jaydin studied the pandinzori around her to make sure none of it was moving.

"Did she talk to you?" Siltadon asked, turning back to them. "Do you now know what she knows? The things I told her?"

"She learned everything she knows from me," Jaydin said. "But Damarin told me nothing about you."

Siltadon seemed to look inward. "Jaydin." She must have been looking at the collective. "The Earth was burning."

"Yes," Jaydin said. Tith had shown her images of it, and she had always been certain it was true. It was something else to hear it confirmed by another kandar. A tevadra who had been there. She almost smiled.

"*You* said that," Siltadon added.

The smile never came. "Did Damarin tell you that?"

Siltadon didn't answer. Jaydin was suddenly wary. What had Damarin told the guardian about her sisters, if anything? About Jaydin in particular? Damarin had learned about Siltadon and World Seven from Jaydin long before she could have heard about it from the tevadra herself. How much had their stories differed?

'I don't like this,' Kadailin said. Siltadon turned towards her and she cringed.

Jaydin looked into the forest around them again. Siltadon had loved the people of this Earth before the restart. She must feel the same about its new inhabitants.

"How have the humans been doing since the restart?"

Siltadon shook her head and looked away. Not the reaction Jaydin had been expecting.

"Where are they?" she asked.

"Gone."

"Gone where?"

"Just—" Siltadon paused. "Gone. World Seven is dead."

"It can't be." The guardian was acting so strangely. "It looks fine. There are trees. Grass. The fire's gone."

"So are the humans."

"What happened to them?"

Siltadon turned her back on Jaydin.

It seemed this Earth's problems were greater than the problems on Derkra. Jaydin wasn't sure what could have happened to the other worlds since they'd left them, but World Seven had been restarted. That should have meant a perfect new beginning, just as it had been when Creator first made the humans and the Earths. It hadn't been long since Tchar closed the shift, not in comparison to the age of existence. World Seven shouldn't have been able to get to this point so quickly. It had taken much longer the first time. The only obvious difference was the absence of kandar.

"Just look at him," Siltadon said, gazing up at Rai's glass branches. "There's no fixing this, no going back. We need to leave this place. Forever."

"Leave?" Jaydin stepped towards Siltadon. "Abandon the Earth?"

"It's dead."

How could the guardian of an Earth say that? Rai's trunk appeared to be strong and dark. He hadn't fallen, despite the glass. There were green leaves there, young branches. He was damaged—and that meant Siltadon couldn't go to him to rest—but could he still grow the Seed? If all the humans were gone—Jaydin had to shake herself when she thought about that—if something had happened to them the world would need to be restarted again. They could still do that if Rai could grow the World Seed. If the Root remained alive below him, all was not lost.

Siltadon wasn't going to be able to help Sandin. Not in the state she appeared to be in and not with her Earth and her father in so much trouble. Tchardin clearly wasn't on World Seven, and Siltadon had nothing useful to say about Damarin. They should shift on. But what was the point of continuing, of trying to save the kandar, if they didn't work on the Purpose when confronted with it? Jaydin couldn't let this go on any longer.

She started towards Rai's trunk. Sandin and Kadailin both moved to stop her but she gave them a reassuring look. Tith had told her everything about the Earths. She must know how to fix this. Somewhere deep in her memory, there had to be an answer.

"You didn't come from another Earth," Siltadon said as she walked away. "You came straight from Derkra. You can take me with you when you go."

"You can't leave," Jaydin said. "This is your Earth."

"But you will leave."

"You are the guardian now and you must stay here forever." Jaydin looked back at the three kandar. Sandin wasn't likely to get what she wanted, but perhaps Kadailin still could. "We're looking for someone. We will go to the other Earths after we leave here."

"You will travel to another Earth directly from World Seven?"

"If it's possible," Jaydin said. "We're certainly going to try."

"You'd just leave me here. With this."

"I can help."

The impressive width of Rai's trunk became clear as Jaydin approached. He truly was magnificent. A World Tree. The first Jaydin would see in person, not just in her mind. She shuddered to think of what state the other Earths must be in if this one had fallen so far since they left it. They'd have a lot of work to do. Hopefully the situations on the other worlds weren't as pressing as World Seven's, or they would never find Tchardin.

She tried not to think of all the humans who must have died on this Earth for the restart to fail. She tried not to think of the waste. They could still save it. They could do that one thing. Miadra and Cotelle were wrong. Damarin was wrong. This was an Earth. This was the Purpose. Jaydin smiled to herself.

"What do you think you're doing?" Siltadon's voice was far behind her now. "Did the kandar learn nothing from World Four?"

Behind Jaydin, past Siltadon, her sisters stood close together. The guardian blocked Jaydin's view of Sandin but Kadailin was clearly visible. She was surrounded in swirling pandinzori.

"Kadailin!" Jaydin shouted. "Stop!"

***

Kadailin felt the pandinzori around her closing in. She shied away from it, even though she knew it was her own mind that drew it to her. She couldn't help it. The thought of all that pandinzori floating freely through the glass leaves of the glass trees was terrifying. She closed her eyes.

Jaydin's voice floated over her but the words didn't mean anything. Sandin's hand appeared in her peripheral vision, a dark space lined in light. It connected with her shoulder and shocked her. She opened her eyes, the threat of pandinzori forgotten for a moment.

"You'll kill us all with that, you know," the guardian said. "You have no control."

Siltadon gave Kadailin an expressionless stare for a moment, then turned to look after Jaydin. The amount of pandinzori that surrounded the guardian was unnerving. She didn't seem bothered by the glass at all. Kadailin tried to avoid looking at her. She turned towards Jaydin instead. Her sister met her eyes and her expression was neutral. Almost like Siltadon's.

Jaydin turned and walked towards the World Tree again. She was getting far enough away now that she wouldn't hear them if they spoke aloud. Siltadon must have realised the same thing.

'You don't know about glass,' Siltadon said, making no effort to keep her words from Kadailin, *'and you will travel from one Earth to another without a second thought. What exactly* do *you know?'*

'Everything.' Jaydin didn't stop to answer. *'My father told me the history of the kandar before I was born.'*

'But he didn't tell you what started all this?'

'The kandar must have lost their way,' Jaydin said. *'Maybe they forgot the Purpose.'*

Siltadon laughed. Sandin crossed her arms beside Kadailin.

'Useless,' the guardian said. *'What does that even mean?'*

The conversation made Kadailin nervous. She looked at her sister beside her. If it was making her nervous, what would it be doing to Sandin, who couldn't hear them speak? She tried to catch the tevadra's eye, but Sandin stared straight ahead, her gaze locked on Jaydin.

Kadailin joined her in watching their sister. Could Jaydin really help the Earth? What could she do with a tree made of glass that would save it? Kadailin hadn't learned much from their oldest sister yet, but Jaydin must have a plan if she would keep them on this Earth long enough to go to the damaged World Tree.

Siltadon stalked away from them, waiting for Jaydin to answer.

"They're talking?" Sandin asked.

Kadailin turned towards her. Sandin continued to watch Jaydin and the guardian.

"They are, but I don't think I should repeat it now." Kadailin looked at Siltadon's back. The guardian had stopped about twenty paces from them. "She'd probably notice. Jaydin would have told her about you if she thought it was a good idea."

Sandin frowned. "She knows I didn't join the collective."

"I guess that's true," Kadailin said. "I'm sure Jaydin will explain it all later."

Jaydin stood before Rai's trunk and ran her hands along his bark. Kadailin shuddered at the thought of doing so. The tree was an abomination. He had to be dead. How could he live with glass growing out of him? Siltadon paced back and forth in the grass ahead of them.

'So you'd never let me leave?' the guardian asked. *'Not even if I can help?'*

'You can help best by staying here. This world will need to begin again, and it will need a guardian.'

'You need me on Derkra. You need me on the other Earths. Rai is dead.'

'I'm not sure yet,' Jaydin said. Kadailin could just make out her red hair against the dark bark as she looked up into Rai's canopy. *'There may still be hope.'*

Siltadon paced more quickly between Jaydin and the two tevadra. She seemed agitated. Kadailin had to remind herself not to grasp at pandinzori again to comfort herself.

'What do you know?' Siltadon said. *'What do any of you know? Stuck on Derkra since your births. What have you done for the humans? For the Earths? What have any of you done in your lives?'*

'I know everything,' Jaydin responded. *'I may not have done much yet, but now that we've returned to the Earths I'll begin to apply my knowledge. The other kandar will do the same.'*

Siltadon looked like she would tear her hair out. Kadailin wondered if Jaydin would be so calm if she knew how the guardian was reacting. Then she decided she would be. Jaydin had always been sure of what she knew. Now she could finally use it.

'The Root is alive.' There was elation in Jaydin's mindvoice. Kadailin smiled at Sandin to let her know everything was fine. *'I think the world can start again. We only need to find the Seed.'*

"There is no Seed," Siltadon muttered. Jaydin was far enough away that she couldn't have heard her. "Not this time. World Seven can never live again!"

Kadailin cringed, the smile quickly gone from her face, but instead of continuing Siltadon went silent. The guardian stopped pacing, then she looked from Jaydin to Kadailin and back again. Her thoughts were loud, but indecipherable. Kadailin concentrated on her seed in the collective.

'Four,' the guardian's mind said. "Four of them who know," she whispered. She walked towards Jaydin. "Two of them are here."

"Where's she going?" Sandin asked.

Kadailin frowned. Her eyes were drawn away from Sandin by the movement of pandinzori. It looked hazy and it seemed to be floating through the trees, towards Rai. It had to be doing that on its own. Pandinzori moved all over Calendrai without anyone to control it, drawn to the kandar or to the trees. It had been moving here when they arrived. She shuddered, watching it. Was it slightly darker than it should be? Slightly more grey in the air? It seemed so purposeful. It seemed to be following the guardian, but that didn't mean it was touched by a mind. It would have reacted with the glass around them if it had been.

Siltadon stopped when she was half-way to Rai and turned back. She looked past the two sisters. Kadailin followed her gaze. The pandinzori there was moving too. The world seemed to vibrate around her. She had to refocus her attention to stop herself from gripping pandinzori. The movement of the light had to be in her mind. The guardian wouldn't do that. No kandar would.

Kadailin was about to turn back when she saw a strip of pandinzori bend to avoid a glass branch. Everywhere else it just floated right through.

"Jaydin," she said, but her voice was barely more than a whisper.

"What?" Sandin asked from beside her. "What's happening?"

'Jaydin!' Kadailin projected to her sister's leaf. *'Get away from the tree!'*

Jaydin turned from where she stood at the foot of Rai's trunk. She looked at Sandin and Kadailin and tilted her head in question as she must have noticed the welling pandinzori. Above her Rai's branches exploded with light.

Kadailin reached for the pandinzori around her, finding she had already taken some of it unconsciously. She pushed her mind outwards, trying to grasp that around Sandin as well. Resistance. Siltadon must be holding it. It didn't matter. Kadailin needed it.

Sandin turned away from the blinding flash and shouted. Kadailin didn't hear what she said. The collective shuddered and Kadailin's mind recoiled from what it could mean. Siltadon was nowhere to be seen and Jaydin had disappeared behind the wall of light. It rushed towards them.

Sandin shouldered her. "Behind you!" she shouted over the roar. Kadailin turned to find that light came at them from every direction. She concentrated, pushed her mind outwards, and forced the resistance away. She had it. She hardened it.

Sandin froze. Her eyes showed panic. Kadailin experienced a strange moment of calm. She felt safe behind pandinzori. She felt protected, encapsulated in it. But Jaydin's words came back to her and she knew it would kill them if she kept it.

The light hit her pandinzori from the front, from behind, from above. From every side. It shocked her, a pulse running through her body like the sensation of another kandar intruding on her aura. The ripple spread to every surface of her pandinzori in an instant. Then she did the most difficult thing she'd ever done.

She let go.

Chapter 36

Sandin opened her eyes and lifted her upper body off the ground. There was pressure on the back of her legs, holding her down. At first she thought it must be pandinzori but it moved as she attempted to rise. She looked behind her to find that the weight on her lower body was Kadailin. Her sister lay motionless across the back of Sandin's thighs.

"Kadailin." Sandin pulled her legs out from under her sister and rose to a crouch. The forest continued in the distance, but its edge was far away now. The earth gaped open in front of them. She turned to look around and found it all the same. Kadailin opened her eyes. She stared at Sandin for a moment, then put her hands over her face and curled into a ball. She didn't say anything.

All Sandin could remember was blinding light. Then shouting. She looked at the ravaged Earth. There had been trees there. Now there were none. The earth was black and furrowed. The green had been torn away. She looked down at her skin but the only strange things about it were the cuts she had gotten from Marr.

"Kadailin." She leaned over her sister and attempted to press their invisible auras together. Kadailin displayed no reaction despite the shock Sandin felt. Her left arm and side glistened with blood.

Sandin remembered Siltadon and was afraid. She had wanted to meet the tevadra so badly, but the guardian hadn't been what she expected at all.

"Where's Jaydin?" she asked. Kadailin made a small noise. The forest stood around them in an irregular circle. The World Tree, Rai, had been there once. Now he was gone. Sandin remembered being held in place. Suddenly it all made sense.

"You touched pandinzori." Sandin pushed Kadailin, tried to roll her over, ignoring the pulsing shock that came from the contact. She grabbed her sister's hands and pulled them away from her face. "You did this, didn't you?"

Kadailin struggled against her.

"What happened? Where's Jaydin, Kadailin! Where is she?"

"I didn't do it," Kadailin said. "I didn't!"

"What about Siltadon?"

Kadailin shook her head. A shiver of dread crept across Sandin's skin.

"I can't sense them," Sandin said, "but I know you can. So you need to tell me. They're out in the forest, aren't they?"

"Jaydin," Kadailin said. "She's gone. Her leaf..."

"No." Sandin shook her sister. "No, that can't be true."

"Siltadon did it. I don't know how she did it, but she took all the pandinzori around us and touched the glass. All at once. It came from everywhere." Kadailin fought to escape Sandin's grasp. "There was nothing I could do! Kandar aren't supposed to kill each other!"

Sandin let Kadailin go. She stood and looked around them.

"I tried," Kadailin said. "I just tried to protect us."

"Why would Siltadon do this?" Sandin asked. Kadailin didn't answer. "What were they saying to each other? Why would she risk her father? Why would she kill herself?" She didn't know how to react to Kadailin's words. "I don't believe you."

How could it not be Kadailin's fault? Jaydin had said she was touching pandinzori. Even Siltadon had mentioned it. Kadailin couldn't control herself, couldn't avoid pandinzori even when she knew it was dangerous. Their eyes met and for the first time Sandin couldn't hold Kadailin's gaze. She turned away.

"She said something about us being two of the four who know," Kadailin finally said. "I don't know what she meant, but she didn't kill herself."

"What?"

"Siltadon's seed," Kadailin said. "It's still bright."

Sandin looked at the ground. She was the one who had insisted they travel to World Seven, that she meet Siltadon. She remembered her excitement when the tevadra had appeared. She had needed to know, needed to talk to the one who could teach her to be kandar. Then she remembered the light and where it had come from. Kadailin wasn't responsible for what had happened. If anything it was Sandin's fault. Siltadon was dangerous, and Sandin had made them come here.

"Jaydin's leaf fell?" she asked again.

Kadailin nodded, her head in her hands.

"And her body..."

Rai was gone. Blown to nothing when his glass branches reacted to the pandinzori around them. Jaydin had stood at his base.

"Jaydin was the only one of us who really cared," Sandin whispered.

Not just about the kandar or the Purpose, but about Sandin. Jaydin had been the only one to stand by her and protect her when she didn't know who or what she was. Now her sister was dead. Her body destroyed. She would never get to rest in Tith and she would never be reborn. She would never meet the humans, or see the kandar returned to the Purpose. If she had a dodenzinn somewhere out there he could be left alone forever.

Sandin dropped to her knees at the edge of the grass. She slammed her fists into the dark earth, raked through it with her fingers. She hadn't learned anything from Siltadon to help her be kandar. They hadn't learned anything useful about Damarin. They hadn't even found Tchardin. And now Jaydin was gone.

***

Tchardin stood in stunned silence and looked around her, trying to get a sense of what could have happened.

The World Tree was gone. His name had been Athol. Jaydin had told her that. He was nowhere to be seen. Every time she had come out on an Earth she had been within sight of its World Tree. The forest she found herself in looked to be short, sparse, yet she could see nothing that looked like a kandaran tree. She'd even considered that he could be small, like Zemko, or tiny, like Irah, but their pandinzori had given them away and there was nothing like that here. There was almost no pandinzori at all, which was strange, given the number of trees. The majority of it hovered around Tchardin.

Whose branches had she touched in the shift that had led her into this world? Was she going to find another empty Earth, only this time without even a World Tree that could save it?

She continued to stare into the canopy. There was another strange thing about this forest. Its trees had brightly coloured leaves. Like Ovaeron's. Some were red and orange and yellow. Some of the trees had trunks that were dark but others were grey, or even white. The leaves of the tree in the shift had been mostly yellow, but some had been red, some green and brown. What could that mean? Rai's translucent leaves had told her he was damaged. Veradon's leaves had been splotched with black, and he was dying. Did these colourful leaves mean the same thing? Were they ruined like the trees of Cens after the fire?

She shuddered as she thought of Siltadon's parting words to her. Damarin must be up to something back on Derkra. What could that mean for the kandar? Her sister had displayed some strange opinions before throwing Tchardin into the shift to World One, and her actions on World Four had been extreme, but it seemed she had gone even further since.

Tchardin was just glad the shift had been open and ready when the guardian made her threat. What could she have done if she hadn't been ready to leave? If Siltadon had truly wanted to stop her? The guardian was definitely stronger than she was. Tchardin hoped World Eight would be different. Better.

A branch broke to her right. A sharp click followed. The forest lit up with a flash. She swung around to find the source of the noise and light. The leaves of this forest were thin near the ground. When she turned she saw a man standing behind them. His back was to her.

Tchardin froze. For each world she had entered she had been unsure of what she would find. Now she knew it could be anything. Truly anything. The worlds hadn't even been made by Creator, who had made the kandar. They had been made by the humans who lived in them. The man who stood in the forest in front of her was a part of that. What could he know about it, if anything?

She needed to know what had happened to Athol. If this man was walking in this forest, the forest where the World Tree should be, he must know of it. Even if he hadn't seen it himself. The humans spoke to each other, told each other their history, as Jaydin had said.

Tchardin extended her mind towards the man's. He stood still, and from the way he held his arms Tchardin thought he must be looking down at something in his hands. She wanted to listen to his thoughts, find out if he knew anything about the World Tree, find out if he knew anything about building the world itself, even unconsciously. While she stared at him he turned in her direction. A name came to her. *Aaron.*

A flash of light filled her eyes. She ducked away from it, her back brushing against a trunk. She felt her camouflage settle over her and noticed the man looked through the trees in her direction. His leaf brought others to the collective. Hundreds of them. Thousands. His mind opened up to her and she knew that the thing in his hands was a *camera*, and that he would make eternal images with it. *Pictures. Photographs.* He crouched and stared into the leaves.

"Uh, hello?" he said. "Is there someone in there?"

Tchardin looked down at her purple dress and wasn't surprised he could see her. She took a step back, making sure to keep her feet quiet on the leaves and branches. Should she meet this man? Or should she run and continue on her way to Derkra?

"Hello?" he said again.

Tchardin pushed through the branches towards him. She brushed the last set out of the way and found herself on a hard path, not unlike the grey ground on World Five that had irritated her feet.

The man watched her warily. She met his eyes and heard his thoughts, saw herself as he saw her. He took in her purple dress, ripped, near to rags. He saw the dirt on her arms and legs and face. He looked down at her bare feet and found them covered in mud. The cut on her forehead had healed, but the body had left a scar. A ragged purple line. There was dried blood in her hair, and a single torn red leaf stuck in it.

"Hello," Tchardin said.

Aaron pursed his lips. She saw him hesitate. He turned away from her to gaze down the path. Then he looked back, and she heard his thoughts on her appearance repeated.

"Are you ok?" he asked. "It's pretty cold out here and you're not wearing any shoes."

Tchardin smiled. This was already a better world.

PART IV

Chapter 37

Tchardin followed Aaron through the forest. The man continued to glance back at her as he walked, as if he expected her to disappear at any moment. Tchardin continued to consider doing so.

"I'm Aaron, by the way," he said, meeting her eyes before turning to look ahead again. Tchardin didn't respond. She still found it strange that humans had to tell each other their names. She had decided not to reveal hers yet.

His thoughts told her he was worried about taking her with him, about how she would react to his interest. Why had he asked her to follow him? There seemed to be many reasons, all confusing to Tchardin. The way she looked had started it. She was in trouble. The state of her clothing had told him it was so. The scar on her forehead could mean she'd forgotten herself, or that someone had tried to hurt her. Her skin was a deep brown and so was his.

Tchardin looked down at her skin. She distinctly remembered it being lighter on World Three, when she had first seen her human camouflage. She wasn't sure about the other worlds because she hadn't paid much attention to it since. Maybe this was something that mattered to humans and her camouflage was adapting to that. Aaron's reaction seemed to indicate it mattered. At least in this case.

The colourful leaves thinned ahead of them, not that they had ever been thick. This forest might have more trees than Cens but it was nowhere near as dense. Only its colour was impressive when compared to the forests of the other Earths. Tchardin was struck again by how little pandinzori flowed through it. Aaron was surrounded by it, as all humans were, but when it left his skin it spread out and disappeared.

It was bright beyond the trees. So bright she had trouble looking past the edge of the forest. The sun on this Earth must be particularly dazzling. Aaron stepped out ahead of her and the light reflected off his thick black hair. Tchardin followed.

She was struck by voices. She sank to her knees and covered her ears, though it didn't help. The voices were loud in her mind and impossible to stop. Once she adjusted to the brightness and saw the world outside the forest clearly she couldn't help but open her mouth in surprise. There were humans everywhere.

"Are you ok?" Aaron asked.

Tchardin barely heard him over the din of thoughts. She looked up to see his mouth moving. She concentrated on his spoken words, tried to push the voices into the back of her mind.

"It's not much farther."

She looked at the multitude of moving shapes ahead of them. She shouldn't be surprised. Aaron had brought thousands of leaves to the collective and his thoughts were not the thoughts of a king, like Tezroi's. She should have known there would be vast numbers of humans on this Earth. More than any she had visited so far.

Her mind spun with the voices. She allowed Aaron to help her to her feet. As they approached the mass of people, lights exploded in her mind. In an instant the number of leaves in the collective had doubled, and the growth wasn't slowing.

Tchardin staggered through the crowd, overwhelmed, almost unaware of Aaron's hand on her elbow. How could all of this have come from two? How could nine hundred kandar ever have helped them? So many humans. If she were ever to see them make the world, if she were ever to see what rendinzori could truly do, this would be the Earth for it.

***

All Sandin could think of was the approaching light. She had to escape those thoughts. They had come to World Seven for her and Jaydin had died because of it, but there wasn't any use in dwelling on that now. The kandar were in trouble. Derkra was in trouble. They had to get away from Siltadon and back to their people. Jaydin would have wanted that. Sandin looked over the ragged, exposed earth that surrounded them, looked into the trees in the distance, and closed her eyes.

Blackness. She concentrated on the emptiness in front of her. She told herself she could use rendinzori. She would. She was going to open the grey shift and take them back to Derkra. Nothing happened. She opened her eyes and looked down at Kadailin. Her sister sat on the remaining grass with her head in her hands. She hadn't moved since they'd last spoken. Sandin frowned.

"You have to open the shift for me," she said. "We have to go back to Derkra."

"The glass," Kadailin whispered.

Sandin had once had the same concern. When they'd first arrived on World Seven she hadn't been sure how they would leave. Now it would be easy, if only Kadailin would help her. "Look around you. There's nothing left, nothing close enough to hurt us."

Kadailin was quiet.

"I don't even care if you point it at Derkra," Sandin continued. "I don't need your help to get us there, but I do need you to get us in."

Sandin could easily sit down in the grass as Kadailin did. She could just give up. When she thought of losing Jaydin she wanted to join her younger sister in despair. But they still had things to do. They shouldn't go to any of the other Earths, not when they didn't know what to expect, but they could go back to Calendrai and join the kandar there. Try everything they could to rally their people and prepare them for Damarin. The kandar were alone now, without Jaydin to guide them, and they would have to do things for themselves. Sandin scanned the edge of the forest. It wasn't safe to stay on World Seven.

"Sandin," Kadailin said. "Look."

Sandin was brought back to the moment by her sister's words. Kadailin was focused on the grass in front of her. There, in the green, were tiny red flowers, exactly like those they had found in Cens. Kadailin held a hand out and in the centre of her palm was a small black spider. Sandin knelt to study it.

The spider had crumpled into a ball but as they watched it in silence it lifted itself again and scurried off Kadailin's palm and into the grass to disappear.

Kadailin met Sandin's eyes. "She brought them to Cens from here."

Sandin shuddered. If Damarin had brought the flowers and spiders back to Calendrai from World Seven, what else had she brought? "Is

Siltadon close?" she asked. Kadailin shook her head. "Is she still on the Earth?"

"Yes."

Sandin had to remind herself that the alternative would be worse. "Let's hope she stays here." She brushed against Kadailin's aura, sending a shock through them both. "We really have to leave. I'll hold you in the shift, take you home to Calendrai. I just need you to open it for me."

"The glass," Kadailin said again.

"It's gone. Too far away to be a threat."

Sandin hated that she needed to stay strong for them. She should be the one so affected, not Kadailin. The younger tevadra had hardly spent any time with Jaydin, but maybe that was why it was so necessary for Sandin to go on. Jaydin would have wanted it that way. She would have expected it.

"Jaydin's leaf," Kadailin said then. "The empty space where it once hung..."

Sandin frowned. She would never know what it felt like to lose a leaf from the collective, or to have one grow there. There were so many things she didn't truly know about being kandar. This was the first time she was glad of it. If she had to feel something in addition to the loss she already felt for her sister, it would be unbearable.

Could she shift back to Calendrai on her own? Kadailin didn't seem able to help. Could Sandin use rendinzori if she tried hard enough? It must be possible. If the humans of World Four could open the shift, Sandin would find a way. But Kadailin had saved her. She had been too far away to help Jaydin, but she had saved Sandin. They had to leave together or not at all.

"Please," Sandin said. "I can protect us from the water, just like you protected me. I promise."

Kadailin looked up at her and Sandin wished she could hear what her sister was thinking. If Kadailin refused to help, Sandin would attempt to use rendinzori again. Again and again until it worked. Then she would take her sister with her.

"For Jaydin," Kadailin finally said. "For Tchardin."

She got to her feet. Sandin moved aside on the small piece of untouched earth, making space for Kadailin to open the shift. She looked out at the destruction that surrounded them, at the trees that were now so far away. An Earth without any humans. Now without a World Tree. With Jaydin gone, she didn't believe they could help it, even if the Root still lived.

"Think of Derkra," she said. "Think of Calendrai and Tith."

Kadailin closed her eyes. Sandin scanned the distant tree line warily, for Siltadon, for glass, for any approaching light, but there was nothing. Only green.

Finally the shift appeared before them. Sandin would have smiled to see it, but she wasn't sure she could smile anymore. Not yet. She walked to the ice and placed her hand against it. Kadailin didn't join her. She turned back to see what kept her sister.

"I don't like the water," Kadailin said.

"I know."

Sandin reached back for Kadailin, and when her sister extended an arm and took her hand, Sandin broke the ice.

Sandin felt in control again. She was massive and powerful. As large as anything could be. As large as existence. She held everything inside her and felt none of it and all of it at the same time. The sensation of detached awareness was soothing after what had happened on World Seven.

But she had to feel something specific. She looked inside herself, looked down, down, closer and closer, until she saw something that moved. Not the gentle movements of branches in the water, but the violence of other, the fight of something that didn't belong. Kadailin. She refocused in her sister's direction.

There were leaves there, close to Kadailin. The vast flow that was Sandin struggled to remember why that mattered. Kadailin's wild current strained towards them, pushing through Sandin, pulling pieces of her with it. The leaves were bright red, like a blaze of blood in the blue. Not the leaves they were looking for. Ovaeron's leaves. Sandin swept Kadailin away from them.

'The water...' a voice came up. *'Don't let us die in the water.'*

'I'll find Tith's leaves.' Sandin's voice echoed inside herself. *'Wait for me.'*

She refocused outwards, trying to hold Kadailin still while she expanded, lessened in intensity. Green leaves. Familiar, comforting shapes. She was looking for her father. She had to remember that. But there were other green leaves, many green trees leaning into the shift, and only one set that was red.

Sandin felt herself relax at the same moment she saw her father's foliage. She tried to leave a part of herself near him to mark his place as she had with Kadailin to protect her, but when she returned to Ovaeron there was nothing there to break the stillness. Only the waving red leaves. Compact as she was, cohesive and whole, she felt fear course through her. Kadailin was gone. The release of tension she had felt wasn't only from finding her father. Her sister had left the shift.

Sandin swirled around the red leaves, growing larger and larger, feeling less and less. She should return to Tith and go back to Calendrai, but she couldn't leave Kadailin in Black Valley alone. Not after she had decided to stay with her. To protect her. She let herself collapse against the leaves and the water tore away.

Sandin was staring at black sand when she came back to herself. Then she remembered where they had gone. Ovaeron towered above her, his black trunk rising from the black sand only steps away. She stood and searched for Kadailin. Her sister was getting to her feet just outside the circle of dark sand. Sandin strode towards her.

"Why did you leave the shift?"

Kadailin stared up into Ovaeron's canopy, his great wide trunk blocking their view of the valley. Sandin knew the false Coralynth was hidden behind it.

"We wouldn't have made it to Calendrai," Kadailin said. "It's too small."

"I would have gotten us there—"

"No. Not through all that water. Tchardin and Cien came out in the water when they tried it, and they were lucky to land so close. If we had come out in the middle of Water Side—"

"I found Tith's branches. I was coming back for you. I would have brought us out at Tith's base just as I did for Jaydin when we returned from Black Valley the first time!"

Sandin was quickly forgetting the sympathy she had felt for her sister on World Seven.

"How will you ever get back to Calendrai from here, if you're so afraid of the water?" she asked. "Did you think of that? You might be willing to stay here with Damarin and her kandar but I certainly am not. Open the shift for me. I'll go alone if I have to."

"It's too dangerous." Kadailin looked away. "I don't want to lose another sister."

The pain of Jaydin's death flooded back to Sandin, but she'd been unwilling to experience it on World Seven and she was unwilling to deal with it now. She pushed it to the back of her mind.

"Do you want to lose Tchardin?" she asked. "We can't help her from here. We can't help any of them from here."

Kadailin didn't respond. Sandin scanned the valley. Her gaze caught on a dark shape in the distance, silhouetted against the yellow valley wall. A devoshai walked towards them. Sandin didn't recognise him but he had to be from Calendrai with colouring like that. What could have happened while they were gone to bring him to Black Valley?

When she turned back Kadailin had noticed him too. Sandin studied her sister's face. It looked like the two were talking. She cursed her flaw again.

"It's the guardian Jaydin told us about," Kadailin said. "Ruon."

Sandin suppressed a flash of dread. A guardian. Like Siltadon.

"He should never have come here," she whispered to Kadailin, but Kadailin wasn't paying attention. Her sister continued to stare at the guardian. "What are you saying to him?"

Ruon joined them. His gaze locked onto Sandin immediately.

"You are not in the collective," he said.

Sandin looked away. At the edge of her vision she saw the guardian smile.

"You must be Sandin. I am Ruon, guardian of World Four and the Shadow of Derkra."

"There is no Shadow of Derkra," Sandin responded. "Cien is the Shadow of Black Valley."

Kadailin stood silent beside her. Sandin wished more than anything she could think some sense into Kadailin's mind without Ruon hearing her. She turned her eyes on her sister and tried to convey meaning with them. Kadailin looked back at her. The look said nothing.

"You cannot see pandinzori, can you?" the guardian asked.

Sandin frowned.

"Then we will do this in a way you can understand."

Sandin was about to run away, sprint across the desert to the water and swim back to Calendrai if she had to, but Ruon moved impossibly quickly. He slid behind her and brought one arm up under her chin, pressed against her neck. His other wrapped across her chest and bound her arms against her sides. In a moment she was trapped. He must be using pandinzori as well as his body because Sandin should be able to match his strength and she was caught as if by stone. He swung her around to face Kadailin, wrenching her body through the air. She struggled still, disgusted at his touch and shocked to find she felt nothing from his aura.

"How dare you!" she shouted, but a quiet voice stopped her from saying more.

"You went to an Earth."

Sandin would have turned towards the familiar voice if Ruon had let her, but she was held fast.

Damarin came into view, walking a wide circle around Kadailin, who had only just begun to react to Ruon's assault. Kadailin grew still and her gaze went to the ground. Sandin hadn't seen the two tevadra together in a long time. The resemblance was uncanny.

"Where's Jaydin?" Damarin asked. "I want to know what she thinks of the humans now."

Kadailin cringed away when their middle sister's gaze fell on her.

"Dead?" Damarin's expression was stoic, but had Sandin heard something in her voice? Sadness? Shock? "Not at rest, but dead? She can't be."

"She is," Kadailin said, still looking at the sand. "On World Seven. I lost her leaf."

"Yet I have not." Damarin turned away from them. "World Seven. She didn't even get to meet the humans."

Sandin strained in Ruon's arms.

"We could never have come this far without her," Damarin continued, "even if she wouldn't be happy to hear it. I would have liked her to see the changes I will make."

"She wouldn't be dead if it weren't for you," Sandin growled.

Damarin turned. She actually looked hurt for a moment. "How so?"

Ruon's grip tightened across her throat but Sandin refused to be silent. "Siltadon," she spat. "The glass."

"Siltadon," Damarin mused, her eyes on Sandin. "Did you go to her to learn about rendinzori? Jaydin would do that for you."

"We were looking for Tchardin," Kadailin said.

"And you didn't find her." Damarin's gaze bore into Sandin. "Rendinzori," she whispered. Then a thought seemed to come into her mind and her demeanour changed completely. "You didn't lose her leaf either," she said, almost sympathetically. "You never had it to begin with."

Sandin struggled more viciously. Not only against Ruon's hold, but against the sadness she felt. It overwhelmed her and she slumped in the guardian's arms.

"To know others only as they appear to be on the surface." Damarin's eyes glittered. "No place in the collective mind. So human." She looked behind Sandin, to Ruon. "I need her."

Sandin met Kadailin's eyes over Ruon's dark skin. "You have to do something," she said, needing Kadailin to find a way to save them. "You have to get us out of here."

"I can't. I can't fight them."

"She's right." Damarin turned to Kadailin—a shorter, less intimidating version of herself. "Tchardin and Jaydin are gone, and you are not strong enough alone. I suggest you come with us."

Kadailin glanced back and forth between Damarin and Ruon. "Where will you take her?"

"There," Damarin answered and gestured towards something Sandin couldn't see. Ruon turned.

Kadailin's gaze swept past Ovaeron's trunk and settled on the false Coralynth. Her eyes were drawn upwards by it and her mouth hung open in awe. "What is that?"

Damarin opened her arms wide towards the mountain. "It's Coralynth, come to Derkra."

"It's not the real Coralynth," Sandin muttered. Ruon brought a hand up over her mouth. She sought to close her teeth on him but he shook her savagely and she desisted. She tried to shout but the sound that formed behind his hand was incomprehensible.

"Of course not," Kadailin said quietly.

"The kandar are no longer bound by the Purpose," Damarin said. "There's no need for the real Coralynth."

Ruon turned away from Kadailin and Sandin's feet were lifted from the ground. He carried her towards the mountain. They headed for a darker space in its side that looked to be the opening of a cave. Sandin struggled one last time against Ruon's impossible grip and gave up.

"Then why bring it here?" Kadailin's voice came from behind them. Ruon turned to face her, bringing Sandin with him. "Why mimic the place of Tchar and Dani and the Purpose if you want the kandar to forget?"

Sandin felt a tiny thread of hope at Kadailin's words. Her sister's eyes were bright again, and she looked to Damarin with the same questions in them as she had when she had looked at Jaydin.

"Some are not so quick to see the truth," Damarin said. "They need to be guided towards it, carefully, slowly. Our Coralynth is a part of that process."

Ruon turned away again, pulling Sandin with him. If Kadailin answered she didn't do it aloud.

Chapter 38

Cien stood slowly from his place on the cave floor and leaned against the bars of his cage. He had finally gotten over his physical revulsion towards the glass that contained him. Some part of his body had been pressed against it since he was thrown there and he was still alive. It wasn't the physical he needed to be afraid of.

Ruon's seed grew bright in the collective. Cien prepared himself for the guardian to appear. He was apprehensive, but at the same time found that he was looking forward to having someone to talk to again. He may have gotten over his fear of the physical, but the fear of his own mind and what it could do to him with glass and pandinzori so near was palpable within him. It wasn't safe to be alone with that.

The guardian's seed grew brighter but no shadow came into the entrance to accompany it. Cien looked around the cave while he waited. The light from the fire appeared to be the same. Nothing had moved. There were spiders in the leaves and on the red flowers, but they didn't come down. He studied the pandinzori that clung to him, seeing it without focusing on it, without touching it with his mind. It had grown, but it looked the same too. He felt stronger, as Ruon had said he would, but nothing else had changed. Why should that power matter when he was stuck in a glass cage? If anything, it was even more dangerous to him.

Damarin's leaf burst into light in his mind. Cien's gaze went to the cave entrance again. They were both coming this time. He shifted against the glass, uneasy. A third leaf began to glow.

His eyes widened involuntarily before he closed them to concentrate on the collective. The third leaf was dim and he realised with surprise that it wasn't a part of the Black Valley collective. He wasn't sure if that was good for his situation or bad. He focused on it and came up with a name. *Kadailin.*

He opened his eyes. Kadailin was one of the sisters. One of Tith's daughters. She was in Black Valley. But why was she with Damarin and Ruon? Kadailin was Tchardin's friend as well as sister. How could she ally herself with Damarin? How could he sense those three kandar and none of the others when they didn't appear in the cave? Perhaps they were somewhere else in the mountain?

Cien closed his eyes again and concentrated on the glowing leaf. Even if Kadailin was with the other two kandar out of loyalty and a shared vision, he had to make her aware of his situation. He had to find a way to tell the kandar of Black Valley, his people, where he was and why he was being held there. This might be his only chance to do so.

'Kadailin,' he said, flinching as he used his mindvoice and grateful when nothing came of it. *'Kadailin, this is Cien. I'm being held in the mountain.'*

***

Aaron guided Tchardin through the chaos. His thoughts were so loud in her mind now they almost felt like her own. He wondered if she needed more help than he could provide. Afraid of the outside world? Was that why she hid in the park? She appreciated his thoughts, despite their eclipsing nature, because they drowned out the others.

Tchardin kept her eyes closed as they walked to avoid feeling overwhelmed. The pandinzori on this world was still scarce, so she was mostly in the dark despite the inconceivable number of people. When she walked by other humans their relative brightness lit up the space behind her eyes so she could see the wonders around her. Aaron directed her.

"Up," he said. "Step up."

They had come to a wall of blackness. She stepped up. And stepped up again. The pandinzori around Aaron extended slightly in front of them and Tchardin saw a set of blocks that climbed. *Stairs.* They walked up the stairs together and came to a door. The voices quieted as they ascended.

"Now," Aaron said. Tchardin opened her eyes to look at him. He was worried. She could see that on his face, an expression she'd never have truly recognised before meeting the humans. “Do you think you can wait just inside the door while I talk to my partner?”

Partner. Tchardin looked at the blue door, then back down the stairs they’d climbed. They were hidden from the crowds of humans now and it was quieter. Thoughts came from behind the door, but there was only one person inside. He lived there with Aaron. They shared the space. He was Aaron’s dodenzinn, perhaps? It seemed to be slightly different. Aaron wanted them to be together forever but they hadn’t made that commitment yet. Unlike the kandar, they could choose who to be with. His mind told her this. She nodded.

“Okay,” he said. “Let’s go then.”

He used his knuckles to rap on the door before opening it, then walked through. Tchardin followed. As she entered the room she was surprised by the amount of pandinzori it contained. While Aaron’s pandinzori had swirled away from him in the forest and in the streets, here it stayed and collected. A rush of light flowed around a corner and Aaron’s partner followed it.

The man had no hair on his head. Every kandar had hair. It varied in length and texture and colour, but it was always there. This man had none. His skin was as dark as Damarin’s in its darkest patches and his eyes and eyebrows were black.

“Bronson,” Aaron said as he walked to the man, and Tchardin assumed that was his name.

She moved to follow him but remembered what he had said about waiting. She studied the room instead. The *apartment*, it was called. It had windows like Irah’s home had, clear sheets of glass that let in the world outside. She was almost used to that by now. There were two other doors she could see and a hall that led around a corner, where Bronson had come from. There were chairs—she recognised them as being similar to the one Irah had made her sit in—and a black box facing them, raised slightly above the floor. Then the leaves grew in the collective and she forgot the room completely.

There were thousands of lights. Her collective contained so many

leaves now she wasn’t surprised one human could bring so many, but she was still in awe. The man's own leaf blazed. He had to be important to shine so bright. His eyes fell on her.

He pitied her. His thoughts on that were clear. He was also incredibly angry. That reaction was more complicated. The two men spoke quietly, but their thoughts helped her hear them.

"I might have a pair of shoes for her," Aaron whispered, "and some clothes. It doesn't matter if they're a little big. That's got to be better than nothing, right?"

"Look at her." Bronson grimaced. "She's fearless. Dressed like that, out in the park like she was. Now, standing in this strange apartment with two strange men? She should be terrified."

"She was. She was afraid when I took her out of the trees."

"But look at her now. That's not good. I don't think it'll help if we give her shoes or clothes and let her leave. She needs *real* help."

Bronson was angry at his own insistence she be afraid. He noticed her staring at him.

"We have to talk about this more," he said. "For now, let her stay here as long as she feels safe. At least she'll be warm."

Aaron's thoughts were of relief. He turned back to Tchardin and motioned her forwards.

"This is Bronson," he said when she approached them. Bronson nodded to her. "We live here together. You're welcome to stay and warm up. I'll get you some clothes."

"And food," Bronson said. "I'm making dinner right now. You can help if you like."

Tchardin smiled at them. She didn't want to talk. Their world was clearly complicated and she only had a surface view of it so far. It was best to be silent until she understood exactly what was going on.

"What's your name?" Bronson asked.

Tchardin stared at him and waited. Aaron shrugged and Bronson frowned. They were beginning to think she wasn't able to speak. Tchardin wasn't sure that was a bad thing.

Aaron placed a hand on Bronson's shoulder. "I have to look at these photos," he said. "Mireille will be waiting for them."

"Dinner should be ready in half an hour if you're hungry. You can come with me," Bronson said to Tchardin. He motioned for her to follow him and together they walked around the corner.

Tchardin looked up from her food to find the two men anxiously watching her.

'She has to be hungry,' Aaron thought. *'Why doesn't she eat?'*

He was worried for her and Tchardin considered putting some of the food in her mouth just to please him. Kandar could eat if they had to, but given her limited experience she didn't think the display would be convincing. Before coming to the Earths she had never thought of what it would be like to mimic the humans in everything, including this. She had to admit she hadn't fully understood the ritual of eating and she still didn't.

Bronson's eyes went to his empty plate and he frowned. Tchardin lifted the delicate white disk they'd set before her and offered it to him.

"No," he said, "that's for you."

She shook her head.

"We'll keep it then. You can eat it later."

She struggled to stand. The table the three of them sat at was clearly meant for two. Aaron had to stand as well to get out of her way. As she escaped from the kitchen their worry was oppressive on her mind.

What was she doing here? She had to think hard to remember. A feeling of belonging was developing the longer she stayed with them. It was just as it had been on World Four, when she had almost come to believe she *was* one of the Sparr, as Tezroi and Jaycee had thought. These men were complex, and their world was the same. Compared to her life as kandar it was overwhelming and threatened to consume her. If they didn't know anything about the guardian and the World Tree she would have to be on her way.

Aaron and Bronson followed her back to the main room. They argued.

"We're not equipped to deal with this," Bronson said. "I told you there were bigger problems here."

"I just wanted to help someone!" Aaron responded. "You're always helping people."

Tchardin walked towards the door. Bronson stopped her.

"Here." He put a hand on her arm and directed her back into the room. He had a small black object in his other hand and he pointed it at the black box near the chairs. It was a *TV*, controlled by a *remote*. The head and shoulders of a woman appeared. Tchardin jumped. Rendinzori, to an extent she had yet to see.

The woman began to talk. Tchardin looked at the TV with suspicion, her thoughts of leaving gone. It couldn't be a real human. At least, if it was she wasn't in the room with them. Bronson went back to arguing with Aaron and Tchardin moved towards the woman. No leaf appeared in the collective and Tchardin couldn't hear any thoughts from her. It must be an image. A moving, talking image.

"Jobs," the image said. "Jobs are ruining everything. The *'nine-to-five'*." The image of the woman gripped the air with her fingers when she said that. "It's just empty purpose, soulless motivation. Get up, go to work. Go home, watch TV. Sleep. Repeat. Why do anything else? Gives people a reason to stop using their brains, to stop feeling things, to stop seeing the fantastic, to stop even looking! If your purpose is a paycheque, what will you do for the world?"

Tchardin sat on the floor to listen. She was mesmerised, but without thoughts to hear and interpret, she was lost.

"You need that paycheque? I hear you. You say the world would fall apart without your work? I hear you. But I say, why did we build it like that in the first place?" Tchardin leaned towards the woman. That was something she did understand. The humans of World Eight had built their world and they were openly discussing it.

"Who started all this?" the woman asked. "We learned to walk on two feet and use our hands and we got bored? Needed something to do? We were better off as animals." She faced Tchardin, her gaze conspiratorial. "All is not lost. We can rebuild it. We have the technology—or rather, we have it and we don't need it."

Bronson walked up behind Tchardin and stood at her shoulder. Aaron had left the room. Tchardin could still feel his presence in the collective but he had gone somewhat farther away.

"I'm doing it," the woman said with enthusiasm. "I'm changing the world. Just you watch, and listen, because I can't do it without you. You need to change too. We all need to change."

"Not that again." Aaron's muffled voice came from one of the other rooms. "We'd die of starvation way before anything changed."

"It doesn't work literally," Bronson said, too quietly for Aaron to hear. He raised his voice. "We can't stop working. At least not right away. I just think maybe, we shouldn't care about it so much. Most jobs aren't important. We should be thinking about how to fix things. All the time."

'Like me,' was silently added. Tchardin turned to stare up at him.

Aaron's head appeared from behind one of the doors. "Like you?"

Tchardin's eyes widened. Could they hear each other's thoughts?

"Like us?" Aaron continued. "We practically *are* starving. My point stands."

"Most of the world is much hungrier than we are. Much colder, much sicker. It could only get better."

Aaron joined them and put his arm around Bronson's shoulders. "The world is a machine and we are but cogs. There are too many of us for the type of lifestyle you want to be possible."

"I don't think that's true." Bronson frowned and his thoughts buzzed loudly.

Aaron pursed his lips. "I'm sorry." He looked at the woman in the TV. "You shouldn't watch this channel. It's not good for you."

"And you shouldn't bring women off the street back to our apartment to make me confront the sad state of our world so viscerally."

They stared at each other for a moment.

"I got her from the forest," Aaron said. "Not the street."

Bronson laughed. The tension left the two men and Tchardin smiled.

"Enough of this then." Bronson pointed the remote at the TV and the woman disappeared. "Are you sure you don't want something to eat?" he asked Tchardin.

She nodded. The longer she went without talking the harder it was to start. Her mind spun with everything she'd heard.

"Can you speak?" Bronson asked. Aaron waited.

Tchardin nodded again.

"But you don't want to?"

Tchardin smiled.

Aaron threw up his arms. "I'm sorry again," he said to Bronson, but he smiled at Tchardin as he said it. "Maybe you'll speak with us eventually. I still have work to do though. You two entertain each other."

Bronson's thoughts said the conversation wasn't over, but Aaron left through one of the doors without acknowledging them. Tchardin was relieved to learn they couldn't hear each other think, or at least that it was difficult for them. She didn't know what she would do if they could hear her. What any of the kandar would do.

Bronson opened his mouth to speak but almost immediately Aaron's shout stopped him.

"Bronson! Come in here. I need to show you something."

"I'd better go," Bronson said, with a look on his face Tchardin expected she was supposed to recognise.

He walked through the door Aaron had left by and closed it behind him. Tchardin stood and quietly followed.

"Look at this," Aaron said from behind the door.

There was a silence during which even their thoughts were quiet and Tchardin wished she had been invited into the room.

"Interesting," Bronson finally said.

"No one's going to believe I didn't alter this picture. Or at the least get a model to pose for it."

"It's beautiful though. She looks like the Tree Man."

"I thought the same. But alive. And real."

For a moment their thoughts went to the forest of the World Tree. Tchardin recognised it even though they thought of green leaves, rather than the many colours she had seen when she came into this world. They thought of the forest because the Tree Man was found there.

"We should get back to her," Bronson said.

The door opened outwards and Tchardin had to jump back to avoid it. Bronson stopped when he saw her, Aaron almost running into him. Tchardin searched their minds for thoughts of this Tree Man. They shared a look. Aaron extended something towards her.

"Just look at this picture," he said. "That's you, there, in the trees."

Tchardin took the offered picture. It was an image of the colourful forest she had been in, contained on a white, leaf-like material. This had to be some other type of rendinzori, but similar to that used on the black box. She studied it for a moment before deciding it was the same material that made up the pages of Jaydin's notebook. There was a woman in the trees in the image, wrapped in shadow. But she wasn't a woman. She was tevadra. Without her camouflage.

"Look at your skin," Aaron said. "Look at the shadows around you. I don't know what could be wrong with my camera to get that, but it's beautiful."

Tchardin looked up at them in horror. Kordic's words came back to her. If they saw her as kandar she was supposed to kill them. She couldn't do that to these two. She was starting to believe she couldn't do it to any human.

"It's strange," Bronson said. "It really does look like—"

"Who's the Tree Man?" Tchardin startled herself with her words, but she needed to get Kordic's out of her mind.

Bronson raised his eyebrows. He seemed just as startled to hear her speak, but he was encouraged as well. Aaron answered her.

"The Tree Man is a body they found in the trunk of a tree around here, a couple hundred years ago. Back when they were still cutting down the big ones. The body looks like this." He indicated the picture.

"It's a hoax," Bronson said.

Tchardin frowned.

"The body doesn't decompose," Aaron explained. "It doesn't rot, and its insides are too simple to be human, or anything animal."

"It's made of fabric," Bronson added. "It has to be. And plastic. It just gives off a weird sense of being real. That's why it fooled so many people. It's also really old. Back when it was found they believed everything they saw."

Tchardin looked at their thoughts as they spoke. Finally she could see him. *Ruslan*. Dead, but mostly intact. Someone on this Earth had the body of their guardian.

"I need to go to him," she said.

They thought she had lost her mind. They had already thought as much, but now they were almost certain. Why would a starving forest woman want to see an empty sack shaped like a person?

She should reveal herself. The words of the woman in the TV decided her. The woman's words about changing the world and the men's ensuing conversation. For the first time Tchardin wondered what it would be like to talk to humans for real. As kandar. As herself. Not the humans of a world like World Four, where they knew the kandar and feared them, but those of a place like this. What could Aaron and Bronson do for their world with the knowledge of a guardian race? Of rendinzori, if they didn't know it? Even if they never shared it with others? Somehow Tchardin believed it would help these two instead of hindering them. At the very least they could help her return their guardian to his father. She wasn't afraid. She closed her eyes and let her camouflage go.

"I need to find the Tree Man," she said, opening her eyes to see the shadows of the room stretch and wrap around her body, to see her skin change to many shades rather than just one. "He's not a hoax, nor is he human. He's like me."

They blinked at her, almost in unison. Bronson's mouth was open. They didn't move but their thoughts were loud.

"My name is Tchardin," she continued in the resulting silence. "I am kandar. Daughter of the trees. Guardian of the Earths. I need to put the Tree Man back in the World Tree for your Earth to have any hope."

"This can't be happening," Aaron said. He turned to Bronson. "This isn't happening, right?"

Bronson looked at his partner. "Uh."

"Look at her!" Aaron practically shouted. "What is going on?"

Tchardin didn't regret her choice but she was beginning to worry.

"I have to sit down," Aaron said.

Bronson stopped him with a hand on his arm. He had regained his composure and his gaze was intense. "This is that moment. The moment where everything changes and you realise the world is more than you could have ever believed or understood."

"We're too old for that!"

"I'm not supposed to reveal myself to humans," Tchardin said. They turned back to stare at her again. "But the Tree Man is kandar, and you'd already seen me. I felt like it was the right time."

Aaron covered his face with his hands. "This is surreal. I have to be dreaming."

"Then I'm dreaming too," Bronson said.

Tchardin watched them react to her. When their thoughts had calmed she spoke again. "Will you show me where his body is?"

Bronson laughed. Tchardin was startled by his outburst. She didn't think there was anything funny about the situation.

"I guess we can?" Aaron looked up at Bronson who shook his head, still laughing. "But it's too late now. Laurence will probably be sleeping and if he isn't it won't be for lack of trying."

Bronson nodded. "Lyudmila would kill us if we woke him."

"Laurence?" Tchardin asked. *Sleeping.* She looked at the windows. The world outside was dark. That must happen quickly. The sun had been bright when she left the forest with Aaron.

"The Tree Man is a part of his collection," Bronson said. "He lives pretty close by, actually."

"It's night?" Tchardin asked, relieved to be able to talk to these humans in a natural way, instead of pretending.

The men just stared at her some more, but their minds told her she was right.

"Not human," Aaron said. "We have to be dreaming."

Tchardin raised an eyebrow. Irah had mentioned dreaming. "But you're not asleep."

"She's right," Bronson said. "I don't think we're asleep, but maybe we should be. Maybe this will have sorted itself out by morning."

"I can't believe it hasn't already sorted itself out," Aaron said. "How is this happening?"

Tchardin got the impression they needed some time. The men could sleep if they wanted to, and they would probably wait until the sun came back to wake up. She walked to the TV and sat down in front of it. She looked back at the men.

"I can wait," she said.

"Uh. Will you be okay to sleep on the couch?" Aaron looked over at Bronson and shrugged. "Or do you want our bed? I don't know what to offer a guardian of the Earth."

"Earths," Tchardin corrected. "And we don't sleep."

"This is too much," Aaron said.

Bronson turned to him. "Are you going to be okay?"

"Maybe?" Aaron sighed. "I guess I'm just glad my camera isn't broken."

Bronson laughed. "I'll make sure she's settled. I'll join you in a minute. If we're not hallucinating we can change the world tomorrow."

"We're probably hallucinating."

Aaron left the room through the other door and Bronson came over to kneel beside Tchardin. He stared at her for another long moment before speaking.

"You'll be okay here then?"

"I will."

"Just...sitting? You don't need something to do?"

"I don't think so. It's no different from Derkra." His dark head was very close to hers. She noticed there were tiny hairs on it, so short she hadn't seen them before. "What's wrong with your hair? You barely have any."

Bronson lifted a hand to his head. "I shave it off. Someday it will go on its own but for now it's my choice. You've never seen that before?"

She shook her head.

"You're just as lost as we are, aren't you?"

"If I was pretending, I never would have asked. I would have listened to your thoughts to learn about it."

"My thoughts?" Bronson's eyes grew unfocused for a moment. "I *do* need to sleep."

Tchardin could tell this was a hard thing for him to accept, but at the same time his thoughts were jubilant. He just needed more, to help him understand.

"I was supposed to avoid you." Tchardin remembered Kordic's words. "I was supposed to stay away from humans, even while in camouflage, but I haven't been very good at that."

"Does anyone else know about you?"

"On this Earth? I don't know. Probably," she said after giving it some thought. If she had found occasion to reveal herself to humans some other kandar must have once. Why shouldn't they have? Kordic only knew one world. This world was not World Three. "Will you tell the other humans?"

"No," he said quickly. "I mean, I want to, but..."

From his thoughts she knew what he would have said. "They wouldn't believe it," she finished for him. He nodded.

She looked at the TV, now quiet. "Could you bring the woman back to speak to me?"

"The woman?" He followed her gaze. "Oh, yes, I think I can do that. She's on most of the time."

Tchardin waited while he stood to get the remote. Then he pointed at the TV again and the face from before appeared.

"We'll take you to see the Tree Man in the morning," Bronson said. "Assuming Lyudmila lets us in."

"I'll find a way to do what I have to do, as long as you can get me there."

"I'm sure you will." He walked to the same door Aaron had left through earlier. "Goodnight, even if you don't sleep."

He closed the door behind him and the apartment filled with the two men's thoughts a moment later. Tchardin listened to them idly as she turned her attention back to the image in the TV.

"I'm doing it," the woman said, her eyes seeming to meet Tchardin's through the image. "I'm changing the world. Just you watch, and listen, because I can't do it without you. You need to change too. We all do."

CHAPTER 39

KADAILIN'S EYES WERE DRAWN to the source of light in the cave. She'd followed the guardian—who pulled Sandin along roughly—and Damarin through the valley to come to this place. A pool of red and orange lay in one corner. Fire. She shivered as images of the burning trees of Cens lit up her mind. This fire didn't move, didn't rush towards them, but it did pull pandinzori into it.

"Liquid rock," Damarin said, following her gaze. "Liquid fire."

Ruon finally took his hand off Sandin's mouth.

"What have you done?" she said when she could speak again. "This is worse than I thought it would be."

The walls of the cave moved. They seemed somehow to be alive. They were covered in vines and those were covered in flowers. The same red flowers they had seen in Cens. The same red flowers they had found on World Seven.

Something tickled Kadailin's shoulder. She turned her head and her eyes widened. A large brown spider descended from one of the flowers. It crawled onto her skin. She knocked it to the ground and backed away from the wall to the centre of the cave.

"You might not want to let them touch you," Damarin said. "They have a somewhat different purpose now than they had when I created them."

Yellow-tinged pandinzori came up from behind Kadailin and swept the cave's walls. The spiders fell, their many branch-like legs gripping helplessly at the air. They were pushed into the fire and their bodies twisted and exploded in sudden bursts of flame. Then the walls were still.

"You brought those to Derkra from World Seven," Kadailin said.

"An unconscious act. One of the first times I used rendinzori without knowing it."

Sandin stared at the walls of the cave with her mouth open. Kadailin's gaze was drawn back to the fire. Damarin moved closer to her and her thoughts were loud. Images grew in Kadailin's mind. The vines, the flowers, the spiders, then burning.

Kadailin gasped. "You set the forest on fire to hide them?"

"Rendinzori is unpredictable." Damarin walked past Kadailin to the cave wall and picked a red flower from the vines. "This fire at least was intentional, but it came from Ruon, not from me."

"I can't believe you burned our fathers," Sandin said. "I can't believe you brought a guardian to our world to burn it further. He shouldn't be here. He's as dangerous as Siltadon."

"We are not his enemy." Damarin smiled at Sandin before turning back to Kadailin. "How human do you think Sandin would be if she'd been born on the Earths?"

"This again?" Sandin shouted. "I am kandar!"

"Would she eat?" Damarin continued, ignoring their sister.

"Kandar don't need to eat," Kadailin said.

"But we can." Damarin handed the red flower to Ruon.

Ruon pried Sandin's mouth open with pandinzori and pushed the flower in. He covered it with a hand again while Sandin fought him. Kadailin ached to stop him but the pandinzori around them was a swirl of yellow and grey, already claimed. She pushed against their control but they were too strong.

Sandin was forced to swallow. She went limp. Ruon removed his hand.

"Why are you doing this to me?" The flower didn't seem to have hurt Sandin, although her lips were now a deep red. "What do you mean to accomplish? Kandar in Calendrai have been eating leaves since before we were born."

"Kadailin," Damarin said, ignoring Sandin. "Would Sandin sleep on the Earths?"

"We can't sleep," Kadailin answered. "Ryten has been trying his whole life. It's impossible."

Damarin didn't respond. She stared intently at Sandin. Kadailin followed her gaze and noticed that Sandin's eyes were nearly closed. Any other kandar would have been concentrating on pandinzori, or the collective, but the expression looked strange on Sandin. Suddenly those half-lidded eyes tried to widen in surprise.

"Yes," Damarin said. "Maybe there was a time when we truly couldn't, or maybe this is only a rediscovered talent, but we *can* sleep."

"Kadailin," Sandin whispered. Her eyes closed. She fell forward in Ruon's loosened grip, and jerked back, opening her eyes.

"And most importantly, Kadailin. Can kandar dream?"

"*Dream*?" Kadailin had never heard the word before. Not even from Jaydin. "What does that mean?"

Sandin's head fell again and she didn't jerk it up this time. Could she truly be sleeping? Could the red flower have made it so?

"I don't know anymore," Kadailin said. "Can we?"

Damarin moved towards Ruon. She ran a hand over Sandin's face. Their auras collided but Sandin was unresponsive. Damarin gestured and Ruon laid Sandin down on the cave floor.

"We shall see," she said.

As soon as Ruon stepped back Kadailin ran to Sandin. They didn't stop her. She lifted her sister's head and shoulders into her lap, ignoring the pulses of revulsion she felt. Sandin didn't stir.

"How do you know she sleeps?" Kadailin asked.

"Miadra has slept in this way, and so have I."

"You slept? You're sure?"

"I did. Once I knew it was possible and how to achieve it I had to experience it."

"Did you"—Kadailin hesitated, afraid of what this could mean for their sister—"did you dream?"

Damarin frowned. "No. Not in the way I believe we'll need to."

"What about Miadra? Did she dream?" Kadailin remembered with horror that Miadra was Cotelle's dodenzinn and that she was dead. But Damarin was alive. It must be possible to survive it.

"Miadra never got a chance to tell me."

"What makes you think Sandin can dream when you couldn't?"

"When I slept I heard only the voices of the kandar. The collective came into my mind and spoke to me. I'm hoping—"

Kadailin didn't need to hear Damarin's thoughts to know what she would say. "That Sandin will dream because she's cut off from the collective."

"Exactly."

"But why?" Kadailin genuinely didn't understand what Damarin was trying to do. "Why do we need to sleep? To dream? What is it?"

"A dream is an image in the mind that comes from nothing. Sometimes a set of images, an encounter, a place. The ability to dream is something the humans have that we do not."

Kadailin still didn't understand. She looked to the guardian but he was watching Damarin intently and didn't seem to notice.

"Dreaming while asleep is just the beginning." Damarin knelt beside Kadailin. "I want to dream when I'm awake. That's what the humans do with their rendinzori." Her eyes lit up. "There's a very powerful woman on World Five, perhaps the most powerful of all the humans in existence. She used to sleep and dream her world had ended. She no longer sleeps and her waking dreams say it isn't so. Both are made true."

Kadailin looked around the cave. "You want the kandar to be like humans? For rendinzori? For this mountain and these flowers and spiders?"

"No," Damarin said, a familiar flash of anger crossing her face. "I should have known you wouldn't understand. I want the kandar to be kandar. It's Derkra that I want to change. The kandar will need to change it, and for that we'll need rendinzori on a scale unknown to most humans. Coralynth was the first step, dreaming is the next."

The pandinzori surrounding Sandin sloughed off her skin.

"You're killing her!" Kadailin shouted. She pulled her sister closer to her own aura, melding them together, fighting the revulsion that spread through her body. Sandin didn't move.

"I don't think so," Damarin said. "Look."

Kadailin didn't know what Damarin wanted her to see. She shook Sandin, shouted at her, but her sister didn't move. Pandinzori swirled around them, more than Kadailin had ever held, more than Ruon had held in the valley when he caught them. It spread out in the cave. It came off Sandin's skin, leaving her, killing her, but the longer Kadailin watched the more shocked she became. The pandinzori that left Sandin's skin was replenishing. It almost seemed to grow there.

"Is she..."

"She's creating it," Ruon said. His first words since they'd entered the cave.

"Impossible." Only trees and humans did that. Kadailin tried to take hold of the pandinzori that grew up around her sister but it was quickly claimed by the guardian.

"I have to go," Damarin said.

Kadailin was desperate. "You'd leave her like this?"

"There's something I must do. We won't know if she's dreaming until she wakes, although I believe she is. There's nothing you can do to wake her. You can only wait. I trust you will remain here with her?"

Kadailin thought of lying, but Damarin would hear her thoughts.

"I do hear them. I won't be here to stop you if you choose to leave, but Ruon will be waiting in the valley and Sandin is helpless like this. Even more helpless than usual. She'll need you to protect her while she sleeps."

Damarin brushed a hand across Sandin's unmoving face and smoothed their sister's hair. '*I thought you were less than us, but you're only different and maybe even more. I will give you what Jaydin could not.*'

Kadailin didn't turn as Damarin stood and walked out of the cave behind her with Ruon. She held Sandin against her body and despaired. There was nothing she could do to help her sister, just as she'd been unable to help Jaydin. The pandinzori that grew around Sandin was available to her mind now but Damarin had been right. It was useless when faced with this. Kadailin closed her eyes and looked to the collective for comfort.

The branches were bare. She hadn't picked up any of the Black Valley kandar's leaves as they walked across the sand, and Damarin's leaf and Ruon's seed had disappeared when they left the cave. The darkness made the absence of Jaydin's leaf less obvious. For the first time since World Seven Kadailin could pretend it was still there, only hidden by distance.

Then she noticed there was one dim leaf lit in the collective. She opened her eyes and stared at Sandin, but it was not her sister she saw. Sleeping couldn't give Sandin a place in the collective. The leaf had to belong to another.

As she focused on it she thought she heard her name.

***

Ryten stood on the shore outside of Cens and looked over the endless water. Unlike a lot of the kandar on Calendrai he had stood like this many times, when he had come out of the forest to stare uselessly at Water Side with Tchardin or Damarin. He wondered how it had looked when they travelled across it.

He closed his eyes and waited. The collective was alive with light, but the four lights he waited for were dark. How long had it been since the rest of the sisters had left them? He could never know for sure, but it felt too long. They should have returned by now.

One of the brighter leaves flashed and Ryten knew its owner was near. He turned just as Torshe walked out of the trees behind him. He and Ocien had been looking for Moradi's dodenzinn.

"Did you find him?" Ryten asked.

"No." Torshe looked unsettled. "Very few kandar even knew her. She must have been one of those that hide in Cens their whole lives. I assume her dodenzinn is, or was, the same."

Ryten understood his meaning. Assuming Moradi's dodenzinn still lived, they might never find the devoshai unless he came into the clearing.

"Where's Ocien?" Ryten asked.

"With Moradi's body, at Tith's base in the clearing."

"And Cotelle?"

Torshe shrugged. "Sometimes his leaf is dark and sometimes light. I assume he travels between Land Side and Calendrai but I haven't seen him since the sisters left."

What could the big devoshai be up to? Torshe turned to leave.

"Wait," Ryten said. "I think we need to do something more. Jaydin's been gone for too long."

"What can we do? We helped them heal the forest and now we wait."

"Jaydin said there were very few kandar in Black Valley," Ryten said, thinking. "If the kandar are going to war again, why should we wait for them to come here? If Jaydin and Cotelle can shift between the two cities we could bring the kandar of Calendrai there."

"And do what?"

Ryten was inspired by the prospect of action, by the possibility of doing something other than pretending to sleep. "Stop the war before it starts. If we bring enough kandar they'll never be able to stand against us; even if Damarin has convinced them she's right. They wouldn't try it."

"Why should our number matter? Are we strong enough individually to fight them? The greater number might only complicate things. It was nearly impossible to fight Marr when I could barely tell if I was fighting you or him."

"We might not be strong enough, but hopefully we'll look it. We've fought with pandinzori and understand the difficulty, but they may not."

Ryten turned away from the water to confront the darkness of Cens. As he stared into the shadowed depth of the forest he realised how great of a mistake they had made.

"But how will we find the other kandar with the forest healed?" he whispered, his excitement fading.

"I believe we can," Torshe said from beside him. "Remember that those of us who remain are the kandar of Cens. We'll find the others in the forest. The same could not be said of the daughters of Tith."

"It will only be easier for us. By no means is it guaranteed. Especially when the forest has changed so much."

"Then they remain hidden and unknowing as they are now." Torshe frowned. "They may be better off that way, as long as Damarin doesn't find them."

"She would find them eventually."

Torshe considered for a moment. "Then we should try, at least. We can't wait for Jaydin to save us, or any of Tith's other daughters. I'll let Ocien know."

They stood in silence at the edge of the trees as Torshe called his dodenzinn.

"She'll begin," he said after a moment. "Moradi will be fine where she is for now."

"Tell Ocien to be careful. Cens has changed."

Torshe nodded. "The forest is difficult."

"Is Buran–"

"Gone. Or at least I can no longer find him or sense him. But strangely I don't feel any loss. Maybe it's as Jaydin said and I will have a new father when it comes time to rest."

Ryten shifted on his feet. He was grateful to Torshe for agreeing to help, but he remembered previous conflict between them.

"I want you to know," he began, "that I truly struggle with the issue of which tevadra is my dodenzinn." He hesitated before speaking his next words. "I still feel strength from more than one of Tith's daughters."

Torshe studied him, his brow furrowed. "And I still can't understand the way you feel towards them. I just knew when I came upon Ocien in Cens. That is how it should be."

"It might even be more than two of them," Ryten said in a moment of honesty. Sandin had always drawn him, and he had thought Jaydin drew everyone with her vast memory but that didn't seem to be true.

Torshe actually laughed, surprising him. "Two isn't enough?"

"I'm just happy it doesn't seem to be all five."

"As am I." The devoshai's laughter faded. "You would follow the right one? No matter who it comes to be?"

"The right one?"

"The one that is right. For the kandar."

"Tchardin's aura is golden. She is my queen even if the other is my dodenzinn."

Torshe nodded. "We should start searching. Ocien has probably found half the council by now."

This time Ryten laughed. Torshe smiled and disappeared into the forest. Despite his reaction, Ryten hoped Ocien hadn't found too many council members. He'd be glad if no one ever found Marr or his allies again. The devoshai's leaf remained dark.

Ryten walked into the trees. He knew Cens, and Cens knew him, but despite its renewed appearance it hadn't fully recovered from the fire. The forest was different now, in layout and in temperament. Sometimes he found himself walking in circles, something that had never happened to him until the forest healed.

An entirely new stretch of trees had been added. From their perspective in the path of the fire this new piece hadn't seemed like it would be large, but once inside the healed forest it was evident it had expanded. Ryten looked through the shadows, trying to orient himself. Nothing was familiar. There were trees he didn't know here. He must have walked into the new section after all.

He thought of Del, and tried to feel his father's location. There was a faint pull in one direction. Ryten's primary objective was to find the kandar but he didn't want to get lost in the newly unpredictable Cens either. He walked towards Del until he recognised the forest again, then he stopped and closed his eyes.

The collective came into his mind. He focused on each leaf briefly, looking for any that were particularly bright. He sensed a devoshai. *Wallan*. He was close. Ryten scanned the branches above. Perhaps he would be better off in the canopy? Then he saw a mass of pandinzori slide through the leaves. He climbed the closest trunk and found the devoshai he was looking for. He was not alone.

A tevadra stood with him. She had to be his dodenzinn from the close contact they shared. Ryten entered their space and was conscious of their reactions as they turned to look at him. Kandar had dodenzinn, sometimes they had friends or partners they went to the Earths with, but they didn't approach each other on a whim while on Derkra. Only Jaydin had been comfortable doing that. The two stared at him.

"I'm sure you've been made aware that the queen is missing," he said.

After staring at him for long enough to imply they were inconvenienced by his presence the two turned away and completely ignored him.

"Damarin is on Land Side, attempting to take Tchardin's place with the kandar there," Ryten said. "The kandar of Calendrai need to stand behind our queen."

The tevadra was called Rahfa. She turned to him and he hoped.

"There are no kandar on Land Side," she said.

"There are," he insisted. "They've been there since the war, left behind when Carrensing brought us to Calendrai."

The dodenzinn exchanged a look.

"Tchardin is not our queen," Wallan said. "Not yet."

"She will be, as soon as we can acknowledge her."

"When the council is called," Rahfa said, "and the queen of the kandar tells us Coralynth is open to us again, and we may travel to the Earths to fulfill the Purpose, we will come. Not before, and not for you."

"But we need you," Ryten said.

Rahfa frowned at him. "We await Tchardin, as queen. Or the council."

Wallan looked into Rahfa's eyes and Ryten could tell they spoke silently. Then the devoshai jumped down from the branch and disappeared into the canopy. Rahfa stood and studied Ryten for a moment more, then she too continued on her way.

Ryten was left standing stunned on the branch. He finally understood why Jaydin had made such a big deal about proper position. Tchardin, as queen, might really be necessary to rouse the kandar. In fact, Ryten was impressed with how big of an impact Jaydin had made despite her lack of position. How had she gotten any of them to listen to her in the first place?

Then a thought came to him. They were asking the wrong kandar. He reached out to Ocien and Torshe in the collective.

'Will they come?' he asked.

'No.' Ocien's voice, faint. *'Though I've only met five so far.'*

'I've seen four, and none will come.' Torshe's voice, closer and clearer.

'I know the kandar we need to talk to,' Ryten thought as loudly as he could to them. *'Meet me by Tith's trunk.'*

Torshe wouldn't like his plan, but Ryten didn't think they had any other choice. At least the kandar he was looking for now were much easier to find than those who hid in the forest.

Ryten stared up into Ahron's canopy in awe. The tree was full of pandinzori, swirling between the bodies of a hundred kandar at least. There had never been so many for as long as he'd been one of them. If he could convince these kandar to travel to Black Valley it might be enough to deter the kandar there. He looked down at the branch they'd stopped on.

"Maxim," he said to the unresponsive devoshai sprawled at his feet, pretending to sleep.

Ryten had been right, Torshe wasn't impressed with his idea, but he had agreed to come along despite his reservations. He stood below them in the canopy, unwilling to be seen to mix with kandar of this type, but he was listening.

Ocien stood beside Ryten. She had no such reservations. When Maxim refused to stir she pushed him with her foot, frowning as their auras blended. The devoshai nearly fell off the branch.

He caught himself just in time, his eyes snapping open. He stared at them for a moment with an outraged expression on his face, then he closed his eyes and his body relaxed again. Ryten was impressed with the devoshai's resolve. Jaydin's thoughts alone had been enough to bring Ryten out of feigned sleep more than once. Maxim was committed to the end.

'You know I've done the same thing myself, Maxim,' Ryten said into his mind. *'There's no point in pretending for me.'*

Ocien knelt beside the devoshai. She reached towards him until their auras collided. Ryten saw the discomfort it caused her plain on her face, but Maxim only rolled away. He fell out of the tree.

Ocien's eyes were wide when Ryten met them. They moved to the edge of the branch and looked down.

'He didn't stop himself,' Torshe's voice came up to them. Maxim was suspended in pandinzori below, stopped in his fall just before he could hit a branch. As they watched, the pandinzori that held him softened. Maxim fell the short distance to knock against the wood. His body made an audible crack.

Ryten jumped down, using pandinzori to guide him. When he landed Maxim was attempting to stand. The attempt failed and the devoshai settled onto his side.

"What happened to me?" he asked when he saw Ryten.

Ocien joined Ryten on the branch. They exchanged a look.

"You fell," she said.

"Amazing." Maxim's eyes were partly closed and he didn't seem able to open them further. "I must have moved in my sleep."

"Enough," Ryten said. "I know you weren't sleeping."

"I was. This time I really was. Truly asleep."

"Impossible. I tried for so long."

"I know. As did I. But this time...it's the leaves," Maxim insisted. "The red ones. If you eat them you can sleep. Just look at all of them. Look up." He gestured above him at the kandar arrayed throughout the canopy. There were so many more than before. Ryten remembered the group as a small one. There had to be a reason for its growth. Maybe Maxim was right.

Ryten wanted to try it.

'No,' Ocien said, for his mind only. *'It's not worth it even if it works. Especially if it works. You've already wasted enough time here. There are more important things than this.'*

"We can actually sleep," Maxim said, failing to hear the tevadra's thoughts. "Don't you understand? We have something to do for the first time since our births."

That was the reason they pretended to sleep. The reason Ryten had done so himself. To have something to do when there was nothing else. Now there were things to do. Ocien was right. Ryten had wasted enough of his life already.

"I have something for you to do. Something that's actually important."

Maxim's half-lidded eyes were keen, despite being stuck that way. "The Purpose?"

"Not yet," Ryten said. "This is about the kandar."

He explained.

Ryten dropped down through the branches to stand with Torshe.

"It worked," the shorter devoshai said when he landed.

"It seems that way." Maxim and Ocien climbed through the branches and tried to wake the others. Ryten had a thought. "Will you watch them? Ensure they don't change their minds, or forget their new purpose?"

"I will."

Ryten steeled himself. "I'm going to shift to Black Valley."

"Is that safe?"

"We're asking them to do it. I should at least try it first."

He pulled pandinzori from Ahron and held it in front of them. He closed his eyes and thought of the magnificent father of all kandar, Ovaeron. When he opened his eyes again the red leaves blazed before him. Remembering what Jaydin had told him he let the image dissolve but kept the feeling of the great tree. He was faced with spinning grey. Tchardin could be in Black Valley. Damarin could be there.

They stood for a moment, watching the shift spin. Then Ryten pushed forward and broke the ice. Water took him.

Chapter 40

Bronson said something but Tchardin didn't hear him. She walked with her eyes open this time and World Eight was too big, too impressive to ignore in favour of words. Even the thoughts of the many humans faded into the back of her mind as she took in the sights, and the new clothes the men had put her in ceased to bother her. Bronson had to repeat his question.

"How exactly does it work?" he asked.

"I'm still new to the Earths." Tchardin wasn't going to explain that the kandar had lost the Purpose, and what she said was still true. "We are to guide you, but I don't fully understand what that means. I'm supposed to learn from your guardian."

"The Tree Man?"

"Yes."

"Great," Bronson said. "We killed him."

"He'll be reborn, if we can give him back to his father." Tchardin remembered Bronson had said the tree was cut down. She shivered. "Or," she added, "to whichever tree has come to replace him."

Bronson settled into silence, his thoughts buzzing. Tchardin turned her attention to Aaron. The man held her hand as he had when they first walked to the apartment from the forest, guiding her. Unlike the clothing, his touch on her skin didn't bother her.

Aaron had been mostly silent since the men woke. His thoughts told Tchardin he still wasn't sure what she was or how this was happening. She was in her camouflage now, out of the apartment, and he seemed calmed by that, but also unsettled, worried he had misunderstood what happened the night before.

"We're almost there," he said now, noticing her staring.

The buildings around them had decreased in height dramatically. Tchardin felt like she had walked through multiple worlds to get here, from the flat greyness of Aaron and Bronson's neighbourhood through a forest of tall buildings to this bright and beautiful place. She had to prepare herself. She was going to see a dead guardian, held in the house of a human. Under glass, Bronson had said. He had told her that this morning when she'd been confronted with a mirror. The men had expected her to want to look at her new clothing. She had been afraid.

Aaron guided her around some small trees with yellow leaves and Bronson's eyes immediately focused on a wide, flat building as it came into view. It must be Laurence's home.

"Do you think Lyudmila will let us in?" Aaron asked as they approached.

"I don't see why not," Bronson answered. "She's let us in before."

"Do you think she'll let us out again?" The rest of the question remained unasked but Tchardin heard it in their minds. Would the woman let them out of the house with the guardian? Bronson didn't answer.

"She will," Tchardin said. Aaron squeezed her hand. They walked up the steps to the door and waited while Bronson knocked. This door was green.

There was a man behind it when it opened. He reminded Tchardin of Kordic in his human camouflage, with much more white hair on his chin than on his head. This must be an old man then. He had circles of glass before his eyes as Ira had worn on World Five. *Glasses*, the men's minds told her. She should have been able to guess that one.

Aaron and Bronson's leaves flashed in the collective, made stronger by their association with this man's leaf. *Laurence* came to her. Surprisingly, many of the other leaves Tchardin had accumulated on World Eight also grew brighter as they clustered around his. It seemed this old man knew a lot of them. Or they knew him. He added many more to the collective as well. An unbelievable number. So many she didn't know how he could know them all. It seemed that no matter how important the humans she met happened to be, there were always others who were greater.

"Oh," Bronson said, "Laurence, where's Lyudmila?"

The old man looked up at the two younger men. His thoughts were loud and confused. They were complex and impressive, but they were tangled. He grasped at them but they evaded him. Aaron and Bronson were distressed.

"Who are you?" Laurence asked. Somehow he must have forgotten those in his collective.

There was conflict in Bronson's thoughts at this reaction. There was something wrong with Laurence that made him confused, made him easy to take advantage of. If the situation were different they would wait for the woman, Lyudmila, to come to the door to speak with them, but they had to get into the house.

"We're here to look at the collection," Aaron said. Bronson glanced back at him.

"Ah." Laurence looked thoughtful for a moment before continuing. "The collection. Yes. It's just this way."

He turned to walk down the dark hall that led away from the door, motioning for them to follow. A part of his mind had been freed. Accessed. He was excited by this. Purposeful. He might not know who the men and woman were, but he had a direction.

"No need to remove your shoes," he said as he hurried away from them. "Follow me."

Tchardin looked down at her feet. *Shoes*. They were terrible things. Aaron had insisted she wear them and Laurence was insisting she continue to wear them. Bronson shrugged and followed Laurence down the hall.

'What's wrong with him?' Tchardin sent to Bronson. She caught up with him and Aaron trailed behind her.

"Disease," Bronson whispered. "It makes him forget."

They turned a corner from the dark hallway into a bright room. It was bright with lights but also with pandinzori. Laurence stood at the centre of it. His mind was clear and pandinzori rolled off him in waves.

There were glass structures throughout the space. They protruded from the walls and the floors and contained shapes of all sizes. Close to the old man was a raised surface covered by a glass box. A withered body with dark, mottled skin was laid beneath it. Tchardin took a step forward without thinking. It had to be Ruslan, guardian of World Eight. This was a *display room*, and it housed the old man's collection.

Laurence smiled and opened his mouth to speak, but instead he paused. His expression became confused and the smile faded from his face. His thoughts began to unravel.

"Who are you?" His eyes darted between them. "What are you doing in my house?"

"Laurence—" Bronson began, but the old man was past listening. He started to shout.

"Lyudmila will hear him!" Aaron said. "We have to leave."

"We need the Tree Man." Bronson walked past Laurence, who flinched away, and shoved the glass box. It didn't move. He ran to grab a chair from against the wall. Tchardin knew what he was going to do next.

"No!" she said. Bronson stopped. Laurence stared at them in terror. "There's no need." She approached Laurence and put a hand on his shoulder. He didn't cringe away from her; instead he turned to look into her eyes.

'Laurence,' she said into his mind.

She didn't show him her true self in the room. She didn't reveal her mottled skin or the shadows that strove to cling to it, but she did show herself to his mind. She showed him her encounter with Aaron and Bronson and her subsequent discovery of the Tree Man and what he truly was. In images, she told him what the guardian would mean to World Eight. Then she thought of Derkra and its significance, of each of the worlds and the humans on them. She thought of the Purpose and the kandar and Creator. She knew he was capable of understanding. His beautiful mind showed her that. Laurence stood still and quiet as he worked over the images she gave him, his thoughts coming together. His eyes glistened.

"What are you doing?" Bronson asked.

"I'm helping him understand. I'm telling him what I told you."

Bronson's eyes widened. "Why would you do that? He probably feels crazy enough as it is!"

Tchardin was surprised at Bronson's reaction. He had reacted positively to her revealing herself to them, and she could tell his relationship with Laurence was strong. Why did he think something that was right for him to know was wrong for the old man?

Tchardin turned her attention back to Laurence. He stood in silence and stared at her. His thoughts were collected now, calm. She was sure she had done the right thing. Bronson was about to speak again when the old man spoke first.

"So a Creator made us?" Laurence asked. Aaron and Bronson gaped at him. "Is there a plan then?"

"A plan?" Tchardin asked, unsure of his meaning.

"What does the Creator want from us?" The old man was silent for another moment, then he laughed. "Why are we here? What is the purpose of life? I never thought I'd get to ask those questions and expect a useful answer."

"I don't know," Tchardin said. "I only know what It wants from me."

"Not such a useful answer after all. The Purpose?"

Aaron and Bronson watched the quick conversation with amazement on their faces.

"We're meant to help you. To guide you and inspire you. To guard you."

"From ourselves, no doubt."

"Perhaps." Tchardin had seen some frightening things on the Earths so far. "I'm still young. It's hard to understand."

Laurence nodded. "It seems vague. To inspire us in some way, guide us without revealing yourselves."

"Laurence?" Bronson said hesitantly. His thoughts told Tchardin this was how the old man should be, that he was acting how he had before the disease took hold of his mind.

"Bronson," Laurence said, "and Aaron. It's nice to see you both, and to meet your new friend."

Aaron looked to the entrance of the room anxiously.

"Lyudmila is out," Laurence said, as if answering a question from Aaron's mind. Tchardin was amazed again to see a human do that. She wasn't sure they were as cut off from each other as the kandar thought. "We should have some time before she returns. She knows I don't normally notice." He turned to Tchardin. "You want the Tree Man."

It wasn't a question. Tchardin nodded. Laurence walked to the glass box that held the guardian's body. He looked down for a moment before speaking.

"I want to know more. While I can still understand. I want to know more about this world, this life. How it all works."

Tchardin had ached to talk about the world since she revealed herself, now that she could communicate openly with humans. Bronson and Aaron had been too preoccupied with the kandar. Laurence was more interested in the Earth, as Tchardin was.

"I don't fully understand rendinzori—" she said.

"Rendinzori?" Bronson interrupted.

Tchardin considered what would be right to say, what would be safe. "It's a power humans have. On some of the Earths it's hidden, but you all have it. If you don't know of it you must use it without your knowledge." Their minds told her they didn't understand. "It lets you do things to the world. Move things, change them. On World Four the humans could bind you, walk through empty air..."

She saw the two young men's minds considering the concept of other worlds, other humans. Laurence had already done so when she'd shown herself to him. His mind went to something called *magic.*

"We have it too?" Bronson asked.

"How can we use it without our knowledge?" Laurence asked at the same time.

Siltadon's words were vivid in Tchardin's mind. "This world grew from nothing to something before the kandar came to you and Creator only began the process." She hesitated. "I believe you made it yourselves."

The men were quiet.

"Interesting," Laurence eventually said.

Tchardin met his eyes. "I also believe you continue to make it, and that our Purpose is to help you do that."

"The world becomes what we want it to be," Laurence murmured to himself. "It becomes what we expect." Tchardin realised the thought had already been in his mind. She had only confirmed something for him.

"Then things could get better?" Bronson asked, intent on every quiet word the old man said. "If we want them to get better, and expect them to, just like that?"

Laurence was silent for a moment, then he snorted. Tchardin sensed anger in him suddenly. "Of course, but that has always been true. The world *is* what we make it, whether through natural means or magical."

"But this changes everything!" Bronson said. "We can help the Earth by putting an empty shell of a person in a tree and after that we just need to want it to get better. If only people knew. It's so simple."

"Nothing would change," Laurence said.

Bronson's enthusiasm didn't dampen. "Why not?"

The old man looked at the floor. "Magic or no magic, secret guardians or not, if everyone on this planet wanted to fix it, truly wanted to, it would be fixed. It might take a while, generations even, but it would happen. Priorities would shift; people would make time, teach their children to make time, make it possible." Now he met the young man's eyes. "But they don't want to fix it. Sometimes they might think they do, but they don't. Not enough of them anyway. This broken system works for too many people who only think about themselves, and it works on so many levels they barely notice it.

"If enough people thought differently, if they could only see..." he trailed off. "I dedicated my life to showing them and I can't do it anymore. I just hope some of them were paying attention."

"I was," Bronson said. "I want to fix it. I really do."

"Evidently we need more."

"What do the kandar want?" Aaron asked.

The three men turned towards Tchardin.

"They want," Tchardin paused to think. "We—" she faltered. "The kandar don't want anything. We want to come to the Earths to help you, as Creator bids us." Damarin wanted something else, but Tchardin wouldn't worry the humans with that. It was a matter for the kandar to deal with when she returned.

"How can you not want anything else?" Bronson asked.

"That's what makes them perfect for the job," Laurence said, studying Tchardin. "Everything a human being wants they want for themselves, even if it's the safety or success of another. That doesn't negate the good we do, but it does define it. It's all about us, all selfish."

"But how can they help us if they don't want the same things?"

"Oh, Bronson," Laurence said. "Live a little longer and you'll come to understand. If they wanted what we want, things could only get worse."

Then the three men in the room shared a thought, and Tchardin saw it too. Powerful humans might rule this world but they couldn't stand up to the kandar. A world built by humans, no matter how wrong they were, was still a human world. Not so a world built by kandar. Not so a world claimed by them. Tchardin came back to herself and wondered about that.

They were very different. Humans and kandar. Laurence saw this as a good thing. The old man looked down at the guardian again. Tchardin joined him in front of the glass, studying Ruslan's withered face.

"I've had the Tree Man for so long now," Laurence said, "and I never knew what I really had."

"His name is Ruslan."

"Ruslan," the old man repeated. "Everyone believed so wholeheartedly that it was a hoax, for good reason, and yet, there was something special about it. Something strange."

Tchardin nodded. She could see why the humans had thought this a fake. Before she'd come to the Earths she had assumed human bodies were different from kandaran bodies, but now that she had seen the complexity of their lives on the worlds she knew that to be true. They couldn't be the same. A human body needed so much. It needed something inside it to deal with the food it consumed, the water it drank. It needed something to control the raised bumps on its skin when it grew cold or afraid. It needed to age and change. By comparison a kandaran body was really only a mind. Tchardin could see why the humans had trouble believing this simple deflated thing had once been alive.

"Take him," Laurence said. "Give him back to the tree. I assume I couldn't stop you if I wanted to, but I give him freely. Maybe I can finally make a difference in this world. It won't change the people, but if it will bring you back to us, that's something at least."

Tchardin looked into the depths of his impressive mind, at the thoughts far below the surface, and knew he had already made a difference. The collective was full of lights that linked to his, made brighter by its presence.

"You've done more than you know," she said. "Maybe not as much as you hoped, not as much as you could have done with more time, but those you spoke to will speak to others, and it will continue."

Laurence looked at Bronson as she spoke those words and Tchardin began to understand their relationship. Bronson had gotten his ideas from this man. Their connection in the collective was strong, and in a way it was the reason Bronson's own contribution to the tree in her mind had been great. It was a fraction of the size of Laurence's but the man was still young. He would gather more.

Maybe that was how the kandar were supposed to do it. How they fulfilled the Purpose. How they could influence so many humans when there were so few kandar. There were likely only six hundred or so kandar remaining and countless humans across the Earths. If they hoped to make a difference they would have to find those like Tezroi and Jaycee, those like Laurence and Bronson, and speak with them, in camouflage in most cases, perhaps not in others. They would have to understand what these people needed and help them make the right choices for their Earths; help those they connected with do the same. The guardians would know who the kandar should work with on each Earth. It was a way to start at least, when she returned to Derkra and the kandar returned to the Earths.

"Lyudmila could be back soon." Laurence walked to one of the walls in the room and pressed something. The glass box lifted off the guardian and slid to the side. "Take him and go."

"What will you tell her?" Aaron asked.

"I don't know. If I were myself I could confound her with words like I used to." He laughed sadly. "Those days are gone."

Tchardin touched the guardian. His empty body felt strange against her skin.

"We'll need something to carry him in," Aaron said. "You can't just sling him over your shoulder and walk through the city."

"A body bag?" Bronson replied. "Like that would be any better."

Tchardin lifted the guardian off the flat surface and did place him over her shoulder. "Show me what you mean," she said, moving away from the glass. They stared at her. "Make an image in your mind."

She laid the guardian on the floor and drew pandinzori to her. She was careful to keep it close, careful to avoid the other glass objects in the room. Somehow it seemed easier to control than it had been before, and she was nowhere near as afraid. The men's thoughts were useless for a moment before Aaron gave her what she needed.

She closed her eyes and saw it perfectly. It was an image of the guardian covered in black cloth, made up of the colours she controlled in her mind. Could she use those colours to create it? Form pandinzori around Ruslan and make the black cloth real? She thought back to Kordic's creation of the rabbit and saw no difference besides complexity. Pandinzori flowed through the image, lines of light behind her eyes. She pressed them against the guardian.

"Well," Laurence said after a moment. "That was suitably mundane for my first experience of real magic."

Tchardin stood and lifted the body onto her shoulder again, this time shrouded in black fabric. She smiled at Laurence and strode towards the hallway. The men said a quick goodbye to the old man as she left and hurried to follow her. Bronson caught her arm just outside the room.

"I should carry him," he said when she stopped. "It'll look strange otherwise."

Tchardin didn't protest. Bronson's mind had told her his reason. It had something to do with his size relative to hers, but deep down in his mind it was also the fact that she was posing as a woman. A woman, again. It didn't make any sense since she was perfectly capable of carrying the guardian and had already demonstrated she could, but she figured it was best to let the humans deal with human perceptions. At least for now.

Aaron waited while she helped Bronson transfer the guardian to his shoulder. A voice interrupted them.

"Aaron? Bronson? What are you two doing here?"

Tchardin turned, startled by the sound. A woman stood in the darkness just inside the door.

"What is that?" the woman asked. "And who is this?"

Tchardin thought of revealing herself again until she caught Bronson's eye.

'Not this one,' his thoughts said. *'Not to her.'*

"Are you taking something out of this house?" Her voice rose to a higher pitch and the skin on her face lightened. She walked towards them. *Lyudmila* came into Tchardin's mind along with a small collection of leaves. "You of all people, to take advantage of him—"

"Let them go, Lyudmila," Laurence said from behind them. He stood in the entrance to the display room. "They have my permission to leave with him."

"Him?" Lyudmila asked, stopping just in front of them. She looked at the object draped over Bronson's shoulder and Tchardin saw understanding in her eyes. "That's not the Tree Man, is it?"

"Lyudmila," Laurence said.

The woman looked back at him for a long moment.

She turned to Bronson. "I don't know how you've convinced him to give you that construct. I would call the police—"

"No," Aaron said, "please don't."

"But I won't," Lyudmila concluded. "You've been good to him over the years, and he knows what he's offering you. Somehow, amazingly, he understands. I just worry about how he'll react when he's forgotten."

"He won't forget," Tchardin said. "Not this."

Lyudmila laughed ruefully and brushed by them, walking to the old man and murmuring to him in soothing tones.

"How do you know?" Bronson asked quietly. His expression was hopeful.

"I just know." Laurence watched them from the brightness of the display room; looking past Lyudmila and seeming not to hear her. Tchardin had left pathways in his mind when she showed herself to him. She didn't believe whatever was wrong with him was strong enough to break them.

"We should go," Aaron said.

Tchardin looked back at Laurence once more before she followed Aaron and Bronson down the hall. She would return to him when she brought the kandar back to the Earths. Maybe more could be done. For such a great mind to be trapped inside itself was a travesty. If the humans had made themselves, why had they made such a thing?

***

"Jaydin!" Sandin shouted across the desert. Jaydin was lost somewhere in the infinity, and because of her flaw, Sandin couldn't find her. As usual she hated herself for it. She had to find their oldest sister before Damarin did.

The world blurred and it felt like she was spinning. There was a bright light in the air. She sat down in the sand to re-orient herself. She lay back and closed her eyes to shut out the light. Why was she searching for her sister? She couldn't remember why she needed to find Jaydin. In fact, she couldn't remember how she had gotten this far out into the sand.

Something took hold of her legs. Sandin sat up in a panic. There were vines all around her, covered in red flowers like blood. They crept up and twined around her body where her skin touched the desert floor. They bled light into the air. She shouted and jumped to her feet.

None of the vines came with her. By the time she was standing they had disappeared. What was she doing again? She was supposed to be looking for Jaydin.

She noticed a forest in the distance and turned to walk towards its red-leafed trees, looking over her shoulder to be sure no vines would follow. Jaydin must be waiting under one of the trees. A dark shape moved between them. Too dark to be Jaydin.

"Damarin?" she asked.

Damarin wanted to use her for something, though she didn't remember what. If Sandin wasn't careful she'd be caught. A voice called out to her.

"Sandin!" It didn't sound like Damarin. "Sandin, you have to wake up!"

"Jaydin? Where are you?"

The world spun around her again and she saw Damarin's face, blurred by light. Sandin tried to react but the sensation that hit her when she attempted to move was strange. She felt like she had two bodies. The body in the desert moved at her bidding, her arm striking out in front of her and hitting nothing, but the body she could feel but not see resisted and the face remained hazy in her vision, untouched.

"Damarin!" she shouted. "What have you done to me?"

Damarin had to be using pandinzori against her. Nothing else could explain this strangeness. Sandin began to feel it, holding her down. She forced herself against it. There was a moment where she felt powerful, felt like she had in the shift. She pushed outwards with all her strength and her sister's face disappeared in a whirl of light.

"Sandin, stop!" the voice shouted. "I'm Kadailin, not Damarin."

Sandin felt her second body better now. She lay on something harder than sand, flatter. She tried to move her mouth to speak but it resisted. "Kadailin?" she tried to say.

Kadailin's face appeared before her again, looking just as much like Damarin's as it always had. Sandin looked behind it into vines and flowers. The light was gone. She remembered where she was.

"Where's Damarin?" she tried to ask. She had to repeat it four times before it worked, before there was an answer. Her body didn't listen to her. It felt heavy and slow.

"She left with Ruon. I've been trying to wake you since." Kadailin's eyes were wide. "Sandin, you moved pandinzori! You..."

Her sister's voice faded. Sandin tried to force her external body to move, but it didn't. Something surrounded her, pressing on her.

"You have to get away from here," she said. "I don't know what's happening to me."

Kadailin frowned. "I won't leave you."

Sandin fell back into the desert. She couldn't find Jaydin anywhere. Perhaps her sister was under these red trees? Jaydin's hair would be invisible against their leaves, but her dark skin would stand out. Sandin didn't remember ever seeing so many red-leafed trees before. She had thought Ovaeron to be the only one.

"Sandin!"

Kadailin appeared, superimposed over the foliage of the tree in front of Sandin. The red leaves slowly faded, and behind her sister was a green wall, dotted with red flowers. Everything shook slightly.

"Where's Jaydin?" Sandin asked. Kadailin was the one shaking her.

Kadailin didn't answer. "Listen to me, Sandin. Damarin is gone and Cien is in the mountain with us. He's calling to me. We need to find him."

Sandin's mind cleared slowly and she regretted asking for Jaydin. She remembered what had happened to their sister. It was amazing she could be convinced otherwise so easily. "Can you sense him? Enough to go to him?"

"I think so. But I'll wait until you can get up."

"No. I can't move."

"I don't want to leave you..."

"Just come back for me after you've found Cien."

"But—"

The red leaves swayed above Sandin's head, then blended together like the leaves of the trees in Cens and she was in an endless blood-red forest, blazing with light. Her dark skin stood out strongly against the white trunks and the red leaves. This was nothing like Cens, in which she had been a master of shadows. Damarin would be able to see her here.

She heard a thumping in the distance. The ground shook. The trees to her right were being felled by something huge.

"You need to wake up," a voice said.

Sandin jumped out of the way as a giant brown spider burst through the trees. She stumbled in the shaking world. A wave of smaller spiders streamed out of the shadows and crawled onto her. Their weight forced her to the ground. She started awake with a gasp, almost hitting Kadailin as she sat up sharply.

"The spiders! Kadailin, the spiders," she breathed, looking to either side of her and pulling her hands to her chest. She was amazed to find they responded. Where had she been a moment ago?

"There's nothing here," Kadailin said. "Damarin killed all the spiders in the cave. You were writhing, and mumbling. I thought you could hear me. You used pandinzori!"

Sandin fought to pull herself together. Wherever she may have been, she had also been here, speaking with Kadailin.

"I was asleep. But I could hear you. Somehow. I used pandinzori?"

"You threw me across the cave, pushed me away from you."

Sandin looked around them. Nothing had changed since Ruon forced her to eat the red leaf.

"I don't see pandinzori," she said. "How could I have moved it?"

"I don't know, but you did. It was the colour of your aura and no one else was here."

An uncomfortable pulse ran through Sandin's body that meant Kadailin's aura was in contact with her own. "You said you found Cien?"

"No." Kadailin sat back, moving away from her. "I stayed with you, but I heard him call my name. I can sense him, barely. He must be in the mountain."

"He might know where Tchardin is. You have to find him before Damarin returns."

"We'll find him together."

Sandin tried to get to her feet but her legs were heavy and unresponsive. Kadailin flinched when she fell to the ground again.

"I can't, Kadailin. Something's wrong with me."

"It's—" Kadailin started. She shook her head.

Sandin felt extremely weak. Worse than she'd felt when Marr attacked her. "It's what?"

"The pandinzori around you, you moved it when you slept, but..." Kadailin's gaze flitted around the cave. "I'll take you with me. I can carry you in pandinzori."

Sandin's eyes began to close again. She tried to force them open but they didn't comply. "I'm going to sleep again."

"No!"

"I can't"—Sandin faltered, her head drooped forward of its own accord—"I can't stop it."

The desert swarmed with spiders. Sandin ran from them. Damarin appeared before her out of nothing. Light swirled around her dark sister and Sandin felt when it froze her movements. Damarin opened her mouth to speak. Sandin shouted and pushed the light away with her mind. She turned it back on Damarin, throwing her into the air, holding her there.

"Sandin, please!"

Was this Damarin or Kadailin? The spiders rushed over Sandin but she was unable to take her eyes off the tevadra she held still in the air. An image of the cave came to her. Kadailin hung suspended against the wall. Sandin forced herself awake.

Kadailin dropped through the leaves and crashed to the floor of the cave. Sandin thought she saw the light that held her sister for a moment before it faded from her vision. Kadailin looked too much like Damarin. She wasn't going to be safe unless Sandin could stay awake.

Kadailin knelt by her. "I can't—"

"Find Cien," Sandin said. "I'll be fine here."

Kadailin seemed to stand slowly, haltingly, as if Sandin could only see some of her movements. "I'll be back soon," she said. She ran to the exit of the cave but turned back before leaving. "Were you dreaming?"

Sandin slumped to the floor. She saw the desert with its red trees behind her closing eyes. She thought she might even see a mountain in the distance. Voices whispered to her. So this was what Damarin had wanted from her. To dream.

"Yes," Sandin said through one of her mouths, hoping her sister could hear her. "I dream."

Chapter 41

The colourful forest swallowed them up and the miasma of human thoughts faded into the back of Tchardin's mind again. She let her camouflage fade away with them.

"Finally," Aaron said. "Everyone we passed must have thought we were trying to dispose of a body."

"Poorly," Bronson said. "If I was dumping a body I wouldn't carry it through the city in broad daylight. Although, given the fact that no one stopped us, that might be the way to go."

"They certainly stared."

Tchardin was barely listening to the men. She hoped to sense the World Tree.

"His leaves are many-coloured, but mostly yellow. I saw them in the shift." A lot of the trees around them had fully red or orange leaves. Fewer of them were yellow. That might help them find him.

"*His* leaves?" Aaron asked. "The tree is male?"

Tchardin considered. "They are all our fathers."

"And your mother?"

"I never had one."

The men smiled at each other.

"Give me the guardian," she said.

Bronson transferred the body to her. As soon as she touched it she felt something new. "I feel a pull."

"The World Tree?" Aaron asked.

"No." Tchardin hadn't seen anything that looked like a World Tree when she exited the shift. And if the story was true, and the guardian and World Tree together had been cut from the Earth, then the World Tree was dead. "The World Tree is gone, but it should be the tree that will replace him. The tree that will become a World Tree when Ruslan is given to him. My sister told me that happened on World Two once. A World Tree was damaged by humans and replaced."

"This is just a park," Aaron said. "How can something like that be here?"

Tchardin lifted Ruslan onto her shoulder and turned towards the pull. She walked off the path into trees and the men followed her.

"It's a forest," she said, and as she said it she realised something, remembering each of the forests that had held a World Tree. "All forests are equal, despite what they look like."

She felt a quality now that reminded her of Cens. It was as if the forest here had an identity. It wasn't just the trees as individuals that made it, but a wholeness, achieved when they stood together. She turned slightly and kept walking. "It has to be close."

The forest ahead of them darkened considerably. Tchardin didn't notice at first, but she felt it on the minds of the two humans. Aaron dreaded what lay ahead. Bronson was excited, but underneath that he was afraid, and perplexed to find himself so. They would have turned back if it weren't for her. She also noticed it was getting more difficult to see where they were going. The trees seemed to grow thicker. Pandinzori surrounded them. It gave her hope.

"That the forest makes you uneasy here is a good thing," she said. "There is a forest on Derkra that feels like this. Alive."

She took one more step and found what she was looking for. Bronson and Aaron both gasped but Tchardin knew it wasn't for the reason she opened her own mouth in awe.

The canopy had lifted up and now the lowest branches were so high they should have stood above the trees she had just left. Looking behind her she saw more of the same. These were kandaran trees. More than she'd ever seen. None of those she saw matched Tith in width or height, but they were so much greater than the average trees of World Eight the effect was just as impressive. Only then did she think to calm the two worried voices that remained behind her.

"Step forward," she said, and at the same time she sent her words into their minds in case they couldn't hear her.

Their anxiety quieted. Bronson appeared behind her. He would have disappeared from Aaron's sight, and Aaron's desperate thoughts confirmed it. Bronson called to him and he quickly followed. They held each other for a moment before confronting what now stood before them.

"I've never seen..." Bronson trailed off in the middle of speaking. He took a couple steps forward and past Tchardin. "Never."

"Is this what the forests on Derkra are like?" Aaron asked.

"No," Tchardin said. "We have nothing as magnificent as this."

Aaron joined Bronson and took his hand. Pandinzori rolled off them in waves. They created it, fed the forest with it. Tchardin found she finally understood. The men were definitely dodenzinn. She smiled. For humans to find their dodenzinn when there were so many of them, in such a great area. It was incredible.

She watched the pandinzori that surrounded them as some of it joined her aura and some entered into the high canopy above. The change in the forest delighted her. It reminded her of Cens and Calendrai. It made her miss Derkra. She needed to go home soon. If she couldn't find her own way from here or from World Nine she would call Tchar again. Maybe the first kandar would answer her then, as Kordic had said she might.

"The tree is definitely here." The guardian's body vibrated softly against her skin, almost as if it was alive. "Stay close to me. If you get too far away you might disappear."

They walked through the trees and Tchardin told the men their names as they came to her. "That's Eskola, Thiaw, and that one is Sisask. I've never seen so many."

"What about this one?" Aaron laid a hand on one of the trunks just ahead of her. The tree had a thick crown of red leaves. Tchardin focused on him.

"That is Kangur."

Aaron looked up into Kangur's impressive foliage. "Is this what the World Tree was like? This big?"

"Probably bigger. The World Trees I saw on the other Earths were mostly larger, although these are certainly kandaran."

"I can't believe they cut it down!" Aaron said. "How do you not have respect for something like that?"

"How old are these trees?" Bronson asked.

"The World Tree was born when the world was made," Tchardin said, "but I don't know how long these have been here."

"We cut down a tree from the beginning of time." Bronson's expression was blank. Aaron's eyes glittered. They remained silent for a moment.

"How can this be here?" Aaron finally asked. "The park is so small."

"These trees are huge," Bronson added. "We should be able to see them from outside. They'd tower over the others."

Tchardin shrugged. "It's a forest. It may have hidden itself so no more trees could be cut down."

"I wish I had my camera," Aaron said. "Even if I never got to share the images."

Bronson put a hand on his arm. "That would ruin it. Better to see this through your own eyes, rather than from behind a lens."

The kandaran trees continued. Tchardin shifted the guardian on her shoulder while she studied them one by one. His new father was close. One of these trees was ready to receive the guardian of this Earth. Then she saw him.

"That's him." She pointed and Aaron and Bronson turned to follow her finger's trajectory. "Zalenth," she said as she approached and his name came to her.

Zalenth rang through the humans' minds. The earth seemed to beat with it. The forest hummed. Zalenth was not the biggest tree in the stand of kandaran trees, but he was beautiful. He had three grey trunks, two joined close to the ground, and one joined beneath it. His leaves were green nearer to the ground, blending into a rich yellow, then orange, then red as they reached towards the sky. She approached the tree with the guardian. As she walked towards him the wood of his central trunk split open and pandinzori swirled around it.

Tchardin walked into the fissure, into the heart of a tree, and stood for a moment with the body. The feeling was euphoric, the colours in her mind coming up to dance in front of her eyes without her needing to call them, her whole body caressed by spinning pandinzori. She couldn't help thinking of Tith. What would it be like to go to him in rest when he called her? Would it be as wonderful as this? Could Zalenth keep her instead of the guardian?

The tree sent her a strong feeling of repulsion. She was almost physically pushed out of his trunk. At first she was angry, but then she came back to herself. This was a World Tree. If she stayed she might become a guardian for all of time and the kandar might never return to the Earths. Her dodenzinn, whether it was Ryten or Cien, or both, would be alone and might never find another half. She had the rightful guardian in her arms. Zalenth was to be Ruslan's father, while Tith was hers. She placed the sack containing the guardian's body on the straining wood and stepped back out of the trunk.

Aaron and Bronson stared at her when she emerged. A riveting crack cut through the air as the trunk closed behind her.

"He will be reborn now," she said in the resulting silence, "maybe not in your lifetimes but eventually. And soon the kandar will come back to your Earth."

"That was amazing," Aaron said.

Bronson wrapped his arms around Aaron and smiled at Tchardin. "I guess we changed the world."

Tchardin returned his smile but she was already thinking of Derkra. She would need to shift on now. She'd done all she could do here alone, and the sooner she returned to Calendrai the sooner the kandar could come back to World Eight. They couldn't know when Ruslan would wake, but the kandar could learn from Aaron and Bronson to start. Perhaps even from Laurence. Tchardin would see them again that way.

A leaf she hadn't seen for a long time grew bright in the collective. Damarin appeared from between the trees behind Aaron and Bronson. She wore no camouflage.

Tchardin must have shown her reaction on her face because Aaron turned around in confusion and Bronson postured. His mind said he was ready to defend them, from whatever threat had made Tchardin's brows knit together and her mouth open slightly in alarm.

"Cens is not unique after all," Damarin said aloud.

Her sister had preceded her on the other Earths. Tchardin hadn't expected to run into her now, so close to the end of her journey. Tchardin's best chance to control the situation might be to pretend everything was as it always had been between them. Damarin wouldn't know what Siltadon had told her, might not know Tchardin had seen her kill the guards on World Four. Throwing Tchardin into the shift could be forgiven, possibly, but she wasn't sure about the rest.

"You've come a long way in distance," Damarin said, "but not so far in judgement. You really think I can't hear your thoughts?"

"I—"

"I thought the Earths would make you better, but it appears that has not been the case."

Damarin's gaze moved to the two men. Pandinzori spiralled off her. An image of the dead guards on World Four entered Tchardin's mind at the same time she remembered both of them were out of their camouflage.

'Don't hurt them,' she said, unsure whether her words were an entreaty or a threat.

"Why not?" Damarin asked. "They've seen me. Seen us."

"They're too important to kill."

Damarin's gaze focused on Tchardin and she could almost feel her sister listening. Tchardin thought loudly of all the reasons humans were so important to her and to the kandar, tried to teach her sister the things she had learned. It wasn't even just humans in general that were important, but each individual human. The extent of their minds, the things they could think and do, each one of them. Tchardin hadn't learned anything about the guards Damarin killed, but she knew they'd been the same. Taken as a whole the humans had to be the Purpose, deserved to be it. Aaron and Bronson stayed silent at her side, aware of the danger they were in.

"I see." Damarin advanced farther into the stand of kandaran trees, closer to Tchardin and the two men.

Tchardin tensed. Damarin's leaf in the collective was still extremely bright. She searched for her sister's intentions. She heard a whisper of a thought, then Damarin's eyes went to Zalenth and her thoughts changed and were spoken aloud.

"The guardian," she said. "How did you find him?"

Tchardin looked to Aaron and Bronson. "They found him."

"Amazing," Damarin whispered, calming herself, "but pointless. He can't help them on his own." Her eyes followed Zalenth's mighty trunks into the canopy. "An impressive forest for the new World Tree to stand in. Why should they have more kandaran trees here than we do on Derkra?"

Tchardin scanned the forest. The number of mammoth trees was uncountable. "The humans must have wanted them."

Damarin's expression hardened. "So you know they can make them?"

"Siltadon told me."

"Of course she did. Being born our future queen always gave you an unfair advantage with the kandar."

Queen. Tchardin heard Bronson's sharp intake of breath. She placed herself between Damarin and the two men. Her sister's pandinzori was frightening but there had to be something Tchardin could do to protect them.

"Do you think it's true of all the worlds?" Damarin asked. "What Siltadon said of their beginnings? Not just the restart?"

"I do." Tchardin gestured to Aaron and Bronson. "Look at them, at their pandinzori. Listen to their minds. There are so many of them here and some I have seen are greater than these two. How could they not build their own world?"

Damarin nodded. "But to build these magnificent trees. You know why they wanted them, don't you? It wasn't for awe, for their beauty or brilliance. Or for their minds. It was for conquest. Dominion. They destroy the earth to build from it. They see the World Tree, a wonder of a size and majesty far greater than they could ever have achieved alone and they take that and corrupt it." She stared at the men now. "Or even worse than that, it may only have been for wood."

"No." Bronson strained towards Damarin but Aaron held him back. "We're not all like that!"

Tchardin glared at them, willing them to hide, to leave, but they stayed.

"Why do you think I would make them?" her sister asked, ignoring him.

"You could never make them. They have minds. They are our own makers. Even if we can make other things, kandar can't make trees. Kordic told me so."

Damarin frowned. "That's why you never will. It's also the reason you shouldn't be the queen of our people." She turned away, looking into Zalenth's massive canopy. "I came to gauge your progress and I am unimpressed. You haven't learned enough here, but somehow the golden aura remains."

Tchardin met Bronson's eyes. She had to leave them, but as long as she took Damarin with her they would be safe. She lined herself up without thinking, opened the shift even as she moved, and charged into Damarin's back.

Tchardin felt a moment of panicked apprehension while they flew through the air, once she thought about what she was doing. Damarin was stronger than she was, always had been stronger. What if her sister stopped them before they went through? Then Damarin laughed, and the ice broke, and the water came out to swallow them.

The water roared. There was confusion for a moment before Tchardin pushed it away. She reformed herself and retreated into a protective sphere of ice. The water around her became calm and blue and infinite. Damarin was nowhere to be seen.

Suddenly the walls of her bubble collapsed. Tchardin struggled to reform it, fighting the water as she had since she'd learned to safely travel the shift. But this was something else. Another sphere of ice encroached on hers. There was a dark shape inside that must be Damarin. Tchardin heard nothing. She pushed back on the breaking ice with her own mind, and for a moment her bubble reformed and Damarin's began to crumble.

Then the wall of ice between them shattered and the two spheres joined. The triumph Tchardin had felt faded as Damarin leapt towards her and the sound came back. Tchardin shouted as she sidestepped her sister's attack and the two spun around each other. The creature who opposed her was not truly Damarin, couldn't be. Its expression was wild and frightening, like nothing she had ever seen on the face of a kandar, its body distorted and unstable, and for a moment Tchardin wondered what she looked like in the shift. Was she a warped image of herself as Damarin was? Then her mind returned to the fight just in time to save herself from being thrown through the wall of ice and into the raging water.

Their bodies collided again and again as each tried to throw the other off balance. She'd never done such a thing on Derkra, or on any of the Earths. There were no auras here. The only feeling that came from the touch of her sister's skin was terror.

Tchardin wasn't sure anymore who was in control of the ice that protected them. At times she felt it was hers and at times Damarin's. She was pushed back against it, hoping it was hers, hoping it would hold, then she had an idea.

Surely she'd spent more time in the water of the shift, her sister being more adept at travelling it. She wrested control of the ice from Damarin and let it go.

Damarin's effigy was ripped away as the water clawed at Tchardin. She fought it with everything she had, but the water, having finally regained her, tore her to shreds. She felt the last of her consciousness ebbing away and struggled against the needs of the water. Where were the leaves of World Nine? She fought to control her vision, to have eyes, rather than the ubiquitous perspective of the shift. Damarin was gone now, but how would she escape? Then the water that was Damarin collided with her and pushed her out of the blue.

Tchardin's strength left her immediately. Only numbly did she feel her body catch and slide, her skin scraping against something until she came to a stop. Her mind ached. It reminded her of Water Side, drifting in the infinity without pandinzori, but this was worse. There was nothing here to cling to, nothing to soften the blow. Her mind was alone. Absolutely. She opened her eyes and saw white, but no light. It took her a moment to understand what that meant.

What place could have less pandinzori than the waters of Water Side?

Chapter 42

Tchardin attempted to bring colours into the darkness behind her eyes to escape her pain but nothing would come. She searched for something already there, anything. At first the black was absolute, then tiny wisps of light grew in it. She opened her eyes and was overwhelmed by the contrasting white. Pandinzori flowed slowly off her skin. For a moment she worried she would die, but her strength seemed to be improving already.

What was this place? She had travelled through eight worlds before it and the only places left in existence were World Nine and Coralynth. But it couldn't be Coralynth. Tchar and Dani may have abandoned the kandar, but Tchardin couldn't believe they would leave their home. So it had to be World Nine. But with no leaves in the shift and nothing around her, how could it be a human Earth?

Tchardin scanned the whiteness and definition slowly came to the land. The ground was flat. It was so flat it created a sense of infinity, like the land on Derkra. A dark grey line stood along the horizon in the far distance. It looked like a building—the first sign of humans on World Nine. There were faint streaks of red around her where she had scraped across the ground. Blood. Various places on the right side of her body mimicked the pattern. There was nothing else to be seen. No sign of Damarin on the land or in the collective. Perhaps her sister had left the shift somewhere else.

Tchardin propped herself up on one elbow and realised the abrasive surface she lay on was ice. It was white on top, but where cracks ran through it she saw it was a deep blue at its heart. She searched the world for a sign of life, for anything: a shred of pandinzori, a person, a tree. She focused on the grey line—the long building—hoping to find pandinzori growing behind its walls, but there was nothing there. Not ahead of her and not behind. If this plane of ice had once been World Nine it was now dead. More so than World Five. More so than World Seven.

It seemed to have no World Tree and no humans. Nothing alive on the face of the Earth. Could the Root of the World itself be dead? What had happened here that could have caused this?

'Tchar?' she thought, looking up into the white sky.

There was no response. If Kordic was right, Tchardin's only chance to leave the final Earth might be to contact the first kandar. She didn't know how to shift to Derkra, and at this point she didn't think she could. The pandinzori around her body was not enough to sustain her and to shift. Some outside source would have to help her or she would be stuck in this dead place until she died too.

Then her searching mind found something in the abyss. It was something strange. A presence, maybe humanity, but faint. It didn't feel like anything she had sensed on any other world. It was something though, and she clung to it in the emptiness. She looked around and noticed her pandinzori had grown. Maybe she would be able to shift on, but to where? Without Tchar's help there didn't seem to be anywhere else to go.

A tiny blaze of light appeared ahead of her, in front of the grey line. She closed her eyes for a moment to confirm her suspicions. It was pandinzori. Tchardin strained to see where it came from. The pandinzori reached out to her and power came back into her limbs and her mind, to save her. Maybe it was a human.

Her mind clearing, pandinzori impossibly billowing around her, Tchardin rose to sit on the ice. The collective pulsed. Then she saw—in the centre of the great blaze of light—that the one who approached her was Damarin.

***

Kadailin peered around the edge of the opening to the cave. Cien's leaf faded as she leaned into the valley and Ruon's seed blossomed into existence. She stepped back into shadow. Pandinzori blew past her, given to the desert by Sandin.

Damarin had threatened them with the guardian. How could Kadailin leave Sandin alone with Ruon in the valley? He would sense her leave the mountain. But they had to find Cien, and Sandin had told her to go. Hidden in the tunnel once more, the Shadow's leaf glowed steadily in Kadailin's mind. It indicated he was somewhere above her. How would she find him when his leaf darkened? She might have to search the entire mountain. That would leave Sandin vulnerable.

She pushed herself to look into the valley again, Cien's leaf fading as she stepped into the light. The scene of normality that greeted her was shocking. Kandar went about as usual in Black Valley. None even turned their eyes to her. Very few of them would possess her leaf, but they must see the pandinzori coming from the cave behind her. Torrents of it brushed Kadailin as it was forced out of the mountain. It spread out to either side of her and wound around the rock. That in itself should have been strange enough to warrant investigation. Jaydin had been right. The kandar didn't care.

Kadailin looked up, searching in the direction Cien's leaf had told her he would be. The pandinzori that emerged from Sandin's cave encircled the stone and rose to meet a second source swirling around the middle of the mountain. Its origin might mark the opening to another cave. Cien could be contained within and he could be close to death, with that much pandinzori coming off him. Or maybe he was dreaming, as Sandin was. Kadailin had to get to him quickly and she had to be wary. If Sandin could use pandinzori against her from a dream, what could Cien do?

Ruon's seed threatened. The guardian must have every leaf from the valley by now. Perhaps he wouldn't notice Kadailin's light up in the collective. She took a couple steps onto the sand, trying to get a better look at the path she'd have to travel. Jagged black rock was very different from the bark of trees and she was going to have to avoid the fire that flowed down it. The pandinzori that blew out of the mountain was sucked inwards by the fire. More pandinzori than she had seen around anything but Tith and his two brothers. Maybe she didn't have to climb.

She took the abundant pandinzori with her mind and hardened it into a protective sphere around her body. For a moment she remembered protecting herself and Sandin from the blast Siltadon had created but she shook the memory away. With one last look at the cave she had come from, and one last scan of the collective for signs of Damarin's leaf and

Ruon's seed—still glowing dimly—she pushed the pandinzori below her upwards, through the air, and towards the mountain.

She soared towards the rock, trying not to get too close for fear the fire would draw her in. Kandar shrunk below her as she dared a glance back towards Ovaeron. The cave entrance loomed, a slender crack in the stone.

A leaf lit up in the collective. Kadailin almost let herself drop from the sky at the shock. The newly bright leaf belonged to the Calendrai collective. She slowed to a stop, focusing inwards to examine the tree in her mind.

Torshe. She opened her eyes, swinging around in her already precarious position to search the valley below. There, at the base of Ovaeron's trunk, was a dark-skinned kandar. He would have been invisible against the black sand if it weren't for his aura. What could Torshe be doing in Black Valley? Another light lit the collective. Kadailin's eyes widened. A second dark kandar joined him. *Ocien*.

Then the collective exploded with lights. Kandar of Calendrai poured onto the sand at Ovaeron's base. By the time there were fifty, Ruon's seed had darkened. He must have left the valley. Sandin would be safe. Kadailin could find out what they were doing once she had Cien. She turned back to the mountain and propelled herself upwards with pandinzori.

The cave entrance neared and the pandinzori that flew from it bolstered her. There was so much she could have hardened a path in it and walked into the cave. She alighted on the lip of the entrance. The tunnel was dark and narrow and she had to duck to walk through.

Just before she entered the rock she thought she felt Ryten's leaf grow bright. She leaned out towards the valley and confirmed that it glowed softly in the collective. She looked for his aura among the milling dark kandar at Ovaeron's base. Cien's leaf appeared as she did so. A voice entered her mind.

'Kadailin!'

'Cien,' she thought his name as strongly as she could.

'Kadailin,' came back in answer, faint, from down the twisting crevice in the rock. *'Don't use pandinzori when you enter here.'*

Kadailin paused. It couldn't be... No, it couldn't be. She started towards him. The leaves of the kandar of Calendrai disappeared from her mind, leaving her alone in the collective with the Shadow. The floor flattened a little way down the path and she heard Cien speak aloud. She turned the last corner into the cave and a wave of debilitating fear settled over her. Cien stood across from her in the dimly lit space, his body striped with shadow. The shadow was created by glass.

"Kadailin!" There was so much emotion in Cien's voice Kadailin was worried.

"I'm going to help you." She was amazed she was able to speak at all. The cave was filled with pandinzori from wall to wall, floor to ceiling. There was only one space free of it. There was fire at the edge of the cave, pulling the light into itself and destroying it. All she could think of was Siltadon and World Seven. "You have to calm down."

"You don't understand what this is like. I need to get out of here right now."

"We'll think of a way." But she didn't think there was a way. "Is Tchardin alive? Is she here?"

Cien pushed his forehead against the panels of glass and looked at the ground. The fingers he pushed through the openings to either side of his face were rigid, forced too tightly against the glass. "I haven't lost her leaf, but she's not here. You need to get me out. Out of this cage. Out of this glass."

Kadailin was ecstatic for a moment before the situation dragged her down again. Tchardin was alive, but she wasn't found, and Cien would have said if he knew where she was. So for now she had to free him. Then they could find Tchardin.

She started towards the glass but couldn't make herself approach it. She thought of him losing it and killing them both. She thought of losing it herself. She almost had with Siltadon. The pandinzori around her seemed to move on its own. She ducked away from it, finding herself on the ground. Jaydin had died. Glass had killed her and now it would kill Kadailin.

"Kadailin, please."

She closed her eyes, steeled herself. It wouldn't be dangerous unless she used pandinzori. She stood, approached slowly, and the severity of the situation dawned on her in truth. There was glass all around him. It wasn't just the bars they would have to deal with but the floor and walls as well. She wouldn't dare approach it with pandinzori. Cien's body was dark, as if he came from Calendrai. He was covered in blood. He stared at her, his eyes intense.

"How?" she asked him. "How can we get you out?"

He threw his hands up in the air. "I don't know! I don't know if Damarin ever meant to free me."

"Damarin put you in there?"

Cien shook his head and his face showed black rage. Kadailin almost took a step back.

"Ruon," he breathed.

She looked away, anxious for a moment that she couldn't see if the guardian's seed was lit in the collective or not. She'd have to hope the kandar in the valley kept him away. What kind of kandar would put another behind glass?

"Could we break the bars without pandinzori?" she asked. "Just enough to get you out?"

Cien shrugged and all of a sudden he was laughing. Kadailin didn't like this at all.

"I've tried to break them." He beat his fists against the thick pillars of glass. He threw his shoulder into them. He left dark blood on the clouded columns where his body touched them. "Without pandinzori..."

The walls of the cave not covered by glass were covered in vines. Kadailin ran to the far wall, flinching both at the sharp feeling of relief that hit her when she put distance between herself and the glass and at Cien's cry when it must have looked like she was abandoning him.

"I'm not leaving!" she said, and flinched again as her concentrated awareness touched the pandinzori around her.

She examined the vines. The wall behind them would be made of rock. She opened her mind to use pandinzori to rip the vines away but remembered at the last moment she shouldn't do so. She would only use it as a last resort and she could remove the vines without it. She pulled them down with her hands. Brown spiders crawled away when they were revealed but didn't frighten her. Compared to the glass and the fire they were nothing.

The leaves and flowers tore away to reveal a rough black surface. Now Kadailin's hands would fail her. If she used pandinzori to break the rock, she could use the rock to break the glass. Cien was still and silent. His eyes were large and unblinking as he watched her. He knew what she was going to do.

"I can do it," she said.

The last thing she needed was to frighten him. She should be far enough away to control pandinzori without endangering them, but she was afraid too, and that frayed her concentration. She focused on the pandinzori in front of her, that between her and the rock, and tried to hold just the slightest bit of it, just enough to push behind the stone and pull it away.

"Please." Cien's voice was wretched.

Kadailin sent the sliver of light through an outwards jutting ridge. It sheared off as if it was never attached. She let go of pandinzori immediately. The large slab of rock fell to the ground and splintered into three pieces. She picked the sharpest of them.

***

Ryten stared up at the mountain that dominated the valley. He could have sworn he saw a tevadra slip into a crack in its side just a moment ago. The same moment he thought he had seen Kadailin's leaf give a quick flash in the collective.

"It *was* Kadailin," Torshe said from his side. "When I came through I saw her standing in the air by the mountain."

Ryten hadn't seen any of the sisters' leaves when he'd shifted to Black Valley the first time to check if it was safe for the kandar to come over. He had only stayed for a moment, threatened by a black devoshai holding more pandinzori than he had ever seen. That devoshai was gone now, but it was strange to Ryten that Kadailin was here when she hadn't been before.

"She propelled herself up there with pandinzori." Torshe indicated the fissure far above them that pulsed with escaping light. "She went into the rock."

"Why?" Ryten asked, more to himself than to Torshe. "Her leaf is dark now."

Torshe shrugged. "Should we go after her?"

"I will. You need to get the kandar organised. Make sure everyone came through and make sure they're ready in case we're attacked." A few of the kandar behind Ryten had lain down in the black sand. "Wake up anyone who's fallen asleep."

He still couldn't believe it. That the kandar could finally sleep, after he had tried so hard and for so long. Even more than that he couldn't believe he hadn't tried it himself yet. He had a purpose now.

Some of the lightly-coloured kandar of the valley watched them. Ryten didn't want to walk by them to get to the mountain, but the air was so full of pandinzori now he didn't think he'd have to. If Kadailin had used it to avoid scaling the burning rock, he should be able to do the same.

He tried to stop himself from wondering if Tchardin was with Kadailin. If one sister could be in that mountain and hide from the collective they all could. That included Damarin. What would it be like to see her again after all of this? To see either of them? It almost hadn't seemed real to him, what Damarin was doing, and that Tchardin was gone. Now he would be confronted with it.

He leapt into the air but fell to the ground again while he tried to wrap his mind around the idea of propelling himself forwards using pandinzori. Instead of trying again he formed a solid platform of pandinzori above the sand. He stepped onto it and balanced while he sent it up towards the mountain.

The light and dark kandar below watched him go, but none moved to follow. As he soared through the air he took in the valley, and the great red leaves of Ovaeron, the father of all of them. That this black mountain had been put into their midst was a desecration.

There was fire on the mountain. Not like the fire in Cens. Not the all-consuming, rushing, reaching fire of the trees, but a steady flowing fire. It burned through the rock below as he moved towards the fissure. Towards the source of pandinzori. That confused him. Why would so much pandinzori be coming from rock when it was supposed to come from trees? He landed and slipped through the opening.

Kadailin's leaf grew bright before he saw her and so did another. The rest of the collective darkened, making the second leaf easy to identify. It was Cien's. Ryten rounded a bend into the cave and found Kadailin holding a large rock above her head. Cien stood before her, striped with shadow. The shadow was created by clouded, blood-streaked columns of ice. But it wasn't ice.

Cien turned to look at Ryten just as Kadailin smashed the rock into the pillars of glass that contained him. She seemed to hesitate at the last moment, shying away from the glass, from what would happen to it, and the rock didn't hit with all the force she was capable of.

Jagged edges of broken glass forced themselves against Cien. Some of the glass came back at Kadailin as well. Ryten had to restrain himself from using pandinzori to protect them, had to remind himself of how to treat the most serious threat the kandar had ever faced. The cave was full of pandinzori, tempting the kandar to use it, to harness it and send it through the glass to unleash its hidden potential.

The world seemed to slow. Cien raised his arms to shield himself and Kadailin jumped back as if expecting that to be the end. She dropped the rock. The two froze like that, waiting for the worst to hit. Ryten came forward and examined the small break Kadailin had made. She stared up at him.

"It's glass," she mouthed.

Cien's upper body streamed red. He seemed to come back to himself and notice the opening in the glass. He stretched to reach through the hole the rock had made. The glass peeled his skin away.

"Stop!" Ryten was shocked at the sight of it. "Wait."

The force of Ryten's voice seemed to clear Cien's mind. The devoshai took a step away from the glass and pressed himself against the wall behind him. Kadailin stared blankly at Cien as if she didn't know what to do. Ryten picked up the rock she had dropped. He gripped it hard in both hands and the rough edges cut him. He held it in front of him and across his body, then he brought it against the pillars.

He crushed them, starting at the top where they were broken and going lower and lower until they were a shattered mess on the floor. Tiny pieces stuck in his hands and arms but he continued until Cien pushed through and past him, taking slivers of the glass with him in his skin.

Ryten was brought out of his task by the current of unpleasantness when Cien's aura brushed his. Cien paced in the cave, his skin dripping blood. Pandinzori swirled around him and he raised his arms above his head as if to embrace it. Kadailin watched him with wariness.

"Have you been in there the whole time?" Ryten asked the devoshai.

Cien turned, his expression at odds with his earlier movement. His eyes were haunted, his lips strained. "First I was in the desert and then the glass. But I haven't seen my people, or anyone since the fire in Cens. I haven't been able to touch pandinzori..." He closed his eyes. Kadailin ran to him.

"It's not safe yet," she said. "You have glass in your skin."

Ryten looked down at his hands, streaming blood. There was glass in them too.

"What do we do about this?" If they left the cave with glass in their skin they would be a liability not only to themselves but to everyone in the valley.

"We have to remove it," Cien said.

Kadailin shot Ryten a worried look. "He's right. Who knows how easy it will be to touch this from outside the mountain."

"But how?" Ryten asked. "We could kill ourselves."

Cien's eyes hardened. "I can do it."

Chapter 43

CIEN WAS FINALLY FREE of his cage. Pandinzori flowed around him and if it weren't for the glass in his hands he could have embraced it and taken down the whole mountain. The power he felt was unbelievable. He had started to understand Ruon's words about it when he saw the glass shatter in front of him, but he wasn't truly free yet. The glass in his skin still held him.

The other two kandar stared at him. Ryten stood across the cave with his arms spread to keep the glass as far away from his body as possible. Kadailin was between the two, her eyes locked on Cien. The tension was clear in their buzzing thoughts. They wanted desperately to leave the cave but knew they would only be in greater danger if they did. Cien examined the shards of glass in his skin. It was time to remove that final hindrance.

"Give me a moment," he said.

"Where are the others?" Ryten asked Kadailin.

Kadailin shook her head and didn't answer.

Cien walked towards the fire at the edge of the cave. A call pulsed in the back of his mind. Ovaeron. From the persistence of the call he almost believed the tree knew he was free and that he was more likely to accept now, after all that had happened to him. He focused on the fire.

He studied his hands as he stood over it. There were splinters of bloody glass in them. The ends of his fingers dripped red into the fire. He knelt there, watching as the pandinzori of his aura was pulled into the bright liquid to disappear. He felt weak as it was pulled away from him, felt a moment of dismay where he thought he would fall in after it. Then a surge of pandinzori seemed to come from nowhere and surround him. The power Ruon spoke of. The power to bring pandinzori to him without having to call it.

Cien held his hands just above the fire, causing the pandinzori around his arms and upper body to thin. He closed his eyes. The darkness of his skin was limned in light. He would have to touch it with his mind, but not just part of it, all of it at once, to avoid drawing out the reaction.

He touched the first, thinnest layer surrounding his skin. He waited but nothing happened. He moved further with his mind, slowly, closer and closer to the glass, ready at each moment to let go. Light exploded around his hands and up his arms to his chest. He let go and opened his eyes. It had only been for an instant and the red on his fingers had redoubled. But his hands were still there. He clenched them in fists and blood flowed freely into the fire. Red on red. He looked over his shoulder to see the two kandar standing completely still.

"Ryten," he said. "You'll need to stand near the fire if I'm to do the same for you."

The big devoshai didn't look happy but the feel of the glass in his skin must have decided him. He walked to Cien and knelt.

"Stand as close to the fire as you can. I need you to have as little pandinzori around you as possible."

Ryten leaned down and lowered his hands to the fire. The pandinzori of his aura was almost depleted, sucked down into the fire in an instant. He slumped and tipped forwards. Cien held him back, tolerating the shock of his diminished aura. He reached out to the pandinzori around Ryten's body until a small flash of light lit it. Then Ryten was likewise freed of the glass. Cien gently pushed the big devoshai away from the fire.

He looked down at his hands and arms and found them drying. Without the glass the cuts healed quickly. Ryten lifted himself off the stone floor behind Cien.

"It's safe?" Ryten examined his arms.

"It is."

Cien looked to the cave opening and found the thought of seeing the valley again terrified him. He was glad to be free of the glass, but to see Ovaeron after everything that had happened? To meet Ruon while free? "We have to find Tchardin."

"We don't know where she is," Ryten said.

"She's not on Derkra," Kadailin said. "Or at least not in either city. She wasn't on World Seven."

"Damarin told me she might be on an Earth, but not which one," Cien said.

Kadailin frowned.

"Where's Jaydin?" Ryten asked her. "And Sandin? Are they still on the Earths or did you come straight here?"

Kadailin looked away. Her thoughts were loud. It seemed the other sisters had followed Damarin off Derkra only to find disaster.

"One is dead and one is dreaming," Cien said.

Ryten's eyes widened. "What?"

"Jaydin is gone," Kadailin said. "It happened on World Seven."

Cien had only met Jaydin a few times but he knew her loss was a great one.

"How?" Ryten eventually asked.

Kadailin held a deep sadness and was reluctant to answer. Cien was surprised Ryten couldn't hear her thoughts.

"Another time," he interceded.

Ryten glanced at him before turning back to Kadailin. "And Sandin?"

"We met Damarin and Ruon in the valley when we came back. Damarin gave her a red flower. Now she's sleeping. Dreaming."

"Where is she?" Cien asked.

"In the mountain."

The image of Miadra covered in twitching brown bodies came into his mind unbidden. "If she was given a red flower she must be kept away from the spiders."

"Damarin destroyed the spiders in the cave."

Cien frowned. "They could come back."

"We should go to her," Kadailin said. "Even without the spiders she's not safe where she is, but I had to find you. I thought I might find Tchardin here too."

"We'll go to Sandin," Cien said, "and we will find Tchardin. Is Ruon in the valley now?"

"No," Kadailin responded. "His seed disappeared when the kandar arrived from Calendrai."

"I think I saw him," Ryten said, "when I first came here. He is small and dark, but not of Calendrai. Surrounded by so much pandinzori..."

"Yes." Cien found it funny that Ryten called Ruon small, but he guessed everyone would look small to the giant devoshai. Everyone except Cotelle. "That would be him. There are kandar from Calendrai here?"

"About a hundred of us came," Ryten replied. "I thought it best, given that Damarin seems to be trying to take over."

Cien nodded.

Ryten turned to Kadailin. "We need to go back to Calendrai to gather the rest of them. They wouldn't listen to us, Kadailin. We need to more than equal the number of kandar here, just in case Damarin has them all."

"Are you trying to start a war?" Cien asked.

"If we have enough, there shouldn't be one."

"I can call the council," Kadailin said. "I'm a member."

Cien cringed at hearing that, but then he wondered if it really mattered anymore. He looked to Ryten to see the devoshai's reaction, but found his face full of fear.

"What's wrong?" Kadailin asked, noticing at the same time.

"It's Marr," Ryten whispered. "I'd hoped he disappeared somewhere and went to rest after we fixed Cens, but he's here."

A spattering of glass shards twinkled on the cave floor, and there was still the glass ceiling and wall behind it. Cien didn't know who Marr was, but if Ryten was that worried he was worried too. Another kandar might not know how to behave around the glass. "If you can sense him he must be—"

A shadow appeared against the cave entrance. The pandinzori before them shifted slightly. Kadailin shouted. Cien took it. All movement ceased.

A devoshai stood in the entrance, silhouetted against the light. Cien held him there with solid pandinzori. He held Kadailin and Ryten where they were as well. It would have been too risky to let them defend themselves with the glass so close by. Cien's controlled pandinzori ended just before the former confines of his cage. He knew the cave so well he could avoid it, as well as the broken shards of the pillars that covered the floor. Marr could still touch the pandinzori there, if he noticed the free space, but Cien should be able to let go of his pandinzori immediately if he did. He hoped Marr wouldn't notice.

"What do you want?" Cien asked.

"I sensed you." The devoshai's eyes turned to Ryten as he said it. Cien allowed his face to move so he could speak. "Kadailin was here, then gone, then here again. You just arrived, then disappeared. Where is Jaydin?"

"There's glass in this cave," Cien said. "You can't touch pandinzori if I release you."

'Don't release him,' Ryten said. *'He'll kill us. Likely on purpose but if not then by accident.'*

"You'd deserve it," Marr responded.

He pushed against Cien's mind. Strong, yet Cien found it easy to resist him.

"I have to find Jaydin," Marr said. "She must be held accountable for all she has done on Calendrai."

"She has been," Kadailin said from behind Cien. "And she did *not* deserve it."

Cien pulled Marr towards him. At the same time he lifted Ryten and Kadailin towards the entrance. The three kandar spun around each other as they moved through the air. Cien released the pandinzori holding Ryten and Kadailin.

"Go down to the valley," he said to them. "Be careful where you touch pandinzori."

Ryten hesitated at the entrance to the cave. "He's dangerous. He tried to hurt Sandin on Calendrai."

"They killed the trees," Marr responded. "Gerrin is gone! They killed him," he implored, his eyes on Cien now. "My father..."

Ryten left the cave.

'What are you going to do to him?' Kadailin asked.

'I don't know yet,' Cien said, but looking into the devoshai's eyes he did know.

Kadailin followed Ryten out of the cave. Cien waited until their leaves faded from the collective, then he turned the devoshai in the air. He had Marr's leaf now, and it helped him hear the devoshai's erratic thoughts. He walked in front of the suspended form in the direction of his broken cage.

Marr could die. Cien could kill him. But what of his dodenzinn? They were nearing the glass. Marr's eyes never left his.

Pandinzori floated against the glass wall behind the devoshai. It was outside Cien's control. Outside what would be safe to claim. If Marr touched it all the pandinzori Cien held would start to react. He made sure he held everything else in the cave. He would have to act quickly.

"If I free you, what will you do?"

"I will find and kill the daughters of Tith, and any other kandar who helped them kill our fathers."

"Why?"

"You didn't hear him scream. The trees shrieked when they were torn from the ground. Screeched like they did during the fire."

Cien remembered the sound the trees had made when the fire took them. He removed his mind from the pandinzori around the devoshai and at the same moment he physically shoved him backwards into the glass. Marr twisted as he fell and found support against the wall of the cave, rebounding off it to face Cien again.

His expression was angry, but the look changed to fear in the instant he realised the floor beneath his feet was made of glass. His gaze swung wildly to the wall behind him, the wall he had just touched, and a wail escaped his lips. Cien looked to the ceiling of the cave, to the place Ruon had opened above him and let the fire fall. If he did the same he could capture Marr behind glass, create a new cage for one who would fight him, and preserve a body that belonged to another kandar. Just as Miadra had said she was doing for Cien. He held pandinzori tightly around him. Marr was frozen in fear. Cien turned away. The devoshai scrambled after him.

"Am I free?"

When Cien turned back to face Marr his eyes met a look of dangerous desperation, something Kadailin must have seen in Cien before she freed him. "You are. I would not trap a kandar in glass, no matter how much it would benefit me or my people. You're free to leave, but you will not kill any kandar when you do."

The devoshai's thoughts said he considered Cien's strength. Marr might be strong compared to the other kandar but he couldn't stand against Cien. Not now. Not anymore.

"Then I'm not truly free."

"You're alive," Cien said. "Go to rest if you want to die, but don't make me kill you here. Don't leave your dodenzinn alone."

Cien turned and strode towards the cave entrance, hoping the devoshai would leave things as they were, hoping he would go back to Calendrai and forget what had happened to him.

"No," said Marr.

Cien recognised a familiar note in that voice. He ran for the entrance. He sensed Marr take hold of the pandinzori behind him, felt the incredible shock as that pandinzori ignited and touched his own. It pressed at his back. Tore at him. He saw the valley.

He jumped and let go.

***

Pandinzori continued to flow from the cave opening high above Kadailin. She remembered how strong Marr had been in the forest, when he had fought her and Ryten. Cien had taken the devoshai's pandinzori in a moment, without a struggle, and held it. He had held Kadailin and Ryten as well. He had held three kandar and all the pandinzori in the cave and had not feared the glass.

The collective in her mind was well lit again with the leaves of kandar from Calendrai. They stood around Ovaeron's base and their eyes were on the mountain. Kadailin glanced at Ryten, standing behind her and braced against the rock. His thoughts were loud and clear to her. He spoke with Torshe across the distance and remembered the moment Cien had cleared his skin of glass, of the precision and speed such an act would require. He noticed her looking at him.

"I could never have done it," he said. "Even with the fire to thin my aura. Especially not with the fire there."

She turned to look up again and as she did a flare of light lit the cave opening. There was a loud roar and the mountain shook. Cien hit the ground in front of them in a shower of black rocks. He was on his feet in an instant and Kadailin felt him take the pandinzori around her to shield the three kandar as rock fell on top of them. She waited, immobile and powerless, as they were covered, descending into darkness.

Then the rocks were thrown off. The light came back even brighter than before and Kadailin saw the reason why. Fire flowed towards them.

The side of the mountain had opened up and burning liquid rock poured towards the valley.

She ran. There was no point in trying to block it. She had seen fire swallow pandinzori in Cens. She would never have enough to stop it. Ryten ran just ahead of her and the kandar that stood around Ovaeron watched them with their mouths open and their eyes wide.

Ovaeron. Kadailin skidded in the sand, trying to turn from her sprint. They'd have to stop the fire before it reached him, stop it before it touched any of the trees. Even if that was impossible she had to try. She had finally regained control of herself when she saw Cien.

The devoshai hadn't run. His back bled onto the sand as he held a wall of pandinzori so thick and high it smothered the fire under it and remained strong. The rush of red cooled to black as Cien's pandinzori was pushed into it, fed to it. The mountain took on a new shape. Then it was over. Cien turned towards the great tree and fell to his knees. Kadailin went to him. Ryten followed close behind her.

"Did you kill him?" she asked the Shadow.

"Marr is gone," Cien said.

Kadailin looked up at the mountain. The place where the cave had been was obliterated. There would be no way to recover Marr's body. "What about his dodenzinn?"

Cien didn't turn towards her when he spoke. He stared past her at the great red tree, his eyes wide. "What about *my* dodenzinn?" he whispered. "We don't know where Tchardin is. Or Damarin. And still, I'm trapped by it. Called by Ovaeron—"

"Ovaeron?" Ryten interrupted.

"The father of all of us calls me—has called me for most of my life. I should have gone to rest long before any of this started, long before Tchardin and Damarin came to Land Side. But I waited for them, though I didn't know what would come. Now that I'm free from the glass I still can't rest until I know which of the two it is. Is Tchardin my dodenzinn, or is it Damarin? It seems to be both, but how is that possible? Will they react equally if I rest? My end could decide this conflict, but which way?"

Kadailin was stunned. The only other kandar Ovaeron had held was Tchar, the first of them. Ryten seemed less shocked. His thoughts told her he focused on something else Cien had said.

"My end too," Ryten said from behind her. This time Cien did turn, wrenching his gaze from the black trunk and crimson leaves. "It's both of them for me as well. I've never been able to figure it out. I'm not called, but if I was I don't know what I'd do."

Kadailin looked back to the broken cave in the mountain. Who was Marr's dodenzinn? Did he have one? If Kadailin were to die there would be no one affected. Perhaps Marr was the same.

"I could rest," Cien said. "That would be easy." He sounded so sure, so cold. "I was almost willing to do it out in the sand. I was more willing to do it in that cage. It's living for them after all this—for whichever one I'm living for—that's so difficult. Living so they can finish whatever it is they need to do. That's the hard part now."

Ryten nodded. Kadailin looked between the two devoshai. They seemed to have found something that united them, something they shared.

"I thought it was Tchardin," Cien said. "I want it to be only Tchardin, but is that just because she was first? If I had found myself drawn to Damarin before Tchardin would I feel differently about her plans? Would it be me instead of Ruon who stood beside her?"

Ryten knelt next to him. "It wouldn't be you. It would have been me long before it was you."

"And would I stand beside her or would I go to Ovaeron to stop her?" He looked to Ryten. "What would you do?"

The two devoshai stared at each other. It was a mutual confusion Kadailin knew no other kandar could understand.

"Damarin is wrong," she said, drawing their eyes to her. "So choose Tchardin and live."

"But we don't know," Ryten said. "We can't just choose."

"Why not?" Kadailin asked. "Damarin is right about one thing at least. Derkra is changing. If you truly don't know which it is, choose the future queen and help her. Choose the Purpose."

There was silence as her words washed over them. When had this become possible? How did dodenzinn discuss ending their own lives to hurt their other half? Kadailin looked back to the mountain. A third of its base was now buried in shattered rock or smooth, solid fire. A terrifying thought came to her.

"Sandin," she said. "She must be under all of that!"

"No," Cien said. "There, look."

Pandinzori still flowed from the mountain. It came from behind the edge of the fallen rocks and climbed the false Coralynth in a spiral.

"That must be her," Cien said.

Kadailin studied the origin of the pandinzori and compared it to the location of the cave she had flown to, the cave that was now just a jagged hole in the rock. She couldn't lose another sister. "We need to make sure she can get out!"

"Cien and I can do that," Ryten said. "You have to go to Calendrai. I'm useless there, as are Ocien and Torshe. You're a council member and the council needs to be called."

"Shift to Calendrai?" Kadailin asked in a daze.

"As soon as possible." Ryten looked down at Cien who stared at the false Coralynth. "If Ruon returns we'll deal with him."

"How?" Cien asked. "Ruon's a guardian. He's inherently stronger than we are."

"You're incredibly strong," Ryten said. "And the kandar are more likely to unite against Ruon than against Damarin. There are many of us now. Even more if Kadailin can get us the kandar of Calendrai's council and the rest of our people with them."

"Find Sandin first." Kadailin saw the sense in Ryten's words but she wanted her sister protected. She was going to have to leave. To shift on her own. "Find Sandin before you confront Ruon. Take her somewhere safe. She can't protect herself."

"I will," Ryten said.

"She'll be sleeping." Kadailin remembered Sandin's burst of pandinzori. "Be careful."

Ryten gave her a strange look. "What's so dangerous about sleep?"

"She used pandinzori on me. Somehow sleep has let her do that. Or the dreaming has. She thought I was Damarin. I'm worried about her." Kadailin looked at the ground. "Pandinzori is leaving her skin. So much of it. More than I've ever seen around any kandar who was called."

Ryten grimaced. He offered Cien a hand and hoisted the smaller devoshai to his feet. They must really have found an understanding if they were willing to tolerate the revulsion of touching. Kadailin didn't think she could touch Cien after what she'd seen. She was afraid of his power, and she worried he would go to Ovaeron and doom Tchardin with him.

It might be worth it for the effect on Damarin, but they couldn't be sure what would happen. The kandar needed Tchardin. Jaydin would have emphasised that.

'Don't let him rest,' she added, only for Ryten's mind. He nodded in acknowledgement.

She turned away from them to open the shift. It formed easily for her now and immediately showed her Tith. She sighed. Her father beckoned her from the other side of the ice, but she knew what she had to cross to get there, and it worried her. All of her previous experiences with it had been terrifying. She let his image fade to grey and took one last look at her devoshai companions and the mountain that held her sleeping sister. Then she reached out to the ice.

***

Clouds of light flowed across the desert. Voices whispered in Sandin's mind, beyond hearing. She strained her eyes and thought she could see Black Valley in the distance, with the peak of the false Coralynth hanging above. Nothing changed when she walked towards it.

So this was a dream. This was the thing Damarin wanted the kandar to have. What would it give to the kandar to dream? It didn't seem like much, but now Sandin knew the clouds of light were pandinzori, and she could see them. That had to be worth something.

She continued to walk towards the mountain but made no progress. At the same time, she couldn't wake up. There had to be something she could do here, in the dream, while she waited for Kadailin to return to her and wake her. She strained to make out the false Coralynth. She didn't just want to see it; she wanted to go to it. And she was there.

The abrupt change in location unsettled her. The hazy darkness of the cave in Black Valley obscured her vision again. The world outside the dream shook violently. Sandin remembered how Kadailin had shaken her awake the first time, but this shaking wasn't caused by Kadailin. She looked through her waking eyes and saw that the cave was empty. Rocks came loose from the walls and fell, or were held up by the vines and flowers. She was waking again, but this time she didn't want to. She focused on the mountain ahead of her in her dream, hazy and fading, the false Coralynth, as out of place as it had been in reality, but different somehow.

The dizziness of waking abated and she was firmly in the Black Valley of her dream. The mountain had changed. It was no longer tall and perfect. A great rent had been carved in its side and the rocks that had occupied that space had fallen to lie at its base. She wondered if the rest of Black Valley had changed. Turning, she examined it. The rest of the valley was still beautiful. Ovaeron's red leaves were brilliant in the light and his nine hundred children stood yellow and white against the sand.

The false Coralynth was ugly and wrong in the desert valley. Its blackness was not like the blackness of Ovaeron's trunk, though both were twisted and jagged. The red it held was not the red of leaves, but of fire, something that should never have come to Derkra. Light covered it, almost as much as surrounded the great tree, but it seemed to come from the mountain's base and not from its height, as it did around Ovaeron.

The light was pandinzori. Sandin wondered if it really looked like that in the waking world. Was this what the other kandar would see in her cave? When Sandin only saw the darkness and the faint light from the valley?

She'd watched Damarin and Ruon make the mountain, but all she'd seen was the blackness and fire coming up from the earth. It must have been magnificent, to see the light bring it up. But now that it was here, could the light take it away?

Sandin didn't know how the other kandar manipulated pandinzori. It was just something they did, something she had known she would never be able to do, something she had never asked about. Looking at the light, at the way it flowed through the air, it reminded her of the shift. She did know how to control the water.

She became the light. The disconnect she felt from her body in the dream was like the disconnect she felt from her waking self in the cave. The part of her that was pandinzori rendered in light was free and could do anything. Just like in the shift, Sandin felt powerful beyond measure. She flowed over the mountain and tried to force it down, back into the earth, but found she was limited in one thing. Her dream body vibrated as if struck and the rock didn't move. Her waking mind lay under it and she couldn't bring it down on herself. The mountain would not go back to where it had come from, so instead she sought to change it.

As she flowed over the mountain—massive, seeing her body standing below from all possible perspectives, seeing herself sleeping inside the cave—Sandin felt its shape against her. She felt its colour and its composition. The mountain was dark and the valley was light. So Sandin brushed away the dark rock and smoothed it. She brought the vines out of the caves and the darkness and made the new surface live. She approached the summit of the mountain with an idea. She would cool the fire.

Something touched her skin. Sandin was drawn back into her dream body and she spun around, but there was nothing to be seen in the valley. She looked up at the mountain. The changes she had made were right for it, but it still burned. She felt the touch again, once on her shoulder and once on her face. Tiny points of pressure. She opened her eyes. She opened her waking eyes. A shadow crossed her vision.

There was a spider on the ground next to her in the cave. Sandin wasn't able to move her head to look, but it seemed many of the vines had fallen with the rocks when the cave shook. The spider must have been hiding behind them. It extended a barbed leg towards her face and she shivered internally as it climbed on top of her. Her vision blurred, her eyes closing.

She forced herself awake, forced herself to move. The spider was at her side now, tentatively tapping her ribs with two of its eight legs, testing. The image of the valley from her dream hovered over her and it was difficult to control the right body. She felt resistance as she tried to move her arm, close her fingers in a fist, but she did it. Her hand slid towards the spider slowly, haltingly. She watched it as if it belonged to someone else. When it rested beside the spider she let her fingers relax.

The spider's body and legs were like thin branches. It would be hard to hold onto if she could even move quickly enough to catch it. The spider put two legs on her chest and touched her with a third. The part of it she assumed to be its face dipped towards her skin. She moved her head slightly, noticing there was a wall near her with jagged black rock showing. She could try to crush the spider against it—red light came to her eyes—or drop it into the fire. Sandin readied herself. Just as the spider rested its third leg on her body she closed her fingers again, on two of its other legs.

She ripped it off her, feeling the barbs in its feet pull her skin where they'd gripped, and whipped it towards the exposed rock with all her strength. It connected with a crack and fell, crawled away slowly on four legs, the others that had hit the wall hanging limply. She dragged herself towards it, thankful her upper body was responding at last, and pushed it into the fire. A burst of steam rose as the spider sizzled and blackened and disappeared.

She lay on her back, out of danger, but she felt her strength leaving her. For a moment she saw the light of pandinzori swirling away. She knew it had to be there. She'd always known that, and because she could now feel it, it seemed impossible to miss. She reached for it, tried to hold it against her skin, clutched at it, but her efforts were wasted. It continued to flow away.

Voices spoke to her in the darkness, almost physical beside the pandinzori that dominated the air. They were like the whispers in her dream, but stronger. Real. They were strange, but at the same time she thought she recognised them. One of them sounded like Ryten. It came from somewhere just outside her vision.

But it wasn't like it always had been. Sandin scrambled up to rest against the leaves on the cave wall. She had to still be dreaming. Ryten's voice was in her mind. She must be creating it, alone in the darkness beside the red light of the fire. Alone in the cave. Her lids were still heavy, the world around her still slightly slowed. She must still be dreaming. Then she heard Cien.

'Do you think she did that to the mountain?' Cien's voice said.

'It seems impossible, but Kadailin said she touched pandinzori, and the pandinzori that wrapped around the mountain came from this cave. We can ask her.'

Sandin looked towards the cave entrance, towards Ryten's voice, although it didn't seem to have an exact source.

'Do you think she'll be asleep?' Ryten asked.

'She couldn't have done that asleep.' Cien's voice sounded unsure. Sandin thought she could hear it out loud now. "Could she?"

And they appeared to her in a burst of light, running through the cave towards her.

"Ryten." Her voice wavered. "Is this a dream?"

"It's not." He knelt before her. He gave Cien a worried look. *'Kadailin was right. Look at her aura.'*

"Were you bitten?" Cien asked. "Did a spider touch you?"

"I killed it. I pushed it into the fire."

'It must have bitten her,' Cien said. *'She looks like Miadra did.'*

"I can hear you," Sandin said. "I don't think it did. Where's Kadailin?"

'What if it bit her?' Ryten asked.

Cien looked away. *'We have to get her out of here.'*

"I'll take you to Kadailin," Ryten said.

Ryten lifted her. As he did she saw their auras collide for the first time. She felt no pulse to go with it, and she looked into the devoshai's eyes and saw genuine concern there.

"Yes," she said, "take me to the valley, to look upon the mountain."

Chapter 44

Damarin approached, her pandinzori beginning to join with Tchardin's. Now would be the time to do it. Now would be the time to shift away, but to where? Where could she go from here if she couldn't get back to Derkra?

Seeing Damarin, somehow strong and surrounded by pandinzori in this desolate place, Tchardin realised it didn't matter where she went. She had to get away. She reached for pandinzori with her mind, reached towards the seemingly infinite amount her sister brought with her, and found it all claimed. While there was pandinzori around Tchardin, her aura was nearly nothing now and she was too weak to wrest any of it from Damarin.

"So this is World Nine." Damarin stopped about ten steps away and scanned the horizon, her pandinzori held in a giant wall around her. "I was right to avoid it until now. I wouldn't have been ready."

Tchardin struggled to lift herself off the ice. Damarin watched her without emotion.

"Just as you are not ready. You've been to them all. What do you think of this?"

"It's—" Tchardin started but found her voice weak. She tried again. "It's terrible."

"No World Tree here. No Seed. Not even the Root of the World survives. This Earth is dead, with no hope of salvation." Damarin examined Tchardin. "No need to cover yourself like a human here."

Sharp pandinzori whipped across Tchardin. It tore at the clothes and shoes Aaron had given her. It tore at her skin. She pushed it away in time to protect most of her body but the clothes and shoes lay across the ice in shredded strips. She was once more covered by only shadows. The fight left her even more exhausted and she slumped down.

"That's better," Damarin said. "Now you look like kandar again."

"I've always been kandar."

"Yet you care nothing for your own people. Maybe it would have been better to leave you in your disguise. It more adequately defined your allegiance."

Damarin looked towards the grey line in the distance. Tchardin followed her gaze but didn't see anything other than grey and infinite ice.

"I care about the humans," Tchardin said, "as should you, but I care just as much about the kandar. I'm going to lead us back to the Purpose."

"The Purpose is a waste of our lives. The Earths are doomed with or without us. They're only holding us back."

"Why are you doing this? Saying these things? You could tell me that at least. Why throw me into the shift? Why not bring the kandar back if you could? The Purpose wouldn't be a waste of our time if we helped the humans be better." Tchardin focused on the grey line, so far away, and tried to see what Damarin was looking so intently at. There was nothing to be seen. "We could have saved this place."

"It was dead before we were born." Damarin turned back to her. "It's not even about the humans or the Earths. You must understand that by now. It's about the kandar. We could be so much more than we are. We could be so much more than the humans if we just let them go."

"But why? Why should we be more than them?"

"Because we're better. Jaydin's words taught me that, though she never meant them to. Seeing the humans and their Earths confirmed it." Damarin's thoughts were silent as she stared down at Tchardin. "I don't know why you've seen them so differently than I did. It could be that I came to them knowing what to expect from Jaydin's stories. Or it could be that I went first to World Seven, when you got to start at the beginning, from a place where humans were still mostly good. I can see why that would be easier."

"You went directly to World Seven after you threw me into the shift?" So she had gone to them out of order.

Damarin laughed. "Is that why you've been travelling them in order? You don't know how to control it?" She paced on the ice. "I'm not surprised you went to World One first—it seems to be the closest, whatever that means in the shift—but I didn't know why you went to World Two from there rather than returning to Derkra. Or why you continued."

Tchardin fought the weakness in her body. Damarin's pandinzori hung just out of her reach. The pandinzori Tchardin had access to seemed to be growing, but it wasn't enough. Not enough to shift. Not even enough to stand. Damarin knelt beside her.

"I travelled to World Seven for the first time long before we left for Black Valley. I rediscovered the shift just after you were born, by accident." Damarin smiled and shook her head. "What would Jaydin have thought if she knew the shift was found by accident?"

Tchardin's eyes widened. "How?"

"I was doubting the Purpose and I needed to get away from Derkra. Pandinzori came to me when I called and I opened the air." Damarin's thoughts buzzed now, her leaf blazing in the collective. Tchardin reached for them but could hear nothing. "When I finally decided to attempt an Earth, Rai's glass leaves drew me to him. I met Siltadon then, for the first time. I've visited her many times since and explored the rest of the worlds. All save this one. I've seen the same things everywhere."

"I can't believe you've been using the shift since my birth. Why did you make us cross Water Side to find Black Valley?"

"I didn't know there would be kandar there. I hoped, but I wasn't sure. It would have been too much of a risk to shift into nothing for nothing."

"We could have died on the water."

"I could have brought us back to Tith from the raft at any point if I needed to." Damarin leaned closer. She was eerily still, as was her pandinzori, and nothing on the ice moved at all while she spoke.

"You want to know why I'm doing this?" she asked. "The humans destroy everything that's given to them. Jaydin's history made that plain. Is that what Creator meant them to be? Is that what It meant us to dedicate our lives to? It never made sense to me. Then Siltadon saw the beginning of an Earth. Two humans—made by Creator—built the rest of their race from the ruin of their old world and they only made themselves worse. They are not truly Creator's children, as we are. Nine hundred kandar, made at the beginning of time, never to change. To guard and to guide and to help. The humans owe their flawed nature to no one but themselves."

That wasn't the way Tchardin had taken Siltadon's words. The humans were magnificent in how they created themselves. The kandar weren't capable of it. "Siltadon's lost her mind."

"Yes," Damarin said. "She probably has. But she speaks the truth when she speaks of the humans. She really loved them once. Jaydin was right about that."

"How could you not tell Jaydin you found a way to the Earths? You know that's all she ever wanted."

"I wish I could have been the first to show Jaydin an Earth." Damarin met her eyes. "But that has been done, and now she is gone."

"Gone where?"

"Gone. Dead."

Tchardin focused inwards to look at the collective before she remembered there would be nothing there. Damarin's leaf shone alone. The desolation hurt Tchardin. "She can't be."

"It happened on World Seven, of all places." Damarin frowned. "I still have her leaf too. It will remain to haunt me forever, a ghost in the collective."

"Why didn't you show her?" Tchardin demanded. She refused to believe what her sister said. "When you found the shift, why didn't you take her back with you? You could have discovered the Earths together. None of this had to happen!"

"It was too late by then." Damarin stood and turned her back on Tchardin. Shadows wrapped her closely. "You know, I was made High Seat just before you were born. Jaydin was finally starting to accept that I might be able to help our people in a real way. She was against it at first, but she was coming around. Jaydin was always smart, if stubborn." Damarin laughed mirthlessly. "She was smiling when the old High Seat gave me her title, waiting to speak with me about what we could do with the power. Then Tith called us to witness a birth. She chose her side when she abandoned me in my moment of triumph, and later—alone at the edge of the island—I opened the shift for the first time."

Tchardin knew which birth Damarin was talking about. "Jaydin wasn't there when I was born."

"I guess we'll never know where she went." Damarin turned back towards Tchardin. Emotion showed on her face for the first time. "Did she ever tell you her purpose? What she believed it to be?"

Tchardin fought the feeling that her middle sister was telling the truth, that the oldest of them—the one who knew everything—was gone. "The Purpose was her purpose, more than for any of us."

"It was, but she always believed she was meant for something else. Something special, something more. Everyone knows Tith told her the history of our people, but he also told her he would give a child to Derkra, a tevadra who would change things. Jaydin thought her great knowledge was gifted to her so she could guide this tevadra on her path. She thought Tith was referring to you. 'Tchar-din'. Named for the first of us. A queen—the first queen since before the war—to change things for our people. To bring the kandar back to how they used to be."

Tchardin hadn't heard any of this before. Had Jaydin's secondary purpose been told to anyone else? Damarin's aggressive tone startled her out of her thoughts.

"Tith was talking about me, Tchardin. How could he not be? And I knew. I knew the first time Jaydin mentioned it that he was referring to me. Long before I discovered the Earths, long before you were born I knew, and she refused to see it. When she told me all the things he told her I knew I was supposed to see the wrongness in them. Tith wanted me to change things, not back to how they once were, but to something completely different." She sighed, looking back at the grey line again. "I waited too long to tell Jaydin that."

Tchardin felt pandinzori growing around her. With Damarin's eyes elsewhere she tried to move it. It was free, hers to command. She let it go, let it lay flat against her as if it were only her aura. The pandinzori around Damarin was still inaccessible.

"Why didn't you tell her?" Tchardin asked.

"I wanted her to see it first. I never wanted to be queen. I hadn't thought of the possibility until you were born. But even before you came to us I'd always wanted to lead, and I wanted Jaydin to support me. We argued constantly, but I would never have come to the conclusions I have without that. If we could only have agreed on one thing, we could have done great things for our people. Together."

Jaydin's knowledge had already guided Damarin to do great things. Their middle sister had become High Seat in Calendrai. She had rediscovered the Earths after generations without them. What else could she have done with Jaydin on her side? But Tchardin also knew the kandar were meant to guide humanity. A focus on themselves would be against Creator's wish, against the whole point of their creation. Jaydin would never have united with Damarin in a way that meant the kandar left the humans behind. An idea came to Tchardin and she stared at Damarin in horror.

Her sister stared back, meeting her eyes without a flicker of emotion. "I know what you're thinking. I had nothing to do with her death. We were set against each other in some ways, but I still wanted her to join me."

It would have been difficult for Damarin to push Jaydin away from the centre of things, but not impossible. It was more than that. Jaydin's support meant something to Damarin. "You needed her to."

Damarin tilted her head slightly in acquiescence. "I was willing to wait for her to understand, but I knew she would never accept that the golden aura was wrong. If *you* had joined me we could have convinced her. I tried to talk to you, to make you see that our world was changing around us, but like the rest of the kandar you were incapable of meaningful conversation. You needed that trip to Black Valley to escape the dullness a life in Calendrai had created in you. So I brought you with me. But still, you didn't see, and I couldn't wait. So I sent you away."

So it *had* been on purpose. Damarin had known what she was doing when she sent Tchardin through the spinning grey to come out on the first human Earth. "You threw me onto the Earths because you wanted me to join you?"

"It also gained me time. I thought if I let you wander the Earths—let you blunder through situations Jaydin's words could never have prepared you to face—not only would you become more interesting, but it would give me time alone on Derkra to change things. I could improve things for our people and set them on the right path without you getting in the way. I hoped you would come to agree with me, but I also knew that if you did not—if you failed in the face of the challenges presented by the humans—you might lose the golden aura. It has wavered before, and who could be more deserving to replace you? What better way to prove I should rule than to present myself as queen with you, alive and changed, beside me?"

"It's stayed with me from birth," Tchardin protested.

"On Derkra," Damarin replied, "where you only had to wait. Wait until quarter life for the kandar to acknowledge you. What could have changed, in such a sterile environment? Here you have been tested."

"And I still have it."

"You do. It perplexes me."

"Maybe you're not what the kandar need. Maybe Tith *was* talking about me as Jaydin suspected. He gave me the aura—"

"But that was my test," Damarin interrupted. "The beginning of change..." Her thoughts were loud but obscure in the collective. "Everything I've done has been for the kandar. You only care about the humans and before that you only cared about yourself."

Tchardin remembered Laurence's words about human selfishness. He had exempted the kandar from it but maybe he shouldn't have. "Humans are the Purpose. We exist to help them."

Damarin let out a burst of laughter, but the sound held no amusement. "Jaydin taught you well."

Tchardin fought a wave of sadness. She couldn't believe Jaydin was gone. She wasn't sure she'd ever believe it when she still had her sister's dark leaf in the collective. Pandinzori swirled around her.

"You can stay here a little longer," Damarin said. "If the golden aura is a thing of the Purpose, then it's no longer necessary. It only represents the past. To rule without it would be change. To make the kandar listen, to make them care without it..." she trailed off. "The desolation of World Nine may finally achieve what the other worlds could not. If you lose the aura I'll have my proof. If you don't, I'll change Derkra without it."

"Damarin—" Tchardin started, but her sister would not be stopped.

"And maybe some time here will finally convince you I'm right. Look at what remains when humans have come and gone. They did this to themselves, just as they have done on all the other Earths. Creator didn't make them like that. They grew out of themselves and they grew wrong."

Tchardin looked at the bleakness that surrounded them. Humans had done this because they lacked guidance from the kandar.

"No!" Damarin shouted. "Even with our guidance they still came to this. How much of the damage was done before we lost them? World Seven never lacked guidance from the kandar and it had to be restarted."

Damarin turned slightly and opened the shift.

"I'm going back to Black Valley to learn how to dream, then I will make Derkra into a place at once like no human Earth and like the greatest of them. It will be beautiful and complex and full of kandar instead of humans."

Tchardin searched the pandinzori that coated her with her mind. She needed to get back to Derkra to warn them. Damarin wasn't just usurping her place as queen of the kandar, she was trying to change the whole landscape of existence. The humans would doom themselves and the kandar would focus inwards on their own lives as they let it happen. To think of all those brilliant minds disappearing forever. Tchardin had only met a few but it had been enough. She couldn't let it happen. If Damarin was planning on shifting from World Nine to Black Valley it had to be possible. Tchardin had to be able to do it as well.

She was weak. Her pandinzori had grown, but it was barely enough. If she could open the shift before her sister left World Nine, she could use some of Damarin's pandinzori to bolster her own. She pulled at the pandinzori around her with all her strength and focused on sifting some away from Damarin. It formed into a spinning circle of grey. The movement made Damarin turn back to look at her.

"So you can leave," Damarin said, her eyes wide. "Barely, but still I've underestimated you."

Tchardin had her hand on the ice by that time. Damarin was a few steps away from her own entrance to the shift.

"I could destroy you easily in the shift, you know," Damarin said.

They stood like that for a moment longer, each poised to enter the violent water. Then Damarin turned away once more. Her expression was pained, as if something gnawed at her thoughts.

"Impossible," she said, looking off to the grey line in the distance. "There's something out there–"

Tchardin broke the ice with her fist and was pulled into the shift.

The water was surprisingly calm. Tchardin floated through it wrapped in thin ice. She could barely move. She was weaker than she'd ever been when the water took her. It was funny that it might finally claim her once she'd learned to protect herself from it.

A tremor ran through her, as if something beat against the surface of the water. But in the shift the water had no surface. She looked around her, not turning her head, but using the curious ubiquitous gaze of the water to help her see. Damarin was nowhere in sight. The water was smooth and calm between the beats. Forever.

The pulsing continued. The film of ice around her weakened with each tremor but there was nowhere to go. She searched for a way out, knowing she wasn't strong enough to handle the water should her bubble break, but even that slight struggle cost her.

There was nothing near enough to hold onto, nowhere to break through the shift and escape. The continued pulsing threatened to shatter the ice and let the water in. Tchardin closed her eyes, summoned the last of her strength, and thought of Tith. When she opened her eyes she saw leaves, just at the edge of her vision, but she also saw that a crack had formed in the ice, white against the blue, and a single bead of water blossomed before her eyes.

The bubble burst and the water rushed in. Her weakened body dissolved and she began to forget who she was, worried she would lose sight of her goal. She had to make it to Derkra. She had to get back to her people. But the water rushed. It rushed forwards and sideways and filled all the space. It wanted to expand, to grow, to dilute. It raged, and Tchardin raged with it, until she was so thin she ceased to exist, and then there was only water.

The water spread, and when it had achieved its own goal, it was calm.

PART V

CHAPTER 45

A BODY RAN UP against something. Only one part of the water understood the sensation. That part was kandar. The feeling came to Tchardin behind her mind where she was still solid. It happened again. She opened her eyes to blue darkness.

She crashed through ice and strong arms gripped her. The water seethed and tried to pull her back with it but she was held still as it receded. She found herself pressed against the chest of a tall white devoshai. He was a giant, taller than Ryten and broad like Cotelle. Nothing appeared in her mind to go with him. The devoshai looked down at her and his face showed more emotion in that moment than most kandar ever did. He appeared to be just as shocked as she was.

"Why would you go in there?" His voice echoed strangely. "It will take everything you are."

"What will?" Damarin and World Nine were gone, but the ice remained. It surrounded them, so smooth and clear it seemed they stood in a tunnel of glass. Tchardin couldn't see any pandinzori but didn't feel the loss.

"The water between the worlds," the devoshai clarified.

"We're in the shift?"

He nodded. How could she still be in the shift? She had thought herself lost. Taken by the water one last time. The devoshai must know the shift very well to create such a large structure within it. She noticed there were cracks in the ice above them.

"You broke me out of it!" The water had dissolved her, destroyed her until she wasn't whole anymore. "How did you see me?"

"It is only your mind that the water takes. Your body remains. It came up against the ice and I thought you might still be alive. So I got you out."

Tchardin pushed off his chest. There was no discomfort from his aura. To be close to him was the same as being close to a human or a guardian. Or to Cien. Or Ryten. The devoshai frowned when she left him.

"Be more careful in the future," he said. "There are only so many of you."

He turned and walked away. Tchardin watched him for a moment, still in shock about her situation, then she ran after him.

"You're Dani," she said in awe. One of the first kandar. The second only after Tchar, born before the guardians of the nine Earths and before the nine hundred. How had she not known right away? It should have been obvious. Who else would know the shift so well and have no place in the collective? He nodded, accepting her naming of him.

She looked down the tunnel in the direction he was headed, excitement mounting. "Does that lead to Coralynth?"

"Of course."

Tchardin turned and walked backwards with him for a moment, trying to sense what lay at the opposite end of the tunnel. "And that to Derkra."

"Yes."

She continued to walk with him, unsure of what to say. No kandar had been to Coralynth since Carrensing brought them to Calendrai. She now stood with Dani facing a path to Coralynth. She might get to meet Tchar. He stopped.

"Why did you not come straight through?" he asked.

Tchardin's eyes widened. Surely he knew the shift was blocked—

"Blocked?"

They stared at each other for a moment, the great devoshai's thoughts silent.

"Must be Tchar," he mused.

"You don't know?" Tchardin was incredulous. "Don't you know what's going on? Haven't you been watching?"

Dani shrugged. "Tchar watches."

His expression grew sullen. This was more than Tchardin could take. Dani didn't even know the kandar were barred from the Earths. How could he have missed it? Generations had passed. He walked ahead of her with his shoulders hunched slightly and his head bowed. He reminded her of Ryten in that moment and she wondered what could cause the second kandar to act that way. Maybe Damarin had a point. Maybe he didn't care. The path continued in front of them as if without end.

"Do you know how to get out?" he asked.

Tchardin shook her head.

"I do not understand how the kandar could forget the shift."

"We've been barred from it! It's not our fault we—"

There was no pandinzori in the ice, but all of a sudden there was an image of the path on Coralynth in front of them. It filled the tunnel from edge to edge.

"You have to pass through the water to get out of the tunnel," Dani said when she grew silent. He gestured towards the image. "There is no more than a curtain of it. It will not harm you if you are quick."

"Just go right through?"

He nodded. "We can go together if you prefer."

She hesitated. Dani was one of the first. Tchardin wasn't sure his impression of the shift would be the same as hers. He said it wasn't dangerous, but the shift was the most dangerous place she had ever been. It was worse than World Seven. Maybe worse than World Nine.

"That is because you have been using it incorrectly. Come."

He held out his hand and Tchardin took it, hers disappearing in his massive grip. They stepped towards the image together and Tchardin shivered as the ice approached. She remembered being torn apart, dissolved into nothing, but she believed the second kandar would protect her. Dani broke the ice in front of them with an outstretched palm and the water enclosed them, and retreated. They stepped out seamlessly onto the path.

The path. It was only a slight depression in the snow but it would lead Tchardin to Tchar or to any of the nine Earths. She turned and behind them was an image of Ovaeron. His bright red leaves were a comforting sight. Dark kandar gathered at his base. Tchardin moved back towards the image. Dani stopped her with a large hand placed gently on her shoulder. He turned her around.

"Coralynth," he said.

She looked up this time instead of down. The path stretched over a hill and disappeared. The perpetually open portals to each of the other worlds hung to either side of it. Images of the World Trees stood to her right and left. Dani gestured for her to look farther. There were two great mountain peaks in the distance, hanging above the swirling snow. They appeared to be suspended over the path, their bases obscured by white. The pit would be in the valley at the end of this path. Would Tchar be there too?

"She is there," Dani said. "You may go to her."

Tchardin walked forward, then turned, looking back at the image of Ovaeron. The dark kandar at his base confused her. Were they kandar of Black Valley, only darkened in shadow? Or could they be kandar of Calendrai, with a natural darkness of skin? Dani stepped in front of her.

"Tchar would speak with you."

Tchardin turned around again. What would the first kandar say? Tchardin would ask her why the kandar had been abandoned, why she had closed Coralynth to them. She could finally answer a question the kandar had been asking themselves since they lost the Purpose.

She walked past the nine portals to the Earths. She saw Karel of World one, enormous and straight-trunked, the Symbol red at his base. Miran, the many-trunked yellow tree of World Two. Zemko, with his bare branches, his roots deep under snow that mirrored that on Coralynth. Tairasyn, dark and reaching in the black forest of World Four. Tiny Irah and dying Veradon. When she passed the shift to World Seven she stopped. Rai was gone. There was a dark hole in the earth where he'd once stood. She remembered what Damarin had said about Jaydin. That Siltadon had killed her.

"You must speak with Tchar," Dani said. "She has things for you to do."

The Purpose. Tchardin was on Coralynth to accept the Purpose of the kandar from great Tchar. She would go back to Derkra—and back to Damarin wherever she was—with word from the queen of existence that the Earths were to be theirs again.

She pulled herself away from the shift to World Seven, shielding her eyes from those of World Eight and World Nine. She slowed as she passed the last. Was Damarin still on World Nine? Or had she shifted to Derkra to continue with her plan? Tchardin turned to ask Dani if he knew but he was gone. In his place was a view of the mountain. She was drawn towards it, cresting the hill to look into a valley at its base. There she saw the pit. It was a large black circle set amongst snowy stones. Steam rose from its surface. A tevadra stood looking into it.

The tevadra was Tchar. Her red hair—the colour of Ovaeron's ruby leaves—was bright against the snow and her white body faded into it. Her skin was the colour her father's trunk had been before he bore her. From her vantage point on the hill Tchardin could also see more of the mountain. It wasn't obscured by snow but by steam. The cloud of steam moved steadily across the mountain and at times Tchardin saw the fire that created it, streaking down the white slope.

A great echoing voice entered her mind. *'It was made for me.'*

Tchardin descended the hill until she was level with the first kandar. She walked towards the pit. It was frightening up close; it appeared not to be water but black stone, yet it seemed to be translucent, empty all the way into infinity. The depth must be immense. The surface looked like glass.

"The pit was made for you?" she asked.

"Yes," Tchar answered, "and the mountain. Coralynth. All of it. For me and by me. Before."

Tchardin struggled to take in the vastness of the place. There had to be a lot she couldn't see. The depression they stood in was surrounded by hills, and past that she could only see the peaks. Coralynth was like Cens. No one knew how big it really was or what exactly it contained.

"When you were human?"

Tchar nodded. Tchardin looked into the pit. She saw only blackness but Tchar studied it as if there was something else to see.

"You did not leave me much time," Tchar said, still looking into the pit. "If you had waited a moment longer until Damarin was in the shift I may not have been able to stop her. The water between the worlds can be unpredictable, even for me."

The darkness of the pit grew cloudy. Tchardin found she couldn't look away.

"You stopped her?" she asked absently.

"I did."

"Why?"

"World Nine needs a guardian."

Tchardin raised her eyebrows in disbelief, finally freeing her gaze from the changing pool. "Damarin would never guard a human Earth."

"I do not intend to keep the part of her that makes her Damarin."

Tchar looked up from the pit and met Tchardin's gaze with the deep black of her own eyes. The darkness Cien had first mentioned the two tevadra shared.

"Yes," Tchar said. "Your eyes were an interesting choice on Tith's part."

She looked down into the pit again and Tchardin was compelled to do the same. The translucent blackness became cloudy immediately when she did so, then slowly it grew as white as the snow around them and Tchardin saw a figure.

"You have to go back," Tchar said.

The figure was dark against the white, the severe contrast making it difficult to discern any detail. Tchardin's eyes adjusted to the image and she knew the whiteness was ice. The figure was Damarin.

"To World Nine?"

"Damarin must die if she is to become guardian, and without you on World Nine she never will."

The image moved in on her sister. Damarin was seated on the ice, her eyes closed. Pandinzori spiralled off her and into the sky.

"Why should I want her to die?" Tchardin asked.

"If she does not die she will remain herself. What would happen to Derkra if she returned when those of you who know her, who oppose her, are all gone? When there is no tevadra with a golden aura to stand in her way?"

"But you've stopped her," Tchardin said, confused. "You wouldn't let her—"

Damarin opened her eyes in the image. Tchardin was struck silent by the cold intensity she saw there. Her sister stood and looked straight up into the sky. The image disappeared. Tchardin found Tchar staring at her.

"The shift should not remain closed for long," the first of the kandar said. "Existence would not like it. World Nine does not like it now. There are things that need to pass through the water between the worlds. Things that even the kandar do not fully understand."

"But you've blocked it for generations—"

"I blocked only the pre-existing paths. World Nine is completely separate from the rest of existence now. That is different."

So that was why the kandar could still access the shift. Why Damarin had been able to rediscover the Earths, and why Tchardin had never before seen the tunnel of ice Dani said was the true shift. In her mind she could still see Damarin seated in the desolation of World Nine, still see the look in her eyes when she had opened them. Tchar turned back to the pit, but this time it remained dark for Tchardin when she tried to follow. She wondered what else the great tevadra saw there. Was she watching Damarin now? What would her sister do with that cold look and all that pandinzori?

"Damarin will destroy us if you free her," Tchardin said.

"You can stop that from happening if you do as I say. I do not hold Damarin on World Nine to protect the kandar. I expect you to do that yourselves." Tchardin was about to protest but Tchar raised a hand to forestall her. "To me, Damarin is simply a step back. The kandar have come far since Carrensing brought you to Calendrai, but not far enough. You never will. Not while remaining on the island. Things may take longer if I free her, but existence will find a way to right itself eventually."

"Why then? If not for us?"

"I hold her because I desire World Nine to have a guardian, as I said. You must help me achieve that. I cannot kill her myself."

How could the great one expect Tchardin to kill Damarin if she wasn't able to do so herself? Could her sister have possibly become so powerful?

"Existence would tear itself apart if I killed one of the kandar," Tchar said. "Just as you were made to guide the humans, so I was made to guide you."

"But we can kill humans. Kordic even told me to kill them if things went wrong."

Tchar frowned. "Yes, you can, and sometimes it is necessary. But they can still fight you. They can overcome you if they must. They have done so in the past, and likely will again."

Tchardin took this to mean the kandar could never stand against Tchar. If the first kandar was set against them they would be destroyed. That made her wonder about the guardians.

"Siltadon—"

"Siltadon is not the one you have to worry about right now."

Tchardin looked into the pit and saw the desert.

"Land Side," Tchar said, her voice showing emotion where before there had been none. She sounded surprised.

The image showed the vastness outside Black Valley. A dark devoshai stood between two dunes in the sand. There was pandinzori around him as there had been around Damarin, though they both stood in desolation. Tchardin gasped. It was Ruon. She turned to Tchar and saw in the first kandar's face a look that confirmed everything she'd worried about the guardian of World Four. Ruon had followed Damarin to Derkra.

"What about Ruon? If we can't stand against you, can we stand against a guardian?"

Tchar shrugged. "That is yet to be seen."

"But you would leave us to it?"

"He is no true threat. He merely wishes to change the kandar. Make them in his image. In that he will never succeed."

"That's what Damarin wants."

"No." Tchar's black eyes pierced through her. "That is not what Damarin wants."

Tchardin held the first kandar's gaze. What *did* Damarin want? She wanted what the humans had, but she wanted the kandar to have it.

Tchar nodded. "Unlike Ruon—who wishes to change the kandar and who *will* fail in that—Damarin wishes to change Derkra. But Derkra keeps you what you are. It is the only thing that can truly change the kandar. Change Derkra and you change its people."

"She would succeed?"

"She might. If you let her."

Tchardin felt trapped. The first kandar wanted to use her and there didn't seem to be any way around it. Tchar smiled.

"So you see, the only way we can both get what we want is if you kill her on World Nine."

"Why me? If you thought I was capable of killing her you should have left me on World Nine in the first place. Why bring me here at all?"

"I did not bring you here. You will remember that Dani broke you out of the shift."

Tchardin frowned.

"You owe me," Tchar said. "Both of you do. Damarin will become one of my guardians. There is something else I need from you."

Tchardin turned away. She no longer felt overawed by the queen of existence. She would be a queen too, and she clearly cared more about her people than this one did. Tchar didn't intend for the kandar to be sent back to the Earths. Tchardin had come to Coralynth by accident and Dani had saved her and admitted her because he didn't know any better. The only thing Tchar had done was stop Damarin, but even that was tied to ulterior motives. Tchardin's respect for the tevadra diminished.

"How do we owe you?" she asked.

"You may not remember your previous lives, but I do."

"What else do you want?"

The first kandar seemed to sense her changed perspective, or hear it in Tchardin's thoughts. Her eyes hardened. "You have the golden aura. The kandar will listen to you. Call them home to Black Valley."

"Why?"

"If the kandar do not return to Land Side and rest, they will never return to the Earths."

"If the kandar on Land Side follow Damarin I can't bring those from Calendrai to meet them. They'll kill each other."

"They will not," Tchar said. "They cannot. They do not know what that means. There were only two kandar on Derkra who truly knew what war was. One of them has lost her leaf. Damarin may think she knows it but only Ruon remains. Wait too long and he may teach it on a scale the kandar have never seen."

Tchardin was definitely being used, and not in a way that seemed to benefit her or her people. Perhaps Damarin had been right about Tchar and Dani. Her sister was wrong about the humans, but the kandar of Coralynth were not what Tchardin thought they should be. She was glad Jaydin had never gotten to meet this creature. Tchar watched her, expressionless.

"Why did you exile us?" Tchardin asked.

"That does not concern you."

"It does. I am kandar and even more than that I will be their queen. How can we fulfill the Purpose if we can't reach the Earths?"

"The kandar are not fit to fulfill the Purpose as they are now. They have not been fit since the kandaran war, since long before it in truth. They need to return to the place they were made, in the valley, at Ovaeron's base, and they need to remain there."

Tchardin felt a thrill of excitement. It was possible to bring her people back to the Earths with Tchar's help. "You'll reopen Coralynth to us if I bring the kandar together again?"

"They need to rest, all at once. When all the kandar are back in Black Valley and each has found peace with their father, I will reopen Coralynth and access to the Earths from it."

Tchardin's excitement faded. If Tchar got her way the kandar of this generation would never visit the Earths. Jaydin would never have seen them if she hadn't gone to World Seven to die. What would it be like to return from Coralynth only to tell her sisters they must rest and leave the Purpose to those they would become? It was sad. It was disappointing. Tchardin looked back towards the hill that hid the path. She was so close to home now.

"You must all rest," Tchar continued, "but before you can join the others Damarin must die on World Nine."

Tchardin ignored the repetition. "How did Dani not know about this after all this time? How did he not notice you had barred us from our Purpose?"

Tchar actually smiled at that. A faint smile—just a slight turn of the lips—that would have fit on the face of any human.

"Time moves differently for us here, more slowly than it does on Derkra for you. Sometimes it does not move at all. You have sat in Calendrai and done nothing for near two hundred human years by World One's standard and you did not realise how long it had been. Dani has done nothing for close to five thousand by World Seven's. When nothing around us changes, that is but an instant." She looked back up the hill and Tchardin followed her eyes. Dani had reappeared there. "He does not remember the years because they did not exist for him. I watch. I have seen the years pass on the Earths, seen the generations live and rest on Derkra. I have waited here alone for so long."

"With Dani."

"On occasion."

Tchardin wasn't sure how to feel about this new side she saw in Tchar. This seemingly human side. She'd always expected that a creature so old and so grand must be very different from herself, but she was still surprised at the first of the kandar. It was almost wrong to call her kandar at all. Maybe the manipulative side had been human too. Tchardin was reminded of Laurence's words. Tchar wanted something. Many things, it seemed. Could she really be kandar? Tchar's smile disappeared.

"How will I kill Damarin?" Tchardin asked. "She's so much stronger than I am."

"That should not matter, but you should know you are stronger than you think."

Tchardin turned away from the tevadra and the mountain. Dani waited at the top of the hill, at the beginning of the path, to escort her to Derkra. She didn't know what she would do, but she did know she wanted to see her home and her people again. Tchar's voice followed her as she walked away.

"Right a very old wrong, Tchardin. Bring your people home, then go to World Nine and kill your sister."

"And if I don't?" Tchardin asked, looking back one last time.

Tchar shrugged. "My answer is the same. You will do this for me, but you must also do it for yourself. I can wait forever if I have to. You know the humans cannot."

Chapter 46

Kadailin stood on Tith's largest, straightest branch and faced the parallel branch from Sirrhon that would house the council. Shadows hung there, waiting to be called to kandaran forms as they assembled. She hadn't seen anyone around as she climbed Tith. Cens must have drawn a lot of them back in.

She looked down at the edge of the forest. It bristled with leaves and branches. Cens was full and whole again. It made her happy. It would have made Jaydin very happy. The body at Tith's base would have dampened the effect. No one had found a place for Moradi yet.

Kadailin had been waiting to call the council because she wasn't sure exactly what to say. Speaking to the kandar was Jaydin and Damarin's strength, not hers, and the council still frightened her. But Marr wouldn't come when called and Damarin's leaf was dark. The majority of the problems the council had given her stemmed from those two. Still, she wished Jaydin was here to address them, for more than one reason.

Kadailin opened her mind to the collective and scanned it. She came to a red leaf, a council member, and mentally pressured it. The leaf vibrated and sent shivers down its branch and through the rest. Kadailin grimly noted the empty space where Jaydin's leaf had been when the vibrations travelled past it. She stepped onto Sirrhon's branch and the shadows came to her. Others slowly joined.

'Kadailin,' a tevadra said. Her name was Siv. *'Do you know what has become of Tchardin and the High Seat?'*

Kadailin nodded. *'When everyone is assembled.'*

The council members filtered in, waiting on the smaller branches that extended from the great one.

'Where is Jaydin?' a voice floated out of the group.

'Where are the kandar who sleep? They leave a hole in the collective.'

'Where is Damarin?'

'Tchardin?'

Kadailin didn't like that Tchardin's name had come last, but she did feel some hope that Jaydin's had been first.

'Where is the Voice?'

Marr. Kadailin pushed an image of the obliterated cave out of her mind and waited. She wouldn't answer until the full council was present.

'I need all of you first.'

The council buzzed with thoughts. Minds reached out to others, those that weren't present. Why had they not come? How were they not interested? Kadailin needed them all. Those who were absent began to appear. She looked at the collective again as one last red leaf grew bright. The voices rose in question and she silenced them with her words.

'Jaydin is dead.' Loud thoughts buzzed. *'Marr as well.'*

'How?' came the voices.

'We would have lost their leaves.'

Kadailin had to strain her mindvoice to be heard over them. *'Jaydin died on an Earth. On World Seven.'* The collective erupted in thoughts of disbelief. *'Marr died on Land Side. Ryten has brought the sleeping kandar of Calendrai to Black Valley—'*

'How can these things have happened?' Kadailin recognised the mindvoice that interrupted her. A devoshai pushed through the shadows to stand in the centre of the crowd. It was Anatoly, son of Ahron. *'How are the Earths accessible to us when we did not know? How did Marr die? How is Jaydin gone?'*

Kadailin met his eyes. *'Damarin is changing things.'*

'What has she done?'

'She brought rendinzori to Derkra. Grew a mountain out of the sand on Land Side. Summoned a guardian from his Earth.'

The thoughts were angry now. All kandar knew a guardian didn't belong on Derkra.

'Damarin held the Shadow of Black Valley far out in the desert and then confined him to a glass cage in her fire mountain,' Kadailin said. *'Ryten and I freed him while our people watched from Ovaeron's base.'*

Anatoly's eyes widened. *'That is unbelievable.'*

'The guardian helps her. She wants to rule the kandar.'

'Does she want to be queen?' someone asked.

'But where is Tchardin?' Another voice.

'Damarin could never take the future queen's place.'

'Tchardin doesn't care. She has been called for acknowledgement twice and has not come.'

Kadailin tried to calm them but their thoughts quickly grew out of control. Some accused the future queen. Some defended her. Some exclaimed their disbelief of everything Kadailin had said. Others praised her for saving Cien. The council shadow reverberated with their thoughts. Kadailin wasn't sure how to get them to stop.

'Council.'

The word was faint but something about the voice struck Kadailin and made it clear over the roar of the rest. She didn't need to search the collective to know who spoke. She turned back to Tith and saw Tchardin standing in such a flurry of pandinzori she was almost obscured. She wasn't alone either. Kandar stood behind her in Tith's branches and their eyes weren't on the shadow. They remained fixed on their future queen. The council slowly turned around Kadailin, their mindvoices quieting. They must have seen the golden aura, then they all turned back—silent—to look at Kadailin.

'Who will address her?' someone asked.

Kadailin hadn't considered that. She was too much in awe of her sister who appeared to have completely changed. The tevadra before them would never have run from Damarin and Marr as they spoke scathing words to her from the shadows of the council. The look on her face made that clear. She was ready to stand in front of them now. But they were gone.

'The High Seat is not here.'

'Nor the Voice.'

'The Voice is dead.'

'Kadailin?'

Kadailin did need to talk to Tchardin, but not in this capacity. The council members closest to her looked at her expectantly. She met their eyes in turn. *'Can you accept her as queen?'*

The council was quiet.

'Look at her aura. She is your queen. You would have acknowledged her before.'

A few voices stirred.

'Her aura is gold.'

'Where has she been?'

'She has been called twice and not come.'

'Look how she draws pandonzori to her.'

Kadailin didn't hear any outright renouncement.

'In Damarin's absence,' she said, *'and in the absence of the Voice, I will address her.'*

Before any could protest that she might need a Voice herself given her close relationship with the future queen, Kadailin started. She didn't expect Tchardin to recognise her. The tevadra who stood before them now was not the one who had disappeared after the fire. Kadailin hoped the council could see that.

'Tchardin.'

Tchardin's gaze quested through the shadowed bodies and landed right on her. Kadailin's eyes widened. Did her sister somehow know who spoke?

'Why do the kandar of Calendrai remain here when there are kandar in Black Valley, separated from us for so long?' Tchardin asked.

'They await the word of the council, which we were about to decide.'

Tchardin's eyes hardened. *'About to? This is the first you've spoken of it? We must go to them now. If Derkra unifies fewer lives will be lost in what comes.'*

Voices in the council repeated her words behind Kadailin. *'What comes?'* they asked. Tchardin wouldn't hear them but Kadailin felt it necessary to enlighten them before they became too difficult to direct. She turned back to them, remembering Jaydin's fears.

'It could be war,' she said.

'Why?' Anatoly asked.

'There are kandar in Black Valley who believe Damarin is right in attempting to change our world.'

'And the queen disagrees?'

Kadailin silently thanked Anatoly for referring to Tchardin as queen, but she wasn't surprised he did. He had long been one of Jaydin's greatest allies in the council. Kadailin contemplated his question. If Tchardin thought lives would be lost it had to be war and it had to mean she would be on one side of it and their middle sister on the other. Kadailin turned back to Tchardin, who waited unmoving on the branch.

'War?' Kadailin asked.

'I don't think so.'

That surprised Kadailin. A few of the council members close to her made sounds of surprise as well. If not war, then what?

'Not war,' Tchardin continued. *'Not so bad as that. But conflict between the kandar. Damarin proposes we abandon the Purpose and there are those in Black Valley who support her. The quicker we react to this threat, to this division, the less likely it is to create great loss. We must unite.'*

'And leave our fathers?' a voice called out.

That one had come from behind Tchardin, from one of the kandar in the branches around her. Tchardin turned to face those kandar.

'It must be done. At least for now.' They weren't happy to hear that. Kadailin worried Tchardin would lose their support. *'I have word from Tchar that as long as the kandar remain in Calendrai we will not enter Coralynth.'*

The kandar outside the shadow were quiet in their shock but the council reacted with thought. From the look on Tchardin's face she could hear their mindvoices buzzing. The shadow failed to drown the council out.

'You spoke to Tchar?' Kadailin tried to keep the disbelief from her mindvoice. Where had Tchardin been for all that time? On Coralynth?

'I first visited the nine human Earths and then I went to Coralynth. There I met Tchar.' Tchardin was assured and still. *'Damarin is wrong. The Purpose is still our purpose. We have only failed so heartily that Tchar won't let us return to it at this time.'*

Kadailin heard something in her sister's voice then, something she had heard before. It seemed her sister wasn't telling them everything. She wasn't sure which part of Tchardin's words to doubt.

'Nothing has changed,' Tchardin continued. *'What Damarin attempts to lead the kandar to is contrary to all that we are.'*

Again it seemed like she was hiding something. Kadailin glanced at the other members of the council but saw no recognition of that fact on their faces. She heard nothing of it in their thoughts. She watched her sister on the branch.

***

Tchardin was certain she was talking to Kadailin. It was easy to hear where the voice originated in the mass of shadows and something about it was familiar. That made her feel like smiling. Everything else made it easy not to. When she had arrived in Calendrai she'd noticed there were leaves missing from the collective. Many leaves. Ryten was gone with them. Had the kandar left Calendrai to travel to Land Side? Maybe she had seen them through the shift on Coralynth—the dark kandar under Ovaeron's canopy. Did they go to support Damarin or to fight her?

Then there was Tchar. Tchardin would use the first kandar's name to rally her people, to convince them to leave the island and return to Black Valley, but she was undecided about what to do with them once they arrived. Damarin's followers, if she had them, would need to be dealt with. The guardian too, if he remained on Derkra. But to have them all rest? Tchardin didn't know if she could ask them to do that.

At least Kadailin remained. She'd be able to tell Tchardin what had happened to Ryten and a large group of her people. They could discuss what to do about Tchar and the Purpose. Tchardin wished more than anything that Jaydin was around to help with the decision.

As Voice, Kadailin's mindvoice was amplified. It was imposing. *'What do you propose to the council?'*

'I propose that all kandar in Calendrai take the shift to Black Valley. I do not yet propose the move be permanent.'

The council hummed with thoughts. Her words had created quite an uproar. She had to remind herself that the kandar here wouldn't be used to the idea of the shift yet, when she had travelled to each of the Earths and fought the raging water between them.

'We will call a vote.'

Tchardin felt the nudge along the obscured collective, fuzzy and undefined so close to the council shadow.

'But first, we will acknowledge you.'

The nudge was insistent. It radiated outwards from Tchardin's leaf. It was a strong suggestion from the council to meet with them but any kandar who saw it would know what it really meant. Many had gathered in Tith's branches while she spoke, before the call went out, but Tchardin still wondered how many kandar would come.

They poured in. She'd underestimated the interest they had in acknowledging a queen. She didn't know how many had come before, or if the numbers had changed between the first and second time she'd been called, but this time they all seemed to come. The collective was unclear, but it was bright, bursting into blaring light as the kandar surrounded her. Would it be enough? Could the kandar that remained acknowledge her in the absence of the rest?

'Part of the collective remains dark,' Kadailin said, as if addressing Tchardin's thoughts, *'but they are not gone from us forever. We will hear those who are here for now and we will hear the rest when they can be asked. Do you, the kandar of Calendrai, acknowledge your queen?'*

Mindvoices rose loud behind her. There was no dissent. Tchardin thought she saw the gold of her aura before her for the first time as the voices coalesced in agreement. Then it was done. She closed her eyes. Acknowledged queen of the kandar at last.

Now to see if it would change anything.

'That is enough,' Kadailin said from behind the shadow. Her voice was loud and clear and it stopped the kandar in their exultations. *'Queen Tchardin,'* she said, and all eyes lay on Tchardin for a moment before she continued. *'Now we must vote. Queen Tchardin proposes that all the kandar of Calendrai who remain here take the shift to Black Valley. There are kandar there who have been separated from us for as long as we have been lost to the Earths. But there is also a conflict. We will face it together if you agree.'*

The voices were more hesitant this time. They hadn't seen the shift yet. Some of them hadn't even known it was found.

'It will be dangerous,' Kadailin continued. *'Not just on Land Side, but the journey as well. The shift is—'* she paused.

Tchardin realised she had to speak before the kandar were dissuaded. There was something she could do to make the journey easier. *'The shift is safe. I learned of it from Tchar and Dani on Coralynth. It's meant to simply be a walk through the water between the worlds, just as it always had been before.'*

The voices of the kandar around Tchardin became more positive at the mention of Tchar and Dani. The council shadow was quiet. Kadailin must be processing that information and discussing it with the rest of the council. Her sister knew the shift was dangerous. She wouldn't know what Tchardin had experienced when Dani saved her.

'I can make it so again,' she added.

'Then you must,' Kadailin answered. *'The shift will be safe. We don't know what we will face on Land Side, but it is our home. Ovaeron is there, and many of our people—'*

She was trying to sway the kandar. The mindvoices around Tchardin told her it was working. Kadailin didn't get a chance to finish before they agreed. Despite its amplification, Kadailin's voice became inaudible over the excitement of the kandar. They thought of Ovaeron, and of the desert, and the valley. They thought of the shift and the Purpose—that which Tchardin had implied they would regain if they went back to Land Side. There was nothing to do but wait until the tide of voices subsided.

When it finally did, Kadailin spoke again. *'It is decided. If Queen Tchardin can make the shift safe for us, we will go.'*

Tchardin turned away from the council to look at her people. They cheered her in their minds and began to move away into the leaves to let the council disband, their thoughts slowly fading with distance.

Tchardin dropped from Tith's trunk to the ground. She felt different, but she expected that had less to do with being acknowledged queen and more to do with the choices she now had to make for her people. The grass of the clearing comforted her. She was back in her home. She walked towards the edge of Cens.

She needed to meet Kadailin to discuss what had taken place while she'd been gone. She hadn't wanted to let on that she knew who she was talking with in the council. She also had to figure out how to make the shift safe. She must be able to build an ice tunnel for the kandar to use, but she wasn't sure exactly how to do it yet.

Tchardin walked towards the place she and Damarin had visited many times before the fire, the place where she had felt Cien and Black Valley calling to her. She looked towards the section of the forest that had been a charred strip of black the last time she saw it and saw trees instead. Thick, green, and shadowed. If she were to create an ice path, the water's edge would be a good place to start.

It was interesting being back on Calendrai. Derkra seemed simpler now than Tchardin had once thought. There were no subtleties to the light as there were on the Earths. The air didn't move. The colours and visual details seemed to be lesser. The kandar were all the same. Their thoughts were dull and uniform when compared to the thoughts of humans. How much would change if she brought them back to the Earths?

Kadailin caught up to her just as she was about to enter the forest. Her sister smiled, but now Tchardin recognised the smile as the lifeless thing it was. Kadailin's expression was no more nuanced than that of any of the other kandar. Tchardin had never noticed how blank their faces were.

They walked through the first set of trees together and the shadows closed in around them.

"Where have you been?" Kadailin asked.

Tchardin almost laughed at the absurdity of the question. "There isn't time to tell it all now. There may never be time for everything I've seen."

Kadailin waited expectantly.

"After the fire," Tchardin said, remembering, "Damarin sent me through the shift. Just pushed me into it without warning. It nearly consumed me, but somehow I found leaves to grasp and I ended up on World One."

"The first human Earth," Kadailin whispered reverently.

"I went from world to world and met humans and guardians. I saw so much." Tchardin found herself caught up in images of the Earths. Even on Derkra she was drawn to the humans. She felt changed by them. Changed in a way none of the exiled kandar would understand. "I could never explain the things I saw to you. You'd have to see them yourself. I travelled until World Nine and from there I went to Coralynth. Dani was the one who brought me there. Damarin remains on World Nine—"

"You saw Damarin?"

"I saw her on World Four but she left before we could speak. She confronted me on World Eight and we went through the shift to World Nine together. Tchar is holding her there." Kadailin walked towards the water. Tchardin followed because Kadailin had always been better at finding her way in the forest. "The first of the kandar wants me to go back and kill her."

Kadailin's thoughts buzzed loudly but she didn't say anything. After a few moments of silence she finally spoke, but she didn't address what Tchardin had said.

"You have to be careful in here now. This is the new part of Cens, where the fire was, and you could walk in circles forever if you don't pay attention."

Tchardin was still in awe at the change. "How did you fix it?"

The forest had gone back to its original depth and strength from before the fire, but she saw differences too. Cens was not as welcoming as it once had been.

"Jaydin told us what to do. We had to—" Kadailin stopped speaking and walking at the same time.

Tchardin looked back at her and heard her horrified thoughts. "You had to kill them after all."

"Jaydin began it. A tevadra was called by a damaged tree and wanted to go to her father. Jaydin saved her, in a way. Torshe and Ocien helped Jaydin clear the trees while Ryten and I protected Sandin from Marr."

"You had to protect Sandin from another kandar?"

"That's not even the worst of what you missed. While we were trying to find Sandin the forest was healed. Jaydin said they never finished clearing the trees, but somehow it came back."

Tchardin had refused to order the kandar to kill the trees when Jaydin told her it was necessary. She should have known their oldest sister would be willing to back up her own words.

"Then Jaydin, Sandin, and I went to World Seven," Kadailin continued, her voice faltering.

Tchardin understood now. "And Jaydin died there."

"How did you know?"

"Damarin told me."

Kadailin looked away. "I don't think Jaydin would ever have believed a guardian would kill another kandar."

"Why did you go there?"

"We thought she could tell us about rendinzori. Cotelle said it killed Miadra, and that Damarin wanted the kandar to have it. He said she had gotten the idea from Siltadon. Of course Jaydin wanted to meet the tevadra who restarted a world. Even Sandin wanted to go. She thought she could learn to use rendinzori."

"Miadra's dead too? And where's Sandin now?" Tchardin still had Miadra's leaf. That reminded her of the empty spaces in the collective. "And Ryten? And all the rest of my people."

"On Land Side. Sandin and I went there when we returned from World Seven. Ryten arrived with his kandar shortly afterwards. Cien's there too. Damarin took him into the desert when you left, then she trapped him in glass."

Tchardin closed her eyes. An image of Ruon stood behind them, his fingers pushed through his glass cage.

"We're near the edge," Kadailin said, bringing Tchardin back to herself. "Can you really make the shift safe?"

"I've seen how it's supposed to be at least."

Kadailin stopped and stared at the dark forest in front of them. Tchardin saw no indication of it being the edge.

"I can't believe you've met Tchar and Dani. I can't believe you've seen all the Earths and met humans." Kadailin turned back to look at Tchardin. "Jaydin would be so proud."

Tchardin inadvertently searched the collective for their oldest sister's leaf before remembering it would be dark. "I still have her leaf."

"I lost it."

Tchardin couldn't help thinking that if things had stayed the way they were before she took the raft to Land Side, Kadailin might not have lost their sister's leaf unless Jaydin died right in front of her. They weren't close enough. They had barely known each other. It seemed Jaydin *may* have died right in front of Kadailin, but even that would never have happened. They hadn't spent any time together.

"How did you become the Voice? I was surprised to find it was you when I spoke to the council. Jaydin would be equally proud of that."

Kadailin smiled. "I'm not the Voice. There is no Voice. I just started talking. I didn't wait for anyone to object."

Tchardin laughed. Kadailin would never have done that before.

Her sister's face grew serious. "When you spoke of Tchar and Dani, I could tell something was wrong."

Tchardin had been working hard since she came to Derkra to hide her thoughts of the first two kandar, of Tchar in particular, but if she were going to tell anyone, it would be Kadailin.

"Humans were more than I could have expected. The Earths were indescribable. But Tchar and Dani were disappointing." She hesitated before continuing. "Once Damarin is gone, Tchar wants us to remain on Land Side. She wants every single kandar to go back to the nine hundred and rest before she'll allow us back on the Earths."

"All of us? Why?"

"I don't know." Tchardin decided to share the thing she had been contemplating since she left Coralynth. "I don't think we have to. I think we could do it ourselves. Build new pathways to the Earths, as I'm going to do between Calendrai and Black Valley. Ask the guardians how to fulfill the Purpose."

Kadailin said nothing.

"I wish Jaydin was here," Tchardin said. "She'd know what to do. I'm happy she got to see an Earth but I wanted to bring her back to them in truth."

Kadailin smiled sadly. "She saw an Earth and met a guardian. That's more than she believed she would get. And you're back safely. That's all she really wanted."

Tchardin had to focus on the tunnel she needed to build. Thinking about Jaydin wasn't helping. She turned away from Kadailin and was about to leave the trees when something on the ground caught her eye. Kadailin's gaze followed hers. It was Jaydin's notebook, partially covered in leaves.

"She left it?" Tchardin asked.

"I didn't know."

Tchardin knelt to pick up the notebook. "She told me she kept it for future generations of kandar, so we wouldn't repeat the mistakes of the past."

Kadailin looked over her shoulder. Tchardin opened the notebook. Tight scrawls of black writing filled the pages. She flipped through them. It was indecipherable.

"Can you?" she asked Kadailin. Her sister shook her head. Tchardin handed the notebook to her.

"I'm going to try to build the path now. Will you bring that to the three brothers for me?"

"And do what with it?"

"Lay it in the council shadow. We'll come back for it when all this is done. Maybe there is a kandar among us who can read it."

Kadailin nodded and slipped into the forest behind her. Tchardin took the last step and found herself alone at the water. She looked over it and felt as if she had never left the island. This was the stretch of shore she had spent so much of her early life on, staring towards Land Side. She and Damarin had left this place on the raft. In truth Damarin had left and Tchardin had rushed to catch up. What if she had let her sister go alone?

Tchardin had needed to go. She had been called too strongly. She felt it now. Even if Kadailin hadn't told her, she would know Cien and Ryten were there. Their leaves had been dark in the collective for so long. It was time to feel the strength of them again.

Tchardin opened the shift easily. It had taken intense concentration before, when Cien first taught her to shift. They had thought Miadra taught Damarin at the same time. Now Tchardin knew more about the shift than any living kandar on Derkra. Perhaps she knew it better than Damarin. An image of Ovaeron's deep red leaves filled the ice in front of her. They seemed darker somehow, as if they harboured shadows that didn't belong on Land Side. She let the image fade to grey.

A hand-span from the ice, she broke it with her mind. The water rushed forward but this time she pushed through it, into it, and put up the bubble of ice around her. She emerged from the water, suspended in a sheath of ice between the worlds.

She moved towards her destination until she saw the tips of Ovaeron's leaves. A moment later she found herself suspended over the great tree in her ice bubble and could exit, but she hadn't left a lasting impression on the shift. She turned in the bubble. Tith's leaves beckoned to her an indistinct distance away in the clarity of the water. She had to extend the ice towards him, create a tunnel like the one Dani had brought her into on the way to Coralynth. She pushed towards Tith with her shoulder. The ice cracked but she willed it not to break. She kept pushing. It cracked further.

She had to make it safe. She stepped back in the bubble and pushed with her mind. The wall of ice extended and ran in a tunnel towards Tith's leaves. It impacted something before it reached them. A network of jagged lines appeared in the clear water. Cracks in ice. The water moved around them and Tchardin was thrown forward.

She picked herself up, expecting to find herself standing on grass, but instead she stood on ice. She hadn't left the shift. She'd been thrown into an existing tunnel. Behind her the tunnel she had been creating extended from the one she found herself in. This must be the old path.

Tchar had said she blocked only the pre-existing paths in the shift, leaving the water between the worlds free to move as it wished. Tchardin had found one of those old paths. It was possible to create new paths, and to access the old ones.

She returned to her new tunnel and closed the connection to the old one with ice. Then she broke the ice wall in the direction of Tith to continue. She pushed towards his leaves and this time she made it there, stopping just as they connected.

Calm descended and she found herself standing in the perfectly formed tunnel. She enjoyed the quiet for a moment. She'd missed the collective while she was on the Earths, but she'd forgotten how loud it could be. When she had gotten enough tranquillity from the tunnel she brought a sheet of ice up in front of her, just as Dani had done to take them to Coralynth. Tith's trunk showed in it. Kandar milled at his base. She broke the ice.

The water fell away and Tchardin stepped onto the grass of the clearing, the collective immediately growing bright.

'Queen Tchardin!'

Mindvoices came to her. Kandar flooded in around her.

'Have you done it?'

'Is it safe?'

'Do we go?'

The thoughts crushed her. She hadn't had so many individual thoughts in her mind since she walked out of the forest with Aaron on World Eight and the human voices assaulted her. The voices around the council had been many but they were united. Here they fought each other.

Something touched her shoulder, the pulse of revulsion from another kandar's aura allowing her to focus on pushing the thoughts out of her mind. She looked up.

"Did it work?" Kadailin asked.

'I think so.' Kadailin removed her hand with a slight flinch. That thought had been for her mind only. Tchardin didn't want the rest of the kandar to know she doubted. "Will you try it with me?"

Kadailin nodded without hesitation. At least she understood the need to look confident in front of the kandar.

'I'm not faking it,' Kadailin said. *'I really believe you've done it.'*

Tchardin laughed. *'When did you get to be as bad as Damarin?'*

'Never as bad as Damarin,' her sister responded, but she laughed as well.

Tchardin opened the shift and brought up Ovaeron's image. The kandar that crowded them mostly became silent, looking upon his ruby leaves for the first time. A few of them panicked as they thought they saw glass instead of ice but their thoughts quickly calmed as the collective reassured them. Tchardin reached out for her sister's hand—as Dani had asked for hers—and broke the barrier. Water rushed outward and swallowed them. A moment later they stood in the ice tunnel. Kadailin dropped to her knees.

"I can't believe this is the shift." Kadailin's voice echoed down the tunnel. It looked to go on forever, as the one to Coralynth had.

Tchardin was pleased to see it had worked. She was reminded again of the possibilities. Could she build these to each of the Earths? Would Tchar block them?

"Do you think this is how Carrensing did it?" Kadailin asked with awe in her voice.

"I certainly hope so," Tchardin answered. "No kandar should ever have to travel it as we have again. This is how we'll return to the Purpose."

Chapter 47

Tchardin stared up into Ovaeron's branches. The great tree was as magnificent as ever after all she had seen. There was something special about him that no other tree had. Not the World Trees of the human Earths, the fathers of guardians. Not even Tith.

Kadailin stood with her as the kandar of Calendrai spilled out of the shift behind them onto the sand. The dim leaves of the missing kandar had grown bright when Tchardin stepped into the valley but the rest from Calendrai had faded. As the kandar came out of the shift the lights returned and slowly the collective began to look right.

"Something's happened to the mountain since I left," Kadailin said.

Tchardin turned to find the city changed. A mass of yellow rock rose from the edge of the valley. It was wreathed in green. Her mouth dropped open.

"It used to be black and burnt," Kadailin added. "I don't know how it came to be like this."

"Damarin made it?"

"She and Ruon pulled it from the earth together. A fire mountain. Damarin named it Coralynth."

Damarin wanted to change Derkra, just as Tchar had said. The mountain was nothing like the true Coralynth. Tchardin couldn't decide if that was good or bad for the kandar. The question was probably irrelevant since it was likely there to stay.

"I have to find Cien and Ryten," she said.

"They might still be looking for Sandin. Come, to the mountain."

Before Kadailin could leave Tchardin noticed two kandar standing in the valley. One was light and one was dark. Pandinzori seemed to fly from them. Cien and Ryten.

"Why isn't Sandin with them?" Kadailin asked, noticing them too. "They should have found her by now."

Tchardin was surprised at the concern in Kadailin's voice. When she'd left Derkra Kadailin had barely known Sandin. Now she sounded worried for their flawed sister.

Cien moved to the side and it became clear there was another aura between the two devoshai. "She's there," Tchardin said. "Lying in the sand."

Kadailin ran towards them and Tchardin followed. She felt a surge of strength as Cien and Ryten's leaves grew in brightness in the collective. The two devoshai turned towards her but Tchardin's gaze was drawn to the tevadra on the ground.

Sandin's eyes were on the mountain. Pandinzori grew from her and spun around the devoshai. It floated loosely above her skin when it left. Tchardin was struck with the image. Sandin looked like a human with her pandinzori like that.

Kadailin ran to their sister and knelt at her side. Tchardin followed.

'She must be called,' Ryten said. The first thing he had said to Tchardin since before the fire in Cens.

"But I'm not," Sandin replied.

Kadailin gasped. Tchardin raised her eyebrows. Sandin had answered Ryten's words. The words he had sent through the collective to Tchardin's mind.

"You heard him?" Tchardin asked.

Sandin propped herself up and tried to turn. The pandinzori of her aura didn't follow her. Movement was obviously difficult for her, so Tchardin went to her knees on Sandin's other side, facing Kadailin.

"I did," Sandin said. "I'm not called. You'd think I would hear Tith if I can hear the collective."

"Then what..." Tchardin watched pandinzori leave Sandin's skin. She stopped because she realised her sister couldn't see it.

"Actually," Cien said, "she *can* see it."

Sandin looked Tchardin in the eyes. "Losing it makes me weak."

Tchardin had to look away. She found Cien and Ryten standing together behind Kadailin.

'How did this happen?' she directed at them. *'She's too young for this.'*

Ryten stared helplessly back at her but didn't answer. Cien frowned. Tchardin noticed for the first time how much of the pandinzori swirling from the two of them was concentrated around him. It seemed mostly to flow from Sandin and Cien.

'I think she was bitten by a spider,' Cien said. *'She insists she wasn't.'*

'A spider?'

'One of the stick creatures Damarin brought to Derkra. They look like tangles of brown or black branches. Miadra was bitten by many of them and died immediately.'

Miadra had died. Sandin said she wasn't called. Tchardin looked down at her sister again. Pandinzori left her. That would kill a kandar, with or without a tree to take her body.

"I changed the false Coralynth," Sandin said. Tchardin followed her gaze to the mountain. "It used to be black and sharp and burnt, and now it's..."

The mountain was lightly coloured. It blended with the sand at its base and darkened as it rose from it. There was fire on it—near the summit—but it didn't appear burnt. Strange bands of green twisted across it. They were not grass, but leaves. Vines covered in leaves.

"I would have done more—" Sandin continued.

"How?" Tchardin asked. "How did you do it?"

"Damarin said I wasn't kandar."

"You *are* kandar," Kadailin said forcefully. "Just as much as any of us are."

Sandin smiled weakly. "Yes, and it's finally being proven. I changed the mountain in a dream and only humans dream, but now..." Her gaze flitted around her, seeming to follow the pandinzori that came off her and didn't return. "This wouldn't happen to a human."

"I knew she was hurting you," Kadailin said.

Again Tchardin was struck by the depth of feeling in the words. Kadailin's eyes hadn't left Sandin.

"I am kandar," Sandin said. "Damarin wanted to use me because she thought I could be more, but there's no avoiding what it's done to me." She looked up at Kadailin and Tchardin, past them to Ryten and Cien. "When I die, none of you will feel anything."

"I will," Kadailin said at the same time Tchardin thought it.

"Didn't you feel when Jaydin died?" Tchardin asked instead.

"I did. I still do. But it wasn't like the loss of a leaf from the collective. Or I don't believe so, from what I saw happen to Kadailin." Sandin's body seemed to shiver and her voice grew urgent. "Don't bring me to Tith when I die. Give me to the shift. I don't belong to the trees. Tith has never been a true father to me. I don't hear him calling. I don't believe I have a dodenzinn and Jaydin is gone forever, never to be reborn. Why should I be?"

The shift? Tchardin looked to Kadailin. The request made no sense.

'You should have seen her in the shift,' Kadailin said. *'Her mind is so powerful.'*

Tchardin had missed a lot. She looked down at Sandin and met her eyes.

"You'll stop her, won't you?" Sandin asked. "Damarin?"

Return to World Nine. That was all Tchar had said she had to do. The rest would come. "I'll try."

Tchardin studied the second oldest of Tith's daughters, now lying flat on her back, barely moving. Sandin's face was the first she had seen when she was born. Sandin's leaf, if she had one, would have been Tchardin's first leaf. The silent kandar—the one with no mindvoice and no place in the collective—was the only one to somehow answer Tith's call to witness the birth of the last of his daughters. The one who would be queen. The one who *was* queen.

Sandin smiled. "I was there because of Jaydin."

"I always wondered why you came."

"She wanted to go to Tith so badly, but I could see that another disappointment"—Sandin paused, looking up at Kadailin, but Kadailin only laughed quietly—"she couldn't handle it anymore. So I went instead and brought you to her."

Tchardin frowned. "Damarin was being named High Seat at the same time. She told me Jaydin left."

Sandin nodded weakly, the movement barely perceptible. "I don't know what happened when she left the council, but I was waiting for her when she came down from the shadow. She was distressed. She didn't like leaving Damarin. I think she always regretted it, just as she regretted not going to you. Tith picked the most difficult time to bring you out onto the earth."

"I wonder if things would have been different if she'd stayed with Damarin," Kadailin said.

Tchardin was sure they would be. She just didn't know how.

"Thank you for saving me," Sandin said to Kadailin.

"I wish I could have saved Jaydin too. I wish I could have stopped Damarin from putting you to sleep."

"I had a dream," Sandin said, her voice faltering. "I got to see pandinzori and I got to hear your mindvoices." She turned to Tchardin. "I can see your golden aura."

"I am finally the acknowledged queen of the kandar." Tchardin knew that would make Sandin happy even if only because it would have made Jaydin happy.

Sandin smiled. She turned to look at the mountain again. The pandinzori that came off her swirled away. Kadailin put a hand on her shoulder and Sandin's aura dispersed. Tchardin found herself waiting for a leaf to grow dark and fall, but there would be no leaf for Sandin.

'Find us when you're ready,' Cien said.

Tchardin felt a slight dampening of her strength and turned to see the two devoshai walking back to Ovaeron's trunk.

"It's just us now," Kadailin said.

For a moment Tchardin thought Kadailin meant to say they were finally alone, but she realised Kadailin meant they were the only remaining sisters.

"And Damarin," Tchardin added. But maybe not for long.

Kadailin smoothed a hand across Sandin's cheek, no aura to repel her touch. "I don't know what's worse. I didn't get to see Jaydin's body. She was just gone. I'm glad I never had to see her like this, but I also feel like she could join us at any moment. If her leaf hadn't fallen I'd never believe she was dead."

Tchardin nodded. Kandar weren't supposed to die like this. They were supposed to go to rest and their leaves were supposed to fall. Jaydin's body was gone, but Tchardin still had her leaf. A ghost in the collective, like Damarin had said. It would never leave her, but it would remain dark forever.

"Sandin didn't have a leaf," Kadailin continued. "If this had happened to her somewhere else we'd never know. This is proof she's gone, but her body is still here and I don't like seeing her this way."

Sandin's body looked almost the same as it had in life. But it looked empty somehow, as if something was missing. Its complete stillness was unnerving. Kandar would die when they lost their pandinzori, but they were supposed to go back to their father before that happened. To rest rather than die. They definitely weren't supposed to be so young.

"We should give her to the shift," Kadailin said. "Like she wanted."

"But why? What would that accomplish?"

"You didn't see her in the water. Or feel her, as I did."

Tchardin felt like her sister belonged in a tree. Belonged with Tith. "It can wait." Kadailin looked up at her. "It can wait until this is all over. We'll keep her body at Ovaeron's base until we have time to decide."

She could tell Kadailin didn't agree, but her sister didn't say anything. When she finally spoke it was of something else.

"You'll go back to World Nine soon."

Tchardin knew what Kadailin was thinking without having to listen to her thoughts. There were only three daughters of Tith left alive and one was marked for death by Tchar herself. But Tchardin also couldn't be sure she would succeed and Kadailin could be left on Derkra alone.

"I've been wondering," Kadailin said. "Why can't Tchar just do it herself? Why does she need you?"

"She's not allowed to kill us. Or, unable, somehow. She said she's meant to guide us, as we guide the humans." Tchardin left it unsaid that the kandar could kill humans if they had to. No reason to distress Kadailin further. "She said it has to be me."

"If you don't come back, I'll never know what happened."

"Maybe I shouldn't go."

"But you will go. The kandar have to return to the Purpose. We need Tchar on our side to do that."

It would be harder without Tchar, but it didn't seem impossible. Not anymore. "I think we can do it ourselves."

"But maybe we shouldn't."

That gave Tchardin pause. "I'll come back, but if I don't you have to take the kandar back to the Earths. With or without access to Coralynth."

"I wouldn't know what to do—"

"Build paths in the ice. Speak with Kordic, guardian of World Three, and learn to be your true selves again. Meet the humans. Find Aaron and

Bronson on World Eight, by the new World Tree Zalenth. Go to Irah and Irah on World Five."

Kadailin shook her head. "You'll come back."

"I will."

Tchardin looked towards Ovaeron. The kandar of Calendrai gathered there. All of them that were awake at this time in their history. There would be some left in the trees in Calendrai, but this had to be enough for Tchar for now. If she chose to obey the first of the kandar she could get the rest as they were born. If she chose not to, at least if the queen of existence was watching, it would look like she might.

"Kadailin," she said. "Find a Black Valley council member and tell them I've been acknowledged. Tell them Damarin is not coming back and that the Purpose will remain our only ambition." She noticed the one lightly-coloured devoshai in the mass of shadows. "Send Cien to me."

***

Cien was aware of Tchardin's presence from across the valley. Her leaf was brilliant in the collective, but it was more than that. The thing that had been missing from his early life on Land Side had been found when Tchardin and Damarin crossed Water Side to come to him. Then Tchardin had left him almost immediately. Now she had finally returned.

He got the sense it wouldn't last long. The two tevadra rose to stand above the body of their sister. Kadailin turned away from Tchardin and walked towards him at Ovaeron's base. Tchardin knelt by Sandin again.

It was hard to tell if Tchardin gave him more strength than Damarin did, or if he felt the same no matter which of the tevadra was near him. He hated Damarin for what she had done to him and what he had seen her do to Derkra, but he couldn't deny she affected him. She was his dodenzinn. Just as Tchardin was. Dodenzinn were meant to be together because they were two halves of a whole. The situation was no longer so simple, because there were more than two of them, but they still needed each other. Cien wondered if there was a way he could have both.

Kadailin joined him on the black sand. "Tchardin wants to speak with you."

She eyed the kandar closest to him before continuing, obviously judging they were far enough away not to hear. He stood slightly apart, his colouring marking him as different. Ryten stood away from him, encapsulated by his own people.

"I've called the Black Valley council to meet with me," she said.

Cien looked around at the hundreds of dark-skinned kandar and agreed that informing the council was prudent.

"Where was she?" he asked. "How did she return to us?"

"She was on the Earths."

"So Damarin managed to send her there after all."

Kadailin nodded. "Tchar helped her return in the end. The first kandar also trapped Damarin on World Nine."

If Tchar was getting involved things were serious. "What will happen here? Have the kandar of Calendrai come to stay?"

"They have. At least for now. Tchardin was acknowledged as their queen just before we arrived. I go to ask your council to do the same."

"They should agree, if you can convince them to accept her over Damarin."

Kadailin must have heard the question in his words or in his mind. "Damarin won't be coming back. Tchar wants Tchardin to kill her."

The finality of the statement shocked Cien. It seemed he wouldn't have both in this lifetime. He focused inwards for a moment and heard Ovaeron's call, still there, as it almost always had been. Perhaps there was still a chance for their future selves to be whole in the right way, when all of this was over.

"Even if Tchardin can't do it the fight will be on World Nine, not Derkra," Kadailin continued. "It's already over for us."

Cien watched Tchardin in the sand. The pandinzori that swirled around her couldn't match what Damarin held. Maybe he was doomed to spend all of time alone.

"She can't win," he said.

Kadailin was agitated. "Then I don't know what Tchar expects of her, but it doesn't matter. She's going and she wants to talk to you first."

The tevadra turned away and walked in the direction of the valley wall. The dark kandar in the dark sand watched her go and Cien couldn't help the thought that she should have hidden herself in some way, as she was clearly headed for the council's meeting place. Then he realised the kandar of Calendrai wouldn't know where it was. And did it really matter anymore? When so many rules had already been broken? The false Coralynth that towered over them was a plain enough sign that things had changed.

She was too far away before he thought to ask her if she knew what had happened to the council's Voice, Cotelle. The devoshai's leaf was dark, but there was a chance he had been on Calendrai. Cien wasn't sure whether the Voice would help or hurt Kadailin's cause if he still lived.

He walked towards Tchardin. Her back faced him as she knelt beside her sister. A slight shiver went through her when the pandinzori around the two of them merged.

"I'm not sure the spider killed her," she said, her eyes locked on Sandin's quiet form. He stopped beside her and similarly looked down. "Did you see the way pandinzori left her? Who's to say she wasn't called? I didn't feel Tith shake the collective, but he could have been asking her back to him. Without a way to reach her, how would she have known?"

"Maybe she would have heard him if he called," Cien said. "She heard us, so why not Tith? Even if she didn't hear him, she could still have died without being called. It's happened to kandar before." They all knew a kandar who lost pandinzori would die, with or without their father, but this was the first time Cien had seen it happen. "The spiders definitely killed Miadra, but Sandin could have escaped them."

"Then it was just this that killed her, like she said," Tchardin responded, gesturing to the pandinzori around them. "She had so much. It left her skin but there was always more. When I first saw her lying here I could have sworn she was a human from the way she looked. Dreaming must have done it to her." Tchardin looked up at Cien. "We also have too much pandinzori. I have more than most kandar I've seen here and you have more than Damarin."

"But I'm not weak. There must be a difference. There must be a reason hers left her while ours stays. I feel even stronger now that you're here."

"I won't be here for much longer," she said, confirming Kadailin's suspicion. "I have to go back to World Nine."

"To Damarin." She looked up at him in surprise. "I don't hear you so well. Kadailin told me what Tchar wants you to do, but I don't understand why she wants it. Why would she interfere with us after all this time?"

Tchardin scowled. "She says everything she does is for the Purpose and for existence. She admits it may not seem that way and it does not."

She didn't continue and Cien didn't push her. She was the queen of their people. The first of the kandar had spoken to her and told her what she needed to do. He didn't ask what she thought would happen if she killed her sister, the one who was also his dodenzinn. What it would do to him and to Ryten, and by extension to Tchardin herself. He left that to her to contemplate.

"From what Kadailin told me you have reason to hate her," Tchardin said.

Cien remembered the pain from the desert and the terror of glass. "I do."

"Do you want her to die?"

There was confusion on her face. She seemed sad.

"I thought I did. But we're supposed to be reborn." He thought of Marr and the fate that had befallen him. He thought of Miadra. Tchardin was silent, her thoughts buzzing just out of his reach.

"What about Ruon?" he asked. "His seed is gone and we don't know where he went, but he could return. Did Tchar say anything about him?"

"He's on Land Side, far away in the desert. I saw him there when I was on Coralynth. Tchar said he's the only kandar left on Derkra who truly knows what war is. She said he may choose to teach us of it."

Cien couldn't hide his alarm. He'd seen and felt Ruon's power many times and he'd been told exactly what the guardian wanted from the kandar on Derkra. Cien's pandinzori had grown and Ruon had told him rendinzori would come to him too, but he didn't want to test exactly how strong he'd become.

"Will Tchar help us?" he asked.

Tchardin actually laughed at the question. Her black eyes lifted to meet his for the first time since he'd joined her. "No," she said. "She won't."

***

Ryten stood near Ocien and Torshe while the two dodenzinn spoke silently together. He didn't join them even though their thoughts were loud, the invitation clear. He had too many things to consider.

Tchardin and Cien stood together with Sandin. Or with what was left of her. Ryten fought a sadness he didn't understand when he thought of her death. Watching the two kandar and seeing the one in the sand made him wonder about the future of dodenzinn. Ocien and Torshe had been sure, and all other kandar were supposed to be as well, but Ryten wasn't. Nor was Cien. Damarin had certainly been conflicted at one point. Whether she was any longer Ryten didn't know. Sandin hadn't seemed to have a dodenzinn—at least not obviously—nor had Jaydin. What did that mean for the kandar they would become? A kandar without a dodenzinn would be weak and solitary, but a kandar with more than one was dangerous. How had this change come about and what would it do when they'd returned to their fathers? Should they return to their fathers at all?

Kadailin walked towards him through the crowd of kandar. Her leaf in the collective glowed more strongly than he'd expected. Of all the sisters she was the one he knew the least. As usual he was struck by how much she looked like Damarin.

"What exactly is going on?" he asked as she approached, drawing her eyes to him. "How did Tchardin get back? Where's Damarin?"

Kadailin moved closer before speaking. Ocien and Torshe made space for her beside Ryten.

"Tchardin showed up on Calendrai while I was speaking with the council. She said she came from Coralynth and had spoken with Tchar. Damarin is on World Nine and will not be allowed to return to Derkra."

"Then it's over?" he asked, before realising the impact of Kadailin's words.

If Damarin was never allowed to return, he would never see her again. The last time he saw her was shortly after the fire in Cens. He hadn't expected to ever interact with Damarin the same way he once had, but he'd at least expected to see her. To resolve his memories of her with what she had done since. Kadailin's expression showed she'd heard his thoughts.

"It's worse than that. The conflict is over, yes—I just spoke with the council of Black Valley, and while some of them are still unsure about the Purpose, they have no leader without Damarin. Jaydin was right when she said the kandar don't care enough. Without Damarin—without even Miadra or Cotelle—they'll do whatever Tchardin wants them to do simply because they can't think of anything else."

"How can that be worse?"

Kadailin looked away for a moment, looked to Tchardin and Cien in the valley. "The conflict may be over for us, but Damarin will have to die. And Tchardin will have to kill her."

She was right. Somehow that was worse. Jaydin had predicted war, had expected the kandar might fight each other on a grander scale, but somehow Ryten found this smaller fight to be much more devastating. Ocien and Torshe listened to them, completely still. He opened his mouth to respond but felt something that stopped him. The collective had changed. A light had been lit in his mind. It wasn't a leaf.

***

Ryten and Kadailin broke free from the mass of kandar under Ovaeron and ran towards Tchardin where she stood with Cien.

"He's coming back," Cien said.

Tchardin's attention was drawn to the collective. Ruon's seed was lit.

"It's dim," Cien said as the two kandar joined them, "but it's brighter."

"I had hoped he left for good," Kadailin said.

"He remained on Derkra." Tchardin remembered she hadn't told her sister any more than necessary in her rush to get the kandar of Calendrai to Land Side. "I saw him in the desert. Tchar showed me in the pit."

"Maybe he'll be like the council," Ryten said. "Kadailin says they won't fight us with Damarin gone."

"They're aimless without Damarin and Miadra," her sister added.

"No," Cien said. "Ruon has his own purpose. He doesn't need Damarin."

The other three kandar scanned the valley wall for any sign of the guardian. His seed remained lit, but it didn't brighten.

Tchardin had seen the guardian's power only once, when he had killed the King of Arkaiyan on World Four, a world where they had their own power, where they used rendinzori directly. The image of Ruon confined in a cage there and the blackness of his thoughts were burned into her mind. Tchar said he remembered the war.

The kandar of Calendrai, her people, huddled under Ovaeron's branches. She looked to the nine hundred and saw the sand-coloured bodies of the Black Valley kandar, those who would be her people. They were newly united. Not yet united in truth.

"I have to stay," she said.

The other three stopped their searching.

"You can't," Cien said. "The kandar need the Purpose and for that we need Coralynth and Tchar. The first of the kandar asked you to return to World Nine. She'll let us go back to the Earths if you do as she says, right?"

Tchardin exchanged a look with Kadailin. Her sister was the only one who knew what Tchar had actually said. The first kandar had never promised to let the kandar go back if Tchardin killed Damarin on World Nine, but she *had* threatened to free their middle sister if Tchardin refused. Tchardin could stay on Derkra and attempt to help the kandar with Ruon, but what if she died doing it?

"You'll stand a better chance against Damarin," Cien said when she didn't answer. "Ruon is monstrously powerful."

"Like you," Kadailin said, her eyes on him.

Tchardin had to admit Cien had the most pandinzori of any kandar in the valley. Most of what surrounded the group belonged to him and more grew from him every moment, as it had from Sandin.

"If Tchar wants you to go to World Nine you should go," Ryten said.

"And you'll come back to us," Kadailin added.

Tchardin looked from one of them to another. "He might not come into the valley."

"He may never come into the valley," Cien agreed.

"You can fight together."

Kadailin and Ryten exchanged a look. Their expressions were worried.

"That's not as easy as you might think," Ryten said. "But there are so many of us it should be difficult for Ruon to overwhelm us if he comes, and we have Cien."

Tchardin looked down at Sandin's body. She could come back to much more devastation when she returned.

"Take Sandin to Ovaeron's trunk. We can decide what to do with her body when all of this is done. Be careful," she added.

She turned away to contemplate the shift. She wasn't sure how she would get back to World Nine. It was the only world she'd visited where she hadn't initiated her own exit from the shift. Coralynth was the same, but a kandar could see Coralynth from Derkra. They could see into and through the ice tunnel that led there. World Nine had no World Tree to search for in the infinite water. If that wasn't enough, Tchar had blocked it completely.

Tchardin opened the shift to Coralynth. *'Tchar.'* The first kandar hadn't been a part of the collective but she could hear if she wished to. Tchardin waited for a long moment. Ruon's seed threatened.

Tchar's image appeared in the shift. Kadailin and Ryten gasped behind Tchardin. Cien was silent. The first kandar stared out at them.

'I'm going to World Nine as you wished,' Tchardin said. *'I need the shift opened.'*

Tchar looked back at her for a moment, expressionless. Then the ice of the shift exploded and the water sucked Tchardin in.

Chapter 48

Tchardin was dragged through the water. It blasted her skin and made it clear she was whole. Tchar was sending her to World Nine. Could she make a path so she could return to Derkra when this was all over? A path the other kandar could travel if they wished to go to the Earth? Tchardin knew the shift now. She knew this part of the shift. She stopped herself.

The water froze around her and she stood suspended in a bubble of ice. She took a moment to appreciate the infinite clarity. If she could create a pathway the kandar might never have to look at this again, even if they didn't go through Coralynth to get to the Earths. The water pulled at her, tried to direct her, but Tchardin fought it. She thought of Ovaeron and moved towards the idea of his leaves. She left the ice behind her.

Red blossomed in the blue. She pushed the ice tunnel she was creating towards the leaves, letting it stop just shy of touching. She held it there—as she had done when she made the pathway between Tith and Ovaeron—and turned away, back in the direction Tchar had been taking her. She kept the ice in her mind, held the path open. The water bore her along until she crashed into open air. She braced herself for the feeling of desolation, for the lack of pandinzori, but as she hit the ground she felt no change. She landed on grass.

She stood, bewildered by the transformation, and found herself surrounded by trees. Despite its changed appearance the eerie sense of emptiness remained. The Earth might look different but it was still dead. There was no World Tree, nor Seed, nor Root. There was only this forest and pandinzori to keep her alive. The collective was as barren as the last time she was there. Only Damarin's leaf was lit.

Could this be what Damarin had done with the swirling mass of pandinzori Tchar had shown Tchardin in the pit? But these trees were real—not made of pandinzori. Kandar shouldn't be able to make trees like this, but Tchardin remembered Damarin saying they could.

She closed her eyes to better look at the collective. Damarin's leaf was dim but Tchardin could guess which direction to go based on it. She opened her eyes and looked through the trees towards her sister. There was white in the distance, between the leaves. It could be the ice. Her shock slowly left her. It seemed only part of the world had changed.

She opened the shift. The spinning grey waited before her. If she was right about the ice tunnel she should be able to see Ovaeron when she thought of travelling to Derkra. She closed her eyes, seeing the great tree's red leaves behind her lids. When she opened her eyes the image before her mirrored the one from her mind. The tunnel remained.

She closed the shift and moved through the forest in the direction of Damarin's leaf. The trees rose to either side of her and made her question where she truly was. They were real trees, with real pandinzori around them. The ground beneath her feet became hard and rocky as she walked. The trees grew sparser. Her eyes were drawn to one in particular.

Maybe kandar could create real trees. Siltadon said the humans did it using rendinzori. It was possible all the trees in this forest had been made by Damarin—if her sister had learned to use rendinzori as well as she wanted to—but this tree was definitely made by kandar. Made of pandinzori. Its trunk and branches and leaves were full of the lines of light Tchardin could take apart just by concentrating.

She backed away from it, into the shadow of the forest, into the thickness of the natural trees. She turned her head, so as not to look upon the uncanny leaves any longer, and saw another tree made the same. She wanted to run away from this change, back to the bleakness and nothing. Instead she ran towards her sister's leaf, through the thinning trees, encountering more and more of the abominations. The leaves on one of them brushed her as she ran and she shivered all over.

A shelf of grey rock spread out ahead and finally the trees disappeared in her wake. A great roar filled the air. There was pandinzori here. Living light burst into the open ahead of her, propelled upwards by something hidden. Then she recognised the sound as that of water falling, as it had when Ruon's earthquake brought a river into Castle Arkaiyan. She approached the source of the sound.

It *was* falling water. A waterfall so wide and violent it reminded Tchardin of the shift. The water was ubiquitous in her view, grey as the rock and jagged, moving downwards, onwards. The closer she got to it the more the water seemed to pull her mind down with it. There was no danger—she was surrounded by pandinzori that could be used to steady her in a moment—but the water's pull felt dangerous. Had Damarin created this too? Tchardin tore her gaze from it and looked across to the other side. It was slightly lower than the side she stood on. The ice lay beyond it. The grey line that had so occupied Damarin's attention could be seen farther in the distance. It was clearer now, more defined. It *was* a building.

The river that fed the great waterfall continued for as far as Tchardin could see. She'd have to cross it if she wanted to find her sister. She lifted herself in pandinzori and flew over the water. She looked down into the churning and rushing depths as she did, feeling the pull and resisting it. She held her body rigid, only relaxing when her feet touched the rock on the other side.

The grey rock ended where it sloped down and the ice began. There was no pandinzori on the ice. It was the same as it had been when Tchardin first came to World Nine with Damarin. Only one thing had changed. The grey building had pandinzori above it now. It was a darker line across the horizon, stretching infinitely in both directions, never-ending. Tchardin would have to cross the ice to get to it. She'd have to weaken herself considerably. But Damarin was there. What could her sister be thinking, now that she could see Tchardin's leaf on World Nine again?

Tchardin held pandinzori around her and stepped onto the ice. Her strength drained away, but she had brought a lot of the light. She held it hard against herself and a curious thing happened. It seemed to be bolstered as she walked. Her body was weak, but she could stand and move. She gained a great advantage from coming to a place where pandinzori was plentiful on this Earth before entering the wasteland of the ice, unlike the last time she had come here. And now, as well, it seemed she may be making some of her own.

The building was a line of light grey columns with darkness behind them. Tchardin assumed there were doors there or some other way of entering. Pandinzori flowed onto the ice from the columns ahead of her.

In some places it rushed out and disappeared. In others it lingered. She focused on the pandinzori that waited for her and tried to ignore the thinning of her own. It certainly was thinning. Most of it would be gone before she reached the building. She wasn't afraid, as she'd been spat out onto the ice with nothing before and survived. Her body could handle this and would only grow stronger. But she did worry about Damarin, and she remembered Sandin. Maybe it was possible to grow too strong.

She ran. It was easy to run on the hard scarred ice. She covered a lot of ground before she weakened and got even farther before her legs gave way. Had she ever believed she could fight Damarin here? Kill her, as Tchar had asked? She slid across the ice on her knees, then on her side. She might believe her strength would return but that wouldn't help her when Damarin didn't need a moment to recover and would never falter. Tchardin lay staring at the grey building and waited.

The truth was she had never thought she could kill her sister with force. Tchar must never have believed it either. Her approach would have to be different if she wanted to succeed. She studied the grey columns. The pandinzori there looked to be coming closer. A dark figure emerged. Damarin. Tchardin got up as the pandinzori reached out to her, giving her strength. Her sister turned and walked back into shadow. The mass of pandinzori followed.

Tchardin struggled to keep up with it. She stumbled through the first set of columns and her strength returned. The light of pandinzori blazed before her. She had to remember how to look past it and see only darkness. The room—if it could be called a room—was massive and seemed to go on forever, columns interspersed throughout the emptiness. Tchardin couldn't see the ceiling of the building.

Damarin stood near one of the columns and looked down at something that lay against it. The pandinzori around her was thrown back. A black void claimed the space in front of her. Tchardin hesitated.

'Come here.' Damarin turned to face Tchardin and the distance between them felt small.

Tchardin considered leaving, but she had come to World Nine to confront Damarin and there was nowhere else to go. The emptiness of the world had once again shown her weakness but Damarin didn't look like she wanted to fight. At least not yet. Tchardin walked towards her sister, her steps on the strange floor echoing through the infinite building.

"It's called the Never-Ending Hall," Damarin said. "That has always been its name, though it once had an end. Now it's truly never-ending."

Tchardin felt pressure on her aura as she approached. The pandinzori that surrounded her stretched out behind her as it did behind Damarin. Her eyes came to rest on the dark object against the column at Damarin's feet. The collective changed. She gasped.

"Yes," said Damarin. "This is a human. Or once was a human. I'm not sure which is true."

Light blossomed in the space. Not the light of pandinzori, but true light, created by Damarin. The object took on a familiar shape as Tchardin came to stand beside her sister. It was a hunched, ragged figure, dressed in dull grey fabric that was full of holes. The face was hidden but the collective told Tchardin this was a woman. Her hands were as grey as the fabric of her clothes, rigid and covered in something dark, like dirt. She repelled pandinzori.

"Alive?" Tchardin asked, though the collective told her it must be so.

"In a way. Did Jaydin tell you anything about World Nine?"

Tchardin studied the human figure. *Flint*, the collective said. That was it. Flint. No explanation of who or what this was came with the name. No thoughts came from the woman's mind. Jaydin hadn't told Tchardin anything about World Nine. They had never gotten past World Eight.

"That's too bad," Damarin said. "World Nine was quite interesting. Now Flint here is all that remains. An example of what happens when humans reach too far."

Tchardin turned to her. "What do you expect will happen when you've gone too far?"

"I'm not human."

"And yet you would create trees."

"I have created trees."

"Abominations, made of pandinzori."

"Some of them," Damarin said. "But I've made real trees too. True fathers who could bear kandar."

"You would create them on Derkra?"

"I will."

Tchar had said Damarin wanted to change Derkra and that by changing Derkra she would change the kandar. The false Coralynth had only been the first step. How could Damarin let the kandar create their own fathers? Create potential fathers that were not true trees, like those made of pandinzori? What would happen to a kandar who went to one of those?

"Sandin's gone," Tchardin said.

Damarin's eyes flickered wider for a moment. "How?"

Tchardin met her sister's gaze and held it. "You pushed her too far."

"Did she dream?"

Damarin's expression was desperate when she asked. Tchardin contemplated not telling her what she wanted to hear, but her fate would be bad enough already. "She did."

Damarin knelt before the ragged figure and lifted the woman's hood to reveal her features. Tchardin took a step back in horror. The skin of Flint's face was the same grey as her clothing, the same grey as the columns. Her lips too, were grey. The most horrifying thing about her face was not the lifeless colour of her skin, but her eyes. Or the absence of them. She had no eyes, only scarred, black holes. Tchardin looked again at the woman's darkened fingers.

"You know how the humans of World Nine reached too far?" Damarin asked. "They wanted to live forever. It seems Flint was the only one to achieve that." She stood, dropping the hood back over the face of the figure. The woman didn't react, didn't move at all. "Ruon may want the kandar to live forever, but I don't. I only want to change things before I rest, so that when I wake again the kandar have everything the humans had and more. I want all the kandar to wake to that."

"But what about the humans who already wake to it? Who are many more than us and only get to live once?" Tchardin avoided looking at Flint, who couldn't look back, who was still alive though she had no thoughts to show it.

"I wouldn't take it from them. I only want Derkra. They may destroy themselves and their Earths without us, but how is that our concern?"

"No one else can help them. We were made for it. They were made for us to guide them."

"So Jaydin said."

"So Tchar says," Tchardin answered, angry now. "So say the trees and Creator before them. Even if they didn't, you've seen the Earths. You've met humans. They may destroy the things around them but without them those things wouldn't exist. If you'd never seen them, if Jaydin had never told you of them or Tith put images in your mind, would you ever have made a thing?"

"I can't answer that. I'm only what I was made to be. Without Jaydin, without Tith, I wouldn't be myself."

"You'll be different when you're reborn."

"The world will have already changed."

"But you'll be different," Tchardin said. "Look at the other kandar. Do they make things? Even with your encouragement, can they truly match the humans? The kandar—dull as they are, uncaring as they are—could guide the humans now. They could go to the Earths and learn to fulfill the Purpose, but they would never be able to do what the humans can do. They're not supposed to. They weren't made that way. If Tith hadn't made you, if Jaydin hadn't shaped you, if you were like them, you wouldn't want this."

"The other kandar will be like me when they're born into the world I envision for them."

"They'll be human," Tchardin said, finally understanding what Tchar had meant about a changing Derkra changing the kandar. "Or so close it wouldn't matter. Closer every time another generation of kandar went to rest and woke again in an ever-changing world. Then what's to stop them from dragging your world down around them? What's to stop the one you become from doing so? The humans need us and we need them. If we become them, who will guide us?"

Damarin stared at Flint in silence for a moment. Then she turned and walked towards the light and the ice. Tchardin followed, anticipation building under her skin. Damarin stopped at the division between inside and out. Tchardin stopped just behind her.

"Tell me something." Damarin's pandinzori flowed out of the building, pushed away by Flint. It floated into the nothing and dissipated there. "Why did you come back?"

Damarin might hear her thoughts if Tchardin tried to hide them, but she also might finally be capable of deceiving her sister. She realised she didn't want to. "Tchar sent me."

Damarin's shoulders relaxed. "So that's why I'm held here."

"She's decided to stop you."

"After all this time? She intervenes for this?"

Tchardin kept her expression neutral but inside she felt the same confusion. Damarin truly was a threat to the kandar and Tchardin doubted there had ever been any so great before her, but why had the queen of existence let things get this bad in the first place? The situation that had shaped the daughters of Tith could have been undone long ago.

"You spoke to her?" Damarin asked.

"I went to Coralynth."

Damarin laughed. "Of course you did. Now Tchar will send the kandar back to the Earths—or to the seven of them that remain alive at least—and you will become the queen Jaydin always wanted you to be." She turned away. "And I will remain here."

Tchardin thought about staying quiet but she felt her sister deserved to know what Tchar was. Part of her also wondered what Damarin would do in her place. "She won't open Coralynth to us. Not until the kandar have gone to rest all at once."

"Then those you rule now would never see what you've fought so valiantly to achieve." Damarin was quiet for a moment. "Do you think they'd care?"

That made Tchardin pause. Would they really care? Outside the daughters of Tith and those they closely associated with, would the kandar really object to going to rest if their queen asked them to? Tchardin objected to it because she knew what the Earths were, knew what they would do for the kandar and what the kandar could do for them. But never having seen them, never having done anything, would the rest of her people really understand what they were missing?

"I care," she said. Damarin's eyes flicked to hers. A thought struck Tchardin. "But we must do as Tchar says."

Damarin turned away again. Tchardin kept her mind quiet as she explored the thought that had come to her. Why not bring Damarin back to Tith? Or to one of the trees of Black Valley? If the kandar were meant to rest then why couldn't their middle sister remain a part of Derkra? Tchar said she wanted Damarin as guardian of this Earth, but the Earth was dead. There was no World Tree for her sister to go to. Maybe Tchar had a way to fix that but Tchardin saw no evidence of it now. Why shouldn't Damarin get to stay kandar? Tchardin wouldn't give in to Tchar's threats. She wouldn't force the kandar to rest, not yet, but she would remember that they had to. Damarin didn't need to know that. If her sister agreed, Tchardin would only have to find a way back to Derkra with her. She had made the path. Maybe Tchar wouldn't block it.

"You could come back to rest," Tchardin said. "Tchar won't let you continue with your plan. She keeps you here, controls you. No kandar can stand against her. Those in the council who followed you have come back to us and look to the true Coralynth to guide them. If you rest you'll be reborn to a Derkra full of kandar who travel to the Earths. Kandar who are fulfilled, who have the Purpose. Your dodenzinn—"

"Yes," Damarin interrupted. "What do Ryten and Cien think of this? If I'm not allowed to return what will become of them? Of you? You will be just as affected by it, if we truly share them as I believe we do."

"I don't know," Tchardin said, only just grasping the far-reaching consequences of Tchar's plan. They were minute compared to the scale of existence and Tchar may have accounted for them in some way. "Just come back to Derkra and go to the trees. You don't have to die here."

Damarin studied the ice. Tchardin followed her gaze and could just see the mist and pandinzori that rose above the great waterfall in the distance.

"Why should I die here?" Damarin asked. "There are no true trees to call me, if you're right about my creations. This Earth is dead and the kandar will never come back to it. I should be able to live here forever if I don't lose my pandinzori. Like Ruon in his glass cage on World Four. Like Flint—with only my own mind and her body to keep me company. Unless"—she took a step into the nothingness—"Tchar didn't just send you to speak with me."

Damarin's pandinzori was prodigious, even when the emptiness around her should have stripped her of it. The absurdity of Tchar's plan came back to Tchardin and her confidence fled. Who could truly stand against her sister?

"Were you meant to kill me?" Damarin asked, but this time it seemed she spoke for herself, not for Tchardin. "Why would she want that? Even if you could do it, what would that achieve?" She closed her eyes for a moment. Pandinzori spiralled off her. "Could this be about Heirrar?"

Tchardin remembered the dead white tree with the broken trunk that stood in the cave in Black Valley's wall. The tree Damarin had named as one of Carrensing's three fathers. One who had held the only tevadra known to have gone to Calendrai's greatest tree, she who became the daughters of Tith.

"Jaydin may not have told you about World Nine, but she did tell me. She told me everything she knew. Her memory—Tith's memory—of the kandaran war was vague, as were the events surrounding Carrensing's life, but she did remember one very important catalyst in that war. Heirrar, grown from the Seed of a World Tree, meant to restart this Earth."

Right an old wrong, Tchar had said. Make Damarin the guardian of World Nine. Tith was their father, but maybe they weren't all meant to return to him.

"So I'm meant to die here," Damarin continued, "and even if I do, there will be no escape. Tchar means to trap me forever, whether I am dead or alive. Whether I am myself or the one I will become."

The pandinzori around her condensed and she shot into the air with it. Tchardin ran onto the ice to watch the brightness of her as she flew away, towards the waterfall and the forest.

'Damarin,' she said.

The blaze of pandinzori came to rest on the other side of the plane of ice. It expanded and spun across the earth and rose into the sky. Tchardin watched it in amazement and terror.

'Tchar would make me guardian of this dead place, worse than Derkra in its desolation, worse in its lack of pandinzori.' Damarin's voice was loud and forceful in the empty collective. *'I'll show her what I would do with Derkra, what I would have given our people. It will only make me more powerful, and when I can, I'll go back.'*

A mountain rose from the earth. It came from beneath the river and lifted its spray up high. Trees grew on its sides as it emerged, breaking the ice into huge pieces that slid down its great height and crashed into the waterfall.

Tchardin launched herself into the air using the thinning pandinzori around the hall entrance, crossing the empty ice and landing at the edge of the waterfall and the foot of the river's new mountain. When she landed the sky lit up in a flash, followed by a massive boom that shook the world. Clouds grew from nothing and roiled against the white. Rain began to fall.

Flashes and crashes filled the air as Tchardin propelled herself up and over the rising landmass in search of her sister. She skimmed the growing height of the trees, the entire mountain flooding with pandinzori. As she crested it she stopped in shock, for on the other side of the mountain a true flood had begun. More mountains had come up around the first and the rain filled the newly formed valley between them. Damarin stood above the rising water, enveloped in pandinzori.

'Damarin!'

Her sister opened her eyes and looked up. *'It's so much easier here,'* she said, her words punctuated by a flash and bang in the sky. *'This world is ready to be made, where Derkra only fought me.'*

The land around them was in constant motion, morphing into the most impressive natural features Tchardin had seen on the Earths. The mountain beneath her feet split open and the great river with the waterfall burst through behind her. She lifted herself above it just in time to escape the torrent. The grey river water was added to that running down all sides of the mountains.

'What good is this?' Tchardin asked. *'The world is dead! None of this matters.'*

'Practice. See how I make it. See how magnificent the limitless desert of Derkra could become or how full the empty waters.'

Damarin looked down at the rising lake in the valley. The water was bright with pandinzori. Something moved within it, lit from below by pandinzori and from above by the flashing in the sky. Tchardin landed on the broken mountain and watched. She didn't see how Damarin was making these things. Pandinzori filled the valley and covered the mountains but it didn't run through them. There were new trees around Tchardin but they weren't made of pandinzori. Could her sister do all this with rendinzori? How?

A moving shadow drew Tchardin's eye as it was silhouetted against the flashing sky behind her. A cat—big like the one in Arkaiyan's pit—lurked in the branches of one of the trees. It bore its teeth at her. She stumbled down the mountain, too shocked at its appearance to fend it off. When she was only a few steps away she saw the water approaching, still rising with the flood of rain and river.

A shadow moved through it towards her and thrust itself onto the shore. Teeth the length of her arm came within inches of her before she stopped them with pandinzori. The creature, which appeared to be mostly jagged mouth, hung suspended just above the rising water. Tchardin didn't recognise this one. Damarin laughed somewhere above her, the sound strange as it could be heard above the thunder of the sky.

'Why fight with pandinzori when you can fight with something better? With the earth and with its animals.'

Tchardin turned to find the cat right behind her. She sent a length of pandinzori through it and it fell to the ground. The water rose and covered the first creature that had attacked her. It slipped back into the darkness. Another shadow moved through the trees towards her.

'Am I not as good as the humans?' Damarin shouted to the collective. *'Is my mind not as complex? Why shouldn't we build our own world? Why shouldn't I build it for us?'*

Something huge came out of the sky to dive at Tchardin. She solidified the pandinzori above her and ran. The creature crashed into it and rebounded off. She came to the crest of the mountain and turned to get a better look but the earth beneath her feet gave way and she fell.

She rolled over in the rock and dirt, tumbling down the mountain towards the ice. When she finally stopped herself she saw the creature come again. It was a dragon. Bigger than Lowren. She felt for the creature with her mind but it was real. No threads of pandinzori ran through it for her to control. Instead she blocked it once again—its great claws scrabbling against the hardened light—and turned to throw herself off the mountain.

She barely controlled her fall, opting for speed rather than safety. She landed at the opposite edge of the river. The dragon followed. Tchardin staggered away, noticing that the plane of ice ahead of her remained untouched. It lay before the never-ending hall and it extended along the edge of the building in both directions, seemingly forever. She moved onto it, gasping as the pandinzori around her was pushed away, but grateful for the protection of the unchanging surface. The dragon came towards her. She readied herself but as it approached it faded. The creature never made it within reach of her, vanishing with a cry as it flew over the ice.

Tchardin looked at the ice and the never-ending hall. For some reason Damarin wasn't affecting this place. Pandinzori hadn't come to it. Even the real creatures were destroyed if they came too close. Tchardin looked back to see her sister disappearing behind the further shaping of the Earth and wondered. Maybe Damarin couldn't change it. Maybe Flint held it like this with her empty mind. What did it mean if she could do that? The Earth here was as lifeless as when they'd arrived the first time, no matter what Damarin did to change the rest of it. How could that help Tchardin?

'Even here,' she said, projecting her mindvoice into the collective, *'even now, a human is still stronger than you are.'*

She waited but there was no reply.

'Look, Damarin,' Tchardin said, *'look at the ice.'*

The movement in the distance ceased. A blaze of light shot into the air. Tchardin prepared for her sister's return.

***

Cien focused on two dark leaves in the collective. Tchardin and Damarin, nearly side by side, given to him at almost the exact same moment when he found them in the sand. The two leaves would be the only indication of what was happening on World Nine. If either of them fell it might mean disaster for him, but he was expecting at least one to fall. He opened his eyes and turned to see Ryten likely doing the same.

The devoshai stood with his eyes closed and his face marked by concentration. Maybe he looked at Ruon's seed instead. It still glowed in the collective. The guardian hadn't come closer nor moved farther away in the time since Tchardin left them. They waited by Ovaeron's trunk for something to happen.

The kandar of Calendrai were spread out beneath the canopy of the great tree. More kandar than Cien had ever seen in one place. Interspersed among them were kandar of a lighter skin colour. Some of those in Black Valley were curious. Cien was worried about the ones who weren't.

Kadailin had talked to the council again. She had returned with no news of Cotelle. Cien still wondered what had happened to the devoshai but he expected never to see him again. The council, leaderless, had been easy for Kadailin to convince of their position. She spoke with Ocien and Torshe now. Something behind them caught Cien's eye.

A tevadra ran across the valley from the direction of the false Coralynth. Those who were nearest to her had started to push back, compacting the kandar around Cien. He moved through them to meet her.

"There's something coming," she said to no one in particular.

"What is it?" Cien asked.

She turned towards him. "I think it's sand. Look."

She gestured to the left of the mountain. The sky was darker there. Sand hung in the air, advancing on the valley. Cien looked at the collective. Ruon's seed grew steadily brighter.

"He's coming," he said. Ryten was beside him in an instant.

"What should we do?" the devoshai asked.

Cien turned to the kandar around them. *'The guardian is returning,'* he said to the collective, not directing his voice at any in particular. *'All those who wish to avoid him should go to the caves in the valley wall.'*

None of the kandar moved.

"I'm not sure they understand," Ryten said.

"They will when he gets here."

The sand screen advanced until it flowed into the valley. It spun in the air, driven by dark pandinzori, whipping against the false Coralynth and tearing the vines on it to shreds. There were kandar between Cien and the mountain. Some of the nine hundred grew there. He reached for the pandinzori around the trees and tried to hold it steady but it was too far from him to be sure. He walked out from under Ovaeron's leaves. Ryten followed him.

"The sand could harm the trees," Cien said. "We have to protect them. Gather the kandar to help."

Ryten nodded and ran back to the group of kandar. Cien ran to the first of the nine hundred and tracked the sand's slow advance. Some of the kandar who stood in its way were familiar to him. Two of them were turned towards it, watching.

'Olexin, Jav, you have to move,' he said to them, holding their leaves in his mind in the collective. *'Go to the valley wall. Go to the caves! Now!'*

Jav turned to look back at him but didn't respond. The sand flowed over them. Kadailin ran up beside Cien in time to see their skin stripped by the thrashing grit. Two leaves fell from the collective. Cien exchanged a look with the tevadra.

"What do you need us to do?" she asked.

"Take some of the kandar and wait in Ovaeron. Don't let anything touch his leaves. Tell everyone to protect themselves from that sand."

Cien looked back at the massed kandar and found that most of them had seen Jav and Olexin's end. Their eyes were wide and their mouths open in surprise. He frowned.

"Get them moving," he said to Kadailin.

Ryten joined him with a group of kandar but Cien found he was so powerful now he didn't need help to hold the pandinzori around any of the trees he could easily see. He took it and held it fast and solid. The leaves on the trees froze. Any kandar in their branches would be stuck there.

"We're going to be fighting each other," Ryten said from his side. "They'll try to protect themselves and they'll be fighting you for control."

"Tell them then."

'Keep the pandinzori around you solid,' Ryten's mindvoice boomed. *'Hold anything and everything you can and protect the trees and yourselves from the sand when it comes. If you feel resistance from another kandar don't fight it.'*

"What if the guardian's the one who fights them?" Cien asked.

Ryten shrugged. Ruon's aura was nearly black. Cien had been told his was grey. It would be hard to tell the difference in pandinzori.

The sky was dark with sand and the false Coralynth was hidden from view. As the swirling mass encroached on the first set of trees it hit Cien's controlled pandinzori and spiralled up into the sky, billowing over the kandar. Cien held on against it, pushing up to dispel the wave that travelled towards Ovaeron. Ruon's seed was bright.

The darkness parted and a figure emerged. The sand stopped swirling but remained suspended. The valley grew quiet. Cien held his pandinzori with all his strength.

'Cien,' Ruon said through the silent anticipation. *'You have grown even stronger, as I expected.'*

'Guardian. Go back to your Earth. Damarin is gone and the kandar no longer follow her.'

The dark figure took a step towards them. Ryten tensed at Cien's side.

'Why should I go?' Ruon asked. *'Damarin is gone and so is your queen. I am the Shadow of Derkra. Should I not now rule?'*

'I am the Shadow of Black Valley, as I always have been, and the Shadow doesn't rule.'

'But I say the Shadow does rule, and I will. You will step aside.'

'I won't,' Cien said. *'I'll stand against you, as will each and every kandar here. Derkra is not for you. Go back to World Four.'*

The sound of Ruon's laughter rolled over the sand to them from across the valley.

'You may have grown strong,' he said when he finally calmed, *'but you are not strong enough. I was not driven by Damarin, only galvanised, and I will not stop just because she is gone. None of you can stand against me as you are. The trees make you weak and so do your dodenzinn. Fight me and I will take them from you. I will show you what you are without them. Watch me and see what you could be, what I will make you when I am done.'*

The sand fell out of the air and hid him. The kandar behind Cien became agitated.

"Calm them," he said to Ryten. "I'll watch for Ruon."

The sand cleared slowly but there was no sign of the guardian. Ryten's thoughts were loud as he talked to Kadailin, Torshe, and Ocien. Cien heard them in the collective as the devoshai tried to get the kandar under control. The earth trembled. Cien's eyes were drawn to the false Coralynth.

Fire burst from the crown of the mountain. It exploded upwards and out, taking the top of the mountain with it in pieces. It almost seemed to hang in the air for a moment, it was so massive.

Cien held the pandinzori above them as a rock the width of Ovaeron's trunk crashed down on top of it and shattered. He pushed the pieces away with his mind, letting them fall past the nine hundred, in the empty sand of the valley. Black grit billowed from the hole in the false Coralynth and filled the sky above. Then it began to fall, masking the bigger rocks that fell with it. Fire flowed from the peak of the mountain in a torrent and cascaded down its sides. The kandar behind Cien screamed and ran.

"Protect the trees!" he shouted. Torshe ran to his side. "We have to stop the fire that's flowing into the valley," Cien said to him. The devoshai's eyes never left the burning mountain. "Take all the kandar and push pandinzori at it. As much as you can. Don't let it burn the nine hundred."

Torshe ran off and Cien focused on the sky. The black sand built up on his pandinzori, making it impossible to see anything above. He could hold pandinzori and block out both the rocks and the black sand but he wouldn't be able to do anything else. Red showed through in places in the direction of the mountain and the light of pandinzori was ubiquitous but there was no natural light left. He was stuck. If the guardian attacked he wouldn't be able to defend them.

'Ryten,' he said, finding the devoshai's leaf in the collective.

'What is this?' Ryten asked. *'What's happening?'*

'I don't know but I have to let this black sand go. Tell the kandar to watch for falling rocks.'

Cien looked up and saw nothing but pandinzori and blackness. He had to stop it and he had to find Ruon. The kandar would have to protect themselves from the projectiles of the mountain while he searched for the guardian. He let go of pandinzori and the sand dropped around them. It coated his skin, more like dust than sand. Lighter. When he brushed his arms he found it abrasive. Now that it no longer collected above them he had expected to be able to see, but that was not the case.

The sharp black dust came down from the mountain so thickly he could only see a few steps in each direction. He brought up the barrier of pandinzori again but it was no help. The dust only built up more quickly. He had to get above the darkness and find the guardian, had to stop the mountain from obscuring their vision. He pushed upwards and away, lifting himself with pandinzori, indifferent to the lesions that grew on his skin as he flew through the sharp particles. A leaf fell from the collective. There would be many more, Cien knew. He tried to ignore the sense of loss it created in him.

It was possible to see what was going on in the valley by closing his eyes and focusing on the light of pandinzori. Auras were visible below him, darting through the darkness, but he couldn't see what was happening with the mountain. He could tell it was ahead of him because bright pandinzori rushed towards it and was swallowed by masses of pure black. Those would be the flowing fires. Even with his eyes closed he couldn't see the rocks that flew through the air to land amongst the kandar below.

Another leaf fell from the collective. Cien flinched. What if Ruon killed them all? Was it worth fighting if they could all die? He approached the mountain. Lines of pandinzori-consuming black wound down its height. He couldn't tell where the wall of rock ended. If he continued to fly towards it he could end up embedded in the mountain. There might be fire behind its surface.

He turned and let go of the pandinzori that supported him, aiming his body at a place where there was no black. The speed of his approach propelled him forwards as he fell and he reached out to find the rock of the mountain.

His fingers took the brunt of the impact. Instinct allowed his arms and legs to absorb the rest of the shock. He solidified pandinzori to hold him while he found places he could grip. The rock was sharper than the bark of the great trees but mostly the same to climb. When he felt secure he turned to look down into the valley.

Through his closed lids he saw the halted approach of the flowing fire towards the trees and the auras that rushed around it. One broad strip had made it to the ground and the kandar swarmed its edges. As he watched, another current of fire joined the first and two more leaves fell from the collective. The guardian was nowhere to be seen.

Cien turned back towards the rock. There was so much fire in the valley—so much that continued to flow from the mountain—he wasn't sure he could stop it. But he might be able to do something about the black dust that fell—sharper and lighter than any sand on Derkra—and the rocks that came concealed within it.

He lifted himself in pandinzori and flew towards the fountain of darkness at the mountain's summit. He stayed close to the rock to be sure he didn't lose it. Jutting edges raked him as he brushed past them, then were sheared off by the pandinzori beneath his feet.

He felt for the false Coralynth as he flew over it—not just the rock, but the entirety of it. He reached for the pandinzori around it in his mind and wondered how Sandin had changed it. How Ruon had made it do this. It hadn't been done with pandinzori or the kandar would have seen it. It must have been done with rendinzori. Damarin had told Cien he used rendinzori once. Ruon had said it would come to him.

He stopped just below the peak of the mountain and opened his eyes. The dust didn't fall as thickly this close to the top. He shaded his eyes against it and looked up. The crown of the mountain was its source, pouring it up and out before it rolled back down to fall in the valley. How could he stop it?

How had he killed Miadra? Damarin had said he used rendinzori against her but the spiders had killed her, not him. He remembered wanting Miadra to die, needing her to feel the consequences of her actions visited upon her person. Damarin also said the spiders had once been harmless. She had created them with rendinzori and Cien had changed them to destroy the Black Valley High Seat.

He closed his eyes and saw the black fire beneath the dust and the pandinzori that swirled into it. He brought up the colours behind his eyes and reconstructed the image as if there was light—real light—he could see by. Light like that bursting through the canopy of the forest Jaydin had shown him on World Four. The light of the sun. The red of the fire grew behind his eyes and a dark grey cloud of dust formed around it, blocking the newly created light. He pushed it away and replaced it with Derkra's blue sky. He climbed the final distance towards the summit and as he did he imposed the image on reality. Rendinzori would make it so.

When he reached the top he opened his eyes. A wide pool of fire extended before him. It no longer fountained into the air and the dark grit was gone. The fire was yellow and orange and red in the strong light and it moved as if alive, its surface churning, pieces of it flying into the air as if trying to escape. It ate pandinzori, pulling at Cien's aura as he stood at its edge. There was no sign of Ruon.

The sky in the valley cleared as the last of the dust fell. Cien looked down from the top of the mountain to see the kandar appearing through the grit, all stained black, the kandar of Black Valley indistinguishable from the kandar of Calendrai. They stood in deep, dark dust and fought the fire. It continued to advance. Some of the nine hundred burned.

Cien searched the sky for Ruon and finally found him standing in the air above the valley. The guardian met his eyes and smiled. Cien lifted himself from the rock with pandinzori and moved towards him.

Chapter 49

Ryten scanned the sky for falling rocks. The air was obscured by grit, but some of the rocks brought fire with them and could be seen to swallow pandinzori as they flew. It was the only indication they approached.

Something crashed through the leaves above and bounced off his barrier of light. He flinched. He hadn't seen that one coming.

He walked slowly towards the blackness of flowing fire in the distance, examining the nine hundred as he went. Their white trunks and yellow leaves were stained, their silhouettes stark against the screen of dirt from the mountain. There were groups of kandar standing around each of the trees that were closest to the edge of the fire, their auras visible through the darkness. They would be waiting in case the fire turned towards them.

There was a line of auras past the trees, blazing with pandinzori as the kandar there sent outrageous amounts of light into the fire to be swallowed. Torshe and Ocien's auras were among them, the dodenzinn standing side by side. Sand sprayed Ryten from his right, the result of another large rock crashing into the valley. He heard shouts in that direction and turned to see auras scattered on the ground. A leaf fell from the collective.

Where was Cien? The devoshai had been able to cover nearly all of them with his unbelievable control of pandinzori before he'd left. Ryten didn't see the Shadow's aura anywhere in the line even though his leaf remained bright in the collective.

Ryten ran towards the kandar battling the fire and took hold of the free pandinzori above them and hardened it, shielding them. He took only that which was easy to take, not wanting to fight any of the kandar who already held some.

'Has it advanced?' he asked, directing his words at Torshe but letting any who were listening hear.

'It continues to advance,' Torshe answered.

'There's no stopping it,' Ocien added. *'We can only slow it.'*

Pieces of the burning darkness tumbled forwards, swallowing the pandinzori beneath them as they fell. The line of kandar took a step back. The fire was visible through the murky air because of its proximity, but mostly Ryten still saw it as the absence of pandinzori. A gap in the light.

'What if it takes all the pandinzori in the valley?' a voice came from farther down the line. *'What do we do when there's nothing left?'*

'It won't,' Ryten said, though he wasn't really sure. *'It can't. There's more pandinzori in this valley now than I've ever seen. Just keep pushing against it.'*

Ryten traced the path of the fire back up the mountain, from near the ground—where he could see it dimly burning—and up as a twisting black line to the height of the false Coralynth. There a black fountain was spitting fire into the light. He thought he saw an aura there, tiny and faint, before his eyes were drawn back down to a second rush of fire.

It burst from the side of the mountain and joined the wide black strip the kandar were fighting. The fire in front of them bulged and flowed forward, heedless of the pandinzori the kandar pushed into it. Ryten stepped back as it came towards him, redirecting the pandinzori he controlled towards it. He might be able to slow it but he knew he couldn't stop it. He turned to run as it loomed above him. Ocien and Torshe were at his side as they fled. Two leaves dropped from the collective and Ryten became angry at their helplessness. Fire didn't belong on Derkra. This unnatural darkness didn't belong.

Branches appeared in the grit, emerging from the haze to either side of the running kandar. The nine hundred. If they had run so far back from the line then the fire would soon hit the trees. Ryten stopped and turned, finding the dusky air lit with more than just pandinzori.

The trees screamed. Cracking trunks and crackling leaves accompanied the sound. Ryten remembered the fire in Cens with terror. There was no water here to quell the burning.

'We have to stop,' he said. *'Turn! Turn back to the trees. We have to stop the fire!'*

Another leaf fell from the collective. Ryten stumbled in the deepening sand. The black grit pooled at his feet and built up around him. Soon they would be buried in it. He searched the valley for the burning trees, seeing auras and vague shapes running all around him. They couldn't do much in this half-light, without being able to see.

He looked up to the mountain and this time he did clearly see an aura. Cien's aura. At the top of the false Coralynth. It looked like the black fountain had stopped and as Ryten watched, the dimness in the sky began to clear. Another aura became visible, floating above the mountain. A darker aura. Ruon's.

Ryten looked back to the chaos that surrounded him. He could now see farther into the distance, see more of the trees in the valley. See Ovaeron, towering behind them. The kandar were clustered around two of the nine hundred. They burned. Ryten ran towards them, slipping at first in the deep, sharp sand. Kadailin was there with the other kandar. They sent pandinzori into the fire on the leaves but it barely affected the flames.

Behind them the line of fire was again suppressed by the kandar. They'd found a way to get it to spread out rather than flow forwards. It moved around the first group of trees in two directions. It had never made it to them.

"How are they burning?" he asked as he came up beside Kadailin.

"The rocks," she said. "Some of the rocks that fall are on fire!"

The kandar continued to push pandinzori into the trees but the damage was already extensive. Ryten knew the burning trees were already dead but if they couldn't stop the fire it could spread to other leaves.

'Can we cover it?' a new voice suggested.

The collective said it was Cotelle. Ryten searched the crowd of kandar for the giant and found him standing near the back, head visible over the shorter kandar around them. Ryten must not have noticed the appearance of his leaf in the confusion.

'Cover it with what?' he asked, desperate for a solution.

'Maybe the sand?'

A wave of light and dark sand crashed over them, sliding off the controlled pandinzori around the tree. The flames it touched yielded to it.

'Put sand on the fire,' Ryten said to the kandar around them. He pushed through the crowd to Cotelle while the kandar complied. Sand

flew through the air and the trees grew dark, their once-white branches scorched and black, but they were no longer alight. *'Use it on the fire from the mountain as well.'* Some of the kandar ran past him towards the two lines of fire. Torshe was among them.

Cotelle stood at the edge of the crowd, his extraordinary height making him visible over the other kandar. As Ryten came up to him he was reminded of his own uncommon size. Cotelle was the only kandar he could look in the eye without bending down. The line of kandar attempting to block the fire had slowed its flow, the advancing wall darkening as sand was heaped onto it. Ruon and Cien streaked across the sky above, the guardian pursuing the Shadow.

Kadailin joined them and took hold of the pandinzori above, hardening it. The falling rocks seemed to have stopped but Ryten was glad to see she wasn't ready to risk it. They stood with Cotelle and watched the pandinzori coming off the two devoshai fill the sky.

"Where did you come from?" Ryten asked Cotelle. "Your leaf was dark on Calendrai and in the valley."

"I had some things to secure," the devoshai answered, his big head following the fight above. "I was in the mountain."

"Can we help him?" Ryten asked. Cien seemed the one pursued and Ryten couldn't tell how easy it was for him to defend himself.

"Not easily," Cotelle said. "They're not like us. They have too much pandinzori." The big devoshai looked away from the guardian. "I know what we can do, but the guardian must not hear it."

"What can we do?" Kadailin asked from behind them. She looked terrified, anxious, and Ryten wasn't sure why. Perhaps she had lost another leaf.

Cotelle looked up to the top of the mountain. "We have to cut through the guardian's pandinzori."

"How?" Ryten asked, following his gaze. "Lift the fire? Drop it on him?" It would be like trying to push water, but not with pandinzori, with hands, fingers spread. "It would swallow the pandinzori used to move it, flow around the edges at best. It would be impossible to control, would take too much power."

Cotelle watched Cien as he flew through the air. Pandinzori seemed to grow from him. Both Cien and the guardian seemed unable to do much to affect the other directly. Instead, they projected cutting sand and huge rocks at each other.

"Cien has enough," Cotelle said. "It just has to happen fast. Fire could crush the guardian. Even if it failed it would reduce his pandinzori considerably."

"And severely reduce Cien's in the attempt," Kadailin said.

Cotelle shrugged. "What else can we do? Look at them. If this doesn't end soon they'll tear the valley to pieces and there will be no kandar left."

Kadailin's expression became determined, the fear fading from her face. Ryen was impressed with how quickly she pulled herself together.

"We'll have to tell him without Ruon hearing," he said.

"I'm very good at not being heard," Cotelle answered.

"Be careful," Kadailin said. "We're doomed if he hears. He'll decide to use fire against *us*."

"If I didn't think this was our only hope I would never have suggested it." Cotelle looked up at Ruon. "I knew he was dangerous but Damarin seemed to control him somehow. Where is she?"

"Gone," Ryten said, remembering that Cotelle had once supported Tith's third daughter. "She's never coming back."

Cotelle was quiet. "And Jaydin?"

Ryten and Kadailin exchanged a look.

"We can talk about this if your plan succeeds," Ryten said. "Otherwise I don't think it'll matter."

***

The pandinzori that filled the sky above the valley was so thick now Cien didn't have to worry about supporting himself as he moved through it. He didn't bother to hold it steady, instead choosing to harden small flat places in it when he needed to put a foot down. He moved across it as if running and only held broad sections of the light to block Ruon's attacks.

The guardian followed him with air that pushed and pulled, sand that shredded skin, and burning rocks that came out of nowhere to crash against him. Cien waited in dread for the moment the guardian decided to send pure fire at him.

Ruon didn't run through the air. Sometimes he darted out, following Cien, but mostly he waited, floating near the side of the false Coralynth. Staying near his mountain and his fire. That fire continued to pursue the kandar below, flowing across the valley towards their bodies and the trees. An endless supply waited above the guardian, at the crown of the mountain.

'Do they know I made you?' Ruon's mindvoice was a whisper, as if he stood beside Cien and spoke only to him.

'I've always been strong,' Cien said.

'But not like this. This is something else. Something I *gave you.'* The guardian stopped moving, stopped attacking. Cien stopped as well, taking the moment of respite to gather his strength, but he was wary.

'Look at them,' Ruon said, gesturing to the kandar running through the valley below. *'Think of the things we could do when all the kandar are as strong as this. When they learn to use rendinzori. When they live forever. We could eradicate the humans and live on their Earths. Destroy all the Earths if we chose to! Fire and glass would be our weapons and could not be used to stop us. No cage could ever hold us.'*

'That's not what we want,' Cien said. *'We're strong enough to do what we must on the Earths. No kandar wants more.'*

'If the kandar are allowed to return to the Earths, you would have them killed or caged? You would have the humans catch them and hold them? Torture them as they tortured me?'

'You did it to me too.'

'Only to show you. Only to make you stronger.'

'Is that what all this is supposed to do?'

The guardian moved towards him and Cien moved away.

'Those who cannot survive this will never be strong enough,' Ruon said. *'This is simply the power of the earth you face. You have not seen what humans can do.'*

Pandinzori came at Cien again, this time picking up sand from the floor of the valley. It swung up in an arc to crash on top of him. He dropped out of the air as it rushed over. A second wave hit him. He solidified pandinzori to block it. He felt the guardian's mind behind the blast, pushing against him, pushing him harder.

'Cien,' a voice came to him. He recognised it but was surprised to hear it. Cotelle. The devoshai was alive. *'Don't let Ruon know I'm speaking to you. Keep it from your mind.'*

It was hard enough to concentrate on avoiding the guardian's attacks. Cien wasn't sure he could listen to Cotelle let alone respond and hide it.

'Don't answer then. You may not need to.'

Cien tried to angle himself to see the devoshai in the valley but found it impossible and gave up.

'Ruon is too strong to fight this way,' Cotelle said. *'See the pool of fire at the top of the mountain?'*

Cien shifted in his defence, dropped even lower in the air. As he fell he looked up to the top of the false Coralynth. He remembered the wide pool of fire—writhing, twisting as pieces of it leapt into the air. The guardian fell slightly to face him.

'You need to drop it on him,' Cotelle said.

Cien had to work hard to keep himself from visibly reacting to the devoshai's words. What Cotelle asked him to do seemed impossible, but there might not be any other way. The whirling sand came back at Cien from the other side. He held on against it.

'I don't know if I can do it,' he said, keeping his mind focused on Cotelle's leaf alone, while working as hard as possible to hold on against the sand. *'He won't stay in the same place long enough for me to hit him.'*

'We'll help,' Cotelle said. *'Wait for us.'*

The last wave of sand rushed past and Cien moved higher into the air, closer to the guardian. He had an idea. If Ruon could stop the fight, so could Cien. He made a platform of pandinzori and leapt to land on it. He faced the guardian, faced the mountain that stood behind him. Ruon rose to meet him, but stopped too, as Cien had hoped. Cien closed his eyes.

'Tired of fighting?' the guardian asked. *'Tired of fleeing?'*

Cien gently touched the pandinzori above the guardian with his mind and found resistance. He reached higher, closer and closer to the mountain. It was difficult to reach for pandinzori he could see but not directly touch with the pandinzori he already controlled. Maybe rendinzori could be used again.

'What are you doing?' Ruon asked.

'Just testing this strength you say I've acquired,' Cien said.

'You are not as strong as I am. Not yet. Not with a dodenzinn and a father who calls you.'

Cien refocused and blocked as Ruon sent a sheet of pandinzori towards him.

'Not as strong as Damarin,' the guardian said. *'You are only using pandinzori.'*

'Should I be using rendinzori?'

'You have before. More than once.'

Cien moved his focus through the pandinzori around the mountain and finally found purchase at the top. The fire was still great there and it sucked pandinzori down into it. Cien tried to lift it with his mind but his pandinzori only slipped under the fire and disappeared, causing ripples that rebounded around the pool. Again the task seemed impossible, but then he thought he saw a way.

He didn't need rendinzori. He didn't need to lift the fire. He only needed to make sure the guardian was close enough to the mountain. Then he could simply push the fire off, send enough pandinzori into it with enough force to cause a wave. He reached for the mass of pandinzori and held it away from the fire. Now all he had to do was wait for Cotelle.

***

Kadailin had an idea. She had thought Cotelle might have the same idea until he brought up the fire. She'd been afraid. The guardian and the Shadow faced off against each other above her and she focused on keeping her idea quiet. If Cotelle's plan with the fire worked, there would be no need to implement her own.

She moved towards Ovaeron, his beautiful leaves blackened by the grime. She would be able to watch the fight better from his canopy and she could check on the kandar who guarded him. Maybe she could even help Cien.

She sprinted across the valley, through the nine hundred. There were kandar in their leaves. She saw more than one fearful set of eyes following her progress as she dashed past beneath the branches. She thought of telling them to join the kandar by the fire but decided against it. More kandar wouldn't help. More minds to grasp the limited pandinzori. It was best to leave them where they were and hope they'd protect the trees they hid in if the fire came.

When she saw Ovaeron's canopy above her she didn't wait to reach his trunk. Instead of climbing she lifted herself into the air with pandinzori and shot up through his branches, twisting as she rose to avoid them. She landed about half-way up the great tree's height and walked as far down a branch as she could, until she saw the two kandar in the sky. Black dust fell from Ovaeron's leaves as she rattled his smallest branches.

She saw other kandar as she walked through. They waited, holding pandinzori in case the fire came to the great tree. Kadailin stood on a branch across from one of these kandar. He nodded in her direction. She turned to watch the fight.

The devoshai and the guardian didn't move now, only stood facing each other in the sky. Ruon had his back to the false Coralynth and Cien hung across from him above the valley. Suddenly pandinzori came up at the guardian from below. Concentrated strips of light flew towards him and disappeared into the pandinzori he held. He didn't react to them as if touched but he did drop slightly in the air. His focus shifted downwards.

The attackers were a small group of kandar in the empty sand, far from the nine hundred, with Cotelle in their midst. Ruon turned to the false Coralynth and pulled fire from it. It streaked down the mountain's side to spill amongst the kandar. Most of them made it out of the way but Kadailin felt the collective tremble as three were caught in the stream. They disappeared under the fire and their leaves shook and fell.

The guardian turned back. Cien's body was rigid in the air when pandinzori hit the pool of fire at the top of the mountain. A great wave rushed across it and flowed over the edge. Kadailin saw the moment Ruon realised something was wrong and turned back to find a fountain of fire falling towards him. The mass of pandinzori that followed it and directed it was incredible. Ruon raised his arms above his head as if to stop it. Pandinzori came to him but the fire fell over him and down in a steady stream.

Kadailin closed her eyes to focus on his seed in the collective. It grew dark but didn't fall. The stream of fire slowed to the point it began to run down the mountain again and the kandar below scattered, abandoning the nine-hundred to the fire's flow. Trees were engulfed—their canopies bursting into flame at the heat of the fire without ever coming into contact with the red that swept beneath them. Leaves fell from the collective. Cien stood in the air and watched it all. He moved lower and Kadailin saw the result of his pandinzori sweeping across the valley, pushing the fire away where he could, throwing sand onto it in great waves, stopping it from spreading through the leaves of the trees not actually affected by it.

Kadailin waited, looking at the guardian's seed. If he was gone it should have fallen. She watched the mountain, watched the fire. It was a good thing she did.

'Cien!' she sent to him as the fire's flow picked up, beginning to run down all sides of the false Coralynth from its crown. *'Watch the fire!'*

Cien lifted his head in time to see the jet of fire that came towards him. This was not the fury of the mountain, not simply nudged in the right direction by an outpouring of pandinzori. This fire flew.

The guardian's seed grew bright as he emerged from a crevice in the side of the mountain just beside the old flow. He followed the line of fire, pushing it, directing it. It twisted in the air as if to wrap around Cien, but instead of trying to stop it the Shadow ducked and dropped in the air. The fire shot past him and splattered across the ground close to Ovaeron's trunk, growing dark and hard as it spread out.

Kadailin cringed. She gave the devoshai across from her a look. The kandar hidden in the dusty leaves would have to protect their father from even more danger now. Kadailin wouldn't be there to help them.

Cotelle's plan hadn't worked and there would be no second chance. It was time to implement her own plan. She jumped out of Ovaeron's leaves and guided herself to the ground with pandinzori. When she landed she ran towards the edge of the valley, perpendicular to the line of fire. Kandar were trying to save the trees there and others were trying to direct the flow. Kadailin's presence there wouldn't help them. She had a plan to stop the guardian and more than anything she needed to keep her thoughts about that to herself.

Cotelle met her when she had almost reached the valley's edge. He ran in the same direction she did. His skin was burned and bleeding.

"Where are you going?" he asked.

"To the mountain," she said, not stopping.

"Why?" He ran beside her.

"If fire didn't stop him there's only one thing left that might."

The big devoshai stopped in his tracks. He nodded and turned back to the fire and the fight. Kadailin continued on her way. She would circle the false Coralynth and come at it from the other side.

***

Tchardin watched Damarin land in the middle of the field of ice, half-way between her and the never-ending hall. She landed with enough force to shatter the ice but made no impression. It resisted her, as Flint resisted her. The void of pandinzori pressed down on her as soon as she landed but it didn't diminish the blaze of her, only compacted it. Tchardin walked to meet her, feeling the loss of pandinzori until she was close enough to Damarin to share hers. Her sister looked in the direction of the hall.

"She's stronger than me because she can do this?" Damarin asked. "Better than me because she can keep things the same?"

Tchardin looked back at the mountains and clouds Damarin had created. "What's out there isn't real, Damarin. This is real. This world is dead."

"And is Derkra not dead? The kandar are as bad as Flint, refusing to build. World Nine doesn't have to stay this way, as I have shown. Only Flint stops it from becoming what it could be. Derkra is the same, but with Jaydin and now Tchar to oppose me."

Tchardin could see what Damarin meant by her words, but she didn't agree. Flint did keep the Earth stagnant and unchanging but none of Damarin's creations had truly brought it back to life either. They were changes to the surface. Beautiful, powerful, but ultimately empty. Flint's ability to oppose Damarin's rendinzori was impressive, especially when she didn't seem to be conscious, but it was just as empty. Both achieved the same thing.

"Just because we can change does that mean we should?" Tchardin asked.

Damarin seemed to lose some of her anger. She raised an eyebrow at Tchardin. "Explain."

"The humans have something we don't," Tchardin continued. "Tchar was human once. Ovaeron must have taken something away from her to make her kandar. The trees must have taken it from all of us. Whatever it was, it let the humans create their worlds around them. It lets them make themselves. Maybe *you* have it. Maybe we could all get it back if we let Derkra change, but I think that would just make us human. Then we could no longer be kandar." Tchardin remembered her conversation with Laurence on World Eight. She almost smiled, thinking about the old man and his ideas, his vast collective. Laurence had said they were perfect guardians because they weren't human. Because they didn't want anything for themselves. "I think Creator had the trees take it away for a reason, so we could fulfill the Purpose, guide the humans. You think that makes us better than them but I'm not sure it does." Tchardin looked at her sister, willing her to understand. "Creator made us different. That difference is necessary. We're different, but we're not better."

"But we're kandar," Damarin said. "We're not humans. The kandar are your people, mine. I believe we're better, but even if we're not, even if the world I create ends in ruin like any human Earth, even if we become so human there's no longer any difference, why should we serve them? Why should we sacrifice so much to help them when they can't even help themselves? Why limit ourselves for that?"

"Creator made us to do it." That answer was starting to feel like rote to Tchardin. Automatic. It meant less and less.

"That can't possibly be enough for you. Not after all of this. Not after you've seen what Tchar truly is."

"You're right. It's not enough, but it is true. I've seen the humans and they are enough. I've also seen the kandar. I think we need them as much as they need us."

"So what will you do when you leave here?" Damarin asked. "Will you rest and make the humans wait? Or have you decided to disobey the first of us?"

"I think we can do it without her."

Damarin looked at her in silence for a moment, her dark eyes revealing nothing. "So do I," she finally said.

Damarin opened the shift. This time when she brought it up Tchardin saw a curved black trunk. It was Ovaeron, though his leaves were no longer red. They were dimmed by something dark, but he was there, in the shift. The path Tchardin had made remained. She felt a moment of panic when she thought of Damarin going through. Going back to the valley in the state she was in now. The panic passed when her sister's fist hit the ice and rebounded off. The surface of the shift didn't even crack.

"I told you," Tchardin said. "You can't go back. Tchar won't let you. No matter how strong you become you'll never be able to leave on your own."

"Can you go back?" Damarin asked. "Maybe she'll keep you here too. What makes you think you can resist her?"

Damarin struck the ice again. When it didn't yield she let the shift go and turned back towards her creations.

"I don't need Derkra," she said calmly, "at least not right now. If I can't leave I'll build this Earth around me and create my own people as the humans created themselves. I'll remake the kandar and this can be our Derkra. I'll start it all over."

She turned to the hall and as she turned Tchardin noticed that the pandinzori around her slid on her skin.

"Damarin," she said softly.

"Flint won't stop me this time." Pandinzori spiralled off her. It came when she called. It came across the ice, despite being pushed back, despite being battered by Flint. "I'll destroy her if I have to."

Pandinzori came to Damarin from the mountains, from the waterfall, and it brought change with it. Grass grew across the ice behind it and Tchardin jumped as it shot beneath her. It stopped at Damarin's feet. Her sister looked down at it and then looked forward. She took a step towards the hall. A wall of earth went with her, the ice fading away in front of it.

Tchardin stepped to the side, away from her sister as she advanced. Great cracks spread through the ice and ran almost to the never-ending hall. The emptiness seemed to push back now instead of just resisting. Damarin's aura began to blow away from her. The pandinzori around her seemed to shiver.

"I don't need pandinzori either," Damarin shouted. "I have rendinzori now. Rendinzori to build a world. To build a people!" She dropped to her knees. Her aura floated loosely above her skin.

Tchardin approached her. Damarin gestured her away with a hand. The collective pulsed at her leaf. It called to Tchardin to attend to Tith, but Tith wasn't calling Tchardin. Tith was calling Damarin. Tchardin was simply called to witness her sister's end. She was amazed at their father's strength, to call his daughter from across the worlds.

"No," Damarin said. "This can't be it."

"He calls you." Tchardin knelt beside her. "You've done too much, grown too great. It's time to rest."

"Why call me?" Damarin asked. "I can't go back. Tchar won't let me."

Tchardin opened the shift and brought up Ovaeron's leaves. It wasn't Tith, but it was Derkra, and there was a path from Ovaeron to Tith now. If Tchar would let her through she might be able to take Damarin back. She touched the ice. Tiny cracks spread from her fingers.

"I can take you back," Tchardin said. Damarin's eyes were on the ice. "But only to rest."

"No," Damarin said. "I won't go to rest."

Damarin got to her feet again and Tchardin closed the shift, afraid her sister would push past her and break through, but Damarin didn't try it. Instead she turned towards the hall. She called pandinzori to her, shaped it around her, and this time it came mostly from her own skin and mixed with the remains of her aura. Tchardin didn't know what to do.

Light blazed across the ice and Tchardin was pushed back, digging her feet into the cracks to find some purchase. Translucent shapes emerged from the maelstrom—dark and light, of all colours—and began to fill the world. The ice broke up and flew into the air, crashing through the hazy shapes and away. Tchardin could barely see Damarin at the centre of everything, but she still stood, a darker shadow against the light. She pushed and Tchardin flew.

The world spun and something came into the Earth. A sense of life, of humanity. Tchardin's skin prickled as she tumbled through the air to land hard on the ice. Something was happening. Could Damarin really make her own people? Without an aura? While Tith called her? Flint's nothing shrank and as Tchardin pulled herself to her feet she thought she saw the never-ending hall begin to disappear. A tremor ran through her. It ran through the whole Earth.

A leaf fell from the collective.

Chapter 50

TCHARDIN LAY ON ICE, the white sky spread out above her. The world felt emptier than it had before. She got to her feet and closed her eyes to look at the collective. Damarin's leaf had fallen, leaving only Flint's dimly lit in her mind.

She had thought for a moment that Damarin won. When the light spread across the ice and the never-ending hall seemed to disappear, she had thought it must be Flint's leaf that fell. But the hall had not disappeared.

She opened her eyes and turned in a circle, looking for her sister. The grass beneath her feet was gone but the changes in the distance remained. When Tchardin turned back towards the hall she saw her.

Damarin's body was surrounded in grass though the rest of the plane had returned to ice. Tchardin walked to her and knelt beside her sister's body. Damarin was empty and unmoving. She had been so powerful, so forceful in life. To see her in this state, as passive and still as this, crushed Tchardin. She would never have wanted this for Damarin. When Tchar spoke of guardianship this was not what Tchardin had seen.

The pandinzori on the ice began to slowly shrink. The created landscape her sister had brought into the world faded with it. Tchardin held back a despairing laugh.

Damarin's magnificent struggle had been made futile when Tchar trapped her here. World Nine was dead. It had been dead for so long it couldn't change. Even Damarin's greatest effort hadn't brought it back. The tree that was meant to be its World Tree was on Derkra and dead as well. Heirrar would never grow a Seed. She didn't know what Tchar had been thinking when she asked Tchardin to come here. Damarin couldn't become guardian of this world. No kandar could.

She opened the shift and brought up Coralynth. The image was not of the path but of the sky. Tchar walked into her view.

"Why did you do this to us?" Tchardin asked. "Did you know this would happen?"

The first of the kandar stared at her but said nothing. Tchardin slumped against Damarin, unnerved by the lack of repulsion she felt when they touched but too devastated to move away.

"What good will a guardian do for this Earth when it's dead?" she asked. "What good is a guardian without a World Tree?"

Tchar's plan had led to nothing but waste. The humans were worth something on their own but a dead Earth was not. A barren plane of ice wasn't worth the lives of kandar. It wasn't worth the life of her sister when she could have gone back to Tith. Tchar waited in the shift, silent and far away. The first kandar's dark eyes, so familiar, bore through Tchardin.

Suddenly she felt something. A tiny flash in the collective. She looked down at her sister and at the grass around her. It was the same feeling of humanity she had gotten when Damarin pushed against Flint, just before it ended. The feeling left her.

She stared at her sister's body. The grass around Damarin drew her focus. Tchardin concentrated on the earth there and felt the flash of life again. Something was alive, deep below them, its pulsing heat striving to wake up the world. She searched the icy landscape for something she would recognise as life but there was nothing. Only the pulse. She looked at Damarin again—at the soil and grass her sister lay on—and she understood. The Root of World Nine had been revived. It was there, where Damarin had fallen.

A World Tree could grow from the Root. Jaydin had told them that. It wasn't likely given the state of World Nine but it was possible. Tchardin looked back at Tchar, her eyes now wide and hopeful. "Will there be humans, if there is a tree?"

The queen of existence didn't answer. Tchardin let the shift close. The pandinzori around her dissipated. She felt the emptiness over the ice extending from Flint, from the hall, outwards to Damarin's created landscape. As the mountains faded, the pulse of the Root weakened. Flint would destroy everything Damarin had made before long. Including the revived Root.

Tchardin was also getting weaker, despite the pandinzori that grew from her. Without Damarin to sustain it she could lose the ability to shift. She looked down at her aura. She would lose the ability to shift soon anyway. She leaned down to touch Damarin and for a moment her arm was bare of the light. Her aura was leaving her.

She opened the shift and watched the grey streak through it once more. Then she brought up Ovaeron. Kandar cowered beneath his branches. The sand around them was no longer light, not only dark beneath Ovaeron's leaves but dark everywhere.

Tchardin held her hand above the ice. Would Tchar let her leave? The ice had cracked before but would it do so now that everything was over? She let her hand drop to her side and closed the shift. She turned back to Damarin's body and felt the pulse of the Root below it.

When she looked up and back the forest was gone. The mountains were gone, the trees, the lake, the waterfall. There were no clouds in the sky, no colour at all. In every direction for as far as she could see there was only ice and white. And there was the hall. The hall persisted after Damarin was gone because it had been there before she came.

Tchardin closed her eyes. The light that remained on the plane of ice became brighter to her. Damarin's body made no impression on Tchardin's vision, empty as it was, with no aura, but the grass around her blazed. Tchardin reached for the remaining pandinzori with her mind, reached for everything she could see and drew it towards herself and her sister.

The Earth was dead but it had a chance to live again. It might not come back right away, but if there was a Root there could be a World Tree, and if there was a World Tree there could be a guardian. If there was a guardian there could at least be a Seed and maybe there could be humans. It wasn't certain but the chance was worth everything. Tchardin wanted the kandar to come back to all nine Earths, not seven. There was nothing she could do now for the others that were failing, for World Seven which may truly have died with Rai gone, but she was here, on World Nine, and its Root was alive.

Alive and buried in earth and ice. Damarin couldn't get to it alone. Tchardin wondered for a moment if it would come up to her sister but the dampening pulse it gave off convinced her that was not the case. Flint pushed against it, would push against any life on this Earth.

Tchardin took her sister in her arms. It didn't seem right to hold her with pandinzori now.

Kadailin would bring the kandar back to the Earths. Cien and Ryten had known what it could mean when Tchardin left Derkra and they hadn't stopped her. She thought of Ruon and the fight that could take place on their world. How would Damarin's fight with Flint and its outcome affect Derkra? How would Tchardin's final decision affect it?

Tchar had said Ruon was no threat, and while Tchardin knew he would be a threat to each individual kandar, she believed the first kandar when she said he was not a threat to existence. Tchardin could stay on World Nine with Damarin. To right an old wrong. To give the world a chance to live again.

Her aura slipped on her skin. She had to act fast. She didn't know if she could refuse if Tith called her and he had called Damarin from across existence. She looked up and formed the remaining pandinzori into a whirling mass of light above them, reminiscent of the image Tchar had shown her of Damarin when she was first trapped.

Tchardin opened her eyes and moved into the circle of grass. She looked into the earth, through it, at what was below. A live Root might grow a World Tree if it had a reason, and what better reason was there for a tree to live than to hold a guardian?

She brought the swirling pandinzori down on them and bored into the earth with it, into the ice around it, cracking it into great sheets. She held Damarin against her as she made her way deeper and deeper, towards the Root that barely hung on, towards the only thing on World Nine that was truly alive. The tree it grew would have to survive Flint. Tchardin could only think of one way to accomplish that.

***

Cien dodged a streak of fire, avoiding the guardian's attack rather than trying to block it with pandinzori. The fire left holes in the light as it sped through and made it more difficult for him to navigate the sky, but the holes would only be larger if he concentrated pandinzori in its path.

Ruon advanced on him slowly. The guardian must know Cien didn't have time to return his attacks now. Cien took heart in the fact that the closer Ruon came to him the farther he got from the mountain, the more tenuous his control on the fire.

A strange sensation entered his mind. The collective trembled and seemed to collapse. Cien was hit with weakness like he had never felt before. It reminded him of his first foray into the sand in search of the edge of the water. Fire cascaded towards him but there was nothing he could do to avoid it. Damarin's leaf fell from the collective. Cien began to fall from the sky.

At the last moment the fire that hurtled towards him changed direction, and all of a sudden the guardian was there, beside him. Cien tried to steady himself but it was unnecessary. The guardian held him up.

"Your dodenzinn?" Ruon asked. "The queen?"

Ovaeron's call blasted Cien's mind. He looked at Ruon, wondering why the guardian had turned the fire, why he waited for Cien to recover. It didn't matter anymore. Tchardin had won. She would be coming back.

Ruon didn't resume his attack. The pandinzori around Cien lost its solidity and he dropped in the air. The world faded around him, and reappeared, and faded as he fell towards the sand. He barely felt the impact as he landed. The guardian descended towards him through a haze and landed on his feet a few steps away. Cien managed to get to his hands and knees before his strength waned again. He waited with his head bowed.

'Dodenzinn make you weak,' Ruon said to all the kandar in the valley. *'The trees who call you make you weak. You can survive without them. I am proof of that. Reject your fathers and you will no longer need them!'*

Cien lifted his head and could just see Ovaeron's branches through Ruon's legs, past a crowd of kandar that gathered in the valley. He lowered his head again, exhausted. He couldn't go to rest before Tchardin returned.

'I have never had a dodenzinn,' the guardian continued, *'but I did have a father. I was unable to answer his call and I only got stronger as a result. Cien, too, does not answer the call, has not answered it since before I came to Derkra. His strength has grown immensely but now the loss of his dodenzinn brings him to his knees. I have no such weakness. You need not have it.'*

Ruon turned back to him. If Tchardin had been strong enough to deal with Damarin she might be strong enough to take down the guardian. Cien had to hope that was true. He couldn't do it himself. Not anymore.

Then the collective rippled, surged, and he lost another leaf. Ovaeron called, shaking his world, raking through the collective. Cien struggled to rise in the sand, his intention not to fight but to run to the father of all the kandar and lose himself from existence. Neither of them were coming back. Tchardin was gone too.

'Now, Cien, rise. You have ignored the call of the trees. You can ignore this as well.'

"Are you sure that's what you want?" Cien asked quietly, so only the guardian would hear him. He wasn't going to fight, but how could Ruon know that? "You want to keep fighting?"

'Not to fight,' the guardian answered. *'I would not have you rise if I could not crush you when you did. You will stand before me and before them. To show them what they could be.'*

Cien shuddered. No kandar would choose to lose a dodenzinn and live. Ruon would never know what that felt like. Cien had ignored the call of a tree—not his true father, not the tree who had given him to the Earth, but Ovaeron, father of all kandar—because he had wanted to give his dodenzinn a chance at life. Now she was gone. Now they were gone. He looked again through the crowd of kandar and could just see Ovaeron's trunk there. Could see it opening for him in his mind. Welcoming him.

"Ruon!" a voice rose above the crowd.

The guardian turned away. Cien knew the voice.

"Guardian!" Cotelle shouted. "I too have lost my dodenzinn and I remain here."

"Yes," Ruon responded. "Your dodenzinn was killed in the mountain."

The kandar would still fight, even if Cien couldn't. He looked down at his hands, partly buried in the grey dust and yellow sand, and saw his aura there, strong as ever. Pandinzori flowed off him, but it still stuck to his skin. The guardian didn't hold him. His strength was returning but there was a hole in him. Would be, until he finally got to rest.

"You stay for power?" the guardian asked.

"No," Cotelle answered. "I stay because my dodenzinn deserves to be reborn into a world that inspires her. That's why I followed Damarin."

Ruon took a step towards Cotelle. Cien got to his knees. Every movement drained him and he slumped over. The red tree burned in his mind.

"All kandar deserve to be reborn," Cotelle continued. "There are many now who won't be."

"You would fight me then? Because of this?" Ruon laughed. "You do not need to fight. You will get your world. You can have the Earths. That is what the kandar deserve. When your dodenzinn is reborn she can have it all forever."

Cien lifted his head with effort and noticed Ryten standing at the front of the crowd of kandar, behind a wide wall of pandinzori. He was easy to pick out because of his height. How was he standing? How did he not feel the same as Cien? He looked for Cotelle. The big devoshai was also easy to see, standing alone on the other side of the valley, nearer to the mountain.

"All you need to do is stay alive and wait for her," the guardian said.

"She wouldn't be herself," Cotelle responded. "Miadra is gone now. She will never come back to me. That is as it should be, as long as those we will become have a chance to be together. But now"—he paused, looking into the crowd of kandar across the valley from him—"because of you, that can't happen for some of us."

Some of the kandar behind Ryten shouted in agreement.

Ruon advanced on them. "More of you stay."

"Yes," Cotelle said. "But not for you. In spite of you."

The group of kandar stirred and broke up. Kandar ran to join Cotelle, some of them slowly, painfully. Cien recognised the feeling of loss in them.

"Ruon," Cotelle continued, kandar at either side of him now. "Those of us without dodenzinn may have lost half our strength, but because of you there are many of us, and we have nothing left to live for."

Ruon's back was exposed as he faced the small crowd of kandar. Cien reached for pandinzori but was too weak to move anything, too weak to take it from the guardian. Cotelle charged at Ruon from his other side. Kandar ran beside him and behind him, joining in the assault. Some leapt over them to attack from the sky. Ruon sent fire at them. A massive cord of red and black twisted through the air above Cien. It pulled at his pandinzori. He slumped down. He was weak and Ovaeron called him. The guardian was busy with the other kandar. He could go now if he wanted to.

But the kandar sacrificed themselves for him. It had to be another distraction, set up so he could end it. He reached for the guardian with his mind but found him covered in solid pandinzori. No matter how hard he tried he couldn't take any of it. Past the guardian Ryten gestured for Cien to join them. The devoshai showed no sign of weakness.

Cien stood and ran, stumbling as he tried to control his awkward limbs, falling and sliding in the black grit. Ryten ran to his side and helped him to his feet, the uncomfortable pulse of their colliding auras making Cien more alert. They ran together.

Ryten gestured the kandar out of the way as they came to the crowd. They left Cien space to run between them and he did, skidding to a halt just behind the first group. He turned to see them close around him and Ryten just as three leaves fell from the collective. Ryten knelt beside him.

"I hope he didn't do that to save me." It was the second diversion Cotelle had orchestrated to help Cien defeat the guardian. The second that had failed. Cotelle's leaf remained, but as Cien searched the collective, more leaves fell. "I couldn't do anything to stop Ruon from attacking them. I couldn't do anything to end it."

"Nothing was planned," Ryten said.

The kandar parted to give Cien and Ryten a view of the fight. Cotelle landed heavily in the sand as Ruon knocked him out of the air with pandinzori. The other dodenzinn-less kandar closed between them, giving Cotelle time to get to his feet. There were about twenty of them left.

"Ruon's playing with them," Cien said. "They don't stand a chance."

"I don't know why they did it," Ryten said.

Watching, Cien thought the answer was obvious. "Their dodenzinn will never be reborn."

***

Kadailin inched along the tunnel of rock. An opening ahead of her revealed a sliver of sky. She only needed to get close enough to see the guardian. If she couldn't see him from there she'd have to move to another tunnel.

She didn't want to move to another tunnel. This tunnel had glass.

She had crawled into it from a hole on the side of the mountain that faced the endless desert. No kandar could have seen her do so. Now her location must be obscured to the guardian and to all the kandar below—her leaf should be dark in the collective as Cien's had been when he was held in the mountain. That part of her plan was essential. If Ruon saw her she'd never succeed. There were other reasons she might not succeed but she tried to keep them out of her mind.

She leaned out of the jagged opening. The base of the false Coralynth spread out below. She shifted slightly and the guardian came into view. He stood on the ground with his back to her. A devoshai knelt behind him. Kadailin recognised Cien's aura. Why didn't the Shadow do something? The guardian faced away from him, towards a lone devoshai in the sand. The devoshai was as big as Ryten and his skin was stained as dark, but she knew it was Cotelle.

Cien's position perplexed Kadailin, but Cotelle's was good. If Cotelle saw the light approaching he would hold pandinzori. That was what Kadailin needed. Others would burn with it but she couldn't think of them now. She was likely to burn herself, but it didn't matter anymore. Too many leaves had fallen already. The guardian had to be stopped.

She backed away from the opening—hoping none had seen her—and ran to the glass. It wasn't far, just a few strides, but it felt like a great distance when she was moving towards something so dangerous. The glass was black and shiny, nestled into the rock at eye height. Semi-circular patterns ran through it and reflected the light from the cave opening. The pandinzori around her seemed to tremble slightly when she looked at it. She closed her eyes tightly and tried not to focus on the light.

If she had to die to destroy the guardian she was willing to accept that, but if she died before the reaction reached him there was no point to any of it. She tried to remember what she had seen when Siltadon blew Rai to pieces. How had the guardian of World Seven done it without destroying herself?

Thoughts of Siltadon brought back images of Jaydin disappearing behind a wall of light and the gaping holes left in the earth when it cleared. Kadailin flinched and forced the images away. If Siltadon had taken the pandinzori around the glass in Rai first she never would have succeeded in taking so much before it reacted. Kadailin had to take the pandinzori closest to the guardian first, then connect it with the glass, as Siltadon had done when she brought threads of pandinzori to Rai.

Kadailin ran back along the tunnel to the cave opening. Cien had moved. Cotelle fought Ruon, joined by fifteen or so other kandar. She had to hurry.

She focused on the pandinzori above them. She didn't have to hold a lot of it if Ruon remained unaware, just enough that it was likely to connect with the active pandinzori around him. She closed her eyes and the valley lit up.

Pandinzori whirled in the air below her, manipulated by so many kandar. There was a tremendous, unmoving blaze of it around the guardian. She reached out with her mind to take some of it—so far to reach, farther than she had ever reached before—and found it impossible. She stopped. Instead, she focused on the light directly in front of her and took a thin strip. Once she had it she extended it, keeping it as thin as possible until it reached far enough away from the mountain that she thought it would be safe, then she reached for a whole swath. Her mind ached with the effort. She reached until she met the resistance of pandinzori already held by a mind. She opened her eyes.

The beginning of the brilliant thread of light shimmered before her. When she went back to the glass she would touch them together and send the reaction down to the guardian. But what if he moved? What if he wasn't holding enough pandinzori when it hit him? He could always let go.

Cotelle fought on below, oblivious to the thread of destruction that hung over the valley. He knew what she was doing. Maybe if she told him to be ready he could help her. The guardian didn't need to hold the pandinzori for the glass to burn it all away, but someone did.

She leaned out of the opening, just for a moment, just long enough to find Cotelle's leaf in the newly lit collective.

'Cotelle,' she said, as quietly and directly as she could. *'Hold pandinzori.'*

Then she backed up into the darkness of the tunnel and brought her thread with her.

***

Ryten stood above the Shadow and readied himself to ask the question he needed to ask. Tith had called one of his daughters. Ryten had felt it, but he didn't know which it had been. He barely heard the battle behind him.

"You lost one of their leaves?"

Cien frowned. "Both."

Both of them. Ryten turned away. He looked quickly at the collective and was disgusted by what he saw. He had lost many leaves before Tith began to call. Then the great tree had stopped, but Damarin and Tchardin's leaves remained. They were dark but still there. They hung by Jaydin's leaf, also dark but not fallen. He didn't understand.

He quickly scanned the rest of the collective and saw something that shocked him even more. Kadailin's leaf was dark too.

"Not Kadailin." How had her leaf not fallen when so many he barely knew had? "What happened to her?"

Cien shrugged. He closed his eyes—probably searching for the darkened leaf. "I haven't lost it, but it is dark."

Ryten turned his focus to the guardian again.

"Weak!" Ruon shouted as he tossed kandar across the valley. There were few of the dodenzinn-less kandar left to fight him, though Cotelle hung on. "Weak before you lost your dodenzinn, even weaker now!"

It seemed he would never be defeated. He was so much stronger than they were. Ryten understood now why Jaydin had been so angry when she met him. Guardians weren't supposed to come to Derkra.

"What if we all attack at once?" Ryten asked.

Cien had slumped to the ground again and lay staring in Ovaeron's direction.

"Cien?" Ryten prompted.

The devoshai looked at him but his eyes didn't seem to register the sight. He shook his head and finally spoke. "It might be our only option now. I don't know what else we can do."

“Could you lift the fire again?”

Cien seemed to examine his body. He lifted an arm to stare at it. His aura stayed with him, despite everything that had happened.

“Cien?”

“I don’t know. I’m getting stronger, but Ovaeron calls me. He really calls me now.”

Ryten looked at the wide strip of fire that came down the mountain behind the guardian, still red and wet and malleable. Could the kandar move the fire if they worked together? If they couldn’t count on Cien they’d have to do it themselves.

“It’ll be more difficult for him to avoid fire on the ground.” Ryten looked back to the Shadow, finding the devoshai’s attention already drifting. He touched Cien’s shoulder, eliciting a shock. “Please, Cien, we need your help.”

The devoshai’s eyes focused. He nodded and turned to look at the mountain. Ryten followed his gaze and noticed a tiny point of light far above them. A leaf in the collective flickered. Had it belonged to Kadailin?

“Something’s happening in the mountain,” he said, looking in the direction of the light he had seen. There was nothing there. Kadailin’s leaf was dark.

Cotelle shouted. The sound came to them across the valley as a deep hum. The words were indistinguishable but the kandar around the devoshai must have heard him. What Ryten did hear was Cotelle’s laugh.

“I think I know what’s going on.” The guardian continued to push pandinzori at the kandar who attacked him. One of those kandar stopped moving in the sand and held steady, surrounded by pandinzori. Another did the same. One of them was swept away by fire, but still the others held on. “If the guardian lets go we have to take the pandinzori above him. Don’t touch the pandinzori here. Only that directly above Ruon. As much as possible. Can you do that?”

“Why?”

Ryten didn’t have time to explain. “Just watch the guardian.” He turned to the nearest tevadra. “Let go of pandinzori. The guardian is occupied and nothing will fall on us. Tell the kandar on the line but don’t speak it in the collective.” She stared at him for a moment, then nodded. “Quickly,” he added.

The tevadra turned and spoke to the kandar next to her. Ryten saw that kandar pass the message on. They must think he had some plan in mind, probably involving the Shadow. He had no plan. He thought someone else might.

"I think Kadailin's in the mountain," he said to Cien. "She—"

A brilliant flash of light streaked down from the false Coralynth. The sand in front of them exploded.

***

Cien pulled himself up in the chaos of running kandar to find a gigantic hole in the valley ahead of him. The kandar who had fought the guardian were gone. So was the pandinzori they had held. There was a void in the valley, empty of light.

"I can't believe it," Ryten said from somewhere above him. "There's no way."

The guardian stood on the only patch of sand that remained untouched. His face and body were burned and his hair was gone, but he had survived where all the others had been obliterated. Pandinzori grew around him.

'Use glass against me?' he said, laughing. *'I am always ready to let go.'*

The fire behind the guardian flowed freely again, loosed from the mountain by the blast. Ryten was looking at the same thing Cien was. The devoshai met his eye.

"Do it," Ryten said.

Cien used the last of his strength to reach above the void and push pandinzori straight down into the fire's flow. He pushed continuously, drawing the light into a long sheet and feeding it to the fire. The liquid fire bunched and cascaded down the path it had made, towards the ridge of sandblasted rock the kandar had created in stopping it.

Cien followed it with pandinzori, pushing it faster and faster until it flipped over the barrier and into the air. Ruon was still laughing when it consumed his meagre pandinzori and engulfed him.

Chapter 51

Ryten lay in the sand and looked at the collective. Ruon's seed had fallen—his body covered in fire he finally couldn't deflect—but so had many leaves.

"Where did it come from?" Cien asked from beside him. "Who thought of it?"

Ryten knew he was talking about the burst of light that could only have come from glass. "I think it was Kadailin." The last of Tith's daughters was gone, her leaf dark in Ryten's collective but not lost. "I thought I saw her leaf flicker and an aura in the mountain before the end. Did you lose her leaf?"

"No," Cien said. "I barely knew her."

Ryten realised that was true about him as well. Kadailin was the last of Tith's daughters he had gotten to know. He still thought he should have lost her leaf. Especially since she was on Derkra when she died, and so physically close. They both should have lost it. But maybe it had something to do with her being in the mountain when the flash lit the sky.

"I have to go," Cien said.

The Shadow of Black Valley lay in the dark sand beside Ryten. He had grown calm once Ruon was gone. He could go to Ovaeron now and no one would stop him. Ryten had hoped he would wait.

"Does your father call you too?" Ryten asked.

"No, Roa does not call. Only Ovaeron."

"Why go now then?"

Cien just looked at him.

Ryten frowned. "They're gone, but you can still live. You seem to be fine. Your aura is intact. You've resisted this long and we'll need leaders to deal with all this."

"I'm surprised I look fine," Cien said. "I don't feel it. This collective"—he closed his eyes and shook his head as if to rid himself of the image—"it's not something I want to look at anymore. The kandar will have to find new leaders."

"What if they're not reborn?" Ryten asked.

Cien would know who he meant. He asked for Cien's sake but he also asked for himself. The devoshai beside him was the only other living kandar who understood his situation. Cien's decision might help him make his own.

"I've thought about that." Cien tried to stand but fell back. Ryten stood and helped him to his feet, ignoring the repulsion of Cien's still-strong aura. "Ovaeron's wanted me since before I met Tchardin and Damarin and he wants me still. I'm sure the one I am to become can deal with the consequences, if Ovaeron wills it."

Ryten helped to steady the devoshai in the deep black grit. Del didn't call him, though all the daughters of Tith were gone.

"Maybe I never had a dodenzinn," he said. "Maybe instead of both, or all five, it was none."

Cien gave him an understanding look. "You're not called yet. You have time to decide what to do. I must go now."

Ryten looked away. He had lost nearly all the kandar he spent time with, those he spoke to. What would be left for him? His father didn't call him and the kandar weren't meant to return to Calendrai anyway. No father and no dodenzinn. What kind of kandar was he?

A leaf grew in the collective. *Janna.* The tevadra had stopped beside them in the sand.

"There are bodies in the valley," she said, directing her words at the Shadow. "Some can go to rest, but some..." she trailed off.

"If their bodies are whole, give them back to the trees," Cien said. "Find their dodenzinn first. If their dodenzinn can't be found..." he also trailed off.

They waited in silence for a moment.

"We'll do the best we can." She ran towards the false Coralynth.

Ryten was glad the kandar of the valley had come up with the initiative on their own. The Calendrai collective was noticeably smaller than it had been when he was born and it had already been severely reduced by the war and the split. How many events like this could the kandar survive, before they became ineffective or disappeared altogether?

Ocien walked towards them from the direction of the mountain. A body wreathed in pandinzori floated behind her. Ryten was afraid the body might belong to Torshe, but as she got closer it was clear the body was once a tevadra. He focused on the collective and found the devoshai's leaf lit. At least those two could still be together.

"Where are you going with her?" Ryten asked when she got to them.

"To Ovaeron's trunk," she answered. "We've decided to put those whose dodenzinn cannot be found there for now. With Sandin."

The floating tevadra's body was pristine. It wasn't even stained with the black dust from the mountain.

"How did she die?" Ryten asked.

"I don't know," Ocien said. "We found her in a cave on the far side of the false Coralynth. We thought some of the kandar might be hiding there. She was just lying in the sand."

"Burn her," Cien said. "If there isn't any fire left, send her to the waters of Water Side."

Ocien frowned. "Shouldn't we try to find her dodenzinn?"

"That's Miadra. It's hard to tell without her aura, but she was always particularly tall and particularly light. And see her eyes? Yes, that's her."

"Miadra?" Ryten asked.

"Cotelle's dodenzinn."

Ryten flinched as an image of the big devoshai shouting and laughing before the explosion invaded his mind.

"He wouldn't want her reborn alone," Cien said.

"Why did he do it?" Ryten asked, not expecting an answer. "Sacrifice himself when he had her body?"

Cien shrugged. "He supported Damarin. Misguided in her purpose or not, she seemed to care about the kandar and I think Cotelle did too."

Cien looked weary as he spoke. Ryten leaned into him to help hold him up. The Shadow opened his eyes wider at the uncomfortable pulse between their auras.

"I was there when Miadra died," Cien said. "Since then there's been a good chance one of them wouldn't be reborn. Cotelle probably figured leaving her in the mountain when he came to us was a good way to ensure she wouldn't be, unless he came back to get her."

"He knew about the glass," Ocien said. "I heard him shout before the light came. He told the kandar to hold pandinzori, to take as much as they could."

"I thought I heard something," Ryten said.

"So there's your answer," Cien said. "Or as good of one as we'll get."

He separated himself from Ryten and limped towards Ovaeron. Ryten followed, nodding to Ocien as he left. She stood in the sand and stared at Miadra's body. Ryten wondered if she was thinking of Moradi, the tevadra they had left beneath Tith when they came to Black Valley. He didn't know if anything would be done with her now.

He caught up with Cien and walked beside him. There was a strange brightness in the sky. Ryten looked up and squinted against it. There was a brilliant white ball hanging in the air above Ovaeron. The light it gave off felt comforting on his skin. The shadows that wrapped him grew darker and massed together. Then it occurred to him that the sky had once been empty. The circle of light was new. Ovaeron threw a vast shadow across the valley towards them. The Black Valley was indeed black now, not only where its dark sand spread from Ovaeron's trunk. It settled into bluish-grey beneath him.

"What is it?" he asked, pointing to the light in the sky.

"It's a sun," Cien said. "Like they have on the Earths. It must have come into Derkra when I stopped the dust from the mountain. I needed real light to be able to see."

Ryten studied the changes the light made to the valley. The kandar of Calendrai wouldn't look so jarring against the yellow sand as they once had, but the Black Valley kandar who walked through Ovaeron's shadow stood out like the white trunks of their trees, outsiders in their own home.

"A *sun*," he said. "How strange."

They entered Ovaeron's shadow and Ryten no longer had to squint. He looked around at what was left of the valley and the kandar, unencumbered by the light. The devastation he saw told him Ruon could have destroyed World Four if he'd wanted to. Could have taken all the Earths himself and killed every last human. They were almost lucky the guardian had felt the need to change the kandar first, to bring them with him, or there wouldn't be a Purpose left to go back to.

Ryten called the collective up in his mind. It had quickly grown to accommodate the kandar of Black Valley. The tree was more difficult to navigate than it once had been. He noticed with interest that some of the branches of each collective meshed with those of the other. But there were so many empty spaces. So many kandar gone. He looked at the dark leaves of Tith's daughters again. Only four, as Sandin had never had one, but he would have those four ghosts for the rest of his life.

Cien's leaf would soon be gone though. Ryten looked up at the father of all of them and was happy to see his branches full of kandar, the red coming back as they shook the dust out of him. The collective pulsed, finally letting them know their Shadow was called to rest. As Cien and Ryten approached the great tree, his trunk began to open.

***

Pandinzori encircled Kadailin in the darkness. When the blast of light had burst from the glass and the rocks had begun to fall around her she had done what she was good at and held on. Now she was trapped in the mountain.

The streak of light had damaged her, but she didn't feel weak. She only felt confused. What should she do to escape? What could she do if she pushed through the rocks and found fire? She had to make a decision and she had to get out soon. There was nothing in the collective to tell her whether her plan had worked. The kandar could still be fighting the guardian in the valley.

She didn't think she'd been thrown far when the rocks fell on top of her. She couldn't be oriented much differently than before she froze herself and began to hang on. If that was true then the opening of the old tunnel should be to her left. She felt in that direction with her mind. Pandinzori responded to her and she slowly pushed it outwards. She only got a small distance before the rocks gave way.

She tumbled down the edge of the mountain, sliding, electing to concentrate on the state of the collective rather than make her fall more comfortable. She was already bleeding from the explosion in the cave. What did it matter if her body got worse? As long as she didn't hit any fire.

The first thing she noticed was the darkness of Ruon's seed. She stopped herself in the air. His seed was dark but it was still there. The last time that happened he was hiding in the mountain. She looked down over the valley and found the massive hole in the sand her blast must have created. The kandar who walked around it appeared to be in no hurry. There was a great, dark strip of hardened fire in the centre of it. She looked back over the collective and found Cotelle's leaf dark as well.

She lowered herself the rest of the way down the false Coralynth and came to a crowd of kandar searching the edge of a big strip of hardened fire. The first of the crowd she encountered turned when she approached. He stared at her. He was from Black Valley—his light colouring making his heritage obvious—and he wasn't a devoshai she knew. His leaf bloomed in the collective and she knew his name was Loam.

"Is the guardian dead?" she asked.

"Yes," he answered, his eyes sliding over her body. "Covered in fire and gone."

She almost smiled, but then she thought of the kandar who must have been sacrificed to end it. She checked the collective to see if Ryten and Cien had survived and was relieved to see their leaves were lit. She checked Tchardin and Damarin's leaves and found them dark. The tree in her mind pulsed as she looked over it. It called her to Ovaeron to witness a devoshai's final moments as himself. Cien was going to rest.

A crowd gathered at the great tree's base. She ran towards him. As she made her way past the groups of kandar in the valley she felt as if they all followed her with their eyes. A shadow descended from Ovaeron and covered her as she approached. He was silhouetted against a strange light. When she drew closer she saw his trunk was opening.

She broke through the last line of kandar to see his bark wrapped back around itself. Ryten and Cien stood before him. Cien turned away from the kandar and walked towards the opening. A few steps from the trunk he stopped and looked back at them with a weak smile on his lips. Then he saw Kadailin.

She rushed towards him. She couldn't let him enter Ovaeron. It could mean Tchardin's death. His eyes were wide when she stopped in front of him.

"You're alive!" Ryten came to her side and she looked from one devoshai to the other with terror.

"Tchardin?" she asked.

The two devoshai looked away when she said it but Ryten shook his head. Kadailin still had Tchardin's leaf in the collective. She refused to believe her little sister was gone.

"Damarin's gone too," Cien said. "You must still have their leaves."

Damarin's leaf hung on in Kadailin's collective just as Tchardin's did, though both were dark. If her sisters were gone those leaves would never fall, nor be lit again.

"I felt Tith's call," Ryten said, "but I still have them too."

"Then how do you know they're gone?" Kadailin asked.

He looked at the ground. "Cien felt them fall."

"Both of them?"

They didn't answer. She turned away from their blank looks and was confronted with all the kandar of the valley. They massed to watch the great tree as he opened. They seemed to be staring at Kadailin, but they must be looking at Cien.

"Kadailin," Cien said gently from behind her. "Do you know why the kandar stare at you?"

"They're looking at you," she said. "Watching their Shadow go to rest."

He shook his head. "No. They're looking at their future queen."

Kadailin frowned. A queen was born, not made. Even if a queen could be made, why should it be her? She was the least of Tith's daughters. But—she remembered with a pang of sadness—she was also the last.

"It's true," Ryten said. "You have the golden aura."

Kadailin looked down at her body, but a kandar couldn't see the colour of their own aura.

'I must go now,' Cien said to the entire collective. *'Ovaeron has been waiting for me for a long time.'*

He walked away from them. When he passed through the opening to the great trunk Kadailin gave up hope her sisters would ever return.

"Wait," she said.

He turned back.

Kadailin hated what she had to say. "We don't know what happened to them. They might not be reborn."

Ryten stood at her side and they exchanged a look. He had probably already brought it up. They almost definitely wouldn't be reborn, since they'd died on another world.

"I don't think it matters," Cien said. "Ovaeron doesn't seem to care and it's my choice. If those I am to be are born alone, I can handle that. They can handle it. I choose to answer the call."

The collective buzzed with thought. Cien walked deeper into the father of all kandar, into the greatest tree in existence. Kadailin looked at Ryten in confusion. He motioned towards the trunk and turned his eyes on Cien.

The devoshai had walked far into the abyss now. As he turned to look back, and the great rent in Ovaeron's bark began to close, Kadailin caught his eye. He smiled, but it was a weary, defeated smile. Kadailin doubted any of them had much more than that left. Ovaeron closed over him and he was gone. A leaf fell from the collective.

"I can't believe he would relegate himself to eternity without a dodenzinn," she said.

Ryten shrugged. "How will we ever know? They could be reborn. We don't know what happened on World Nine. Everything he said"—Ryten sighed—"I don't think he wanted to leave them alone, just in case."

A thought occurred to Kadailin. "The ice path."

"What do you mean?" Ryten looked around. She ignored him.

The kandar had focused their multitude of eyes on her again. She stared back at them and opened her mind to speak.

'Make yourselves one collective,' she said. *'Join into each other's minds until the kandar are one whole again instead of two parts. The two councils will meet and a new hierarchy will be built within them including kandar of both cities. When I've been acknowledged we will go back to the Earths.'*

Voices rose from the collective.

With an afterthought she added. *'I will call a vote to make Ryten the Shadow of Derkra beside me.'*

The collective went crazy. She made her voice as loud as possible and said, *'I have not been acknowledged, true, but I will be.'*

They raged for a few moments longer then quieted and slowly they began to disperse.

"You'll take us back?" Ryten asked.

"It's what Tchardin wanted."

Kadailin didn't want to be queen. She'd never thought it possible, but the golden aura would help her achieve what Tchardin had started. She remembered what her sister had told her about the ice paths, and what she'd said about the guardians. World Three would be first, to meet the guardian there. They would avoid World Seven and hope Siltadon never left it. Kadailin thought they should avoid World Nine too. But maybe not. There was one thing she had to do before any decisions could be made.

"Sandin." She turned to look for her sister's body and walked towards Ovaeron's trunk. Ryten followed her.

Sandin's body lay amongst a silent gathering of others, eerily empty and still. More dead kandar than the leaves Kadailin had lost because not all of them had been a part of her collective. They were light and dark skinned. Of Black Valley and of Calendrai. Kadailin moved through them and tried not to focus on who they used to be.

Sandin lay closest to Ovaeron's black bark. Her body was relatively untouched, having been under the protection of the great tree's leaves when the dark dust filled the air, but there was still a thin coating of grit on it. Kadailin looked down on her dead sister—one of four, the only one to leave a body—and wondered how they had come to this.

"We'll give her to the shift," she said. "Like she wanted."

Ryten didn't protest so she opened the swirling grey. She didn't think it was worth trying to give Sandin back to Tith. Her sister hadn't wanted that and Kadailin had to admit she could see why. Tith hadn't called Sandin at her death, had never spoken to her before it. Ryten said he had called once for Tchardin or Damarin. Kadailin wondered if they'd ever know which it was.

Ryten lifted Sandin's body into the air with pandinzori. Kadailin didn't direct the shift to anything. She didn't think that would make any difference. Instead she left it swirling and featureless as she and Ryten shared a look. He lifted Sandin towards it while she broke the ice with pandinzori. The water reached for them and found Tith's silent daughter. Her body was pulled back with it when it retreated. The shift disappeared.

Kadailin was still. She'd been thinking about World Nine before she remembered Sandin's body. She opened the shift again. She'd only seen two of her sisters die, though all four of them were gone. "I need to know what happened to them. I need to know how it ended."

She looked at the swirling grey of the shift and thought of World Nine. She didn't know what it looked like but thinking about it should be enough. It had worked for Jaydin and World Seven. Jaydin had brought up the blankness of the shift and somehow that had brought them to Rai, but this time Kadailin was hoping for more.

The shift changed. The spiralling grey transformed into a rigid line of dark grey surrounded by white. When the image settled both Kadailin and Ryten gasped.

"She made a path," Kadailin said.

The dark grey line stretched across the image and there was a tall kandaran tree in front of it. His boughs rose high into the air and gracefully swept towards the ground from varying heights. For some reason there was no colour to him. Kadailin moved to break the ice.

"No," Ryten said and reached for her arm. "We've done enough—"

They went through together, fighting the sheet of water that descended on them, but stepping into the tunnel in the shift a moment later. Kadailin ran ahead, desperate to find out what had happened to her sisters. Ryten followed her. He didn't protest now that they were in the shift. Kadailin assumed he was just as curious as she was. Just as desperate to know.

Kadailin ran to an image of World Nine at the end of the tunnel of ice. It showed the desolate landscape dominated by the strange tree. She waited for Ryten to catch up before pushing through the barrier.

They tumbled onto hard ice together. A sense of loss hit Kadailin and the collective grew dark. Only Ryten's leaf was lit. Kadailin scrambled to her feet and looked up. The tree's closest branches were only steps away. Ryten's aura brushed hers as he moved to stand with her. She noticed for the first time that there was almost no repulsion from him, but the realisation barely registered. She was too focused on the tree. Pandinzori spiralled off him and his strange appearance was even stranger from close up. He was entirely made of ice.

The thick, opaque branches curved high into the air and delicate strips of ice hung from them and cascaded to the ground. They were lined with oval leaves the length of her arm, also made of ice. Kadailin spun around, taking in the plane of ice that surrounded them. The tree was the only thing she could see other than the dark grey line in the distance behind him. She turned her focus back to the tree, wondering if he was really alive. She caught a glimpse of his thick trunk through an opening in his branches. There was a dark streak in it near the ground, showing through the mostly clear ice.

"What is that?" Ryten asked.

Kadailin moved hesitantly closer. The emptiness of this world was like nothing she had ever experienced. Even the empty collective in the false Coralynth was nothing compared to the desolation of this Earth, but the strange tree was alive, despite being made of ice. She felt it from where she stood.

The dark streak in the centre of his massive trunk grew clearer as she approached. She ducked under the hanging leaves—not truly leaves as they were rigid and would never move—and walked right up to him. His name came to her. *Banda*. It was the first time a World Tree had spoken to her. Her eyes widened as she got close enough to see through his trunk. Ryten joined her.

"Amazing," he said.

Kadailin nodded. The dark streak was a body, encased and obscured in the mostly translucent trunk. Just one body. She turned away and looked over the emptiness. Which sister could he hold, and what had happened to the other?

"I guess Tchar got what she wanted," she said, finding nothing of note in the limitless white. She turned back to Banda and the darkness inside him that must be Tchardin or Damarin. "It seems World Nine will have a guardian after all."

END OF BOOK I

Thank you!

Thank you so much for reading! It's been a long journey from imagining up these worlds, characters, and this story to publishing this book and getting it into your hands. If you have a moment, please take the time to rate or review DAUGHTERS OF TITH on Amazon, Goodreads, or any of your other favourite book review sites. This will help it reach more readers and facilitate the creation of its sequels so you can continue to learn about the kandar and their Purpose as guardians of the nine Earths.

ACKNOWLEDGMENTS

THE STORY YOU'VE BEGUN with this first book was written by childhood insomnia. Fantasy books filled the hours when I could get away with reading all night. The rest were filled with this.

To Mike, my little brother, for being my first reader and critique partner. If you didn't copy everything I do I'd probably be on this journey alone.

To Ragnar, my husband, for helping me find time to work around our three small children. For being a first reader, and for letting me read all my work out loud to you.

To Windy and Ralph, my parents, for supporting me and not only cheering for this book but also reading it! To my mom, for being a reader. For leading by example in that and all things so I could be the same. To my dad, for talking to me about big ideas and making me want to change the world.

To my kids for the future date they can read this and know what I was doing when I spent so much time on the computer.

To Taya—and later to the whole of the Fantasy Book Twitter discord—for helping me navigate the indie publishing journey from decision-to-publish to actual-physical-book-that-exists.

And to my beta readers and early readers listed here. You gave me the confidence to give DAUGHTERS OF TITH to the world instead of putting it in a drawer.

Thank you Anna M, Anna-K, Gabby, Stacey, Tom, Phil, Patrick Ffrench, RJ Taylor, Thea, Dominique, Gavin, Gerrit, Shannon, Colleen, Anne, and Manny.

Three Trees

Children of the Trees: Book II

Children of the Trees will continue in *THREE TREES*, expected in 2025...

THREE TREES takes place before DAUGHTERS OF TITH and tells the story of the kandaran war. Updates will be available on jpatriciaanderson.com.

www.ingramcontent.com/pod-product-compliance
Lightning Source LLC
Chambersburg PA
CBHW020533310726
48979CB00014B/2311/J

* 9 7 8 1 7 7 8 2 8 8 1 3 5 *